HUNGER

HUNGER

the vampire legacy

KAREN E. TAYLOR

[redacted]

KENSINGTON BOOKS
www.kensingtonbooks.com

KENSINGTON BOOKS are published by

Kensington Publishing Corp.
119 West 40th Street
New York, NY 10018

All Kensington titles, imprints, and distributed lines are available at special quantity discounts for bulk purchases for sales promotion, premiums, fund-raising, educational, or institutional use.

Special book excerpts or customized printings can also be created to fit specific needs. For details, write or phone the office of the Kensington Special Sales Manager: Kensington Publishing Corp., 119 West 40th Street, New York, NY 10018. Attn. Special Sales Department. Phone: 1-800-221-2647.

ISBN-13: 978-0-7582-6870-9
ISBN-10: 0-7582-6870-X

First Kensington Trade Paperback Printing: July 2011
10 9 8 7 6 5 4 3 2 1

Printed in the United States of America

Contents

BLOOD SECRETS

Dedicated in loving memory to my mother,
Leona Gallagher, who must be pleased
to know that her many attempts to encourage
a creative spirit finally paid off.

Acknowledgments

So many people helped with the completion of *Blood Secrets* that it's hard to mention them all, but I'll try. Thank you to Cherry, my agent, and John, my editor at Zebra; to Cheri, Elise, John, Pam and Randy for their proofreading talents and continuity checks; to Lori, my favorite writer / hair stylist; to the ladies of the neighborhood (Debbie, Debi, Karen, Kristi and Pauline) because they asked for more; to Ed and Celeste, whose suggestions and criticisms always went down easily with rum and Coke; to my father, Will, my brothers, Dave and Larry, and Dave's wife, Candy, for their loving support; to my children, Brian and Geoffrey, for (sometimes) being quiet at the appropriate moments; and most especially thank you to Pete, for being there, for doing the laundry and for keeping me in line.

Chapter 1

I stood at the window, staring at the late night streets. All too soon there would be those first tentative walkers, anonymously muffled against the chilled morning air. They would be joined by others, growing bolder and more confident in their destinations. I thought myself thankful I would not have to join them.

I turned and surveyed the room. The remains of the work of the last month lay strewn around the suite: discarded papers and sketches, emptied wine bottles and brimming ashtrays. "God, what a wreck," I said aloud. The echo of my voice, in a room that had been so long silent, startled me. For the past month, I had lived on room service, solitude and my work.

The final results of this feverish month were neatly stacked and labeled for my secretary Gwen to pick up in the morning. Gwen was anxious to see the new summer line; her enthusiasm was almost overwhelming. It was her wide-eyed approach to life that caused me to hire her. All city people must have seemed odd to her then. In our initial contact I must have appeared as one of them; powerful, polished and no less eccentric or inapproachable. If after ten years she realized my life style was more bizarre than most, she let no condemnation of it affect our friendship.

The answering machine light beckoned me, but I decided that the phone messages could wait until after I showered and slept. It was far too long since I had attended to personal needs, so immersed was I in my designs. I laughed to myself about how I would appear to the fashion world at this moment. Disheveled and unkempt, I couldn't be that same person known for her elegant and romantic fashions, her fastidious attention to details. "You're old enough to know better," I addressed my mirrored image and appraised the damage done as I removed my jeans and shirt. I distrusted mirrors; one of my greatest fears, especially after one of my extended work periods, was that I would fade away to nothing. I was pleased to find that I was not as insubstantial as I felt; I was perhaps thinner and paler than usual, but still very much alive. I turned out the light, removed my contact lenses and stepped into the shower.

Some light filtered into the room from the hall, just enough so that I could see small tufts of steam rising. A hot shower had always been an almost religious experience for me; I enjoyed the feel of the water flowing over my body, relaxing, caressing and renewing. A new twist, in these later years, was the almost pitch blackness of the bathroom, a condition once made necessary by my extremely light-sensitive eyes. Now with new and improved contacts, I could shower in the light, but I had found the combination of darkness and water so intimate and sensuous that I could not bear to violate their union.

Afterwards, I wrapped myself in a towel and prepared the suite for my sleep. The outer rooms would need to be left single locked only, so that the hotel staff could get in. Whoever has tomorrow's shift will have quite a job, I thought to myself, remembering the condition of the room, but shrugged the guilt away knowing that sleep was what I needed most.

Picking up my lenses from the bathroom, I entered the bedroom and triple locked the door behind me. Only I had a complete set of three keys in my possession; the hotel had one of them, Gwen had a second and Max had the third. Privacy in sleep is essential to me. I closed the blinds, pulled the heavy drapes shut and crawled into bed. It was almost sunrise.

"Please, God, no dreams," I prayed. I felt my body relax, and I slept.

My slumber was burdened by interruptions that day; I felt, rather than heard, the sounds of life all around me. The cursing of the maid cleaning the outer rooms, Gwen's tentative knock and entry, the rustling of pages and her call of "sleep well," as she left, the traffic from outside and the elevator bell further down the hall, even the insistent whirr of the telephone answering machine; all these noises filtered into my sleeping consciousness. I wondered if people in a coma felt this way, semi-aware of life continuing around them, but powerless to make a response. I envisioned myself, lying on my back on the bed, eyes wide open yet seeing nothing, seemingly dead. A moment of panic ensued; if I should die, how long would it take to be discovered? Almost as soon as the thought entered my head, I dismissed it. I was not dead, and although there was a time when I desired death, it would not come now.

Eventually the sounds ceased and sleep came, magically deep. When I finally awoke, I perceived that the sun had already set. The noise from outside seemed sharper and more distinct; the smell of the air crisp and cold. The alarm clock read 6:30 P.M. I stretched, yawned, and listened to the wind buffeting the windows. As I listened, I became aware of my growing hunger. Once recognized, it threatened to overwhelm me, an engulfing need that must be met soon. It had been too long, I knew. I needed music and talk, a drink, a man. I would find all these things at Max's.

Unlocking the bedroom door, I went into the bathroom. In the medicine cabinet, I found another pair of lenses, dark amber, as close to my original eye color as could be found. They would be fine for tonight, enough to shield my eyes from headlights and barlights. My needs urgently prodded me as I washed, brushed my teeth and applied my makeup. My hair, snarled from the day's sleep, took longer to comb than I wished. The blood in my veins pounded the count of each endless second. It took no time to choose my clothes; I knew what it would be. "Black leather," I smiled to myself. "For Max."

Before I called the doorman to arrange for a cab I checked the mirror. The black leather jeans were supple and tight, like a second skin, but the lace blouse softened the effect. I wore high heels to enhance my height of 5'3"—I liked to look people in the eyes. My hair, a deep auburn, almost mahogany, curled around my face and fell below my shoulders. My skin was pale, almost translucent, but the makeup helped to disguise this pallor. One final critical glance in the mirror told me that I looked good, even better than I should. I removed my coat from the closet, the one I called my wolf coat; the fur was shaggy and coarse and the color was a shadowy gray. It was a huge fashion success for me last season. I put it on and went for the phone.

I was surprised that when I picked it up there was someone already on the other end. "Yes?" I said, my voice rough and my manner abrupt.

"Deirdre, where have you been? I've been trying to reach you for weeks. What's the use of that damn answering machine if you never listen to the tape?"

"Sorry, Max," I said indulgently. "I've been working."

"Your obsession with your work will kill you one day. I know you haven't been taking care of youself. Get over here now and I'll fix you up. But hurry, we close early tonight. It's Thanksgiving, you know."

I didn't know. "I'm calling the cab now," I said, hanging up and then dialing the doorman.

He greeted me as I got off the elevator. "Miss Griffin, the cab will be here in a few minutes. I'd advise you to wait in the lobby as it's a very cold night."

I didn't mind the cold, but I smiled my acceptance at his suggestion. The smile was all the encouragement he needed. "You've not been out for a while. Are you well?" He had perfected the obsequious manner, courteous yet subservient, and the hotel patrons tipped him well.

I was no exception. In fact, I had become even more generous with the staff since I began hearing the whispers about me. Innuendos and speculative comments about aspects of my life had begun to filter through partially closed doors. This always made me nervous, almost paranoid, so I tipped well. I discovered that people would be unlikely to ask questions or turn on you if you did. "Never bite the hand that feeds you," I murmured to myself.

"Miss Griffin?" he questioned. "Are you okay?"

"Yes, I'm sorry, Frank, I was thinking of something else. I'm fine. I've just been working too hard."

The cab pulled up to the front door; he ushered me outside and into the backseat. I thanked Frank and instructed the driver, "The Ballroom, please."

Over ten years ago, Max had purchased a small nightclub in midtown. He had christened it the "Ballroom of Romance" and had retained me to provide the decor. Thrilled at the prospect of leaving a bad situation, I jumped at the chance. We decided on a Victorian approach; lace and hearts, black and white silk wallpaper, heavy fringe on the small lamps adorning the walls. The dance floor was surrounded by the bar and individual heart-shaped tables. It became one of the most popular clubs in town, an instant success for Max and for me. My services were suddenly very much in demand and after several years of interior design work, I was able to move into my first love, clothing. I could never quite believe my good luck, and always suspected that Max was much more involved in my initial jobs than he would admit. Over the years we had become the best of friends; he became my sole confidant and knew everything about me. His understanding of my needs and desires and his sympathy for my problems were boundless. I would have married him, but he never asked.

"Hey, lady, there's a crowd. Want to go somewhere else?" I came out of my reverie at the sound of the cabdriver's voice.

"No thank you," I said with confidence, consulting the meter. "They're expecting me."

"Suit yourself," he said after I paid him.

There was a crowd, even on Thanksgiving. My stomach tightened with an anxious anticipation; I hoped Max told them I was coming. I should not have worried though, for Larry was there to greet me at the door.

"Miss Griffin, so nice to see you." He smiled, and as his handsome face lit up with that smile, I regretted my promise to Max not to fraternize with his employees.

"Thank you, Larry. It's nice to see you, too."

"We have your regular table reserved. Just follow me." He parted the crowd and I watched the way his body moved as he walked in front of me. The smell of his cologne floated back to me and I inhaled it appreciatively. Of course, Max was right; I came here too often to get involved with the help. So, although tempting, Larry was off limits.

"What a shame." I sighed as I sat at the table. Then, loudly enough to be heard over the music, I ordered my usual—a special burgundy Max kept reserved for me. I lit a cigarette while I waited, and began to watch the dancers. The dance floor was crowded with the usual types: mostly rich and bored young people anxious to show off their latest fashions and their latest lovers. Some, however, were people who had saved for months to be here this evening. I could tell who they were by their clothes and by their obvious delight of finally being here. They were continually glancing around, to find any celebrity they could. They must be disappointed, I thought as I looked around the club myself. Since it was Thanksgiving, the most famous and glamorous had better things to do. Still there were a few, who like me had no family or friends with which to celebrate the occasion. God, I thought bitterly, how I hate holidays.

The band changed to a slow plaintive love song. One of Max's rules was that out of every musical set only two songs could be fast. The rest had to fit the club's theme—romance. "People come here to grope and grab," he told me in one of his cynical moods. "They will do things on the dance floor they would never do anywhere else but in the privacy of their own homes." He was right, of course. You could almost feel the heat exuding from the dancers. Some couples barely moved, so engrossed were they in the fit and feel of each other's bodies. Other nights this exhibitionist behavior offended me; tonight it merely intensified my mood. Max would come through for me, and provide a vibrant young body I could grasp and caress, while anticipating the final moment of rapture and release. I could, for a short time, be like one of the people on the dance floor.

I jumped, startled by the hand suddenly placed on my shoulder. I spun around in my seat to find Max standing there, an apologetic look on his face and my wine in his hand. He set the wine on the table, and brushed the hair from my neck to deposit a light, teasing kiss on the nape of my neck. I shuddered and he moved away. "Please don't," I said, smiling to remove some of the sting of the words and the shudder, "you know how ticklish I am."

"Sorry, love. I was just thinking how lovely your neck is. You should wear your hair up." He sat in the chair next to mine, a challenge in his eyes. I didn't want to rehash the same old arguments tonight, didn't want to get involved in the discussions of how Max thought I should dress or style my hair, or even live my life. I looked away and ground out my cigarette. He received no response; my silence was answer enough.

"I know," he said, sounding chastened, "you like it that way. Let's just drop it, shall we?" I looked up from my study of the wine. He was dressed in a black tuxedo impeccably tailored and correct, accentuating the lean but muscular body underneath. His teeth were white and even, and his hands, resting on the table, were strong. His dark hair, I knew, was becoming streaked with grey at the temples, although his face showed no sign of aging. It saddened me to think of Max growing old; how could I survive without him?

"You've been away too long, Deirdre." His teasing manner was gone and his concern for me showed on his face. "You should stop doing this to yourself. You look ghastly. I know your work is important, but you've got to live a little, too. If you're not careful, you'll lose your touch. I don't think you can exist very long as a hermit."

"No, I suppose not," I admitted to him. Sometimes, I felt that Max knew my needs better than I did. "So, what do you have lined up for tonight?"

"A tasty little number that I think you will enjoy immensely. I'll bring him over and introduce him now." With a graceful ease, he rose from the table, hugged me briefly and left. I watched him work his way through the crowd, speaking to several people on the way. Max was a lot like me; he too had many acquaintances but very few friends.

I drank my wine while I waited for his return. The wait seemed long, but in reality was only a few minutes. He soon arrived, bearing two glasses of wine, followed by my partner for the evening.

"Deirdre Griffin, meet Bill Andrews." Max never showed any jealousy of the men he introduced to me. They were carefully screened by him, he knew all about their careers, their habits, their personal lives. I knew that he had spent hours behind the bar questioning this man, delicately prying into his life. He was most likely married, or engaged, but looking for one night of excitement. Max and I both knew that no commitments would be formed; the way he set everything up ensured it. And I wanted it that way.

I smiled up at Bill. "It's nice to meet you," I purred, playing my part to the hilt. "Max has told me so much about you."

"And he told me about you, but he should have warned me how beautiful you were. I might just fall in love." The words were insincere, I knew; I had heard them all before, too many times. Suddenly I was overwhelmingly tired, sick of the entire situation, the seedy little drama acted out weekly here in the Ballroom of Romance.

"Deirdre?" Max was glaring down at me, an expression of warning on his face. "Are you feeling okay?"

I looked at the two of them standing there expectantly and suppressed my unexpected emotional reaction. "I'm fine, thank you, Max." I smiled at Bill and gestured to the chair recently vacated by Max. "Please, sit down."

As Bill did so, Max politely excused himself with a twisted smile. "Well, I've got a business to run. Enjoy yourselves."

Now that we were alone, I had no other option but to proceed as I normally would. I looked over at Bill and smiled again, hoping that my sudden disgust hadn't been too obvious. This was my life now and I could never turn back. It is too late, I admonished myself, for an attack of conscience. Too late to worry about how this evening would affect his life, his family. Too late for anything but this.

He returned my smile and I realized what a good choice Max had made for this evening; he certainly knew my taste in men. Youthful and attractive, but not devastatingly so, Bill Andrews was pleasant, unassuming and waiting for me to make the first move. I usually preferred being the predator, but tonight, for some reason beyond my understanding, I had no taste for the hunt. Maybe Max was right; I was losing my touch. I reached for another cigarette and as he lit it for me, I saw his wedding band gleam in the flame. In that instant, my heart hardened and I abandoned my rueful thoughts. He was just another bastard looking for some action. And, I thought vehemently as I gave him an appraising stare, he would get some.

He cleared his throat and pulled at his tie; my silence had unnerved him. Seeking to repair the damage, I smiled my most inviting smile and gestured towards the dance floor. "Let's have another glass of wine before we join the crowd. I hate to dance sober, don't you?" He agreed with a laugh that relaxed us both. We began to engage in the typical small talk that leads to seduction, my flattering attention to the talk of his career, his compliments on my appearance and body. By the time we finished our wine, we had moved closer together, our knees making contact under the table. His hand brushed my thigh and remained there; I could feel the heat of his touch through the leather. "Time to dance," I said provocatively, took his hand and led him to the dance floor.

Making an effort to seem slightly drunk as we began to dance, I leaned against him and he held me tightly and possessively. I made no effort to pull back from him. This was what I wanted now; it was no longer just acceptance of the inevitable. I had become intoxicated, not with the wine, but with the flesh of this man. I put my head on his shoulder so that I could better savor his aroma, the cologne he wore, the muskiness of perspiration, the acrid smell of wine on his breath. I could feel his heart pounding next to my breast, the rhythm matching my own heart and the music. As he became more aroused he whispered in my ear, "Sweet, oh, sweet." He kept repeating it like a prayer to a goddess. His hands were caressing my back and I was trembling with the urgency of my own need.

"Come with me," I said, and he followed obediently.

The corridor outside the bar had a few secluded rooms known only to those intimately familiar with the place. I led Bill to one of these places; a lounge, seldom used, with a sturdy lock on the door and a comfortable oversized couch. The music from the band could be heard softly in the background and the bar was equipped with the burgundy I liked. I poured two glasses while he removed his jacket and loosened his tie. Sitting next to him on the sofa, I handed him his wine. He drained it in one gulp, then seemed embarrassed, so I followed suit. This was always the most awkward time, reestablishing the ardor that had developed on the dance floor. Bill was no different than the others; he seemed nervous, unsure of how to proceed.

"You know," he said, hesitating and staring at the floor, "I've never really gone in for this type of thing before. I mean, I know it's a line, but I've been a faithful husband for over five years . . ." His voice trailed away.

No, I will not lose him now, I raged inside and I cupped his face in my hands. "Bill, look at me," I ordered, and he snapped his head up, surprised at the tone of my voice. "We will not do anything here tonight that will affect your future life. I don't want your tomorrows, I just want you tonight." Our eyes made contact, and when I saw that his guilt and confusion were beginning to fade, I made my move.

"Relax," I smiled seductively, "just relax a little. I can give you an evening you'll never forget. You won't regret it, I promise." Passion began to flare again, in his eyes and in his body.

"Kiss me," I whispered, not wanting to lose the moment. He turned to me abruptly, almost violently, as if he needed the momentum to carry him past his doubts. His mouth was hot on mine, evidence of a desire almost as deep as my own. He kissed my eyelids, my ears and my neck, all the while sliding my blouse over my shoulders. I helped him out of his shirt and tie and soon we lay, naked from the waist up on the couch. He made a move to take off his trousers, but I stopped him.

"Let's take it slow," I suggested.

Lazily I caressed his shoulders and back, feeling the tensing of his muscles; his skin burned beneath my cool hands. His hands busied themselves with the unfastening of my leather jeans. I permitted this and welcomed first his hand and then his kisses in the soft curve of my stomach. He began to move back up my body, concentrating on one breast and then the other, until he again returned to my mouth.

After the kiss, I buried my face in his neck. Now, I thought as I heard the blood pulse in his veins, Oh, please, now.

I nipped him at first, savoring the moment, my low moans echoed by his. Then when my teeth grew longer and sharper, I could hold back no longer. I bit him brutally, tapping the artery and was rewarded by the flow of his blood: hot, salty and bitter. He shuddered violently and fought to push me away, but his resistance was futile. Finally his struggles ceased and his body grew limp as I continued to draw on him, gently now, almost tenderly. I drank a long time, slowly, relishing the feel of my own body being replenished, then I withdrew.

Arising from the couch, I caught sight of myself in the mirror. No longer pale and haggard, my skin glowed with life and my eyes shone, victorious and demonic. A few drops of blood were trickling down my chin; I wiped them away with the back of my hand and turned from my reflection in disgust.

Chapter 2

I knew that I had taken more blood from Bill Andrews than usual. He lay unconscious and pale. Dear God, I thought in horror, I've taken too much. He'll die. I frantically felt for his pulse, and was relieved when I found it, faint but steady. He would be weak for a few days and bear a small bruise, but he would live.

I lifted him from the couch and put his shirt back on. He was not a small man, but I am much stronger than an ordinary person, especially after feeding. I dressed myself, walked to the bar for a glass of wine and lit a cigarette.

I watched him as I smoked, waiting for a sign of his awakening. Eventually his eyelids fluttered and he looked at me, puzzled and still slightly dazed. I discovered some time ago, that people in his state were highly suggestible and, whenever possible, I used this to my advantage. I again cupped his face in my hands and made eye contact. "You don't know me," I said softly and insistently. "You had too much to drink, found this room and passed out." He nodded vacantly and I knew the suggestion would work. "You will sleep for a while, then be awake and alert when you hear a knock at the door." His eyes slowly closed and he began to snore.

I went to the door and opened it. The noise from the bar was subdued and checking my watch I discovered that it was past closing hour. I could hear the faint clash of glasses and knew that the staff was hurriedly clearing tables so they could get home early. Bill should make his exit soon, I decided and knocked upon the door.

"Mr. Andrews?" I queried.

"Yes, that's me." He sat up and looked around. Seeing me, he smiled weakly and with no recognition in his eyes. "Sorry, I must have passed out here," he said sheepishly.

"No problem," I countered. "Max asked me to find you—we're closing now. There will be cabs waiting outside if you want one."

"Thank you, I will." He collected his tie and jacket, checked for his wallet and with a final vague smile, walked slowly down the hallway to the exit. I heard Larry say goodnight to him then waited until I heard the cab drive away. I collected my coat and left through a side door.

I did not need to take a cab. The cold was exhilarating and I was so full of stolen life that I wanted to walk and run and dance in the darkened streets. The night was my element. I, of all people in the city, could walk in its beauty without fear.

The next afternoon I ventured into the streets again, this time with more risk. The exposure of my flesh for just a few seconds to the sun would result in a severe burn and extreme sickness. It had happened a few times and was not an experience I cared to repeat. Still, the day was overcast and I had been rejuvenated through the feeding of last evening, and so, armed with sunglasses, gloves and a large hat to shield my face, I was relatively safe. Perversely, I enjoyed taking the risk, merely for the human feel of walking in the daylight.

As I walked I noticed that the store windows had been decorated for Christmas and I felt a wave of sadness at the season's too sudden approach. The trappings of today seemed so garish compared to those of my youth: the softly glowing candles, the handmade decorations and the warm red fire, all against a backdrop of pure white snow. There was always snow, and ebony night skies, so beautiful and icy that they could make you laugh for joy. Now all was neon and glittering, even nativity scenes seemed gaudy, embellished with flashing lights. Christmas was, for me, a dismal time made bitter by memories, parents long dead, friends aged or aging, and others, more dear, irretrievably lost. A tear slowly snaked its way down my cheek and I brushed it away impatiently; it would be blood-tinged, I knew, and would stand out angrily on my face. With the practice of all too many years, I pushed my emotions aside, replaced them with considerations of here and now.

The walk to the office was short, only five city blocks. I entered the building, showed my I.D. and signed in. Once on the elevator, I removed my gloves, hat and sunglasses; any light that would reach me now would be artificial, and my lenses were more than adequate protection. The elevator jolted to a stop on the 29th floor and opened to the glass doors of our reception area. Griffin Designs had exclusive use of the top two floors.

Gwen was talking to the receptionist as I walked in. She smiled a warm welcome, but the other woman jumped guiltily, murmured a good afternoon and immersed herself in some work behind her massive marble desk. This desk was my favorite piece of furniture, supported as it was with two large onyx statues of griffins, but it was really too decorative for my personal use, so it stood here, to impress our customers. I laughed inwardly at myself; I was no different from the doormen of the world, I just made more money.

Gwen began filling me in on the details of yesterday and today as we walked together to my office. "The pattern makers have been working all day and have some preliminaries for you to see. The fabric suppliers have been contacted and I expect the swatches by courier almost immediately. The models have been called and will be here next Friday for their fittings, and the seamstresses will report on Monday for their twelve hour shifts. I promised the usual bonuses, okay?" She glanced at me for my approval.

"It's nice to see you too, Gwen, only slow down a bit please," I laughed. "Give me a chance to catch my breath."

"Sorry, Deirdre, but I just get so involved." She shrugged. "Coffee?" Knowing my answer, she filled a cup and handed it to me.

"Thanks, Gwen. Let me have ten minutes to settle in, then we can start." I walked into my office, but left the door slightly ajar. Sitting down at my desk with a happy sigh, I warmed my hands on the mug of steaming coffee. It felt good to be back here again, to be among people for reasons other than those which usually drew me to them. I lifted my briefcase to the top of the desk and began to unload its meager contents; a newspaper, a sheaf of notes, and the phone answering tape I had not found the time or inclination to review. Any important calls would have come in to the office; the calls on the tape were most likely from Gwen. She often used the machine for leaving notes on items she might otherwise forget, knowing that she would ultimately be the one to review them. The other calls would be from Max. I smiled to myself; Gwen had once confessed to me that she thought that he and I had one of the most romantic relationships. She would be horrified to discover the truth of it—that Max was practically a pimp and my payment was in blood, not money. Unaware of this darker side, however, she seemed to get a vicarious pleasure in hearing his voice on the phone. I pushed the tape over to one side.

The newspaper was tempting, but I didn't succumb. Later, after working out a thousand details: fabric, color, and accessory selection, work schedules and pricing, after the office had emptied of all personnel, I would curl up and read it all, not missing one item or advertisement, saving the crossword puzzle until last. Setting the newspaper down, I turned my attention to the summer line.

Fashion is a risky business; keeping a reputation and clientele in today's variable climate is difficult. I had established Griffin Designs at a time when all others were showing tailored suits and dresses, and took a chance on more feminine clothes. It had paid off; my first show, consisting entirely of evening clothes, gowns with bustle detailing, low necklines and billowing skirts with yards of elegant, old-fashioned fabrics, received rave reviews from most of the fashion critics. I had one particular article, written at that time, framed and hanging on the wall of my office; the headline read—"Deirdre Griffin Shares Her Secrets of the Night." I think I kept it there as a reminder of my true nature, lest I get too involved in the little human world I had created for myself. Too soon, it would be ended; I had perhaps another year, maybe two before it was noticed that I hadn't changed, hadn't aged a year since my debut as a "young" designer. Then I would have to create yet another identity, pursue some other career to fill my time. How many more lives, I wondered; how many more years?

Gwen charged in, bearing a fresh pot of coffee and three pages of notes accumulated during my absence from the office. The names of clients who were patiently waiting for my personal attention to their wardrobe problems and fittings, and others who were not so patient and would have to be cajoled and flattered, all were listed and prioritized for my consideration. Gwen had, for all her faults, an organized mind and a great business sense; I trusted many of the more important details of Griffin Designs to her judgement. Some others in the office might complain of her incessant chatter, and her dressing in bargain basement chic; I knew, however, that I could leave the office in her care for a month, and still have a viable business when I returned. I liked her talk—it filled my silence; I admired her for her unconventional approach to fashion. She was the closest I had come to having a girl friend since my school days.

We spent the next four hours struggling over sketches and schedules, setting up appointments for the next week, and arranging the final details for our show in two weeks. Although I had established my business on evening attire, we had branched out over the years into office and casual clothes. The options for materials and accessories seemed limitless, but we finally reached the end of the list. We paused at last and became aware of the eerie quiet surrounding us; we had been so engrossed that we had not noticed the gradual cessation of noise from without. Gwen jumped and glanced at her watch. "Oh, no," she wailed. "I'm so late and Nick will be worried. Can we finish tomorrow?"

I nodded. "We were almost through for this evening anyway. I'll be in early. Have a good time."

"Thanks," she said, running out. "See you then." I heard the ladies room door squeak once, then twice; she had made a hurried check on hair and makeup before meeting her fiance. She and Nick were only recently engaged and were planning to be married in May. I had talked her into a late evening ceremony, on the pretense that it would be more elegant, so that I could attend. Although I didn't care much for Nick, I envied her that May wedding. The elevator bell rang, and the doors thumped shut as she descended to meet a future I could never have.

I stretched and rose from the desk to make a tour of the office. I switched off all the lights on my way to lock the front door, except for the reading lamp on my desk. I would read the paper and then go to bed. I was tired suddenly; the elated feeling of last night was gone. Ordinarily, I needed to feed only once a week, but after a month's abstinence, I would have to do so four or five times over the next few weeks to regain my full strength. Tomorrow was Saturday and a good night at the Ballroom—I would feed again.

Pouring myself the last of the coffee, now lukewarm and grainy, I sat back down. I read the paper from back to front, pausing in the middle to glance at the first few crossword clues, to peruse the fashion pages, then on to the real news of the front section. It held no interest for me this evening, until, while reaching into my desk for a sharpened pencil, a headline caught my eye. "Local Attorney Found Dead." The picture looked familiar, although for a moment I couldn't place it, then I read on.

"William W. Andrews was discovered lying dead on his apartment house steps early Friday morning . . ."

The pencil snapped, driving slivers of wood and lead deep into my palm. Beads of blood, so preciously bought, dropped onto the paper, almost obscuring the words. I wiped them off gently so that I could continue to read.

". . . police have declined comment on the case, only saying that it is currently under investigation. Inside sources have indicated that foul play is suspected . . ."

I clenched my fist, ignoring the pain in my hand. "No," I said, then louder still, "No!" until my voice reverberated in the empty building. It should not have happened; I've had many victims, but, to my knowledge, never been the deliberate cause of their death. I can't believe it, I thought. There must be some mistake! But the picture and the name were his. I looked back at the article; no further details, other than funeral arrangements, were supplied.

I got up and paced the office, pulling the small shards of pencil out of my palm and grinding them into the carpet. My mind replayed the events of last night, searching for any blame I might hold in this death.

I had fed on so many over the years; if pressed I could not even give an accurate count. So much blood stolen through the passing years, so many bodies to sate my appetite. But none of them had suffered any lasting effects from my presence. Some may have had odd dreams or nightmares, some may have been unaccountably repulsed, or even strangely attracted, by a woman of my height and build. Perhaps they suffered headaches or dizziness for days afterwards. But when my victims were left alive, they stayed alive.

Like all the others, Bill Andrews was alive; he got up and walked out of the club unaided. He should not have died, and it did not have to be my fault. He could have been robbed and shot, or had a heart attack; there are so many ways that people can die. He was alive when he left, I insisted again, and there was no way that I could be connected to him or his death. I wanted desperately to talk to someone, and considered calling Max. But gradually the initial shock began to wear away and I decided that it could wait. I was just too tired.

When our offices had been constructed, a small living and sleeping area had been included. The entrance to these rooms was hidden behind draperies hanging in the rear of my office. This area was the only place I ever felt completely secure; no one knew of its existence. I would sleep there tonight.

I locked the outer door of my office and entered the secret retreat. With the closing of the inner door, a security system was armed; it would alert me to the presence of someone outside. The door itself had three sturdy bolts and these I secured. I turned on the light and glanced around; it had stayed relatively clean in my absence, as it was completely sealed off from the outside with no windows or doors other than the one, no dust could filter in. There were a few cobwebs and probably more than a few spiders but it made no difference. If there was any home for me, it was here.

The area consisted of a bedroom and bath on the upper level with a spiral staircase leading down to the living area and small kitchen. The kitchen was not really necessary but the refrigerator did hold a supply of my favorite wine. I poured a large glass for myself and sat down. The lack of windows was compensated for by a great variety of art prints and originals scattered on the walls. My favorite was a little–known Van Gogh acquired at auction many years ago for a ridiculously small sum. It was a wheat field on a sunny day, and the colors were so vibrant that I was often tempted to lay my cheek against it, as if to feel the warmth of its sun. All of the pictures were landscapes in daylight; it helped to alleviate the otherwise tomb-like atmosphere. If tradition and necessity dictated that I must dwell in a crypt at least it was decorated to my liking.

I finished my wine and climbed the stairs. Finding a nightgown in the closet, I changed, sat on the bed, and turned out the lights at the master switch on the wall behind the headboard. I removed my lenses and settled in for the night. The walls were well insulated so that sounds from within my rooms were not heard, but a mike installed outside insured that I would hear the first sounds from without. I pushed the thoughts of Bill Andrews' unfortunate death far from my mind, and prayed, as usual, for a dreamless sleep.

Chapter 3

It rained in the night, a cold November rain pounding insistently on the roof. The sound filtered into my consciousness and began to shape the dream again. I tried to fight it, to force some other into its place, but even as I fought, I knew this dream would win.

I am wearing a cotton print dress, too thin for the weather, but it accommodates my expanded waistline; I am seven months pregnant. I struggle with the voluminous skirt, now soaked at the hem and pull my shawl closer about my shoulders. It had gotten cold and begun to rain while we were inside; he drapes his coat around me while the coachman gets our carriage. After I am settled into my seat and warmly wrapped in a wool blanket, he gives the reins a shake and we begin the long ride home. The horses are skittish, dancing sideways for a few steps before they are calmed by his steady control. He looks at me and smiles.

"We could have stayed the night. Loretta readied the spare room for us."

I snuggle against his shoulder. "I know, but I long for my own bed. And you would have been up all night talking incessantly about the possibilities of war. It is better this way."

"I suppose so," he admits, "just so you feel fit enough for the trip."

"I am fine." A rumble of thunder interrupts the steady rhythm of the rain, the horses start and whinny, then go on. The baby kicks hard against my ribs and I make a little grunting noise. He reaches over and with a mischievous grin, pats my stomach, proud of our unborn child. Our marriage, unlike many others of the time, is a match of love, but it had been a long ten years before the baby was conceived. At twenty-eight, many of the women think I am too old to carry a first baby full term. But we will prove them wrong, I think, my husband and I.

Our eyes meet for a second, and I read his love for me in them. I feel warm, despite the chill in the carriage, and realize that I have never felt so happy. Wanting this moment to last forever, wanting time to stop, I smile, stretch up to kiss his cheek, and recoil from the blinding glare of a flash of lightning.

There is a deafening crash, much louder than the previous thunder and a tree plummets onto the back of the carriage. With a sickening lurch, we topple over and crash to the ground. The horses rear and scream with fright, then drag us further down the road. Eventually they slow and stop, still restive but standing now. The only sound is the stamping of their hooves, their labored breathing and the relentless downpour of rain. I try to push up on the carriage door, but the once-warming blanket is now soaked and clings tightly to my arms and legs. It is hard to distinguish my tears from the rain, but soon all sensation drains away and I faint.

On awakening, I feel a small trickle of blood flow down my face. More disturbing is the gush of warmth between my legs; my water has broken and labor has started. And he is gone. He must be here. But where? I wonder, seeing nothing but the rain, hearing nothing but the restless shuffle of the horses. I call his name and begin to cry, in pain and fright.

The carriage door opens and two strong arms reach in to ease me out. He is back, I think and sigh in relief. His embrace is comforting and I relax into it. I try to speak but he quiets me, whispering words of reassurance and love. He is kissing me, caressing me and it feels so strange, so wrong. I push away from him and peer through the rain and darkness into eyes—not his. These eyes are deep with hunger and desire, not love, and yet they seem to draw my soul from my body. His mouth finds my neck and I shudder. The tension builds in my body as he drinks; I grapple with him, pulling at his shirt and ripping it in my panic. When my teeth graze his shoulder, I bite down hard, in fear or passion or possibly both. He is startled at first, then laughs, low and cynically, as his blood washes down my throat. I am being carried away by the rapid currents of this stream; I am drowning.

I am alone, shaking and cold, lying by the side of the road. Yards behind me lies the crumpled body that had been crushed beneath the carriage. I do not recognize it, cannot seem to acknowledge the grief I should feel. My mind is filled only with the other man. As I drift into blackness, his last words, tender yet somehow bitter, echo in my mind. "If you survive, my little one, we will meet again."

The hospital walls are white and chilling. The nurses and

doctors speak in rustling whispers and shake their heads in frustrated reaction to my case. With time, I come to understand that my husband is dead, the child was stillborn and there is no hope of others to follow. My own health they describe as precarious; they don't understand how I survived the ordeal. I wish I hadn't, I keep thinking before sleep comes and the walls wash into darkness once more.

I was extremely disoriented upon awakening, a combination of the dream and the dawn. I could sense the rise of the sun, although I would never again see or feel its warmth. Since the accident, my instincts had become sharpened, finely honed to those of a predator. My senses of smell, hearing and touch had intensified, and although my daytime vision was impaired, my night vision was excellent. I required little light to see. I felt deep within me the change of the seasons, the phases of the moon; my body was attuned to the earth in a way I would never have imagined.

It was this adjustment that caused me distress now; my physical being screamed danger from the dawn and even though my mind knew I was safe here, my body fought its awakening. I tossed restlessly, trying to resolve the dilemma until my body accepted the wisdom of the mind and I arose.

I took my typical shower, scalding water in utter darkness, and felt considerably restored. I dressed in clothes I found in the closet; faded jeans and a soft, comfortable oversized sweater. I towel dried my hair and pulled it back into a ponytail. It would be out of the way and I could style it later before my night at the Ballroom. I appraised my image in the mirror and thought that I looked even younger than usual. After my change, I had not aged, my body had been permanently frozen at twenty-eight. Many years ago I quit looking for gray hairs and crow's feet. "Every woman's dream come true," I scoffed at myself as I walked away.

I padded downstairs in stocking feet, found a pair of boots in the coat closet and left my sanctuary for the office.

It was still early and there was no sign of Gwen. I was pleased because I had something special that I had designed for her in conjunction with the summer line. It was a wedding dress, patterned after a ball gown from the late 1860s. I hoped it would please her, it was unconventional enough for her taste, yet elegant and romantic. I envisioned it in ivory moire satin, with pearl and lace trim, but had included several fabric choices in the initial planning so that she could pick what she liked best. Gwen had asked me to help her shop for a gown some time ago; I knew she was hoping I could do more than that, but hadn't wanted to presume upon our friendship. I never even hinted that I would provide the dress; she would be surprised.

As I put the last touches on my final sketch, I heard someone unlock the front door. After a few seconds, I recognized the footsteps; it was Gwen, switching on the lights as she came down the hall. I had been working with only the small lamp on my desk not wanting to put in my lenses until absolutely necessary. Now I realized that in my haste, I had left them in my small apartment. I couldn't function without them in full artificial light, so I would have to return. Quietly, hurriedly I slipped into the entrance, retrieved the contacts and paused, listening. There was no sound from without; I pushed the door open, and came through, gently closing it behind me. I breathed a sigh of relief, thinking that I had not been discovered. I could hear Gwen at the coffee machine; she always made that her first chore of the morning. I quickly inserted my contacts and went into the hall.

"Good morning." At the sound of my voice, she jumped, whirled around and dropped yesterday's coffee grounds on the floor.

"Deirdre, I didn't know you were here. Why can't you turn on the lights when you get here? How can you stand to be in this place in total darkness? It gives me the creeps to think of it. This city is full of weirdos and worse, just waiting to . . ."

"I know, Gwen. I'm sorry I startled you," I interrupted, all the while inwardly pleased that my secret was still safe. My current lifestyle was making me too complacent and trusting. It was not good. "The security here is very thorough. I don't think those weirdos you keep lecturing me about could get past the front guard. Anyway, I've not been afraid of the dark for years." I helped her clean up the mess I had caused and while the coffee was dripping I invited her into my office. "I have something to show you, that I hope you'll like."

"Oh, Deirdre," she gushed after seeing the sketches, "it's beautiful. But . . ." she hesitated.

"But what? Don't you like it?"

"I love it, but I thought you always said you wouldn't get into a wedding line."

"I'm not, dummy, you are. Did you think I would let you walk down the aisle wearing anyone else's dress? Just think of the scandal it would cause if you were reported wearing anything but a Griffin gown. It would be very bad for business." I was touched by her reaction, but did not want to let it show.

"Thank you so much." She practically flung herself over the desk to give me a small hug. "The gown is wonderful." Suddenly, I felt her stiffen. "Deirdre, there's someone here, behind the curtain." I could hear the tension in her whispered voice.

"Don't be silly, Gwen." I turned around and saw what had scared her. The door that I had tried to close so quietly had not latched properly, but swung open behind the drapes. It did look a bit like a person standing there, if you didn't know what it was. Now I would have to reveal one of my best kept secrets. Gwen was someone I trusted, yet I still felt like a fool and cursed myself for my carelessness. "Welcome to my other life." I tried to smile as I pulled back the curtain, exposing the entrance. "You didn't really believe that I slept on the office couch all those nights, did you?" I pitched my voice to sound its most reassuring and reasonable.

"No, I guess not, now that you mention it. But why the secrecy? Lots of people who work in a position like yours have this sort of arrangement." She had recovered from her fright and seemed to be enjoying my embarrassment.

"I like my privacy. Let's keep it between us two, please, I don't want the models thinking they can use it for their own personal dressing room." There was almost enough anger in my voice to stop any further discussion.

"Since it's important to you, Deirdre, my lips are sealed. But I want a guided tour some day, okay?" She was smiling, thinking, I supposed, about the midnight trysts she imagined between Max and me happening right here through the walls of our office. She wouldn't mention it to anyone, I felt sure. And it did not seem out of the ordinary to her; it probably only added to my image in her eyes.

We kept quite busy that day, working through to the late afternoon. Gwen went out to pick up some lunch at one point and, as usual, I declined. I could eat solid food on occasion, but I generally took in only liquids. It was all a poor substitute for my mainstay. Now and then, I did enjoy a rare steak; as a rule I stayed away from most other foods, especially the type Gwen would bring back for lunch. It was assumed that I followed a stringent regimen of diet and exercise and had often been asked to share my secrets with readers of the women's magazines for whom I had granted an occasional interview. I always demurred on the question, laughing to myself at the havoc that would be created by my truthful answer. And, horribly enough, there would be people sick or obsessed enough to try to emulate my lifestyle.

The sun was setting as Gwen and I prepared to leave. We had made enough progress on the line and show to both earn a day off tomorrow. Beginning Monday, the next two weeks would probably be non-stop work and worry, so it was best to start in well-rested, and, I thought to myself, well-fed. I let her go ahead of me, so that I could straighten up a few things in my office and apartment. I looked at the clock and decided that I should call Max. I wanted to let him know I'd be at the club tonight; I also wanted to discuss Bill Andrews' death with him. Thoughts of the intimacies shared that night, the feel of his warm body pressed against me, juxtaposed against my vision of him now, lying cold and lifeless on a table in the morgue, had plagued me during the day. I still believed, I needed to believe, that I had nothing to do with his murder, but I wanted Max's confirmation and reassurance.

I dialed the phone and lit a cigarette while I waited for an answer. It was not long in coming.

"Good evening, and thank you for calling the Ballroom of Romance. How may I help you?"

It was Larry. I was a bit surprised because I had dialed Max's private number. "Larry, this is Deirdre Griffin. Is he in yet?"

"Hello, Miss Griffin. How are you tonight?"

"Fine, thank you. May I speak to Max?"

"Well, he's not here right at this moment. But he sort of expected you to call and asked me to give you a message." He hesitated, but I didn't feel much like being put off tonight and my irritation showed.

"Go ahead, Larry, I'm listening," I said sharply.

"I don't understand him, you know. I guess I don't understand much of what's going on." I could tell he was stalling, holding something back he didn't want to tell me.

"Larry, please, just give me his message. He can talk about whatever it is tonight, when I get there."

"But that's just it. He asked me to tell you not to come here again. He said he was very upset about what happened last night. I didn't know that anything happened last night."

I suddenly felt that he was fishing for information, that his confusion was not entirely real. "I didn't think so either." I hoped to sound cool and unconcerned, but I began to shake inwardly. What was wrong?

"Miss Griffin," he began tentatively, "I'm sorry I was the one to tell you. But you know how insistent Max can be. He's had me sit in his office since I got here, just on the chance that you might call. I don't know what else to say, except that if he doesn't make it up with you, he's a damn fool. You're a remarkable lady, and even if he doesn't know it there are plenty of other men around who would be thrilled to be with you. You know, I always thought that you and I could—damn, Max is coming. I've got to go now. I want to see you again . . ."

I could hear Max's voice faintly in the background; then the phone was slammed down.

I hung up on my end. What had happened? I had no reason to doubt that Larry was telling the truth and yet, I also had no reason to think that Max would cut me cold. Unless, of course, he believed that I had killed Bill. That must be it, I thought, but he should know me better than that; he should know that even if I had, it was inadvertent. I felt betrayed. I loved Max, as much as I could feel free to love any human, and somehow had thought it was returned.

I glanced down at my hand and noticed that my cigarette had burned down to the filter. I angrily crushed it out in the ashtray. Smoking was indicative of my constant attempts to be human; it was a habit I had acquired many years ago to appear more normal, to try to fit in with the crowd. Apparently, like my relationships, it was an empty gesture. Maddened, I shredded what remained of the pack, put on my coat and left the office.

"Never again," I thought out loud on the way down in the empty elevator. "I will not rely on another. I will stay true to my nature, a hunter, a lone predator. I don't need anyone; I don't want anyone." I felt a new strength, a resolve in my very being, that was never there before. For so many years, I had been frightened, guilty, and apologetic; that would end now.

As I walked out of the building and slowly made my way to the hotel, I began to make my plans. I would still feed this evening; I needed the strength, physically and psychologically. I could see now that I had lived like a pampered pet for years, Max's pet, to be thrown a morsel now and then, to be caressed and played with. Now I would reawaken my feral instincts, stalk my own prey and take what I wanted. There were many places in the city where people walked alone, where my food could be easily obtained. I was never afraid to prowl the parts of the city where the undesirable and unwanted lived. There were homeless people on park benches, people who had nothing to lose, no reason to guard against thieves, no value to anyone but me. And I would steal less from them than others had, only a little blood, something that they would gladly give for just a few dollars. Before I met Max this was how I lived, and I could do it again.

I spun through the entrance to the hotel, deep in my plans for the night, and nearly ran into someone waiting by the door. With surprise, I noticed it was Larry. Despite my resolve, I felt my spirits rise. Max had sent him to apologize, Larry had misunderstood his message and he wanted to set it straight. I smiled encouragingly at him, but he kept his head lowered. His expression was rueful.

"Miss Griffin?" I turned around and saw that Frank was on duty again. He looked at Larry and continued. "He said he had to speak with you, that it was important. I was just about to ask him to leave when you came in. Do you know him?" Frank always took his responsibilities as doorman and guard seriously. I had never had anyone call for me, and I imagine he found it rather unusual.

"Thank you, Frank. I do know him, it's fine." Turning to Larry, I said quietly, "Do you have time to come upstairs? I'd like to talk about this in private."

He smiled at me, too brightly, I thought. "Yes, I'd like that." We boarded the elevator and rode silently, both staring at the lighted numbers above the door. The elevator stopped at my floor, and as we walked down the hall, I found his closeness exhilirating. Surely he was not off limits now. I imagined I could hear his heart beating, circulating the precious blood through his veins. By the time we arrived at my room, I was trembling with anticipation and nearly dropped my keys. He took them from me, and without a word, opened the door and escorted me in.

I took off my coat, walked to the bar and poured myself a drink, to steady my nerves. When I turned around, Larry was staring at me, with a look of surprise on his face. "You look so different, Miss Griffin," he said, sitting down on the couch. "Younger or something."

"Not quite the elegant lady of the night you're used to, am I?" I indicated my clothes with a gesture and made a slight curtsy. "Let's just drop the Miss Griffin, shall we? Please call me Deirdre. Can I fix you a drink?"

"I'd better not, I've got to be back to work in a bit. If Max knew I came here he'd fire me." His mouth set into a frown incongruous for his years. "And unfortunately, I need the job."

I was disappointed that he was apparently not here to apologize for Max, and yet, just the closeness of this man, this human with his aroma of blood and sweat, was enough for me to forget my hurt and concentrate on my hunger. I would have to act fast on this and satisfy my need before he had to return to the Ballroom. I knew he wanted me, I could read it on his face. It would be easy enough to seduce him, to feed on him, and then to implant the suggestion that he had spent a rather disappointing time in my bed, that his visit here was not something he'd like to repeat. I felt a rush of power, and said a thankful prayer that my first independent victim in years was so neatly delivered to my doorstep.

I moved slowly toward him. "Well, what did you want to talk about?"

"Oh, I don't know." He stood up for a minute as if to come closer to me. I leaned forward, but he moved back, suddenly seeming uncomfortable and uneasy. Then I smiled and he relaxed, sitting down again and casually laying his arm over the back of the couch. I admired his handsome form clad in the Ballroom's uniform tuxedo. On Max the suit seemed like a second skin, on Larry, it was a cocoon from which his lean, youthful body struggled to emerge. I longed to unbutton his shirt, undress him completely and enjoy his blood. Take it slow, I advised myself. Don't scare him away.

"Are you sure you won't have a drink, Larry?"

He checked his watch, "Well, yeah, I guess a small one wouldn't hurt."

As I filled a glass for him, I was aware of his gaze following my every movement. Slowly I walked across the room and handed him his drink.

"Thanks." He gave me a nod and took a sip. I sat down next to him and waited.

"I thought maybe you could help me out."

"And how could I do that?"

"Well, you could answer a few questions for me. I've been trying to understand what goes on with you at the Ballroom. Max has always maintained that you belonged to him; that no one at the club was to touch you. But then, he's always setting you up with other men, total strangers, some of them real sleazeballs, and you always go along with it." He looked at me, with a odd, almost pleading look, wanting answers I could never give him.

"Larry, it really is not what you think."

He gave me a sharp look. "How can you guess what I think it is? Just answer my question, what happens between you and the men he brings in? Once a week, almost like clockwork you're there, not good enough for the staff but just fine for anyone else he can drag in. And what about this Andrews guy? He's dead, did you know?" At my nod, he continued. "I thought you might. The cops were there too, talking to everyone, looking for you."

"But I didn't have anything to do with . . ."

He didn't let me finish. "That doesn't matter," he said with a shrug. "What bothers me most is Max's reaction. When he heard, he was furious, ranting and breaking things. He doesn't even want to hear your name, and asked me to keep you away. He should know you by now! How can he turn on you like that? You, of all people, you're so beautiful and, well, he should want to protect you, worship you . . . like I do." This last was said quietly so I could not hear, but I did and looked at him intently; he stared at the floor, his cheeks flushed.

"How old are you, Larry?"

"I'll be twenty-five in January." He seemed defensive, avoiding my stare. "Not that much younger than you."

"Looks can be deceiving. I'll be thirty-six on my next birthday," I lied. I reached over to him and taking his hands in mine, made eye contact. "Take my advice, please. Don't try to get involved in any of this, not with Max or me. You'll just wind up getting hurt." I dropped my eyes but remained holding his hands. "Whatever goes on at the club," I smiled my most convincing smile, "and even my relationship with Max, well, that is all over now. So let's not discuss it, okay?"

"But what goes on, Deirdre? What happens that's so awful you can't talk about it?"

I realized that I had perhaps underestimated him. He was

young, true, but not stupid and certainly not unobservant. And unfortunately for me, not a good choice for feeding. Taking his blood now would only raise more questions in his mind, cause me more problems than it would solve. "It doesn't matter, Larry," I said with certainty, meeting his eyes with as much determination as I could muster. "All that is over. Just forget about it. Forget about it."

He stood up and shook his head briefly, confused by the forcefulness of my command. "Well, I guess I'd better get back. Thanks for the drink."

"I am glad you stopped by, Larry." I took his arm and walked him to the door. "It was so very nice of you to be concerned for me. But if you have to go, you had better go now. I would feel just terrible if I got you fired. We can get together some other time, dinner on your day off, maybe?" I didn't want to alienate him, but if I spent much more time in his presence I could lose my control. Fortunately, he seemed not to take my comments as a brush off.

"I'd like that, Deirdre. May I call you?"

I smiled my warmest smile. "Anytime, Larry. I would be happy to talk with you again." On impulse I stretched up to kiss his cheek. He turned his head to meet that kiss, and folded me in his strong, muscular arms. His tongue probed my mouth, tentatively at first and then with more purpose, his warm hands molding the flesh of my lower back. He was so ardent that I almost relented and, regardless of the danger involved, almost sunk my sharpening teeth into his neck. As I was about to make my move, he pulled away, abruptly. Surprisingly, he was blushing.

"I'm sorry, Deirdre, I didn't want to, I mean, I'm not ready to . . . See you later." He ran from the room and down the hall as if I had bit him and was pursuing him for more. The elevator door closed and I closed my own.

I was shaking still from my unsatisfied need, when suddenly I began to laugh, sounding slightly hysterical. "It seems the great huntress may have found herself a virgin," I said to myself. "The best blood of all, so the books say, and she let him get away." I poured myself another glass of wine and as I drank it, I calmed down. In another few minutes I would leave and find myself a more appropriate victim.

Frank gave me a curious look as I left the hotel, but I ignored the questions in his eyes, and walked out into the night.

It was early evening, and there were many clusters of people, pursuing their own interests, shows or dinners or drinks with friends. These could be no help to me, but not too far away were dark streets avoided by most of the city's dwellers. Gwen's weirdos walked these streets, or at least I hoped so; my conscience seldom rebuked me for feeding on these. I sniffed the air and enjoyed the stabbing sensation of cold entering my lungs. It would snow tonight, a thin white covering that would too soon be grey or black with the morning's traffic. I turned off onto a less traveled street, and began to grow uneasy; was I being followed? I looked behind me, but there was no sign of movement. I thought I could hear faint footfalls echoing my own, but when I stopped the sounds ceased, even as my own did. I brushed off the feeling; I was letting the events of the last few days influence me. There was no one there, and even if there were, I knew I could handle them. After all, I was hunting for just such a person.

Then, in the darkness ahead, I perceived a shadow against a wall. Had my night vision been less than perfect, I would have walked right by without noticing him. I heard him breathe a small sigh, his patience and silence had paid off, or so he thought.

Whether he desired my purse, my body or my life, I never had the opportunity to find out.

I walked past him, as if I did not know he was there. He came up close behind me and grabbing my arm, whirled me around. "Hey, baby," he said, and then spoke no more. I flung myself at him and fastened upon his neck. He struggled, but I drew his blood quickly and violently, quenching my dark thirst. As he grew quiescent in my arms, I fed slower, savoring each drop. It was ecstasy; it was hell, it was life. I pulled myself from him, shuddering when the withdrawal was complete. He was unconscious, but his pulse was strong, much stronger than Bill's had been last night. Ordinarily, I would have taken more, but I felt safer only taking exactly what I needed.

I left him lying where I had found him. When he came to in a few minutes, I would be gone. Chances are, he wouldn't remember the incident, and due to the darkness of the alley he would probably not even recall my face. And I doubted that he would report the attack to anyone; after all, who would believe him?

As I turned away and began to walk back down the alley, I heard a stifled gasp coming from where he lay. There, I thought with satisfaction, he was even stronger than I thought and was already reviving. I hurried back to the more populated streets, and passing a store, peered in the window at my reflection. Other than my shining eyes, there was no telltale trace of my activity. I removed a tissue from my pocket and wiped my mouth anyway. I fluffed my hair around my face and headed back to the hotel. I was glutted with blood and would want to sleep soon. It had been a successful hunt, I thought, and moved languidly through the streets. Snow had begun to fall; I raised my face to the night sky and felt the brush of flakes on my cheeks, like the tentative touch of a baby's hand: so beautiful, so pure, and so soon gone.

"Did you have a nice walk, Miss Griffin?" Frank asked as he greeted me at the door.

"Yes, it's a lovely evening. Good night." When I got to my room, I completed my evening rituals; the locking of the door, the pulling of the drapes. After tonight's feeding, I should sleep well and wake tomorrow, refreshed and renewed. I turned off my restless and questioning mind, fell upon the bed and slept.

Chapter 4

My sleep was disturbed by the ringing of the phone. Someone must have switched the ringer back on while cleaning the room and the unknown caller was desperately trying to avoid the answering machine. The phone would ring four times, then stop; this pattern repeated every five minutes or so. I half remembered hearing this as I slept and wondered how long it had continued. No matter, I was awake now; I had slept through the entire night and the next day. The sun was setting as I left my bed and I felt a new strength flow through my body. I had experienced this feeling many times before in my life, but it always left me in awe. I was young, strong and prepared for life. I felt like I did indeed possess the powers my kind were purported to have: flying, shape changing, dissolving into a mist, none of these seemed out of my grasp tonight. This wonder of my existence had kept me sane through my many years and lives; without it, I would have persisted in finding a way to die.

The phone rang again as I unlocked the bedroom door and entered the bathroom. I let it ring; they had been calling for a while, they would call back. I inserted my contacts, turned on the lights and sat in front of the mirror to brush my hair, which seemed electric and vibrant, with a life of its own. I could feel each stroke of the brush tingling from the roots to the ends. As I applied my makeup, I noticed that the feeding of last night had revitalized my skin; it was firm, smooth and without blemish. I felt perfected in every way, and ready to conquer the world.

As I dressed, I planned the evening. I would begin to stake out new territory, visit a few of the newer clubs that had opened. Although last night had provided satisfactory sustenance, it had not given me the contact I had grown to appreciate through years of feeding at the Ballroom. I still needed the interplay, the seduction; I wanted to ignite the spark of desire in a man's eyes. I hadn't the companionship of others like me and although I knew that at least one must exist, all I had of him were the small fragments of a dream I would like to forget.

This time when the phone rang, I answered it.

"Deirdre, don't hang up, please."

"I received your message, Max," I said coldly. "I won't be back."

"No, wait. Let me explain. You owe me that, after all these years." He sounded sincere enough, and yet I did not want to fall into the trap of trusting him again.

"Do it quickly, then, and get it over with. I have plans for this evening."

"Deirdre, love, I made a mistake. I'm only human, you know."

"And you know I'm not. Now get on with it, or let me go." I doubted he had much to say at this point.

"Look, I can't talk about this over the phone. Come and see me tonight and if I can't make a reasonable apology you have my blessing to go for my throat."

In spite of the anger, I laughed. "Too bad you didn't make that offer last night, when I really needed it. You could have saved me a bit of trouble."

He didn't laugh. "I'm truly sorry, my dear. Please come tonight. It's important."

Wearily I agreed. "Only for a moment or two, and only because I want to hear your excuses. I'll be there."

Despite Max's attempt at reconciliation, I still wanted to pursue the plans I had been formulating. After a brief stop at the Ballroom, I would catch a cab and get a recommendation from the driver on some of the newer night spots in the city. I didn't have to feed this night, I might even be able to wait a week for my next victim, but I needed to know what alternatives I had.

I walked to the club; the snow from last night had completely disappeared and the night was bitter cold. The skies were clearer than normal and the light of the moon bathed the streets in a soft glow. I felt like I was on a holiday, somehow. I had no hunger to drive me, no needs to satisfy; tonight I could be merely human.

Larry must have been off this evening, the doorman was a stranger to me, but since it was early, and a Sunday, I had no trouble getting in. I mentioned that I was here to see Max, and he nodded. He had been expecting me, he said. Max had some urgent business that had just come up but I was to wait in his office. As I was escorted to the room, I thought that the urgent business was probably nonexistent, a ploy to throw me off balance, a chance to get me thinking about Max in familiar, comfortable surroundings. As I settled into the couch, with a glass of wine from a newly opened bottle, I struggled between anger at his self–assurance and tenderness at being completely accepted by him. He knew me so well; how could any of his ploys fail to work?

Max and I had met during the mid-60's when I had been working as the night shift waitress at a truck stop. It had been one of the more ideal jobs for me, so many people passing through at all hours of the night, so many warm, anonymous bodies to take in the darkness.

I can remember the odors and the tastes of that time vividly: the warm fumes of gasoline filtering through the summer nights, the musty smell of marijuana that clung to the uniforms of the other waitresses, the odd and individual flavors of the blood of the drivers that passed by the truck stop regularly. Buddy had been the truck driver that night. He came through the stop once a month and always asked for me to deliver his coffee. He was dark–haired and only slightly overweight, with the plump, youthful face of a cherub. Some of the girls complained of his body odor, but he suited me just fine, and his blood had, I imagined, a sweeter flavor than most. He never complained like some others about the sharp nip I would give him during our love play and he never missed what I took.

I struggled back into my tight, pink uniform, and as I got out of his truck, he jumped out and gave me a small swat on the behind. "You serve the best coffee in the tri-state area, darlin'."

"Thank you, Buddy." My eyes danced as I reached up to kiss him. I adjusted his collar to hide the fang marks on his neck.

"Go easy on the hickies next time, honey. The last one you gave me lasted two weeks and the missus got suspicious." He was smiling as he said it, proud, I thought, of our monthly liasons.

"I just can't control myself around you, Buddy." I gave him another kiss, this one on the cheek and watched as he got back into the cab. "Drive carefully, and see you next month."

I watched him drive away and looked at my watch. It was time for me to go off shift. I would sleep well this night.

I stopped off to deposit half of Buddy's tip in the cash register. As I walked out, Max walked in; our eyes met as we passed in the doorway. Just for that one second, I was overwhelmed with a sense of unity, a recognition of a soul within that could speak to mine. Then he blinked, the feeling faded and we went our separate ways. I thought about him as I drove to the isolated trailer in which I made my home; thought about the many years spent in a fruitless search, trying to discover someone who could share in my life, allay in some way the dark loneliness within which I existed. No spark had ever flared, until now. Not for the first time, I cursed the ill chance that made me what I was. If I could have endured the sunlight, I might have been able to stay and cultivate a relationship with this man. I was sure that, like all the others, he would be gone by tomorrow night.

When I arrived at work the next evening, however, he was waiting outside the door, and softly called my name. I smiled broadly for the mere joy of his presence.

"How did you know my name?" I asked curiously.

His voice was deep and cultured and seemed to caress my ears. "Well, for one thing, I asked your friends about you last night. And it's written as plain as day on your uniform." He chuckled a little at my expense, but somehow I didn't mind.

"Yes, I guess it is." I glanced at the name embroidered on the cheap dress, embarrassed because I had forgotten it was there. In reality it was no more my name than any of the others I had carried over the years. But here, at a tiny truck stop in Kansas I was known as Diane Gleason. "But," I said with a smile, "your name isn't."

"I'm Max," he said briefly. "Max Hunter." Then after a small pause, "Do you think you could get tonight off? I'll only be in town for a few more days, and I'd like to get to know you."

One of the oldest lines in the book, I thought, but it didn't matter. He seemed so perfect.

I went into the diner and got permission to take the night off. Sincc I usually had nothing else to do, I had covered for the other waitresses more than a few times; now they could return the favor. Besides, Max had made quite an impression on them last night, and they were happy to oblige when I promised a detailed report on him the next day.

He drove me to my trailer so that I could change my clothes. I half expected him to make his move then, but he waited politely in the car until I came out, dressed in jeans and a black suede shirt, fringed and strewn with sequins. It was one of my favorite garments, but I seldom had a chance to wear it. I caught his admiring glance as I got into the car and felt that the long evenings cutting and stitching had all been worth it.

"You have a good eye for clothes, Diane. That's very attractive." He reached over, to touch the material, I thought, but instead he stroked my cheek gently, moving his fingers softly to the base of my neck. A sweet chill ran through me and I moved toward him, waiting for his next caress. It didn't come. Instead he pulled away, leaving me confused and disappointed.

"Where shall we go?" he asked innocently, as if the contact had not been made.

I laughed at his question. "There isn't much open after dark around here, but just keep driving. We can find something to do eventually, I'm sure." He ignored the innuendo and did as I suggested.

We drove around most of the night, stopping at a few bars, or private clubs as the law liked to call them, along the way. Mostly we talked and laughed, sharing stories of our lives and our hopes for the future. He was traveling across the country from California to the east coast, I found out, and hoped to open a restaurant or club if he could get the financing. He thought that I was something of a gypsy, moving from town to town, never staying more than a few years in any one place.

"How can you ever establish a home for yourself that way, Diane Gleason?" He was still making fun of the name on my uniform and we laughed, as if it were the funniest joke ever told. I found him charming and attractive, so different from the men I met at the truck stop, and began to wonder if I could make a mate of him. Shortly before dawn, he brought me back to the trailer, and after making arrangements to meet the next evening, kissed me quickly, his lips hard and demanding on mine.

"Would you like to come in?" I asked breathlessly.

"You are beautiful, Diane, and so alive. Who would ever have thought . . ." His voice trailed off as he buried his mouth in my hair.

"Thought what, Max?"

He held me at arms length and looked at me intently, then smiled. "That I could find a girl like you in a place like this." He kissed me once more and let me go. "I've got to go, now. Till tomorrow." He got into his car and sped away.

"Till tomorrow," I repeated as I entered my trailer.

The sun was rising as I pulled the drapes and laid down on my bed. Long after I should have been asleep, I thought about Max and the evening we had spent. Formulating plans for converting him into a creature like me, I tried to remember the procedure from the countless books I had read. My own transformation was hazy, veiled in a disturbing dream, and so could offer no solution. I fell asleep composing the words to my proposal. I would offer him endless youth and life; he and I could be united forever.

We spent the next few nights together. I took a week's vacation from work, something I hadn't done in the past two years. We must have put hundreds of miles on his car, doing nothing but driving and talking. Just being with Max made me feel more human than I had in years; I was young and vibrant again, the long lonely times finally behind me. On our last night together, we found a deserted country road, miles away from everything.

We lay in a field, staring at the night sky. Thinking how I wanted to preserve the moment forever: the silence, the stars and his presence, I sighed, almost involuntarily.

"I have to leave tomorrow," he said abruptly; his words were a brutal interruption of the quiet night. "There's no way around it."

Something in the tone of his voice angered me, a detachment, and coldness I had never heard before. "Well, you needn't sound so damned happy about it," I snarled at him. "I knew you would only be here tor a while. You owe me nothing."

"On the contrary, my love, I owe you a lot. You've renewed me, taken me away from my own selfish pursuits, made me feel that life may be worth living, after all. But even at that, I have to leave." The words were properly sincere, but the voice was that of a stranger. "You could come with me, I suppose, but I have never been able to sustain a lasting relationship with anyone before; I care too much about you to give you less than you deserve. It's better to end things right now."

I studied his profile in the moonlight, trying to etch it into my memory as I considered his words. The proposal I had rehearsed night after night would not come; I was too proud, too unsure of him. I could take him by force, change him as I had been changed, perhaps, but I wanted a willing partner, someone who could move gracefully into my existence. That partner would not be him. My perception of him as eternal companion began to fade, replaced by the vision of his face in twenty or thirty years, aging and grayed. Max would become one with all the others, those whom I touched and those who had touched me, only to be claimed by their final lover—death—while I lived on. With that thought, I let go of him, reluctantly, yet completely, condemning him to his fate and me to mine.

"Hell, Max," I said quietly and tenderly, "in the whole scheme of eternity, it can hardly matter."

"Ah, eternity," he said, giving a low laugh. "What must eternity be like?"

"Terrible," I said as our eyes met, "yet beautiful when filled with times like this."

We turned to each other then and made love in the cool night air. It seemed a bitter union, desperate and futile. Mentally we had both accepted the inevitable separation; physically we clung to each other in a desperate attempt to postpone the parting. We were joined in an animal mating; instinct took over, leaving no room for intellect or emotion. We were merely two bodies, taking from each other, insatiable yet dispassionate. In the final moments when our lovemaking grew frantic, our peak very near, I realized that I had been crying for some time, a silent outpouring of blood-tinged tears, flowing down my face, soaking my hair and the dark earth beneath me.

When it was over, we drove in silence back to my trailer. Max came in for the first and last time, and lay down on my narrow bed as I prepared for sleep. I drew the drapes, slowly undressed and crawled in beside him.

"Max," I said and could say no more.

"Hush, my little love, sleep now." He crooned and rocked me; I relaxed and slept in his arms like a child.

When I awoke the next evening, he was gone. He left a printed card on the pillow with his address. Almost as an afterthought, the words "Love, Max" were scrawled in red ink.

I could not cry, all my tears had been shed during our lovemaking. I dressed and returned to the life I led before we met.

We had kept in touch over the years, Christmas cards from him and change of address notices from me. When my luck ran out in a small southern town, where a persistent sheriff had grown too curious about my nocturnal activities, Max had answered my distress call with a plane ticket, a new life and a new identity. After I arrived in Manhattan, I had offered him no explanations and he had asked no questions.

I broke down one night about three years later and confessed to him the horrors of my life. Max needed little convincing, he had already observed some of my more telling habits: that I never went out into full sunlight, never consumed solid food, how weekly I would choose a man from the dance floor of the Ballroom and return from the encounter revitalized and strengthened. He was curious, not frightened, and his only stipulation to belief was that I allow him to observe a feeding. When this had been done, he laughingly admitted that I either was a vampire or gave an amazingly convincing imitation of one. It was at this point that he began screening potential victims and directing them my way. I accepted his assistance out of the love I still felt for him. But even with my confession, or perhaps because of it, our relationship never progressed further than friendship. It was almost as if that one night of love had never happened.

A loud knock on the door interrupted my thoughts and I was jolted back into the present. "Come in," I called softly, wondering why Max would knock. When the door opened, my question was answered. A stranger stood there looking rather ill at ease, and yet oddly sure of himself. He was not the normal type that frequented the club, he looked older than most of the patrons, probably in his late forties. He was tall, fair and well built, but rather nondescript, I thought, until my gaze rested on his face. He had a strong, hawk–like nose and eyes bluer and more intense than any I had ever seen. A tough customer, I thought to myself as I rose from the couch to greet him.

"Hello, you must be looking for Max. He should be here in a few minutes. Sit down and I'll see if I can find him for you."

"Actually," he said slowly and deliberately, looking me up and down in an appraising manner, "I've already seen him. It's you I want to see, if you're Deirdre Griffin. I was told you'd be here."

"Business or pleasure?" I asked him, smiling my most seductive smile. As a peace offering from Max, he was not really my type, nor was he necessary tonight, but it was a nice gesture. "How can I help you, Mr . . . ?"

"Detective Mitchell Greer, Miss Griffin. And most definitely business." He gave me a stern look and flashed his badge briefly. "I'd like to ask you a few questions about Thursday night and one of the customers here. I believe you were acquainted with him." He settled commandingly into the chair behind Max's desk, leaving me with two obvious options. I could remain standing before him like a schoolgirl called to the principal's office or I could sit in one of the side chairs like a prospective employee to be interviewed and grilled. I liked neither of these options, so I walked to the bar and poured myself another drink, mostly to steady my now shaking hands. I lounged against the bar and waited for him to continue.

"Bill Andrews, did you know him?" he asked, all the while studying my face with those incredible eyes.

I saw no reason not to tell most of what had occurred. There was, I felt, still no way that I could be connected to his death. No one, especially not this man, could believe in what I am. And perhaps, if I were subtle enough in my prying, I could discover the true cause of Bill's death, and salve my conscience.

"Yes, Detective Greer, I met him here that night. We drank and danced, as I remember. Then he took a taxi home; he had overindulged a bit. I read about his death in the paper the next day."

He seemed surprised at the openness of my answer. "And just how well did you know him, Miss Griffin? I suppose he was a regular here."

"No, he had never been here before to my knowledge. I can't even imagine how you knew he'd been here at all."

He reached into his pocket and pulled out a pack of matches. "He had these in his coat. His wife said that he didn't smoke, and that they had never been here together, so we assumed he had been here that night and met someone. An employee here said that you and Bill were together, and Max Hunter confirmed that the two of you had left the dance floor together." He smugly put the matches back into his pocket.

Max? I thought. Why would he willingly give my name to someone in a situation like this? He of all people knew that one night in jail, or one day, could easily kill me. I tried to keep the anger at bay, but when I spoke, my response was scornful and more a reaction to Max than to this man. "I guess that is an example of brilliant investigative work. Nice job, Detective." I bared my teeth in more of a grimace than a smile.

Astonishingly, he smiled back, a disarming sort of smile that made him look years younger. "Well," he admitted sheepishly, "it's not exactly brilliant, but it gave us the only lead we have. To be perfectly honest, we can't really discover much of a motive in this case and we were hoping to find one here."

I softened a bit toward him, and then realized that that was probably his intention. "I really wish I could help you," I said stiffly, "but I'm afraid that I am just as puzzled as you. I did not know him very well, we had only just met that evening, you see. He did not seem to be the sort that would be involved in anything that would result in his death."

"He also didn't seem the sort that would be involved with someone like you. But apparently he was. You and he were reported to have slipped away to some back room here at the club. Would you mind explaining what transpired between the two of you?" His smile had gone and he was again an uncompromising inquisitor.

"I do not care for the tone of your voice or the implications you seem to be making, Detective. Someone here should be able to back up my statement that he took a taxi home, alone. In view of that fact, I can't see that what happened between the two of us is any of your business."

He gave me another of his sharp, appraising stares. "It is my business when what happens is against the law."

"And exactly what are the charges? Drinking? Dancing without a license? Corrupting the morals of an attorney?"

"Miss Griffin, this is not a joke. While certainly not as serious as some crime, prostitution is still against the law. And it's my job to enforce that law. You'll find that I take my job very seriously.

I must have stared at him in shock for a few seconds. Prostitution? And all the while I thought he was questioning me for the murder of Bill Andrews. I began to laugh, softly at first, then loudly and for a long time. "I'll have to thank you for this, Detective, when I recover," I said between bursts of laughter. "I haven't been so amused for a long time."

He seemed confused by my outburst, then a shy smile brushed his face. "Another great piece of investigative work, huh? The evidence seemed so overwhelming, you coming here so often, meeting so many men. Well, it just didn't look right."

I guessed this was as close as he would get to an apology and I was so relieved at not being suspected in the murder of Bill Andrews that I let him off the hook.

"Trust me," I said still smiling, "my morals may not be impeccable, but I do not take money in return for my favors." Not in this lifetime, anyway, I added silently. "For one thing, I don't need to."

He looked at me in puzzlement, so I went on. "In my business I make a profit of around seven figures a year. I own Griffin Designs." When his confused expression did not clear. I explained further. "I'm a fashion designer, women's clothes. You must be a confirmed bachelor not to have heard of me."

"Divorced, actually," he admitted reluctantly. "I'm sorry I misunderstood; it's been a long day and I'm very tired."

"Well then, if there's nothing else I can help you with . . ."

The phone rang and he answered it without hesitation. I found myself admiring his forcefulness—here in Max's office where the furniture, I knew, cost more than he would make in a year, he was at ease and in command. Mitchell Greer was not a man easily intimidated or impressed by the trappings of wealth.

"Yes, this is Greer," he said. "What's up?" As he listened intently to the caller, all traces of amusement vanished from his face. "Another one? Where?" he questioned. Then, "Who was it? That's strange, otherwise it matches the m.o. pretty well." He ran his fingers in a tired gesture through his hair. "I'll be over as soon as I finish up here." He hung up the phone with a bang.

"I'm sorry I was so unreasonable with you, Miss Griffin, but this case has me bothered. After all my years on the force, I've still never quite gotten used to the violence." He gave me a wan little smile. "Thank you for your time tonight. Send me a bill if you want, I enjoyed your company."

I was more concerned with his telephone conversation, than his attempt at humor. "Can you tell me what is happening? I live in the area and if there is a maniac roaming the streets, I would like to be prepared." My eyes searched out his, made contact and held him there, hesitant and undecided about how much he should reveal. Had he been just slightly more forceful he might have been able to avoid my questions.

"I shouldn't really say anything, but I can't see what harm it would do. There's been another murder, but it doesn't seem to match, somehow. This one was a prostitute that frequents the area—there must be a connection somewhere but I just can't see it. It's just so odd, that they both died the same way."

"Can you tell me," my eyes were locked on his, "can you tell me how they died?"

"Damndest thing I've ever seen," he admitted, pulling away from my gaze and walking slowly to the door, "no signs of violence, no large wounds, but every drop of blood was drained from the bodies."

I felt a surge of excitement, and lowered my eyes to hide it from him, but he was not looking at me.

"Good night, Miss Griffin." He closed the door softly behind him.

I sank to the couch in amazement. Finally after all these years here was a sign of another of my kind—in the same city, the same area in which I operated. While I might have been responsible for the death of Bill Andrews, however improbable it seemed, I knew nothing of the girl. No, it had to be someone else like me and I would find them.

Plans began to race through my mind furiously; could I investigate the murders myself without becoming too obvious about my interest? I knew from past experiences that it didn't pay to get too deeply involved with the law—maybe Max could . . .

Max—in my reaction to the information supplied by Detective Greer I had forgotten about Max and his recent role in the investigation. What game was he playing? Did he feel pressured to put me under suspicion to protect the club? To protect his reputation? Would it be bad for business if people were afraid to come to the Ballroom, due to too many murders in the neighborhood?

At that moment the door opened again and Max entered. "Deirdre," he called tentatively, "are you still here?"

"Afraid that Greer took me in for the murder of Bill Andrews, Max?" Suddenly I was angry, totally enraged, out of control. Before I knew I had moved, I was across the room, slamming the door and grasping his shoulders in a grip designed to hurt. I dug my nails in and felt the material shred beneath my fingers. "You bastard, Max. You knew he'd be here; you set me up for this. Why else would you have called me, pleading with me to see you tonight? Greer needed a murderer and you delivered one to him. Well, it didn't work, he doesn't suspect me."

He flinched and I realized I had drawn blood. I could feel its warmth oozing onto my fingertips, the thought that I had gone too far with him intensified my anger. "I could kill you very easily right now. Unfortunately, I would be a serious suspect in that murder." As I pushed him away I noticed a gleam in his eyes. I walked to the door, trying to calm myself, wondering at the deepness of my rage. I didn't want him dead, just frightened and in my control. In a gesture designed to unnerve him, I proceeded to lick the traces of his blood from my hands. He watched me, with a look of fascination on his face. Then, to my surprise, he turned his back to me, took off his jacket and began to unbutton his shirt.

"Care to finish what you started, my dear?" He turned around and I saw deep ruts in his shoulders, each surrounded with drops of congealing blood. I turned my head away in answer, disgusted at my behavior. "No? Well then, let me just clean up a bit and we'll talk about it all." I looked at him again and saw that he had wiped the blood from his arms with his shirt. He discarded both the shirt and jacket into the wastebasket and went to the closet behind his desk to get new clothes.

"No, Max," I said desperately, anxious to leave him. The taste of his blood lingered in my mouth, the smell of his blood in the air. "There's been enough talk for one night. I must go now." I left the room and closed the door behind me. Leaning up against it, I tried to catch my breath. What was happening? I wondered, how could I lose control so quickly? If he had shown the slightest trace of fear I would have been on him in seconds, my teeth imbedded tightly in his neck. I recalled the gratifying feel of his torn flesh beneath my fingers and shivered.

"Damn," I swore softly, then hurried down the hall toward the exit, to put as much distance between us as possible. Soon I was running, as if pursued by all the demons of my past and present. The doorman hailed a taxi and I rode into the comfort of the night.

Chapter 5

The roses began to arrive at my office on Monday afternoon, bouquets of massive, deep-red blooms overwhelming in their fragrance and their beauty. Every day that week another arrangement was delivered, each one more spectacular than the previous. No cards were included but I knew who had sent them. They all had Max's signature, a single pure black rose embedded amid the profusion of red. He had once, in an uncharacteristic, poetic mood, referred to me as a "rose clad in black." The mood had passed quickly and soon he was his cynical self, but the epithet had remained. Ever since, any gift or message he sent was accompanied by a black rose. He was, I knew, seeking forgiveness and a reconciliation. The first I could grant, given time. But the second seemed to be a risky venture. The passion and anger that he had inspired frightened me, more than I cared to admit even to myself. Yet, as the week went on, and the flowers continued to arrive, I began to soften towards him, the emotions I felt subsided. Perhaps I had misjudged him; he really had not had a chance to explain, maybe I did owe him that chance.

In actuality, I spent very little time worrying about Max and our relationship. Even the thought that there might be another of my kind prowling the city was pushed into the back of my mind. The week proved to be as busy as I had expected and I immersed myself in the work. I could lose my identity in the designs, following and coaxing the ideas and drawings into something with texture, something with a tangible beauty. By Friday evening, when my office was overflowing with flowers, all delicately displayed in tall alabaster vases, a similar array of colors decorated the rack of finished garments in the dressing rooms.

The show was now only a week away and we had made great progress. I worked like one obsessed and had expected no less of my employees. With the prospect of a free weekend ahead of them they had matched my long hours with few complaints and were now tired but relieved that the rush was behind us. The tasks that remained for the next week were the final fittings, some accessorizing, and the staging of the show itself, mostly work for Gwen, myself and a few of our top seamstresses.

When everyone else had left the building, Gwen entered my office bearing two cups of coffee, one so diluted with sugar and cream it lost all resemblance to its origin, and for me, one black and steaming. I took it from her appreciatively and gestured to one of the office chairs. She flopped down with a sigh.

"Tired?" I questioned, needlessly, for even in the dim light I could see the dark circles beneath her eyes.

"Tired doesn't even come close to describing it, Deirdre. I don't think I could move from this chair, even if the building were on fire. But you, you still look as good as you did first thing Monday morning. Come to think of it, you still look like you did almost ten years ago. However do you manage it?" Her tired eyes squinted at me.

"Clean living, Gwen," I joked. "I don't eat junk and I work like a dog. It's the Protestant work ethic, you know."

"Whatever it is, it sure works for you. I feel like I've aged twenty years in the past five days. I had an argument with Nick about it; he wanted to go out tonight, but if I let him see me like this, the wedding would be off."

"You're such an ass, Gwen; he loves you very much, tired or not. Go home, take a hot bath, chill a bottle of wine and invite him to your place. You can spend the entire weekend in bed if you're so tired."

"Deirdre, if I didn't know better I'd think you were jealous. Don't you and Max have plans? I just assumed that with all these flowers you two had something special going on."

"I hate to disappoint you, but there is nothing between Max and me, there never really was. Part of my secret is having no serious involvement with anybody." I smiled indulgently at her. "But you are already involved, so my advice comes too late. Go home, Gwen, and have a nice time."

She rose slowly from the chair and was walking to the door, when the intercom on my desk buzzed. We jumped in unison, having both supposed the office was empty. I answered and the front desk receptionist's voice filled the office.

"Miss Griffin, I'm sorry to bother you. I just came back upstairs to get something and found someone here waiting for you. Should I send him back?"

"I'll be right out to get him," Gwen broke in. She turned to me. "Nothing happening, huh? Finally I get to meet the great Max." With no trace of her professed exhaustion, she rushed out of the office and down the hall.

Unlike Gwen, I was not so sure that the visitor was Max. He had never before made any attempt to see me outside of the confines of the club, yet, given the precarious course our relationship had taken, he would have a better chance of making his explanations in person. Perhaps it was logical for him to make his appearance tonight.

I didn't have long to ponder the question, for I could hear Gwen's chattering approach my office.

"You're not anything like I pictured you, but it's nice to meet you. I'm sure Deirdre will be thrilled to see you. She's so maddeningly private about her life, she never even told me you'd be stopping here tonight. But I knew something was up, when all those beautiful flowers started to arrive. Here we are." She was so excited about the visitor as she escorted him into my office, I felt it was cruel to disillusion her but it was necessary.

"Gwen," I said as sharply as a slap and watched the smile fade from her face, "meet Detective Mitchell Greer."

"Oh, God, I'm so embarrassed." She flushed a bright red. "I'm sorry, Detective, I thought you were someone else."

"Obviously," he said with a kind smile, "but thank you for the greeting, anyway. People seldom meet me with such enthusiasm."

"No, I bet they don't," she started, then blushed more deeply. "I mean, or I didn't mean . . . oh, shit . . ."

"Gwen," I said reassuringly, "you're tired. Just go home, I'll see you later." With a muffled good night she scurried through the door and we were left alone.

I cleared my throat. "Your visit is such a surprise to Gwen and me. I have very few friends and none ever come here to the office. She just jumped to conclusions about who you are. I apologize if she embarrassed you." I knew it sounded as if I were babbling, but it seemed a good way to cover the nervousness I felt in his presence. "We were just about to leave for the night; had you come a few minutes later you would have found an empty office." I sat down behind my desk and began to restlessly shuffle papers around. "Sit down, please, and let me know how I can help you."

He glanced around the office for a few seconds. "Thank you," he said, sitting down, then abruptly, "Who died?"

I stiffened at his question, until I saw he was studying the flowers. "It is a bit excessive, isn't it?" I said with a small laugh, but supplied no further information. "Now, I hate to be rude, but it has been a long week and I am very tired. Can we get on with it?"

"Get on with it?"

"Yes, get on with it. Ask me your questions and then let me get out of here."

"Well," he began with infuriating slowness, "there is one very important question I'd like you to answer. Are you hungry?"

"Hungry?" What was he getting at? "Actually, I have been so busy this week, I can hardly remember my last meal. So, now that you mention it, yes, I am very hungry. Why do you ask?" His line of questioning worried me; there was no way for him to know of my habits and yet he was so unnerving. I rose from the desk and walked across the room to the flowers. Absently, I plucked a few of the drooping blooms, showering the credenza with a flood of scarlet petals.

He began to laugh. "No wonder you have so few friends, Miss Griffin. Don't you recognize a dinner invitation when you get one?" His face was lit with a mischievous smile and I could see that he was enjoying the situation.

His grin was infectious and I found myself smiling back. "Actually, I get very few dinner invitations and accept even fewer, so I never know how to react to them." I hesitated for a while; if this was a friendly gesture on his part, it would do no harm. If it was part of his investigation, still I could get more details on the progress of the case from him than from anyone else. He could be an invaluable help in tracking the murderer for me. "Yes," I replied at last, "I would like to have dinner with you. And since I assume you are not on official business, please call me Deirdre."

"Fine, if you'll drop the detective and call me Mitch. What would you like to eat? I know a place not far from here that's wonderful. Nothing fancy, but they serve good steaks and some seafood." He looked at me for my approval.

"A nice rare steak would be great for me. Just let me freshen up a bit and we can go."

As we rode the elevator, I wondered what on earth possessed me to accept the invitation. There was something about Mitch that intrigued me, but I was hardly in any position to begin or pursue a relationship with anyone. And my idea of a dinner date hardly coincided with his. But as the doors opened into the lobby and I met his eyes and matched his smile, I felt strangely content with the situation.

A car was parked at the curb, a rather dingy sedan of indeterminate color, but unmistakably his, as the placard in the window proudly proclaimed "Official Police Business".

"Business?" I questioned, giving him a sidelong glance as he opened the door.

"Well, no . . . I forgot to take it out of the window. Besides," he said wryly, tossing the sign into the back seat, "it was easier than finding a parking spot."

"Not above the law are you, Detective? While it may not be as serious a crime as some, illegal parking is still . . ." I mimicked the tone he took as our last meeting and he laughed, a nice honest sound.

"Okay, okay, let's drop it. To be perfectly truthful, I did start out on police business. It seemed a good idea to verify your identity, so I did some checking before I came up to your office."

"Did I check out satisfactorily?" I inquired, trying to establish a casual tone.

"Most definitely," he asserted. "You are Deirdre Griffin genius designer: hardworking, successful, ambitious and extremely wealthy." He maneuvered his car carefully into the early evening traffic, then gave me a shrewd glance. "And there may have been a few more adjectives used that I left out."

"I assume they were not all complimentary. Who provided you with this wealth of information?"

He glanced at me briefly, then gave a small shrug. "The usual sorts of informants: doormen, security guards, landlords and, uh, the editors of several fashion publications."

"Who, no doubt, were more than happy to supply you with all the details of my criminal activities. So, with what shall I be charged?" I felt secure in the knowledge that none of the mentioned persons could have anything incriminating to say about me.

"Other than asking an exorbitant amount for your clothes, and getting it—nothing, I'm happy to report." His voice lost all traces of humor. "Still I find it interesting that very little of your private life is known to anyone."

"Why should it be known?" I could hear the anger creeping into my voice. "It is private, after all."

"Don't get me wrong, I didn't mean to offend you. It's just that . . ." He hesitated for a second, considering his words. "You seem to live your life like a phantom, touching no one, leaving no impact on those around you. You hardly seem real."

"I'm real enough," I murmured, thinking myself a fool for accepting this date. He was too perceptive, too keen and I felt as if I was walking along a steep cliff merely by being with him. I glanced at him as he concentrated grimly on his driving. We sat in an uneasy silence; I turned my attention to the lights of the city flowing past the window.

I barely noticed when we stopped at the curb, until he reached over and gently touched my arm. "Deirdre," he said softly, pausing again to collect his thoughts. "I'm sorry. Don't be mad." He turned to look at me, his face seemed expressionless in the dark car. "I guess I just find it hard to believe that someone like you, with everything going for you—looks, talent, wealth—hasn't ever been married or pursued a serious relationship. It doesn't add up."

"I was married, once." My voice sounded small and lost. "He died." I looked out the window, trying to shake the fear and sadness. "I never talk about it."

"Oh, God," he began. "I'm . . ."

"Forget it," I interrupted. "I'm starving. Let's get that steak you promised. And please don't apologize any more tonight."

"Fine with me; let's go." He opened the door and came around to escort me out of the car. We walked down the dimly lit street to the restaurant, his arm comfortingly draped across my shoulders.

"Do you really enjoy that bloody mess of a meal?" I jumped guiltily at the question. Mitch was grinning broadly and pointing to my dinner plate. "You could send it back to the kitchen and have it cooked, you know."

I looked down and saw the small piece of remaining steak sitting amid a pool of red fluid that even the most dedicated gourmand would hesitate to call "au jus".

"It is cooked," I protested. "Well, anyway, it's warm. Have some, you might enjoy it." I offered it, and laughed at his grimace. "I should think, Detective, that with your job you would be better accustomed to the sight of blood."

"Blood, yes. But not to the sight of someone making a meal

of it." I caught my breath, but he went on happily, not noticing. "You really should have had the fettucini, it's much healthier. All this garlic is good for the digestion."

I crinkled my nose in distaste. "My digestion is just fine, thank you." I pushed my plate aside and poured myself another glass of wine. The waiter came to clear the table and offer coffee and dessert. The restaurant had been crowded when we entered, but was now empty except for us and an elderly couple who had just been seated. When the waiter returned with pie for Mitch, coffee for us both, and the tab was paid, we were left virtually alone.

"Thank you for the dinner," I said sincerely. "It was nice of you to ask me."

"My pleasure," he said. He reached across the table and took my hand. "Next time, I'll pick some place a little fancier."

"This place is just fine. I didn't expect fancy," I said noncommittally. There would be no next time. He was human, not someone I could afford to get involved with. Still, I felt a twinge of sadness about using him to track the other. I had discovered over dinner that I liked Mitch, and thought that I would miss his sharp eyes and dry humor when it was all over. I inadvertently sighed at my own thoughts.

"Do you want to go?" he asked solicitously. "It's not late and I have tomorrow off for a change. I thought maybe we could go somewhere and talk, or just drive around, or . . ."

"Go to your place?" I finished the thought with a smile.

"Well, now that you mention it, yes." He still had hold of my hand and pulled me up from my seat with a boyish eagerness. I did not resist, but allowed him to steer me out of the restaurant and into the car.

As it turned out, Mitch's apartment was no more than three blocks from my hotel. He lived in an area midway between the exclusiveness of where I lived, worked and fed, and the terrible poverty on the other side. Undoubtedly I had passed this street in my search for a victim less than a week ago. I must have given him a doubtful look as we exited the car; he was quick to reassure me. "It may look like no-man's land, but it's really quite nice and relatively safe. Besides you're in the protection of one of the city's finest, remember?"

"I was just surprised at how close we actually live to one another." Clasping my arm in his, we walked up the steps to his building, a rather typical, nondescript stone structure.

"So near and yet so far, right?" he joked. "I know where you live. My brilliant investigative work again, remember? I only hope you don't feel too far below your league." He was still smiling, but I noticed a look of doubt enter his eyes.

"Now that is just plain silly, Mitch. I may be rich now, but I came from very humble beginnings and have had my share of hard knocks, believe me." I moved closer to him as we climbed the few stairs to the entrance.

When he opened the door on his apartment, I discovered a small place, tastefully decorated and painstakingly neat. The walls were lined with bookshelves on all sides, crowded with an amazingly diverse selection of books. A complete set of Shakespeare stood next to a row of cheap detective novels, science fiction mingled with astronomy and pure science volumes, legal textbooks competed with famous erotic works. He watched as I studied this array. "I read a lot," he said casually. "Can I get you a drink?" He was heading toward a small kitchenette, while removing his tie and loosening his collar.

"Wine, if you have some, please," I replied, settling into what looked like his reading chair. Several books were stacked on the small end table and I perused his current reading material.

"Cabernet, okay?" he called from the kitchen.

"That would be wonderful." I picked up a small volume of poetry on the top of the pile. It opened of itself to a dog-eared page and a marked passage. I read it softly to myself.

In the desert
I saw a creature, naked, bestial,
Who, squatting upon the ground,
Held his heart in his hands,
And ate of it.
I said: "Is it good, friend?"

"It is bitter—bitter," he answered;
"But I like it
Because it is bitter,
And because it is my heart."

I laid it back on the table, and in doing so jostled the stack. On the bottom was an obviously new copy of a book extremely familiar to me. I pulled it from the table and held it in my hands; the price tag, still intact, did nothing to obscure the title, which flashed at me in blood red letters, *The Annotated Dracula.* As I hurriedly replaced it, my pulse racing, Mitch returned with the wine and glasses.

"Not my normal nightly reading," he said, pouring us each a glass of wine, "but I must admit I found it rather fascinating. Have you read it?"

"Yes, some time ago," I admitted, "but surely this sort of thing is completely ridiculous. You can't think that the recent murders were actually committed by a vampire." The dreaded word, that I tried to avoid even in my own thoughts, seemed to hang heavy in the air. The voice that said it sounded high-pitched and slightly hysterical.

He looked at me with the intense gaze that so unnerved me. Every instinct cried out that this man is a danger—strike, Deirdre, it urged. Strike, kill and flee. The blood thirst, which no amount of rare steak could assuage, welled up within me. I will take him, I thought, without mercy, as an enraged wolf will take even an armed man, savage and quick. I moved in his direction, feeling my teeth enlarge, scenting the blood beating in his veins. I saw myself reflected, wild and feral, in his eyes; somewhere within me, a voice called for caution, but I ignored it. God, how I wanted this man's blood.

Then, thankfully he dropped his eyes and began to laugh. "You're really spooked by this, aren't you?" he said, still laughing. "No, of course I don't think we have a real vampire on the loose. But we may have someone who *thinks* that he is. I just didn't think it would hurt to bone up a little on the legends, just in case I could find something that might trip our man up."

"And you think it's a man?" I rose from the chair and walked to the window, trying to compose myself.

"We're not entirely sure, of course. But it seems unlikely that it's a woman. Both victims were tough, each in their own way. Andrews worked out quite frequently, and the girl had street smarts, a real scrapper. I just can't see a woman being able to subdue either one of them long enough to drain their blood."

"How was the blood drained?" My voice sounded casual again, curious but not too eager. I had managed to submerge my desires, for the moment, and turned away from the window and sat down again.

"We don't really know yet; a syringe perhaps. Although our 'vampire,'" I cringed at the word, "was cautious enough to leave the obligatory bruises and fang marks on their necks. But that could be easily faked, I suppose. Pathology is working on it."

I made a sort of noncommittal grunt and he gave me an appraising glance. "You know, I didn't bring you here to discuss police business." He offered me a glass of wine and I accepted it, gratified to notice that my hand was steady.

"Why did you bring me here, Mitch? To be perfectly honest, you seem to be above pursuing a one-night stand and you've already discovered that I'm not the type to sustain a relationship." I felt betrayed by the situation that forced me to remember and echo the hurtful words once said to me in a dark field, under a clear night sky. Regardless of what could be assumed from my seemingly promiscuous behavior every week at the club, I had not made love without feeding since the night I heard similar words issue from Max. I was not even sure that I could perform sexually now *without* the taking of blood. A silence fell over us as I occupied myself with draining my glass and refilling it. His wine had not been touched.

"You sure don't pull any punches, do you?" His voice sounded harsh, but his eyes were kind. "I think you give yourself too little credit and me too much. But let's just say that I brought you here because you're the first woman I've reacted to since the divorce and I wanted to prolong our evening." He turned and went to a small stereo system on one of his bookcases. "Would you like to dance?" he asked with a shy smile.

"That I can do," I said and as I entered his arms and we merged with the music, all awkwardness vanished. The thoughts of guilt and deceit, death and blood all fell from me, leaving me with only a body that enjoyed the rhythmic closeness of another and a mind that relished the thought that the neck so warm above my mouth need never be violated by my hunger.

The night sped by, occupied as we were with dance and conversation. A bond had begun to grow between us, incongruous as it seemed. Mitch, I discovered, was a complex and fascinating person. His natural reticence dissolved with the wine we drank, and he told me of his private life. He talked of his earlier aspirations of a career in law, and how that was abandoned due to the financial aspects of an unexpected pregnancy. "I was thrilled with the baby," he explained, "and I didn't mind leaving school for him." Two years ago, his wife filed for divorce. "She said she was tired of struggling with the problems of being a policeman's wife, tired of waiting for the late night call to say I'd been killed or injured." They'd had no other children but the son, Chris. Mitch's eyes shown with a quiet pride when he spoke of him. "He'll graduate from law school this summer," he said with a rueful grin, "so the cycle will be complete." They kept in touch by phone and letters and occasional visits. "I'd like you to meet him next time he comes in; he'd really think old Dad hit the big time."

"Have you?" I asked, getting up from the couch and making a halfhearted attempt to tidy up the wine glasses and bottles that had accumulated during the evening.

"Who knows? Stranger things have happened." He smiled at me as I went into the kitchen.

Once there, I glanced at the clock and saw it was nearly six. "God, Mitch," I called to him, "how did it get so late? I've really got to go."

"Stay and watch the sunrise with me?" He came up behind me and rested his chin on my shoulder. His voice was soft and scratchy in my ear. "I'd like to see the sunlight in your hair."

"I can't, Mitch. You may have the day off tomorrow, or I should say today, but I have details to take care of that can't wait. I stayed too long as it is, and although it has been a lovely evening . . ." I could not remember what time sunup was, but I knew it was close. I had to leave soon.

"I've had too much wine to drive you, but at least let me walk you back to your hotel." He moved to get his coat.

"That would be nice," I said, considering the situation, "but let's make it the office instead. I can catch a few hours sleep on the couch until Gwen gets in. It's only a few more blocks, can you stagger that far?"

He laughed. "I imagine so, if you can."

"Never fear, Detective. I can drink a lot more than I have tonight and still find my way home in the dark." I moved toward the door and he followed.

On the streets we walked arm in arm, silent once more, but no longer uneasy with each other. The sky was dark and cloudy with no sign of the impending dawn, but I could feel my body's warnings begin. I quickened my step involuntarily and he looked at me questioningly.

"In a hurry?" he asked abruptly.

"Yes," I answered simply and we were quiet once more until we were within a block of the office.

"God damn it, Deirdre, slow down, will you." He pulled my arm sharply as we stood at a corner. "I have some questions to ask you."

I winced from his tight grip and he lightened it a bit, but still kept hold as if he thought I would run away. "Can't it wait, Mitch? I have to get some sleep soon or I'll drop."

"No, it can't wait. It's important."

"Isn't it a little late to be discussing police business, Mitch? I can't think what else would be so critical that it didn't come up earlier." My fear of the approaching sunrise forced me to speak sharply.

"Don't be so damned jumpy, not everything I do or say is connected with my job. I'm a man, too and I want some answers." His eyes searched mine and held them for a second, then fell away to study the empty street.

He paused for a long time, avoiding my gaze. I waited as patiently as was possible for me.

Hurriedly, he blurted it out. "Who sent the flowers?"

"What?" I could hardly make the connection.

"The flowers that were overflowing in your office. Who sent them?"

"Max."

"That's it. Just Max?"

"Yes, Mitch, he sent the flowers. What else do you want me to say?"

"Why?"

I sighed before I answered. "We had an argument and they were his way of trying to apologize. That's all." I could feel the precious minutes before dawn ticking away.

"Who did Gwen think I was when I came in last night?" He met my eyes again for a while before looking away.

"I suppose she thought you were Max. Look, Mitch. I can't see where all this is leading, but I really do have to go."

"This is where it's leading," he said and pulled me to him roughly. His lips met mine with a hunger and urgency so deep, I began to realize what my victims must feel with my kiss. As when we had danced earlier that evening, I responded to him without thought for my condition. It had been more years than I cared to remember since I had been kissed like this by someone I liked, someone I had no intention of feeding upon.

He broke away first and we were both breathless and shaken. "I'm sorry, Deirdre," he said, studying my face. "You can be so damn contrary at times. All I wanted to know was, who's the competition?"

"After that kiss, you should know you have none." I put my hands up and caressed his face. It was stubbly. "But," I laughed, "you need a shave and I need some sleep. Can we go now?"

"Certainly," he said, extending his arm. We slowly walked the last block to my office building and entered the lobby. The security guard nodded to us, he was a regular and recognized me. He gave Mitch a sleepy look, then returned to his paper.

Suddenly I felt awkward again, like a school girl, until Mitch gathered me into his arms. It was a brief kiss, for we both could feel the guard's surprise and interest.

"Can I see you tomorrow?"

"I don't know," I said honestly. "Call me later and we'll talk. Good night." I gave his cheek one final caress and went to the elevator.

"Good night," he said softly and walked out the door. Before the elevator began its rise, I could see the street already lightening with the dawn.

Chapter 6

While my own personal library was not nearly as extensive as Mitch's, it was interesting to note that we possessed at least two books in common. One was a small volume of Stephen Crane's poetry, with the same page and passage marked. Another was *The Annotated Dracula*. I also possessed a much older copy of the original text of *Dracula* by Bram Stoker. In my mind, I referred to these as my survival manual; the poetry to keep me sane and the other to keep me alive.

When I had awakened in my hospital bed following the accident, I had no actual knowledge of what had occurred. I knew, merely, that I had lived and that all I loved had perished. My mind was filled with odd desires and visions, but the medical profession at the time was not concerned with mental soundness. They healed my body to the best of their abilities and sent me back into the world.

I returned to an empty house, the house in which I had been born, and four years later, in which my mother died giving birth to a still-born boy. It had always been filled with light and love, but now seemed too dark, too lifeless. It had never been empty before; I had shared it with my father, who with his exuberance and joy made it into a home. When I married it was to this house we returned after our wedding trip; so that even with my father's peaceful death two years later, I had not been alone.

I found I could not sleep through the night; I would rise within an hour of retiring to pace and stalk the empty rooms until, close to dawn, I would fall into bed and sleep through most of the next morning and afternoon. The smell and taste of food were repugnant to me; I had always been slender, but four weeks following my release from the hospital, the mourning clothes I had worn for my father's death hung on me like meal sacks, without the aid of heavy corsets. My face grew gaunt; my moods black and despairing. I would sit in the rocking chair in the parlor, hugging my emaciated arms to myself, humming odd bits of lullabies and popular songs.

One morning, too tired to climb the stairs, I remained huddled in the darkened parlor. I knew I would die if I stayed in that chair, and I wanted death to come, waited impatiently for its arrival. But my vigil was interrupted by a knock on the door.

"Go away," I tried to call out, but discovered that my voice was scratchy and hoarse with disuse. My visitor opened the door and entered, giving a gasp of surprise at what she probably supposed was my corpse. I turned my head to her and gave her a skeletal grin. "Good morning, Mrs. Blake," I croaked, "so nice of you to call. How are you today?"

She had been carrying parcels, direct from the market, which she dropped, scattering their contents on the hallway floor.

"Oh, my poor dear." She came rushing to me, and crushed me in a bosomy embrace. "I had no idea you would be so . . . well, you look so. . . . Honey, when I walked in I just thought you were dead." She held me out at arms' length and clucked her disapproval. "Hasn't anyone besides me stopped to see you, to take care of you?"

"I think people did knock. I just never answered the door and they didn't come in." Her presence began to revive me, warm me; she was so alive.

"Well, never let it be said that I let a closed door keep me from doing my Christian duty." She began to bustle around the room, neatening and straightening.

I suppressed a giggle at the accurate summation of her personality. "Daddy always said you were a good . . ."

"Hush, child," she interrupted, peering at me with watery blue eyes. "Your daddy always said I was an interfering old busybody. And maybe he was right, but I can't just sit here and let you waste away, if only for your mother's sake. Now, have you seen the doctor?"

I shook my head. "He can't help me, just let me die."

"I'll do no such thing and I won't hear any more talk of dying. Now, we'll get you cleaned up and dressed and off to the doctor."

She half carried me up the stairs, bathed me and dressed me as if I were a child. I succumbed to her attentions and let myself be coddled and comforted. It was such a joy for me to hear a human voice again, and Mrs. Blake provided a more than adequate amount of talk.

As she helped me back down the stairs, I stumbled and fell, face forward into her neck. "Oh, Mrs. Blake," I whispered, half fainting, "your perfume is wonderful."

"Perfume? Bah! What call would an old biddy like me have for wearing perfume? While you're at it, have that doctor check your nose, too."

We reached the bottom of the stairs and she realized that the parcels she had carried in were still strewn on the floor. "Let me just put these away for now. When we get back, I'll make you a nice supper." She gathered everything and went into the kitchen, returning with a look of disapproval. "I can see no cooking's been done in that room for a month of Sundays. You need some looking after, that's a fact."

"Thank you, Mrs. Blake," I said meekly and allowed her to hurry me to the doctor's office under bleak, overcast skies.

* * *

After a thorough examination, I sat in a cold, uncomfortable leather chair awaiting his verdict. He sat across the desk, fingertips touching, and tapped his two forefingers against his lips. "I can't find anything physically wrong with you, other than the fact that you are close to starvation. My advice to you is go home, eat a good dinner and try to start your life over. You can't grieve forever." He gave me a patronizing smile and pushed his chair back. "Have the dreams stopped?"

"Dreams? What dreams?" I said confusedly. "I don't remember any dreams."

"It's probably just as well. You had some rather terrible dreams while you were in the hospital, brought on, I believe, by the shock of the accident. If you can't remember, then you must be getting over it." He got up from the desk and stood over me. "Now, Dorothy, I want to talk to you, not as a doctor, but as one of your father's friends. This part of the country is no place for a woman without a man to protect her, especially now, with the whole place in an uproar over the coming war. You should give some thought to marrying again. No, certainly not right away," he amended, seeing the shock his words caused, "but later on. You're relatively young and attractive; that, plus the money your father left you, makes you eminently marriageable. In fact, I have a nephew in Lawrence, a widower with four children who could use a wife of your breeding and background. Why don't I talk to him and see what can be arranged."

"Thank you, Doctor." I looked away from him, trying to hide my distaste at the suggestion. I had no desire to be married to a stranger, raising some other woman's children when I could have none of my own. But I deferred to him as was appropriate for the times.

"That's a good girl," He patted my arm in a fatherly gesture, seeming well pleased with himself. "Now go home and eat something. Come back in a month or so and we'll see how you're getting along." He escorted me out of the office.

* * *

Mrs. Blake babbled indignantly all the way home. "I know his nephew, my dear. Already balding and round about the middle. His wife died in childbirth, you know, delivering their fourth baby in as many years. Shameful, the way some people carry on. And telling you to go home and eat; why, I could have told you the same thing and saved us all the time. Oh, no," she cried suddenly, interrupting herself, "speaking of time, I promised Frances I'd meet her at the church this afternoon. We're setting up for the social tomorrow night. I guess if you need me, I could stay on a bit, but you know how Frances is. Oh, dear, I'd never hear the end of it."

"I'll be fine, Mrs. Blake, don't worry about me. In fact after this walk I feel a great deal better." I lied about this, the sun was burning my eyes and skin and I felt weaker than before. But I had had enough company for the day and longed for my solitude again. "Don't keep Frances waiting, she'll never forget it." I smiled at her wearily and my words seemed to reassure her.

"If you're sure you'll be fine . . . now, mind you, cook up some of that good food I left you. There's a roast, some new potatoes and some milk to mash them with."

"Thank you." Impulsively, I gave her a small hug.

"There, there, child. It will all come out right, just you see. I'll be over tomorrow to see how you are." She saw me to my front door, then hurried away, bewailing her lateness.

I dutifully went into the kitchen and began to make preparations for my dinner. I put on a pot of water to boil the potatoes and turned my attention to the meat. It had sat while we were gone, and as I unwrapped the butcher paper my nose was assailed with the odor of blood and meat, slightly gamy, but still good. Suddenly I was ravenously hungry. I couldn't wait for the roast to cook in its entirety, but decided to cut a slice for pan frying. In my haste with the knife, I nicked the tip of my finger and put it into my mouth to suck the wound.

The first taste of my own blood almost knocked me senseless, but I continued to draw on the small cut until it was dry. Disappointed, I picked up the knife to cut myself again, until I saw the half-carved roast still on the table. This should suit me, I thought to myself as I picked it up and brought it to my mouth. I bit into the meat and pulled what blood I could from it. When the juices were all drained, I was left with a grayish husk, which I nevertheless devoured, tearing it with my teeth, teeth that suddenly felt odd, too large for my mouth. They interfered with my chewing of the raw meat. I discarded what was left of the roast, mostly fat and gristle, and went in search of a mirror to look at my teeth.

I don't know what I expected to see in the mirror but what I saw surprised me. There was no demon, no shadowy image, only my face staring back at me. But this was not the face I wore that morning. It was blood spattered from my struggle with the roast, but through the blood I could see that the gauntness had gone, the hollows beneath my eyes had been filled, and my skin had regained some of its normal coloring. I pulled my upper lip back to examine my teeth, the canines seemed longer, sharper and I felt them cautiously. Then even as I watched they seemed to diminish back to their normal size. I shook my head to dispel the image and whispered softly.

"God, what is happening to me?"

I thought back to my pregnancy and remembered the odd whims and cravings that went with that period of my life. This, also, I rationalized, was probably no more than a passing phase, something that would not continue. And, though mentally confused, I realized that for the first time in over a month, I felt physically well. The severe lassitude had gone, replaced by such a wonderful feeling of wellness and wholeness. I attacked the household chores with a fervor I had seldom felt before, and when I collapsed into my bed shortly before dawn, the house was fit for viewing by a thousand Mrs. Blakes.

Unfortunately, the bizarre meal of that day and the shock of health and activity that followed had an adverse effect on my sleep. I began to dream, slow, winding dreams that carried me far down the corridor of my life.

I walk down a hallway. It is dark with many doors on each side. I slowly open the doors, one by one. I enter a room which contains the coffin of my mother; I know it to be hers because I am so small, I have to be lifted to see her face, pale and lifeless. I run from the room into another, to find my father, lying in his bed, motionless. He is dead, too, I know and I touch his cheek in a soft farewell before I leave. The next door I open carefully, knowing who is here. This coffin is sealed, but I try to open the lid. I had been denied a last view of this face and I want to see him again. Tears stream down my face, and I struggle with the heavy wood, scratching at the casket lid to no avail. My fingernails break and bleed, blood is flowing from my hands in concert with my tears.

The odor of blood fills the room. I put my fingers up to my mouth and suck. Suddenly, I am not alone. I can see no one, but feel a breath, hot on my back, and an urgent mouth pressed to my neck. I push away and run the length of the corridor. It seems endless and I run forever, laughter pursuing me, chasing me down to the final door.

This door I open in trepidation to find a wondrous sight. I am outdoors, on a clear summer night, in a sweet smelling field. I lie down on the grass, slightly wet but still warm from the day's sun. I admire the stars; they are bright and beautiful and seem to speak to me of peace and contentment.

"This must be heaven," I whisper, afraid to break the mood, when suddenly the sky grows dark.

An enormous black overwhelms the stars; it shifts its form, coalescing into the shape of a giant bird, man-sized and elegant. It hovers above me, as if in homage to my prone body, silently asking permission. I smile and stretch my arms to it; it descends upon me and I caress its wings, glossy as silk.

I feel no shame as I realize my clothes have disappeared, for it covers my naked body with a rustling sigh. It—no, he—is dark and beautiful like the night, my skin against the ebony feathers is the pale white reflection of the moon, the stars. The coming together seems as natural, as inevitable as the tides. I welcome even the pain of his penetration, giving myself entirely to this creature of the night. We are one. His beak grazes my breasts, closing upon the nipples, and I gasp. He smells of blood, a perfume so intoxicating I almost faint. But his movement within me quickens and my body responds. "Oh, God," I cry as he fills me with the blackness of the sky.

He gazes at me, with wise crow's eyes and promises future delights, then rises from me on strong wings. There is no feeling of emptiness when he departs, just a serene acceptance of this mystery. My thighs are sticky and warm. I lie there for what seems an eternity when suddenly above the soft night noises, I hear a strange tearing sound. I turn on my side, as curious as a child to witness this new event.

The giant bird is systematically stripping the flesh from the bones of two bodies, one full-grown, the other piteously small. I want to cradle these two, bring them back to life, but I cannot move, cannot call out. I gasp and the bird stops its mutilation and turns to me, laughing. It is his laugh, the laughter of the corridor, but the face on the bird is mine . . .

"You must kill it," I shrieked. "Kill it before it grows larger." I realized I was grasping at someone's sleeve, my head burrowing into a warm lap. I open my eyes to see the broad, friendly face of Mrs. Blake, concern in her eyes. "Oh, it was so horrible," I began haltingly. "I didn't know. It was so beautiful, so dark, but so evil. How could I know? And I let it touch me and then it was tearing the flesh from their bones . . ." My mind stopped in mid-thought. "I can't seem to remember it all, but it is important. I must try to remember."

"Now, now, dearie, it seems to me you should just forget it. It was only a bad dream, after all." She looked at me critically. "How do you feel now?"

As my fear dissipated, I relaxed and stretched, considering her question. "Actually, I feel good." There was a note of surprise in my voice; I could hardly believe my physical state. "Better than good, I feel . . ." I paused, searching for the right word. "I feel reborn, as if this last, terrible month has been washed away." To emphasize my words I arose from the bed and led her in a wild, whirling dance through the bedroom.

She was flushed and breathless when we finally stopped. "Well, child," she puffed, "you certainly seem fit enough. I knew a good meal and a good sleep would set you up righter than rain." She beamed at me and nodded her head, taking full credit for my recovery.

"That's right, Mrs. Blake. You can tell them all that you did it, you and that beautiful, beautiful roast you brought."

"Well, I did have the butcher cut it special for me. I brought you another just like it, I did, when I saw that you had eaten the other." At my look of shock—had she watched me eat it?—she laughed. "You see, child, I let myself in earlier, you were sleeping like a baby and I didn't like to disturb you. But I did think I could help out with the cleaning and such. You beat me to it, though, didn't you?" She didn't wait for an answer but continued. "Hard work is a good cure for what ails you. Anyway, what I meant to say was that I noticed when I was in the kitchen that you'd eaten it all. So I ran out and got another. It's cooking right now, can't you smell it?"

Now that she had called it to my attention, I could indeed smell it; the nauseating smell of roasting flesh permeated the air. I would have to get her out of here, or she would sit down with me and force me to eat every bite. My mind raced, trying to come up with an excuse for her to leave, when I thought back to our conversation yesterday.

"What time is it?" I asked.

"Oh, about half past five. You slept a good long time."

"But Mrs. Blake," I said in mock horror, "don't you have to be at church tonight?"

"Goodness, yes I do! Seeing you put it clean out of my mind. But will you be all right? I don't want to leave, somehow. You seem good now, but yesterday," she clucked her tongue, "well, I don't mind saying you gave me quite a scare there." She rose. "If you're sure . . ."

"I'll be fine," I said reassuringly, restraining myself from giving her a push. "Have a nice evening."

I waited no more than a minute after I heard the door shut behind her, to rush down the stairs and try to salvage what was left of the meat.

It was almost completely cooked, I discovered as I cut slice after slice, frantically looking for small patches of red flesh. I nibbled on one small piece, pink in the middle, but it tasted like clay. I opened the kitchen door and tossed it, pan and all, into the small yard. Then I opened the doors and windows wide to clear the odor and sat down on the porch steps.

The sun was setting and the autumn air growing chilly, but I did not feel the cold. I stared into the approaching night as if answers could be found there, in the darkness. Suddenly, I sensed the stealthy approach of something nearing my house. I tensed and listened, relaxing when I picked up the soft padding of paws and the quiet breathy pants. The creature slowly came into view. It was a dog, a stray by the looks of the ribs showing through its fur. I could still smell the odor of the roast in the air; it was this that had brought him so near. "You have it, dog," I said quietly. "It does me no good." He sidled past me and fell to devouring the meat savagely.

When he had finished, he looked at me questioningly, with a half wag of his tail. "No, boy, there's no more. Come here." Surprisingly, he came right to me, and with one sniff of my opened hand, he settled in on the porch with me.

He rested his scruffy chin on my knee and I scratched his pointed ears. "It's a strange world, dog," I confided to him, "where a mongrel like you can eat a fine meal, while I have to go hungry."

He gazed at me with trusting eyes and his tail thumped with a hollow sound on the wooden porch planks. I began to cry, silent tears streaming coldly down my cheeks in the night air. He hunched over close to me, offering what comfort he could and I buried my face in his soft fur. Instinctively, without thought, I pushed aside his thick hair with my tongue and sank my teeth into his neck. He snarled softly, whined, then relaxed as I was rewarded with the thick, salty flow. I took no more than two or three swallows, when, in horror at what I had done, I jumped away from him. He stared up at me, with adoring eyes and weakly wagged his tail again.

"My God," I whispered to the quiet night. "What have I become?"

I stood on the porch for a long time, staring into the darkness, searching my mind for answers to my questions. Finding none, I entered the house, softly closed the door and went upstairs to my father's room, where most of our books were kept.

My father had been an avid reader of the horror literature of the time; by the time of his death he had accumulated quite an impressive collection, from potboilers to literary classics. One of my fondest childhood memories was his reading aloud from Shelley's *Frankenstein* or from one of Poe's short stories; I can still hear his voice echoing through the house quoting some dramatic passage. But he had other books which he would not read aloud. "Not suitable for a young lady," he would say, putting those particular books aside, not permitting me to see them. It was these forbidden books that drew me to the shelves in his old room that night.

I opened his door, with a small shiver of anticipation, remembering the dream of that afternoon. The bed was empty, of course, but all else was as it had been when he was alive. The books on the shelves were dusty, but on the top shelf I found the one I sought. Opening the book, I began to read.

"CHAPTER 1—How graves give up their dead, And how the night air hideous grows with shrieks!" . . .

I completed it that night, huddled in a corner. When I was finished, I sighed and hugged my knees to my chest. If the whole idea wasn't quite so ludicrous, I thought, it would make sense. So many things were explained: the odd hunger for blood, the sharpened teeth, the aversion to food and sunlight. I stood up and began to pace the room.

It's ridiculous, I thought again. How could such a thing happen? There had been no demon materializing; no beastlike creature perched on my window sill. I could remember nothing that could explain this situation. But with a sudden shock, I recalled the dream, the hungry mouth fastening on my neck with a terrible desire, the mocking laughter, the man-sized black evilness that claimed my body and soul in a star-lit field.

"It was only a dream," I whispered, shaking with fear. "Nothing more than a dream."

I went to the window and pulled aside the heavy drapes. The sun was just beginning to rise and I looked at the lightening sky with hope and relief. "So," I said aloud, "it can't be true." But even as I said it, I felt the rays of the sun burn into my exposed skin, reddening and blistering it as I watched. I had not the courage to endure the pain; I drew the drapes shut again and collapsed, crying on the floor.

It took many months for the horrible realization of what I had become to sink into my consciousness. I defied the conventions that had been established for one of my kind. The walls of the house abounded with mirrors and crucifixes; the first infallibly reflecting my image and the latter evoking, not the loathing and fear that would be expected, but rather compassion and a yearning toward the redemption they represented. Standing at the window, I would greet the dawn until the pain of my burning flesh could not be tolerated. Upon waking the next evening, I would discover that the burns had healed, leaving no trace of their ravaging of my skin.

Some compulsions I could not deny: the sleep of the day and the call of the night, together with the taking of blood. With each dose of blood, my powers of night vision, hearing and the heightened awareness of the world surrounding me increased along with the intolerance of light, especially sunlight.

The dog continued to make his visits to my back porch once or twice a week and we fed each other, until one night he failed to come. I wondered about his absence; we had become companions of a sort and the relationship was satisfying for both of us. But my worries over the dog were soon replaced by others more pressing. The first was how to keep my bizarre transformation from Mrs. Blake; the second more profound and unsettling. I was beginning to suspect that the blood of animals could not completely fulfill my hunger; eventually I knew I would have to turn to humans for my sustenance.

* * *

Mrs. Blake died of pneumonia that winter; her death solved both of my problems. Though it was not of my doing, I deeply regretted both her death and my feeling of relief when it occurred. She had been good to me and had helped me through those bad months; yet her visits had become troublesome. Her presence in a room would make me frantic with rage and lust. I could smell the blood within her veins and it would take every shred of control I had to keep her at a distance. She was confused at my seeming coldness toward her, which I could not explain. And when I received word of her death, it was too late for explanations. I could not attend her funeral, for the day was sunny though cold and I could not risk prolonged exposure. Instead, I visited the graveyard that evening, bearing with me roses cut from my now overgrown garden.

The night was frosty, and the grass in the cemetery crunched beneath my feet as I wandered, looking for her grave. When I found it, I tenderly lay the roses on the fresh–turned earth. "Mrs. Blake," I said softly, then "Anna" for there was no need for formality now. "Anna, rest well here with the others I loved." I sat for a long time there, leaning against the adjacent headstone and content to have the cold air dry my tears. I heard footsteps behind me and stood up quickly. A man stood there, gaping in astonishment at my apparent rising from the grave.

He shook off his apprehension with the help of a flask he held clutched in his hands. "Li'l late ta come callin', ain' it, girlie?" He slurred the words and I could tell from his appearance and the smell on his breath that he was quite drunk. He gave me a crooked, leering smile. " 'm closin' the gates now."

"I am sorry," I said. "I missed the funeral and just wanted to say goodbye."

I suddenly remembered Mrs. Blake once mentioning the unsuitableness of the new caretaker. "Oh my dear," she had said. "Why old Mr. Jones picked such a man, I'll never know . . ." Now I understood her distress; he stood in front of me, swaying slightly in the wind. I walked past him and he lurched toward me.

"No need ta rush off," he said, grasping my arms. "I still got a li'l lef' in my bottle, we can say g'bye together." He gave a little drunken laugh, his breath hot and foul in my face. "Mebbe, we can say h'lo, too."

"No, thank you. Please let me go." I struggled with him until he began to nuzzle my ear and my hair. My mouth fell against his neck and time seemed suspended. I could feel the rapid beat of his pulse against my tongue. There was no thought, no effort that went into the bite. Suddenly, the taste of his blood was in my mouth, tinged with alcohol, but tangy and bitter and wonderful. I could feel the liquid flowing into my body even as I felt his pulse falter. Feeling satiated and drugged, I pulled away from him.

His eyes fluttered open and looked on me with confusion. "Wha' happened?" he said. "Who're you?"

"Nobody you know," I insisted. "You are drunk, go back and sleep it off. I will close the gates."

To my surprise, he moved away from me like a sleepwalker, shaking his head and muttering to himself. I watched him make his way back to the small brick building that was the cemetery office. He did not look back, he seemed to have completely forgotten me.

Quietly, I slipped out through the front gates closing them behind me. A euphoria engulfed me as I walked home; the night seemed alive to me, I felt welcomed to its darkness.

Shortly after that night, I had packed what little belongings I cared to take. Clothing, books, letters and papers, it had made a small bundle in the hallway of that empty house. I had made arrangements with the family lawyer to sell the house and the furnishings; he would forward those proceeds to me along with the profits from my father's business, a trading post and general store which I had inherited after his death. I was going to make a new start, I had told him, and would let him know where to send the money when I was settled. I was excited at the prospect of a new life somewhere away from my memories, not knowing at the time that it was just the first of many trips down that corridor of rooms, filled with death and loneliness.

Chapter 7

I had spent most of the day in memory, sitting quietly, motionlessly, considering my past. As I rose from my apartment couch, I noticed that the sun had already set. With scarcely a thought for what I was doing, I went upstairs and began to dress. I decided to abandon my normal black for this evening. Instead I pulled from the back of the wardrobe a dress I had made last year and never worn. It was a winter white velvet, with a scoop neck and a wide, full skirt. To liven it up I added a wide, red belt and a pair of red high heels. Surveying the results in the mirror, I was pleased with my appearance. The white seemed to brighten my hair and compliment my pale skin.

I left my apartment, locked the door and entered the office. The overpowering odor of roses filled the room and I smiled when I thought about Max. It was inevitable, I supposed, that I would have to see him again. Although he had never before attended one of my shows, he had sent the card back this time with a response of yes. If he did put in an appearance, it would be better to work out our problems before that night. After all, he had really done me no harm, and was responsible for my meeting Mitch. At the thought of his name, I gave a small sigh; how ironic it was that Max should be the one to introduce me, albeit indirectly, to someone who moved me as he had over twenty years ago. This time, however, I had no delusions about the outcome of any relationship with a human, and I had no intentions of changing Mitch, or anyone else, into a creature like me. The bitterness and hatred I felt for my unknown sire were still fresh and strong, even after all these years. I had no desire to foster the same emotions in someone I loved.

I called for a cab from the office phone and headed for the elevator. As I was closing the front door, the phone began to ring. I went back in to answer it.

"Deirdre, you're still there." At the sound of Mitch's voice my heart gave a curious little jump.

"Hello, Mitch. I was just leaving."

"Well, I can't talk long anyway. I wanted to see you tonight, but Chris came into town today. How about dinner tomorrow night?" He sounded enthusiastic, boyish.

"I don't know . . ." I began evasively.

"You have other plans?" he interrupted sharply.

"No, no I don't." God, I thought, how I hate to do this. Not only did I genuinely care about Mitch and want to see him again, he also provided me a chance to find the other vampire in the city. But he was dangerous, curious and quick–witted, and it would be too easy to fall in love with him. I could make my own investigations into the other of my kind easier than I could afford to begin a relationship with Mitch.

"It won't work out between us, Mitch." I tried to convince him as I tried to convince myself. "There is no way that it can." I was sure that he could hear my voice wavering. "I am sorry."

"Damn it all, Deirdre, you're wrong and you know it. What we felt last night was real." He paused for a long time, then continued, softly. "Give me a chance, please. Just one more night, and then if you still feel the same, I won't bother you again. Scout's honor."

I could hear the teasing in his voice, thought of our conversations last night, how I had enjoyed his company. How in his arms I found a release from my existence, how he made me forget for a while my struggle with the lust for blood. How for a few seconds, in the pre-dawn streets of the city, I had been human again.

"Oh, what the hell. Pick me up at the hotel at eight." Even as I said it, I knew instinctively that I had made the right decision. "But promise me, no more all-nighters. I have a busy weekend ahead of me."

"I'll be there. Oh, and Deirdre?" His voice acquired serious overtones.

"Yes?"

"You said you were on your way out. You aren't going to see Max, are you?"

I lied. "No, I am not going to see Max. Why do you ask?"

"Well, the flowers and all that. He always seems to be lurking around in the background." His voice took on a defensive note. "I can't believe he's not in the running, that's all."

"The running for what, Detective? I am not a trophy."

"Sorry, Deirdre. I guess I'm a little insecure."

"Only a little?" I snapped at him sarcastically. I could imagine the cold glint in his eyes and instantly regretted my harsh tone. "Mitch, you have no need to be," I said gently. "I . . . I will see you tomorrow. Goodnight."

I stood for a while after he hung up, the phone cradled against my chest. Then I hung it up quietly and went to the lobby to catch my taxi.

The streets were crowded and the traffic heavy, so I stared out the window as we slowly made our way to the Ballroom. The idea that there may have been others of my kind prowling the streets was intriguing, and I studied all the people we passed in the hopes that I would find a sign of their presence. Not that I would recognize another from their appearance; the only way I could be sure would be to see them feeding. And surely, they would guard their secret as well as I did mine, by hunting cautiously and covering all evidence of their existence. But they had not done that. With the two corpses left behind, they had left a calling card for any with the wisdom to identify the facts. I wondered at those deaths; even at my most voracious, I had never killed. I must find the other, I thought. I could learn from him; perhaps I could find in him someone that could share my life.

The answers to my questions were not found in the streets. Everyone looked. normal, human and busily involved in themselves. When we stopped at a light, however, I noticed a familiar figure crossing in front of us. I hurriedly paid the driver and got out of the cab. My heels made a clacking sound on the sidewalk as I tried to reach him. Catching up with him, I gently touched his arm. He spun around and the snarl on his face changed into a smile of recognition. It seemed a genuine smile, not his customary sneer, and I knew that he had forgiven the harsh words and hasty action of our last meeting.

"Hello, Max. How have you been?" I gave him a small hug and was surprised to have it returned with fervor.

"Deirdre, I'm glad to see you." He held me out at arms' length and smiled at me again. "You look wonderful. Were you coming to see me? Or just prowling around?"

I looked up into his eyes; they were dark, fathomless. "Max, I never gave you a chance to explain about the police. I'm sorry about that. Now that I have had time to think, I realize it wasn't your fault. At the time, I felt trapped; I thought you had turned me in to protect yourself and the club."

"That would be a logical assumption on your part, my dear. After all, I suppose I could be considered an accessory to at least one of the murders, if you did them. Did you?" He had an odd expression on his face, a mixture of curiousity and indulgence, as if I were a young relative discovered in some small indiscretion.

"No, of course I didn't. And even if I did, Max, I would hardly stand here on the street discussing it." I looked up at his face, the lights of the street highlighting its sculptured lines and felt a surge of anger at his complacency, his distance. "Now you can answer a question for me. Why did you feel it was necessary to mention my name to the police in connection with Bill Andrews?"

"Deirdre, calm down. I could hardly deny it, when so many other people at the club saw the two of you together. And," he added, justifying himself, "I did ask you to stay away for a while."

"But you begged to me come that night, knowing that the police would be there."

"I didn't know they'd be there that night; they don't really make appointments in advance, you know. And I thought that they had finished their questioning the previous night." He reached over and touched my cheek. "Besides," he added with a twisted smile, "can I help it if I just can't do without your presence? I missed you."

"Damn it, Max. It was only one night. You can quit your little game, now." I had never been able to ascertain why Max did the things he did, now was not the time to start. And since the policeman in question was Mitch, he had really done me a favor of sorts. The anger drained away and I smiled up at him. "Anyway, it doesn't really matter at this point. Shall we go?" I clasped his arm and we continued the walk to the club.

Larry stood guard at the front door and moved the crowd away so that we could enter. Max gave him a slight nod of greeting and I noticed how Larry's bright smile darkened and his fists clenched. I had not given much thought to Larry since his visit to my hotel. Now all of the anger and confusion he had expressed that night came back to me; I regretted that he had gotten involved, even remotely, in the sordid events of my life.

"Damn," I swore under my breath as Max propelled me down the hall toward his office. He lifted an eyebrow ever so slightly as he opened the door. I removed my coat and flung it over his couch while he opened a bottle of wine and poured two glasses.

He handed one to me. "You look radiant, Deirdre. Maybe it's the dress or the color? So virginal, so innocent; it should go over well with the police." He drained his glass abruptly and poured another. His face reflected his normal cynicism with a small trace of excitement.

"I thought it was time for a change, Max. No one can stay the same forever." I settled on the couch, demurely smoothing the velvet skirt.

"Not even you, my little vampire?" He came across the room to sit beside me and draped his arm carelessly on the edge of the couch, his fingers lightly grazing my shoulders. "No," he said shaking his head. "You have changed. You seem more confident, more at ease. As if something has finally touched you, made you aware of yourself."

A smile crossed my face and I thought of Mitch. I knew at that moment that I loved him. God help us both, I did love him and although it would go no further, I could still hold one warm time to my heart as I faced the loneliness and coldness of my unending life.

The change in my expression had not escaped Max's attention. "Ah," he said, leaning back, "it has happened then. I envy you this moment of revelation, my dear. Enjoy the exhilaration, it can make a life such as yours worthwhile indeed." He clinked my glass in a silent toast and we sat companionably for a few minutes. Then he rose, setting his glass down, and stared down at me. "Just promise me two things, Deirdre." He continued without waiting for my response. "Stay away from Larry. He asks more questions about you than he should. You do know that he is obsessed with you, don't you?"

"I surmised that at our last meeting."

"Only at your last meeting? I have known it for years; I'm surprised you've never noticed." Max crooked an eyebrow and gave me a slight smile. "He's been working here four years now and in all that time he's never so much looked at another woman. To be truthful, I don't think he's ever had a woman."

"I guessed that, too."

He looked at me questioningly, then continued. "According to the other employees, he spends most of his free time at the library, or someplace like it. Doing research, he says, but nobody knows why or on what."

I really didn't care to know what Larry did. "So, maybe he's a scholar. I can't see that it matters much. But you could tell me what kind of questions he asks about me."

"Where I met you, and how long ago, that sort of thing. He wanted to know your family background, whether you had ever married and how old you were."

"And you told him?"

He smiled. "Rest assured, I gave him a varnished version. Nothing that could make him more suspicious of you. But he seems to know more than he should. Watch out."

"I can't think that he would be much of a threat, but I'll steer clear of him."

"Don't underestimate him, my dear. He seems to be in a frantic state these days; I wouldn't be surprised if he might decide to follow you on one of your nightly walks. There are things he should probably not see."

I met his eyes firmly. "I said I'd stay away from him, Max. And the second promise?"

"No more dead bodies to be traced back here to the Ballroom. You may still feed here and I will continue to help, but be more careful. Neither you nor I need the hassle of police investigations."

"Oh, it wasn't all that bad." Even to myself I sounded smug.

"Don't be flippant about this," he said angrily. "You walk a dangerous line, my dear, and I don't want you to fall."

"There is no need for you to remind me of the peril." I grew angry at his continued patronizing and for once I decided not to let it alone. "I have lived with it since before you were born and, forgive me for saying so, I will do so after you are dead and buried." Even as I said the words I wanted to take them back. Instead, I reached out and touched his hand in unspoken apology.

Unexpectedly, he threw his head back and laughed. "You don't have to be afraid of mentioning my pitiful life span," he said. "I have come to terms with it." He pulled me to my feet and gave me a strong, affectionate hug. "So, then, it's agreed? You'll be more discreet and not leave any more bodies to be traced back here?"

"I am afraid I can make no guarantee of that, Max. You see, I did not kill Bill or anyone else. I don't even know who the second victim is."

"Oh, but you do. The girl was Linda, surely you remember her—the petite blonde, worked here as a waitress. I fired her several months ago for providing, shall we say, extra services to the customers."

"Oh my God," I exclaimed. I did indeed remember Linda, pretty little Linda who always had such a lost way about her. We had often sat together and talked on nights when the club was slow and I was not on the hunt. We had a common bond; I had for many years worked her profession.

"So you *do* remember her. It's not really important, you know. What difference does one less tramp make to this city?"

"How can you say that?" I was horrified at his attitude. "Linda was a nice girl, just a little misled. I liked her."

"Of course you did, my dear, just as you like all humans—food for the superior species. I told you before, it all makes no difference to me, just leave my club out of it."

"But, Max, I didn't kill them."

"If not you, then who?"

"That is what I'd like to find out. Don't you see what this whole thing means to me? Finally, I have proof that someone else like me exists. If I could find them . . ."

"You could swap stories about the old country, trade recipes, compare family trees?"

"Max, I am serious. This is important to me. I have searched so long for someone like me."

"And when you find the mystery vampire, what do you do then?"

I thought for a long time. Although for most of my life, I had been waiting for just this situation, I was psychologically unprepared to face it. I shrugged, "I don't really know. Maybe they could answer some questions for me; how I became what I am, what the scope of my powers are, and is the process reversible?"

"The chance of finding the person who changed you is probably not very good, Deirdre. And who else would be able to answer those questions?"

"Why would the chances be so bad? I have travelled around for over a century now; this is the first indication I have had that I'm not alone in my fate. I don't exactly think the city is teeming with us; there would be more signs."

Max gave me an intense look. "And when you finally confront your creator?"

"First I will ask him why. Then I will kill him."

"I'm surprised at you. That intent makes no sense, coming from the woman, who only a few seconds ago was bewailing the death of a cheap little hooker. Don't you see how unrealistic you are being?"

"Maybe I am. But that is the way I feel. And if given the chance, I will do it." I smiled at him, cynically. "I *do* promise to be careful, though, so you need not worry about me."

"Oh, I won't. Now, let's change the subject. Did you come only to see me or are you hungry?" He gave me a twisted smile and waited for my answer.

I glanced at him for a moment and then looked away. I wondered for the first time in our relationship, did he feel that I was using him? I hoped he knew me better than that. "Max, I came to make up for what went on last week. You must know that I . . ." With my realization of the love I felt for Mitch, the words I would have said blithely last week would not come. ". . . care for you deeply." I hoped that the hesitation was not noticeable. "Now that apologies have been made and accepted and we're back on familiar ground . . ." My voice trailed off and I looked at him for reassurance.

He gave me none, but walked to his desk and began to occupy himself with his silver–plated desk set, turning the letter opener over and over in his strong hands.

"Max," I asked plaintively, "what's wrong?"

"Nothing," he said. "I was just thinking—silver for werewolves, wood for vampires."

"What on earth?"

"Forgive me, my dear. You aren't the only one who entertains morbid thoughts on occasion." His voice grew thick with emotion, but when he looked into my eyes, I was surprised at his lack of expression. "Actually, what I was really thinking was that not too long ago you would have said you loved me." Not hearing my small murmur of denial, he continued. "You have changed, you know. You are stronger, more self-sufficient than you were." He set the letter opener down and walked around the desk to hold me. "I am happy it happened. I have been hoping for this day. It's what I want most for you, for us. But I'll miss the lonely little thing you were."

Tears began to stream down my face, soaking into his coat. "Max, I do love you," I began.

"Don't waste it on me," he interrupted. "I'm a heartless bastard as you are so fond of reminding me." I looked up at his chuckle. "Besides, you're ruining my jacket. Now tend to your makeup; I have someone I want you to meet.

From David Leigh's walk it was apparent that he had spent a long time at the bar. He and Max seemed friendly; this in itself was unusual. But, when after the introductions, Max sat down at the table to have a drink with us it became obvious that this was not David's first visit here. They discussed sports, football mostly, while I occupied myself with watching the dance floor. Finally, just as the conversation was turning to basketball, I looked up from the dancers and gave a long audible sigh.

"Deirdre, I'm so sorry," Max apologized. "Dave is a long-time customer, he's been coming here for years. We were just catching up a little." He rose from the table and turned to go.

"See you soon, eh, Max." Dave stood up and extended his hand.

"Count on it," Max said, shaking his hand and clapping him on the shoulder. "Oh, and watch out for Deirdre, she's a killer."

"Very funny, Max," I said dryly. "In that case, guard your neck. Now go and run your business."

With a bow and a little mock flourish of his arm he left us alone.

"That old Max is one hell of a guy," Dave said, watching him walk out of sight.

I grinned at him. "Hell is often one of the words that come to my mind."

"I get the feeling I shouldn't ask what any of the other words are."

I nodded my head. "It's best that way."

"What was all that about killing and Max's neck?"

I shrugged. "His idea of a joke in very poor taste, I'm afraid. I would really rather not discuss it."

He smiled his agreement. "Well then, what do you want to talk about? I get the impression that sports is not your forte."

"Tell me about yourself," I prompted him with a smile.

He was an auditor from out of town, making frequent business trips and staying over here for about two weeks at a time, before moving on. He had struck up an acquaintance with Max five years ago and visited the Ballroom as often as possible. They had just hit it off, he explained, and became good friends over the years.

"I think he must know every important detail of my life. I always felt I could tell him anything, you know. And after a few drinks, I usually do." He looked over at me and laughed. "But I guess you could tell that, huh?" He took another drink of his beer. "I know a lot about you, too."

"Me?" I jumped, jostling my wine glass and spilling a few drops on the white linen cocktail napkin.

"Well," he amended, "maybe not a lot. But Max has mentioned you a number of times. Your talent, your career, your looks." At this last statement, he looked rather embarrassed. "I think I must have made a big deal out of being introduced to you. But now that it's finally happened, well, I don't know."

"Don't know what, Dave?" I asked, blotting up the drops of wine with my fingertip.

"Don't get me wrong. You are everything he said, and more. It's just that, well, I'm a big talker, in a lot of ways. I think Max must have misunderstood my intentions. I miss my wife and family while I'm on the road, and I do get lonely. But I wasn't really looking for female companionship, if you get my meaning."

"I do, indeed, Dave and there is no need for you to be embarrassed." His confession made the whole situation easier for me. I had decided early on in our conversation not to feed on him. It didn't seem right, since he was actually a good friend of Max's. And I discovered that I actually liked Dave, not as a potential lover, but as a friend or a brother. "And, I'll be honest with you; I was not looking for any involvement either. Although I am enjoying our conversation, you're easy to talk to. Would you like to go somewhere quieter?" The band had returned from their break and the noise was deafening.

"Fine with me, Deirdre. It does get a bit loud, doesn't it? Let me get another beer before we go."

I grabbed his hand, stopping the gesture toward our waiter. "I'll take care of that," I said, rising from the table. "We can drink from old Max's private stock. Come with me."

It must have appeared to be the same old scenario to the staff. As we made our way past the bar I noticed quite a few knowing smiles; Max gave me a half salute as we passed by. I led the way down the hallway to the lounge area.

Once inside, Dave gave a whistle of approval. "Nice digs," he said as he made his way to inspect the stock in the refrigerator. He selected an imported beer and settled on the couch. I sat in a chair a safe distance away; I wanted to stay as far from him as possible so that I would not be tempted to feed. It had been a week since I had taken blood and I needed it tonight. But it would not be his. We had been talking for some time when a knock on the door interrupted us. Because I had not planned to feed, I had not locked it. "Come in," I called. "It's open."

Larry stood hesitantly in the doorway. "Deirdre," he said, his face flushed, "there's a, uh, a phone call for you."

Dave gave a small shrug and picked up his jacket. "I've got to get going anyway. I have an important meeting first thing tomorrow morning." He came over to me and made a move to shake my hand. "I enjoyed meeting you and hope to see you again."

I avoided his hand and stretched up to kiss his cheek. Larry stiffened and then relaxed as Dave walked to the door.

"Wait," I said to Dave and walked over to him, laying my hand on his arm. I rummaged around in my purse and came up with a small, crumpled card. "Next time you are in town, stop by my office. Bring your wife, she can pick out anything in the shop she would like."

"Thanks. I think she'd like that. Good night."

"Good night, Dave." I smiled. "You take care."

He made his exit and I looked at Larry who had stood silent during our conversation. "Well," I said sternly, "what's this about a phone call?"

He hung his head and would not meet my eyes. "There's no phone call," he admitted.

"Then why on earth did you interrupt us? That was a close friend of Max's. We were just getting acquainted. What's the problem, Larry?"

"Deirdre," he said quietly and made a step toward me. His arms hung limply at his sides; his hands clenched and unclenched in nervousness. "I just wanted him to leave."

"Why?"

"You lied to me," he began, "when you said that all of this was over. You made me believe that you and I could be together. Then I see you and Max come in tonight like old friends. And when I took my break, all the guys were joking about it; about how, only a week after that guy was killed, you were at it again." His voice broke in anger.

"At what, Larry?" I asked softly and urgently as I stared into his eyes. "What do they say about me?"

He fidgeted under my gaze but the contact held. "They say you're Max's whore." He spat the last word at me in a defiant gesture and sat down on the couch.

I moved next to him and stroked his hair. "Larry, that is not true. I don't work for Max, nor do I belong to him. What I do, I do for myself. Can you understand that?"

"I understand, better than you think, Deirdre," he said, shaking his head. "I know you're not what you seem to the others. But I don't like them to say those things about you; it demeans you. They shouldn't be allowed to say those things; if they only knew you like I do, they wouldn't."

Max was right about Larry, I knew—he *was* obsessed with me, but I saw no harm in him. I just couldn't believe he would do anything to hurt me. "Poor kid," I whispered to myself and held him in my arms.

Eventually he pulled himself out of his despondency and raised his head. His eyes seemed to glow with strong emotion. "Don't hate me," he begged. "I love you."

"Why would I hate you?"

"Because I'm weak and inferior and I have no control . . . because I can't stop myself from . . . hating all the others."

"Jealousy is a normal reaction," I assured him. "And love

and hate are strong at twenty–five. How could I hate you for being what you are?" I got up from beside him and moved to the chair I sat in previously. "Larry, I want to be honest with you; I also want to be kind. In this situation I cannot be both. What do you want from me?"

"I want you to love me back," he said in a choked voice, sounding at least ten years younger than he was. "I want to be with you forever."

I gave him a sharp glance. "Why do you say forever? Nothing lasts forever."

Although his head was down, his eyes glinted up at me. "That's what people say who love each other, I'll love you forever, they say. And I will."

I shook my head and mastered the impulse I had to comfort him again. It would do no good. Instead, I looked him coldly in the eye. "I can't do that, Larry. If you wanted a friend, a sister, even a one-time lover . . ." His eyes glittered angrily. ". . . I could give you that. But I cannot return the gift of your love. I am sorry."

He rose slowly from the couch and squared his shoulders. Methodically, he walked to the door and reached for the knob. His hand stopped, he spun around and confronted me. "You are what they say." His voice was awful in its quietness and its rage. "No, you're worse than they say. I know what you are and who you are, Dorothy," he hissed the name at me and I recoiled. "Hell can't come too soon for you. But before that, I will get what I want." He softened a bit and reached out to stroke my cheek. "I would have been good to you. I could protect you, take care of you, give you anything you ask, give you all you require." He licked his lips. "And I know what you require. But, no, you say you can't, you're sorry. You will be sorry one day, I'm sure." He pulled away abruptly, making his brief touch feel like a slap, and left the room.

I stood staring at the door and raised my hand to my burning cheek. "Dear God," I said in the emptiness of the room. "What does he know about me? How could he know the truth?" I had to find Max, discover exactly what he had told Larry. Maybe he had mentioned my original name, saying that I had changed it for professional reasons. Larry could know nothing about me, I rationalized, and even if he guessed at the truth, who would believe him? Unless, of course, he was the vampire doing the killing. I dismissed that idea almost as soon as I thought it; it seemed too unlikely. Surely I would feel some sort of rapport with another of my kind, some recognition, some spark would flow between us. And as for his being my transformer, that could never be. I would know him.

I gathered my belongings and went to Max's office where I had left my coat. I was surprised to discover his office was empty and the lights were out. I stared for a while at his desk, then, on impulse, turned to the employee directory. Finding Larry's name, I wrote down his address and phone number, folded the paper and carefully put it into my purse. If things got too hot, if he really *did* know something, I would have to take action against him. Shuddering slightly as the thought of what action I could take, I left the office and closed the door.

Walking slowly through the bar, I studied the faces of the patrons at the tables, hoping to find Max drinking with David Leigh. They were not there. But when I questioned the bartender, he shrugged and said that Max was probably around somewhere. Did I want him paged? I nodded and turned away, pulling on my black leather gloves while surveying the tables and the dance floor.

"Miss Griffin?" The bartender beckoned me with a smirk. "No answer from Max. But if you're looking for your other friend, he left just a few minutes ago. Maybe you can catch up with him." His manner was unpleasant, sneering and I swallowed the urge to slap him across the face.

"Thank you," I replied with a false grin, while looking him deep in the eyes. He shifted uncomfortably until I dropped my gaze. "I might just do that. Please tell Max that I need to speak with him as soon as possible. Good night."

When I got out to the street, I saw no one I knew—there was no sign of Max, Larry or David Leigh. Just as well, I decided, if I couldn't find Max, I was in no mood for conversation with anyone else. Right now, I needed to find a victim so that I could be fed and rejuvenated before I met Mitch tomorrow.

The streets were full of people: couples, singles and large groups, bundled up against the evening air, their laughter rising up in billowy puffs. It was still relatively early and a Saturday. I would need to find a less populated street. After wandering aimlessly for a while, I found myself admiring for once the displays in store windows. The normally angry thought of celebrating yet another Christmas was softened now by images of spending the time with Mitch. I smiled so broadly about the idea that a couple I passed were shocked into returning my smile. With a half-embarrassed nod they hurried away on their business, reminding me suddenly of my own purpose tonight. My smile died, and I walked on with more determination.

Three blocks past the club, I turned into a side street. I could sense someone's presence at the end of this alley and went forward eagerly to meet them. He was sleeping and took no notice of me as I settled down next to him, pushed the baby–fine blonde hair away from his neck and fed.

When my teeth pierced his neck he stirred, moaned and went back to his fitful sleep. Not even my withdrawal awoke him. As always, when I had finished I checked his pulse and found it strong.

I turned to walk away, when I actually looked at him. What I saw was pathetic. Dressed only in ragged jeans and a lightweight shirt; he wore shoes, but no socks, and was shivering uncontrollably in his sleep. He seemed no more than fifteen or sixteen, most likely a recent runaway for he was better fed than some I had seen. He would survive the feeding, I felt sure, but the cold would kill him. Shaking my head, I took off my coat and removed the label by tearing the lining with my still sharpened teeth. Wrapping the fur gently around him, I tucked some money into his shirt pocket. Oddly enough the warmth woke him, and he stared at me out of eyes that belied his years, eyes shadowed with fear and despair.

"You will be all right," I whispered confidently to him. He answered me with an angelic grin that almost made up for his desperate eyes. "There's a shelter just two down blocks down the street," I pointed in the right direction. "Go there for tonight. I have given you some money; do you have a home to go back to?"

He nodded, getting to his feet slowly, my coat still draped around him. He made a move to take it off, but I stopped him.

"Keep it," I urged, "and get a bus ticket for home tomorrow. Don't spend another night on the streets, please." I began to walk away.

"Lady?" he called after me and I turned back to face him. "Thank you." He smiled his choir boy smile again. I nodded to him and watched as he went in the direction I had shown him. His walk was youthful and strong, and I was confident that the small price I had extracted from him would not matter. His blood had had no taint of drugs or alcohol; if he took my advice, he would survive this night of cold and vampirism with no more than a small mark on his neck and a warm memory of someone who had helped him recover his life.

I lingered on the streets no longer, but returned to the office. I worked on the upcoming show throughout the night and at dawn retired to my apartment. The feeding had sated me physically and I felt uplifted from my contact with the boy. I slept dreamlessly, to awaken Sunday evening, as the sun was setting.

I lay in bed for some time, savoring, as always, the feelings of youth and strength that followed a feeding. The darkness and quiet of the room enveloped me, calming the nerves tortured by the past few weeks. I wanted to lay there forever, avoiding the world outside. Next time, I thought languidly, I will choose a more peaceful life. I had accumulated enough money to make it possible, for at least a few decades, to live somewhere with no job, no commitments, no complicated relationships.

"Oh, God," I said sitting upright in bed and reaching for my contacts. "I forgot I have to meet Mitch." I hurriedly consulted the clock, it was only a little before seven. I would have time to get back to the hotel and dress before he picked me up. I threw on some jeans and a shirt and ran down the spiral staircase. I put on my boots and searched the closet for a coat to replace the one I had given away. I put on the first one I found; it was an ankle length black velvet cape. I seldom wore it, even for me the effect was too theatrical. It flapped annoyingly around my legs as I rushed down the hall to the elevators. I burst into the lobby, called a quick good–night to the startled guard and sped to the hotel.

When I reached the front door, I was only a little breathless and was happy to see that it was just turning seven. I slowed down, and entered the revolving door.

Frank was at the desk and jumped a bit at my entrance. "Hello, Frank," I said gaily. "How have you been?"

He stared at me uncomprehendingly at first, then said, "Fine. Uh, Miss . . ."

"I really am in a hurry, Frank," I interrupted. "If someone named Greer stops in for me, send him up, please. Thanks so much." Without a pause, I headed for the elevators, when a hand on my arm stopped me. I spun around and found myself facing two uniformed policemen. "Can I help you, gentlemen?"

The taller of the two spoke. "Are you Deirdre Griffin?" At my nod he continued. "We'd like you to come with us, if you would. We have some questions to ask you concerning a recent homicide."

"Recent homicide?" I repeated stupidly. "But I have already told Detective Greer everything I knew about Bill Andrews."

"Not Andrews this time. We have a new one."

"A new one?" I felt a sudden stab of fear. Although I was not the killer, I had known the other two victims. If this third one was also known to me, it could create a very uncomfortable situation. One night in jail, followed as it would be, by the rising sun, and I would be dead; the fact that I was innocent would not matter then. I should have left town as soon as Bill Andrews died; instead I had stayed around, playing human, and this was where it got me. "Damn," I swore softly under my breath and glanced over at Frank as if in appeal. He looked away and busied himself at the hotel register.

"That's right, Miss Griffin." The policeman gave me what I thought was a chilling smile. "And we have reason to believe you can help with identification. Come with us, please."

And although it was not the police escort I had expected that evening, I accompanied them to the station.

Chapter 8

I sat in silence in the back seat of the police car, considering my alternatives. There was not much time to plan since the police station was only five blocks away. As the car pulled up to the curb, I cleared my throat loudly. The driver turned around.

"Yes, Miss Griffin?"

It was too dark to make sufficient eye contact, so I simply said, "What are the charges, officer?"

"You must have misunderstood, Miss Griffin," he said with a half smile. "We are not making any charges, we only want you to answer a few questions, and as I explained before, help us with an identification of the corpse, if possible."

He was toying with me, I thought, but I nodded and decided to play along. "I will be happy to cooperate in any way I can; I'm just not sure what help I can give you." I got out of the car and went with them into the station. As we entered the lobby I turned to the nearest officer. "May I make a phone call? I have a . . . an appointment tonight; I'd like to let them know I'll be a little late. This won't take long, will it?" I looked at him for confirmation.

"It shouldn't, but you can call if you want." He gestured to a telephone across the lobby. I walked there, checked for the number in the book and turned my back on their curious stares as I dialed.

The phone rang ten times before Mitch finally answered.

"Hello," he sounded brusque, hurried.

"Hello." I did not want to say his name out loud here.

"Deirdre, I was just coming to get you. What's up?"

"I wanted to let you know that I'll be detained for a while. Something important has come up."

The tenseness in my voice did not escape his notice. "What's wrong? Where are you?"

"At the police station." From his muffled exclamation, I could tell he knew nothing about this situation. "Don't worry, they tell me it won't take long."

"What the hell is it all about? I swear I had nothing to do with this, Deirdre." He sounded confused and angry, very angry. "I'll be right there."

"No, I will be fine, just wait . . ." I had no chance to finish; he had already hung up. I said goodbye to the empty receiver for the benefit of my listeners and walked back to them.

"Shall we go?" I addressed them with more confidence than I felt.

We rode the elevator down to the basement level, and exited into a gray, dimly-lit hall. I recoiled visibly as the doors opened, for my heightened senses reeled with the overwhelming reek of death and decay. God, it was foul; the smells of formaldehyde, disinfectant and rotting flesh permeated the air. Coughing and gagging in an uncontrollable reaction to this assault, I leaned against the wall in an attempt to calm my retching stomach and my mind travelled back to a time and place I never desired to visit again.

The casualties of the first battles had been worse than anyone had ever expected. Men who marched out proud and resolute returned torn and wounded, both physically and mentally. All too soon the tents set up for the injured were overcrowded; cots and blankets with the bodies of maimed and dying soldiers overflowed onto the pathways of our encampment. I remember the early days of that war as smoke-filled and alive with pain and suffering.

I had elected to take night duty in the medical tents; few of the other women wanted the task for it was at night that the moans of the dying were loudest, during the day the sounds of battle would block most of the cries. Beginning at sunset, I would carry my lantern through the rows of men, stopping to administer what was most needed: water, food or morphine. By the time I would reach the second tent, my skirts would be soaked to the knees, sodden with muddy water and blood.

It was in the second tent that the worst odor lingered. Here we kept the most severly injured and the dying. Those men who had lost limbs were the lucky ones. Even though they might be feverish or delirious, minus an arm or a leg, they still stood the best chance of living. But the ones with the belly or groin wounds were fated to die, a horrible, clawing death that tore them apart with the pain. The smell these soldiers exuded seemed almost tangible; a mixture of bile, feces and gangrenous flesh combined with sweat and blood. Most nights I would have to stop my rounds before entering the second tent, so that I could empty my stomach. Even if there was nothing in my stomach, I would still be possessed with the uncontrollable urge to vomit. I continued on because I was needed, but I never adjusted to the odors of death.

Dimly I became aware of the person beside me, the officer had his arm around me and was supporting me. "I'm sorry," I gasped. "It's the smell." Soon the nausea passed and I was able to stand erect and gain control over my body.

The officer shrugged apologetically. "It gets some people that way. I guess I've just gotten used to it."

The other man addressed me. "We're sorry, Miss Griffin, but this trip is necessary. Let's just get it out of the way as quickly as possible. Will you be okay?" He pulled a small vial from his pocket.

"You may put away the smelling salts, please. I promise you I won't faint." We walked slowly down the corridor, our shadows undulating on the walls. I stopped outside the morgue door.

"Before we go in, can you tell me what to expect? Who is it?"

"We don't know, we hope you can tell us."

"Why me?"

"He had something on him that belongs to you. Are you ready to go in?"

I nodded and nervously drew in a deep breath of the foul air. He pushed the door inward and turned on the lights. They led me past carts and tables, some still containing bodies, their shapes distorted by the bright light and stark white coverings. Our destination was soon reached, a small examination room in the back.

We entered and with no preliminary warning the sheet was stripped away. The body was naked and gray, the skin waxen; and the neck was badly bruised. The fangmarks were apparent, but were not mine. Even if I could have believed that I fed on this man and had forgotten, I knew that I left no such marks. They were wider than mine, coming from a larger mouth and they were torn and stretched, as if worried by an animal. But no animal left these marks. I reached out and touched a hand, it was cold and flaccid. Choking back the tears that threatened, I gently replaced the sheet over the face.

"Miss Griffin," the officer's voice sounded soft in that brutal environment, "did you know him?"

"Yes. His name is David Leigh. I met him last night."

"We have a few more questions to ask. Would you like to go back upstairs now?"

"Yes," I nodded gratefully. "Thank you. This is all very disturbing."

He turned out the lights and closed the doors as we walked back. Waiting for the elevator, I glanced at the clock.

"We will only take just a little more of your time, Miss Griffin. Your, um, appointment won't have to wait long."

Before we got off the elevator, I discovered that my appointment was waiting in the lobby. I could hear his raised voice through the opening doors. ". . . and why wasn't I informed that you had taken me off the case? There's no need . . ."

The man he was talking to mumbled something, then fell silent as we appeared. Mitch turned around and our eyes met. I could read his concern for me underneath the anger. He came to my side and grasped my arm. "Are you okay, Deirdre?"

I smiled. "I'm fine, now, thank you."

"Can she go now, Lieutenant?"

The lieutenant looked to the officers. They shifted uneasily. "Actually, Mitch, we weren't quite done."

"Let's finish it up, then. But I want to stay with her. I trust that there are no objections."

The lieutenant shrugged, walked off and Mitch escorted me to a small room, the other officers trailed behind us. He sat down next to me, across the table from the other two. The silence grew uncomfortable until I turned to Mitch.

"Could you get me a cup of coffee or something?"

He hesitated briefly, then got to his feet and left the room.

"I don't really want to cause any problems for you," I said, smiling. "Maybe we can finish this before he comes back."

They sighed their relief. "It is a bit difficult with him here," one admitted. "Just tell us what you know about this guy."

"His name was David Leigh," I repeated while one of them began to take notes. "I met him at the Ballroom of Romance last night. He's a good friend of Max's." They didn't seem to recognize the name. "Max Hunter," I prompted. "He owns the club." The one taking notes nodded and I continued. "Dave was an auditor; I don't remember for whom he worked."

"Local guy?"

"No, he was from out of town. He came to the city frequently, though. He's known Max for about five years. If you need any more personal information, you might check with him."

"When we found him his wallet was gone. Of course that's not at all unusual; in fact if it were still on him, that would be strange. But he had your business card in his coat pocket. Had you made plans to meet again?"

I grimaced inwardly thinking how all this could have been avoided had I not given him my card. "No, no plans as such. I told him to bring his wife to town next time he came; I offered to have some clothes made for her."

"Why? I can't believe you make that offer to everyone you meet."

"Oh, I don't really know. I am a bit eccentric; but I liked him, he seemed like a nice guy."

"Do you know any reason someone would murder him?"

I didn't hesitate. "Quite honestly, I did not know him well enough to make that judgement. But offhand, I would say no. None of this makes any sense at all."

"One final question, Miss Griffin." He gave me an apologetic look. "You understand I have to ask this one. And I hope you understand you don't have to answer it, at least not without the advice of counsel." He hesitated, then looked directly into my eyes. "Did you kill him?"

"No, I did not."

As we held eye contact, I felt his doubt of me lessen and fade away entirely.

"One more thing, Miss Griffin," the officer taking notes interrupted, "we may need to talk with you again; don't make any plans to leave the city for a while."

"I understand. Will that be all?" At their nods of affirmation, I stood up. The door opened and Mitch walked in bearing a tray with four cups of coffee and set it on the table. I selected a cup for myself and took a sip. "If you don't mind, I will drink mine on the way out. I do have an appointment, you know. I hope he won't mind waiting a while; I still have to get ready." I felt sure that Mitch wouldn't want our personal relationship made common knowledge at the station. But the knowing smiles exchanged between the two officers made me think that my caution was unnecessary.

I gathered up my cloak and couldn't resist a theatrical swirl as I settled it on my shoulders. "Good evening, gentlemen."

"Wait," Mitch called as I left. "I'll walk you out." He strode beside me, we went out the front door together and on to the street. He looked around and seeing no one, gave me a brief kiss. "I'd wait forever," he whispered, "but if you're not ready in an hour . . ." I laughed at his feigned threat. He gestured for a cab and when one stopped, he helped me in. "I just want to do some checking on what's going on. And I want to get myself reinstated on the case. I won't be long." He gave me another kiss, closed the door and the cab moved away.

Upon my return to the hotel, I gave Frank a curt nod and went directly to my room. I had not been there for a week now, but it was clean and sterile for my arrival. I entered without turning on the lights, dropped my black cloak on the floor and shed the rest of my clothes on the way to the shower. I made the water hotter than usual, to wash away the reek of the morgue that still lingered about me.

I dressed with great care, selecting a forest green sheath with a high neck and a low-cut cowl back. I wore a thin gold necklace, gold button earrings and pulled my hair up from the sides with combs, the rest of my hair rippled down my bare back. I applied my makeup carefully and tried to coax as much color into my pale complexion as possible. For a finishing touch I changed my contacts to a pair tinted deep green to complement the dress. I checked the clock and discovered that Mitch's prescribed hour had elapsed. He would arrive soon.

One hour later I still sat in the near darkness of the room. I rose from the sofa, went to the window and pulled the drapes aside. The streets were still crowded with people hurrying to their various destinations, but I saw no one familiar. A shadowy figure walked below my window, it might be Mitch, I thought, feeling a rush of anticipation. But as I watched, he passed the hotel entrance without a backward glance. It was not him. Disappointed I closed the drapes, then went to the bar and opened a bottle of wine to kill the time, to calm my nerves as the minutes dragged. There was work on my desk that I wanted to finish sometime this weekend; I turned on the light and tried to review the plans for the show, but I could not concentrate and kept checking the clock in disbelief. I put aside my work, switched off the light and went back to the sofa, the wine and the darkness.

Sometime after midnight I abandoned all pretense that he would show. I had waited over three hours listening for the phone, a knock on the door or even a set of approaching footsteps. I drank the last bit of wine. He wasn't coming, I decided.

"Damn him." I flung the crystal goblet against the wall, taking a perverse delight in the destruction of the delicate glass. Then I rose from the sofa and began to remove the clothing I had so carefully donned earlier in the evening. I kicked off my shoes, tossed the dress into a corner of the bedroom, removed my jewelry and the combs from my hair. Wrapping myself in a black silk robe, I found a broom and swept the broken crystal into a corner; the hotel staff could clean the rest tomorrow. Just as I was opening the next bottle of wine, and pouring another glass, the phone rang.

"Miss Griffin?" Frank's tone was uncertain.

"Hello, Frank. What can I do for you?"

"There's someone here to see you. Detective Mitchell Greer. What shall I do?" I could sense an excitement in his voice; this would probably be one of his most memorable evenings here, with policemen and detectives hauling out residents at all hours.

"You've certainly had one hell of a night, haven't you, Frank?" I spoke more sharply than I had intended to. But after having led such a secretive existence for so long, I was growing steadily more angry over the intrusions into my life.

"Excuse me?"

"Oh, damn it all, Frank, just send him up."

"If you want, Miss Griffin." He hung up the phone.

I had a few minutes before Mitch would arrive, so I mussed the covers on the neatly made bed and ruffled my hair into a mass of tangles. There was no reason to let Mitch think I had waited patiently for his arrival. Let him think I had been sleeping, that his lateness had not bothered me.

When he knocked, I closed the bedroom door and turned on the lights in the second half of the suite. I answered the door, pushing the hair out of my eyes and affecting a sleepy smile. "I'm sorry," I began. "I fell asleep. I can be ready . . ."

"Forget about it." He slammed the door, pushed past me and stalked into the room. He picked up the bottle of wine and gestured with it. "Don't you have anything stronger than this?" He rummaged around behind the bar.

"I think there may be a bottle of scotch. Try the bottom shelf."

Even before I finished speaking, he found the bottle along with a glass and some ice. He threw the cubes savagely into the glass and filled it to the top. Then he sat on the sofa and glared angrily into his drink. "Well?"

"Well, what?" I responded as angrily as he had. "You're the one who didn't show up when expected. I do not like to be stood up."

"That's not what I mean and you know it. I've got three dead bodies, two of them tied directly to you. I jeopardized over twenty years standing in the department, almost got removed from a very important homicide case, one that I now feel personally involved with. I believed you when you told me you knew nothing about Andrews' death. And I believed you when you told me you would not be seeing Max Hunter. Then I discover that you slinked off to him last night and met some unlucky chump who just happened to turn up dead with your business card in his pocket." He drained his scotch and went to the bar for another. "What will you try to make me believe next, Deirdre? That you're not involved? That it's all just a coincidence? I'm sorry, but I've been at the job for far too long to believe in coincidences." He stood at the bar, glaring at me and swirling the ice cubes in his drink.

"Mitch, I . . ."

"I wasn't done yet. Let me finish. To top it off, as if all that isn't enough, I believed in you." His voice softened now almost to a whisper. "I really thought we might have a chance together. I fell for you, hard, and I got the feeling it was returned, regardless of your promiscuous habits. And what did it all get me? Nothing but lies, from the beginning to the end. But before I leave here tonight, lady, I will get the truth from you."

I summoned what dignity I could, clasped my robe tighter around my body and pulled myself upright. "I did not lie to you, Mitch. I knew nothing about Bill Andrews' death and I know nothing about David Leigh's. Yes, it is all a coincidence, and I'm sorry that you can't believe that. There are stranger things in this world than coincidence. I want to help you, I really do, but I'm not sure what I can do."

"Well, for starters, you can explain why, although you told me you weren't going to, you went to Max's club last night. It couldn't have taken you more than ten minutes to get to where you said you weren't going."

"What is it about Max that bothers you? I have already told you that he is not a threat to you in any way. Max is an old friend, that's all."

"But you met him after you said you wouldn't."

"I ran into him on the street, Mitch. It wasn't planned or arranged. It was just by chance that I saw him at all." He gave me a sharp glance. "I know, I know, you don't believe in that either. Give me the benefit of the doubt, Mitch. Even criminals are thought to be innocent until proven guilty."

He met my eyes finally and a small smile began to play on his face. "I guess I've been a little too rough on you tonight, huh?" He took one sip of his drink and then another. "It's just that the job is getting to me, the press is clamoring for a solution and we're no closer to that now than when Andrews died. And there's something about Max that really gets to me, his attitude, his lifestyle, something. I don't know. When I spoke to him tonight, he was polite and solicitous, but I had the feeling he was laughing at me, taunting me. And when he speaks of you, I get angry—just hearing your name on his lips—well, I can't really explain it. He talks as if he owns you, protects you, as if you were his child, or his wife."

"I am neither, Mitch. He oversteps his bounds a lot, and he interferes with things when he should stay out. But for all that, he is still my friend."

"How close a friend?"

I sighed and moved over to him. He looked up at me, his eyes locked on mine. "Mitch, there is nothing between Max and me, now. You must believe me."

"I do, but . . ."

"Jesus, Mitch, will you just drop it? I do not want to spend the rest of the evening talking about Max. Do you?"

"No, not really." He drained his drink, got up from the couch and set his glass on the bar. "Look, I know it's late, but would you like to go out for a while? Maybe we could take a walk or have dinner? Are you hungry?"

I shrugged. "Whatever you'd like, Mitch. It doesn't make any difference to me. Let me change first, though." As I walked past him on the way to the bedroom, he touched my arm and turned me around to face him.

"Deirdre, I'm sorry." He held my arms in his gently, then rubbed his hands up and down the sleeves. I felt my stomach tighten in anticipation and smiled up at him.

"It's okay, Mitch. Actually, I am flattered that you like me enough to be so jealous. Just don't mention his name again."

"I promise." He tightened his grip on me and his eyes lit with desire. I thought to myself, before his mouth came down to mine, that this night would make up for those countless others.

For what could have been seconds or years, the kiss continued. He slid his hands under my robe; they felt grainy against the soft skin of my back as he drew me closer. His arousal was evident and I arched my body into his. He held me tightly with one arm, while struggling to remove his coat with the other. He switched arms, and removing his coat entirely, exposed his shoulder holster and gun. I reached a hand up lightly to touch it.

"I don't think you will need this now, do you, Detective?"

He agreed with a smile that lit up his eyes and draped it and his shirt over the back of a chair. He reached for me again, and as I went to him, the silk robe slipped over my shoulders. I dropped my arms and let it fall.

"Deirdre," he whispered into my hair as he lowered me to the floor. "You make me crazy." I twined my arms around his neck, drew him down to me and silenced him with a kiss.

Chapter 9

We lay sated and exhausted. Mitch rolled over, leaned on one elbow and smoothed the hair from my eyes. "God," he said, his voice somewhere between a laugh and a moan. "I'm getting too old for this."

"Oh, really? I hadn't noticed."

He smiled. "No, not for that." He laughed for real this time. "I mean making love on the floor, like a couple of kids."

"I do have a bed, but you seemed so eager I hated to spoil the moment." I stood up and he followed me. He wrapped his arm around my shoulder.

"You're cold, let's get you under the covers."

I stopped in the bathroom and removed my contacts, then turned out the lights and entered the bedroom. From his breathing I could tell that Mitch was already half asleep; I could feel his body warmth emanating from the bed, could almost hear the beating of his heart. I could even smell the blood in his veins, beckoning me.

"This will be harder than I thought," I whispered to myself as I tried to slide into bed beside him without disturbing him. I settled in and he rolled toward me.

"What did you say?"

"Oh, nothing important." He rubbed his hand up and down my thigh, massaging and caressing. "Mitch," I admonished him gently, "you have to work tomorrow. Don't you think you should get some sleep?"

"As if I could, now."

I caught my breath and my body relaxed under his ministrations, but my mind raced. I had conditioned myself for many years to look at sexual play as a prelude to feeding. I felt my canines grow in anticipation and when his mouth replaced the hand on my thigh, I moaned aloud.

That sound was all the encouragement he needed. He teased and nibbled until I began to thrash and flail in arousal. When I thought I could stand no more, he plunged into me deeply.

"Jesus," I cried and he fell upon me heavily, pinning me to the bed. My mouth was resting against his shoulder, then his neck which I kissed and suckled, not biting, not yet. I couldn't let this happen, but it was happening, the hunger for blood had awakened within me and I couldn't stop. I didn't want it to stop. I flung one arm around his neck and pulled him to me tightly. I was ready, I needed only his blood.

Time stopped; all the universe seemed to be waiting for this one moment. My mouth opened as if of its own will, my head fell to the side, my teeth contacted flesh, and hot, sweet blood filled my mouth and throat. I swallowed frantically and realized from a sharp pain in my shoulder, that I had turned away from him, that I had bitten myself.

"Thank God," I whispered reverently, as orgasms overcame us and we shuddered in our pleasure.

Finally, he reached over and turned on the light. I hid my eyes with my one arm, keeping the shoulder I had bitten pressed to the bed. "Turn it off, Mitch," I complained.

"I just want to look at you," he explained. "You're so beautiful." I squinted up at him and he smiled, reaching over to touch my lips.

"Deirdre, you've got blood on your mouth." He wiped it away with his finger.

I felt myself blush, warming with embarrasment and fear. "I guess I bit myself," I said as casually as possible. "I'll probably be all puffy tomorrow."

"God, I hope so." He snuggled next to me. "That was incredible, you know?"

"I know."

He rolled onto his back and stared up at the ceiling. Comfortable silence enveloped us, and I traced a shadowy scar down the right side of his body. He jumped and laughed and took my hand. “That tickles.” He raised my hand to his mouth and gently kissed my fingertips.

“Where did you get it?”

“I interfered in a knife fight.”

“Did you stop it?”

“Yes.”

“Good.” We lay silently again and I thought he had fallen asleep. I closed my eyes with a sigh and began to drift.

His voice brought me back. “Deirdre?”

“Yes?”

“What was he like?”

“Who?”

“Your husband. The one you never talk about.”

“Oh.” I paused, collecting my thoughts, wondering just how much I should tell him.

He mistook my pause for a reluctance to talk. His voice was tentative, soft. “You don’t have to tell me, if you don’t want to. I just wanted to know what kind of man could make a woman like you close herself off from life.”

“I don’t mind talking about him, really. It just seems there is no point in it. I mean, he’s dead and I’m alive and there’s nothing I can do about it.”

“He meant that much to you, then?”

“I loved him. But there are times when I can barely remember his face.” I had never talked to anyone about this, not even Max. It was hard to separate his death from the awful transformation that had overtaken me at the same time. In my mind, it was all the same. “But then I have a dream that brings it all back.”

“That must be awful.”

I was silent again for a time. I could hardly recognize the voice as mine when I began. “I was there, when he died. I almost died myself. It was raining and the carr . . . the car . . . he lost control of the car and we overturned. I don’t remember too much after that.” I shuddered and continued in a whisper. “But when I woke in the hospital they told me he had died.” I was amazed at how much pain was in my voice, amazed at the tears

I brushed away. It had been, after all, more than a century ago. "I was pregnant; I lost the baby. They said I couldn't have any more."

"I'm sorry." He looked over at me, his eyes intense with shared pain. "But I'm glad you didn't die."

I gave a small smile and touched his cheek. "I'm glad, too." I knew then I could not admit that until I had met Mitch, I still wished I *had* died, or at least had been allowed to live a human life following the accident, to die of natural causes. Suddenly I was overcome with anger at the person who had caused my existence, the one who I, justly or not, held accountable for my life as it was. Because of him, I had lived long enough to meet and fall in love with the one person who could have replaced my dead husband. And because of him, I could never have Mitch the way I wanted to.

"Damn," I swore and punched the pillow angrily.

"What's that all about?"

"Why is life so complicated?"

"It seems good enough to me right now." I looked over at him and he was smiling. "After all, here we are, you and I. We seem to be doing just fine."

"I suppose so."

He reached over and turned out the light, then pulled me close to him and kissed me. "Deirdre." His voice was trembling. "This is probably not the right time to say this, and I don't want to scare you off, but I love you."

"As you get to know me better, Detective, you'll discover that very little in this world scares me." It wasn't true, I was frightened of him, of life, of what this relationship could mean. Then I realized a sarcastic answer was uncalled for in this situation. "Mitch," I tried to soften my reply without making the committment I knew he wanted to hear, the one I had no right to make. "I didn't mean it like that. Why would I be scared of you? Thank you."

"My pleasure, good night." He rolled over and was asleep in what seemed seconds. I listened to his rhythmic breathing, and mouthed the words I wanted, but did not dare to say.

"I love you, Mitch."

* * *

"Deirdre, if you're there, pick up the phone, please." Through the closed bedroom door, I could hear the pleading in Gwen's voice on the answering machine. Mitch was still sleeping; I reached over and touched his hair gently, then rose from bed to take the call. She was in the midst of her frantic message when I picked up the phone and interrupted her.

"Hello, Gwen."

"Oh, Deirdre, thank God. Where have you been? Do you know what time it is? I've been so worried."

I glanced at the clock, it was after nine. I should have been to the office by 7:30 at the latest. "Sorry, Gwen. I was sleeping so soundly that I didn't hear the phone."

"I find that hard to believe; it's never happened before. What's going on?"

"Nothing is going on. I was tired, that's all." I permitted myself a small reminiscent sigh, remembering why I had been so tired. Mitch entered the room with a sheepish smile, searching for the clothes he had discarded the night before.

"Deirdre," Gwen continued. "When will you be coming in?"

"Don't open the drapes," I warned sharply as Mitch headed in that direction.

He shrugged, then went for the light switch. "Is this okay?" he asked sleepily.

"Yes, that will be fine." I braced myself against the glare, I had forgotten to put my contacts in. "No, Gwen, I wasn't talking to you."

"You have someone there with you, don't you? Who is it?" Her voice acquired the curious, voyeuristic quality it always had when she talked about my personal life.

"Never mind that. What's the weather like?"

I could visualize her confusion as clearly as if she had been in the same room with me. "The weather? Well, it's clear and sunny, a really beautiful day, and not too cold, but what has that got to do with anything?"

"Nothing, it doesn't matter. Can you handle the office today? I won't be coming in." I spoke absently as I watched Mitch pick up clothing from the floor. He had found his shorts and put them on, then came up behind me to wrap the robe around my shoulders.

"You're as cold as ice," he said quietly as he kissed my neck and wrapped his arms around my waist. I giggled softly in reaction.

"Deirdre, are you still there? What the hell is happening?"

"Nothing." Mitch's nuzzling was becoming more intense. I reached my hand back to caress his face. "Can you take care of everything for me today?"

"I guess so, but what will I tell everyone . . ."

"Tell them I'm going on a picnic." I hung up the phone.

"Picnic?" Mitch questioned as he kissed my arm and hand, easing the robe back off my shoulders. "You want to go on a picnic?"

"Not really . . ." I began, when he interrupted.

"What the hell?"

I turned my head to see what caused his reaction. He was staring at my shoulder; it displayed the remains of a nasty bruise, greenish blue but already beginning to fade although it had been formed only a few hours ago. "Did I do that?" He sounded horrified. "Oh, Deirdre, I'm sorry. I never meant to hurt you."

I felt myself flush; I had inflicted the wound myself, of course, but I could not tell him that. Instead, I pulled the robe tightly around me. "No, Mitch, you didn't cause that. It's an old bruise."

He looked at me oddly. "Funny, I don't remember any bruise there last night."

"And I don't remember you paying very much attention to my shoulder." I gave him a bright smile which he returned. "Now, be a love and order us some coffee from room service." I headed for the bathroom. "I'll be just a few minutes."

The water in the shower was as hot as possible to warm my cold skin, the heat it gave would have to last as long as Mitch was there. As it cascaded over my naked body, I enjoyed its touch, but not as much as his. He had been a wonderful lover, considerate yet passionate, gentle yet urging me to newer and more violent pleasures than I had ever known. Soaping my breasts, I thought of him touching me there, his mouth and his hands on my body, a body that responded as it never had before.

I gave a small, throaty laugh when I thought of how ridiculous I was acting—almost as if I were a bride or a novice in the sexual game. Over the hundred plus years that I had lived, I had exchanged sexual favors for blood or for protection. Or, as in Max's case, as a way to try to keep someone with me. I had known more men than I could count in so many various ways, love, hate, anger and fear. I had even married and truly loved someone who also loved me. But no one, and I felt slightly disloyal to my dead husband as I thought this, had touched me as Mitch had done. With no one had I felt the excitement, the total joining of two persons, as I had with him.

I turned the shower off and stepped out of the stall. I dried and, wrapping myself in a large towel, went to the bedroom. As I dressed I examined the bruise on my shoulder; it was already yellowing with age and healing. It had to be kept secret, I thought in a panic, Mitch couldn't see that it was substantially better. I pulled on a pair of jeans and put on a tight-necked sweater. He would have to leave, as soon as possible. I could not take the chance of him finding out the truth about me—he meant too much to me for that. And I knew there would be no second chance for me, if he knew the truth. Imagining his face, his repulsion if he knew what I was and how I had to live, I shuddered. He could never know, I realized, no matter how compelled I felt to tell him, to unburden myself in confession, to throw myself into his arms and sob out my sordid, monstrous past. For a monster I was, and I must never let myself forget it.

A silent rage built up inside me and I longed to scream, to lose myself in a primitive reaction. A man that I loved was right through the door, a door that I could easily break into splinters. A body that I knew and could never forget, lived and grew old almost before my eyes. The blood that pulsed through his veins was precious because it was his. And I could never have it, never share it or his life.

I sat staring in the mirror, brushing my hair. For once I took no delight in my reflection, my eternal youthfulness. I would give it all up for one grey hair, one wrinkle, any sign that it might someday be possible to lead a normal life. If I could not have that, I would prefer that the old myths were true, that a creature such as I would have no image to mock, no daily reminder of what I had become.

"Damn." My voice was a whisper; it would not carry to the other room. Calmly, easily, I took my hand and pressed on the mirror. Harder and harder I pushed, until I felt the glass give way under my touch. I arched my hand and flexed my nails until tiny cracks began to form and spread, making soft, tingling noises that I knew only I could hear. I applied pressure until the entire surface cracked. My reflection was distorted into a thousand images, broken and malformed, lined and twisted: a portrait of the vampire.

I pulled my hand away, picked out a few specks of glass and gently sucked the blood from the wounds. Mitch could never know, I decided again with more fervor. I had to send him away.

But before that happened I would have to use him. Not for his blood, but for his mind, his analytical sense. He had to find the other for me, and I would follow from there. I needed others of my kind, I needed to find the one who had done this to me. And I would kill him. Or he would kill me. At this time, the outcome mattered little. Only the knowlege, only the discovery. The love I felt for Mitch would have to be submerged, buried as finally as my other loves, as deeply as my humanity.

There came a gentle knock at the door and I rose quickly from my seat. "I will be right out," I called, forcing cheerfulness into my voice.

"Breakfast is here," Mitch said complacently. "Come on out—you should be as hungry as I am."

"So, where do you go from here?" I had made a show of eating a danish; in reality I had broken it into small pieces and pushed them around on my plate. Mitch had not really paid much attention to me, there was nothing wrong with his appetite. I had, however, finished the pot of coffee and called downstairs for more.

"What do you mean?"

"Where do you go on the case?"

"You don't really want to discuss that, do you? I had the feeling from the other night that it bothered you, a lot, and that you'd prefer not to know anything more about it."

I reached over and took his hand. "It's important to you, isn't it?" He nodded. "Then it is important to me. Maybe it would help to discuss it with someone who has no previous experience with this sort of situation. I could provide a fresh, new viewpoint."

He gave me a sidelong look as he finished his coffee. "I don't know, Deirdre, I shouldn't discuss police matters with you. It's not standard operating procedure."

Although I knew I could coerce him into talking, I wanted his willing cooperation. Rising from the table, I walked behind him and began to massage his shoulders and back. "I only want to help you, Mitch." My fingers kneaded his flesh, coaxing the tension from him. "And remember, I have a bit of a personal involvement here; after all, I did know two of the victims."

"I remember. I don't like it, but I remember."

I said nothing, but kept the steady pressure of my hands on his back. He moaned appreciatively and rolled his head back. "Relax, my love," I crooned softly. "Just relax. Everything will be just fine."

"When you say that, I can almost believe it. But honestly, we don't know how to proceed. We have no evidence, no clues, no suspect, no blood." His voice drifted off and I hugged him to me in silence. When I heard the elevator bell ring, I put my head down and kissed his ear.

"There's our coffee, I'll be right back."

I went to the door and collected the tray. When I turned back, Mitch had gotten up and was inserting his gun into the shoulder holster. I poured more coffee in both cups and smiled over at him. "If you have to leave soon, at least help me finish this."

He accepted the offered cup and sat back down. "I don't really have to go till this afternoon. It's just," and he indicated the weapon, "I feel naked without this, somehow."

"That's fine with me, I like you that way." I glanced at him, the blue of his eyes began to intensify with a reawakening of passion. How easily I could fall back into the delusion that ours could be a normal relationship. It must not happen. I could not allow it. So instead of going to him and accepting his embrace, I sat down at the table across from him. "You must have some sort of clue," I said without preamble. "How could three people be murdered without any evidence about who had done it?"

"What? Are you back on that subject again?"

"I am only trying to help you. As I said before, a fresh perspective might be just what you need."

He shrugged. "You may be right, Deirdre. I don't really know what to think of all this. And neither does anyone else. Let me hear what you have to say."

My mouth twisted into a strange sort of smile. "Do you watch movies?"

"Movies? Well, sure, but I don't really see what that has to do with anything."

"I think that right now you are all at the point where the wild–eyed doctor comes bursting into the station with the facts that everyone has been ignoring."

"Those facts being?" He had a condescending look on his face that made me feel resentful of his calm, predictable world. I hardened myself to his response; perhaps unfairly, I decided that here was a man who could look an unpleasant fact in the eyes and still deny its existence. I was wasting my time, thinking I could use him to track down the vampire. But for the sake of the love we had shared, and for my own selfish motives I said what I needed to say.

"The fact that modern man is too stubborn and obstinent, ignorant of anything outside his self-centered definition of the world. The fact that myths and fables might all have a core of truth, however they have been distorted over the centuries. And the fact that what you may be dealing with is indeed a supernatural being, or at least a superhuman species, about which you know nothing."

He searched my face for a long time, trying, I thought, to find some trace of humor. There was none. His mouth twitched as if he was controlling a smile or a laugh. I poured myself another cup of coffee, my eyes never leaving his. Then the ridiculousness of the situation caught up with me. I was right about the movies, it was the doctor who should bring forth the theory; never once had a vampire tried to convince the authorities of her existence. It didn't play right, it didn't feel right. I gave a weak smile at the thought of my foolishness. "It was only a thought, Mitch, just an idea that I thought might open you up to a new way of looking at the murders."

Even with my smile, he didn't laugh. "You really believe this, don't you?"

"I do, Mitch."

"I don't suppose you have great-grandparents that came from Romania, do you?"

"Of course not."

"I do." He looked embarassed to make the confession.

"You do?"

"Yeah, but don't tell anyone I admitted that. I'm already the butt of too many jokes at the station for my dedicated involvment in this case."

"Then you agree with me?" I couldn't quite believe it.

Finally he laughed. Oddly enough, I did not resent it; it had no ridicule in it, just the good-natured sound of two people enjoying a rather inane joke. "Now wait a minute, I didn't say I believed you. I don't, but I'm not as narrowminded as you seem to think. It makes perfect sense to assume that our murderer believes himself a vampire; in this case, that belief is enough to make it true. I have three bloodless bodies and one madman responsible. The fact that he doesn't fly through the window in the shape of a bat, or that he doesn't live forever, really makes no difference. In his mind, he is a vampire. Therefore, I go to find a vampire." He smiled wearily. "That's why everyone at the station is having a heyday at my expense. But that's also why I will solve this case."

"Oh." I got up from the table and walked to the window. Through the glass I could hear the city sounds below, feel the warmth of the winter sun and wondered what Mitch would think if I pulled the drapes aside, how he would explain the irrefutable facts when I began to smoulder before his eyes. Would he think that it was only my belief that I was a vampire that caused my death?

"Deirdre?"

At his quiet question, I turned around. He had put his coat on and moved to the door.

"Let's go." He smiled and held out his hand. "I know a perfect place for that picnic you said you wanted to go on."

"I don't want to go on a picnic."

"But you said . . ."

"I just wanted Gwen to quit pressing me on when I would be in at the office. I don't want to go anywhere."

"Fine by me." He moved toward me and reached an arm around my waist. "We'll just stay in. I have two hours before I'm due at work." He pulled me closer and began to kiss me; I pushed him away gently.

"Mitch." I felt his magnetic draw on me, wanting nothing more than to spend another two hours in his embrace, but I needed sleep, and I needed to protect myself from his inquisitive nature. And with every second spent in his presence I felt the urge to feed grow stronger, even though I had fed only two nights ago. "I'd like you to leave now." The tone of my voice was cold and commanding.

He looked at me with shock. "Why? I thought that you and I could spend some more time together. I love you, and I suspect you love me, too, although you're too stubborn to admit it."

"I'm afraid that you may have just jumped to one conclusion too many. I never said I loved you."

"But last night was so good, so wonderful between us, I just assumed that . . ."

"You assumed that because we had a wonderful night of sex, that I would swoon into your arms at the next opportunity? It was wonderful, I admit, and I would like to see you again, soon. Just not today. Call me later in the week and we'll talk."

"The hell we will." His eyes flashed angrily and I knew I had gone too far. "There's nothing to talk about, really. I confused you with someone who had a heart and feelings. Now I see that you were using me for what you use all men for."

I smiled sadly, he would never know how wrong he was about that. "Mitch," I started to explain, "I'm sorry but I'm so tired. I need some sleep and I need to sleep alone. I want you to leave, but I do want you to come back."

"So you can lead me on again? Let me believe we might have a decent relationship and not just a one–night stand? Forget it, lady, I won't be back." He slammed the door and left. I locked it behind him, went to the bedroom and fell on the bed.

Chapter 10

When I awoke at 4:00 A.M. well-rested and refreshed, I checked the machine in the hopes that there might be a message from Mitch. There were a few calls but none from him. I was not particularly surprised. It was possible, I thought, that I would never hear from him again, except perhaps in an official capacity. So be it, I thought and dressed for the office.

In the lobby, Frank was preparing to leave; I called to him and he came to my side immediately. He looked curious, I thought, and probably hoped to have some explanation of the previous evenings events.

"Yes, Miss Griffin. Is something wrong?"

"Not at all, Frank, but the mirror in my bedroom is broken. Please have it replaced before I return." I thanked him, nodded him a curt good morning and hurried out the door lest he try to catch up and walk with me.

The sky was cloudy with impending snow and the wind howled down the empty streets. Small bits of litter blew around and the cloak I was wearing whipped about my body. But it was still night; I reveled in it and felt sadly deflated when the walk ended and I arrived at the office building.

I signed in, rode up in the elevator and unlocked the doors. My footsteps echoes through the dark, empty rooms. I opened the door to my office, placed my briefcase on the desk and turned on a small light. The cloying scent of dying roses filled the air. I turned toward the credenza to dispose of them, when I noticed a body lying motionless on the couch. A cold shock spread through me, until I heard the soft breathing and recognized the form. It was Gwen; how she came to be sleeping here in my office, I would discover later. She looked exhausted and pale, so I let her sleep and went about my work quietly. With the exception of sighs and a few sleepy murmurs she slept soundly for the next three hours while I busied myself with the finishing details for Friday's show.

While I was discarding the dead flowers, and arranging those that had survived in one of the vases, Gwen awoke and looked around in confusion. She sat straight up when she saw me. "Good morning," I said softly with a smile.

"Hi," she said groggily. "Have you been here long? I didn't hear you come in; you should've woke me up." She pushed her hair away from her face with both hands, then giggled as it fell back to cover her eyes. "Boy, I must be a mess. I guess I'd better go home and clean up, but we have so much to do. And I just don't think I can face the subway now."

"Why don't you use my rooms, Gwen? You can shower and change. Check the closet—there should be something that would fit you in there."

She beamed at me. "You mean it? Wow, that would be great.

Ever since you told me about it, I've been dying to see inside. Are you sure you don't mind?"

"If I minded, I wouldn't offer, would I? You go and I'll make the coffee." I reached into a desk drawer, removed the key and opened the door.

"Thanks a lot, Deirdre. What a day we had yesterday without you. I'll fill you in when I get out." She smiled mischievously. "And I'll tell you about my weekend if you tell me about yours." With that provocative comment, she entered my apartment and closed the door.

I left the office and went to the coffee maker, shaking my head and grinning. Gwen could be so outrageous at times; I would miss her companionship when the time finally came for me to leave. And that time was coming soon, I knew. The masquerade would not last much longer—I only hoped to have enough time to discover the other vampire before I had to leave.

I was pouring my second cup of coffee when Gwen finally emerged, dressed in a black suede skirt and white blouse. She stood and studied me for a moment, as if in expectation. I motioned for her to sit down. "Now, shall we get started?"

"You bet!" She smiled at me impishly, as she settled into her usual chair. "You go first, okay?"

"What?"

"You know, tell me about your weekend." She leaned forward in her chair. "You met someone, had someone there with you when I called Monday morning, didn't you? Tell me all about it . . . did he spend the night? Was he any good?"

I felt my face grow flushed. "Gwen, I really don't think . . .

"Deirdre, you're blushing. I don't think I've ever seen that happen before. He must have been good."

"I really don't wish to discuss it, if you don't mind, Gwen."

"Honestly, Deirdre, you can be so Victorian at times. I thought we were friends; you can tell me about it. It won't go any further than me, I promise." She made a small crossing motion over her heart and the gesture was so childlike and endearing I couldn't resist sharing with her.

"Well, since it looks like no work will get done until I oblige that insatiable curiousity of yours, I have no choice. Yes, Gwen, I met someone and he spent the night." I leaned back in my chair and closed my eyes to recall that night. When I spoke again my voice was soft and distant. "It was wonderful, wild . . ." I said no more but clasped my arms to myself, thinking of his strong, warm body enfolded around me.

Gwen interrupted my reverie with a small sign. "Wow," she said, in a hushed voice. "I guess you'll be seeing him again. Who is he? Or is that a big secret, too?"

I opened my eyes and focused on her smiling face. "You met him Friday night."

"The cop?" Her eyes widened in disbelief.

"Believe me, I was as surprised as you are. Everything clicked into place with him. I can't really say why. It seemed right, that's all."

"Seemed? Why the past tense?"

"I don't know, Gwen. I can't see it going any further; we're too different." I gave a sigh of regret. "Can we drop the subject, please?"

"Sure, Deirdre. No problem. But if you like him, and I think you do, you should give it a chance. Differences can be overcome."

I laughed at her naive statement. "Not our differences, I think. You don't know the half of it. And," I interrupted her objections, "I don't want you to know. You should not be involved."

She took my reprimand good naturedly. "Okay," she agreed. "Now it's my turn. Guess where I went Sunday night."

"Nick's place?" I questioned tentatively.

"Oh, no. We had a horrible fight Saturday." She grimaced in remembrance. "He can be so impossible at times. We're not married yet, I told him, and if he keeps up his nonsense we may never be."

"I hate to hear that, Gwen."

"Well, there's this girl he works with, he talks about her all the time. I don't have any proof, of course, but I think he's been sleeping with her. So when I confronted him, he didn't deny it. Didn't admit to it either, but I know him well enough to know that something's up." She sniffed a little and wiped the beginnings of tears angrily from her eyes. "That son of a bitch, I deserve better than that and I told him so. He laughed and said I was welcome to try. So I did. Sunday night I got all dressed up and went out by myself. I called a cab and asked him to take me to the hottest club in town. You know, a real meat-market type. And you'll never guess where I ended up."

I felt a strange foreboding at her words. I nodded slowly and answered her. "I think I know, Gwen. You went to the Ballroom of Romance."

She was disappointed that I guessed correctly, but did not let it dampen her enthusiasm. "Yeah, what a great place. I thought for a while I wouldn't be able to get in, it was really crowded. But I remembered you once said you went there a lot, so I mentioned your name."

"And did it help?"

"It sure did. They gave me the royal treatment; I didn't even have to buy a drink all night." She gave me a sly smile then continued, "And I met some friends of yours."

"Oh?" I glanced at the clock—soon the other employees would begin to arrive. I wished she would get on with her story. There was work to be done. And the delving into my personal life was making me extremely uncomfortable.

"Why didn't you ever mention that your Max was the owner?"

"Didn't I? I suppose it never seemed important. So, you finally met Max."

"Yeah, briefly. He came over to our table and introduced himself; he's real nice and so handsome. But he didn't stick around."

I permitted myself a small smirk. "No, Max doesn't stay very long. Who else did you meet?"

Gwen looked away dreamily and toyed with a strand of her hair. "Oh, Deirdre, he's so cute and he doesn't seem to know it.

I guess he's shy or something. But after a few drinks he really loosened up. Said I was the answer to his prayers; isn't that sweet?"

I suppressed a shiver. "Who, Gwen?"

"Why, Larry, of course. I think I could really fall for him."

A warning went off in my head. "Gwen, I don't mean to presume, but I think you should stay away from Larry and the club. It is not the best place to be these days and you might get hurt." I thought of Larry and his vow of revenge. "Don't you think you should give Nick another chance? I can't believe you would give up on him so quickly."

Gwen looked at me defiantly. "I never realized you approved of Nick so much. I always had the feeling that you hated him. You wouldn't happen to be just a little jealous that I got along so well with Larry, would you?"

"Jealous of you and Larry? No, it's not that. You're free to do whatever you want. But promise me you'll be careful. Don't get involved so soon with someone you just met."

She shrugged and avoided my eyes. "Okay," she agreed reluctantly. "I'll be careful. But I'm not as inexperienced as you think. And I can't see that your advice has done you much good." She seemed to be thinking out loud and instantly regretted her comment. "Oh, I'm sorry . . . I didn't mean . . ."

I laughed a bit and the tension fell away. "Don't worry about it. After all, you are probably right. Now, can we please get to work?"

The days and nights of that week seemed endless, yet when I awoke in my office apartment early Friday afternoon I could scarcely believe that the day for which we had prepared so many months had finally arrived. The line was good, I knew, and the clothes would sell.

I showered and dressed and went into the office. Everyone had been given the day off to prepare for this evening, so when the phone rang I picked it up and was surprised to hear Gwen's voice answering. "No, she's not in right now, may I take a message?"

As I began to put the receiver down, the caller spoke and my spirits lifted when I recognized the voice. "I've got it, Gwen, thank you." There was an awkward silence after the click that signalled Gwen's hanging up. "Hello," I said tentatively and somewhat breathlessly. "Mitch, are you still there?"

"Yeah, I'm here. Deirdre, I want to see you again." He sounded hesitant, fearful of my response. "I didn't really mean the things I said to you. I'd like a chance to start over again. Will you be home tonight?"

"Tonight is the night of the show. But we could meet afterwards." I told him where the show was being held and the time it was scheduled to start. "I'll leave word at the entrance that you should be admitted."

"Thank you. And, uh, Deirdre?"

"Yes?"

"Well, I wanted to call you sooner, but I just didn't know how to approach you again. I'm really sorry for what I said. There are no excuses for it, I know that. It's just that our relationship flared so suddenly, it's overwhelming. I can't imagine where it will lead. But I do know that not a moment has gone by that I haven't thought about you."

"It is the same for me," I admitted gently. "I'll see you tonight."

I hung up the phone softly and stared at it ruefully for a few seconds. There was a knock on the door and Gwen walked in still wearing her coat.

"Surprise," she said breezily. "I know you gave me the day off, but I didn't really want to stay home. Nick keeps calling and I don't want to talk to him. I want him to sweat it out for a bit. Besides, I wanted to show you the dress I'll be wearing tonight. I hope you don't mind."

"Why would I mind? Bring it in."

"Don't have to, I'm wearing it. She pulled off her coat and stood before me awkwardly. "Do you like it?"

I gave her a long, appraising stare and motioned for her to turn around. The dress was an amazing creation—swirls of bright, primary colors, each color sewn on individually in a seemingly haphazard manner. It was sleeveless with large bows of different colors forming the straps. The low cut bodice was formed into an empire waist, then fell straight to her knees. The back dropped to waist level and the skirt was gathered and flowing. The look was avant garde, modern; the complete opposite of the Griffin Design look.

"Gwen, it's lovely, it really is. I like it very much and it suits you, but . . ."

"But what?" she questioned petulantly.

"You know you can't wear another designer's creation to our show. It just doesn't look right."

"But it's not another designer's. Not really." She looked embarrassed, but continued. "It's mine, I made it." She sat down with a flop on the sofa. "I was hoping that you'd let me wear it, see what people think. And then maybe you would let me do a few things for the next show; you know, something light and frivolous."

"You designed it?" She heard the delight in my voice and brightened up a bit.

"Yeah. I wanted to show you that I could do more than answer the phone. Do you really like it? Can I wear it?"

"Gwen, please wear it, it's wonderful. And yes, you may do some things for the next show. I'm thrilled that you want to do that; I was going to suggest that you get more involved."

"Great!" She beamed her delight. "I was hoping that you would go for it. Thanks so much."

"Now, why don't you go home and get some rest before the show. You'll probably need it."

She rose from her chair and began to aimlessly shuffle the papers on my desk. "I guess so, but . . ."

"But what, Gwen? Is something wrong?"

"Not wrong, exactly. It's just that I don't want to stay at home. It's Nick, he's getting so forceful; I'm half afraid of what he might do. I feel safer here." She paused for a moment and then haltingly continued. "Do you, ah, I mean, could I please use your rooms for the weekend? I don't want to impose, but I really need to do some thinking and this would be the perfect place to do it. No one would bother me and Nick couldn't find me. Besides, I figured you might have other plans for the weekend; I mean, since you got a call from your policeman, I thought you'd have better things to do than hole up here all weekend."

My plans for the weekend had been exactly that. But Gwen was so earnest, I felt I couldn't refuse her.

"I would be happy to do it, Gwen. And it's no imposition. Go home and pack a few things for yourself. You can move in after the show tonight; I will leave the key in the top drawer." I gave her a wry smile. "But no wild parties."

"Deirdre, thank you. How can I ever pay you back?"

"Just get yourself back to normal. I need you alert and with your wits together first thing Monday. We will have a lot to do."

"You bet," she agreed. "See you at the show." In her usual headlong fashion, she rushed out of the office.

After she left, I checked the clock. It was still early; over four hours before sundown. Four long hours in which I was virtually confined in this place. With a sigh, I moved as aimlessly through the office as Gwen had: rearranging the chairs, picking loose threads from the carpet, restacking the papers on the desk. I fought the strong, but deadly, urge to open the heavy draperies and observe the street below. I felt trapped, hungry and restless.

"Damn," I swore softly to myself. I entered the apartment and opened a bottle of wine to fill the remaining hours.

Chapter 11

As I drank the wine, I thought about meeting Mitch this evening following the show. Although I had accepted the fact earlier in the week that I might never see him again, and even acknowledged to myself that it would be better if I did not,

I still could not control the rush of excitement that filled me when I thought of him, the fluttering of my stomach when the phone rang and I would answer, hoping it was him. That the relationship was doomed to fail had no real impact on my thoughts. I wanted him, I loved him and could no more control my emotions than I could change the circumstances of my life. "Oh, what the hell," I said as I drained the last of the bottle. "I might as well enjoy it while it lasts." So I would see him and continue to see him as long as I could. With that decision reached, I felt relieved and turned my attentions to preparation for this evening.

After careful deliberation and discarding the usual graceful sweep of full skirts, I chose a gown designed for last year's line but never shown since it did not fit the Griffin image. It was a black, strapless sheath slit to mid–thigh for ease in walking. I had carefully embellished the hem and side slit with red sequins and rhinestones in a flame-like pattern. When I moved the light reflected and danced giving the impression that the dress was indeed on fire. As a final concession to Max, I pinned my hair up in an approximation of a Gibson Girl. I frowned at it in the mirror, wondering how long the countless pins would hold, but decided to leave it up. My shoulders looked almost white against the black of the dress; I did not want to distract from their marble appearance. The final adornment was a pair of small ruby earrings and a matching necklace that had belonged to my mother. After one final glance in the mirror, I covered it all with my cape and went through the office and downstairs to meet the limousine hired for the evening.

We arrived early enough to avoid the press and the public. The show was being held in one of the most exclusive hotels in town. Two of the ballrooms were reserved for the show itself, one large room was to be partitioned off into small dressing areas; a smaller area outside the ballrooms was set aside as the reception area. I walked through this area, noticing with pleasure that all was elegant, understated and dignified. I held my breath while opening the main doors; the preparations this week had progressed well, but the area had still been unfinished yesterday.

I let my breath out in a relieved sigh. It was perfect, exactly as I had envisioned it. The walls had been covered with heavy grey paper, printed to appear as rough hewn stones. The gilt hands grasping candles that lined the walls were shamelessly borrowed from Jean Cocteau; the theme of the show was one that he himself had borrowed: "Beauty and the Beast." I thought that I would probably lose points for originality on this initially, but the theme was maintained throughout the show. The macabre backdrop was only one element. The models themselves would carry the message that beauty and the grotesque were often separated by a very thin line.

Removing my cape and draping it over my arm, I slowly walked down one of the center aisles to approach the runway. As I stepped on the platform, I jumped when one of the hands moved, then laughed inwardly at my apprehension. They had been designed to move almost imperceptibly, in sequence; the technicians were merely making their final test. I laughed again when I noticed that we had lost the fight with the fire marshall; the hands held electric candles, not the real ones I had wanted to use. I shrugged off this last problem; it was not noticeable except here on the stage. All that mattered was that the desired mood be set.

Stepping through one of the side doors, I entered into the dressing areas, squinting against the bright lights. When my vision cleared, I made a mental count to find that all the models had arrived. Some were giggling in nervousness; others sat quietly while the last touches of makeup were applied.

"Good evening, ladies."

When they all turned to face me at my greeting, the effect was chilling. I experienced a moment of apprehension that perhaps I had gone too far. I studied the models individually; each wore a gown, characteristic of Griffin Designs with the romantic touches of lace, ruffles, satin and velvet. But each model had received an added touch, a flaw in their perfect appearance. On some it was subtle: excessively long nails coated in black lacquer or sharpened white canines peeking out from beneath blood red lips. For others who were willing to take more of a risk, we had ordered full theatrical makeup transforming them into various wild animals: one posed as a serpent; another, a cat; a third, a large black raven. Those who did not wish to take part wore full or half-masks, to hint only of the grotesque beneath. The overall effect was nightmarish, almost hallucinogenic.

"Well," I addressed them slowly, "they will either love us or hate us, but this will be a show that won't be forgotten soon. I'm very pleased, thank you all." I glanced at the clock. "Forty-five minutes until the show, ladies. Good luck."

As they all turned away to complete their preparation, I motioned one model, the serpent girl, to me. "Janie, you look wonderful," I complimented her, knowing that she had planned on doing her own makeup. She smiled at me as I continued. "Have you seen Gwen anywhere in this chaos?"

She knew the rules about staying in the area prior to a show and looked away, hesitating slightly before she answered. "She's here somewhere, Miss Griffin. Should I look for her?"

"Janie, I know you two are friends, and I know she'd tell you where she was going. Save the mystery for the show and tell me where she is."

"Sorry, Miss Griffin. She sort of asked me to cover for her. You see, her date came early and she wanted to spend a little time with him alone. She's not been gone long, no more than five or ten minutes. Everything here is pretty much in control and . . ."

"Don't worry, Janie, she won't get in trouble. Where is she?"

"In the bar," Janie confessed in a lowered voice. "She should be back real soon now."

"Thank you, Janie. I'll get her." I smiled at her reassuringly. "Good luck."

I left the dressing room and returned to the platform. The hands followed me as I walked the runway. I glanced in the direction of the control booth. "Perfect, gentlemen," I called to them as I strode out of the room.

Two of the hotel staff members were stationed in the reception area and I questioned them about whether there was a back route into the bar. I did not want to meet with any of the crowd that had begun to gather in the lobby. Following the directions given, I rushed down the back hallways and cursed Gwen all the way there. The only good thing in all this, I thought, was that it seemed to represent a reconciliation with Nick. I didn't think she would have asked anyone else to attend. And while I did not like him much, I far preferred her keeping company with Nick than with Larry or anyone else she would find at the Ballroom of Romance. There were too many unanswered questions concerning Larry. I didn't trust him, not with Gwen.

When I entered the bar, I saw her immediately. Her bright swirls of color stood out from the primarily dark evening attire of the other clientele. She was sitting facing the door engrossed in conversation with someone I immediately assumed to be Nick, from the possessive way his arm encircled her shoulders. I approached them and she glanced at me in surprise. "Oh, hi," she said, not meeting my eyes.

"Gwen, I hate to interrupt your reunion but we really do have to get the show started. You and Nick can get cozy afterwards . . ." I stopped abruptly as he turned around. Of course it wasn't Nick. His build and hair color were similar but I should not have been fooled. I suppose I saw what I had wanted to see.

"Hello, Larry." I smiled to cover my broken composure, the skin crawled at the base of my neck and I repressed a shiver, remembering his disclosures at our last meeting. "How nice of you to come this evening."

He rose slowly and looked me up and down, leeringly. "Deirdre, what a pleasant surprise. We were just talking about you, weren't we, Gwen?" He nodded at her briefly then turned his attention back to me. "You look beautiful as usual. Who's the lucky man tonight?" His voice was calm and pleasant, but the sneer on his face distorted and twisted the words. I looked quickly at Gwen, but she did not seem to notice as she stood up awkwardly and began to collect her coat and purse.

"We really need to leave, Gwen. Nice to see you again, Larry." I turned and walked out of the bar.

Gwen caught up with me a few seconds later, breathless and apologetic. "I'm sorry, Deirdre. I know I should have stayed with the others. But when he sent the message that he was here, I wanted to see him for a bit. Everything was going fine, with the show, I mean, and I didn't think a few minutes away would hurt. He's just so nice." When I made no reply, she continued, "It won't happen again, I promise."

I stopped abruptly and turned to her. "Gwen," I said softly, looking into her eager face. "I don't begrudge you a few minutes to yourself, I really don't. God knows, I give you precious little time to pursue your personal affairs. And I do not want to interfere with your life or your choices. But before you get more deeply involved with Larry, you and I need to talk. Do you two have plans after the show?" She nodded and tried to look away, but I grasped her chin and turned her face toward me. "Cancel them," I ordered peremptorily. "I do not want you to see him again until we talk about this. Please listen to me on this, it is very important. You must not see him again." She nodded again, this time her eyes were locked on mine. I hoped the command would take.

I released my hold on her and she swayed as she stood, still dazed. Then she relaxed and shook her head briefly as she stared bewildered around her. "What are we doing hanging around here? Let's get going," she said, beginning to move down the hall, "or they'll start without us."

The show went well. The macabre treatment was tolerated by most, enjoyed by some and the designs, the most important part after all, were well received. Following the show, those with invitations remained behind for a small reception. Although I normally hated these affairs, I forced myself to attend and exchange pleasantries with my guests. After talking to a succession of nameless faces, accepting compliments and answering questions, I went to claim a glass of wine. Unfortunately, at the bar, I was cornered by a writer for a prominent women's publication. She wanted to discuss the social and psychological ramifications of the fashion industry. I smiled and nodded and managed to make the proper replies, all the while searching for the easiest way to excuse myself from her company. She provided the perfect opportunity by asking about Gwen, who had been given credit in the program for being both my assistant and co–designer. "Have you never met Gwen?" I questioned. "You really must meet, she is a wonderful help and I couldn't function without her. I'll find her and send her over."

I looked around and saw Gwen deep in conversation with someone in the far corner. I weaved through the crowd, nodding and smiling and arrived in time to hear a familiar voice quietly advising her. "Don't forget what I have told you, my dear. It's very important."

"Hello, Max." I gave him an apologetic smile for the interruption. "May I borrow Gwen for a moment?" He nodded his agreement and I pulled her to one side. "Gwen, here's your chance to earn your large bonus."

"Huh?" I wondered how many glasses of wine she had drunk. "What large bonus?"

"The one you will get for helping me out." I explained the situation and she agreed readily. "Tell her anything you like, but keep her talking and away from me. Thank you." I gave her hand a small squeeze and sent her on her way. This was a situation she would have to learn how to handle in the future.

Max drew up closely beside me. "You look elegant, Deirdre. So, you finally decided to wear your hair up. It's very becoming."

"Just for you, Max. And I see that you have finally found someone else on whom to bestow your fatherly advice." I gestured in Gwen's direction.

"She's a sweet thing, Deirdre. I was merely offering my opinion on her present choice of company. You know she had been seeing Larry, don't you?"

"He isn't still here, is he?" I glanced around the room.

"No, he's not."

"Good. I tried to warn her away earlier, but I'm not sure that she listened."

"Perhaps she'll take my advice more seriously than yours."

"I also have a problem with Larry; what exactly did you tell him about me?"

He looked at me and smiled. "I told you, my dear, a brief, varnished story. I told him where you were from initially and what your name was before you changed it to Deirdre Griffin."

I was instantly relieved and laughed. "Thank God, Max. I thought he knew everything since he called me Dorothy. I don't mind telling you I had a few rough moments worrying over it."

"Not surprising." He moved closer to me. "But you know I, of all people, would never betray you."

"Do I?"

"Of course you do. Now, enough of that topic. Don't you want to know what I thought of your show?" He smiled mockingly.

"I don't know, do I?"

"You should, my love." He reached over and began to toy with a strand of hair that had escaped the pins. His breath was warm in my ear and I suppressed my shudder. "What a revelation for you to make. It was wild and exotic and, if I may say so, extremely arousing. You aimed straight for me, didn't you? Romance, with the element of danger. I'm reminded of a vast sky, a wide field, and a certain young waitress . . ."

"I was not that young then, Max, and I'm certainly not now." I spoke harshly, because, as usual, his presence and his words had a disquieting effect on me.

He continued on, undaunted. "Why did we never repeat the experience? We could now, you know. I closed the club tonight in honor of your show. We could go there now, we would have the whole place to ourselves. Deirdre, Deirdre come with me." His voice was low and urgent and so persuasive that I felt myself weakening. I, too, remembered that night so many years ago with tenderness and passion. He felt my resistance subside and pulled me closer to him. And yet, as I looked into his shining eyes and felt his hands grasp at my bare shoulders, I remembered other nights spent in loneliness and despair, feelings that had been caused in part by him, feelings he had not eased. My mind turned to the time I had spent with Mitch and I drew strength from that remembrance.

"No, Max," I said softly but sternly. "I will not go with you. It's too late for that."

I pushed him away and he stared at me, breathing heavily. "It can never be too late for us. I want you. Come with me now." His voice grew louder and we were attracting curious stares from the other guests.

"Damn you, Max. I said no."

He wrapped his hand tightly around my arm. "It would be different this time, Deirdre. I wouldn't leave you. We could be together . . ."

He was interrupted by another hand laid roughly on his arm, prying his grasp away from me.

"I think she said no, Hunter. You can proceed at the risk of harassment charges. The choice is yours."

Max gave a low laugh. "Ah, Detective Greer, I believe." He gave Mitch a quick, contemptuous glance and then looked back at me. He said, whispering so that I only could hear, "I congratulate you. Such a quick worker. The bodies are scarcely cold and already you have a staunch supporter on the force. I see that my concern for your naivete was needless." Once again his face became expressionless and inscrutable and his voice was pitched normally. "Forgive me, my dear, for my forcefulness. I'm afraid I may have had too much wine. Good night."

He quickly kissed my cheek, nodded to Mitch and walked out the door. Mitch and I stood in a small circle of silence separated from the noise and laughter of the reception. "Thank you." I spoke quietly so as not to break the spell and lifted my hand to caress his cheek. He pulled it to him and kissed the palm.

"I hate that son of a bitch." His vehement comment was so out of place with his gentle gesture that I had to laugh. He looked at me questioningly.

"I could have handled him, but it would have been uglier and taken longer. Thank you again." I linked my arm in his and led him to the refreshments. "Would you like a glass of wine?" I asked, taking one for myself. He helped himself to a glass and a small plate of *hors d'oeuvres*.

"No dinner," he confessed sheepishly. "You look wonderful."

"Thank you. So do you." He looked elegant and only slightly out of context in his tuxedo.

He shrugged. "I figured fancy dress was required, so I rented this. Unfortunately, I was held up and got here too late to see the show. How'd you do?"

"Fine, thank you. It seems to have been a success." I smiled up at him warmly. I was so glad to see him that even this stilted conversation seemed wonderful. "I missed you, Mitch."

He seemed distant, distracted. "What? Oh, I missed you too." He looked around at the thinning crowd. "Look, I know I just got here, but it seems the party is breaking up. Could we go somewhere else?"

"I don't see why not. I want to have a talk with Gwen before we go, though. It should only take a few minutes."

"Your secretary?"

"Yes, you remember her. You met her last week."

"Yeah, I know her. She was on her way out when I came in. I said hello but she seemed to be in a hurry."

I felt alarmed by this hasty departure. Gwen usually stayed until everyone had gone home. "Was she alone?"

He nodded. "She was when I saw her."

"Good, then she will be safe." He looked at me sharply but I offered no explanation. "Where would you like to go?"

"Anyplace other than here," he stated flatly. "Although it's a waste of a rented tux, I'd like to have some privacy." He looked deeply into my eyes and smiled for the first time this evening. I hoped that this signified an evening of more than conversation.

"Fine, I'll go get my coat. I won't be too long."

By the time I reached the dressing areas, most of the models had gone. Only a few remained, removing their makeup. I was pleased to see that one of these was Janie. I congratulated her on her performance, then inquired after Gwen. "Did she tell you why she left in such a hurry?"

Janie thought for a moment then answered. "I think she was upset about something you had said, and something, someone, I think she said his name was Max, had told her. She said she needed to get away and do some serious thinking. I reminded her of our party later on, but she said she couldn't come."

"Did she leave with anyone?"

"No, I don't think so. She said that the crowd was bothering her and she wanted to be alone. She didn't seem herself, though. We're all a little worried about her." She looked at me for reassurance.

"I'm sure she'll be fine, Janie. She's been having some trouble with Nick, you know." She nodded in agreement. "Thank you. And have a good time at the party tonight."

"Would you like to come, Miss Griffin? You'd be welcome." She looked at me slyly. "After all, we're going to send you the bill."

I smiled at her. "No, I don't think this time. I have other plans, but thank you." With a final goodbye I walked out of the room.

I found Mitch at the food table filling another plate. "Sorry I took so long, Mitch, but I see you made good use of the time."

"These are really good, you should have some."

I laughed at his suggestion. "No, thank you, I have to watch what I eat." I reached for his free hand and held it. "Would you like to go now, or maybe you'd rather stay here and eat?"

He looked intently at the plate and then at me as if deciding between us. "No," he said in his deliberate fashion giving me the slow smile that made my pulse race. "On second thought, these aren't all that good." Setting the plate back on the table, he took my cape from my arm and wrapped it around my shoulders. "Come on."

As we came through the hotel door, the limo driver jumped out and opened the door. Mitch looked at me in surprise.

"Well," I said, "if you would rather drive, we could send him back."

"Actually, I had to walk here tonight, that's one of the reasons why I came so late. My car is in the shop. I saw the limo when I came in so I assumed it belonged to someone rich and famous."

I gave him a contented smile. "I am, at least for now. Get in."

As we got settled, the driver turned around inquiringly and I glanced over at Mitch. "Would you like to drive around for a while?"

He shook his head. "We should, I guess. I mean, here I am, dressed for the part, with a woman like you, in a car like this, but . . ."

"I'm entirely in your hands, Detective," I teased as I curled up next to him. "Whatever you'd like is fine with me."

"I'll remember that," he replied with a suggestive smile, then leaned forward and gave the driver his address.

Chapter 12

We didn't speak much on the ride to Mitch's apartment. I sat quietly next to him, enjoying his presence. He rested his chin on my head and caressed my arm. We arrived all too soon.

After opening the door, the driver asked whether he should wait. "No, thank you," Mitch said. "I'll get her home from here." I nodded my head in agreement and he drove away.

We mounted the stairs to his apartment in silence. "Here we are," he said lamely as he opened the door and escorted me within.

"So we are." I surveyed the apartment; it was actually neater than the last time I had visited. The bookshelves were dusted and there were tread marks on the carpet left behind from a recent vacuuming. "Were you expecting company? Everything is so clean."

"I was expecting you," he said bluntly.

"Oh." I went to look at the books. "You seem to be pretty sure of me." I tried to make it sound casual, offhand, but failed.

"Why do you have to be so defensive? I only meant that I was hoping you would come." He looked away angrily.

"I'm sorry, Mitch. It has been a hell of a week and I am more than a little on edge."

"I know," he answered. "I'm a bit jumpy myself."

I gave him a shy smile. "Then why don't we start over? Your apartment looks very nice. Thank you for inviting me."

"My pleasure. Can I get you something. Some wine, maybe, or a cup of coffee?"

"Wine, please."

He went to the kitchen and I followed him. I watched him uncork a bottle and pour two glasses, noticing that his hands were shaking. "Did you say that you hadn't had any dinner?"

"It doesn't matter. I'll survive." He handed me my glass and looked at me. "Would you mind if I changed my clothes? I feel a little overdressed."

"Why would I mind? And while you're changing I will fix you something to eat."

"You?"

I smiled at his surprise. "Yes, me. I do know how to cook, you know."

"How could anyone who looks as good as you do in that dress know how to cook?" He still looked doubtful. "And why would you want to?"

"I like to cook," I confessed, laughing, "and, what's more, I learned how from some of the best short–order cooks in the country. I may be a little rusty, but I think I can still scramble a few eggs without poisoning you. Go get changed." I half-pushed him out of the kitchen and he laughed and left.

I found a towel and wrapped it around my waist as a makeshift apron. Opening his refrigerator, I saw what I needed and started. In spite of my comments to the contrary, I had not cooked in an ordinary kitchen for more years than I wanted to count. In fact, I thought, the last time was probably shortly after the change.

The domestic tasks were strangely comforting. Beating the eggs, warming the skillet, setting a place at the table, all these brought back memories of happier times. For once I was not saddened by these thoughts but smiled contentedly and began to sing, softly at first, and then more confidently. *"Into the ward of the clean, whitewashed halls, where the dead slept and the dying lay, wounded by bayonet, saber and ball, somebody's darling was borne one day."* Mitch walked in just as I reached the chorus *". . . Somebody's darling, somebody's pride, who'll tell his mother where her boy died."*

"Sounds good," he said appreciatively, smiling at me from the kitchen entrance. "No, don't stop, keep singing, please. It's good to hear that old song again. I haven't thought of it or even heard it for years. You know, my mother would sing it to me at bedtime, she told me that her grandmother sang it to her. But I'm sort of surprised that you know it."

"Oh," I said offhandedly. "I know a lot of songs."

"Then keep on singing."

"I couldn't, not now." I felt myself blushing. "Besides, your dinner is done." I gestured at the table. "Sit down."

I served him and after he shook salt and pepper on the eggs, he began to eat immediately and hungrily. With his second forkful he seemed to recover his manners. "Aren't you having anything?"

I lifted my glass of wine and took a sip.

"No, not that. Aren't you going to eat? I don't think I've seen you eat anything since that night we had dinner. Are you on a diet or something?"

"Yes," I smiled, enjoying my secret joke. "A very controlled diet. And I'm afraid eggs aren't on it. But I'll take one bite if it makes you happy."

"It would."

I turned around and got myself a fork from the drawer, then reached over and took a small bit from his plate and put it in my mouth. I chewed it and swallowed, trying not to gag. It caught in my throat and I began to choke. Mitch jumped up immediately, gave me a large thump on the back, stepped back and gave me an appraising glance. "You okay?"

"Fine," I said, trying to laugh. "Too much pepper."

"Sorry," he said, sitting back down. "I like it that way."

I finished my wine to wash the egg taste out of my mouth and refilled my glass. He looked up at me, with a question in his eyes, but his mouth was full and he shook his head. At that moment the phone rang, and I jumped. He motioned for me to get it.

"Hello?" The young man on the phone sounded confused, as if he had the wrong number. "Is, ah, Mitchell Greer there?"

"Yes, he is. Hold on a moment." I held the phone out to him with a smile, hoping that this would interrupt his chain of thought on my seeming inability to swallow even the simplest piece of food. "It's for you."

"No kidding." He wiped his mouth and took the receiver from me.

"Hello?" His face brightened. "Hi, Chris. Where are you calling from? Why didn't you reverse the charges?" He listened for a moment. "You're in town again? You were just here last weekend. I hope you're not neglecting your studies."

I could hear the caller's youthful laugh and voice quite clearly. "I hope I didn't interrupt anything, Dad. I didn't know you had company."

"No, no, you didn't interrupt. We, or well, I was just having some dinner. Hold on a second." He held his hand over the receiver. "It's my son, Chris," he said. "Would you like to meet him?"

"Yes, that would be nice; he's in town?"

He nodded and went back to the phone. "Why don't you come on up?" He smiled at me and took my hand. "There's someone here I'd like you to meet."

I would have recognized Chris as Mitch's son immediately. They had the same nose, the same eyes with the same appraising manner. He shook my hand warmly then gave his father a sly wink. "You're right as usual, Dad."

"Right about what?"

Mitch looked embarrassed and gave Chris a sharp look. "Excuse him, Deirdre, he's a bit of a smart ass." But he smiled when he said it; Chris went to him and they exchanged a brief but forceful hug. "I can only guess that his studies haven't reached the part about confidentiality." Mitch gave him a playful push away and Chris smiled at me.

"Nope, they ain't teached me that yet. Besides," and he turned to Mitch again, "I don't think Deirdre would mind knowing that you described her to me in minute detail. I thought he was exaggerating, but now that I've seen you myself . . ." He rolled his eyes and I laughed at him.

"Cut it out, kid, I'm old enough to be your mother."

"I doubt it," he said, looked at me again and dropped his joking manner. "But you're dressed to go out. I didn't mean to spoil your evening."

"We *were* out," Mitch informed him. "We had just come in."

"Then let's go out again. What would you like to do, Deirdre?"

I shrugged. "Whatever you'd like. What would you two do, if I weren't around?"

Mitch laughed. "We usually hit the pool hall for a few games and beers. Not exactly your cup of tea."

"Oh, really? And how would you know about that?" I teased Mitch lightly. "Pool and beer sound good to me."

Chris looked at me in shock. "In that dress? There'd be a full-fledged riot."

"No, of course not. But I could change, if we made a stop first."

Mitch looked doubtful. "If you really want to . . ."

"I do," I insisted. "It's been a while since I've played, but I don't imagine the game has changed."

"Shall I rack them up again, Chris?" I finished my beer and smiled over at him.

He shook his head and looked at Mitch, who gave a disgusted snort. "Not bloody likely, Deirdre. You've already skunked us six games to nothing. I have a reputation to keep up here."

"Dad really hates to lose." Chris seemed to be enjoying himself.

"You get out of here, rat, and get us another beer." Mitch

laughed as Chris left the pool room. He moved toward me and put an arm around my waist.

"I am so sorry, Detective, have I ruined your macho image forever?"

"Are you kidding? The fact that you're the best looking woman to ever enter this place has made my name legend."

"Be honest," I laughed. "I'm practically the only woman to ever come here." I looked over at the rest of the patrons with a small grimace; they were a pretty rough crew, the pool hall was not in the best area of town.

"You're probably right." He looked around, the crowd that had gathered while we played had dispersed, and while most went into the bar, some were still loitering by the doorway. Mitch lowered his voice so that I was the only one who could hear him. "Still I wish you had worn something a little less, well, tempting." I had dressed in my black leather jeans and an oversized sweatshirt that kept falling down over one shoulder. "Not that you don't look great, you understand. I know most of these guys and they're usually a decent lot, but every once in a while they get a little rowdy. In a place like this, someone like you can be a time bomb."

"But I'm with you, and I can take care of myself."

"I guess so." He gave me a sharp look as I pulled at the neckline of my shirt. "Where's your bruise?"

"Bruise?" I couldn't remember at first. "Oh, that. It's gone," I said lightly. "I'm a quick healer."

"I still don't remember you having that earlier in the evening. I can't believe I would have missed it."

"Damn it, Mitch, it was dark and you were otherwise preoccupied. Next time, maybe you should take inventory beforehand." I smiled at him invitingly. "Assuming, of course, that you want a next time."

"Are you crazy?" He pulled me to him and held me tightly. "It's all I've been able to think about this week." He lifted me off the floor and kissed me. I locked my arms around his neck, enjoying the feel of his body pressed to mine. When the kiss was done, I sighed and nestled into his shoulder, my head deliberately turned away from his neck. I wanted him so desperately, not just his body, but his blood. I wondered what it would be like to take a willing victim, not someone I had stalked and hunted, but someone who wanted to give themselves totally to me.

The tingling in my gums signaled the extension of my canines and I gave a sharp intake of breath. At the same time, there was a muffled cough at the door; Mitch let me down abruptly and spun around. Chris stood there, three bottles of beer in his grasp and a wide grin on his face. He looked so much like a younger version of Mitch that I smiled back despite my embarrassment.

"Beers?" he said, holding them out like an offering to the gods.

Mitch laughed. "Carry them into the bar, son, I think we've had enough pool for one night."

We sat down at a small table toward the back of the room. We talked for a while about Chris' studies, but I was distracted by an oddly familiar figure sitting on the other end of the bar. He kept staring at us, at me in particular. Suddenly, I placed him with a sickening twist of my stomach; it was the man I fed on in the alley two weeks ago. Mitch had his back to him, and Chris was too involved in detailing his expectations of the law boards, so neither of them noticed. I glanced at my watch, yawned conspicuously and quickly finished my beer. Sensing my impatience, Mitch looked over at me.

"Would you like to go now?"

I nodded. "It has been a long day and I'm very tired. So if you don't mind . . ."

"Fine, but I need to make one phone call before we leave. I'll be back in a minute."

After Mitch left, Chris stood up. "It's been really nice to meet you, Deirdre." He reached out, shook my hand and gave me the Greer smile. "But I get the feeling that you two would like to be alone for a while. And I know Dad well enough to know that he wouldn't tell me to leave even if he wanted me to. So I'll do the decent thing and quit cutting-in on his time." He looked at me intently then smiled again. "I'm probably way out of line for saying this, but I hope you stick around for a while. I haven't seen him this relaxed for years. You're good for him, I can tell," he flushed slightly, "but don't you dare tell him I said so."

"I promise. Good night, Chris."

"Good night."

Chris wasn't out of the bar for more than a second when the man appeared at the table. I didn't have a chance to move before he grabbed my arm. "Hey, baby," he said in a voice that made my identification a certainty. "Don't I know you from somewhere?"

"I don't think so." I tried to brush him off but he held on.

"I'm sure we met, and not that long ago, neither." He rubbed his neck absently with a glazed look. "I couldn't never forget a babe like you."

"Excuse me, you must be mistaken."

He pulled me to him roughly. "Now I know. We had an appointment in a dark alley. You left too soon, as I remember it. Now that your friends is gone, maybe we can finish up."

"Leave me alone," I hissed at him. "Take your hands off me."

He laughed, and tried to kiss me. I looked around and noticed that no one was watching. Our conversation had been quiet and his invitation was probably nothing out of the ordinary for this place. Mitch was nowhere to be seen and I didn't want to wait for him to reappear. If it were an ordinary night, if I were on my own, I would simply accompany him to some dark place and feed on him again, this time being sure to implant the thought that he didn't know me. But I had no time for that now. Instead, I looked him full in the face and smiled. My teeth had grown and I saw a look of doubt and fear enter his eyes. "Next time a lady says no, you really should listen." I picked him up by the front of his shirt and tossed him on to the table next to us. He and the table collapsed with a loud crash and the sound of breaking bottles; by this time I was sitting down again and staring at him, like the other customers. No one looked at me and no one went to help him up. There was a lot of raucous laughter and some good natured joking about how Sammy couldn't hold his liquor. He lay without moving and I thought for one moment that I had killed him. Then just as Mitch was coming in to see what all the commotion was about, he moaned and rolled over.

"What's happening," he said as he rushed to my side. "Are you okay, Deirdre?"

"I'm fine—he's drunk." I indicated the man rising uncertainly to his feet. "Let's get out of here."

"I'm scared, Deirdre. I guess it all boils down to that. It's been a long time since I felt this way about anyone, and eventually even that got hopelessly screwed up. I don't want that to happen this time." Mitch had haltingly begun to apologize for our argument last week and I tried to console him without giving him too much hope for a lasting relationship.

"I know, Mitch." We arrived at the door of my hotel; he held back to allow me to go through the revolving door first. I did not enter, but pulled him to one side, away from the entrance. The things that needed to be said, should be said privately. "It's been a long time for me, also. And although I do care for you, I can't make any promises."

His eyes reflected pain, but he gave me a small grin. "I can wait around while you make up your mind though, can't I? Just don't take too long with it. I'm not getting any younger."

"Who is?"

"You, for one."

"Why do you say that?" I questioned him sharply, seeing my angry reflection in his eyes. "I'm not getting younger, either. How could I?"

"Whoa, calm down a bit. It was a compliment. Most women like to hear that they don't look their age." He pulled me to him, kissed me and I responded as usual. When it was over, he held me close. "You're a strange one, Deirdre. But somehow, I like it."

"Coming up for a drink?" I moved away from him and he followed me through the door.

Once on the elevator, he kissed me again, teasingly this time. When he bit my lower lip I jumped back and wiped my mouth.

He had drawn no blood. The doors opened on my floor and we entered the room.

"Help yourself." I indicated the bar and walked back to the bedroom. I set my key down and started to take off my shirt when suddenly he was behind me, his arms wrapped around my waist.

"Don't mind if I do." His voice was scratchy in my ear. I watched in the mirror as he undressed me. Each piece of clothing was removed gently and slowly until I stood naked before him. The new mirror displayed my reflection, unflawed and whole once more. Mitch and I might have been any human couple, any two lovers wrapped up in each other. My skin seemed to glow, it was so white beneath his tanned, calloused hands. He examined me, with his hands and his eyes. "Not a mark," he whispered in a voice full of awe. "You're perfect." He leaned his head on my shoulder and made a face at the mirror. "And then there's me . . ."

I turned around and unbuttoned his shirt; I could not match his unhurried pace, I wanted him so much. Two of the buttons dropped to the floor, sheered off by my sharp nails. He looked at me, smiled and carried me to the bed.

Shortly before dawn, he got up and began to dress. I lay, watching him and he jumped when he turned around and saw that my eyes were open. "Sorry." He finished zipping his pants and came to sit next to me. "I didn't mean to wake you."

"Do you have to leave?"

"I've got to get home to change, then get to work. What are your plans for today?"

I stretched and reached a hand up to his face. The sun would be up soon, and I fought back the lethargy that dawn always caused. "I'm going to stay right here and wait for you to come back."

He laughed. "And if I don't?"

"You'll be back." My voice was low, throaty and I rubbed my head on his arm.

"Damn straight, I will." He kissed me, then stood up and

smiled down at me. "You have to sew the buttons back on my shirt."

I blushed and threw a pillow at him. "Sew on your own buttons, Detective, I only remove them."

"And I'll be happy to do it, if you'll tear them off again."

"Promise." Through the heavy draperies I could feel the sun rise. "Oh, and Mitch?" I fought to keep my eyes open until he left. "Take the key with you. You can let yourself in."

He took it from the dressing table, tossed it up in the air and caught it. "See you tonight, then. Sweet dreams."

Only after the door shut and he was gone, did I realize that I had allowed myself to violate one of my most important rules. My sleep that day would be undefended by the normal locks and safeguards. But the thought brought no alarm and no fear. My eyes closed and my body relaxed. I trusted him, I loved him and I held his face in my mind as I fell into the deep crevasse of sleep.

The corridor winds endlessly, a mist rising from the floor. I walk slowly, my footsteps echoing loudly in this silent place of death. Here are the same coffins, the same loves buried out of my reach. I do not attempt to open them, not this time, but quicken my steps to reach something, someone or some answer, waiting I know at the end of the hall. There are more coffins now, they seem uncountable. I wonder why they are here, why I am here.

"They are the fruits of your sins, Deirdre." The voice pulses in my ears. "They died so that you might live forever.

"Who are you?" I call but my voice is lost in a loud clattering. The lids of the coffins, pummelled from within, fall to the floor, shattering into spinters.

"Look on them and rejoice. They are your children, they are your soul." I stand in horror as they rise from their caskets, surrounding me, grasping at me with sharp fingers. I know them all; I recognize the faces, the eyes, the mouths whispering, hissing, speaking all of my different names.

"Diane," a rasping voice calls to me. "How about some more coffee, darlin'?" Buddy's face is bloody and twisted into a lewd grin.

"Dorothy." A rotting soldier dressed in tattered navy rags reaches out to me. "Dorothy, it hurts bad. You can help, help me."

"I just might fall in love." Bill's voice is little more than a croak and although his body has not yet begun to decompose, his walk is choppy, uncoordinated. He lurches toward me.

"No," I scream, pushing them all away. They are weightless and fall to the floor with soft thuds. "No, I will not claim these. Their deaths are not mine." I run from them, tears clouding my vision. The door is near. I see a figure, a man, guarding it. His face is obscured and he does not speak, but dissolves into nothing as I reach him. Where he had been standing, is now a pool of blood. I kneel down, I reach into it, it is deeper than I had expected. I raise my hand to my mouth and drink; I lower my head and lap at it; I am compelled to take it all. Then it is gone and I sit back on my heels, sated and dazed. As I begin to rise, I notice a shred of fabric where the pool had been. I pick it up to wipe the blood from my face and hands. The colors are bright and swirled. "No," I scream again. "Not her, she is not dead."

"Too late, too late," the voices of the dead whisper through the air. They overwhelm me and I cannot seem to resist. They lay me down on the floor and wipe away my bloody tears with icy hands, caressing and stroking my hair and my face, warming their rotting bodies against mine. A darkness overtakes me; their soft words lull me. "Hush, hush," they say. "It's only a dream, it is all just a dream."

Chapter 13

I tried to shake off the hands gripping my shoulders. The voices changed, blended into one, deep and familiar. The words, however, were the same. ". . . it's only a dream, Deirdre. Wake up, please." I realized that these hands were warm, living flesh and the room was no longer dark. I opened my eyes hesitantly and squinted at the light. Mitch's face came into view and I threw my arms around him. He returned my embrace and held me until I stopped trembling. When I calmed down, he held me out at arms' length and stared into my eyes. "Well," he said in a shaky voice, "that must have been one hell of a nightmare. Do you want to tell me about it?"

I shook my head. "In a bit, maybe. But not right now." I ran my fingers through my hair and glanced at the curtained window. "What time is it?"

He smiled. "After six. You must have slept all day; I came in around four and tried to wake you, but you were practically comatose. I have to admit, it scared me a bit. You opened your eyes and looked straight at me. But you didn't focus on me, or even acknowledge that anyone was here. You smiled, moaned and slowly closed your eyes again. It was pretty spooky. Do you always sleep so soundly?"

"Only when I am very tired. And it's your fault."

"Yeah, I remember." He was grinning boisterously, his eyes sparkled and he seemed inordinately pleased with himself. I wondered what was so amusing, until I realized that I was naked and quickly pulled the covers up around me.

"Did you have a good day?" I asked as casually as possible.

"Not too bad," he said slowly. "It was interesting at least. Some really strange things are happening these days."

"Such as?"

"As if the murders weren't bad enough, now we've had a

break–in at the local blood bank. And of course, since I'm the 'vampire' cop, I got the job."

I dropped my gaze, not wanting him to see the interest his words had caused. Breaking into a blood bank was a possibility that always intrigued me, although I had never tried it myself. It always seemed too risky; if you got caught you would have to explain why, and probably spend time in jail. Much easier to obtain it the way I always had. Still, it was one more indication of the other's operations. Or perhaps there was more than one; how ironic it would be after searching for over a century to find a community living in the same city. But I didn't actually believe that theory; although I sometimes longed for companionship of my own kind, I would never want to share my hunts or my territories.

"Deirdre, you're not listening."

"What? Oh, sorry, Mitch. I was just thinking how it might all fit in."

"If you had been paying attention, you would know by now. As I was saying, we actually have a few suspects now, based mostly on the testimony of an eyewitness near the blood bank. You might be interested to know that you are acquainted with one of them."

"Who?"

"I'm not sure I should divulge that information."

"Jesus, Mitch, don't give me the policeman line on it. I want to know. It might be that I could be threatened by him, also."

"Actually, the department was afraid of just that. But I let them know that I would hold you in protective custody."

"I guess that's as good a name as any for what you've been doing," I said dryly. "Now tell me who it is."

"We're not positive of course and I really shouldn't tell you, but I don't see that it can hurt. It's Larry."

"Larry?" It would explain why he was so curious about my past, it might even explain his obsession with me. But somehow I just couldn't believe that he was a vampire.

"Yes, Larry Martin, the club doorman. You do remember him, don't you?"

I shook my head.

"You don't remember him?"

"Of course I do, Mitch. But he is not a vampire." I was sorry as soon as the word was out of my mouth, Mitch did not believe in vampires.

He smiled but did not laugh. "Yeah, well, whatever he is, he's associated with all three of them. He was the last person seen with Andrews, knew the hooker and was reported to have quarrelled with Mr. Leigh."

"What about the other suspects?"

"I'm putting my money on Martin. He has a history of instability as long as my arm; he's been in and out of institutions since he was fourteen. Based on what we've uncovered about him so far, he's one sick dude."

"Do you think I could," I shifted uneasily and the blankets slipped away from me, "do you think I could speak with him?"

"If we had him in custody, sure." He looked at me intently. "Look, Deirdre, I can't concentrate on anything if you're like that. Get dressed," he jokingly ordered as I covered myself again, giving him a shy smile. "And come on out. I brought us some dinner."

I dressed quickly and left the bedroom. Mitch had spread the dinner he brought on the bar. It was from a variety of fast food places. "I didn't really know what you'd want, so I brought a lot." He patted the barstool next to him. "Sit down and eat."

I laughed a bit and crossed the room. I selected a roast beef sandwich; it at least had the dubious distinction of being slightly rare and I thought I could eat enough of it to satisfy him. I pulled the meat from the bun and began to eat.

"Too bad Gwen's not here," I said after the first mouthful. "She would love the assortment. You should see some of the junk she brings in . . ." At the thought of her I grew serious, fearful at the remembrance of my dream. The abrupt change was not lost on him.

"What's the matter?"

"Oh God, Mitch, the dream," I began disjointedly with a

shiver. "She was in my dream. I didn't see her, but I knew she was in danger."

"You hinted at something like that the night of the show. Why would Gwen be in danger? What has she got to do with any of this?"

I ignored his comments and continued, thinking out loud. "She wouldn't have gone with him. I warned her and she promised not to see him again. Even Max warned her. She should be safe."

He looked at me sternly. "Who didn't she go with?"

"Larry. She met him at the club last Sunday. I'm afraid she developed a crush on him. She was with him before the show, too. But he left after that, I'm sure of it."

"How can you be so sure?" He, too, was growing concerned.

"Everyone said she left alone, even you said so. And Max said that Larry had gone, long before that."

"But you warned her, you say, to stay away from him. Would she listen?" Suddenly, his eyes narrowed in concentration. "But you had no knowledge of him being a suspect until tonight. Why would you warn her away? What the hell is going on here?"

I looked at him in confusion for a minute and shook my head to clear it. Of course he had no idea of what had occurred between Larry and me, no comprehension of the truth that seemed to hold us all entangled. "He just seemed unstable to me and I did not want her to get hurt. She'd had a fight with her fiancé, you see, and she was on the rebound. I did not like the thought of her being with Larry. Neither did Max, he said . . ."

"Spare me the thoughts of the great Max," Mitch snarled as he said the name. "Anyway, it can hardly matter. I seem to remember that Gwen lives clear across town and Larry was last seen in the area of your office. So their paths shouldn't have crossed at all."

"But she wasn't going home, Mitch. She was going to stay at my place for the weekend."

"Your place?" He smiled, not comprehending. "But we are at your place. And she's not here, so she must be at home."

Once again I had forgotten how little Mitch knew of my life. "She was staying at my apartment at the office."

"You have an apartment in your office?" He stopped for a moment. "I didn't know." He gave me a suspicious look. "But then apparently there's a lot I don't know. We'd better get over there."

We hesitated only a second, he to throw on his coat and I to put on my shoes. We rushed out of the hotel to his car, a regulation police–issue this time. "My car's still in the shop," he explained as he started the engine and turned on the siren. "I don't like to drive marked cars ordinarily, but this one'll help. Buckle up."

We sped the two blocks and pulled up in front of the building just as an ambulance was leaving. One other police car was parked at the curb. Mitch pushed through the small crowd that had gathered around the doors and we entered. As we approached the two policemen inside, I noticed that they were the same two who had questioned me last week. They both nodded at me in embarrassed recognition; one of them addressed Mitch.

"Well, Greer, I might have known you would show up. How do you manage it?"

"Never mind," he snarled at them. "What happened here? Is she okay?"

"She?" He shook his head. "We came on a call about the security guard. The guy coming on to the next shift found him slumped at his desk. Someone gave him a pretty rough knock on the head. He should be okay, though. What's this about a woman?"

Mitch gave me a angry look. "I have reason to believe that Miss Griffin's secretary is in the office. We're concerned about her safety."

The policeman shook his head again. "We checked all the floors and found nothing unusual; there were no signs anywhere of a break–in. We think it was an attempted robbery; but the guy got scared after hitting the guard and cleared out."

Mitch nodded slowly. "Mind if I check it out?"

He smiled, "No, you will anyway. We were just about ready to leave. Want some help?"

Mitch considered this for a moment. "I might need the back–up," he conceded. "It won't take too long, I hope."

The four of us rode the elevator in silence. I noticed the few curious glances they gave first to Mitch, and then to me, but chose to ignore them. My whole body was tensed in fear and I silently urged the elevator upward. When it arrived at the top floor, I hurried out and unlocked the door. The office looked exactly as it had when I had left; there were no signs of struggle or unusual activity. I led them back to my office and when I opened the door, I saw that everything here also looked normal.

Mitch turned to me. "Well," he said curtly, "where's this apartment you told me about?"

With a doubtful look at the other policemen, I went to my desk and found that the key was gone. Gwen, of course, would have taken it in with her. Silently, I walked to the back wall and pulled aside the draperies to expose the door. "There's only one key," I said shakily, "and Gwen has it now." In what I thought was a futile gesture I turned the knob; to my surprise the door opened easily and we walked in.

Mitch glanced around, walking quickly over to one corner of the room and retrieved a multi-colored garment that was lying on the floor. "This is Gwen's, isn't it?" he asked, handing the dress to me.

I rubbed the material absently, "Yes, she was wearing it last night. Maybe she's still sleeping." As I said it, I knew it wasn't true. The apartment was too empty, too silent, to be occupied. And suddenly the smell overwhelmed me, the smell of blood and death. "Gwen," I called, my voice wavering in a hopeless attempt to deny the obvious. "Gwen, are you here? It's Deirdre." There was a note of hysteria in my voice.

Mitch walked over to me and gave my hand a quick squeeze. "She might not be here at all." How could he say that, when the odor was overpowering. "Shall I check upstairs?"

I nodded, my hand over my mouth, and he walked up the staircase. There was a long silence, an audible gasp, then he called out. "She's here." But even before he spoke, before his pause, before his quietly whispered, "fucking maniac," I knew what he had found.

I sat down on the couch, her dress crushed against my face and began to cry silently. Both of the policeman dashed up the stairs. A few seconds later one of them came back down and his face was yellow with shock. When he asked for the telephone, I gestured at the doorway. As he began to make his phone call, I rose slowly from the floor, and dropping Gwen's dress back on to the floor, I mounted the stairs.

Mitch tried to stop me from entering the loft, putting his arm around me. "You probably shouldn't see this," he said and attempted to lead me back downstairs, but I broke away and pushed past him.

I expected to see Gwen, grey and drained, like the body of David Leigh. I had imagined her as I walked up the stairs, waxen and doll–like. What I saw rocked me back, causing even me to choke back the contents of my stomach.

The room was covered in blood, the ceiling, the floor, the bed, everywhere I looked. I could smell its sweetness, turning rancid now from exposure to the air. Where it had pooled, the blood had clotted over, thickened and crusty. I must have gasped or cried out, for Mitch came to me again and tried to move me away. I ignored him and walked to the bed. I stared for a moment at the uncomprehendable shape lying there, someone had pulled a sheet over it, and the center was peaked as if a tent. Danger, my mind whispered, danger, but my hand moved as if by its own volition to pull aside the sheet.

It was Gwen, her skin was heavy and solid, her small naked body pitiful, lying in the brown stain of her own blood. And emerging from her chest was a large wooden stake; her back was arched, actually raised an inch from the bed where the other end protruded. Her eyes were open and her hands tightly grasped that horrible implement of death, as if she tried to wrench it away in her last moment of life. "Dear, sweet Jesus." I was glued to the spot; I could not take my eyes away from her.

This was something I had read about, something I had envisioned so many times. But it was worse than I had ever imagined, and it was wrong. The body should have been mine.

Pulling my gaze away from the stake, I reached over and gently stroked her tousled hair, closed her eyes and carefully pulled the sheet back over her. I looked into Mitch's eyes. I could tell he shared my grief and horror, but I did not want his comfort.

"Get him," I said, my voice stony and harsh, "you find the bastard that did this. And when you do, he's mine, do you understand? He's mine. I'll tear him apart."

Both Mitch and the other policeman looked at me in shock. "Deirdre?" Mitch softly approached and I permitted him to put his arm around me and lead me back down the stairs. "Do you want me to take you somewhere?" He helped me to the couch as if I would break in his arms. "Your hotel, maybe? Or my place? I'm afraid it'll take some time to get this all taken care of."

"No, thank you. I would like to wait if I may." I wiped my hands over my face to remove my tears. "This was meant for me," I said to myself. "It should not have been Gwen, it was meant for me. If I had known, I could have stopped this." My voice sounded dead and emotionless.

"Deirdre," he clasped me to him roughly, "don't do this. Don't blame yourself. It happened, there was nothing you, or anyone else, could have done to stop it. How could you know? You're only human." He tightened his grip on me and gave me one brief kiss before turning away.

"How I wish that were true, Mitch," I said softly as he climbed the stairs.

The entire investigation took several hours. I sat motionless for some of the time, staring at the art on the walls. It gave me a point of focus other than the activity in the loft. But that focus was shattered when the morgue employees arrived to bundle Gwen up in a zippered plastic bag. I stood up and walked toward the kitchen. "I'll just make some coffee now, if anyone wants it." I spoke to no one in particular and no one answered, but the task enabled me to turn my back on the awkward package, that was once my friend, being carried down the stairs.

The smell of the coffee drew them to the kitchen, one by one. Disinterested and mechanical, I served them all. Mitch was the last to arrive. I fixed a cup and handed it to him. My hands were steady again and he gave me a sad smile. "You doing okay?" he asked.

"As well as can be expected, I suppose." I tried and almost succeeded in returning his smile. "Will you be much longer?"

"No, not too much. But you can help with something, if you would."

"You know I will do whatever I can, Mitch."

"We need to fingerprint you; we'll need to be able to tell your prints from the others we found up there. So we can get a positive ID."

The thoughts of leaving a permanent trace of my existence with the police department made me shiver involuntarily. But I knew I could not refuse, nor did I want to. I needed to identify the murderer, not only for revenge but for my own personal safety. I knew what Gwen's death meant. Somebody knew who and what I was. Somebody who was enjoying the game he was playing with me. Somebody who wanted more than my death. "Larry." I whispered his name with loathing.

Mitch said nothing, but sat watching me, his cup of coffee grasped between his hands.

Finally, I nodded to him. "I will allow the fingerprinting, but you may find it to be a futile gesture."

"You don't think we'll get him?"

"Oh, I am sure we will." I laughed, low and threateningly and he inadvertently drew away from me. "We will find him. But after I'm done with him there won't be enough left to identify."

"Jesus, Deirdre. I know that this has been a shock to you, it would be for anyone. Even if you didn't know her. But you can't do anything about it. Let us do our job."

I looked at him defiantly. He stood up and grabbed my arm,

pulling me roughly to him. "I don't want you involved. I know she was your friend, I can even imagine how you must be feeling. But you must stay out of this; he will be taken care of, I promise you."

"Fine, Mitch. I'll play by your rules, for now. But if he gets away, or gets released on some technicality, I will track him down and I will kill him."

He stared at me in disbelief. "Deirdre, you're in shock and slightly hysterical; later on you will feel differently. You can't expect me to believe that you would be capable of . . ." His voice trailed off.

"You'd be surprised what I am capable of, Mitch." His eyes held a mixture of doubt and confusion, suspicion and fear, as if I had changed in his eyes. I found the emotions he reflected discomforting and saddening. "But then again," and I smiled when he relaxed at my softened voice, "maybe you know me better than I think. Let's get this over with."

When all of the prints had been taken, and all of the evidence examined and photographed, the policemen left. Mitch and I sat in an amiable silence at the kitchen table, finishing the rest of the coffee. He rubbed his hand over his eyes and combed his fingers through his hair. "Tired?" I queried gently.

"I feel like I haven't had a good night's sleep for months. I didn't get much sleep last night, as you well know," he said with a good–natured leer. I blushed slightly and lowered my eyes. "And I don't think I'll get much tonight." He placed his hand over mine at the table. "Unfortunately, it won't be for the same reason."

"What else do you need to do tonight?"

"At the very least, I have to go to the station and file a few reports. We've got an APB out on Larry, but he may not turn up for a while. The lab guys will take care of the prints and the evidence. I hope that after the paperwork is done, I'll be able to go home and get some sleep."

"May I accompany you to the station?"

"That would be a good idea, since I'm supposed to have you

under protective custody. Even if that weren't the case, I won't let you out of my sight until Martin is arrested."

I shivered again, the picture of Gwen impaled was imprinted on my mind. "Make it soon, Mitch."

He said nothing, just looked at me sadly.

"Can we go? I don't want to stay here any longer than necessary. I may never stay here again."

"I don't blame you," he agreed. "It is a shame, though. This place is very nice." He walked into the living room and began to turn off the lights. As he passed the wall of pictures, he stopped and surveyed them. "These are wonderful. But I don't recognize this one. I mean, I know it's a Van Gogh, but I don't believe I've ever seen this particular picture."

"You probably haven't, Mitch. I, well, it's sort of a family heirloom. We acquired it at an estate auction, quite a bargain, I was told."

"It's the original?" he exclaimed in astonishment. "You have an original Van Gogh and have the nerve to tell me it was a bargain? It must be worth a small fortune."

I shrugged. "It is, I'm sure. But the picture was bought during the Depression. Times were hard, people were anxious to recoup their losses, even if it meant selling something as precious as this." I wanted to tell him how precious it really was, how I had risked my life in the daylight to acquire it. How when I looked at it, I felt almost human again.

I had fed for five straight days prior to the auction, trying to build up my strength for the ordeal. Fortunately the day was overcast and the estate shaded with large trees. I had sat under one of these trees, swathed in yards of material. The bidding had been almost as fierce as the ravaging of the sun's rays. But I was determined to get it and get it I did. And though I lay in bed, burnt and shriveled for a week afterwards until my skin finally healed, I never doubted for a minute that it had been worth the cost.

"Deirdre." I tore my gaze away from the painting to see his eyes warm with concern. "Let me get you out of here."

I nodded and accepted his support. He reached for the light

switch but took one final look at the wall. "It's so beautiful," he said as we left the room.

I couldn't lock the door—the key had been taken away with Gwen's effects; I merely adjusted the curtain to hide the entrance once again. As I did this, I realized that I would never return here, not to sleep, not even to work. Gwen's death had cruelly severed any ties I had with this place. The office would be closed and the business sold. I could leave this portion of my life now with little regret.

As we slowly walked to the elevators, I studied Mitch's profile in the near darkness. He had come to mean so much to me during the few days we had spent together. I could hardly visualize what my life would be like without him when I finally had to leave. For I would have to go, I knew, and as the elevator car began its downward journey, I sighed. He gave me a sad smile and put his arm around my shoulders, drawing me closer. I would miss Gwen desperately, though I truly believed she was in a better world. I would miss the daily grind of the fashion industry, the hectic deadlines and even the demanding clients, yet there were other ways I could fill my time. But as for leaving Mitch. . . . I sighed again as the doors opened and we went to the street to his car. Oh, God, I thought, leaving Mitch will be one of the hardest things I will ever do.

Chapter 14

It was just after midnight when Mitch completed his work at the station. Then I persuaded him to return with me to the hotel to gather some of my clothes and personal effects. By the time we finally arrived at his apartment it was after one. That he was exhausted, mentally and physically, was apparent from the way he dragged up the steps, stumbled in the door and slumped on the couch. I set my case down in the hallway and sat in a chair facing him.

"What happens now?" I asked quietly, hating to disturb him.

"What?" He sat up straighter and looked at me. "Oh, I'm sorry, Deirdre. I'm absolutely beat."

"I know," I said sympathetically. "Is there any way I can help?"

"For now, no. I need to get some sleep. We've got men out looking for Larry now and all of his normal haunts are under surveillance. If he shows up, they'll let me know."

"And if he doesn't show up?" I somehow felt there was more that could be done and the question sounded sharper than I had intended. I glimpsed a flash of anger in his eyes.

"Then, tomorrow, we try to flush him out. I can't do anything else about it tonight. And neither can you." As suddenly as it arrived, the anger died and he smiled wearily. "You should get some rest, too, if you can. There will be plenty for you to do tomorrow." He walked over to me and lightly held my arms. "Right now you can help me most by just staying here, with me. Will you be able to sleep?"

I nodded. "I think so. You go ahead. I'll be in a little later."

He gave me a lazy kiss and hug and turned to go, unbuttoning his shirt. As he walked down the hall I watched him with a tenderness that still surprised me. I wanted nothing more tonight than his presence. I would forego for a while my plans of vengeance and do as he wished. With a sigh I picked up my suitcase and followed him.

He had discarded his clothes into a rumpled pile. After I folded each garment and draped them over a nearby chair, I quietly slid into bed next to him. He was asleep already, his breathing was slow and regular. I could not get the picture of Gwen's corpse out of my mind. I replayed the night over and over, receiving no answers, no comfort. "Damn," I swore and turned over roughly. Mitch jumped in his sleep and lifted his head to regard me with sleepy eyes. "Go back to sleep," I soothed him, staring into his eyes. "Everything will be fine."

Nothing is fine, my mind raged and the promises I had made to him and to myself about not getting involved dissolved into the picture of Gwen, staked to my bed. I reached over and took his face in mine. Smiling, I strove to touch his mind with mine. "Everything is fine, Mitch," I repeated again. "Sleep now, I will be with you tonight, all night. I will not leave, I will stay with you all night. Sleep now."

He relaxed and his eyes closed. "Sleep now," he murmured. "You will be here." I released his face and he rolled over and went back to sleep. Ever so quietly I slid from his bed, dressed in the black pants and sweater I had packed, smoothed on my black leather gloves and went out the door.

The night was glorious, clear and cold, with no moon. The streets I traveled were dark and shadowy and took me to an alley behind Larry's apartment. Easing around the corner, I saw the car stationed outside; the shadowy figure inside lit a cigarette and I could smell the rich tobacco from where I stood. I did not need the lowered hum of the radio to identify Mitch's surveillance team. But there was only one in the car and I realized that there must be two.

Where was the other one? Silently, I listened to the sounds of the night, the traffic noises, the muffled sounds from within the surrounding buildings. With an effort of will, I blocked these sounds and tuned them out. There, there he was. I heard the quiet breathing of a man standing just inside the entrance. He stamped his feet, and the scratchy sound of knit gloves rubbing together drifted back to me.

From the personnel file in Max's office I knew that Larry Martin lived on the third floor. I assessed the back walls of the building, laughing silently to myself. Too bad, I thought, too bad that I can't turn into a bat or a mist. Then I could be in and out with no one the wiser. But I thought I could manage the climb.

Somewhere in the back of my mind, a voice urged me to back off, to walk down the dark, beautiful streets and return to

Mitch and the warm bed that awaited me. But I had become reckless with the rage at Gwen's death, almost as if her death had set me free of the final restraints of humanity. That's not true, my mind prodded, if you care that much you are still human.

"Nevertheless," I whispered to the night sky, "I will go." I slipped off my shoes and set them at the side of the wall; I removed my gloves and put them into my pocket. A thrill of excitement, akin to the hunt and capture of a victim, enveloped me. My senses vibrated, my teeth enlarged. A severe hunger and restlessness overtook me and I began to climb, slowly at first and then with more confidence, my fingers and toes clinging tightly to the coarse surface of the bricks.

Before I knew it I was halfway up the wall. My balance was superb and I scaled the rest of the distance effortlessly. It was a simple matter to complete the climb, find an open window and ease myself in. As my feet touched the floor, I suppressed the impulse to laugh—so easy, it was so easy.

Walking down the hall, I found his apartment. I suspect I could have identified it even had the number not matched that found in Max's personnel file; Larry's familiar odor permeated the hall directly outside the door. I put my gloves back on and rashly turned the knob, not caring if he were inside or not. The door was locked but I twisted the knob again, harder this time; the lock broke and the door opened. I looked up and down the hall before I entered—no one had seen me.

Closing the door softly behind me, I glanced around. It was empty, as I knew before I had even taken one step inside. There were only three rooms, I checked the kitchen first, grimacing as a roach ran over my bare foot. The bathroom, next; there was nothing here that would indicate his involvement. If there was any evidence, it would have to be in the main room, that served as both a sleeping and a living area. "But not for long," I bared my teeth at my reflection in the window as I passed.

His bookshelves held a large assortment of paperback books. I took a second look at these and was not really surprised to find that every one of them were vampire novels; he had them all, from the classics to the tawdry. Most of them, I had read and discarded for their uselessness, but from their worn appearance I could tell that Larry had read each one thoroughly several times.

There were two stacks of books, horizontally arranged on the end of one of the shelves; the fact that they were out of line with the rest caught my eye. I moved one of the stacks and saw behind it not the wood of the case but the leather binding of a larger book. Pulling it out, I almost dropped it in shock. The cover was black, blood–red letters emblazoned the surface with the name, Dorothy Grey. My hands trembled and I longed to tear off the confining gloves, but I knew that I did not dare.

The first page held an old, worn picture, in sepia tone. A group of union soldiers, stern and unsmiling, stood around a tent. It could have been any encampment in that war, but I knew these men. Some had died in my arms, some I had even helped along their way. Looking closer, I saw myself, gaunt and glassy eyed, peering out from within the tent. Underneath the picture Larry had written, "The first appearance of Dorothy Grey, The Angel of Death."

"Jesus, he knows." I slid down to the floor, grasping the scrapbook to my chest. "How the hell could he know?" I frantically rifled through the pages; many of my lives and identities were charted here, names, towns, occupations. Oh, he had missed some, but those he had captured were correct and completely damaging. What had he planned to do with this, I wondered, what possible purpose could it serve for him? None, now, I affirmed, for I would take it with me and burn it.

The last few pages he used as a journal, and when I read them, his purpose suddenly became clear. He was searching for eternal life; he wanted to become a vampire. Nowhere did Larry explain how he learned the truth about me, but his aspirations were plainly expressed. His obsession with me went further than love or lust; beyond all of that, he longed to live forever, longed to walk the night, powerful and invincible. I was merely the key to his desire.

I snapped the book shut and stood up again, searching the room and finding a backpack. I unzipped it, emptied its contents onto the floor and put the book inside. As I did so, a scrap of paper fell out. On it was written simply "the blood is the life" and the address of the blood bank that had been robbed.

I let the paper lay where it had fallen. On impulse, I crossed the room and went back to the kitchen. The roaches scattered from the light as I opened the refrigerator. Inside were a dozen bags of blood, neatly labeled and stacked. I wondered if he thought that he could become a vampire simply by drinking the blood or if he were merely stockpiling in the event that I fulfilled his desires. He will never get to use them at all, I thought and removed all but two of them, and, hoping that the plastic would resist punctures, stowed them into the backpack along with the book. Then with a grim smile, I found a piece of paper and a pencil. "My dearest Larry," I wrote, "thank you for dinner. Watch for me, I will be back." I felt a deadly rush of satisfaction as I taped the note to the refrigerator door and left the apartment.

Getting back into Mitch's place was no problem, but as I quietly shut the door and set the backpack down on the floor, I realized that I would have to leave. I glanced at the clock; it was already after five, too much of the night had been lost at Larry's apartment. After checking to see that Mitch still slept, I began to make my plans. The evidence that I now possessed must never be seen, especially by him. And Larry must die. I had never killed before and the decision was anathema to me, but there would be no choice in the matter. For now, though, I had to seek safe harbor. I could not return to the hotel or to the office; Mitch would most certainly look for me there. And I could not allow myself to be found, not yet.

I walked back down the hallway and stood above Mitch's bed. The lights from the street shone in through the window and illuminated his sleeping features. "Damn it, Mitch. It would have been easier to have never met you." Even as I said it, I knew it was not true. No matter the outcome, my love for him was real and uplifting, a memory I could cherish in however many countless years I had remaining. There would be other lovers in my future, but none like him.

He rolled over and spoke. "Deirdre?" He was still half asleep.

"I'm here, Mitch."

"Why aren't you in bed?"

"I have to go to the bathroom. Relax, go to sleep."

When he settled back in, I quietly picked up my suitcase and left the room; if I stayed any longer, I would be lost, in more ways than one.

I did stay long enough to write another note. Taking care to write in block letters so that the paper left at Larry's would not be connected, I wrote: "Mitch—although your protective custody is wonderful, I find I must get away. Please don't worry about me or try to find me. Trust me, I will stay safe and I will contact you as soon as I can. I love you."

The sky was becoming cloudy when I went back to the streets. I hurried three blocks away from Mitch's apartment and went into a convenience store to make a phone call.

"Answer it, damn it. Answer it," I urged, as the phone rang for the tenth time. Finally, on the twentieth ring, a surprisingly alert voice answered. "Yes."

"Max, thank God you're there."

"Deirdre, to what do I owe the honor? I would have thought that after our last meeting, it would be a cold day in hell before you called on me again."

"If so, then I guess Satan is skiing right now. Max, look, I really need your help."

"My help?" His voice took on a grieved tone, but I could hear the humor underlying it. "And what about the intrepid Detective Greer, his shoulders are not as broad as you thought, eh? Or maybe he discovered the truth about you and threw you out on your blood-sucking ass." I had mistaken the humor, these last words were spoken in a hiss, as if through clenched teeth, and Max never stooped to vulgarity unless angered.

"Jesus, Max. I'm serious, I need your help. Can I count on you or shall I call someone else?"

"And just whom would you call, my dear? It seems to me

your options are very limited. They must be, for you to come to me."

He was right, I realized in shock as I ran through a very short list in my mind: Gwen, dead; Mitch, unapproachable; Larry, unthinkable. No, there was only Max now. There was always the option of checking into a hotel, but I needed to talk the situation over with someone. And given the circumstances, that person could only be Max. I sighed.

"Max," there was a pleading in my voice that made me cringe, "I have backed myself into a corner and don't know how to get out. We have been friends for so many years, and I need your help. As far as the other night, well, maybe we could make amends and start over."

"An interesting concept, this starting over. But you don't need to beg, you know." There was a pause and he gave a low chuckle. "Of course you can count on me, Deirdre. Have I ever let you down before?"

I gave a small humorless laugh. "Several times that I can think of, but that doesn't matter. All I need is a safe place to sleep tomorrow. Then I'll be on my way."

"Deirdre, my love, I would be pleased to have you stay with me. When can I expect you?"

"I'll be there in ten minutes." I hung up the phone.

The Ballroom of Romance was closed and dark when I arrived. It seemed so odd, I had never seen it this way. Even before it had opened, there had been a crowd of builders and contractors working through the night. Now it had a forlorn and sinister appearance, that was not in any way alleviated by opening of the front door. Max, looking extremely disheveled, shirtless and barefooted, stood in the unlit doorway, and beckoned me in.

"Did I wake you? I'm sorry, but I wouldn't have bothered you if it wasn't crucial."

He shrugged and led me back to his office. "It is never any bother for you." He began to open a bottle of my favorite wine. "Would you care for a drink?"

"Yes, why not? But first, I am very hungry."

He gave me a twisted smile. "I'm afraid I have no one available at the moment. Shall I send out? Or would you like to open my veins?"

I sat down on his couch, threw my head back and laughed. "A fair offer, I suppose, but this time I brought my own." I reached down, unzipped the backpack and held out one of the bags.

"You are getting enterprising in your old age, Deirdre. Of course, I heard about the robbery but really had no idea you were behind it." He took the bag from me and gingerly balanced it on his hand. "Theft doesn't seem your style."

"I did not rob the blood bank. Tonight I dine on the generosity of our good friend Larry."

"Larry? What the hell is he doing with stolen blood? And you saw him; he gave that to you?"

"Not actually, no. Although he once suggested we have dinner together. So I suppose you could say I decided to take him up on the invitation. Is it my fault that he wasn't at home when I called?"

"You broke into his apartment?" Max made no attempt to hide his amusement. "Moral little Deirdre? The one who is always concerned with the right and wrong of things? Shame on you, my dear. And what would Detective . . ."

"You leave him out of it." I snarled the words and took the blood bag from his hand. "I have a very interesting story to tell you, Max. But first things first."

I walked to the bar and selected a large glass, then walked to his desk and removed a pair of scissors from the top drawer. Clipping the end of the bag, I poured the blood into the glass and held it up admiringly to the light. "To your health."

He had put on a shirt and was buttoning it, but stopped to watch intently while I drank. The amount in the bag was only slightly more than I would normally take from a living victim. It was not an unacceptable substitute, but by the time I reached the end of the glass, it was cool and thickening. Next time, I thought, it should be warmed. Still I tipped it back again to get the very last drop from the bottom of the glass, before I went to the bar to rinse it out and refill it with the wine Max had opened.

When I sat back down, he tucked in his shirt and glanced at the clock. "We have an hour or so before dawn, you are fed and my blood is safe, perhaps now you would like to tell me what's happening."

In answer I reached again into the backpack and pulled out the scrapbook. "Larry has done more than provide a meal; he has also given me this." I smiled bitterly. "At least now we know what he's been researching."

His eyebrows raised when he saw the name on the cover. "May I?" He reached his hand out and I gave the book to him.

Slowly, Max turned the pages, reading each entry completely. At some he paused and laughed, others he read intently. He spent a lot of time on one page, not reading, just staring. I leaned over to see what it was. "Diane Gleason," he said, meeting my eyes. "You were so young, then."

I gave a snort of indignation. "Young? That's the second time you have referred to me as young. At that time, you must remember, I was already a hundred years old."

"No," he said sadly. "Your whole outlook was young. You were vibrant, carefree and utterly enticing. You did what you wanted, when you wanted and everyone else be damned. You had no ties, no ambition, just an endless lust for new horizons. What happened to that spirit?"

"If I remember correctly, it got abused by many people, including you. It was you who left, without so much as a spoken goodbye."

"Are you still angry about that? You're the one who's so quick to remind me it was a long time ago. And we are still together, we are still friends, as you call it."

I got up and poured us both another glass of wine. He continued his reading, acknowledging my offer of the wine with a quick gesture to the table next to his chair. I set it down and walked over to look out the window. Neither of us spoke until I saw the sky begin to lighten with the dawn.

"Max," I began. "The sun is almost up."

"I know, my dear." He stood up and handed the scrapbook back to me. "We'll talk more about this tomorrow evening. You can sleep in the back lounge; no one will bother you, I promise." He smiled and with a gallantry strange for him, held out his arm. "Come, I'll walk you home."

He picked up my suitcase, opened the door and escorted me out, my hand lightly gripping his arm. I suddenly felt comfortable with him again, he was no threat to me. His knowledge of what I was had not impacted our relationship, perhaps it had even intensified it. True, he was not Mitch but that was for the best. There was no place for me in Mitch's life, and all the love that I felt for him would not change me. With Max, there was still, if not the spark, then a chance that we could once again. . . . I shook my head and wondered at the direction my thoughts were taking. I love Mitch, I asserted, no matter how badly it might all turn out.

Max smiled at me as he opened the door to the lounge. It was a sensuous, knowing smile as if he had read my thoughts of him. And perhaps he did; he was perceptive enough to pick up my body language, my renewed ease in his presence.

"Well, here we are."

I walked in, placed the book on the couch and turned around. He carried my case in and put it on the floor. "Thank you, Max. It was good of you to take me in."

"Think nothing of it, Deirdre." A shadow fell over his face for only a moment before it was replaced with his usual cynical expression. "I suppose my spending the, er, day with you is out of the question?"

"I am so very tired, Max. It has been a rough night."

"Ah, well then." His gaze fastened on my lips and he moved toward me. I expected him to grasp me and kiss me; instead I felt his lips graze my cheek lightly. "I hope you don't mind using the couch. Sleep well." He walked out and closed the door.

I went to the window and pulled the curtains closed. They were heavy, well-insulated and should provide the proper protection. Then, after locking the door, and opening the suitcase, I began to undress. The nightgown packed had been for Mitch's benefit, black silk, with a plunging neckline and a billowing skirt. I felt silly wearing it here, with no one to see it, but it was all I had.

Max had thoughtfully set out a blanket and a pillow on one corner of the couch. In spite of his earlier protests on the phone, I felt that he was probably pleased that I had turned to him. He had done his best to make me feel welcome and comfortable in what was an awkward situation for the both of us. I laughed when I remembered the time he had introduced himself as my Renfield to a confused victim. He was more than that to me, of course. I had never thought of him as my servant, but, and I wondered again about my thoughts in the hall, we could never rekindle our intimate relationship. Even if I had not met Mitch, I had to move on, I needed to move on, and there would be no place for Max in my future.

I looked at the phone hanging on the wall. How easy it would be to call Mitch and let him know that I was safe that all was well and that I loved him. Crossing the floor, I picked up the phone and dialed his number, but hung up before it rang. You have no place for Mitch, either, I reminded myself and lay down on the couch.

Many years of practice, many years of life had taught me that no problems could be solved in sleeplessness. Once again, I cleared my mind of all thoughts, pleasant or otherwise, and fell asleep just as the sun rose.

Chapter 15

When I woke it was almost an hour to sunset. I dressed, went to the bar and opened a bottle of wine. Then I sat down and began to read Larry's scrapbook.

The hardest page to get past was the first; that civil war photograph that I can remember being taken as vividly as if it were yesterday. Here I walked in my real life, my own time. And although I was a vampire, I did not yet think of myself as an ageless freak, a walking anachronism. It took the erosion of my soul by many years to do that, the frantic passage of time and man's progress. In this time, there was no progress, or if there was it was a slow and gentle evolution, unnoticed as days rolled one into the other. It was my era and I still ached for it.

But not for the war; although Max often laughed saying that such a time must be a paradise for vampires. I grew to know death, to live with it during this time, but I never gained acceptance of it. Each lost life was deeply mourned by me, who could never die.

They were young, younger than me; they were my lovers, my brothers. They would come to me for advice, to read me that long–awaited letter from a wife or mother. They would come to me in fear and dread, facing impending battles and skirmishes, and I would offer comfort where I could, with my body mostly, giving some of them the only chance they would have for a woman's love. Looking back, I am amazed that I had no qualms about this, being a woman of that time, marrying as a virgin and expecting no other man in my life than my husband. But he was gone and I was damned. And their need of me was great, so great that it often engulfed my own. The grasping hands, the suckling mouth, the young, strong bodies desperate for the touch of life on a field of death.

I gave what I could, and when they returned wounded, bloodied and dying I nursed them with a gentle patience. The field doctors knew that they could rely on me no matter what the situation, I had no delicacy that could be offended and strength enough for the necessary tasks.

After the first two battles, we had tents devoted to the dying and wounded. Here at night I walked, carrying a softly glowing lantern, the quiet swishing of skirts announcing my presence. For the recovering soldiers I had a smile or a soft greeting. The feverish I soothed with my cool hands and voice, sometimes reading until they fell asleep. For the dying, and it became painfully easy to recognize those who would not survive the night, I offered a release from pain and a slow draining into a quiet death. Angel they called me then, even those who in passion had called me devil and witch, with their hands entangled in my hair and their bodies joined to mine.

Out of the group photographed, only one was still alive when I left. As I traveled from camp to camp, and battle to battle, I often thought of him, wondering who would comfort him, who would ease him into death. Soon each soldiers' face became blurred for me: there were so many, so many.

Damn Larry, I thought, brushing aside the tears that were flowing. I was violated, raped by his capture of my essence on these pages. His matter-of-fact captions, the cold stating of facts, names and occupations, reduced my life to nothing but blood and death. And it had been more than that, I knew. There had been friends and laughter, good times intermingled with the bad. I turned the pages and lingered over some: a newspaper photograph of night-shift steel workers during World War II, including one Doreen Gallagher; the employment records of Deborah Garrison who worked in an all-night diner as had Diane Gleason; the police log on Dorothy Grey who made her reappearance as a prostitute in the sleepy, southern town from which Max had finally rescued her for reincarnation as Deirdre Griffin.

I had to admire Larry for his dedication to this task, even while hating him and questioning his motives. It cannot have been an easy job, tracing and tracking me through the decades.

The gaps, bitterly notated by him as turning up nothing, gave me a grim laugh. Most of these were times when I went into hiding, living in some cases as an animal, dirty and homeless, occupying caves or abandoned shacks, running from my previous lives. Running, not in fear, but in regret and sadness for times and people that grew old and died. I hoped these gaps had worried him, tortured him, and stolen from him some of the satisfaction he must have felt for pinning me down so accurately.

The last page I ignored; his plans and aspirations I had already read the previous evening. I needed no reminder of the twisted mind that was trying to force me into doing something I had never done, something that I now had no wish to ever do. He would not become a vampire at my hands; I would kill or be killed before I allowed someone else to share in what he called the gift of life. For me it was nothing but a curse, an unnaturalness, a perversion of the beauty of humanity.

I closed the book, put it into my suitcase and locked it. By now the sun had set and I was free to go. Opening the door, I walked down the hall toward Max's office when suddenly I ducked into the adjoining room. From here the angry voices were audible and easy to identify. "Okay, Hunter, I'll ask it again. Where is she?"

"And I will tell you again, Detective. If she had wanted you to know, don't you think she would have told you?"

"I know she must be here, I can feel it. I must see her, you must tell me where she is. Her life is in danger . . ."

Max laughed, long and loud. "Deirdre is perfectly capable of taking care of herself, I assure you. If you only knew how ridiculously unnecessary your protection is, you would laugh too."

"And was it ridiculous for Gwen?"

"Gwen?" Max's questioning tone was sincere; I had not had the time to tell him about Gwen.

"Deirdre's secretary. Your psycho employee drove a stake through her heart."

"A singularly horrible way to die. But what has that got to do with Deirdre?"

Mitch's voice acquired a deadly patience as if he were speaking to a child. "Don't you understand? He means to do the same to her. He's left messages for her, taunting her, threatening her. And if he finds her she'll die, can't you see that?"

"Of course she would die, anyone would." Max was hedging now; playing this scene coolly, uncertain of what I had revealed to Mitch. "But he has to find her first, doesn't he? She is not easy to be found, if she chooses not to be."

"You don't care, do you? Deirdre tells me that you are her oldest and dearest friend, yet you would just stand by and let her be killed. How could you not care, not love her?"

"Love?" Max was angry now, his voice cold and frightening. "I knew it would come down to that, when you came here. You and all the others, mooning and slobbering over her, begging for an introduction, singing her praises, her beauty, her charm. She is beyond you, Greer, beyond all of you. And you could never keep her, never hold her to you for any more time than she wants to be held." His voice quieted and sounded now more sad than angry. "Don't you think I know that? I have lived with that fact since the day we met."

There was a long pause; then I could hear the clink of ice cubes in a glass and the pouring of a liquid. What the hell were they doing, toasting my death? Silently commemorating a woman they both loved and lost?

Mitch was the next to speak; his manner seemed different, as if over their drinks he and Max had reached some agreement. "Sorry, Hunter, I just wasn't thinking. What do you think I should do? How can I protect her if I can't find her?"

"Wait," Max advised. "Just wait. She'll return, perhaps here, perhaps at her hotel. I assure you, she won't be hurt. Larry doesn't want her dead."

"I wish I were as sure as you. If you hear from her, please let me know." Another brief pause and he continued. "Here are my numbers, at the station and at home. Call anytime."

I heard the door open and listened to Mitch's footsteps heading down the hall and out into the bar. I waited for a minute, but when they did not return I knew he was gone. I left the room and went next door to Max's office.

He was sitting at his desk and did not look up when I entered and locked the door behind me. "I trust you slept well, my dear. Your friend Mitchell Greer was looking for you."

"So I gathered," I said dryly. "He was quite vocal about it."

"Ah, you heard. Then I need not relate the event in all its pathos for you, do I?"

"You did quite well, Max. Never saying too much, not letting on that you knew anything about me or my whereabouts. I found your last statements quite touching."

"They were not meant for your ears, Deirdre." The usual scorn was back in his voice, and his face, when he lifted it to me, held his normal smile. "But they were at least effective in removing him from my office. I assume he's still lurking around, however, so if you don't want to meet him, be careful."

"I will."

"Does it give you pleasure, Deirdre?" He asked it with an agreeable smile, as if asking about the weather.

"What?"

"How you manage to enslave every man you meet, with a kiss or a look or a promise. Larry is now wanted for murder—a murder that your presence caused him to commit. And as for Greer, well, you've known him for less than two weeks now, already he would kill for you or die for you. I know his type, incorruptible and clean, he cannot be bribed or coerced and would never allow his personal feelings to interfere with his job. And yet you have managed to tear him down, rip through the veneer and reduce him to an almost savage state. And you pride yourself on your morals, your conscience, on how you have never taken a life. But he will love you until the day he dies and never realize that to you it was just a pleasant way to pass the time."

I stared at him in shock for a moment. "But, Max, I thought you knew." I hesitated. "I was sure you could tell."

"Tell what?"

"That I love him."

"Love, again? First Greer and now you. And where can you hope it will lead?"

"It will lead nowhere, but I can't help the way I feel. This is real, this is now. Tomorrow can take care of itself."

"Spare me the saccharin. I don't know what your plans are, but you may stay here as long as you wish. As one of your oldest and dearest friends, I could never deny you. Make yourself at home; I've got to get to work now."

"Well, damn," I said as he walked out. Nothing was turning out as I had expected.

I wanted to scream or throw something, in an effort to release the pain that Max's words had caused me. Instead I walked over and sat at his desk, glancing at the few papers on its surface, idly flipping the directory that held names and numbers of employees, suppliers and important customers. All the time my mind was racing, considering the truth of his words.

What he failed to realize, I finally decided, was that the situation was as painful for me as for anyone else. I loved and the loss of that love would hurt me deeply, perhaps even more than it would Mitch. For he could return to his life, and as he aged, the pain would lessen, eventually ceasing with his death. I, on the other hand, carried with me every loss, every love, magnified and multiplied like the links in Marley's chain.

"Damn," I said again and jumped when the phone beside me rang.

"Ballroom of Romance," I answered, my voice surprisingly pleasant and calm.

There was a pause at the end of the line. "Hello," I said. "May I help you?"

"You know you can." My pulse jumped at his voice—here was one at least that gave me reason to continue for a while in this life. Or gave me hope of release.

"Larry."

"Did you get my message?"

"Yes. Did you get mine?"

"Loud and clear, Dorothy. I want to see you. I want . . ."

"I know what you want, Larry. You won't get it."

"But you will meet with me?"

"Yes."

His breathing quickened and I could feel his impatience over the line. "Tonight, midnight, in the cellar of the Ballroom."

"How charmingly melodramatic, Larry. You can expect me."

I hung up the phone. Here was the final test, I thought. Could I kill him, to protect myself and avenge a friend? Or would I allow him to take the life, that, despite my disgust and despair, I had tenaciously clung to for so many years? I checked the clock—there were four hours to wait.

Max had left the office door open, I could hear the band begin to play, the voices of the people gathered. I walked through the kitchen, pushed open service doors and stood at the end of the bar. Mitch was still there, standing by the main entrance, his eyes scanning the dancers. I felt that the next four hours could very easily be spent watching this man who had so unexpectedly come into my life, giving me one more chance to feel my humanity.

"Wine, Miss Griffin?"

I nodded absently to the bartender, never taking my eyes from Mitch's shadowy form. The band had finished playing one of my favorite songs, and I wondered how long it would take him to find me among the crowd. The bartender brought my drink; perhaps it was the movement that called his attention to me, perhaps he could sense me the way I could him. It didn't seem to matter; he had found me, and after my flight of last night, I wanted to be found. Before the night was over, I would be a murderer in fact, or dead; these last few hours were best spent with him.

Ignoring the drink before me, I crossed over to the band and whispered my request. The leader nodded and began the song again as I reached Mitch's side. I put my finger to my lips and led him to the dance floor.

"Where have you been?"

"Quiet, Mitch. I'm here now." Nestling my head against his shoulder, I closed my eyes and began to hum softly. His body relaxed and responded to mine, and we danced.

When the song was over, he held me for a time and looked down into my face and smiled. I could still see anger in his eyes, anger at my desertion of him last night, but the relief at finding me alive finally won out. He kissed me and we danced one more number before we returned to the dark corner of the bar.

"Your regular table is ready if you'd like, Miss Griffin." The bartender nodded his head toward Max who was standing at the other end of the bar, watching us with an amused expression on his face. "We weren't expecting you tonight, but now that you're here, Max says everything's on the house." He picked up my wine and a bottle of beer for Mitch and showed us to the table.

"What does he mean, not expecting you?" Mitch asked after we were seated.

"I usually call ahead to let them know I'm coming. It's always so crowded . . ."

"No, Hunter knew you were here all along. I could swear he did."

"Contrary to what you believe, Mitch, I do not report to Max or anyone. I come and go as I please. And if this is another excuse to start your usual tirade about Max, I do not want to hear it, not tonight."

"Actually, Max and I have come to an understanding."

"Oh?" I smiled wryly. "That must have been quite a task."

He looked at me and shook his head. "What I should have said is that I have come to understand Max. He loves you, you know."

I laughed. "Max loves me? Are we talking about the same person?"

"I'm serious, Deirdre. I still don't like the guy, he still makes my skin crawl, but I have no doubt of how he feels about you. And I feel sorry for him. Almost as sorry as I feel for myself."

"Why should you feel sorry for yourself?"

"Because, oh, hell, let's just forget it, okay?"

I took a drink of my wine and dropped my eyes. "Max doesn't love me. He may have wanted you to believe he did, for whatever devious purpose he had in mind. He's like that, a manipulator, not happy unless he's pulling someone's strings. But he knows me too well to love me."

Mitch reached over and took my hand. "I love you. What on earth could make you think that if someone knows you, they couldn't love you?"

"How well do you know me, Mitch? Do you know where I was born, what my parents' names were, what I wanted to be when I grew up?"

"You know damn well you're too bloody secretive for me to know anything about you. But if you'd like to play twenty questions, I'll start. Where were you born?"

"Fort Leavenworth, Kansas."

"Your parents' names?"

"Robert and Eleanor Grey."

"Grey? Then Griffin was your husband's name?"

"No, I changed it for professional reasons."

"Well then, Deirdre Grey, what did you want to be when you grew up?"

"A nurse. And the name is Dorothy."

"Dorothy? Okay, I can live with that."

I smiled over at him. "I really do prefer Deirdre after all this time."

"Fine with me; you don't seem much like a Dorothy, anyway. Now, I know all that and I still love you. What can be so awful about you that I wouldn't love you?"

"Look, I'm sorry I even brought this up. It doesn't matter."

Suddenly his eyes clouded over with anger. "It does matter, and I've decided that I like this game. Let's continue, shall we? Why did you leave me last night when you knew it was important for you to stay? You did promise to stay. Where did you go and what did you do?"

"I felt trapped. I needed to walk. I told you, I'm not used to reporting in to anyone. And although I hate to say it, that includes you also."

"But your life was in jeopardy, didn't you realize that?"

"My life is only in jeopardy in your mind, Mitch." I gave a

small derisive laugh. "Larry won't hurt me. I'm perfectly capable of handling him."

"Why is everyone trying to convince me that you're Wonder Woman or something? Max said pretty much the same thing, earlier. And I will tell you what I told him. Don't you think Gwen thought the same thing? You see where it got her."

Poor Gwen, I thought sadly, in over her head and she never knew it. "Gwen was different. She was sweet, innocent and trusting. I am none of those. When I next meet Larry, I will be fully prepared to do what needs to be done."

"When you next meet Larry I will be with you. And hopefully he will be behind bars at the time."

"Then there's no need to discuss it, is there?"

He shrugged. "Let's get out of here, anyway. I don't like the thoughts of your being so visible and accessible."

I laughed. "Calm down, he's hardly likely to jump up from between the dancers and drive a stake through my heart right here, Mitch. This seems to be as safe to me as anywhere. But if you have to go, don't let me stop you."

"I don't have to go, I'm not on duty now. Just on alert. And if they need me, they know where I am."

I finished my wine and, as if on cue, a waiter brought me another glass and Mitch another beer. He raised his eyebrows in disbelief, "Is service always so good?"

"For me it is. Let's dance."

Later in the evening, Max came over and sat with us for a while. It seemed odd to have Mitch relaxed around him, he even excused himself to go to the bathroom, leaving us alone. I checked the clock, there was an hour to go.

Max saw my glance. "Going somewhere, my dear?"

Hurriedly I spoke, while studying the door for Mitch's return. "Actually, I have another appointment at twelve. It shouldn't take long, but I would prefer him not to know about it."

"And you'd like me to cover for you? Draw him away from you so that you can leave and come back, with him none the wiser?"

I nodded. "Can you?"

"Hasn't he informed you that he and I are comrades-in-arms now? It is so rarely that I get to make a friend, this duplicity could spoil our relationship." He smiled at me, enjoying my discomfort.

"Jesus, Max. You know as well as I that that's all just something you dreamed up. You and Mitch, friends?"

"Yes, well, then I will do as you ask. Will 11:45 give you enough time to get where you are going?"

"No problem."

"And where are you going? With whom are you meeting?"

"It's all very mysterious, Max," I said with an impudent grin. "Our very dear friend called for an assignation in the cellar at midnight."

"Happy hunting, Deirdre, and be careful." He rose as soon as Mitch returned and lightly kissed me on the cheek.

"What are you hunting, Deirdre?" His forehead had a little crease of worry that I hadn't noticed before.

I reached over the table, took his hand and pressed it to my face. "Why, you, of course."

Chapter 16

Max had never done anything in a small way before, so it shouldn't have surprised me the lengths to which he went to fulfill my request. Promptly at 11:45 the fire alarm rang; panic began to grasp the people in the club. Mitch could not resist getting involved, to calm everyone and organize an orderly exodus from the club. I slipped up to the service doors, waited for the staff to leave and opened the door in the kitchen that lead to the cellars of the Ballroom of Romance.

As I descended the steps, I took the time to unscrew the light bulb and throw it to the floor. Its delicate shattering would have announced my presence but for the sound of the fire alarm still blaring upstairs. I had as long as the alarm continued, I knew, before Mitch would come looking for me. Make it last, I prayed when I got to the bottom of the stairway. I have things to say that I don't want him to hear.

The fact that I had never been here before was to my disadvantage, but I thought that well balanced with the lack of direct lighting. My night vision was perfect; Larry could hardly say the same. I walked down one of the rows of shelves and positioned myself up against the wall, so that I could see him enter. Then I collected my thoughts, and began to plan my method of attack.

I would try to reason with him first, I decided. If I could convince him that his quest was futile, that what he asked for was not a blessing and not a gift, then I could wipe his mind clean of any remembrance of me and what I was. I would need to draw his blood for that, so that the suggestion would go deep enough to block everything. Fine, I thought, and smiled into the darkness, my canines enlarging. He could then be turned over to the police and brought to justice for the death of Gwen. I trusted Mitch enough to know that he would be punished, perhaps even with the death penalty.

If none of that worked, I still had no doubt of my capacity to control him or overpower him. He was merely a human and I was what I was.

The alarm upstairs still continued and was, I realized blocking any sounds I might have heard of his arrival. An uncontrollable chill possessed me. He could be here, now, and I might not know it. And what if all his posturing, all his ambitions were simply a front for his true intentions, to rid the world of a vampire? All of my plans allowed for some sort of interplay between us; what if he arrived stake in hand and prepared for immediate murder? Could I stop him then?

In all my arrogance and complacency, the idea finally took

hold; I may have made a mistake in accepting this meeting. Everything was conspiring against me, it seemed: the earsplitting alarm that took away my enhanced hearing, the fact that my opponent might know more about how to handle this situation than I.

It is not too late to run, my mind urged. I had come down early, he might not be here yet. Choking back my brief spell of panic, I took a step forward, heading toward the stairs. Under the blaring siren I could hear nothing but the low thudding of feet on the floor above. One of the thuds sounded close at hand and I shrunk back into my corner. But it was not followed by any other sound. I waited for a minute, alert and listening; all of the sounds seemed distant and non–threatening.

Now, I thought, I can make the stairs and get Mitch. Once Larry was in custody, I would be free. It was unlikely that any of his wild stories about me would be believed; I possessed the damaging evidence. Larry, on the other hand, was defenseless and likely to be taken for a raving lunatic, guaranteeing his incarceration for some time to come. With a breath of relief I edged forward, listening, watching.

Suddenly the screech of the siren stopped, but it was too late for my escape. Larry had made his approach, silently and stealthily, now I felt his warm breath on the side of my neck. Whirling around, I faced him and he caught my wrists in his hands. I made no move, assessing the strength of his grip on me; he was stronger than I would have thought possible. And although I believed that I could break free should I wish to, I knew that when he held me, he could hold nothing else. No hammer, no stake.

My arsenal of weapons was always available. I smiled seductively at him, trying to meet his eyes. "Larry."

"You're early," he said in a husky voice.

"As are you." I tried to move closer to him, attempted to get my teeth on his neck, but he locked his arms and held me away from him.

"No tricks, Deirdre. I don't trust you, not yet. And I know you can do nothing to me if I don't look into your face." He moved his arm up, still gripping my hand, and stroked my cheek with his fist. "Such a lovely face, too."

"Then look at me, Larry." My voice was pitched low and urgent, a request to a lover.

"No."

I tried a different approach. "Larry, what you want, I have never done before. I don't know how to transform you; I don't even know if it is possible."

"It's possible, and you will do it."

"No, it is not a good thing. You don't want my life; it was forced on me, I had no choice. All those lonely years, Larry, you just can't visualize how horrible it can be. You're young, you have a good life ahead of you. Don't throw it away for this, it's not worth it. Believe me, I know."

His laughter echoed in the room. It sounded hollow, evil. "It's what I want. I've got nothing ahead of me now, don't you think I know that? If you don't transform me, here and now, they will catch me and try me for murder." He laughed again and I shivered. "Then my good life consists of jail or death."

"You shouldn't have killed them, Larry. It was wrong."

"Them?" He shook my hands. "I only killed Gwen. She served her purpose well, of course, and for that I'm thankful."

"And her purpose was?"

His voice was calm, reasonable in his rationalization. "She made it possible for me to get you here, alone, with what I want."

"I would have come. You didn't need to kill her! And it did not need to be that way." I shuddered slightly and he laughed.

"But it was the most effective way of getting my message to you. Besides, let's be honest here, compared with all the others you have murdered over the years, what's one poor silly girl like Gwen?"

"I have never killed anyone."

"Never? I find that hard to believe. And I know for a fact it's not true."

"How could you?"

"You have my book. Did you wonder where that first picture

came from? It's been in my family for generations, along with the story of the beautiful lady who bled and killed wounded soldiers. Always at night, always with a smile. My great-grandfather inherited the picture and the story from his father. He's the one on the far right. And I always assumed the story was embellished over the years, magnified to scare the children. But when I met you, I recognized you immediately. Then I stayed quiet, followed you, watched you. It wasn't hard to draw the conclusions I did. Or to track you over the years; all it took was belief. No one would think to look for a vampire, no one believes in you."

I made no attempt to justify my actions for him. His mind was made up and until he met my eyes or allowed me close enough to feed I could only stand there, trapped by his strong hands.

"But I believe," he said, the tenderness of his voice at odds with the tense, violent stance of his body. "And I will be one. You must do it, take me and change me. I can fill the years for you, Deirdre. You will finally have someone who loves you, to stay with you forever."

"But . . ." I was about to say I didn't want him, could never love him. He felt my reluctance and tightened his grip on my wrists. I changed my tactics again. "But, Larry, my love, you must let me close enough to change you. I can hardly do it at arms' length."

He gave me a doubtful look, then shook his head. A lock of his hair fell over one eye and he impatiently brushed it aside, using his hand, still holding my wrist. I took advantage of the contact and stroked his hair and cheek before he dropped his arm.

"Oh, Larry. You don't understand, do you? I was only testing you, I had to make sure that your resolve was strong, your desire true. Because the whole time that you were watching me, I was watching you, wanting you, grooming you for immortality. Trust me, my love. You won't be sorry." I laughed, low and sexy, and he sighed with longing. "But you must let me get close to you. You'll like it," I purred. "It's an incredible experience. Better than love. Better than anything you can possibly imagine.

I have so much to teach you, to show you. What would you like to know? Shall I tell you of the beauty of the nights, the feeling of being free and secure in a world of people who exist only to satisfy your every need? Shall I tell you of the power of life and death, the crisp touch of teeth to tender skin, the warm flow of life. Or shall I tell you of love?" My body writhed as if in remembrance. "Shall I tell you how a vampire makes love, or shall I show you?"

He said nothing, just stared down at me, still avoiding my glance. The only sign that he was weakening was the glistening of sweat on his forehead.

I turned up the heat some more. "Just imagine, Larry, your senses are heightened, your pleasure is enhanced, your endurance and strength are unimaginable to a human. You will be able to call women to you, all women, any woman you want. They will worship your perfect body with their bodies and their hands and their mouths."

His breathing was labored now, his tongue darted out to lick his lips.

"Oh, Larry, think about it. Even a single touch can drive you to a sexual frenzy that is humanly impossible. And love with another vampire, oh, Larry, I can't find words to describe it. You must let me show you, let me show you."

He said nothing, but his arms began to tremble.

"You will let me do it, won't you, Larry?" I spoke eagerly and earnestly and felt my words hit him. "You must let me do it, Larry. I can feel it now, your blood and my blood, intermeshed, blending together, as our bodies . . ." I let my voice trail off in a low moan.

His arms loosened and relaxed; I moved up to him, rubbed my body against his and he groaned. "Now," I whispered, "now," and I sunk my teeth deeply into his neck.

I was right, I realized as I let myself be carried away in the flow of his blood, it was incredible. His hardened penis pressed urgently against me, he was willingly giving himself to me, not pushing away but welcoming my bite, pulling me deeper into him. Almost, I wished I could take him with me.

Almost, except for the image of Gwen, naked with her blood spattered about my bed. Poor silly girl he had called her. I removed my bloodied mouth from him. "Bastard," I hissed; all the rage in my soul was contained in that whisper and he rocked back from the sound, even as I positioned myself for a slashing bite.

He stared at me, his eyes glazed over. Then his hand shot out, and gripped my wrists again. God, he was strong. I had read about the strength of madmen, but had never realized its truth until now. He whipped me around and pressed me up against the wall, his eyes glinting dangerously in the darkness.

"I should have known better than to trust you, Deirdre," and he reached behind him, stooping, still holding me against the wall. I struggled but his grip held. "I came prepared." And he held up a wooden stake and a mallet that he had hidden. "There are more ways than one to get your blood. I can just as easily drink it from your dying body. And although, you'd be gone; I can still find other women, younger, more beautiful than you, who'd be happy to take your place."

"Larry, it doesn't work that way."

"No, I won't listen to you. It must work, it has to." He pinioned my body against the wall with his legs, placed the stake over my heart and raised the mallet.

"No," I screamed, dodging away from his strike, and heard my scream's echo from the stairs, seconds before a searing pain flashed in my shoulder. He missed, I thought, confused as the hammer dropped from his hand and the stake clattered to the ground. Then he fell, and took me with him, his legs still gripping mine. Larry was dead and his blood was flowing over me, soothing the pain in my arm.

"Oh, God, Deirdre." Mitch rushed down the stairs. "Oh, Deirdre," he cried again.

"Mitch, I'm not hurt. He's dead, just get him off of me."

Quickly, Mitch rolled the body from me. I pushed my hand against the wall and stood up. My whole right side was drenched in blood, some of it mine. But I would not tell him that, the hole left by the bullet that had passed through Larry, would heal quickly. Too quickly for explanations.

"Jesus, look at you."

"It's okay, Mitch. I wasn't hit, all this is Larry's."

"Are you sure?"

"Of course I'm sure. Why would I lie about it?"

I took a step toward him, but my legs were trembling and I couldn't move. He came to me then, held me tightly and whispered into my hair. "I almost lost you, do you know what that would have done to me?" He lifted me up and kissed me.

"Mitch," I said when he finally released my mouth, "thank you."

"For saving your life? Gee, lady, it's all part of my job."

"No, not that. Well, for that too. But mostly, thank you for loving me."

"Oh, that. No problem. Now let's get you out of here and cleaned up. I can take your statement later."

"Don't you have to stay here?"

"Yeah, I guess I do."

I reached up and kissed him again. "Put me in a cab, you can finish up here and then meet me back at my hotel."

I saw the doubt enter his eyes and he shook his head. "I don't know, Deirdre."

"The person you were protecting me from is there." And I pointed to Larry's body, trying to control my shudder. "I don't think he is likely to follow me, do you?"

"No, but . . ."

"And I would really like to get away from this place, not just the cellar, but the whole club. I'll wait for you at the hotel. Don't be too long."

He put his arm around my shoulder and helped me up the stairs. Only about half of the clientele remained after the fire scare. They milled around uncertainly, but when the band resumed playing they went back to the bar or their tables. Max was nowhere in sight. On the way to the door, we passed a coat rack and Mitch removed the closest coat wrapping it around my blood-spattered clothes.

The doorman signalled the cab and when it came, Mitch helped me in. "Are you sure you'll be okay?"

"I'll be fine. I need a shower, some rest and a chance to think." I reached into my purse and handed him my hotel key. "Let yourself in again."

As the cab drove away, I waved, but he had turned away and was walking back into the building. I watched the set of his shoulders, the determined stride and smiled to myself.

At the hotel, I got an extra key from Frank and went to my room. Shuddering at the clammy, sticky feel of the partially dried blood, I stripped off my clothes and noticed the two small holes in the right sleeve. Although I had been shot, the bullet had passed clear through. In front of the bathroom mirror, I probed the wound, tenderly at first and then with more firmness. It was clean, with no bone chips or debris; it should heal cleanly and quickly. My white skin had a rosy glow, due to the thin coating of Larry's blood and mine. I shivered when I thought how close I had come to dying and how it would have been of my own doing, as surely as if I had held the stake and raised the mallet. Had it not been for Mitch, I would have been as dead as Gwen was. But with one possible exception. Would it have been my body lying in blood on the cellar floor, the one in which I lived, the one to which Mitch had made love? Or would it have been a skeletal wreck, as all the unnatural years accumulated in minutes? Or perhaps only a small pile of dust and ash?

I shuddered again as I stepped into the shower, allowing the hot water to wash away the unclean taint of blood that covered my body. Through my folly, I had at least learned one thing; that my life was still precious to me and the next time I decided to risk it by confronting a madman, I had better come prepared with more than my ego and body to protect me.

Mitch was not long in arriving, but even so, I was ready and waiting for him. Knowing that he would have questions for me, questions that I could only in part answer truthfully, I had rehearsed my answers, my responses, as I prepared for his entrance. And of course, I realized as I applied the make–up to my pale complexion, there would be his anger to deal with, the anger that he had not expressed at the club from the sheer relief of finding me alive. But he'd had plenty of time to think since then, to wonder why I had done the things I did. He would be furious that I had attempted the meeting alone, that I had told Max, and not him, of my intentions. So I dressed in self-defense; the red silk of the caftan rustled when I walked, calling me back to more elegant days, making me, I thought, more vulnerable. But no woman of those times could have felt comfortable in such a dress, the silk was thin and, since I wore nothing underneath, it clung to my body, accenting my breasts, outlining all my curves.

I admired the result in my mirror when I heard the key turn in the lock. I hoped that my appearance would keep him sufficiently distracted; that way he might not notice that my answers were less than satisfactory. I hated the thought of deceiving him, seducing him away from his job, but I had no alternative. He must never be allowed find out the truth.

"Deirdre," he called. I was right, the anger had set in. His voice was full of it, cold and uncompromising again, like the first night we met. But what had passed between us, I hoped, would keep us together, if only for a while.

"Hello, Mitch." I came out of the bedroom and went to him. "You're earlier than I expected."

He shrugged. "There was less to do than you might think. And since you were the one involved, most of the work revolves around you. Do you feel up to answering a few questions?"

I nodded. "There's not much to tell, really. Larry called, earlier that evening, and said he wanted to meet me." I sat down on the couch and smoothed the red fabric over my legs. "I, I guess it was stupid of me, but I thought I could get him to turn himself in. I never really thought he would try to hurt me, and I thought he might listen to me."

"Why didn't you tell me? Max knew about it, I suppose that's why he set off the fire alarm. And we were together the whole evening, you and I, and you gave no indication of your plans. Did you think I wouldn't help you? You knew what he was capable of, you saw what he did to Gwen, why on earth wouldn't you tell me, take me along?"

The lie I had practiced came easily to my lips. "He said," and I allowed a tremor to creep into my voice, "he said that if I didn't meet him alone, that he would start killing everyone who knew me. I did not want to risk it, I have so few friends, and he knew about us. You might have been next."

"Damn," he ran his fingers through his hair and looked at me. "And for some strange reason, you thought you could control the situation better than I could? Jesus, Deirdre, that makes no sense at all."

"I never said it made sense. I'm just telling you what happened."

"What did he say to you? Did you talk or did he just jump out at you, brandishing his stake?"

I winced at his sarcasm. "We talked for a bit; he said that Gwen didn't matter. I was angry when I heard that, I couldn't help it. I swore at him. Then he turned on me; I didn't expect him to. And suddenly you were there and he was dead. That's all."

"And how long were you there? I seem to remember you disappeared right after the fire alarm went off. I didn't make it downstairs until about twenty minutes later."

"I waited around for him. Then when the siren went off, I thought I would just leave, come and get you. But it was too late, he was already there."

"So your conversation took about five or ten minutes?"

"I suppose so. Jesus, Mitch, I was frightened and I didn't have a stopwatch with me."

He gave me a rather grim smile that did nothing to break the tension between us. "When I got to the top of the stairs, I heard him say something about how he didn't want to listen to you. How it must work, it has to work. What was he talking about?"

I lowered my eyes. "You heard that? Well, your guess is as good as mine. He was crazy, deranged. That much should be obvious."

"Deirdre." His tone of voice was harsh; he leaned forward on his seat as if he could catch the words I wouldn't say, pull the information from my mind.

"Mitch?"

"You know," he said in a hesitant way, "I would not have expected you to be a hostile witness on this. You're holding back on me, I can tell. Why?"

"Damn it, Mitch. Don't you understand what I went through with Larry? I was almost killed, staked down like some exotic insect. And you expect me to give you a blow by blow description of everything that happened. How am I to answer for the ravings of a madman? Obviously, if I knew what motivated him, I probably would not have been there in the first place."

"Damn straight."

"All right, it was stupid to meet him. We both know that. But I was doing what I thought was the right thing. And I will be damned if I will let myself be put on trial for it. It's over now, Mitch. I'm alive, and you have Gwen's murderer. It seems to me that everyone should be happy about this; you and I and the whole damn department."

"Okay, okay." He smiled at me, a real smile this time, one that lit up his eyes. "I didn't mean to be so rough on you, but every time I think of how you set yourself up for this, how if I had just been one minute later . . . I don't like the thoughts of your being dead."

"Trust me, I don't like it much either."

"No, I guess not." He stood up, reached for my hands and pulled me into a brief embrace. "I've got to get back now," he said regretfully. "There's a lot of paperwork involved in closing this one out. I suspect, given Larry's background and penchant for vampire lore, that we'll pin them all on him. We suspected him anyway in the original three and even though Gwen's murder doesn't match up, it's all in the same vein."

I groaned slightly at his unintended pun. He held me out and smiled at me again.

"Sorry, it's not really a joking matter. But we still have one situation to explain before we're done."

"That being?"

He looked into my eyes and held my hands. "There were fresh bite marks on Larry's neck, similar to the others but with a smaller span. But don't you worry about it, Deirdre, I'm sure there's an answer somewhere. I'll call you tomorrow. Good night."

He kissed me on the forehead and slammed the door behind him.

Chapter 17

Knowing that I would get no sleep after Mitch's last remark, I dressed and went to the office. There was work to do; not just the preparation for filling the orders from the show, but also something that I dreaded, packing up Gwen's personal items and returning them to her family. It was my responsibility, one that I could not shirk.

After I checked in with the guard, I bought a newspaper and rode the elevator alone. For once, the darkness of the rooms frightened me and I turned on all the lights as I made my way to my office. I pulled the curtains aside, and opened the door to my apartment. The room smelled heavily of disinfectant with only a slight undertone of blood. Taking a deep breath, I slowly walked up the spiral staircase to my loft bedroom. I was glad I had accepted Mitch's advice and his recommendation of a cleaning service. The sheets had been stripped away and were gone, the walls and ceiling had been sponged off, but the mattress and carpet, although damp from their cleaning, still showed the faint brown stains from Gwen's blood. I shuddered and went back down the stairs, making a mental note to get them replaced before I sold the business.

At my desk, I made a list of prospective buyers for Griffin Designs; all the thrill I had in this business dissolved with the death of Gwen. I could not continue, did not need to continue. The money I had made in the past ten years, along with that netted from the sale, would be tucked away into some bank account with a different name for my use later on. I would be well provided for and could devote my time to the tracking of the other vampire in this city; I did not believe that Larry was responsible for Andrews and the others. Let the police postulate on how the murders were done, with their theories of syringes and pumps—I knew the truth of it. And I would find him.

But I would have to be quick. I knew that now; Mitch was too discerning and our relationship could never continue. He was sharp and intelligent, and sooner or later the proof would overwhelm his disbelief. Already he was raising questions that he should never have thought to ask. Thank God he had more sense than to believe the superstitions of his Romanian ancestors, otherwise the next time the stake was at my heart, he would be wielding the mallet, not shooting the one who was.

I laughed humorlessly; how ironic, I thought, that Mitch should be the one with the roots in the old country; I was merely a Kansas pioneer with bad luck.

Getting up from my desk with a sigh, I went down the hall and got two boxes from the storage closet, then stopped off and started a pot of coffee.

Gwen's presence was still very much alive at her desk. As I packed, I almost expected her to come bouncing down the hall, berating me for interfering with her possessions; I felt like an intruder here, more of the ghost than she would be. Oddly enough, I did not believe in ghosts; I had seen too many die in my lifetimes, none had ever returned to speak to me or to punish and torture me. They were dead and I hoped in a better place, one that perhaps I would never attain.

There was something belittling about the two packed cartons that represented Gwen's work here. I moved them to one side, planning on delivering them later tonight at the funeral home. Gently, I pushed in her chair and whispered a goodbye.

After splashing my face with cold water in the bathroom, I filled my mug with coffee and went back into my office and closed the door. I read the paper, noting the time and place of Gwen's viewing, then continued to make notes on the work I had ahead of me. When I glanced at the clock I realized that it was only a little after three. None of the calls could be made until tomorrow morning. I was not hungry, but restless, and dawn was still four hours away. In the outer office, I pulled aside the drapes and looked out on the city. Spreading my arms, I leaned against the glass, my cheek on the window pane. The surface was cold and I could hear the slight howl of the wind. Here and there people walked, cars drove by and the sky was dark, with a small crescent moon just beginning to show. I walked out of the office, leaving the lights blazing and the doors unlocked, heedless to everything but the beckoning streets, the beckoning night.

That night I remember as being my last in that city. Perhaps it was just the last time I felt I belonged there. That night was for closing the doors of the corridor of my waking world. And I walked all the streets that for ten years I had considered my territory.

The Ballroom of Romance was dark when I passed; I envisioned Max at his desk, deep within the club, reviewing his books, totalling the receipts of tonight. I wondered if he was angry or amused at this evening's events. I was tempted to ring the night bell but thought better of it and moved on.

Around the corner, there was a small coffee shop. It was open all night and the lights were bright. Few people were inside, but outside three women lingered, looking cold and lonely in their short skirts and high heels. One of them was a friend of Linda's, I had met her once and the three of us had sat in the diner over coffee and cigarettes. She recognized me and waved, but I shook my head, turned around and headed back the other way.

As I passed the office again, I looked up. Where I had left the curtains parted a thin slot of light shone. I should go up and turn them off, I thought, but continued my walk. Not pausing at the hotel, nor acknowledging Frank's wave, I quickened my pace. Before I realized it, I was outside Mitch's apartment building. I stood in the shadows and looked up to his windows. They were dark, was he sleeping or just not home? I longed to climb the stairs and open the door, to curl up into his arms and remain there until dawn. Further up the street was the alley where I had fed on the runaway, the alley where I had surprised the man called Sammy, and the pool hall to which Mitch, Chris and I had gone. I looked at my watch, it was still early, just a little after four. What the hell, I thought, I could use a drink.

Some inner sense warned me before I pushed open the door. I peered through the window and saw Mitch—there was no mistaking his profile and the way he sat in his chair. He was at the table we had occupied that night, and was talking earnestly to someone who looked familiar. I moved away, but not before the man looked up and recognized my face as I recognized his. Sammy stood and pointed, but I was gone before Mitch could turn around. I pulled off my shoes and ran silently, through the alleys and side streets, not slowing until I was back at the office. Outside the doors, I glanced up and down the street and saw no one. I put my shoes back on, and calmly entered the lobby. The guard looked up and smiled at me.

"It's only you, Miss Griffin. Back so soon?"

"Yes, I'm afraid so. It's getting too cold to walk."

"You shouldn't be out by yourself anyway. As you well know, there's some strange goings-on around here." He hummed slightly to himself and then went on. "I read in the paper that they got the scum that killed Gwen. A real shame, that was, she was a sweet girl. I was off that night; I hate to think of it. Maybe if I'd been here that guy couldn't have got in."

"You mustn't blame yourself." I reached over and patted his hand, wishing I could take that advice myself.

He grasped my hand. "Thank you, Miss Griffin. You get upstairs now and get warm. Your hand is as cold as ice."

I smiled at him and moved away.

"Take care, now," he called as the elevator doors closed.

* * *

The pre-dawn hours dragged and when the staff finally arrived, their shocked expressions and reddened eyes told me that the news of Gwen's death had made the rounds and taken its toll. At ten, overly conscious of the empty desk outside my office and the dismal pall that hung over everyone, I sent them all home with pay for the next two days. Switching all but my private phone line to the answering service, I called my attorney and outlined the plans I had to sell Griffin Designs. He had tried to talk me out of it, as I knew he would.

"But, Deirdre, think of all the money you'll be losing. You built the company up from nothing and now that you are showing a good profit, you want out?"

"That's right, I want it sold. Quick and dirty. Can you handle it?"

"Well, sure we can handle it. But don't you think you should think about it? It's a pretty big step for you."

"I have thought about it. All I want is enough to live comfortably for the next ten years. And the provisional two-month stay for the employees with the new owner. Is that unreasonable?"

"No, it's a steal. I can think of several people right now who would jump at the chance. Even for much more than you're asking."

I laughed. Of course the higher we sold for, the bigger his percentage would be. "Get what you can for it, Fred. I'm fed up with the business; I just want out."

"Okay, you're the boss." He hesitated and I knew what he was going to say. "Deirdre, I was sorry to hear about Gwen. The whole thing was pretty horrible, huh?"

"Yes." My answer was curt, to forestall any discussion of the event, but I suddenly remembered that he and Gwen had dated for a while, before Nick came into the picture, and softened my response. "But they tell me, for what it's worth, that it was probably quick; that after the initial blow, she would have died instantly."

"Even so, it was horrible."

"Yes."

"Well, I guess you'll be going to the funeral home. If I don't make it, please give my condolences to her mother."

"I will, thank you. Give me a call tomorrow and let me know how everything is going on the sale."

I hung up the phone and checked to see that everyone had gone home, then locked the front door and turned out the lights.

Going back to the loft, or even the apartment was out of the question, so I curled up on the couch in my office, closed my eyes and slept.

The cab driver spoke very little English, and although he had no trouble finding the funeral home, he could not understand that I wanted him to wait. After repeated attempts to collect his fare, and my attempts to get him to stay, I finally gave in and paid him. Unceremoniously, he dumped the two cartons and me on the steps of the building. "Damn," I swore, watching as he drove away, "now how the hell am I going to get home?"

"Don't worry about it."

I turned around and jumped when I saw Mitch walking out of the door. "What the hell are you doing here?" I was shook up enough—funeral homes upset me terribly—and I didn't really want him around, looking over my shoulder, asking questions, especially after seeing him last night at the pool hall. It didn't take much imagination to recreate the story Sammy must have told him.

He gave me a suspicious glance. "Sorry, I thought you might want some company. I knew you would be here tonight, being as this is the only night viewing."

"And what is that supposed to mean?"

"Nothing." He walked past me and picked up the cartons. "Do these go inside?"

"Yes, thank you." I followed him up the steps and in the door. He put the boxes down in the corner, next to the sign that announced the names of the dead. There were four others, in addition to Gwen DeAngelis. Seeing her name there was a shock, it was so final and seemed so matter of fact. I must have stared at that sign for a long time because finally I became conscious of Mitch's hand on my arm. I shuddered slightly and looked up at him. "I am sorry," I said in a hushed voice. "I hate these places."

"Most people do." His voice was harsh and I lowered my eyes. "Look," he said in a softer voice, but tightened his grip on my arm, "I've already been in and made my condolences. If you'd like to go alone, I'll understand and wait outside."

"That would be nice, Mitch, but you needn't wait."

"I'll wait," he said.

"But I may be a long time," I explained hoping he would just leave. "It could be hours. In fact I'll probably stay until closing."

"Take as much time as you like. I'll wait. We need to talk."

I looked up at his face again. It held no expression, not anger or distrust or even love and his eyes were cold. His words echoed in the empty hall like a death knell and I knew then that there was no avoiding our confrontation.

"Well then, I'll see you later." I moved from his grip and went into the viewing room.

The first thing I noticed was the profusion of flowers and was thankful their fragrance balanced out the smell of death that was so pervading at the entrance. They also helped to alleviate the smells of life; even so, in a crowded, hot room with so many humans gathered together, I could always scent their individuals odors, some sweet, some bitter, all intriguing to me. But masking it was the overpowering scent of the funeral baskets, and I thought that I could stay without losing my control.

Gwen's mother was the first person I recognized out of the sea of people. She stood guard next to the casket, a small, dark haired woman dressed in black, worrying the beads of a crystal rosary in her hands. Mrs. DeAngelis was a woman, strong in her faith, who had already buried her husband and two sons. But Gwen had been her favorite, and I knew this death would break her heart. She looked up, our eyes met and, giving me a sad smile, called me to her.

I slipped through the other mourners and reached her, but

said nothing. Instead, I hugged her against me, giving and taking comfort. Finally, she broke away and gently led me to the kneeler in front of the coffin. I knelt, my head down for a time, then lifted it to look at Gwen's face.

She looked better than I had imagined she would. The undertaker had done his job well, applying color to her bloodless skin. Her hair, I noticed with an irreverent smile, had been styled, not the way Gwen liked it, a mass of unruly curls that often hung down in her eyes, but as her mother liked it, smooth and sculptured. On the occasions I had accompanied her to her mother's house, Gwen's hair had often been the topic of heated but unmistakably loving discussions. I resisted the urge to reach out and toussle it slightly; instead I stood up and laid my hand on her cold ones and leaned down to kiss her forehead.

A tissue was pushed surreptitiously into my hand, I used it to wipe away my tears then turned to Mrs. DeAngelis.

"I'm so sorry," I said simply, not being able to produce anything to justify this death.

"I know, my dear." She twisted the rosary in her hand again and her voice became distant. "She was a good girl, she never did anything to deserve this." Her fingers caressed the silver crucifix attached to the beads. "I know the Lord has His own reasons, but why He needed to take her now, and this way, I'll never understand." Her words were angry and drew attention from the people gathered. A young man, tall and well built, rushed to her side, giving me a dark look.

"Mother, you've been standing all day, let me get you a chair." He walked her across the room and sat her on a sofa. She was crying helplessly now, and I made a step in her direction. The man stopped me and gestured for several ladies to sit with her. When she was settled in he came back over to me.

"Hello, Nick."

"Deirdre." There was anger in his voice, directed at me. "I'd like to talk to you outside, if you don't mind."

"But," I looked over to where Mrs. DeAngelis sat, "I can't just leave her like that."

"Of course you can. What's it to you, anyway?" He took my

arm and led me, not too gently, through the people and out of the room.

He looked around to see if we were unobserved, then hissed at me, "This is all your fault, you know."

"My fault?" I knew that it was, that Gwen would still be alive if she had not been associated with me. But how had Nick reasoned that out?

"You had no right to take her away from us, from me. I know you never liked me, never thought I was good enough for her; but I loved her and you had no right to introduce her to your friend or to interfere with our plans."

"But, Nick, I never introduced her to anyone. She met Larry on her own; I had nothing to do with that. I tried to talk her into going back to you, to try to set things straight."

"There was nothing to set straight. We were going to be married."

I looked at him intently. "That's not what she said."

He met my gaze defiantly for a minute, before his anger faded and was replaced with sorrow and guilt. "I know we had a little disagreement, but I never really expected her to go out and pick up some other guy. Why would she do that?"

"It just happened, Nick. There was nothing anyone could have done about it. And she loved you, you know that, don't you? She loved you very much."

"Did she?" He began to cry silently, with just the horrible trembling of his shoulders and his head to indicate it.

"Of course she did." I gently touched his shoulder. He didn't push me away so I wrapped both arms around him and held him tightly while he cried. I could feel the tension in his body slowly relax and when he stopped, his face, though tinged with tears, was lighter somehow.

"I'm sorry," he said, disengaging himself from my embrace, "I didn't really mean to take this out on you. I know it wasn't your fault, or mine even. I just feel so helpless without her."

"As do I, Nick. And if it is any consolation, the bastard that did this to her is dead too. No parole, no life sentence; just a nice cold slab in the morgue. And no one deserves it more."

"Jesus," he said, in a surprised tone, "you really hate that guy."

"I would have killed him myself, if I had been able to." Perhaps it was the look on my face, or the determination in my voice, but Nick shivered slightly.

"Remind me never to get on your bad side, Deirdre." He gave a shaky little laugh. "I don't think I'd like it much."

"Probably not. Do you feel better now?"

He thought for a moment. "Yeah, I don't know why, but I do. Thanks, I wasn't able to cry before."

"Well, I think you should probably go back in now."

"Yeah, you coming?"

I shook my head. "I don't think so."

"Will you be at the funeral tomorrow?"

"No. Look, I brought some of Gwen's things from the office. They're in those boxes." I pointed. "Can you see that her mother gets them?"

"Sure. See you around?"

I smiled and kissed his cheek. "Maybe, who knows?"

Nick left, and I stood for a moment watching until he disappeared into the crowd, then walked out the door and into the fresh night air. As promised, Mitch was waiting.

"Who was that guy?"

"Guy?"

"You know, the guy you were practically necking with in the hall."

"Damn, Mitch. You've got a real problem. That was Gwen's fiance, Nick. Didn't you meet him?"

"Oh, yeah," he said sheepishly. "I guess I did. I'm sorry Deirdre, I wasn't thinking."

"Obviously."

My dry comment drew the first smile out of him that evening. "Let's get out of here and get something to eat."

"Okay, but I'm not very hungry; I ate before I came."

His smile disappeared. "Well, humor me anyway. I would guess we could find something you can choke down."

I looked at him sharply, but said nothing. He opened the car door for me, closed it behind me and got in behind the wheel.

"Where to, lady?"

"Your choice, Mitch. Remember, I am humoring you tonight."

"Just see that you remember it." As I watched his unsmiling profile, he pulled the car out of the parking lot and turned onto the street, and I thought that it was going to be a long night.

Chapter 18

We went to the same restaurant he had taken me to before. We had the same waiter and ate the same meal, but the atmosphere was charged with the unspoken between us. All of my attempts at conversation were brushed off with a shrug or a one syllable response. Eventually, I quit trying and concentrated on my steak and the second bottle of wine. Mitch had turned from a witty and exciting companion to a sullen child, and ordinarily I would have gotten up from the table and left, never to see him again. But even in the tense silence, I realized that I still loved him; enough that his anger, combined with the events of the last few days, finally reduced me to tears. I excused myself and fled to the ladies' room.

When I returned I was more composed, having reached the decision that our relationship was now at the point I had always feared. No longer would I try to salvage what we had; instead, I would cut my losses and get out. It seemed best, but when I sat back down, he looked over at me with concern on his face and love for me in his eyes once again.

"Are you okay?" he asked, and touched my hand across the table.

I pulled away and noticed the extra glass, now half empty, on the table. I picked it up, sniffed and set it back down. "Scotch, Mitch? On top of all that wine? Do you think that's wise?"

"No, but at this point I don't much care." He took another drink and looked away. "What's happening with us?"

"Us?" I laughed more shrilly than normal. "After tonight, I don't think there will be any us. You were the one who said we should talk; so here we are, let's talk. Or let's just give it up."

"But that's the problem; I don't want to give it up. When I'm away from you, I have all these doubts and questions. Nothing about you or your reaction to situations makes any sense to me. I've never seen you in the light of day, never seen you eat anything substantial. And I have heard some pretty unsavory things about you from various people." I gave him a questioning look and he continued. "But I don't really want to talk about any of that. It can all be explained, I'm sure." He glanced at me, with a sheepish smile. "Nothing about you is as it seems, but when we're together, nothing else matters but you."

"You certainly have a strange way of showing it."

He shrugged. "I've been fighting you all evening, but I didn't realize it until I made you cry. I know these past few days have been rough on you, and you've taken it all pretty well, considering. I should be treating you better than this, we both know that. But everything seems so uncertain. I just don't know what to do, what to say."

"So you say nothing."

"Exactly." When he touched my hand this time, I did not pull away. I closed my eyes and began tracing the outline of his hand with my fingertips, softly touching his fingers, his close trimmed nails and the callouses on his palm. When I reached the soft part of his wrist, he shivered and I raised his hand to my mouth and kissed it. I opened my eyes and looked him square in the face.

"Pay the bill, Mitch, and let's get out of here."

Frank was there to greet us at the door of the hotel, nodding his head in acknowledgement. "Miss Griffin. Detective Greer."

I smiled at him as I passed and he gave me a wink that seemed very out of character. When the elevator doors closed on us, I burst out laughing.

"What's so funny?"

"Frank. He winked at me."

"So?"

"So, you've ruined my reputation, Mitch. Less than a month ago I was a mysterious, unapproachable resident. All anyone knew of me was the little they read of me in the papers or magazines. They may have gossiped about me behind closed doors, but wink at me? No one would have dared. Now suddenly I am an ordinary person, carrying on a perfectly ordinary affair." I laughed again and he still looked puzzled. "I'll have to move."

The elevator doors opened and we walked down the hall. Mitch was still unamused by my predicament. "Why?" he asked, his expression petulant. "Because all of a sudden you have a personal life? It's really nothing to be ashamed of, living like an ordinary person."

"But I have never been . . . oh, never mind, it is not important." I opened the door of my room and he walked in ahead of me.

"Besides," he said, "I don't really think that what you and I have could ever be called ordinary." He took off his jacket and his gun holster and hung them over a chair, then turned around and smiled.

I stood against the locked door and lazily began to unbutton my dress. "Mitch, you have never said anything truer in your life."

He watched until I reached the bottom button and dropped the dress on the floor. Then he crossed the room, his eyes intense and blazing, took me in his arms and switched off the light.

He lay sleeping with his head pillowed on my breast, one hand lightly grazing my hip. I could not sleep, but had stayed perfectly still for what seemed hours so as not to disturb him. Eventually when he stirred and rolled over, I slipped out of bed and pulled aside the heavy drapes.

The night curled in perfect darkness, the slivered moon and the stars were blotted out by thick clouds, rushing through the sky. Dawn was perhaps two or three hours away and I felt the night calling to me. For there, in the dark, I would find what I needed. I had drawn no blood, mine or his, when we made love, but the desire to feed had arisen strongly. To lie next to him now, with my hunger full and strong, would be a great mistake.

I turned and looked at Mitch; his skin seemed to shine faintly in the darkness. Sighing, I quietly pulled my robe from the closet, put it on and gently closed the bedroom door. Once in the other room, I went to the small refrigerator under the bar, remembering an opened bottle of wine that would help alleviate, though not fully satisfy, my thirst. When I opened the door, I also saw what else I had stored there: the nine remaining bags of blood I had taken from Larry's apartment.

"Damn!" I reproached my carelessness. Mitch could have seen these, easily, had he decided he wanted a drink. Thank God he had not. Looking over my shoulder at the still closed bedroom door, I listened carefully. Mitch's regular breathing reassured me. I stood the blood bags against the back wall, supporting and hiding them with the bottles inside, adding additional ones from the bar. I left the scotch in the front, should Mitch awaken and decide he would like to have a drink at some point in the evening. Hopefully, he wouldn't ask me why I was now storing the liquor in the refrigerator.

With my glass of wine poured, I sat down on the couch. With each sip I visualized the blood, remembered its taste and texture. My body trembled and I broke into a sweat, trapped where I sat. I could not go to the bedroom—my desire to feed was too strong now. And I could not risk using one of the bags for fear of Mitch discovering me. But, he was, after all, in a deep sleep, wasn't he? And I was practiced in stealth and silence. I should be able to feed and return to the bed and he would never know. And yet, should he awake and find me, what then?

My body made the decision for me. Getting up from the couch and opening the door, I dislodged one of the bags. The bottles clinked very faintly and I froze, but there was no accompanying noise from the bedroom, only Mitch's rhythmic soft snoring.

Knowing that I could not drink it cold, I went into the darkened bathroom and turned on the hot water. This might wake him, but it was such an ordinary noise, it would not seem unusual. I held the blood under the faucet and the water splashed out, soaking me to the skin. Swearing under my breath, I slid out of the wet robe and pushed it into the corner of the room. When the plastic of the bag became pliable and the liquid inside seemed the right temperature, I removed it from the sink, then realized that I had brought no scissors with which to cut it, and no glass from which to drink.

I might have laughed but frustration had taken hold. I had to feed, I thought. I had to! The bag was awkward in my hands, but I held it to my mouth. The plastic was more resistant to my bite than human skin. But eventually I managed to puncture it, somewhat messily, then drank with ease.

The taking of blood, even in this fashion, is a rapturous event; I become aware of nothing more than its nourishing flow, the heat of the liquid warming my throat, my stomach, my whole body. Except for sleep, it is probably the only other moment that one of my kind is defenseless and without protection from the outside world. There is only the blood and the drinking of the blood; nothing else, at that moment, exists.

When the light flicked on and Mitch entered, I was at the peak of this experience. My eyes fastened on him, still glowing with the hunger and it took me more than a minute to recognize his presence, to realize what had happened. My naked body was exposed in the glaring light, tiny rivulets of blood trickled from my mouth, and elsewhere there were small splashes of blood from my clumsy attempts to puncture the bag.

Mitch stared at me, his face white with shock. The half-empty bag dropped from my hands onto the white-tiled floor. Two small fountains spurted up from my fang marks, then settled down into a small spreading pool.

"I see," he said, his tone flat and emotionless. "Oh yes, I finally see."

He walked out and closed the door behind him. I stood motionless staring at myself in the mirror. Turning on the water again I scrubbed at my face frantically to wash away the traces of blood, then struggled into my wet robe. By the time I left the bathroom, Mitch was dressed and putting his shoulder holster back on. He did not look at me when he buttoned his jacket, nor when he crossed to the front door and kicked my discarded dress out of the way. I shivered for a moment and wrapped my arms around myself.

"What," I croaked, my voice scratchy and hoarse, "what will you do?"

Mitch looked at me at that moment, and I wished he had not. Then without a single word, he opened the door and left.

Chapter 19

For the rest of the night I sat in the darkness, shivering in my wet robe. When I felt the rising of the sun, I threw off the garment and stood naked by the window, my hand on the curtains. How I longed at that moment to open them, to see for the first time in over a hundred years the colors of dawn. I remembered the other times I had been caught by the sun's rays, the agony of burned flesh, the weeks of painful recovery. This time there would be no recovery, if I exposed myself I would not retreat, but allow the sun to burn away all traces of my life.

My hands trembled as they reached for the cords, then jerked away. They moved forward again. "Coward," I whispered. For I was afraid; not of my contemplated death, nor even the pain. That was the easy way out; that was the cowardice. No, I was frightened of where my life would lead.

With a conscious effort I turned away from the window. I would see this through, I decided, and even though I could very well be dead at the end of this day, it would not be by my own hand. Mitch would return, I was certain, for answers or justice. Or both. And I knew that if his justice meant that I must die, I would let him kill me.

Oddly enough, my mind was eased by this decision. I went to the bedroom and dressed in jeans and a shirt, nothing fancy or sexy to distract him from his purpose. I cleaned the blood from the bathroom floor; combed my hair and brushed my teeth, but applied no makeup. No need anymore to pretend to be human; no need to disguise myself. He would see me as I really was.

Halfheartedly, I began to straighten up the room. I started to make the bed, and when I picked up the pillow on which he had slept, I held it to my face. The case smelled of him and I closed my eyes for a moment and remembered the love we had shared. Then I set the pillow back down and covered it up.

When the phone rang, I was removing the liquor from the refrigerator. The sound shocked me and one of the bottles slipped from my hands and shattered on the floor. As I went to the phone, there was a pounding on the door. "So soon, Mitch?" I said softly, then picked up the phone.

"Hold on a minute, please," I said before the caller had a chance to say anything, walked across the room and unlocked the door. He was there, as I knew he would be, and I motioned him in.

"Hello, Mitch, I was expecting you."

"I'll bet you were."

"Look, I've got a phone call, I'll be with you in a minute. Sit down." From the tone of my voice, he could tell nothing of my excitement or my fear. It was as if he was paying a social call and my attitude caught him off guard. He went to the couch and sat down while I returned to the phone.

"Yes?"

"Miss Griffin?" It was the daytime doorman. "There's someone on his way up to see you. I know you don't usually have visitors, but Frank said that lately you've been seeing this guy and, well, I hope it's okay."

"It's fine," I said calmly and I could hear his relieved sigh. "I was expecting him. Oh, and could you please send up some coffee and danish?"

"Right away."

I hung up the phone and turned to Mitch. "I've ordered us some breakfast. Have you eaten yet?"

"No." He gave me a strange look. "Have you?"

I shook my head. "Just coffee for me, of course. The danish is for you."

"Thank you."

"I have a mess behind the bar to clean up. Do you mind?"

"No, go ahead. We can talk when the coffee gets here. I didn't sleep real well last night and I could use the caffeine." He ran his fingers through his hair in the gesture I had learned he used when tired or confused. I smiled at him for a moment then ducked behind the bar.

"I hope you won't want a drink anytime, Mitch. It was the scotch that fell." I sopped up the liquor with a few paper towels and pushed the broken glass aside. When I stood up again, he was staring in my direction.

"So, how did you sleep?"

I laughed. "I don't sleep much at night, Mitch. I thought you had figured that out by now." There was a discreet knock at the door. "Coffee's here," I said and went to collect it. Setting the tray on the bar, I looked over at him. "Cream and sugar, right?" At his nod, I prepared a cup for him, poured one for me and settled down in a chair facing him. He took a sip of his coffee, and I jumped up. "Did you want a roll?" I asked and moved toward the bar to get him one.

"Damn it, Deirdre, this is not a social call and you know it. Quit playing the hostess and sit down. We need to talk."

"Sorry." I sat back down, cross-legged, and took a drink of my coffee. "Now I guess you can read me my rights and get on with it."

"What? Why would I do that?"

"For the first three murders, I would guess. Even though I had nothing to do with them, I must be a prime suspect now that you know."

"I know nothing, except that you need help."

I looked at him in surprise. "Help? Why would I need help? Any help I received now would only be about a hundred years too late."

"Deirdre," his voice was soft, reasonable, "I know that you think you're a vampire. But there are doctors who specialize in this sort of sickness. You could take treatment and be cured of this obsession after a while."

"Obsession? Sickness?" I laughed. Even to me it sounded hollow and hysterical. "You know that I only *think* myself a vampire? Oh, Mitch, that's priceless! After last night, after everything you've discovered about me, you still won't believe."

"How could I believe it? I've spent time with you, made love to you. Damn it, even after last night, I'm still in love with you. But you're human, you're real; I can touch you, see your reflection in a mirror. Just because you're disturbed, and believe in legends and folklore, doesn't mean that I have to."

Suddenly I was angry at his lack of belief. "Ever the skeptic, aren't you, Detective? What if I could offer you proof?"

"And what sort of proof would that be? Can you change into a bat or a wolf? Dissolve into a mist? Crawl down a wall?"

"No, but I can give you proof even you cannot doubt." I got up from my seat and knelt in front of him. Taking his face in my hands, I looked into his eyes and kissed him slowly and passionately.

He did not pull away from me, instead he held me for a moment. "What was that for?" he asked, almost smiling.

"Because you won't want anything to do with me in a few minutes. And because I love you." I gave his cheek a final caress and stood up. "Now stay there and pay attention."

He folded his arms with a smug expression and watched me. I looked around the room and saw the broken glass by the bar. I picked a piece of it up; it was long and jagged and glinted in the light. He looked alarmed and reached for his gun.

"Don't move," I commanded and he dropped his hand. "Proof number one," I said harshly. "Regenerative powers." I quickly slit both of my wrists with the glass.

"Deirdre, no!" Mitch gasped as he saw the bright blood flowing down my hands.

"No doubt, you have seen more than a few suicide cases." He was still riveted to the couch by my command but he nodded and I held my arms out to him. "These would be fatal wounds, wouldn't they, if I didn't get prompt attention?"

He looked away from me. "Let me call an ambulance, please. You didn't have to do this. Let me help you."

"Look at me," I ordered and he did. "I do not need help with this." I rubbed my wrists on the side of my jeans and held them out for his inspection again. The blood had congealed and the cuts, although obviously recent, were already healing. "Touch them," I said gently and moved toward him. He ran a trembling finger over the wounds. "By tomorrow," I said matter-of-factly, "there will only be small scars. Within a few days, there will be no sign that this ever happened." I turned my back on him and went to the window. "You see," I said bitterly, "I have tried this little trick before."

When I looked at him again, his face was ashen, the expression in his eyes, bleak. "Deirdre, I'm so sorry, I had no idea . . ."

I smiled reassuringly. "It's okay, Mitch, it really is. Now, if you'll let me continue."

"No more, please," he interrupted. "I believe you."

"No, Mitch, I don't want you to have any doubts at all. We'll do this my way." I stood back and opened the heavy draperies about an inch. "Test number two," I said, taking a deep breath, "sunlight." I thrust my hand into the ray streaming into the room. It began to smoke immediately, but before the smell of burning flesh became overwhelming, I withdrew my arm and shut the drapes again. "Damn," I said, walking to him. "That really hurts."

He reached up to me and gently took my hand. "Will this heal, too?" he asked in awe as he surveyed the damage. The skin was blackened and withered in the small area that had been exposed.

"Yes, in a day or two." I pulled away from him and sat back in my chair. "Now just let me rest up a bit and we'll go for number three."

"Is that really necessary?" His voice now reflected fear and although I could not determine if he was afraid of me or for me, I could see the belief in his eyes.

I responded with a weak smile. "I had hoped it would not be. The next one is the worst of all."

After several minutes of uncomfortable silence, Mitch spoke again. "Deirdre, I hate to ask, but I have to know. What's test number three?"

"Oh, that," I said disparagingly. "It's the test of immortality."

"How can you prove that?"

"Quite simply, I take your revolver and shoot myself through the heart." I shuddered slightly and went on. "It hurts like hell, but only for a little. As long as the bullet goes clear through there are no serious complications."

He stared at me in horror, then dropped his face into his hands. The minutes ticked by, seeming like hours. I made an attempt to clear our cups, but found that my hands were shaking, so I sat back down again and studied his body for some sign of what would happen next. Eventually, he raised his head. "Oh, God," he said quietly, then wiped his eyes and looked into my face. His expression was strangely composed, his voice calm and confident, as if knowing the worst about me had strengthened him in some way. "Thank you. This explains so many things for me. And it must've been hard for you to tell me all this."

I nodded. "At least now you don't think I'm crazy. Of course, I am crazy," I gave him a little smile, "for telling you this. I could have let you believe what you wanted to believe. But I thought that you would try to drag me off to see a doctor this morning and that would not only have killed me, it would have been a shock to your comfortable theory. So now instead of killing me accidentally, you can be fully aware of your actions."

"Kill you? Why would I want to do that?"

I laughed again. "I can think of several reasons, offhand. I am an inhuman monster who should be exterminated. I am a damned soul who should be released. I am a drainer of blood, a leech on mankind. And then you have your three murders."

"No," he said with a sidelong glance at me. "I have four murders."

"Four? But surely Gwen doesn't count in that number? Larry should account for her death."

"No, I wasn't counting her." He gave me a curious look, partly surprise, partly relief. "You really don't know, do you?"

"Know what?"

"Last night there was another murder. Like the first three. And the time of death has been pinpointed during the time that you and I were, ah, otherwise engaged. So, even if I suspected you, which I did not, you would be free on this."

"Why don't you suspect me? I could have left quietly and come back, you never would have known."

"No." He looked at me sharply. "I would have known. Besides, you may be a, well, what you are, but you are not a killer. You have lied to me about many things, and now I know why you did. You are secretive and crafty, but I know you, maybe better than you think. You could not kill anyone, not like this. Oh, you might be capable of murder, in passion or anger, most people are, but not in cold blood and not repeatedly."

"Thank you. What will you do now?"

"Damned if I know. This is all a little hard to take. And to believe. Oh, I do believe you," he said quickly. "You don't have to give me any more proof. But all along, I've been believing that the person we wanted was deranged. Now I've learned that he may be a true vampire," he winced as he said the word, "how on earth am I going to catch him or make anyone else believe what we are looking for?" He glanced at me in an appeal for help.

"I do not know, Mitch. If the question had arisen one month

ago, I would have denied the existence of others of my kind. In all my years, I have only had proof of one other, the one who made me what I am. However, I'll be more than happy to help you any way I can."

"Why would you help? Isn't that against your code or laws or something?"

"I have no code or laws for dealing with others. I've never met anyone like me. But I want this one."

"Why?"

"Because, if he is the one who changed me, I want him dead. If not, I would like to ask him some questions. You see, I was changed into what I am by accident, I believe. I had no one to guide me, no one to teach me what I needed to know to survive. Somehow, I blundered through and lived."

"How long?" He looked at me sadly for a minute. "How old are you?"

"I was born in 1832, changed in 1860. I've stayed the same since."

He laughed. "You're over a hundred years old? I can believe a lot of things, but not that."

"Truly, Mitch." I walked into the bedroom, and retrieved Larry's scrapbook from the closet where it had been hidden. I came back and handed the book to Mitch. "My life story, or almost, as compiled by Larry Martin."

His hands shook as he took it from me. I poured myself another cup of coffee and watched him read. There were no sounds in the room but the rustle of slowly turned pages.

When he had finished, he looked over at me with regret in his eyes. "You haven't had it easy, have you? All that moving about, for fear of discovery. All the things you've seen, war, poverty, the deaths of people you've known."

"Living forever is not exactly what it is cracked up to be. But short of taking a long walk in the sunlight, there's not much I can do about it."

He rifled through the pages again, pausing with the book open to the photograph on page one. "Where did you get this?"

"The night that Gwen died, I left your place and broke into Larry's apartment."

"But it was under surveillance. No one saw you go in."

"Of course they didn't. I climbed up the back wall and went in a window." I smiled at his expression.

"But there's no way in, in the back. The fire escapes are on the sides of that building."

"I know. I climbed the back wall."

"Oh, I didn't think you could do that."

I laughed. "Actually, it was the very first time I had ever tried. It was amazingly simple. Larry wasn't there, but you know that. I found the book, borrowed some of his private stock, and left."

He nodded, putting the missing pieces in place. "We found the other blood and your note. But we didn't know who it was from. We couldn't figure that one out, or how the lock on his door got broken. I guess you did that, too."

I nodded.

"But there were no prints."

"I have been dating a detective, remember? I wore gloves."

"Oh, of course, you'd been printed that night." He stared at me for a second. "And you knew he had killed Gwen, but still you went to meet him. Obviously, he knew what you were and he came prepared to kill you. I still don't understand why you didn't let me help you."

"Be reasonable, Mitch. I didn't want you to find out about me; he would have told you then and there and been happy to do it. And I really thought I could handle him. But he surprised me; he was much stronger than I would have thought."

"And the marks on his neck?"

"The bite marks are mine." I said it softly, but he shuddered anyway. "Larry wanted me to transform him. I finally managed to convince him to let me close enough to him so that I could take his blood." Mitch's face paled and I continued quickly. "You see, when I take blood, I'm able to plant suggestions. I hoped to take enough to weaken him, and then wipe away any remembrance of me and what I am. After that was accomplished I planned to let him go; you would have caught him eventually and my secrets would have been safe."

"What went wrong?"

"Everything went wrong that night." My voice lowered. "I discovered that I was not as invincible as I thought. It was a sobering experience."

He sat and thought for a while. Then he got up and poured himself another cup of coffee and took a danish. "Want one?" he said, holding out the plate.

"Not really, Mitch. You forget that I don't need to take food. In most cases, I can't even swallow it."

"Oh, yeah. It's easy to forget." He looked at me sheepishly. "I just can't think of you as what you are; I guess I should be frightened or horrified. And I am, a bit. But mostly, I feel sorry for you. Does that make any sense at all?"

"Perfect sense, to me. I'm still the same person I was yesterday and you and I are bonded together, to some degree."

A sudden flare of anger entered his eyes. "You mean you can control me, control my feelings?"

"No, Mitch." I walked over and took his hand in mine. "I don't control you, nor would I want to. I'm not sure that I could; you're very strong in your own right. And I haven't taken your blood."

His free hand went to his neck in a protective, involuntary gesture. He dropped it with an embarrassed look when he realized what he had done. Averting his eyes, as if in the presence of some perversion, he asked softly, "Why didn't you take any blood? Don't you have to?"

"Not always." I smiled reassuringly at him. "And I wouldn't take yours. But that first time we made love, well, do you remember the bruise on my shoulder?"

"Yeah," the realization of the situation dawned in his eyes, "at first it wasn't there. I knew it wasn't. And then it went away much too fast."

"Exactly, and now you know why. I did that to myself. For so long, the taking of blood has been the only intimacy I've had, the only one I thought I needed. I can't fully explain the feelings

I get when I'm feeding; there's the survival factor, the needs satisfied, but there is also a union with my victims, however unwilling they may be. There is a sexuality apart from sex, a power and a fulfillment . . ." I broke off as he dropped my hand and gave a shudder of distaste. "But you're different." A note of pleading entered my voice. "You touch a part of me that has been repressed for over twenty years. I couldn't sully that experience by taking your blood. So I turned my head, and drew my own."

"And the other times?"

"I fought the urge. I don't want to hurt you, Mitch. For what it's worth, I love you. So you're in no danger from me in that respect."

He left my side, went over to the window and peeled back the drapes slightly to look outside. Although I was out of reach of the sunlight, I instinctively jumped back. Lost in his own thoughts, Mitch took no notice and went on, quietly as if to himself. "Shit, I really can pick them, can't I? The first woman I've allowed myself to love for years and she turns out to be a . . ." His voice broke and he turned back to me with an odd pleading look in his eyes.

"You can say it, Mitch. I don't care much for the word myself, but in this case it is appropriate. And you have used it before."

"But not about you. And not for real. I don't want to say it. Jesus, I don't even want to believe it. Right now I need to get out of here, away from you. I've got a lot of thinking to do." He walked to the door.

I found I could not move toward him. "Mitch," I said in a soft, choked voice.

His name stopped him and he turned to me. Quickly he gathered me in his arms and held me.

"I'm so sorry," I whispered.

"So am I, Deirdre." He kissed me gently and held my face between his hands. "I'll be back," he promised and walked out into the hall.

I stood against the door after he left, until I heard the elevator close and start its journey downward. Then, bearing the weight of many years, I locked the door and went into the bedroom.

Chapter 20

I slept fitfully that day, and when the phone finally woke me at three, I got up to answer it, expecting that it would be Mitch. I was disappointed to hear my attorney's voice, but he had good news for me.

"I've got a buyer."

"So soon? You sure didn't waste any time, Fred."

There was a pause on the end of the line. "But you said you wanted it over quickly."

"I did. I just didn't think it would happen so soon. That's great." I tried to put enthusiasm into my voice and failed.

"The deal isn't final yet, of course, so you could still change your mind."

"No, I won't change my mind. Tell me about it."

He talked for some time, going into details that were not terribly important to me; I only half-listened to him, thinking instead of the conversation Mitch and I'd had that morning. He had taken it better than I thought he would, and that confused me somewhat. Maybe I had underestimated his grasp of the situation or the depth of his feeling for me. Could it be possible that he would still wish to continue our relationship, knowing what he did about me? And even at that, how long could either one of us expect it to last? I sighed and Fred was startled.

"Deirdre?"

"Hmmm?"

"You aren't even listening, are you? If you're so uninterested, why did you ask me to call you?"

"I am sorry, Fred, please continue."

"They'd like to meet over lunch, tomorrow. Can you fit that into your schedule?"

"No, lunch is out of the question. What about dinner, tonight?"

"Tonight? Jesus, Deirdre, you don't know what you're asking. It'll take us at least another four hours to get the contracts reviewed and typed. I work fast, but not that fast."

"Did they meet my two conditions?"

"You weren't listening—I knew it! Yes, they met your conditions and upped them a bit. They're very interested."

"Then get it ready for tonight. We can eat late, say around nine or nine-thirty. The office is still closed today; tomorrow when I go in I want to inform the staff of what's been done. After everything else, I don't want an office full of hysterical women, worried over the rumors of a sale. You know how fast this kind of situation gets broadcast on the gossip mill. Can you handle it?"

"Well," he thought for a moment, "if I take everyone off what they're doing now, yes, we can probably make it."

"Great, arrange for whatever bonuses you think are necessary. And make reservations for us at The Imperial. I'll cover the bill."

"Fine with me," he said. There was a trace of a smile in his voice now.

"And bring your wife. That should make up for all the long hours I force you to work."

"I should hope so. Well, I'd better go. Are you sure you don't want to go over the details again?"

"No, I trust you. If you say it is a good deal, I can believe it. Oh and Fred?"

"Yeah?"

"Reserve an extra seat for dinner. I might want to bring a guest."

"You, a guest? I can't wait. You really are full of surprises these days, Deirdre. See you tonight."

I laughed to myself when I hung up the phone. Poor Fred. I guess I had given him a harder job than I should have, but I wanted that portion of my life ended as quickly as possible. There was really no sense in continuing; I didn't need the money or the hassle at this point. I felt a sudden lightening of my mood. The worst was over, things could only improve. Mitch had been told the truth, I could look him in the eyes with no dishonesty or lies. I had faced off someone who wanted me dead, and had lived through the attempt. My time would be my own again, to use any way I wished. When the other was found and dealt with, I was free to begin an entirely new life, or stay in the old for a while. That decision would depend on Mitch.

I rang the police station and found him at his desk.

"Greer speaking." His voice sounded hurried and distracted.

"Mitch, I'm sorry to bother you, but I wondered if you would be free tonight for dinner. The Imperial at nine?"

"Whew," he said, surprised at my request. "I'd better check my bank book first."

"Don't be silly; I'm paying. It's actually a business dinner but I would like you to be there, if you can make it." I suddenly realized that I was making a big assumption. Just because he didn't rant or rave this morning or attempt to kill me straight out didn't mean that he would want to see me again, ever. "I mean," and my voice was soft, less confident now, "that is, if you can stand to be with me after today."

"Hell, Deirdre, for dinner at The Imperial I'd go out with Jack the Ripper."

"That is not very funny, Mitch. If you don't want to go just say so."

He gave a small chuckle. "My, aren't we touchy today? Of course, I'll be there. Should I rent another tux?"

"That's up to you. And thank you."

"No, thank you. How could I turn down an offer like this?"

"No, you know what I mean. You've taken everything well."

His voice changed, soured slightly. "What choice do I have? And when do you want me to pick you up?"

"Why don't you just meet me there? I'll take a cab."

"Fine, see you at nine."

After a leisurely shower, I stood in front of my closet and tried to decide what to wear. Had my choices been limited, the choosing would have been easier. As it was, the rod was crowded with clothes for all occasions. Some were dismissed as too casual, others were too formal, or had been worn before at some other fashion industry function. Finally, I was down to ten dresses that would be appropriate. Of these, eight were black. "Deirdre," I said to myself, "you have allowed yourself to get into a rut," and eliminated all but the remaining two. One was red; too blatant, I decided. But I hesitated over the last one. It was velvet in the same deep forest green color I had chosen to wear for Mitch the night he had shown up three hours too late. Maybe it was a bad omen. Then again, it was a color I had always loved—it had been the color that my husband had always wanted me to wear.

I pulled it from the closet, removing its protective bag and laying it on the bed. It had been packed away with a sachet and the scent had remained fresh. Holding the fabric to my face, I sniffed deeply.

Lily of the valley—it had been my mother's favorite flower. And although she had died while I was very young, I still associated it with her. My father had tended her garden beds religiously until the day he died, keeping the roses, azaleas and lilac bushes pruned and proper, but this flower he allowed a free growth and it flourished. On a warm day in May its odor would permeate the yard and the house. Somehow it seemed appropriate to meet Mitch this evening wrapped in the fragrance that was, to me, the scent of love and a symbol of loyalty and faithfulness.

When my makeup and hair were complete, I slipped the dress over my head and struggled with the zipper. Then I smoothed the skirt over my legs and stood in front of the mirror. With a shock, I realized that this dress was similar to the one I had designed for Gwen's wedding—it fell off the shoulders, had a rounded bodice and pulled to the back in a small bustle. But unlike Gwen's, this dress was unadorned, with no pearls or lace, allowing the elegance of the fabric to speak for itself. I wore no jewelry, except for a small pair of emerald stud earrings and had inserted the contact lenses that matched the color of the dress.

After one final check on my appearance, I worried for a second about the ironies of fate that had caused me to clothe myself in remembered deaths, but shrugged it off and collected my cloak.

I was early in arriving at the restaurant, two hours early the maitre'd informed me with an apologetic smile.

"I am very sorry, Miss Griffin, but Mr. Carlson made the reservation for ten. I hope you will not be too inconvenienced."

"Not at all. May I wait in the bar?"

"Certainly."

I removed my cloak and gloves; he took them from me.

"I will check these for you if I may."

"Thank you." I reached in my purse and gave him a tip. "I'm expecting a Mr. Greer around nine; please see that he finds his way to me."

He nodded and I crossed the hall and entered the bar. It was brightly lit and elegantly decorated as one would expect from a restaurant of its class. But for all of that, I felt out of place and disoriented. I had spent too many nights at the Ballroom, in its comfortable darkness and ambience, to view this place as anything more than an overpriced waiting room. Still, I thought to myself with a smile, as I claimed a table from a couple leaving for their dinner, at least here I did not have to contend with sneering bartenders and overbearing owners.

The service was good, the wine list better, and soon I was securely ensconced with a bottle of burgundy of excellent vintage. After admiring the color and taking my first sip, I began to reevaluate my opinion of The Imperial. Perhaps I should begin to branch out and bring some of my business here. Of course, I wouldn't receive quite the same personal service that the Ballroom offered and would have to make contact with victims on my own. That would not be a bad thing, I thought, looking around curiously at some of the men lounging at the tables and bar. They were young and healthy and could provide amply for my needs. As I continued to glance at the prospects for future reference, I felt my mouth curve in what must have seemed a devilish smile.

Quite accidentally, my eyes made contact with an older-seeming man standing at the edge of the bar. He intercepted my smile with one of his own, and I looked down at my wine in embarrassment. You'll have to be more subtle than that, I chided myself, if you want to succeed at this game. I was severely out of practice. To further my disadvantaged feeling, when I looked back up again, he was standing at my table, smiling down at me.

"Excuse me," he said, his voice betraying a slight Germanic accent, "you are Deirdre Griffin, are you not?"

"Yes." I did not return his smile, but gave him an assessing stare. I couldn't remember ever having met him before, although it was possible that he was a former victim. I'd had many. That thought was distressing; if I had fed off this man and could not recognize him now, I had stayed in this city too long. "Do I know you?"

"No, may I join you?" Despite the coldness of my greeting, his smile did not subside.

"Actually, someone is meeting me."

"But in the meantime, a lovely lady like you should not be drinking alone." He reached over and lifted the bottle of wine, reading the label. "An excellent choice, and one of my favorites. Perhaps I should have the waiter bring another glass."

I gave him my sternest look. "Look, I hate to be rude, but I don't know you. And I am not generally in the habit of . . ."

"But of course you are not," he smoothly interrupted me. "And I am afraid that I have been having a little joke on you. You see, we have a mutual friend. He has had the bad manners of never introducing us, so I thought that I might rectify his mistake. I am Victor Lange."

"And our mutual friend?"

"Max Hunter."

At the mention of the name, I relaxed but smiled in resignation. And I thought I would be avoiding his manipulation tonight. I gestured to the chair. "Please sit down, Mr. Lange."

"Victor, please."

As he sat the waiter came over with an empty wine glass. I was surprised at the fast service and said so.

"You must come here often. I think that waiter just read your mind."

Victor threw his head back and laughed. "Miss Griffin, you really should step out of that dive that Max runs and take in the rest of the world. Yes, I do come here often, as you say. I own the place."

"Oh." I took a drink of wine to cover my chagrin.

"But you mustn't be embarrassed. I am afraid that I did rather mislead you. Did you think I was trying to pick you up?"

"No." I looked at him again and smiled. "Well, yes, I did. I am sorry to have misunderstood."

He nodded sympathetically. "It is quite understandable. It must happen to you often."

I shrugged and finished my wine. He filled the glass for me, drained his and then stood up abruptly. "I believe this must be the gentleman you are waiting for. What will he want to drink?"

I looked up and saw the scowl on Mitch's face as he came toward us. "Scotch, on the rocks, I'm afraid."

Victor said a polite good evening to me, nodded to Mitch as he arrived at the table and left. I stood up and gave Mitch a small kiss on the cheek.

We both sat down again, and the waiter brought the scotch. "How did you know I would want this?" he asked, taking a sip.

"From the look on your face, my love." I reached over and stroked his cheek. "Bad day?"

"No, not too bad." He hesitated and frowned and I waited for the inevitable question; it was not long in coming. "Who was that?"

I laughed. "Mitch, I really hate to say it, but you are so predictable. That was Victor Lange, he owns The Imperial."

"Do you know all the restaurant owners in town? Or does it just seem that way?"

"No, I only met him this evening. He's a friend of Max's."

"Oh, Max." Instead of his usual disgruntled expression at the mention of the name, Mitch smiled. It was not entirely a pleasant smile, but it was a good sign.

"What is so funny?"

"You may not find it funny, but I got a kick out of it. Before I came here tonight, I stopped over at the Ballroom and slapped a citation and a pretty heavy fine on Hunter for setting off a false fire alarm."

"Mitch, you didn't, did you?"

"Yeah, I did."

Our eyes met and we both began to laugh simultaneously. "I'll be willing to bet the price of tonight's dinner, that he wasn't happy about it."

"Deirdre, that's got to be the biggest understatement you ever made in your life. He was livid. I wish you could've seen his face." He laughed again thinking about it. "I'm afraid it wasn't a pretty sight."

"Too bad, you two were just starting to get along."

"Yeah, well, he canceled that out by letting you go down to his cellar alone. He's a smart son of a bitch, I'll give him that. He almost talked me out of the citation. I think he knew that it was more a personal matter than anything else."

"He'll sue you for police harassment."

"I doubt it." Mitch looked over at me and smiled. "But even if he does, it'll be worth every penny. So, who are we having dinner with tonight?"

"You mean besides Jack the Ripper?" I gave him a stern glance, but his eyes danced. He was enjoying that little insult, so I let it go, relaxed and answered his question. "My attorney and the people purchasing Griffin Designs."

"You're selling the company? Why on earth would you want to do that?"

I could not tell him the entire truth; the fact that I wanted to be unencumbered and with cash available should I decide to move on soon, I kept to myself. "Mostly it's because of Gwen. Yesterday I found that I could hardly tolerate the place. It made my skin crawl. I keep seeing her, dead and bloody, in that loft. I don't think the image will ever fade."

"But you could just move into a different building."

"Yes, I could do that. But truthfully, it is time to get out. I have been in business for ten years now—in that time most people begin to age. I have not. Fashion is a high profile industry and although I have managed to avoid publicity more than some designers, I could not continue for too much longer without it being extremely noticeable. I just can't take many more chances than I already have."

He took a long drink of his scotch, his mouth twisted into a frown. "Then you'll be leaving town?"

"Not necessarily. If I don't have to run Griffin Designs, I can fade into anonymity again, staying another five or ten years if I wish."

"And do you want to?"

I took a deep breath and reached over to touch his hand. "That all depends on you, Mitch."

"On me?" He looked surprised and I laughed at him.

"Yes, on you." I began to say more when the waiter came to the table. "Miss Griffin, Mr. Greer, the rest of your party is here. Shall I seat you?"

Mitch stood up and moved my chair back. "Well," he said in a thoughtful manner, extending his arm to me, "I guess we can talk about that later."

Introductions were made at the table; I had never met the woman who was purchasing the company, although I had heard of her. Betsy McCain was what I considered the epitome of the modern business woman, intelligent, brassy and high-pressure. I disliked her at first sight. Conversation with her merely reinforced my initial impression.

She was accompanied by two attorneys and two assistants. With the exception of the lawyer seated to her right, they had little to add to the discussions. I felt that she had merely brought them along for a free meal. But after I realized that the purchasing price was twice what I had asked Fred to get for me, I thought she was entitled, even when all five of them ordered the most expensive items from the menu.

She, at least, made no pretense about how she planned to run Griffin Designs. "We will modernize the entire place, of course," her eyes reflected the glitter of the candles, "and any of the employees who cannot adapt to the situation will be welcome to leave after their two months are up." I knew then that she meant to replace them all. "And the clothes themselves will have to be updated." She reached over and laid her hand on my arm. "Not that what you have on isn't a lovely dress, Deirdre," she was practically purring at this point and I could smell the champagne heavy on her breath, "but today's woman needs clothes that represent her place in today's world."

I looked over at her. She wore a navy blue tailored suit, probably the same one she had worn to her office today. With the exception of her skirt, it was identical to the ones' worn by her attorneys. She had at least made an attempt to dress it up for this evening with jewelry, gold necklaces and bracelets that clinked together harshly with every gesture she made. I smiled at her sweetly. "No, there isn't much room for romance in today's world, is there, Betsy?"

"Romance?" she snorted disdainfully. "It's a rough world out there. We need to dress like we mean business, all the time. Any woman in the marketplace should know how to go for the throat when necessary."

Mitch was in the middle of a drink of champagne and he made a small choking sound. I glanced over at him and winked, then turned back to her. "I do know what you mean, but I'm afraid I never developed much of a killer instinct over the years. Perhaps you could give me lessons sometime?"

Mitch choked again, turned it into a cough and excused himself from the table. She, of course, was oblivious to the irony of the situation.

"That would be a real pleasure, I'm sure. I could never figure how someone as young and inexperienced as you could make a profit anyway." I was glad Mitch left before this last comment; he would probably be under the table in hysterics by now. Fred caught my eye warningly—he knew me well enough to sense my dislike and was probably worried that I might call off the deal.

"Even so," I said noncommittally, and signaled for the waiter. "More champagne, please. Now, shall we sign?"

Mitch returned after we had completed the deal. He seemed to have regained his composure, but his eyes were still laughing. I took his hand and held it for a minute, the new owner of Griffin Designs caught the gesture and leaned forward over the table with an eager smile. "So, Mr. Greer, what do you do for a living?"

"I'm a detective."

"Oh, how fascinating. Just like Mike Hammer, it must be exciting."

"Actually, I'm with the police department."

"I see," she said with a bit of a sneer in her voice. "And how on earth did you two meet?"

"Murder investigation." Everyone at the table grew silent and stared at Mitch. The waiter brought our meals; after we were all served, he spoke again. I could hear the repressed laughter in his voice. "Deirdre was my main suspect." Unconcerned he took a bite of food and a drink of champagne. "Still is, as a matter of fact. I go with her everywhere, so that when she slips up, I can get her."

I smiled sweetly on my dinner partner again. "So, you see, Betsy, I probably don't need those lessons after all."

Fred started the laughter, and the others joined in, nervously at first then wholeheartedly. The tension dissolved and eventually even Betsy participated.

"Bravo, Deirdre. Maybe we're not as different as I thought."

Chapter 21

The new owner and her entourage left shortly after I paid the bill. We had reached an uneasy truce based on a grudging respect due to our verbal sparring. We made plans to meet the next week to tour the facility and take an inventory. She would not actually take control of Griffin Designs until the first of the year. That gave me time to start on the orders from the show, get everyone into the routine and then bow out gracefully.

Fred, his wife, Mitch and I lingered at the table with after-dinner drinks and coffee. Betsy McCain had not been out of the restaurant for more than a minute before we all began to laugh.

"Good God, Fred, where did you dig up that ghoul?" I wiped tears of amusement from my eyes.

He shrugged. "You never specified we had to sell to someone you liked. She was interested enough to double the price; I figured that was a good deal."

"And it was, of course. Sally," I nodded toward his wife, "would you like some more coffee?"

"No," she said with a shy smile, checking her watch. "Everything was wonderful, though. Thank you so much for inviting me. But I think we'd better get going, don't you, honey?"

Fred stood up and agreed. "We promised the sitter we'd have her home by one–thirty or two at the latest. It was interesting, Deirdre." He shook hands with me and then turned to Mitch. "Nice meeting you, Greer. Maybe we should all get together some time, without the sharks."

"You could come over for dinner some night," Sally urged. "You haven't even seen the baby."

"I would like that," I said, giving her a small hug. She smiled and they left.

Mitch and I sat back down and he poured us each another cup of coffee. "They're nice people, Fred and Sally I mean."

"Yes, did you have a good time?"

"Well, I don't know that good could describe it accurately. But as Fred said, it was interesting." His face lit up in a mischievous grin. "That Betsy is something, isn't she?"

"I am sorry about that, Mitch. I had never met her before, but her money is good."

"Did you know that when you went to the ladies' room, she moved over next to me?"

"And?"

"Well, I'll just say that she definitely lacks subtlety. I think she was hoping that maybe more than your company was up for grabs. She must have drunk more champagne by herself than all the rest of us put together." He laughed again, remembering her actions.

"Or," I moved closer to him and put my hand gently on his leg, "maybe she just knows a good man when she sees one."

He leaned in to kiss me.

"Excuse me," the accented voice broke in on us and we jumped apart. "I don't wish to interrupt but I wanted to know if you enjoyed your meal."

"Victor, yes, thank you, everything was wonderful."

He turned to Mitch. "Mr. Greer, I am Victor Lange. I did not have a chance to meet you before." They shook hands and Mitch looked at his watch. "Deirdre, we'll have to go soon, too. Just let me make a stop first; I'll be right back."

As he walked toward the men's room, Victor apologized. "I always seem to be breaking in at the most romantic moments. I am sorry."

"Don't worry about it; this is not the place for it anyway."

"No, but you'd be surprised what goes on, sometimes. I'm afraid I did the same to Max just the other night."

"Max?"

"Yes, and it was even more embarrassing than that. I called the young lady he was with by your name. She was like you, same height and build, but I see now that her hair was different. Yours is its natural color, is it not?" I nodded and he continued. "Hers came from a bottle, I'm sure. You see, he had described you to me and I was so sure. Quite an unfortunate incident."

"How odd." I had never known Max to be with another woman. I was not jealous, but why had he never mentioned his involvement to me?

Victor gave me a curious look, and at that moment Mitch returned. "Ready?" he asked. When I stood up, he turned to Victor and shook his hand. "Dinner was excellent, I enjoyed it very much. You live up to your reputation."

"Thank you, we try to." Victor beamed from the compliment. "But I'm afraid that our chef was very distraught with Miss Griffin here, when she refused his special garnish for the steak."

Mitch caught my eye with an amused look. "But I thought it was wonderful. It had a garlic base, didn't it?" Victor nodded. "Oh, well," he said as he wrapped an arm around my waist, "you have to understand that Deirdre is a purist. Good night."

We stopped by the coat check room, then waited outside for the valet to bring Mitch's car around. I grabbed Mitch's arm, shook it and began to giggle.

"What?"

"A purist? And that crack about me being a prime suspect? You were wonderful. It stopped them all in their tracks." I gave him a sidelong glance. "You had a good time, didn't you?"

"Yeah," he said with a slow smile as he helped me into the car. "You know, I didn't expect to and I'm sort of surprised to admit it, but I really did."

He pulled out into traffic, stopped for a red light and turned to me. "I thought maybe we could go back to my place, that is if you're not too tired." His voice sounded tentative, unsure.

"That would be fine, Mitch. I slept some today. But what about you? Don't you have to go to the station tomorrow?"

He scowled a bit. "Today, after you called, I checked the calendar and realized that I've had only one day off since Thanksgiving. And I haven't had a decent night's sleep either, so I took tomorrow off. If they need me, they know where to find me. I plan on spending the entire day in bed." The light changed and he drove, reaching over and taking my hand in his. "But I wouldn't mind a little company."

I said nothing but smiled and tightened my grip on his hand.

When we arrived at his apartment, he took off his jacket and tie and threw them on a chair. "Get comfortable, if you'd like," he said. "I have something I want to talk about before we go to sleep."

"Did I leave any clothes here?"

"No." He frowned at me. "You packed everything up and cleared out, remember?" Then he shrugged and made an effort to smile. "But you can borrow my robe. It's on the hook on the bathroom door."

I found the green terry cloth robe where he had said it was, carefully removed my dress and hung it on the hook. Putting on the robe, I looked at myself in the mirror. It seemed odd that although the robe covered more than the gown, I felt naked in it, somehow more vulnerable than before. Then I realized why that was, this would be the first night Mitch and I had spent together since my revelation to him of what I was. Tonight there would be no lies between us, he knew the worst of me. For the first time in so many years, I had nothing to hide and I felt defenseless. As I walked out the door, though, I caught the faint odor of the robe. It smelled like Mitch; I rubbed my cheek appreciatively on the sleeve and savored the aroma. Everything would be fine.

He was in the kitchen making coffee. I stood silently in the entrance for a time and watched him. After a while he became aware of my presence and turned to me.

"I thought that after all that champagne, coffee would be nice. Or I could open a bottle of wine."

"Coffee is fine."

"That looks better on you than on me," he said, wiping his hands on a towel. He fixed a tray with mugs, cream and sugar. "Let's adjourn to the living room." He picked up the tray. "You bring the coffee, okay?"

I waited a minute for the water to stop dripping, then carried the pot into the other room and set it on the tray. Wordlessly he poured our cups and fixed his, his eyes never leaving my face. I took a small sip of mine, then put it aside waiting for him to make a move. He cleared his throat and began haltingly. "Deirdre, you must know that yesterday morning was one of the strangest times I've ever had." He stood up and began to pace, touching books, straightening a lamp shade. Finally he sat down and took his mug in his hands, but did not drink. "I've always had a conservative nature," he continued. "People kid me about it sometimes, how I won't read my horoscope or play the lottery. I don't believe in luck, coincidences or the supernatural. So what you had to tell me really shook me up. When I left I had no intention of ever seeing you again."

I looked away from him and began playing with the robe belt, wrapping it over my fingers. "But I am here," I said softly as if to myself.

He either didn't hear or ignored my interruption. "As the day went on, I began to see things differently. I started to think of you in another light. Not as a blood–crazed lunatic, but as a victim, too. I even did a little research on the areas you said you had been in over the years and found no records of murders similar to the ones we've had here. Intuitively, emotionally, I guess I knew you were innocent. But me, I needed definite proof."

I glanced up at him to see him take a drink of his coffee. When he looked at me, I turned away. He slowly rose from his seat and sat down next to me.

"Deirdre, I want to be honest with you. It's not an easy thing."

"I know. Please go on."

"I agreed to meet you tonight with the sole purpose of talking the case over with you, enlisting your help. If what we are dealing with is a vampire, and now I must believe that it is, then your firsthand knowledge on the subject will be extremely helpful."

So that was it. I could help him solve his case and then go on my way alone. I stood up and walked away from him. "I'll help you anyway I can, Mitch. You should know that by now. But some other time; now I would like to get dressed and go home. You don't need to walk me back, I'll catch a cab." I started down the hallway.

He stopped me halfway there and backed me up against the wall blocking my escape. "Why don't you ever let me finish?" he asked with a wry grin. "Are you always this hasty?"

"Yes, but I prefer to call it caution. And I don't usually have a problem exercising it. Let me go, Mitch." I could easily break away from him, but I wanted his concession.

He did not give it. "Deirdre, how could anyone live as long as you and still not understand other people? I thought that age was supposed to give you a certain perspective. It hasn't done you much good, has it?"

"I'm still alive, aren't I?" I snarled. "That should be good for something."

He smiled. "It is good, you know. It saved you for me."

I glanced at him, startled.

"When I thought of you, my intentions were strictly business. But when I spoke to you and saw you tonight, I realized that, despite all my plans and despite what you were, I wanted you here tonight and damn the consequences." He stepped away from me. "And now, I've finished. Do you still want to leave?"

"I never did," I said in honesty. "If I did, you wouldn't have been able to stop me."

He moved me up against the wall again, gently this time. "I knew that, Deirdre. Will you stay?"

"For a while, Mitch, gladly."

I awoke shortly after noon the next day to find Mitch, fully dressed but lying on the bed beside me. He propped himself up on one elbow, carefully considering me. "Good afternoon," he said with a gentle smile. "Did you sleep well?"

"Fine, and you?"

"Like a baby. Chris was right, you are good for me."

"Chris told you he said that?"

"Yeah, he called the next day. He's really quite smitten with you."

"He is a nice kid, Mitch, but don't you think he's a little young for me?"

He reached over and brushed my hair over my face with a devilish smile. "Yeah, probably, but come to think of it, Deirdre, so am I." Before I could respond, he jumped up from the bed and retrieved a paper bag that was sitting in the corner of the room. "Here," he said abruptly, "these are yours."

I looked inside to find a pair of jeans, two or three shirts, some underwear and a bra. "Thank you. Where did you get them?"

"I stopped by your hotel and picked them up for you." He reached in his pocket and handed my key back. "I hope you don't mind."

"Not at all."

"You get dressed. I have some coffee ready."

I smoothed the hair from my eyes. "Sounds good, but is it safe?"

He shot me a quizzical look. "You've drunk my coffee before and lived to tell the tale. Of course it's safe."

"No, I mean is it daylight? Are all the windows covered?"

"Oh!" he said, walking out. "I'll check." I heard him pulling drapes shut, then he called to me. "All clear, I think."

"Thank you." I dressed quickly and cautiously stepped into the living room. "This should be fine."

He was standing at the window with his back to me, his hands still on the drape cord. "It seems a shame. It's such a glorious day."

"Glorious for you, maybe, but deadly for me." His shoulders slumped a bit. "Let it be, Mitch."

He spun around, stung by my comment. "I wouldn't open them. How could you think that?"

"That's not what I mean. I know you wouldn't hurt me. But you should quit tearing yourself up over this situation. It is not worth it. I can't change, no matter how much you or I might wish it."

"But maybe you could. I've been doing research in the area for weeks since this case started. Did you know there's a recently discovered disease that they think may have cause the myths of vampirism to arise? Propheria, I think it was called." He looked at me hopefully and I hated to disillusion him.

"*Porphyria*. I know all about it, Mitch. I paid one of the researchers on the subject good money to examine me and then forget about it."

"And?"

"Sorry, my darling. They could find no trace of it in my system. They did however find out some facts that interested them greatly. My metabolism, my DNA structure, all sorts of details that they wanted to study." I gave a small laugh in recollection of the situation. "I had one hell of a time getting out of the office intact and with all my files."

"How did you get out?"

"Oh," I said casually, but locked my eyes on his, "I talked them into it."

He shuddered slightly as my gaze held him. "I believe it." Then he smiled at me as I dropped my stare. "You must teach me to do that, Deirdre. It would be very handy in my line of work."

"No doubt," I agreed glibly. "But I don't think it can be taught, only acquired." I grew serious considering the matter. "And not without great cost." An uncomfortable silence filled the room as we studied each other, both trying to fathom the other's thoughts.

"Okay, I'll drop it," he said at last. "Now, how about that coffee?"

The hours passed quickly in his company. We sat and talked about commonplace things, carefully avoiding any mention of recent events. He received several phone calls that I presumed were about the case, but made no comment on them, and I asked no questions. It was a peaceful time, unlike the frenzy of passion or anger we usually experienced. Sometimes he would reach out to me and gently stoke my hair or shoulder. I was grateful for the ordinariness of the situation. We could have been any other couple on their day off. It was a comfortable feeling, one that I fervently wished could continue.

In the early afternoon, the phone rang again. Mitch went to it with a shrug and a smile for me. He answered it, talked for a while and then hung up. When he turned back to me he was not smiling. "Nothing, we've got nothing on this case. Everywhere we turn, we come up a blank. How the hell am I supposed to solve this, when I have no witnesses, no clues, no idea of who might be doing it? At least with Larry, I had something concrete. But for this one, he could very well be made of mist, it's that hard to track him." His voice raised in frustration.

"You said last night that I could help you. What exactly do you have in mind?"

"I don't think you should get involved, not anymore. It could be dangerous for you. I keep picturing you in Gwen's place, or like the girl in the morgue."

"What girl in the morgue?"

"The one they brought in, you know, the fourth murder. There was something about her that . . ." He stopped and shuddered. "Anyway, I think it would be best for you just to stay out of it. I can keep you safe here until everything is over."

"Mitch, you cannot keep me locked away forever. And you cannot always be around to protect me. Sooner or later I will have to feed, and should you be around, well, let's just say you could become very anemic over time. Neither of us want that to happen."

"Well, I did bring your supplies over with me in addition to the clothes." He gave me a shy smile. "I put it in the vegetable drawer."

I laughed. "Good place for it, but that doesn't solve the problem."

"I know. Everything you're saying is true. It's just that the thought of losing you makes me crazy."

"Fine, let me help you and it will all be over sooner. I don't believe that the other vampire would harm me in any event."

"I seem to remember that that's what you said about Larry."

I smiled. “Then the odds that I am right will be better this time. Let me help, Mitch.”

He finally reneged. “Actually,” he admitted sheepishly, “there’s really no danger to you on this. I just want you to come along with me while I talk to everyone again. Maybe there will be something you can pick up from them, recognition maybe, I don’t know. But if we start now, we can finish by eight or nine, get some dinner and come back here.”

“Now?” I questioned, glancing at the clock. “The sun won’t set for hours. But,” I said quickly seeing the disappointment on his face, “I could leave at sunset. Will that be soon enough?”

“I guess it will have to be. I don’t have a choice anyway, do I?”

“No, and neither do I.” I went over to him and gently touched his arm. “Nothing of importance is likely to happen in the next few hours, considering that the person we’re looking for also can’t go about in daylight.”

He brightened briefly. “Yeah, I guess I hadn’t thought of it that way. I’m just not used to this confinement. When I want to go out, I go.”

I wrapped my arms around his neck and kissed him. When I was done, I looked up at him and smiled. “We have some free time, Mitch. Do you know what I’d like to do?” I moved away from him and started backing down the hall, slowly unbuttoning my shirt. “I’d really like to have a shower.” I laughed at the look on his face and tossed my shirt to him.

His face lit up with a playful grin. “I hope you don’t mind sharing?”

“Not at all,” I replied. “And I hope you like the water hot.”

Chapter 22

When we eventually emerged from the shower Mitch laughed. "Damn, I feel like a lobster. How can you stand it?"

I shrugged as I wrapped myself in a towel. "It warms me."

"I should hope so," he said with a wry grin, as we went to the bedroom to dress. "It damn near parboiled me."

I sat on the edge of the bed to brush my hair. "Let me do that," he said and took the brush from my hand. He knelt behind me and began to brush, slowly at first, and then with harder strokes. It felt so good that I leaned back into him, contentedly. He continued for a while, then stopped abruptly, threw the brush across the room and buried his face in the mass of hair at my neck. "Oh, Deirdre," he said, making my name into a low, passionate moan, then made a grab at the towel that covered me. He flung it to the floor and pulled me down on the bed next to him.

I looked into his eyes, so blue and intense. "I thought we had to go out," I teased him softly.

"Later," he said and kissed me.

The phone rang and he jumped from me. "Let it ring," I urged, twining my arms around his neck and pulling him back.

"Shit," he swore as he rose from me reluctantly. "I can't just let it ring. It might be important." He reached over, picked up the phone, then covered the receiver and took one more kiss before answering it. "Yeah," he said brusquely into the phone, "this had better be good."

I could hear the voice of the caller, low, urgent and somehow familiar, but did not pay attention. Instead, I occupied myself with lazily tracing the muscles in Mitch's now tense arm until he brushed me off and sat up straight.

"Look, Hunter, I thought I made the situation plain last

night. She's with me now. I'll take care of her. You should just leave her alone."

"Damn," I swore quietly and Mitch gave me a sharp look. I could hear Max's cynical laugh and comment quite plainly. He, too, had raised his voice. "Calm down, Greer. I only want to talk to her. I know she's there."

Mitch put his hand over the receiver again. "It's Max," he snarled, handed me the phone and stalked out of the room.

"Damn it, Max. Your timing couldn't be worse. What do you want?"

"I spoke with Victor Lange today. He said you had dinner at the Imperial last night."

"That's right. And?"

"It was brought to my attention that I just might have some information for Greer, if he would be interested."

I looked up and Mitch was standing in the entrance of the door glaring at the telephone. "What the hell does he want?" he said in a voice loud enough to be heard.

"Tell him what I said, Deirdre."

"I don't much care to be caught in the middle of this, Max. Why don't you just talk to Mitch, if that's what you want? Or maybe he should listen in on the extension." I wasn't sure with which one of them I was most annoyed.

"An excellent idea, Deirdre," Max agreed. "I do have something of importance to say to both of you."

"Pick up the extension, Mitch," I said, exasperated. He went to the kitchen and we maintained silence until we heard the click from the other phone.

"Now, isn't that better?" Max said sarcastically. "All cozy and together again."

"Get to the point, Hunter. We have better things to do . . ."

"I'm sure you do." Max's voice was smooth, insinuating. "So I'll make it quick. I didn't wish to interrupt your afternoon. But it was important that I talk to Deirdre. When I couldn't find her at any of the usual places, I assumed she was with you." I could hear an uncharacteristic sadness in his voice. Mitch must have heard it also, because he awkwardly cleared his throat. Max continued without acknowledging him. "Be that as it may, even if she weren't there, I would have called to give you some information." Max paused and I could hear a faint tingling of ice against a glass.

"Get on with it, Hunter," Mitch said and Max laughed.

"He's so abrupt, my dear. I must admit, I don't quite understand the attraction, but it must be considerable. You don't know how lucky you are, Greer. She's been through hundreds of men since I've known her and never gone back for seconds." He laughed again.

"You bastard . . ." Mitch started.

"It doesn't matter, Mitch," I cut in. "Don't let him get to you. He does it only for the reaction. Isn't that right, Max?"

"Just so, my love. But my advice to you, Greer, is to make hay while the sun shines. Some night she'll fly away and you'll never get her back." There was still a trace of cynical laughter in his voice.

"Spare us the dramatics, Hunter. I heard them all the other night. Just get on with it."

"Fine, I won't waste your time any longer. Today in conversation with Victor Lange, I suddenly realized that I had important information on your case. If the two of you were to stop over at the club tonight, I'd be more than willing to share it."

"What exactly is going on?" Mitch sounded angry. "You gave no indication earlier that you knew anything about this. I know you have been questioned and had nothing to say. I could charge you for withholding evidence, or . . ."

"Don't threaten me, Greer. It will do you no good. Let's just say that I became aware of something of importance to you and I wanted to do my civic duty.

I laughed at that comment, coming from Max. Responsibility, civic or otherwise, was never one of his strong points.

"Deirdre, you wound me." I said nothing and he continued. "You will come, won't you? Together?"

Mitch broke in quickly. "I'll be there, Hunter. But I don't see the need to drag Deirdre into this. She'll stay here. Last time she was at your club, she was almost killed, no thanks to you."

"Deirdre will come with you, won't you, my dear? Otherwise the deal is off. I'll expect you both after sundown."

"We'll be there, Max."

I hung up the phone and Mitch came back into the bedroom. "What do you suppose this is all about?" he asked me and I shook my head.

"It's hard to tell with Max. It may even be his idea of a practical joke."

"It's not funny."

"Not to you, maybe or even me. But Max is different; I don't really think he means any harm. It is just the way he is."

"You have too high an opinion of that man, Deirdre. I could believe almost anything of him. He's just too damn smooth."

"Let's not waste our time talking about Max. We'll find out soon enough what he wants. And until then," I checked the clock, "we have about two hours before sunset. Do you think we could pick up where we left off?"

"Absolutely," he said, crossing the room and smiling the smile that lit his eyes.

Afterwards, we both fell asleep and the dream found me swiftly and mercilessly.

It begins at the side of the road; I leave the carriage and the frightened horses, I step over the body there without question to follow the dark figure that beckons just out of my reach. With every step that takes me nearer to him I grow in strength, but even that is not enough. Still he moves ahead and I struggle to catch up, to match a face to that form and voice that haunt me through dreams and wakings. I am running now, wearing the green velvet dress. It is dirty and stained, the hem sodden and thick with blood and tears. It catches around my ankles and I stumble. He turns around to watch me. His laugh is as dark and unimaginable as his face.

"Come," he urges. "Hurry," he calls and the words are carried on the wind as if from a long distance away. I pull myself from the ground and follow for what seems like miles, never tiring and yet always behind. Soon he leads me down a street I recognize to a house, my house, my father's house. The air is heavy with the sweet scents of the garden but I cannot stay. I must find him.

He has entered the house, I know; the door swings slightly ajar in the wind. His footsteps echo in the upstairs hall and I ascend to meet him. The corridor is long and shadowy, but the dead are not here. "At rest," I whisper. "Have you gone to rest?" There is no answer, all is empty and hollow.

The doorway at the end stands open and I see the starlit sky, the open field. I enter and he is not there. "Show yourself," I scream defiantly, angrily and am answered with a wild rustling of wings, stirring the warm evening air. I feel his presence behind me, his breath is hot on my neck and my hair begins to raise. I do not turn around. "Are you here then?" I ask quietly.

"I am here."

"I would see your face."

"There is no need, little one. It has been before you for years and you did not see."

"I would know who you are."

"But you know me, Deirdre. Better than any other. We are one. Why do you deny me?"

I feel the silken touch of his wing on my neck. It is smooth as before and dark. I tremble at the touch and clench my fists in anger. With his lightly deposited kiss and my ensuing shudder there can be no doubt. For I do know him now, but as I turn around to confront him, he is already dissolving into the darkness. There is only the brief glance of confirmation: the moonlight shining off the sculptured lines of his face, the lifting of an eyebrow, the cruel twist of his mouth, a mouth that had lied and comforted, kissed and tortured, a mouth and a hunger that had killed many and destroyed me—Max's mouth, Max's hunger.

And then he is gone.

Chapter 23

I awoke alone with his name echoing angrily in my head. Mitch must have risen without waking me. I dressed quickly and walked out of the bedroom. Mitch was sitting at the kitchen table, finishing a sandwich. He looked up at me, smiled and finished swallowing. "Sleep well?"

"Fine." I stared at him for a minute, as he stood up and put his plate into the sink. When he turned around he gave me a puzzled look.

"What's wrong? You look shook up."

"Bad dream." I said simply. "Are you ready to go?"

"Yes, if you are."

We walked out of the apartment and got into his car. As he began driving, he turned to me. "Are you sure you're all right? You look like you might be getting sick or something."

"No, I'm fine." I reached over and touched his thigh gently. "Mitch," I asked casually, "what was that you said yesterday about the girl in the morgue?"

"Who?"

"You know, the fourth murder victim. Something about her disturbed you."

"Yeah, she reminded me of you. It bothered me a lot." He smiled and put his hand on top of mine. "But I'm okay now. All of that helped me realize that it didn't matter what or who you are. I knew that I still loved you, if I could get so upset about seeing the dead body of someone who just looked like you."

"In what way did she look like me?"

"Well, she was about your height, your build and her hair was almost the same color, other than that . . ." He stopped abruptly and gave me a sharp look. "Why? Is it important?"

"No, probably not." It really didn't matter at that point; I was still overwhelmed by the identity of the man in my dream. I began to think about our relationship over the years. How could I have been so blind? That first spark of recognition at the diner in Kansas should have told me. So many things since I had known him should have told me. The way he controlled and manipulated me, the way I could never stay angry about anything that he did to me, the way I always came crawling back to the sanctuary of his presence. "Damn," I whispered to myself.

"What did you say?"

"Nothing, only do you think you could drive a little faster. I'd like to get this over with."

He looked at me questioningly, and said nothing but increased his speed as much as possible. The streets were congested with cars and pedestrians. It took us over twenty minutes to travel the remaining six blocks. The whole time I stared out the window, clenching my fists so tightly that my nails broke the surface of the skin. I opened my hands, eight perfect crescents of congealed blood marked the palms.

Mitch parked his car out front and when the doorman tried to stop him, he showed his badge. "Police business," he said and the doorman let us through. We shouldered our way through the crowd in the bar and eventually made our way to the hall that led to Max's office.

Before we reached the door, Mitch stopped in his tracks and grabbed my arms. "Deirdre, what the hell is going on here? All of a sudden, it's like you know something I don't. Care to enlighten me?" His voice was tense and nervous.

"How could he take me in so completely?" I spoke as if to myself. "All these years, and I never knew him, never knew who he was. And now, it's so obvious."

"What's obvious, Deirdre? Who are you talking about?"

I shook my head. "I've been a fool. I suppose I didn't really want to know." I broke away from Mitch and began walking again. He stood still staring for a moment, then caught up with me as I reached Max's closed door.

I pulled him into a fierce embrace. "I love you," I said as I stretched up and kissed him, forgetful for one moment of all that waited for me, behind the door.

"And I love you, too. But this hardly seems the time or place . . ."

"There may be no time, later." I looked deeply into his eyes. "Wait here, Mitch," I pleaded. "I'll handle this by myself."

"Handle what?" he started, but the door opened.

Max stood there, elegant as usual. His features seemed more cruel, more inhuman than I could ever have imagined them. His eyes blazed as they met mine. "What a delightful surprise. You're right on time. Please come in."

I ignored him and kissed Mitch again, slowly and lingeringly. "Stay here," I said to him again when we had finished.

Max laughed. "How touching, Deirdre. But you have me all wrong. I don't intend to hurt him, not if he gives me what I want. And he will, you know. Please come in, you're both most welcome."

" 'Enter freely and of your own will?' " I quoted to him. "Don't you think that just may be a trifle melodramatic, Max?"

He smiled at me and nodded. "Perhaps it is, my little one. But at least you finally understand. That's good. Although I had wanted to reveal myself to you at my own time, when I spoke with Victor, and he told me he had informed you about my escort the other night, well, I realized that it wouldn't be long before the two of you began to put everything together on your own. And so now you know who and what I am. I'm glad; it will make everything so much easier."

Mitch looked at both of us, in confusion. "I don't understand. Would someone just tell me what is going on here?"

"Dracula welcomes Jonathan Harker to his castle," I said to him gently. "Chapter two, I believe." Max nodded and I continued. "I thought you had done research, Mitch."

"Then," he said in disbelief, "Max is also a . . . just like you."

Max's sardonic laughter echoed in the hallway and I felt a chill run up my spine. "So you found the courage to tell him, my dear. And he still stands with you. That's good." Then he turned to Mitch. "Yes, Greer. I'm also a vampire. But you'll find that, unlike some," and he gave me a surprisingly gentle glance, "I'm not afraid to say the word, nor to use the powers I have. But it is most inappropriate to discuss this here in the hall." He motioned us in and we obeyed.

The power he was exerting over us seemed insurmountable and when he gestured for us to sit down, we did so mechanically and without question. Mitch, I noticed briefly, was busy surveying the surroundings, but I could barely take my eyes away from Max. "You and I have a few scores to settle, Max," I said through clenched teeth. "Let Mitch go. He can't hurt you."

"Oh, but he already has. He has taken you and loved you. And made you love him. That cannot be allowed. I'd wager that he wouldn't hesitate to kill me now, if he could. Isn't that right, Greer?"

"You son of a bitch," Mitch snarled and reached into his coat for his gun. He was no match for the other's reflexes. Max moved across the room in a blur and gripped Mitch's arm, twisting until the gun dropped. Then, with a small smile at me, he continued to twist. Mitch gave a moan of pain and I could hear his bones breaking, accompanied by a wet, tearing sound. One of the bones had broken through his skin and my nostrils flared. The room was now filled with the scent of blood.

"Max!" I pleaded with him. "Please stop."

"Anything you say, my dear." Max flung him into a corner of the room as if he weighed nothing. Mitch's head hit the wall and his moaning ceased. I ran to him, searching for the pulse in his neck.

"Still alive?" Max inquired. When I nodded, he shook his head. "He must be stronger than I thought. It makes no difference, I suppose. He can live, for now."

"So help me, Max, if you kill him . . ."

"Oh, but I won't kill him, Deirdre." He looked amused. "I wouldn't even dream of it. Once again you have misjudged me."

I managed a low, bitter laugh. "Misjudged you? No, I don't think so, Max. Underestimated. maybe. But you're capable of anything, aren't you?"

He thought for a moment. "Let's just say that I rarely fail when I set my mind to something. Besides, when one is faced with eternity, as are you and I, a few lives don't matter."

"How can you say that?" I was horrified. "That's inhuman."

"Ah, but then, isn't that the point? We are inhuman."

"Thanks to you, I am. Would you care to explain that?"

"You, I'm sad to admit, were a mistake. I never intended to turn you into a vampire. I've found over the years that women make very poor initiates. They just don't have the cruelty, the ruthlessness that is needed." He gave me a tender glance and walked gracefully to me. He took my hand and kissed it gently. "You don't either, my love. But you had a will to survive and that carried you through. I admired you at the time for the fight you put up. I admire you now. You are one of my best creations."

I stiffened and pulled my hand away. "You have other creations? Where?"

"All over the world, I believe. I keep in touch with a few of them, still. Some are more successful than others, but none turned out quite so well nor half so beautiful as you. I have retried the experiment over the years, you know. Taken someone unwilling and forced my blood upon them. They all died, hideously with the first sunrise. But you had the instincts and the wit to survive." He moved closer to me and fastened his eyes upon me again. "When I met you at that diner in Kansas, I could hardly believe you were the same person. The fact that you had lived for so long, on your own, unguided and untaught, surprised me. Even those with the best of teachers fail and die, usually within fifty years of their transformation." He reached over to me and laid his hands on my shoulders. "But there could be no mistaking you; the blood we had shared called to me. And to you, although you did not know enough then to recognize the bond that held us together. I almost told you, the night we made love, but you weren't ready yet."

"Ready for what?" I asked and a moan interrupted us. We both looked over to the corner where Mitch lay and found him sitting up, rubbing his head with his left arm. His right arm dangled uselessly at his side. I tried to move, but Max's grip tightened.

"Ready to join with me, forever."

"I would never do that, Max. You represent everything I hate, everything our kind has been reviled for over the centuries. There is no need to kill, no hunger so great that would necessitate the death of the victim."

Max threw back his head and laughed. "Oh, Deirdre, you are so young, so innocent yet. Look at her, Greer. Is she not magnificent? The face of an angel and the kiss of a devil. A body captured and preserved at its peak of maturity and passion. Yet in vampire terms, she is still only a child, little more than an infant. She has yet to realize one-tenth of her powers, powers of the body and mind which I have bequeathed to her." He gave both Mitch and me a humorless smile, frightening in its inhumanity, then grasped my face in his hands. "And still you talk of needs and hunger as if the thirst for life could be measured in pints. There was no need, I kill simply because I can."

A faint sound from Mitch's corner interrupted him. Max turned and went to him. "I don't think you will need that radio, Greer. Give it to me."

As Max's hand neared him, Mitch clutched the unit tighter. "You won't get away with this, Hunter," he said grimly, his mouth contorted with pain. Quickly Max reached over and wrested the box from his grip. He looked down on Mitch, an expression of disdain on his face.

"Can you stop me?" he sneered derisively as he reached down and took hold of Mitch's knee. Small beads of sweat began to form on Mitch's forehead and once again I could hear the sound of breaking bones. He let out one labored breath as Max continued, "Are you man enough to take me, Greer?" He turned away abruptly and began to laugh.

"Damn you, Hunter," Mitch said with a grimace. "Get on with your story. I'd like to hear your justification for four murders."

Max laughed again, still looking down at Mitch. "Justification? Why should I need justification for any of my deeds? And why would I provide it to such as you? I could explain to Deirdre, for she might come close to understanding. There are times, lately, when the blood is not enough, when I need the total quenching of life. It was not premeditated, not planned; the deaths simply happened. At such times I have no control, but it makes no difference."

Mitch stared at him, as did I; his total lack of shame for his deeds appalled us. "Before you go any further," Mitch told him in a tight, pained voice, "I must inform you that anything that you say can be considered a confession at this point and it will be used as such."

Max turned to me. "I begin to understand your attraction, my dear. He is a very determined man, even when helpless. He would do well as one of us, don't you think, Deirdre?"

I said nothing but I gasped. "But, no," Max went on, "that would probably be unwise. And you seem to like him human, so human he will remain." He lowered his voice, all traces of humor vanished. "The span of his human endurance I leave up to you."

He strode over to me, held me in his arms. His eyes were crazed, maniacal, striving to draw me into his madness. I looked away, but stood limp and passive in his embrace, not wanting my struggle to inflict further torture on Mitch. "I want you, Deirdre." He whispered to me now, an urging, demanding whisper that caused a chill to travel through my body. "I have always wanted you. You will grow stronger, you will cast away your petty morals. I will teach you to revel in death, as I do." His voice was deep and passionate, his words echoed in my brain. He began to caress my back, his hands strong on my yielding flesh. "Look at me," he commanded and wrapped my hair around his hand, drawing my head back roughly. Our eyes met and I knew I was lost. Then Max kissed me, his lips burned on mine, his eyes blazed into my very soul and I thought he would never stop. I did not want him to stop. Mitch whispered my name in anguish, but I still could not take my eyes from Max.

"Soon, my little one, you will learn that human lives are worthless, next to the power we possess. The power of life eternal, savagely drained. And the power of death. That night at the club, when I said you had changed, I thought that you had finally awakened and come into the power that is yours by right." He smiled at me and I saw that his canines had grown sharper and longer. "I know now that was not the case. That you had only been in love. In love," he repeated with scorn and grasped my face roughly between his hands again. His face glowed with a fury and a love that I had never seen before. "You have no idea what that word means, until you taste what I have to offer." Somewhere in the back of my mind a voice was crying violation and rape, but I was again drawn into him against my will, and when he bent his head to drink at my neck I welcomed his kiss.

"Ah," he said as he withdrew his bloodied mouth. "She walks in beauty, like the night."

I caressed his cheek and smiled. He kissed me again, I could taste my own blood on his tongue and was deeply aroused. "Tell me more," I urged huskily. "About our power."

"We are gods, you and I. They can mean nothing to us; they are here for our sustenance, nothing more." He spoke insistently. "Your initiation has been delayed for too long, little one. But now your time has come. You will be my mate, my love, my passion through all eternity." He turned me in his arms to face Mitch. He was struggling to rise from the floor, to reach us, to stop us. "Look at him, Deirdre," Max commanded. "Look at your human lover. Pitiful, isn't he? You could break his neck with one blow. You could crack his spine easily, without a second thought. But we don't want him dead, not just yet, do we?" I looked at Max questioningly, I was a child in his hands. "Go to him, Deirdre. Take him, he is yours. Take all of him. I suspect he'd rather suffer his death at your hands than at mine. But just to show what a good sport I am, Greer, I will let you die in private."

Max laughed and gave me one more kiss, still holding my gaze. "Soon, my love, we will begin our life together, we will roam the earth together, the night will be ours." He closed the door softly and I walked slowly toward Mitch.

"Deirdre," he said weakly. "You have to stop him." I knelt down next to him, took his uninjured hand in mine and stroked his hair. "He's crazy, you know that. He's got you under some sort of spell, don't you realize that?"

"Don't worry, Mitch," I said. "Everything will be fine." I was startled by the expressionless tone of my voice; he heard it too and tried to crawl away from me. The horror on his face was terrible and yet somehow gratifying. I remembered what Max had said, that he was mine to take completely. I smiled, knowing that my canines were exposed to his view.

His face grew ashen with fear. "Deirdre," a note of pleading entered his voice. "You don't have to do this. He can't make you kill me."

"Oh, but he can, Mitch." I lifted him gently in my arms.

"Look at me, Deirdre. Really look at me." I heard him as if from a distance, but the words made no sense. The veins were throbbing in his neck, calling me, pulling me. I put my mouth on him, nuzzling and licking the skin, his scent was fear and blood.

With one final burst of strength he grabbed my chin and pulled my face up. His eyes drew me; I could read fear there, but beneath it I could see his love for me still. "I love you," he whispered and I heard the truth in his words. "And I will love you even as you do this."

I shuddered and began to lose some of the urgency of Max's words. "I love you, Mitch, and I won't hurt you. It will be painless, I promise." He shook his head weakly, the desperate grab had drained him. "If I don't," I continued in a panic, "Max will. You know that. He won't be kind."

"I don't give a damn about the pain, or even my death. But I don't want him to turn you into someone you're not. You can't be like him, Deirdre. It would kill you eventually." He looked at me again, his eyes that intense blue I so loved. Somewhere, deep inside me, his words were being heard.

"You are not afraid of me, then?"

"No," he said, never taking his eyes from mine. "I know what you are, but I am not afraid. I trust you with my life and my soul. You won't hurt me."

Tears began to stream down my face and I knew that the battle had been won, if only temporarily. "But I don't have the strength to fight him, Mitch. He's fed on me and he is strong, fortified by my blood. He's weakened my body, knowing that my mind will follow. When he returns, he'll force me to kill you or do it himself. You must leave."

He tried to smile. "I can barely sit up, Deirdre, how could I leave?" He looked at me again and shook his head. "No, there is only one way, you must take me, take my blood. Take it all if you need, my death won't matter if you can rid the world of that madman."

"No, I won't."

"You must. I want you to. It's the only way out for you. And you're all I have now. I don't want to live, knowing that he will always be there, to corrupt you, to twist you into a creature like him. You must kill him and you must take my strength to do it."

"Are you sure, my love?"

"Yes, now do it quickly, before he returns."

I kissed his mouth and slowly moved to his neck. "Now, do it now," he whispered and I sank my teeth into his skin; he never even flinched, but sighed and smiled as his blood flowed into my mouth, warming and strengthening my body and my resolve.

When I had finished, I gently stroked the hair from his pale face. "Forgive me, Mitch," I whispered to him. His eyes fluttered weakly but I hoped that he would hear. "I never meant for this to happen." I kissed his cold lips and rose from the floor.

I quickly surveyed the room. It was exactly as I remembered it; how many nights had I sat here with Max, drinking and laughing? And yet how changed it was, now. It had acquired a nightmarish quality and I knew that I would never be free of the dreams that had occurred here tonight: dreams of love, passion and death. "Max." I called his name aloud and it echoed around the room. "Max!" I screamed it in fury and paced around the room. I tossed a barstool at the wall to see it shatter into pieces. Picking up the largest splinter, I turned it over in my hands. It was one of the legs, about two feet long and the end that had broken was sharp and pointed. "Max!" I screamed again, knowing that he would hear. "Come and see what a god has done."

He burst through the door, and saw me, my arms hidden behind my back. His eyes took in the crumpled heap that was Mitch and lit with a devilish glow. "Good, Deirdre. You have done well. Come to me and I'll reward you. Tonight you will feed on me."

I moved toward him, slowly and sensuously. He closed the door and leaned against it. He looked at me; then loosened his tie and unbuttoned his shirt. His neck exposed, he beckoned to me. "Come to me, Deirdre," he said forcefully. "Tonight is our wedding night. I will share my essence with you once again."

I felt a moment of panic as I came closer to him—his power over me was still formidable. Had I taken Mitch in vain?

But at that second, Max closed his eyes, reached for the light switch and turned it off. His power over me was gone and I found him in the dark, as he once found me. I kissed his neck; he gave a low, passionate moan. "Put your arms around me," he said huskily. "Hold me close to you." I could feel his heart beat next to me. I placed one hand firmly on his shoulder, pinning him to the door. "Now your other arm, Deirdre. Ah, I have waited so long for this, so long for you."

"So have I, Max, although I never knew it until tonight. Thank you." I bestowed one more kiss on his neck, then his mouth. He was silent in expectation. "Now," I said quickly and he caught his breath in passion. I brought my other hand from behind my back. The stake found him quickly; I used all my borrowed strength and drove it deeply though his heart. The force of my blow lifted him from the floor and impaled him firmly on the door. He gave a choked cry and flailed his arms about in an attempt to free himself. One of them caught the switch and the lights blazed on.

The sight was horrifying: Max writhing, blood spurting from his chest, his lips foam-flecked and his face grimacing in pain and surprise. When he tried to grip the stake, to remove it, I pinioned his arms to the door. His eyes frantically searched about the room for release; finding none, they fastened upon mine. I could not fathom their expression; was it disbelief, fear or hatred? Perhaps it was even relief, or love. No matter, he held me there as compellingly as I held him. His mouth moved, but no sound emerged. Was he saying my name, pleading with me?

Tears began to flow down my face, but still I held him, and was forced to watch the life slowly drain from him. And as he died, I saw the years accumulate, not in his face or body, but in his eyes. "Dear God," I whispered softly. "How many years, how many centuries?" I loosened my grip upon him in horror at what I had taken away from him and from myself: the knowledge, the capacity to survive for so many years. He struggled no longer, but continued to draw me into his eyes. I shared his pain and despair, his triumphs and conquests; somehow I was pulled into him, deeply pulled into him and felt his power and his pain enter into my own body and soul. Mentally, I staggered back from the invasion, no longer sure that I could hold him or my resolve. No longer sure that I desired his death. But before I could loosen my hold, before I could repair the damage I had inflicted, his eyes glazed over and his mouth fell open in a ghastly grin. His bloodless lips curled back, exposing his teeth, still sharpened, startlingly white. "Deirdre," I heard his whisper in my mind. Then, as abruptly as the slamming of a door, he was gone.

I let go of his arms and they dropped limply at his sides. His body swung gently back and forth and small drops of blood ran down the length of the stake into the expanding pool at his feet. I wiped my hands on my pants and turned away.

"Is he dead?" The voice was weak but undoubtedly Mitch's. I went to where he lay.

"Yes," I said wearily. Speaking was an effort; I was tired and shaken. "He is dead." There was no happiness, no triumph in my voice, but Mitch did not notice.

"Good!" He tried to smile at me but failed. "What a night, huh?" His eyes closed once more. I walked slowly to the desk, and called for an ambulance. Then I sat down next to him and cradled his head in my arms until I heard the sirens. When they arrived, I kissed Mitch and felt for a pulse in his neck. It was there, but so faint that I could have missed it. "Please live," I urged him. "I have enough blood on my hands. I don't want yours." I rose then, carefully opening the door that still held Max impaled and lifeless, and fled into the blackness of the night without turning back.

Chapter 24

During the three weeks Mitch spent in the hospital, I completed my plans for departure. The transfer of Griffin Designs went smoothly. Other aspects took longer: the transfer of my funds to Swiss accounts, travel arrangements and living arrangements at my new destination. But by sundown, New Year's Eve, I was packed and ready to go. Most of my effects had been sent on ahead so all I had was a small travel case, plane tickets and a passport with the picture and name of a stranger. The name I could get used to, I had before; but I looked with doubt at the picture and its image in the mirror. I had cut my hair short and dyed it a deep brown, almost black. It was very chic, very modern and I hated it. But I looked sufficiently unlike Deirdre Griffin to proceed with a new life. That, I told myself again, was all that mattered.

I called the lobby and asked Frank to get a taxi for me in about half an hour. My flight would not leave for almost three hours, but I saw no need to linger. The rooms had already acquired an impersonal feeling; it was strange to consider that soon someone else would be living here. I made a final tour to make sure that I had left nothing behind. I was in the bathroom, when there was a tentative knock on the door.

"Come in, Frank," I called for I assumed he was here to get my bag. "The door is open."

"Deirdre?" The voice was not Frank's; my heart rose then fell when I realized the confrontation I had tried so hard to avoid had come.

"Mitch?" My voice was tremulous, betraying emotion best kept under control. I walked out of the bathroom and into the hall. Mitch stood, glancing around the room, taking in its emptiness and the packed bag at the door. As I entered he looked at me in shock.

"What on earth did you do to yourself?" he questioned sharply.

Nervously, I ran my hand through my too short hair. "Don't you like it?"

"No."

"To tell you the truth," I said with a wan smile, "I don't like it much either. But it keeps the publicity hounds at bay. How are you?"

"Fine." He looked anything but fine. His right arm was in a cast as was his left leg. His face was unusually pale, from the loss of blood, I assumed, but his eyes were as blue and intense as ever. And at this moment they were angry and defiant. I found I could not answer his gaze; I looked away.

"Would you like to sit down?" He grunted an agreement and hobbled across the room on a cane. After he was seated, I walked over and sat facing him.

"You're leaving." It was not a question and I could not lie.

"Yes," I said simply. "It seems best that I do."

"Oh." The single word held such anger, such reproach that I choked back any words of explanation I might have made. Instead, I rose from my chair and went to look out the window. A heavy silence descended on the room. When I finally turned around he was still staring at me, but some of his anger had been replaced with resignation and sadness. I would have preferred the anger.

He began to speak hesitantly. "I thought you might like to know the outcome of the other night. I just stopped by to let you know that you'll not be questioned or held accountable in any way for Max's death."

"Thank you. I was wondering what happened after I left." My voice softened on the last word.

"I know why you left, Deirdre. And I don't blame you." He glanced over at me, and gave the nuance of a smile. "At least not too much. I spent three weeks flat on my back rationalizing the situation, knowing that you wouldn't have left me without good reasons, knowing what those reasons were."

"Mitch, I . . ."

"And still you won't let me finish. I took the blame for Max's death, self–defense in the line of duty. Actually," and he gave me a cold–blooded grin, "I prefer to think of it as credit, rather than blame."

"But you were so weakened, so beat up. How could they believe you had done it?"

He shrugged. "The files are full of cases of people performing under duress. It won't be investigated fully, anyway. I heard his confession. There's no family or friends to press any charges and the precinct is happy to have the case successfully solved at last."

"I am glad, Mitch, that it turned out well for you."

"There is one thing that bothers me, though." His voice softened and he looked up at me from his seat at the couch. "Why didn't you come to see me in the hospital? I thought you would do at least that for me."

"But I did come, Mitch. The first few times they wouldn't let me in. After that I bypassed the nurses' station and came in after hours." I thought back to those dark nights when I sat by his bed, holding his hand as he tossed and turned in delirium. "You were asleep, but I was there."

He gave me a smile, genuine now. "I knew it. I knew you'd been there, it couldn't have been a dream. But when I asked the nurses they didn't know who you were and swore there had been no visitors. How'd you manage it?"

I gave a little laugh. "You shouldn't have to ask that, Mitch. I managed, that's all."

My confession relieved the tension somewhat. "You could

have come when I was awake, you know. They do have visiting hours at night."

"I know, but I wasn't sure what sort of welcome I might get. After all, you were there, in part, because of what I did to you. I was afraid you might not want to see me."

"Deirdre," he stared at me with his blue eyes, "you're a fool. If you don't realize how I feel by now . . ." He broke off as he again considered my suitcase by the door. "But I guess you don't, since you planned on leaving without a word to me. I guess I've just been wasting my time." He sounded bitter and my heart felt torn.

"I am a fool, Mitch," I said and knelt on the floor in front of him. Reaching up, I took his left hand in mine and held it to my face. "I had no right to get involved with you, and certainly no right to fall in love with you. But I do love you and nothing can change that now. Not my leaving, not your anger."

"Then don't leave," he urged. "Stay here, Deirdre. Marry me. How can I convince you that I don't care who or what you are." He gave me a long, appraising stare then chuckled and reached over and tousled my hair. "I don't even care what you've done to yourself." He grew serious again. "All I care about is being with you. I love you. I don't doubt that you'd like to get away from here. That's fine, we could go together, start a new life for the two of us. Marry me, Deirdre," he repeated urgently. "Say yes."

I sighed and shifted my position slightly so that I could rest my head on his uninjured leg. I gave no answer, no sign of the wavering I felt. Instead, I rubbed my cheek on his knee, considering his words. We could leave together. Another plane ticket could be purchased, another passport obtained. My new home could accommodate two quite easily. I allowed myself to envision a future with Mitch, our lives shared and our loneliness abated. It was a gentle dream and I sighed with the sweetness of it.

"Deirdre," he asked, his voice low and intense, "will you?"

The phone rang and I got up to answer it without a word.

"No, Frank," I said, still gazing at Mitch. "I'm not ready

now. Ask him if he'll wait a while; if not, you can call another." I gently put the phone down.

"My cab is here," I said nervously and dropped my eyes. "I don't know what to say, Mitch."

"That's an easy call," he said, smiling uncertainly. "Just say yes."

I tried to return his smile but began to cry instead. "I can't. It wouldn't work." I saw him through a glaze of tears. "You and I both know that it wouldn't. The first few decades would be wonderful, but after that . . ." I brushed away the tears and continued. "How could I bear to see you grow older every year, knowing that I never would? How could I bear to see you sicken and die and know that I could never join you after death? And how could you endure what I need to do to survive? Your love cannot change what I am: a creature of night, doomed to prowl and hunt for my sustenance." I shook my head and repeated, "It wouldn't work."

"But there's another way," he insisted. "You say that you can't change, but I can. You could change me, turn me into a vampire. Maybe, after the other night, you already have." I read fear in his eyes when he said this, but there was also a trace of hope. "Then the decision would have been reached; it would be out of our hands. You'd marry me then, wouldn't you?"

"Yes, but you must know that's not the case, Mitch." I saw the hope fall from his eyes. "You would need to have my blood to make the change and I won't give it." I crossed the room to him and took his hand again. "You're asking me to give you something that I have always considered a curse. For so many years I searched for the phantom that caused my life; I hunted him as surely as I hunt my prey. And yet now that he is gone," my voice quavered and I groped for the right words, "I thought I might go back to what I was before, when he died. But the change in me was too deep, too long-term; I will always be what I am. Max's death has freed me from many things, and one of these is the hope for a normal life. I have accepted that fact, I can live in that knowledge now. I can even accept the fact that I will meet my final death in the same manner. But I do not want that death to be at your hands."

"Deirdre," he protested, "I would never do that, I love you."

"And I loved Max," I replied. "Not the way I love you, it's true. But for many years he was my only friend, my only contact with what I thought was the human world. And yet I hated him," I blazed into anger. "Hated him enough to kill him. He changed me, in more ways than one; discovering that I was capable of murder, no matter what the circumstances, was terrifying. I can live with that, I have to, but I will not lead you, or anyone else, down the same dark paths I have had to follow." I could read pain in his eyes and the anger suddenly drained out of me. "Mitch," I pleaded with him, hoping he would understand. "I couldn't bear for you to hate me someday like that. Leaving, as hard as it is, and never seeing you again, is easier to bear."

He started to protest again, but I put my hand gently over his mouth. "Do you really want a life like mine? Never to walk in the sun, to exist in the night only. Is that what you want, Mitch?"

He met my eyes with a fervent glance. "I want you, Deirdre. And if this is the only way . . ." He struggled to rise from the couch and when he did he put his arm around me and held me close to him. "Deirdre," he breathed into my hair. "Damn it, I don't know." There was uncertainty in his voice. "I haven't really thought it through, I guess. But the thoughts of losing you have made me half-crazy. I don't know what to do." He moved back to study my face. "Look, promise me you won't say no right now. So much has happened to both of us. Would it hurt to postpone the decision? That would give us both some time to think about it. Could you do that?"

I considered his words, his proposal. Over thirty years ago I would not have hesitated; he was the answer to my dreams at that time. Even with my new-found resolve, the prospect was beguiling. To share my endless years with him. . . . I sighed and he relentlessly pressed his case.

"Give it—oh, let's say—six months," he urged, "or a year at

the most. This would be different than what occurred with you and Max. I would do it willingly, and you could teach me, help me. We would have each other."

"No, Mitch," I began, shaking my head, but his eyes met mine, searching, pleading. I smiled at him finally, reluctantly, and gave in. "Oh hell, Mitch, I have all the time in the world. Six months or sixty, it all means nothing to me. But I will not encourage you in this. The decision will be yours and yours alone. Do you understand?" His eyes lit again with hope; I looked away. "Now I have a plane to catch."

He pulled me to him again in a fierce embrace that made him wince in pain. "Oh, Deirdre," he said, "will you still leave? How can I let you go?"

"With love, Mitch." I kissed him a final time. He stroked my hair and cheek, then slowly began to walk away. "Mitch," I called to him and he turned. "I left something for you. It will be delivered to your apartment tomorrow." I thought of the parcel I had instructed my attorney to give him after my departure. He would appreciate its significance. He looked at me questioningly. "It's the Van Gogh," I explained. "The only sunshine you and I will ever share."

He gave me a quiet smile and I found that I had nothing left to say to him. Instead, I opened the door and watched as he limped down the hall to the elevators. The bell rang, and he got in. As the doors began to close, he stopped them with his hand and stepped out slightly for one last glance. He gave me one of his boyish, exuberant grins. "See you in six months," he said confidently. Then the doors shut and he was gone.

Smiling weakly, I covered my hair with a thick scarf, picked up my bag and turned out the lights. Taking one last look at the rooms, I closed the door. "I hope not, Mitch," I said to the empty hall. "I hope not."

Epilogue

The summer sun sets late in my new home. I have adjusted to the life well, but my internal clock is still set to another time, another place. I shower, dress and go down the stairs. The day's mail lies strewn in front of the slot in the door. I pick it up and glance through it, finding nothing of interest except for a small envelope from that other place. The writing is bold and masculine and my heart jumps at the return address. I have waited for months to receive this letter. I open it with trembling hands. The message is short; I can tell through the folded page that it is no more than three lines. Before reading it I hold it to my heart, not really knowing what I want to find. Then I carefully unfold it; I can delay no longer.

"Deirdre," he writes, "I do love you, but you were right after all. There's no way I could live your life. I hope you can forgive me." He has written nothing else except for his name; what more could he say? A single tear drops on the signature; I wipe it away and his name dissolves to a black blot on the white page. I fold it gently and place it on top of the rest of the mail.

The streets of London are dark and shining. I raise my face to the night sky and let the rain wash away the traces of that one tear. Then, purposefully I begin to walk, my footsteps echoing off the weathered walls surrounding me. Five blocks away is the pub at which I now work. It is a homey little place that serves a decent port, and does a good business in the tourist trade.

Life goes on, I think to myself and quicken my steps. I can hear the laughter, the singing, and as I near the bar, I can smell the scent of blood and flesh. The door swings open and I trade the darkness of the night temporarily for the lights of the pub.

Faces turn to greet me, some familiar, some strange. I make my choice for the evening and give him an encouraging smile as I make my way through the crowd to my position behind the bar. So life goes on.

BITTER BLOOD

Dedicated to Pete with undying love

Acknowledgments

The support network for the Vampire Legacy novels is seemingly endless. Once again, I'll try to mention everyone involved. Thank you to: Cheri, Elise, and John, for their invaluable proofreading, often on short notice; to Paul, whose expertise on cemeteries and the seduction of barmaids was very helpful; to the ladies of the neighborhood (again); to Sherron for her promotional advice, and to my editor, John Scognamiglio, at Zebra Books, and Cherry Weiner, my agent. But the real stars are my family, for their support, their love and understanding. Thank you all.

Chapter 1

I shook the cold rain from my heavy woolen cloak as I entered the pub. That the place was nearly empty was not surprising. Although the sun had been set for nearly half an hour, it was still early, too early, for most of our regulars and certainly too early for the tourists. Two men, hunched over their bitter ale, glanced at me from the bar. To my acknowledging nod, they gave a brief grunt of greeting and returned their full attention to the contents of their mugs.

Idly, I moved behind the bar, still groggy from my nightmare-interrupted sleep. I gave the counter a cursory sweep with the dishcloth, then poured myself a large glass of port. Sipping gratefully, I leaned back into the shadows, my eyes greedily searching the dark street outside for passersby.

Business had been bad recently. And while I did not need the money, I did miss the tourists. The wine helped, but it would not be long before I had to feed, at any cost. The hunger possessed me fully, its grasp stronger, more savage each waking moment, seeming to grow proportionately with the intensity of the dream. Two years ago I had sought freedom from that grip to discover too late that there would be no deliverance for me, only a deeper traveling into the inhuman soul—mine or his, it made little difference.

A light touch on my arm drew me, shuddering, out of my thoughts and back to the present.

"Someone walking on your grave, Dottie?"

I looked up at the ruddy face of my one-time boss, now my partner and smiled slightly. "I imagine so, Pete," I said, reaching below the bar to hand him a crumpled pack of Players. He followed the same routine every night before leaving the pub. He would smoke one cigarette, drink a glass of stout, and count the money in the drawer before making his way home to wife and family.

I poured him a drink and handed it to him as he sat on his stool, counting the day's take. The cigarette dangled from his upper lip, and he squinted up at me through the thick smoke.

"Thank you, darlin'. What did I ever do before you came?"

I laughed. "You lost money, just the same as we do now. How was business today?"

"Could have been better, Dot. But you know how I'm not one for complaining." He shut the cash drawer, stubbed out his cigarette, and reached for his coat on a hook behind the bar. "Now, you, I worry about. Tending this bloody place night after night—it's not right for a young thing like you. Close up early tonight, Dottie, and go out and have some fun. Get some roses back into your cheeks."

I reached over and protectively pulled his lapels up closer to his neck. "Pete, you are a dear, but I really enjoy the nights here, with no crowds, no pressure. And in any event, I don't know anyone here well enough to go out with them."

He gave a brief, angelic smile, but the feigned expression of innocence did not fool me; try as he might, he could not disguise the glint of mischief in his eyes.

"Now, and that reminds me," he started in his slow, matter-of-fact way, "bless me if there wasn't a young chap in here a little earlier, asking after you." He began to rummage through his pockets, absently patting and prodding them. "Seems to me, I wrote his name and number down somewhere. A Yank, did I tell you that? He said he knew you in the States. Awful anxious he was. Now, if only I could find that paper . . ."

I folded my arms and leaned against the bar, waiting for him to complete his act as patiently as was possible. Pete, for all of his sixty-plus years, was more of a child than I had ever been, a lover of surprises and practical jokes. Finally he produced a wrinkled, grubby piece of paper with a flourish, and I held my hand out to receive it.

"Thank you, Pete. Have a nice evening."

"You too, darlin'." With a wink he left, whistling an old music-hall tune as he went through the door.

I shook my head and regarded the paper, folded and lying in my trembling hand. There was only one person who knew my current location. Two years had not been enough time to forget him, or the taste and feel of him, yet those years had merely reinforced my reasons for leaving.

Mitch was better off without me; I had believed it then and I believed it now. I was not the same woman I had been; I was changed and not, I thought, for the good. My desperate strike for freedom had failed. I had not driven away the dark spirit. Instead, by giving him death, I had allowed him entrance to my soul and will. Sometimes in my loneliest times, I held him close, savoring our shared passion and pain. We were one in his death, as we had never been in life—it was his whispering voice I heard during the hunt, his cynical pleasure I felt when I fed.

I did not hear the door open—its cheerful little bell had not announced a customer—but suddenly he was there, leaning across the bar, one eyebrow raised and a sardonic smile on his face. "How lovely you look tonight, my dear. How about a drink for an old friend?"

"Dammit, Max. Get the hell out of here."

His body wavered and shimmered, dissolving instantly into the shape of one of our regulars, very surprised and slightly belligerent. "All I want is a drink, Dot, then I'll leave you alone."

"Oh, God, I'm so sorry. I thought you were someone else." I gave him a bright smile and pushed a glass in his direction. "This one is on the house."

He took the drink and my apology good-naturedly. "Thanks. You don't seem too chipper tonight. You feeling all right?"

"I am fine, thank you. Just a little tired, that's all."

He shrugged and moved away from the bar to sit at a table, joined a few minutes later by a few of his friends. I shoved the note unread into my apron pocket and tended to the business of the pub.

* * *

Later that evening my long wait for tourists finally paid off. A group of six, loud and embarrassingly boisterous, arrived one hour before closing, quickly driving out the regulars. I singled out the likeliest candidate, tall and broad-shouldered, with a bold look in his eyes that caused my body to tighten in anticipation. I smiled at him as I took their orders and served their drinks, offering him a glass of port. When he questioned me, I leaned close to him. "For later," I whispered, "for endurance." He drank it in one gulp, shuddering slightly at its bitterness, and immediately asked for another.

"He's ours now, my little one," the cynical voice in my mind prodded. "Don't wait too long."

I did not. So desperate was I for this man that I issued last call almost immediately. My invitation to him to stay and help close up was met with unabashed approval from his friends, and soon we were alone.

I locked the door, dimmed the lights, and walked back across the room. He joined me behind the bar as I was counting the money in the register. "Aren't you afraid I might steal that?" he questioned with a crooked smile as he helped himself to another glass of port.

I laughed, low and sensually, as I put the night's profits in the safe. "There's not enough here to even be tempting." I gave him a warm, appraising glance. "And somehow I don't think that you're interested in my money."

"You sure are right about that, babe." He crossed over to me and put an arm around my waist. "When you're finished here, let's go back to my place." He mentioned the name of his hotel and I nodded my agreement, leaning closer to him.

His grip tightened. "I don't think I caught your name . . ."

"Dorothy . . . ah, just Dorothy. And yours?"

"Oh, I get it. No last names, right? Then I'm Robert, Robbie to my friends."

"It's wonderful to meet you, Robbie. You'll never know how much."

"But I'll bet I can guess." He pulled me closer and kissed me; my teeth grazed his lip, drawing one intoxicating drop of blood.

I savored it and probed with my tongue for more. My hands were wrapped about his waist. I slid my nails slowly up his spine and he shivered, took his mouth away from mine, and looked down at me.

"God." He was breathing heavily, and small beads of sweat appeared on his brow. "You really want this bad, don't you?"

I moaned in answer, and his face grew fierce, full of passion. His hands grasped my waist and he lifted me onto the narrow counter behind the bar, pushing against me forcefully and insistently until I encircled his body with my legs.

He kissed me again and slid his hand down the back of my jeans, kneading the flesh of my lower back. His skin was so warm, so alive. I had to have him now.

"Wait," the voice inside urged. "Let's play a little first."

"I don't want to wait," I protested aloud, and reached up to loosen his tie and unbutton his shirt.

"Neither do I." He lifted my sweater over my head and threw it on the floor. While he nuzzled my breasts, he struggled unsuccessfully to untie my apron. With an exasperated sigh he spun it around on my waist and began to unfasten my jeans. I pulled his shirt off and he ground his groin into mine. Putting my tongue to his skin, I traced a delicate path to his neck and gently nibbled there while he eased my pants down around my knees.

There was a pounding in my head and my gums tingled, signaling the growth of my canines. I was ready; it had been too long, entirely too long. The pounding increased, louder and more demanding.

Abruptly, he pulled away; I lost my balance and lurched up against him.

"What was that?" His voice was angry, suspicious.

"Nothing," I purred, wrapping my arms tightly around his neck. "Come back to me, make love to me."

"No way," he said, wresting himself away from me and putting his clothing back into order. "There's someone at the door."

"They'll go away. I need you, Robbie."

"Forget it."

I was trembling with my unsatisfied need. Quickly I fastened my jeans, put my sweater back on, and walked over to him, where he was putting on his coat. Gently, I laid my hand on his arm and rubbed my head on his sleeve. "Robbie, please, what's wrong? We can go somewhere else if you like, please . . . you can't leave me like this."

The knocking at the door continued, more urgent now.

"Nothing doing, babe. I've heard about this scam before. How much would it have taken to pay off that guy out there—the witness to your 'rape'—five hundred, maybe an even thousand? No thanks, you may be the sexiest bitch I've seen in this country, but you're still too rich for my blood." He pushed me away from him and opened the door. "She's all yours, pal," he said to the figure standing hesitantly in the doorway. "I barely touched her."

"Damn," I swore under my breath as the door slammed. The little bell jangled, discordant in my ears. I rubbed my hands along my jeans. "Well?" I addressed the man whose shadowed face was unrecognizable, even to me. "This had better be damned important."

"Deirdre?" The voice sounded embarrassed, and vaguely familiar. "What was that all about?" He stepped forward into the dim light of the room.

Instantly, I knew who he was—the mysterious Yank visitor that Pete had told me about, whose name and number were on a crumpled piece of paper in my apron pocket. And it was not Mitch. Disappointed at that realization, I understood that my dread at meeting him again would have been overruled by my strong desire to see him, hold him, make love to him one more time.

"Hello, Chris," I said to the man who had inherited Mitch's features and build. He had aged in two years, I thought; lines of worry creased his face and he looked like he hadn't slept in weeks.

"Deirdre, it is you, isn't it? I barely recognize you."

"Yes, it is I, in the flesh," I said with no trace of a smile. Were my changes so apparent, even in the darkness? My hair was still almost black, but I had let it grow to its original length. That could not have made much of a difference to him. And although I had not aged, I knew that my mirror revealed me to be harder, coarser, debased somehow by my inhuman instincts.

"Your eyes look funny, they're . . . well, they're almost glowing." I could hear fear in his voice, a reluctance that had never been there before.

"Don't be silly, Chris. The light in here is deceptive." I reached over and turned on one of the switches behind the bar. "There now," I said reassuringly, squinting slightly against the glare, "is that better?"

"Yeah, I guess so." He paused for a moment, and when he continued, his tone was slightly sullen. "I hope I didn't interrupt something important. That guy sure shot out of here like a bullet. And do you always wear your apron backward?"

I reached down to my waist, twitching the apron around to its proper position, but ignored the unspoken questions about Robbie's presence. "Would you like a drink? On the house, of course." I smiled at him, but he refused to meet my eyes.

"Sure, why not? I'll have a beer."

I motioned him to a table. "Sit down," I said, opening two bottles of beer from the refrigerator, "and I'll join you."

He watched me intently as I walked out from behind the bar and sat down next to him. Without a word he took the bottle from me and drank, quickly and furtively, as if to fortify himself against some dire event. His hands, I noticed with surprise, were shaking. But then, so were mine.

"Now, maybe you would like to tell me how you came to be here and how you knew where to find me. Did your father send you?" The emotion I tried to disguise in my voice was not just frustration over the interrupted feeding.

"No." His voice sounded choked, overhung with anger and grief. "No, he didn't send me. But I found your address while I was sorting through his papers and knew that I should come to see you . . ."

My heart sank. He was dead. I could feel it. I could see it in Chris's face. Jesus, I wailed inside, Mitch is dead. He died and I could have stopped it, but I didn't. I had the power to keep him with me forever, and I did nothing.

"Mitch is dead." My voice, flat and toneless, did nothing to express the despair that the stating of those words caused.

"Oh, no," Chris was quick to protest. "It's not that, honest. It's just that, well, he's bad off, Deirdre. I don't know what's wrong, nobody does. But I think he's dying." He took one more drink of his beer, then set the bottle back on the table softly. His eyes finally held mine and his voice, so much like Mitch's, fell gently on my ears.

"And I think that only you can save him. You must save him, Deirdre. Come back to him."

Chapter 2

"So"—I motioned Chris to a seat on the dark-patterned sofa in what I once would have called my parlor—"what exactly is wrong with him?"

My voice wavered on the last word, and he looked up at me with a start. He had been occupied in studying the room; I could almost see it through his eyes. The furnishings were pleasant enough, though somber in tone—the room large and well-proportioned, the windows draped in heavy burgundy velvet. But the room itself was impersonal, no photographs or mementoes were displayed, as if its inhabitant had no life. It was a cold room, silent and dreary, like the rest of the house, with the feel, if not the actual appearance, of emptiness and decay. A fitting residence for one of my kind, I thought, but gave him a small, forced laugh.

"Pretty dreary, isn't it?"

He shrugged. "No, it's very nice, really. Just not what I imagined." Chris still seemed uncomfortable with me or with his mission, I couldn't tell which. Perhaps it was just embarrassment at meeting his father's lover after two years, at being alone with me, in this house, lacking Mitch's presence.

I did the best I could to make him feel at home. "You know, Chris, I hurried you out of the bar and over here without giving you a chance for another drink, or maybe a meal. Are you hungry?"

He gave me a quick smile, reminiscent of the younger man I knew. "Yeah, you know me, always hungry. How about you—"

He stopped abruptly and the smile dropped from his face, replaced by a painful grimace.

I covered his embarrassment. "I haven't been shopping for food in several days, but I could probably find something . . ."

"Deirdre, you don't have to do this."

"But you're my guest; I want to make you comfortable."

"No, I mean you don't have to lie to me, pretend to be something you aren't." He look at me then, and the knowledge of what I was seemed to reflect in his eyes.

I took a few steps back, retreating closer to the doorway, not wanting to threaten him in any way. "So, he told you. And made you believe it."

He jumped up from the couch, his hands clenched. "Yes, I believed it. I had to believe it. It's true, isn't it?"

"Yes, Chris, unfortunately, it is all true. But I fail to see how any of this will help your father. You say he is dying; can you tell me why?"

"Dammit, Deirdre, don't you understand?" He screamed his anger at me, and I withdrew from him further. "I already told you, no one knows what's wrong. If anyone knew why, they would stop it." Suddenly his anger was replaced with sadness; he sat back down on the couch with a flop and lowered his voice. "Shit, the last time I saw him, he didn't even know who I was. Just sat there in the crazy ward, humming some old song, in his damned institutional pajamas, his damned institutional slippers. He won't even talk about it anymore; it's like he's already given up, already let them devour him, from the inside out."

"Who?"

He gave me a cool, intent stare so like his father's, I wanted to cry.

"The ones like you, of course. The other *vampires.*"

He fell silent and rested his head in his hands, rubbing his eyelids. When he finally looked up at me, his face was flushed. He had said the word with such vehemence that it seemed an obscenity echoing in the room. Perhaps it was obscene to him; it was to me. I stood within the doorway and regarded him solemnly.

"There are no others like me. There was only Max, and he's dead." Even as I said it, my voice wavered and the doubts I had felt over the past two years began to reassert themselves. Was Max really dead or had he somehow survived? The thought was absurd. I knew he had died; he had died by my hand. Had I not felt his life drain from him, slowly and painfully? His presence in my current existence was spiritual only. My dreams and visions of him were merely mental aberrations, a guilty conscience, my own self-induced punishment for his murder.

Tense and nervous, I gripped the doorframe, my nails gouging out pieces of the woodwork. "No," I said now with more conviction. "Max is dead and buried. He can't be the cause."

Chris wasn't listening to me, wrapped up as he was in his own thoughts. "Dad used to visit his grave, did you know that?" He gave me no time to respond, but continued bitterly. "But how could you know? You very conveniently disappeared off the face of the earth. Oh, I know why you did it." He gave me a quelling look to forestall the protest I had begun to make. "Even Dad said he understood your feelings. I guess you can justify anything if you try hard enough."

He paused as a distracted look entered his eyes and a sad smile of reminiscence crossed his face. "He used to go there every day and read the tombstone you so generously provided. He even made sure that your daily gift of roses was received.

Dad always said that as long as those kept coming, he knew you were still alive and might come back someday."

I edged slowly into the room and sat down in a chair facing him. He barely noticed my presence. Nervously, I plunged a hand into my apron pocket, came upon the half-smoked pack of cigarettes, and lit one without thinking, simply to give my trembling hands something to do. Chris looked over at me, and his small smile disappeared.

"All those roses for that dead son of a bitch, and nothing for my father, not even a letter or a call. He loved you, Deirdre, loved you more than you'll ever know or deserve, and you gave him nothing."

Nothing. I sat and considered his words as I smoked my cigarette. How simple the situation must seem to him from his perspective of youth. Reality was much more complicated than Chris wanted to see; the moral and ethical reasons that drove me to this country, the decisions of life, death, and immortality were more important than my petty loves.

"Love be damned." Max's voice rang inside my head. "We're hungry. Take him," the seductive tones urged. "He's young, healthy, and would make excellent sport. His blood is rich, his skin tender. We must feed now."

I crushed out my cigarette and stood up, moving slowly toward Chris. He raised his eyes to mine, and was caught in my gaze. I walked over to him, gripped his shirt-sleeves, and pulled him off the couch. We were so close that I could see the throbbing of the veins in his throat, smell the salty odor of his sweat and blood.

"Yes," the voice hissed. "*Yes.*"

His eyes began to glaze over. "Chris"—the whispered words seemed to force themselves from my throat as I reached one hand up to stroke his cheek—"did your father not warn you of vampires? Or are all Greers born idiots, thinking to tame the supernatural with their talk of love? It didn't work with your father and it will not work for you. And you, my dear boy, will pay the penalty he owes me."

That dark voice, echoing in this room, startled me. Did I

speak the words? I couldn't tell from Chris's appearance, for although his eyes were opened wide in terror, his gaze was uncomprehending. His fright could easily be due to my proximity or his contact with the inhumanity of my stare, which suspended him—a prisoner to my hunger. With an extreme effort of will I drew my eyes away from him and closed them tightly, to seal the death and corruption inside.

As his labored breathing began to return to normal, I stood, blind and swaying, still holding on to his shirt. Finally I eased my eyes open and caught his bewildered stare. "No," I said, shaking my head, my voice muffled slightly by the growth of my teeth. "No, I will not."

I released him, and moving to the window, pulled open the heavy draperies. Just a glimpse of the dark night streets helped to soothe my nerves and calm my internal tremors. I knew then that it was not just Mitch who was being devoured from within. Perhaps with my return, we could both be healed.

"Deirdre?" He sounded hesitant and confused, obviously with no memory of what had just occurred. "What's wrong?"

I pressed my hands against the cool glass and sighed. "Nothing, Chris. Do you have a return ticket?"

His answering nod was reflected in the window; I turned around and gave him a weak smile. "Cash it in. I'll make arrangements for us both."

"Then you'll come back? You'll help Dad?" The sadness that had haunted him all evening was replaced suddenly by a look of hope, of happiness.

I wished fervently that I could capture some of his youthful optimism. "Yes," I said deliberately, "although I can't promise that I'll be able to help or cure him. But I will come back."

I was not sufficiently recovered or prepared for his headlong rush across the room and his exuberant embrace. "Thank you," he said into my ear. "Thank you."

I took a deep breath and held it, then pushed him away from me, so quickly that he stumbled, grasping the top of a chair for support.

"Never, never do that again," I spat out at him through my bared teeth.

His eyes widened at the sight of my canines, and he paled. "I'm sorry . . . I didn't think . . ."

"You had better start thinking." My voice was harsher than I intended, and he cringed. "You interrupted my feeding tonight and I'm hungry, very hungry. You must understand who you have recruited for your cause. I am not an angel of mercy, but an angel of death. Don't forget that, ever."

He nodded and looked at me helplessly. "What should I do?"

"Tonight, go back to your hotel room and lock your door. Get a good night's sleep and call me tomorrow at sunset. We'll make our plans then."

He walked to the door, removed his coat from the rack, and put it on. The dejected slope of his shoulders wrung my heart. I hadn't meant to be so hard on him.

"Chris," I called softly, and he turned to me. "I didn't intend to frighten you. You're safe as long as you keep your distance." I smiled again, and he relaxed at the disappearance of my fangs. "Sleep well."

I allowed myself ten minutes before I followed him out onto the street. At this hour most of the bars and restaurants that I normally frequented would be closed, but it was imperative that I feed now. When I thought how close I had come to taking Chris, not once, but twice, I knew that I had to find someone quickly. Fortunately, I knew exactly where to go.

The hotel lobby door was unlocked; I slid past the sleeping clerk and consulted the guest register. I avoided the elevator, taking the stairs instead. Once outside his door, I stopped and listened carefully. He was in there, sleeping and alone. I knocked on the door tentatively, then louder, until his slightly drunken voice rasped out. "Who's there?"

"Room service," I called seductively. "Open the door."

I heard his cursing, the rustling of bedclothes, and the click of a light switch. He opened the door a mere crack, but wide enough for me to insert my hand and push it open. "What the hell?" He was wrapped in a towel, his hair falling slightly over his forehead, his eyes still unfocused.

"Room service, Robbie." I moved closer to him and shut the door behind me. "I want you," I whispered, "and there are no witnesses here. No scam, no rape. Just you and me. How about it?"

His eyes, confused at first, lit in recognition. He'd had quite a bit more to drink since he left me; I could smell it, heavy on his breath. His inhibitions were gone, and a broad smile crossed his face as he dropped his towel. "Sure, babe, come on in."

"I already am in," I said, leading him to the bed.

"So you are," he began, but I pushed him down, violently. "Hey," he protested, "that hurt."

"I don't want to hurt you, Robbie. Just lie still and I'll give you an evening you'll never forget." I straddled him, and he raised his hands and joined them behind his head.

"I'll bet you will." He was with me now, ready, and watched with a lazy smile as I removed my clothes. He reached for me. "Not yet," I warned, and turned out the light.

He shifted under me, and rolled me over, resting his weight on his arms. I could see his smile gleam in the near darkness.

"Now?"

"Now."

He entered me abruptly and I gasped, startled at his suddenness. But it didn't matter; I hadn't sought him out for the satisfaction of sex; I had come for his blood.

"Is it good?" he asked, his breath warming my ear.

"Good," I purred through my clenched teeth, "but I know how to make it better." Growling, I pierced the surface of his neck, and his blood flooded into my mouth and throat, spreading its rejuvenating warmth. Greedily, I drew in that precious liquid and he groaned, the pain of my bite overridden by his passion. I drank, overwhelmed as always by the miracle of stolen life, almost unaware of his continued frantic thrusts, his incoherent grunts, until he reached his climax, silently shuddering.

I continued to pull on him, long past satisfaction, for the

mouth that drank was not entirely my own. Two hungers were being fed, one much darker and deeper than mine. The pulse of my victim slowed, the naked flesh bearing down on mine grew flaccid and unresisting. With alarm I felt his heartbeat falter, I forced my mouth away from his neck, rolled him over, and switched on the light.

He was so pale, so lifeless. Even as I told myself that I had gone too far, I heard the insatiable laughter in my mind.

"That was good, my love. But why stop so soon? He's strong; there is more to be had."

"Any more and he would be dead." The disgust in my voice was not directed at Max alone. If this man died, I would be the one left with the blame. Brushing my hair back, I laid my head on his chest. To my relief, his heart was still beating; he was young and would probably be strong enough to live.

I sat up and slapped Robbie's face, none too gently; his head bobbed back and forth on the pillow. Finally he sighed, opened his eyes, and looked at me.

"Don't go," he said weakly. "That was wonderful. As soon as I get my strength back, we could do it again."

I looked down at him in loathing. The entire situation was pitiful, and the fact that he was begging for more, ludicrous. I wanted to laugh, but the sound that escaped my lips was more of a choked sob. I brushed my bloody tears away and began to get dressed.

When I was fully clothed I sat next to him and took his head into my hands, relieved to see a natural color returning to his skin. The glance he gave me seemed aware and alive.

"I'm feeling better now. Let's do it again." His voice had regained some of its strength and I felt reassured as I met his eyes.

"We can't do it again, Robbie. We never did it at all. You see, it was all a dream."

"A dream?" he repeated stupidly.

"Yes, it was just a dream, and tomorrow you won't remember it or me. Do you understand? You don't know me; you've never met me. I'm just a dream."

"Just a dream."

He was asleep before I closed the door. I hoped that the suggestion would take hold, but it really made no difference. Tomorrow night at this time Chris and I would be out of the country. Soon I would be with Mitch.

Tears began flowing again as I took to the streets. I hurried through the night, wrapping my cloak tighter around a body that never felt the cold, in the futile attempt to warm the soul within.

Chapter 3

I didn't turn on the lights when I arrived at my house; instead, I locked the door and climbed the stairs, dropping my clothing as I went. In the shower, I set the water at its hottest and attempted to purge my mind and body of all their contacts that evening: the remains of sex and the taking of blood, the tears, the thoughts of Mitch and love.

The room filled with a billowy steam, obscuring the pale moonlight. I watched it curl and dance, tried to imagine what it would be like to merge with the mist, to transform myself as legend said I could. Before he died, Max had hinted of powers as yet undeveloped and undiscovered within me, beyond human understanding. But in the past two years I had made no attempt to cultivate these mysterious powers; the thought of abandoning what little humanity I had for the unknown terrified me absolutely.

The idea entered my mind that now might be the time to experiment, in an attempt to reach my true powers. But as I ran hands over my naked, tangible flesh, feeling the familiar curves of breasts and thighs, I denied the seduction of those thoughts, taking comfort in what I still had. This body, although corrupted by its appetites, was untouched by age and death; I would fight to keep it as it was; it was all I had left of my lost human life.

"And so you deny your birthright and refuse my gift." From out of the mist he came to me, his white, undead flesh glistening with drops of moisture. His face was tender, almost loving, and he reached his arms out to me, forgiving, pleading.

"Oh, Max." I gasped the words. "I'm so sorry. I didn't want to kill you, but you gave me no choice."

He smiled at me, the pointed tips of his canines showing briefly, his hard, muscular body gleaming through the steam. His left side bore a scar, presumably unknown for one of our kind, a small, jagged cut marring the perfection of his skin.

A part of me wanted to touch him, feel the tissue that had somehow formed over his death wound, but instead I backed away from him, putting my hands up in denial. "You gave me no choice," I repeated, my justification sounding hollow even to me.

He threw his head back and laughed, as if his death were of no importance. "I know, little one." His voice was steady and smooth, reassuring. "I asked too much of you; it was too hard a test. Just come to me now and I'll make it right for you."

I took a step in his direction and he caught me in his arms. His eyes glinted in the mist, revealing his true intentions. His mouth came down on my neck and with his bite he infused me with the chill of death and of the grave. I felt the heat of my body flow into him; his every touch burned my skin with an intense cold. Crying out in pain, I slumped against the shower wall, feebly pushing him away as I slid down into the tub.

When I opened my eyes, he was gone and the water had run cold. "Damn," I swore, shivering as I stood up and turned off the tap. I wrapped myself in a large towel, went into my bedroom, and lit the fire laid in the hearth.

The flames soon gave the room an appearance of warmth and normalcy, but still I sat, shaking and trembling with the spiritual cold he had inflicted upon me. Tonight had been one of the strangest I had spent since Max had died. True, I was accustomed to his presence in my mind, had come to expect his appearance during the hunt and my feedings. But he had never seemed so real before, so alive. And he had never touched me, except in dreams, nor had he attempted to touch the living through me. Was the arrival of Chris the catalyst, the final event that unbalanced my mind? Would I eventually go mad, out of control, to be hunted down and killed like a rabid animal? I felt sane, but no doubt so did a thousand others who justified their actions by the authority of the voices in their minds.

"Damn you, Max," I said aloud. "You're supposed to be dead. Why don't you act it?"

There was no answer; my phantom chose his own time. I laughed at my own fancy; I knew Max was dead. I did not believe in ghosts and I did not truly believe that he had taken possession of me. I thought myself to be a rational, relatively modern creature, however ridiculous that seemed, and knew that there must be a rational explanation. Both for me and for Mitch.

"Mitch," I whispered, "I'll be there soon." I sat staring at the flames, and the thoughts of him calmed me and the unnatural chill finally subsided.

Relaxed, stretching my body before the fire, I did something I had not allowed myself to do for two years. I called his features to mind, his intensely blue eyes, his hawklike nose, the small wrinkles that formed on his face when he smiled. I remembered his hands, their strength and slightly rough texture, molding themselves into my cool skin; his body, scarred but beautiful, lying warm and alive next to mine. I could taste him now, his flesh and blood, hear his voice in love and in anger. Why did I ever leave him? And when I returned, would I have the strength to leave again?

"Damn," I swore again, and went to the window. I could sense the approaching dawn, and knew that I must sleep. From force of habit I pulled the blinds down, closed the heavy drapes, and climbed into bed, wrapping the covers around me. The warmth of my rejuvenating body enclosed me, and I focused entirely on the life and vibrancy now coursing through my veins. Oblivion came quickly, and I slept.

* * *

The cemetery gates swing open soundlessly. The gravel paths pull me forward and I follow as if in a trance, allowing them to lead me to the grave that I long, and dread, to find. In my tightly clenched fist I hold a rose, his rose; the thorns drive themselves deeply into the flesh of my palm. My blood, so long ago violated and invaded, contaminated beyond redemption, drips onto the earth, blackening its once-pure surface.

There is no need to call his name; the blood calls for me, drawing him up close enough to draw me down. The moist smell of rotting flesh assails my senses, so much death and corruption surrounds me. I open my mouth to scream, but it fills with the soil of his grave and I drop deeper into his domain, helpless in the power of his grasp.

Suddenly my limbs are free, and I am cleansed from the stench of the grave. I hover, disembodied, in a clear, starlit sky over an expansive field. It smells green and young and beautiful, and I inhale its fragrance deeply.

But I am not alone. Above me hangs another shape, darker and more defined. It swoops; I struggle to avoid it before it merges with my soul. Too late, the shock of penetration overcomes me and we are one. I am forced to see through his eyes; his voice, my voice, speaks words of reassurance.

"Do not fight me, my love," it advises. "It will be made right."

Far below, unaware of our approach, lies a body reveling in the warm spring night. She is naked but unashamed, and like the aroma of the field, she is young, beautiful, and wholly desirable. We circle above her, then descend with the currents of the wind, slowly spiraling down, until she senses our nearness and opens her eyes.

She smiles and opens her arms to us. I want to warn her, to call to her to run and hide, but the lightning shock of recognition makes it impossible for me to speak.

"But see," his voice urges. "See how it was for me."

And I am in his mind; I see how I was, for it is my human self who lies before us on the altar of our hunger. She draws me to her and I want to take her for myself. She is so young, so alive, and her knowledge of that life is childlike and pure. Oh, how I long for that innocence again, and so I claim her. And in that claiming, that rape of myself, the innocence is lost.

Her tears are mine as I break through the surface of the grave and lie panting, sobbing, on the violated earth.

When I awoke the next afternoon it was shortly before sunset. I shook my mind clear of the dream images; already vague and fading, they left only a faint residue of sorrow and bitterness. With a sigh I turned myself to the tasks ahead of me.

I remained in bed and phoned the airport, reserving two one-way tickets on the next flight back to America. The departure and arrival times were perfectly timed. On my previous trip I had been forced to take a private jet to avoid any touch of sunlight; on my return, it seemed, the night would fly with me. Even with unexpected delays, we should still arrive in the evening hours, allowing me ample time to find a secure daytime resting place. I wondered with a fleeting smile if my old suite of rooms would still be available.

When the travel arrangements were made, I got up from bed and went to my closet. Most of my clothing was unsuitable for this trip, designed as it was for the seduction and capture of my unsuspecting victims. It was always my habit to start each segment of my life with a new identity; everything from my existence as Deirdre Griffin had been discarded, traded in for clothing to fit my new persona. Finally, I removed two pairs of jeans and a few loose-fitting sweaters and threw them onto the bed, along with my pairs of contact lenses and the few personal items that were always with me: several old books, some letters, and, a relatively new acquisition, the scrapbook detailing my life compiled by Larry Martin. I did not look through the book, but placed it on the bottom of the suitcase, shuddering at my remembrance of our final confrontation.

Poor, maddened Larry, who in reaching out for immortality, demanding vampire's blood at the cost of my life and his sanity, had ended his life with Mitch's bullet through his heart. I had not escaped unscathed: the shot had gone straight through

Larry and grazed my shoulder. He had died, pinioning me to the floor with his body, his blood staining my clothes and skin. My physical wound had healed quickly, but for some reason his death still haunted me. Not as much as Max's did; still, I knew that I shared the responsibility of guilt, perhaps even carried the largest portion. Larry would never have lost control of his emotions or his mind but for me. I led him along the path to his death as surely as if I had pulled the trigger myself.

Yet, I thought, rationalizing the event once more, had he lived, I would now be dead. Mitch's arrival had saved my life, and now I would attempt to do the same for him.

Covering the book with my clothing, I closed and locked the suitcase, then dressed. When I checked my image in the mirror, I laughed softly to myself. If Deirdre had any friends remaining, they would hardly recognize her in this outfit: black leather miniskirt, black knee-high boots, and black lace hose. And although the effect was softened slightly with a pale peach angora sweater, I doubted that my fashion-designer acquaintances would approve. But Mitch might, I thought with a mischievous grin as I surveyed the view of my body from the back.

If, my mind cautioned, he could be healed; if he could be returned to his former self; if he wanted me back in his life. I only had Chris's word on the endurance of his love; there had been no contact between us since the day I received his letter telling me he could not accept the conditions of my life. And although I fully understood his decision, knew it had been his only logical choice, my feelings for him remained unchanged. Even after two years of trading my body for sustenance from strangers, I still felt his blood in my veins, calling to me, crying for his presence.

I jumped nervously when the phone rang, then picked it up.

"Wake-up call." Chris's voice sounded cheerful and normal.

"Hello, Chris. Pack your bags, we leave at nine tonight."

"Great. Somehow, I knew you'd help. He'll get better, you'll see. Just having you there should make a huge difference to him. He's missed you so much."

"Well," I said noncommittally, "I suppose we will see about

that soon. Just meet me at the pub around seven; we can leave from there. I have a little business to conclude."

After hanging up with Chris, I neatened the bedroom and bath and went downstairs, gathering, as I descended, the clothes I had discarded on the stairs last night. Rolling them all into a ball, I threw them into the front closet, found my cloak, and wrapped it about my shoulders. After checking to see that the back door and the windows were locked and secure, I put the one extra front-door key into my pocket, picked up my suitcase, and went out onto the street. I looked back at the dark house for just one moment, wondering if I would ever return. This place had never seemed like home to me; I could leave it with no regrets, no memories. It had been nothing more than a stop-over—a rest from my travels.

When I arrived at the pub, Pete and several of our regulars were playing darts. He looked up at me, and the smile on his face faded slightly when he saw my suitcase. He left the game and came over to me.

"Going away, Dottie?"

"I'm afraid so, Pete. You see, that young man who stopped by yesterday is Mitch's son."

He nodded knowingly; he had no idea of what my life had been before I had arrived at his door in response to his advertisement for a barmaid, but I had mentioned Mitch and our attachment.

"So he wants you back. Not that I blame him, he should have sent for you a long time ago. He's a lucky fool, this Mitch of yours." He picked up my suitcase and set it behind the bar. "And when do you leave?"

"Tonight." I shrugged off my cloak and hung it on the hook, replacing it with an apron. "You see, it's an emergency and too complicated to explain right now, but when I get back, you can have the whole story."

He returned my smile. "I'll hold you to that, darlin'. And what am I to do while you're gone? Where could I find as good a partner or as juicy a barmaid as you?"

"I'm sorry, Pete," I began, but he laughed and gave me a fatherly pat on my behind.

"Now don't you worry one minute over what I'll be doing. Sure and I'll miss you, but I'll manage fine. As long as you don't want to cash in your half of the business."

I matched his lighthearted tone as I opened the cash drawer and looked at the small amount of money it contained. "What, and miss out on all this profit? No, Pete, you will not get rid of me that easily."

"Good, then you can return to your Mitch with my blessings. But you be sure to tell him now that I said he should make an honest woman out of you."

I reached over and gave him a small hug. "I don't think there's much of a chance of that, but thank you for saying it." I handed him the extra front-door key. "Look after my place while I'm gone."

He nodded and turned his back to me for a minute, busying himself at the bar. When he turned around his eyes were slightly wet and he held up a full glass of stout for a toast. "Listen, boys," Pete's voice echoed in the nearly empty room, "our little Dottie's going away." His announcement was met with laughter from the customers. We hadn't made any attempt to keep our conversation, so they had overheard every word. Still, it was just like Pete to make this an occasion for celebration. "Drinks on the house."

By seven o'clock the party was getting out of hand. Pete was leading the growing crowd in a second rendition of "Knees Up, Mother Brown" when Chris entered. The bell on the door clanged in a tone of finality, and the singing stopped. I introduced Chris and made my good-byes quietly, with a word for each of the regulars and a long kiss for Pete that caused them all to hoot and applaud. With a courtliness that belonged to another age, he solemnly consigned my suitcase to the waiting cabbie, and clapped Chris on the shoulder.

"Take care of our Dorothy, young man. And Dottie, you come back soon, darlin'."

I hugged him one more time and got into the cab. Chris moved around to the other side and slammed his door. As we drove off, I turned and gave Pete a final wave, watching until he went back inside, then settled into my seat and sighed.

"Deirdre"—Chris reached over and lightly, tentatively, touched my arm—"are you okay?"

I looked at his young, eager face and felt a poignant wave of sadness. "Over a hundred years of good-byes—you'd think I would be used to it by now. But every time it hurts."

"Oh."

The cabbie gave a small chuckle. "If you're a hundred years old, lady, then I'm the Prince of Wales. The airport, right?"

"That's right, Charlie," I said with a forced cheerfulness. "We need to make a nine o'clock flight."

Three hours into the flight, when most of the passengers were asleep, I became aware that Chris was watching me, the window reflecting a thoughtful expression on his face. We had eaten dinner—rare prime rib for me, seafood for him—and drunk numerous glasses of wine; our conversation had been commonplace, merely a relating of personal events happening over the past two years. We both avoided the mention of Mitch, or the plans we should be making for our return. After our meal he had occupied himself with magazines and a paperback detective novel, a taste he and his father shared, I noted with a small smile. And I had watched out the window, thinking of nothing but the clear black sky and the clouds below us, billowing and curling.

I turned away from the night and smiled at him. "It is a beautiful night for flying, don't you think?"

He nodded. "Yeah, but planes always make me a little nervous. How about you?"

"Nervous? No, I feel perfectly at home right now." I spoke mostly to put him at ease, but realized as I said it that it was true. The overhead lights were dimmed, with only a few reading lights to illuminate the darkness. Well fed and rejuvenated, my body was satisfied, and my mind content to contemplate nothing but the warmth of the cabin, the faint human scent of the passengers, and the night sky outside. "I could fly like this forever."

"Well," Chris said with a wry, almost bitter smile, "I'm glad someone is enjoying themselves."

"Chris, I'm as worried as you about Mitch."

He looked down at the book on his lap, folded down the corner of a page to mark his place, and slid it into his coat pocket. "Deirdre, we need to talk about this before we land. There are things you need to know."

"Fine, Chris, go ahead."

He threw me a doubtful look and glanced around the plane. The passengers nearest us were sleeping, but he lowered his voice to a near whisper anyway. "I know you insist that there are no other vampires, just you and Max, but you must know that's impossible. There have to be others."

"I don't deny their existence, Chris. Of course I know that somewhere there must be others. I just can't see that they would have any relevance to Mitch or me."

"That's exactly what Dad thought—until they began coming to him at night, tormenting him, deviling him." His eyes darted restlessly before returning to me. "I, well, I don't quite know how to say this without it sounding callous or hard. I don't really mean it that way, honest, But that's why Dad didn't contact you himself; he was determined to take it on, to keep it from you so that you wouldn't be involved in any way."

"Involved in what, Chris?"

He clenched his fists, and his voice grew louder. "But you are involved, aren't you? And in taking the responsibility for your actions, my father is being punished. It's your place, Deirdre; you're the one they want. So, I came to get you, hoping that you would still have enough humanity to respond."

"And I did, it would appear." I reached over and laid my hand on his trembling arm. "I'll help all I can, you know that."

"Yeah," he said, shrinking away from my hand, "and that only makes it worse, somehow. You see, I haven't really brought you back to just save Dad. The others, they want the one who killed Max, and right now they think it's Dad. But when you arrive, I don't see how even you can hide your involvement." Chris looked at me, his eyes shining with unshed tears, his face showing fear and guilt. "Oh, God, I'm sorry. They want you dead, Deirdre, and I've brought you to them."

Chapter 4

I began to laugh, softly at first, then louder, with only a small trace of hysteria. Chris looked at me in disbelief, and a stewardess rushed to our seats.

"Miss, ah, Grey"—she consulted her passenger listing—"we'll be landing in less than three hours. Would you like another drink? Or maybe a pillow or blanket? Most of our passengers find that resting is a good way to pass the time."

"I understand," I said, still choked with laughter. "I am sorry, and yes, I would like another glass of wine. Thank you for asking."

Her arched brows told me she thought I had already had enough, but she dutifully fetched my drink. After she left I took one long sip and, sufficiently calmed, turned to Chris. The expression on his face had changed from guilt to embarrassment. I smiled in my most reassuring manner, but he relaxed only slightly.

"Look, Chris, I think it is very sweet of you to be concerned about me, but I can take care of myself. And if I can't"—I shrugged—"well, I'll deal with that if it happens." I turned my face to the window again. "It wouldn't be that great a loss, after all."

He wasn't meant to hear my last words, but his ears were sharper than I thought.

"How can you say that? Doesn't your life mean anything to you at all?"

"Chris," I sighed, forcing my gaze away from the night sky, "I'm old and tired. I have led an interesting life, if you can call it that. I've lived through three major wars, and more historical events than you can remember. Everyone I have ever known or loved has died or will die, while I go on virtually forever. And what sort of legacy do I leave? A few dresses on a rack somewhere, a couple of pages in some lousy scrapbook, or maybe just a hazy memory locked inside the head of some man I met in a bar, someone I subsequently and cold-heartedly drained of a portion of his blood so that I could live?" I shook my head slightly. "No, Chris, it would not be that great a loss."

"But what about Dad?" His tone of voice was indignant and belligerent, his expression and question displaying such a youthful ignorance that, unexpectedly, I grew angry.

"What about him? He wants no part of me, a fact he made quite plain in the letter he sent less than two years ago. I would be a sorry fool if I believed anything else."

"Oh." Chris gave me an odd look; he opened his mouth and shut it quickly, as if he wanted to say something else then thought better of it. He shook his head instead. "Why did you agree to come back with me?"

I sat quietly for a moment, listening to Max's laughter echoing in my head. "Now's the time, my dear, to give him the speech. You know, that one about how the future doesn't matter, about how you have to be with the man you love. You were quite eloquent about it once, if I remember correctly."

"Just stay out of it," I murmured, turning my face to the window.

"What?"

I looked back at Chris and gave him a half smile. "You are right, Chris." Laughing softly at my own folly, I continued. "It seems a shame that over a century of living did not make me smarter, but where your father is concerned, I am a fool.

Now"—I reached over and gently smoothed his hair—"settle back and get some sleep. I have some thinking to do."

It was raining when we landed in New York, a cold rain, soft but insistent. Due to a technical problem at the gates, we had to walk from the plane to the terminal, and although the airline supplied umbrellas, we were still completely soaked by the time we got inside. The airport was crowded; somehow I had managed to forget just how many people lived there. We arrived at the baggage claim, and I was trembling, not with the wetness of my clothes and hair, but with the overwhelming presence of so many humans. My senses were deluged by the odor, the jostling, the warmth of these living bodies all pressed together. I leaned against the wall and rubbed my hands over my face, feeling faint and exhilarated at the same time.

"You okay?" Chris came over to me, our suitcases in hand.

I nodded weakly. "Can we go now?"

He led the way through the airport, and eventually we burst through the front doors into the night. I sighed my relief; he hailed a taxi and we got in.

"Where are you staying?"

I looked over at Chris. "I haven't made any arrangements yet. I had thought I might go back to my old place."

He reached into his pocket and handed me a set of keys. "Dad's place is empty right now. Why don't you stay there for a while?"

I looked at the keys and hesitated.

"Go on," he urged. "Why spend the money for a hotel? I'd feel better knowing that you were there. Besides, I live just a few blocks away; it would be more convenient."

"Fine," I agreed, "but just for now."

When we arrived at Mitch's apartment, Chris walked in with me and opened the door. It was exactly as it had been when Mitch lived there. Except for the musty, unoccupied odor that lingered in the air, it was as if he had just stepped out for a moment.

"I hope it's okay." Chris glanced around doubtfully. "I cleaned up the best I could."

I looked at the room, the books neatly lined up, the tables dusted, the vacuum cleaner tracks on the carpet, and felt a small shiver of déjà vu. "I see that you Greers are all the same."

"What?"

"Oh, nothing." I gave a small laugh at his confusion but did nothing to explain myself. The similarity to his father was almost uncanny; the neatness, the expectation of my arrival was so much like Mitch's attitude that I could almost feel his presence.

"Well"—Chris moved nervously toward the door—"if everything is okay, I guess I'd better be going. I'll call you tomorrow and we'll go see Dad."

"That would be fine. Call around sunset. I assume there are visiting hours at night?"

"Seven to nine," he informed me. "We should probably leave here no later than six."

"Great. See you then. Good night."

He closed the door and I heard him go down the stairs and out the front door. The cab door closed, the motor surged, and he was gone, leaving me alone with my memories.

For a time I wandered through the apartment, studying the rows of books, amazed once more at their variety. Idly, I ran my finger down the spines of the books, then went into the kitchen. The refrigerator was empty except for two bottles of wine. Silently thanking Chris for his forethought, I poured myself a glass from one and carried it and my suitcase into the bedroom.

This room was also clean—too clean, it seemed to me, but I restrained the urge to open my valise and throw the clothes about. Instead, I opened the closet and looked at the rows of Mitch's clothes. A faint smell arose from them, and I closed my eyes for a minute to isolate the aroma, to breathe it in more deeply, to fill my lungs with the odor of him.

"Damn." I turned away from the closet and left the room. All at once I felt restless and trapped, and knew that I could not sleep there that night. Tomorrow during the sunlight would be soon enough. I picked up the phone and called a taxi.

* * *

The cemetery gates were locked and the graveyard was surrounded by a tall, heavy fence. Smiling to myself about the old joke, I reached down and grasped the padlock in my hand, looking up and down the street to see if I was being observed. There was no one in sight; I had sent the cab driver away, and who else in their right mind would be visiting a cemetery at night? Who, indeed, I thought with a small laugh, pulled the lock apart, pushed open the gates, and closed them again behind me.

Walking quickly, I passed through the older section, where the tombstones were tilted at odd angles and the ground gently rounded. As if from a great distance, the noises outside the gates seemed muffled and indistinct. Even the sounds of my passage were muted; the scratching sounds of my boots on the gravel were no more than a whisper in the night.

I had received directions to the grave site when I had purchased the plot, and as I entered the newer section, I recited the landmarks to myself. "Three trees clumped on the right, two benches and a water faucet, then the third grave to the left." It turned out to be nothing like my dreams, but then, I thought with a shrug, what is?

The granite marker stood tall and proud, bearing the simple inscription over which I had commiserated for much too long, especially when one viewed the final result: his name, the date on which he died, and one word, "Father." I had considered many inscriptions—some were humorous, some slandering or sentimental—but realized finally that my feelings about Max were too confused, too convoluted, and had settled for that one relationship. It made little difference that somewhere else lay another much loved under that same title; his earthly remains had long since gone to dust, and Max, I reasoned, was truly the father of the creature I had become.

I stood for a long time, contemplating his grave. I waited for his voice in my mind, his step on the path, the emergence of his grasping hands. There was nothing but silence. Feeling oddly at ease, I sat down on top of his grave and leaned against the tombstone. The grass was icy and the stalks pushed themselves into my stockings, but the earth remained still and I was alone.

"Max." I addressed him solemnly, my quiet voice forcing strange echoes from the surrounding stones. "I want to make peace. We have paid for your death. Both Mitch and I have paid. Let it go. Let *us* go."

There was no response, not even a glimmer of his presence. I laughed softly at myself, for I already knew that he chose his own time, his own appearances. But still I sat for some time, thinking, weighing the actions of my past, searching my mind for any alternatives that could have been chosen over his death. I came to the same conclusion as always: He had given me no choice; his death had been unavoidable. And although I regretted the deed and missed his presence as acutely as I would a piece of my own body, I knew finally that, given the same situation, I would kill him again.

I rose from the ground slowly and with a sigh. This was as much peace as I would realize, tonight or any other. There was nothing here for me; there never was. I brushed away the dead leaves that had adhered to the back of my cloak. As my hands touched them, they crumbled, but the brittle crunching sounds they made did not disguise the approaching footsteps. I stiffened and remained standing with my back to the path, not really wishing to face this apparition.

"Deirdre?" There was surprise in his voice, and recognition. "It is you, is it not? It's been a long time."

Inwardly I relaxed. The slightly accented voice seemed vaguely familiar, but it was not Max's. I turned around.

I knew that we had met before, but I could not quite remember his name. He was distinguished, handsome and his clothing spoke softly of old money. I pulled my cloak together and folded one arm over it, ashamed of my own apparel, suited more for the life I led in England than the one I had led in America. But I gave him a gracious smile and extended my other hand to him. "So nice to see you again, Mr., ah . . ." I felt myself blushing, wishing I could remember his name.

"Lange. Victor Lange."

Even before he said it, his name and the situation surrounding our meeting came back to me. The recollection caused me to shiver slightly; he had been the one to give me the final clue that enabled me to discover who Max really was. I regretted his role in the affair; eventually Max would have dropped his shield and let me know himself. Perhaps his death could have been avoided. I looked at him with an uncertain smile, wondering if he knew he had been indirectly involved in the killing of his friend.

He took my hand and raised it to his mouth. His lips moved delicately over my knuckles and he laughed. "But of course you wouldn't remember me; we met only once, and that, briefly."

"I do remember you, Mr. Lange. After all, it's been only two years. But I am surprised that you remember me."

He dropped my hand and smiled at me. "How could I ever forget someone like you? Besides, I've been waiting for you. Max said you would come here sooner or later. I walk here often, watching for you."

I jumped, startled. "Max said?" I questioned him, my voice raised to a higher pitch than normal. "But Max is—"

"Dead," he interrupted, his charm lost suddenly in the flare of anger. "A most regrettable occurrence." His eyes glittered in the moonlight and, I, barely aware of my reaction, backed away a few steps from him. He noticed my movement, and his expression and voice softened. "Forgive my poor use of the language, I didn't mean to alarm you. Max never actually said it to me. It was merely a part of the stipulations of his will: that I should watch for you after his death."

"His will? But what has that to do with me?" I gave him a suspicious glance. "Or you, for that matter?"

Victor threw his head back and laughed loudly. "How like Max to not tell you. He was always such a secretive bastard, wasn't he? I won't keep you in suspense any longer, Deirdre. I am executor of his will and you, well, you are a very rich lady."

"Rich?" I shrugged slightly. "I was rich before. How much did he leave me?"

"Everything he had, my dear. You are his sole heir."

I stared at him in shock for a second, then repeated in disbelief, "His sole heir?"

Victor nodded, smiled, and took my arm. "I knew he hadn't told you, although I advised him to many times over. Max always insisted that he had all the time in the world, that he would explain everything at the right moment." He began to walk back down the path, gently urging me along.

"Well," I said, hoping that the bitterness I felt did not show, "that moment never came."

"No." His tone was noncommittal as he pushed the front gates open, giving first the padlock and then me a quick, curious glance. "Careless of the caretakers to leave these unlocked."

"But so convenient for late-night visitors."

He gave me a shrewd look, then smiled and patted my arm. "You can't imagine how good it is to see you alive and well. When you disappeared after Max's death, I was very worried."

"Why would you be worried?"

He did not answer the question right away. "I left town on business the very night he was murdered. By the time I returned, Max was buried and you were gone. Without a trace, I might add. I'm afraid I may have jumped to the wrong conclusion, not that it matters at this point."

I looked at him expectantly, but he seemed deep in thought. "And that conclusion was?" I prompted Victor.

He shook his head briefly and gave a small, angry laugh. "It does seem ridiculous now that I consider it again. I rather thought that Greer had killed you also. And hid your body."

"Mitch Greer? Why on earth would you have thought that?"

Victor shrugged. "As I said, it doesn't matter at this point. What is important is that you are here now, and safe. We'll need to get together sometime soon. I have many papers for you to sign. Where will you be staying?"

"At a friend's apartment." My privacy was still a major concern, and I saw no need for Victor to know where I would be. Especially that I would be at Mitch's place. There was too much I did not know about him and his anger at Max's death was still strong; the vehemence with which he said Mitch's name proved it. "I'll call you at the Imperial, if that's suitable."

"Fine." He waved and a car pulled up to the curb. The driver emerged, nodded to us, and opened the back door. Victor motioned for me to enter, but I shook my head.

"I think I'll just stay around for a while and go home later. It's a lovely night."

He glanced at the sky and smiled his agreement. "If I were thirty years younger, Deirdre, I would be pleased to stay and keep you company. But watch yourself; this is not exactly the best neighborhood around."

I stood on the curb and watched as they drove away. After they were gone from sight, I glanced back once more at the quiet cemetery, then began to walk slowly in the direction of Mitch's place. Three blocks away I hailed a taxi and rode back home.

Chapter 5

To my surprise, I did sleep that night and the rest of the next day as well. And although I dreamed, it was not of Max. Mostly I dreamed of Mitch, of the days and nights we had shared, of sunlit times together that were pure fantasy. All the same, I knew how he would look in the sunlight, his eyes lightened, squinting slightly, his hair reflecting shimmers of gold and silver. They were peaceful dreams of laughter and love, with no taint of blood or death. I woke with a smile on my face.

Stretching luxuriously, enjoying the smell of the clean sheets, I tested my hunger response. When thoughts of biting and drinking aroused no response, no growth of the canines, and no inner raging, I knew that I would remain sated for the next few days. I had fed only two nights ago and fed well.

I shuddered slightly at the thought of Robbie, his urgency,

and my own needs. Having remained celibate for more than twenty years until I had met Mitch, it had been alarmingly easy to fall back into promiscuity. His final denial of me, and the presence of Max, had pushed me into my old ways: the trading of sex for blood. And although each time I found myself repulsed, sickened by the bartering, I did have the feeling that this way was more honest, more fair. My victims got what they wanted, as did I. But it had never occurred to me how I would explain the situation to Mitch—I had never expected to see him again.

I rose and dressed in jeans and a sweater and went out to the kitchen to pour myself a glass of wine. I had almost finished it, when the phone rang.

"Hello." My voice was tentative; I felt like an intruder here, without Mitch. I need not have worried, however, for it was Chris, right on schedule.

"Hi, it's Chris. Did you sleep okay?"

"Fine, thank you."

"Well, I just wondered; I called last night when I got home, but there was no answer."

"I went out for a walk."

"Oh." His voice sounded tense and disapproving. I guess he assumed I was out feeding already.

"Just a walk, Chris, nothing else."

"Oh." The intonation was different this time, embarrassed maybe, or apologetic. I laughed slightly, thinking that actually he had made the adjustment to the truth about his father's lover fairly well considering the enormity of it all.

"Something funny?"

"No, Chris, not really. Will we be leaving soon?"

"Yeah, I'll be by in about fifteen or twenty minutes." He paused for a second. "But that might not be enough notice, I'm sorry. Can you be ready?"

"Of course. See you then." I hung up the phone and rushed into the bathroom to apply my makeup and contact lenses.

After I had coaxed some color into my pale complexion, inserted a pair of green lenses, and brushed my dyed black hair, I stepped back and studied the results in the mirror. "Not too bad," I said aloud with only a bit of a frown, "but first thing tomorrow night I need some clothes and a new dye job."

"I don't know, my love, I've gotten used to the color. It makes you look more the part."

There was no reflection in the mirror, but when I swung around, Max was leaning in the doorway, his lips curved in the condescending smile I remembered so well. The outline of his body was hazy though, and when I looked at him straight on, he seemed to fade in and out of my vision.

"Go back to hell, where you belong, Max." I pushed past him as if he weren't there. And he wasn't. Still, my breathing had quickened and my pulse raced slightly. Hurriedly, I picked up my cloak and bag, turned out the lights, closed and locked the apartment door.

Chris was waiting, parked a few yards down the street. He blew the horn when I walked down the steps and waved to me. I waved back and got into the passenger side.

"You okay, Deirdre?"

"Yes, why?" My voice was raspy, and I coughed to cover it up.

"Well, I don't know, you look a little pale."

"Is that supposed to be a joke?" I snapped in response.

"Oh, no, not really. Forget it, okay?"

He drove in silence for a while, concentrating on the traffic, ignoring, as much as possible, my presence in the car. Finally he cleared his throat and glanced over at me.

"You know," he began hesitantly, "I seem to keep saying the wrong things to you. I don't mean to make you angry; it's just sometimes I don't know what to say. I've never been in the presence of someone like you."

"But you have, Chris. We spent some time together before I left town. Can you remember how you treated me then?"

"Yeah." A reluctant smile crept over his face. "We played pool. You skunked Dad every game. He really hated to lose." The smile faded. "But it's all different now that I know."

"It shouldn't be, Chris. I'm exactly the same person I was then."

"Are you?"

"Yes," I said, but my voice lacked conviction. "Yes," I said again, stronger this time, and with more defiance. "I am the same."

"Okay," he agreed, turning into the parking lot of a large hospital. "If you promise to not be too touchy about it all, I'll try just a little harder to forget."

When he finally found a parking space, he turned off the engine and the lights. I reached over for the door handle, but his touch on my arm stopped me.

"Deirdre, before we go in, I think you should know a little of what to expect."

I nodded. "Tell me."

He looked out the window intently; his voice was soft and pained. "He probably won't know you, most likely won't even acknowledge your presence. Dad hasn't spoken coherently for about two months now; he eats only when they feed him and he has absolutely no contact with reality. A total withdrawal from everything around him." He sighed and continued. "We've tried all sorts of stimulation for him, but nothing works. Physically he checks out okay; other than looking like hell and having lost about thirty pounds, he's in excellent health. But mentally, he's gone." He choked on the last words, and I could see the glistening of tears in his eyes. "He may never get back to normal, never be what he once was. But if we can get a reaction from him, just one reaction, they think they might get somewhere."

I closed my eyes, letting the blackness enfold me wrapping myself in the starkness of Chris's words. One of the first things that had attracted me about Mitch was his sharpness—the alertness in his eyes, the feeling that he was totally alive and a hunter, akin to me. The fact that he might spend the rest of his life in an autistic state was unthinkable, obscene. I wanted to cry, wanted to rage and scream against this fate forced upon him. And I knew that should he prove unredeemable, those who had driven him to this extremity must pay with their lives.

Wearily, I put my hands up to my face and sighed. Was I always to be at odds with the others of my kind; would I never find rest from revenge and murder? When I lowered my hands and opened my eyes, Chris was staring at me, expectantly waiting for some sort of response.

"Dammit, Chris, I told you before I can't work miracles. You tell me that for over a year and a half he's been in the care of some of the best psychiatric experts in this city and yet you seem to expect that I can succeed where they have failed. Don't lay this entirely on my back; his case just might be as hopeless as they all think."

"But don't you see, it's not entirely hopeless—it can't be. He's holding on for something. He's still alive, and where there's life there's—"

"No," I interrupted. "Don't preach that adage to me. I've been dead so long, I've forgotten what life is like. But I will try, Chris. I will do my best to get a reaction."

"It may take a while, and a lot of visits. It could be months or even years." He looked over at me questioningly, pleading for my understanding, my cooperation.

"What the hell," I said vehemently, repeating words I had said to his father not long ago but somehow an entire lifetime away. "I have all the time in the world. Shall we go in?"

I hate hospitals; so many memories are evoked by their appearance and odors, recalling death and war and sickness. This place was no different from others I had been in: It had the same sickly-sweet disinfectant smell, the sour odors of sweat and urine. But it was clean, sterile, and almost cheerful in an infantile way. Brightly colored posters and prints decorated the otherwise stark white walls, and the nurses' station at which we checked in was gaudily trimmed for an early Valentine's Day.

Most of the patients were aged, tired, and confused, walking the halls in a shuffling old-man gait, mumbling soundlessly to themselves. I shuddered at the sight of them, at the ravages of time, disease, and unkindness. Knowing that most of them had been toothless babies long after I had reached the age of sixty made me feel uneasy, guilty; I yearned to run back down the hall and hide in the darkness of the night.

Chris must have felt my hesitation, for he put a gentle hand on my elbow and steered me into a central room. A nurse greeted him by name and with a smile. I ignored their quiet conversation, concentrating instead on a search for Mitch. He wasn't there; I couldn't feel the slightest suggestion of his presence. Then as I half turned to Chris and the nurse, hearing her say to him that no, there had been no change while he was away, I saw him, and the shock of his appearance sent a terrible chill through my spine.

I had already observed the tall, too slender form standing at the grated-over window. He had laid his face against the grill, and his hands were splayed out beside him, grasping at the wire, scratching to get out into the night. His hair was totally gray and my eyes had passed over him, almost discarding him, until he turned to the side and I saw his profile.

"Dear God." I gasped at the change in him and took a few tentative steps toward him. My movement attracted his attention for just one second; his haunted, nonfocused eyes touched mine, then flew away. He shuffled over to a nearby chair, and as he walked, he spoke, the words too quiet for me to hear. But there seemed a familiar rhythm to the movement of his lips, and I looked over at the nurse questioningly.

"Go ahead," she urged me, "try to speak to him. He's not violent."

The room seemed endless, but eventually I stood right in front of Mitch. He remained staring at the floor, and I discovered that he was not speaking, but singing.

" 'Into the ward of the clean, whitewashed walls . . .' "

"Mitch."

There was no response from him, but the song continued. " 'Where the dead slept and the dying lay . . .' "

"Mitch," I said, louder this time. "It's Deirdre. I'm back. Can you hear me?"

His eyes moved from the floor and fastened on my face; there was no recognition, no spark to show me that this was the man

I loved. But his voice grew more agitated, louder, as he sang the next lines. " 'Wounded by bayonet, saber, and ball, somebody's darling was borne one day.' "

I knelt in front of his chair. His eyes followed me and he jumped and shivered as I grasped his warm hands between my cold ones. I did not speak this time, but sang with him instead.

" 'Somebody's darling, somebody's pride, who'll tell his mother where her boy died?' "

After the first four words his voice faltered and stopped, but I continued, feeling slightly foolish. His eyes darted nervously, trying to avoid my face, but eventually I drew them back to me and still holding on to his hands, gently urged him out of the chair. He was trembling violently under my touch, but that merely encouraged me, and I spoke his name again.

"Mitch."

This time I connected. I knew he heard me and understood; his hands tightened on mine and he whispered my name. Then before I could react, he quickly dropped my hands, formed a fist, and silently punched me on the jaw, striking me with such force that I fell to the floor.

As I pulled myself up, shaking my head and gingerly feeling my jaw, I saw him running from the room, pursued by a nurse and two orderlies.

I stood, swaying in the air slightly, oblivious of the uproar Mitch's action must have been causing around me. The noise level in the room rose and as if from a long distance, I could hear the laughing and crying and shouting of the rest of the patients in the room. But my eyes were fastened on the door through which he had disappeared.

What the hell did you expect, you fool, I thought. A passionate embrace, a warm welcome-back kiss? His eyes had been the eyes of one who looked on hell, and I had helped to put him there.

I looked over to where Chris stood, open-mouthed, staring at me. The nurse who had been talking to us came over with a piece of gauze, dabbing at my bleeding lip, making her apologies over and over. Irritated, I shrugged her away and gave Chris a small, bitter smile, wincing somewhat with the pain.

"Tell me, Chris, was that enough of a reaction for you, or shall we try again?"

Chapter 6

"Oh, my God, Miss . . ." the nurse began.

"Griffin."

"Miss Griffin, I would never have expected that to happen. No one here would have. Mitch has never shown any tendency toward violence the entire time he's been here. I just can't imagine what got into him."

"I did."

She gave me a strange look. "What?"

"Never mind, it doesn't matter."

"I hope you understand that we can't be held liable for this event; I mean, if we thought he would hit you, we would never have let you approach him. It's not a case of negligence, and I sincerely apologize for your discomfort. Shall I get a doctor for you?"

I laughed. "I don't need a doctor, thank you. And I promise I will not sue you. I believe I finally got what was coming to me."

Puzzled, she cocked her head at me, obviously wanting more information. I chose not to elaborate; her obvious fawning was beginning to anger me.

"Think nothing more of it." The finality in my voice drove her away, and I went out into the hallway to find Chris.

Since there was no sign of him, I assumed he had gone to Mitch's room; I found a small waiting area and sat down. Picking up a newspaper, I began to catch up on current events. I was thoroughly engrossed in the crossword puzzle when a shadow fell across the page. "Jesus," I swore under my breath, afraid to look up, not knowing who it was. Mitch, come to take another shot at me, perhaps? Maybe my very own personal ghost, here to gloat over my disastrous choice of loving a human? Who it was made no real difference to me; I had no desire to see or talk to anyone else this evening.

"Just go away and leave me alone." I sounded surly even to myself, but didn't care. "I've had trouble enough for one night."

"I'm sure you have, but it's important. Please?"

And because I did not recognize the voice, I glanced at the speaker. He was tall and dark with a fresh-scrubbed sincerity in his face, his jacket and stethoscope identifying him immediately.

"Ah, one of the resident white-coats. I told the nurse I didn't need a doctor."

"Miss Griffin." He smiled broadly, ignoring my bad temper. "I'm John Samuels, Mitch's doctor. My friends call me Sam."

He extended his hand and I reached up to shake it. "Dr. Samuels," I said coolly, "what can I do for you?"

His smile faded only slightly. "You may have already done it. I just wondered if you could spare a little of your time and talk to me about Mitch. There's so much going on here, I can't tell you how excited we all are. He's talking again—a little disoriented, true, but that's to be expected—but, good God, he's talking clearly and lucidly."

His enthusiasm was contagious. Reluctantly I returned his smile and agreed. "I have nowhere else to go, Doctor, and nothing but time on my hands. I am at your disposal."

"Thank you."

I rose from the chair; he smiled and escorted me to his office.

As he settled in behind his desk, I sat uncomfortably, glancing casually around his office. He gave me a long, appraising look, then reached into the top drawer, extracting an ashtray, a pack of cigarettes, and an engraved gold-plated lighter.

"I won't smoke one now," he said with a guilty look. "It just calms me to have them here." Then he laughed. "I know, you think that as a doctor I should have more control, more sense, don't you?"

"I think nothing of the sort. You are human; you may do as you like."

"Why did you say that? 'You are human.' What does that mean?"

I shrugged. "Oh, you know what I mean." My voice sounded relaxed and even, betraying none of my inner turmoil. "It has been a rather extraordinary evening, as you well know. As for me"—I smiled encouragingly—"I don't mind if you smoke, provided you share."

"Fine." He offered the pack, I took one, and reached for the lighter. "Allow me," he said graciously, and quickly struck the flame. I cupped my hand around his as I lit the cigarette, inhaled deeply, then sat back and looked at him.

"Miss Griffin," he began tentatively, "your hands are shaking."

"So?"

"Well, if I had a suspicious mind, I might begin to wonder why you are so nervous and so hostile."

"How fortunate for me"—I couldn't hide the sarcasm in my voice—"that you do not have a suspicious mind. Can I be honest with you, Dr. Samuels?"

"Absolutely, but call me Sam, please."

"Well then, Sam, I do not like hospitals or doctors. It's nothing personal; I am sure you are very good at what you do, I would even be willing to believe that somewhere beneath your charming bedside manner lies a real person." I took another drag on my cigarette, then reached forward to flick the growing ash away. "Right now, however, I would like nothing more than to leave. It seems quite apparent that my presence is a disturbing influence on Mitch." My voice broke on his name and I looked away from Sam's intent gaze.

"And you were hurt by his reaction, surprised?"

"Not surprised." I paused for a minute and thought. "Not at all. The entire event merely confirms what I suspected."

He said nothing, but reached over and lit a cigarette for himself. He kept the lighter in his hands and tapped it on the desk, turning it over, reading the inscription. Finally he looked up at me. "Well?"

Suddenly the anger and frustration I had been reining in since I arrived exploded. "Dammit, he threw me back into the world almost two years ago, forcing me to live the kind of life that even you, with your undoubtedly keen insight into the human psyche, cannot imagine. His son coerces me back with the story that only I can save him. And then to be met with such hatred, such pain." I pressed my fingers against my eyes to prevent the flow of tears. "I never meant for him to be hurt." My voice softened, and Sam leaned forward to catch my words. "I wanted him, I loved him. Love him, more than I have ever loved any man, and this is what my love did to him." I lowered my hands and balled them into fists.

"Miss Griffin." The doctor's voice was compassionate, warm, and I relaxed. When I opened my hands, there was a slight smell of burnt flesh, and I looked down with surprise at the stub of the cigarette crushed between my fingers. I dropped it into the ashtray.

His concern for me showing in his face, Sam stood up and moved toward me. "Did you burn yourself?"

"No."

"May I see?"

"No." Petulantly, I put my hands behind my back.

"Miss Griffin . . ."

I looked at him for a minute. "Oh, what the hell. Call me Deirdre. If I stay here much longer, you will manage to worm out all my deepest secrets." I smiled at him, honestly this time, for I was beginning to like him. "Damn, you are good at this doctor thing, aren't you?"

He flushed at my praise and sat back down at his desk. "Yeah, I'd like to hope so. Do you feel better?"

"Yes, I think so."

"Then maybe we can start over. Deirdre"—he nodded at me—acknowledging my permission to use the name, "how long ago did you and Mitch meet?"

"Two years ago, just a few days after Thanksgiving."

His head jerked in surprise. "Is that all?"

"Yes, why?"

"No reason, I just had the feeling that your relationship was of longer term than that."

"Does it matter?"

"Not really. And you left the country when?"

"New Year's Eve."

"The same year?"

I nodded and he reached over and put his cigarette out. "So you knew each other only a short time."

His statement seemed like a question. "Love at first sight?" I suggested in reply with only a small tinge of sarcasm.

"Could be." Sam met my eyes, and I saw a cautious admiration begin to form. "Do you mind my asking how old you are?"

I tried to evade the question, but quickly searched my memory for the last recorded age for Deirdre Griffin. "What possible difference can that make?"

"None, I suppose. I hope I didn't offend you."

"Not at all, Sam. I'm thirty-eight."

He looked unconvinced. "I'd have guessed from your appearance that you were younger, but your eyes are older, somehow. You're an interesting case, Deirdre."

"Case?" I jumped up from the chair.

"Oh, sorry. I didn't mean that, it's just an expression we use around here. Please sit down again."

"Actually, I would like to leave now. I would be happy to come back and talk again sometime if you think it will help Mitch."

"Even if it doesn't, I'd like it."

"Are you flirting with me?"

He hung his head. "Yeah, I guess I am, maybe just a little."

I extended my hand. "Well, I'm flattered. Thank you."

Before Sam could shake my hand, Chris entered the office. "Deirdre, I'm so glad I found you. It's wonderful. He's better, really better. He wants to see you, wants to know if you're still here. I told him I'd find out."

I sighed, knowing that I could not face Mitch again, so soon after his initial and forceful rejection of me. "Tell him I'll come back tomorrow night. I have to go now."

"Wait!" Chris came after me. "I'll drive you home."

"No, you stay here with your father. I'd like to be alone."

Some habits die hard. For one of my kind, they can often be the only things that keep you alive. So I was not really surprised to discover that my walk led me that night to the Ballroom of Romance. More amazing was the fact that the club was still in business and open.

There was no crowd waiting at the door; its popularity as a night spot must have waned during the years I was away. The doorman was unfamiliar to me; his expression of bored disinterest was apparent as he pulled open the entrance.

Inside, everything was exactly as it was when I had left. The tables, the bar, the dancers—nothing had changed. I caught myself scanning the dance floor for someone I knew and stopped immediately. Who did I expect to see? Max? Larry? Dead, they are dead, I reminded myself, and would not return. Pushing gently through the group of people standing near an empty seat, I laid my bag down on the bar and ordered a drink.

I thanked the bartender for the prompt service when he brought my wine. At the sound of my voice the man tending the other end of the bar turned and glanced at me; his eyes narrowed, as if to focus more clearly in the dim light.

"Miss Griffin?" He recognized me and came over. "It is you. I thought so. Long time no see, huh?"

"Yes, it has been a while. How are you?" I could not remember his name, but I remembered quite plainly the scornful attitude he had shown me in the past. Now, however, he was pleasant, courteous, and respectful.

"Fine, thank you. Can't complain, I suppose. Can I get you something?"

I pointed to my full glass and shook my head. "But you can do me a favor, if you would."

"Anything for you, Miss Griffin. It's nice to have you back."

I listened for a sarcastic note in his voice and found none. I smiled at him; it was nice to meet someone I knew before who had no ulterior motives, no hidden resentment, no open hatred. "Well," I began, "I would like to look around a bit, you know, for old time's sake."

"Be my guest." He threw his arms wide in a welcoming gesture. "You're the boss."

"Thank you." I picked up my wine and headed toward the door that led into the offices and lounges behind the club. This too had not changed. I had a strange feeling that if I waited here long enough, I would see a younger Deirdre walk these halls, her intended victim in thrall, willing to follow, to give her what she wanted. I shivered slightly, then walked without hesitation to Max's office.

The room was dark, but I did not bother to put on the lights. There was no need; my night vision was good enough to see that it was exactly as Max had kept it. And I knew this room so well, I could find my way through it blindfolded.

I closed the door and leaned my face up against it. They had replaced either the entire door or the wood panels within it, for there were no gouges in the wood to show where the makeshift stake had entered, no indication that a living being had once hung impaled there, spewing its life out upon the floor. Even the carpet was new; there had been too much blood spilled for the stains to be removed. Nothing in this room gave any sign that a baffle for life had been waged within its walls; it was sterile and empty. But still I searched for his presence; surely he would be there if he were anywhere.

"Max." I whispered the name at first, then said it louder. There was no response. I took a drink of my wine and walked across the room to sit on the couch. "Dammit, Max, just like always. When I don't want to see you, you come around, and when I would like to talk, you're unavailable. It seems to me you're even less reliable dead than alive."

I set my glass on the table, kicked off my shoes, and lay down on the white leather sofa, staring at the ceiling. Unexpectedly, I began to cry, my sobs quiet, absorbed by the dark, lonely walls.

I cried for myself, for Mitch, for all those I had loved now dead, and I cried for Max.

When I finished, I curled up into a ball and slept.

A soft moaning in the corner wakes me. Rising from the couch, I go to him, but it is too late. Mitch is dead, his face stretched in pain, gaunt and aged, his skin white and bloodless. The fang marks on his neck are mine.

"Deirdre." Max's voice causes the fine hairs on the back of my neck and arms to rise. I make no movement, but stand with my back to him, trembling.

"Deirdre." The name is a command; I am his, I always was. I turn around.

"You are dead, Max," I say, and look upon him. The flesh on his bones is shredded, rotting and decayed. His finely sculptured face is now nothing more than a skull, but the mouth opens and talks.

"Deirdre, come to me. I am not dead."

I move forward one timid step. "Not dead?" I see the stake piercing his rib cage, see the wood of the door behind him splintered with the impact of the killing blow. "No." I cannot deny the evidence of my eyes. "You are dead."

"Not dead, my love, for you still live and I am with you." One skeletal hand grips the implement of his death, but the other beckons. "Come to me."

My legs walk toward him, my body obeys him. But my mind is screaming, I am screaming.

His arm grips my shoulder and pulls me to him, the opposite end of the stake is positioned over my heart. The point penetrates my flesh, breaking the bones, the ribs, and finding its rest deep within my chest.

"Peace," he whispers as he holds me close, lovingly. "Peace and death."

There is not peace for me, no death; there is only the unavoidable pain and the sound of my voice, shrill and sharp, screaming.

"You are dead."

Chapter 7

"Deirdre?"

Disoriented, and feeling drugged, I sat up from the couch and saw the figure of a man outlined in the doorway.

"Max?" I whispered the name.

"I think you were having a bad dream." The voice was reassuring and I relaxed. "Close your eyes and I'll turn the lights on."

When I opened them again, Victor Lange stood there, smiling at me. "They told me out front that you were here. Did I disturb you?"

Standing, I smoothed my clothes. "No, actually I am very happy to see you. I was having a nightmare."

"Want to talk about it?"

"Not really." I met his eyes briefly, then turned away. "What are you doing here?"

"Oh," he said casually, walking around to the desk and setting his briefcase down on the top of it. "I stop by from time to time to check over the accounts. I trust you have no objections."

"Objections? Why would I object?"

Victor looked at me with amusement; he turned the latches on his case and the lid sprung open. "Because you own the Ballroom now. Or at least you will when the papers are signed."

"I own the Ballroom." It took a moment for the fact to sink in, then I laughed, a sharp, scornful laugh directed at no one but myself.

"Do you mind if I ask why you find it funny?" Victor's voice had lost its pleasant tone, acquiring instead an angry, resentful edge, as if I were laughing at him.

"Honestly, Victor"—I choked back the rest of my merriment—"it is nothing you said. It is just that, well"—I thought for a minute, then continued—"the entire situation seems ludicrous to me. That Max should leave me the club, and that this room, a room I never wished to see again, along with everything else he owned, belongs to me. That the employees here, most of whom treated me as if I were a leper, should now be employed by me. And that, somehow through his death, Max found a way to bind me to him forever." That final word wavered in the air. Suddenly, I did not want to laugh.

Victor gave me an odd glance, then proceeded to shuffle through his briefcase. After he had gone through the entire stack of papers he shook his head and looked back at me. "I'm sorry," he said with a gesture toward the desk, "but I don't seem to have the necessary papers here for you to read. Perhaps you would let me give you the gist of his will. There's no intent to bind you in any way; there are, in fact, certain provisions should you not wish to accept his possessions. But before we discuss that, I'd like to clear up one misunderstanding. Max left you everything for one simple reason: He wanted to take care of you."

I made a small sound, a derisive chuckle.

He came out from around the desk and, standing in front of me, gently clasped my chin in his hand and moved my head up to meet his gaze. "Max loved you more than anything in the world." Victor's eyes seemed for a second to glaze over with pain and sadness. Then they cleared and he smiled. "You should be flattered and comforted to know that he chose you. That above all others, he chose you to receive his legacy."

I pulled away from him, uncomfortable with his direct stare. Walking over to the table, I picked up my half-filled glass and drained it. I did not like the thoughts of any of this. Max's legacy to me was nothing more than an infinity of loneliness and estrangement. It could not be sweetened by material things; love could ease it, but that seemed something I would never achieve. When I spoke again my voice was small and tight. "And if I do not want his legacy?"

"As I said, there are provisions. His estate was to be held for you for twenty-five years after his death. Had you not turned up by then, all of his assets would have been transferred to an organization know as The Cadre. The same is true if you refuse.

But I urge you to consider this carefully; you'll be turning your back on an enormous fortune. Something that could support you quite luxuriously for centuries."

"Centuries?" I gave a nervous laugh. "That would be fine, if I could only live that long."

"Ah"—Victor smiled—"just a figure of speech, you understand. I merely wish to impress upon you the vastness of his wealth."

"Oh."

Victor walked over to the window and pulled the drapes aside, looking out. "We'll have snow later on tonight," he remarked flatly, then turned back to me. "And although I know that you're a night owl, I'm afraid that it's getting a little late for me. Can we make arrangements to meet tomorrow, or the next day? I'll bring the papers and you can review them at your leisure."

"That would be fine," I said, cautiously studying his movements. It bothered me that he seemed to know more about me than he should, but it was obvious that he had been a close friend of Max's. And despite his many flaws, Max had never once risked the exposure of what I was. "Trust him," the voice in my head whispered, and I complied. "When would you like to meet again?"

"Here, tomorrow night, say around eleven. I still have The Imperial to run, you know."

He went to the desk and retrieved his briefcase. "May I escort you somewhere?"

I nodded and walked with him out of the office. When we reached the door to the bar, I turned to him and disengaged my arm from his. "Actually, Victor, I think I would like to stay here for a while, in the club. I could use another glass of wine and some company."

"I'm sure you could." We went into the bar, and he took my hand. "Good night, then, till tomorrow."

Although I had told Victor I desired company, it was not really true. Being present in a crowd of humans was enough for me. But as I started my fourth glass of wine, a man stopped at my table. I looked up at him, taking in his expensive suit, manicured hands, his unnaturally even teeth exposed in a seductive smile.

"Hi." For an opening statement, it was unimpressive.

"Hello." I tried to be cordial, but resented his intrusion on my thoughts.

"Are you Deirdre?" At my nod, he pulled up a chair and sat down. "Fred sent me over, said you might like to meet me."

"Fred?"

"You know, the bartender."

I looked over to the bar and the man I had recognized waved at me with a knowing look. "Oh, Fred." I gave a small, sardonic smile; he was trying to make up for his past rudeness now that I was his boss. So much for the lack of ulterior motives.

I shrugged and looked the man over again. Fred must have learned a lot from watching Max arrange my meetings; he certainly had a feel for the kind of man I preferred. And although I should not have been hungry, my appetite awakened instinctively. Maybe I should give Fred a raise, I thought, and smiled at the man again, this time warm and welcoming.

"Did he happen to say why I might want to meet you?" The question was abrupt, but my voice was low and husky and he took no offense.

"No, just that you're new in town and seemed lonely."

"Make that newly back in town, and you would be right. And lonely? Well, you are here now, so how could I be lonely?" I wet my lips and crossed my legs under the table, lightly brushing his leg with my foot. "Would you like to dance?"

His name was Ron Wilkes, an attorney with an elegant condominium in the best part of town, a wonderful stock of wine, and an enormous round bed complete with red satin sheets. After we spent an hour consuming two bottles of his best Merlot, he seemed extremely drunk. I feared that he might pass out before he got around to seducing me, but he eventually led me to his bed.

When it was all over, I lay on my back, his head nestled on my shoulder and his arm heavy on my stomach. I wiped my mouth and stared at the mirrored ceiling, trying not to recall how long it had been since I had made love to a man who was not drunk, trying not to recall who that man was. It did no good. Mitch's face was etched on my memory, his body permanently bonded to mine. I sighed and Ron stirred briefly.

"Deirdre," he murmured, and reached his hand up brushing against my nipple.

"Ron, I have to go now." I shifted away from him, but he pulled me back.

"Don't go just yet." He was still strong, still aware—I had taken only a small amount of blood, more a token than a meal—and he was not as drunk as I had thought. Pushing himself up on one elbow, Ron gave me a sleepy smile. "That was wonderful."

Looking up at his face, I felt a strong surge of guilt. Coming here with Ron had been a purely instinctual reaction. I had not needed his blood, had not needed to feed. It had been unfair of me to use him this way; he had not deserved it. His only mistake was being in the wrong place at the wrong time. And my mistake was in not taking enough from him to leave him open to my suggestions. I decided that I would have to bluff my way out of this one.

"Yes," I agreed languidly, stroking his hair, working my way down to the small mark at the base of his neck. He flinched slightly and I gave a nervous laugh. "But I am afraid you'll have to keep your shirts buttoned for the next week or two. I got a little carried away."

He fingered his neck delicately and gave me a searching look. "You bit me?"

"Yes." I could see the blush creep over me through the mirror.

"I thought so." I tensed at his words, but there was no fear or alarm on his face, just a satisfied smile. He plumped one of the pillows, rolled over, and sat up, drawing the sheet over us both. "Actually, it was a unique feeling. Very erotic. And well worth it."

I laughed, relieved. "I'm glad you think so."

"Would you like to do it again?"

I found his blasé attitude rather shocking. "What, bite you?"

"Among other things, yeah."

I sat up and threw back the sheet. "Some other night, Ron. I really do need to leave."

"Okay. Can I call you?"

Gathering my clothes, I shook my head and began to get dressed. "I'm staying with a friend right now, and I forget the number. But I have your card; I'll call you."

"That'd be great." He got out of bed and went for his clothes. "Let me drive you home."

I zipped my jeans and smoothed the sweater down over my hips. "No, it's late and you need your sleep. I'll take a cab."

"If that's what you want." He came over and gave me a small hug and a kiss on the forehead. Then, with his arm still around me, he walked me to the door. "See you soon, huh?"

Victor's weather prediction was correct. The streets were slick and the sidewalks lightly dusted with newly fallen snow. By the time I reached the brownstone in which Mitch lived, my cloak was almost completely white, and, since I had no body head to melt it off, practically frozen stiff. I hung it over the shower in the bathroom and pulled a chair up to the window, watching the snow until the sky began to lighten. Then I pulled the drapes closed and crawled into Mitch's bed.

My deep, dreamless sleep was interrupted shortly after three the next afternoon by the insistent ringing of the phone. I ignored it at first, but still it kept ringing. Finally I dragged myself from the bed and answered.

"Deirdre, did I wake you?"

My pulse jumped at the sound of his voice.

"Mitch." I whispered the name, fearing that it might not be him.

"Hi."

I smiled, thinking how he always paused in conversation, collecting his thoughts and choosing the words carefully. I waited and he continued. "Look, I'm, well, I'm really sorry about last night. I don't quite understand what happened, what could make me do that to you. I barely even remember it, except that they're all talking about it here."

"I'm sure they are." A trace of amusement crept into my voice and I laughed, rubbing my jaw in remembrance. "It was quite a greeting, Mitch."

"Yeah." He paused again and I closed my eyes, imagining him, not as I saw him last night, but as he was before. I could almost see him run his fingers through his hair in a tired gesture, almost see the glint in his blue eyes. "They said I knocked you flat. Are you okay?"

"I'm fine, Mitch, not that it much matters. But how are you?"

"I don't know. I feel normal, I guess. They tell me I've been here for over a year, and that seems right. I can remember most of what went on, but almost as if it were a dream, or something that happened to someone else. And when I woke up this morning I barely knew where I was. The whole thing is so strange."

"We need to talk about this, Mitch. You must try to remember what happened to you so that we can fight it, so that it won't happen again. Can you arrange some privacy for us this evening? This isn't the sort of thing we want to discuss in the presence of your doctors."

"Well . . ." His voice was evasive, uncertain. "I'm not sure that they'll leave us alone. I think they're afraid I might hit you again. But come anyway, come as soon as you can." There was a pleading in his voice that twisted my heart.

"I'll be there by seven. And Mitch?"

"Yeah?"

Taking a deep breath, I began, rushing my words together, to say what I didn't want to say. "I don't want to make this situation any more difficult for you. I am pleased that you seem to be doing better and will do anything I can to help you. Anything at all. But be assured that when you are fully recovered you won't need to worry about my presence. I'll go and let you live a normal life again."

"Deirdre, I . . ."

"No, Mitch, you know this is how it must be. Don't deny it. There's no place in your life for me. We both know that." I let my tears fall unchecked, but was pleased that there was no sign of them in my voice. "I'll see you tonight."

I hung up the phone before he could say anything more. Rolling onto my stomach, I buried my head in the pillow. It was totally absurd for either of us to believe that our relationship could have any better an outcome than it had two years ago. Nothing had changed; I remained what I was and ultimately Mitch would not be able to live with the truth of my existence.

"Then why are you here?" Max's deep voice resonated in my mind. "There are many others to be had and much sweeter blood to drink. You're still so young, so naive; let me show you what awaits you."

Suddenly my mind was filled with a whirl of exotic images: men and women as carnal vessels of lust and hunger, flesh pressed against flesh, bodies and limbs intertwined, the salty flavors of skin and sex, the forbidden rush of blood, the flooding of the blood, overwhelmingly sensual in its taste, its power.

"Let us go, my love," he urged. "Let us go now. We could leave tonight; I know of places we could go where no one would ever find us. Places where we would be treated as gods, places where we could establish our own dynasties. There is nothing for us here. *Nothing!* But the world outside is waiting and if we leave I can be with you always, to teach, to experience, to live."

My body responded as if he were there; his breath was hot on my neck, his fingers tracing the bones of my spine. I could feel his strong hands grasp me, his nails penetrate my skin, his hungry mouth fasten on me. Max's passion and urgency were mine. I writhed and shivered in torment under his dominance.

I rolled over again, my back arched, my breath escaping in quick, frantic gasps. "No!" I cried, pressing my fingers against my eyes until hot red spots appeared beneath the lids. But still the images continued, flowing through my senses. I pressed harder, as if to tear the thoughts from my mind. Finally, the pain brought me back to myself and drove him away. Then, when my blurred vision returned and the red spots faded, I got up from the bed. Trembling, I walked down the hallway and stepped into the shower.

Chapter 8

After the shower I wrapped myself in a towel and went back into the bedroom. Opening my suitcase, I looked over the clothes I had brought with me. None seemed suitable, so I went to the phone and dialed a number I remembered well.

It was picked up on the first ring, the voice crisp, professional, and unfamiliar. "Griffin Designs, Ms. McCain's office."

"I would like to speak with Betsy."

"May I tell Ms. McCain who is calling?" The tone of voice was curt and the last name was emphasized, as if I had no right to use the given name. The secretary's attitude annoyed me, and I had no desire to publicize my presence, but I supposed it could not be helped.

"Deirdre Griffin."

There was a slight pause, as she remembered me. "Of course, Miss Griffin. I'll put you right through."

Before I could even react to the change from rude to gracious, Betsy McCain's brisk voice burst through the phone.

"Deirdre, what a surprise. I'd no idea you were back in town. How are you?" I was surprised at her warmth; we had become acquainted only at the sale of Griffin Designs, and although by the end of the deal we had each admitted to a grudging admiration of the other, I would never have considered her a friend. Still, her reception of my return was welcoming.

"Fine, Betsy. And you?"

"Better than ever." I heard her take a sip of something, and she continued. "Business has been hectic, but wonderful. Your last show was so good and we had all those orders to build on. I'm afraid I did have to make some changes though. And I've not been able to capture the Griffin romance, or so the critics say." Her voice had a brittle and sly edge. "I, er, I don't imagine you'd consider signing on for a while as a consultant, you know, just while you're here?"

"No, I'm sorry. I won't be in town for too long."

"Too bad. Anyhow, what have you been doing?"

I almost told her the truth and smiled as I imagined what her reaction would be. Well, Betsy, I've been in Europe, draining the blood from tourists. Remembering her as cold-blooded and calculating, I suspected she might even approve. I laughed at the thought. "Oh, nothing of much interest, traveling mostly. But I wonder if you could do me a small favor."

"Anything, Deirdre. I still feel a little guilty, but only a little, mind you, that I bought you out so cheap. I don't mind returning the favor, provided it is a small one." Her statement was not entirely humorous, and I admired her honesty.

"Well, you see, I came back in a bit of a rush and wasn't able to bring much with me. I need some clothes—you know my taste and size—and a hairdresser. And I would like them to come to me. I realize this is a little unorthodox, but I'm expecting some rather important calls and don't want to leave my apartment." The lie came easily to my lips; I was accustomed to covering up my lack of daytime appearances. "I would be happy to pay extra for your inconvenience, of course."

Betsy barked out a short laugh. "No inconvenience, Deirdre, but of course you'll pay extra. How soon would you like all this?"

"Is this afternoon too early?"

"No problem." She took another sip.

"And while you're at it, could you send some coffee along? I haven't had any time to shop at all."

"Okay, decaf or regular, ground or whole bean?"

"Ground, I guess, the other doesn't matter."

"Fine. Now, where are you staying?"

I told her and expressed my thanks. "You're a real life saver, Betsy. It's wonderful of you to do this."

"Oh, hell, Deirdre, it's not often that a fashion great comes to me for help. I'm delighted, I really am. See you soon."

By the time the doorbell rang, I had managed to dress and brush my teeth, but had no opportunity to apply any makeup to liven my pale complexion. It really doesn't make any difference, I thought as I cautiously opened the door to four women, one of whom was Betsy McCain.

She was exactly as I remembered her, dressed in an extremely tailored suit, her short, dark hair perfectly groomed, her handshake firm.

"Jesus, Deirdre, what the hell have you been doing to yourself? You look like death warmed over."

I laughed. "You haven't changed, Betsy. Still as blunt as ever, I see."

To my surprise, she looked embarrassed and a slight blush crossed her face. "I'm sorry, I didn't mean anything by it."

"I know. And you are right, I do look terrible." I turned to look at the women she had brought with her; one of them made a move to open the drapes. "No," I said, harsher than I intended. "Don't open those. I have a headache"—I lowered my voice a bit—"and the sunlight makes it worse."

Betsy gave me a quick look, then nodded at the women. "We have some extra lights in the car, bring those in." Then she glanced over the apartment with an amused smile on her face. "Not quite what I would expect of your place, Deirdre. It's nice, but somehow it's just not you."

"Mitch lives here."

"Oh." Her eyes sparkled at the mention of the name. "I remember, he's that sexy policeman you were dating. Are you still seeing him?"

"Yes." I didn't feel inclined to relate the story to Betsy McCain. She seemed friendly enough, and although it would be a relief for me to have someone to confide in, I knew I could not indulge in that luxury. My last female friend had been brutally mur-ered, a direct cause of our relationship. "And I'll be seeing him onight. So you'll have to work magic."

Betsy stood smiling behind me as we both looked into the mirror. My hair was as close to its original auburn as was possible, my nails manicured, and makeup had coaxed a delicate color into my complexion. She had brought with her eleven outfits, mostly dresses, and for that night we had chosen a winter-white wool sheath. It was, I thought, too short and too tight, but Betsy assured me it was a perfect fit.

"Well," she said over my shoulder, "what do you think?"

"Much better."

"Much better, my ass. You looked like a hag when I came and now you're gorgeous. I doubt that your Mitch will be able to control himself."

I began to laugh. "I hope you're wrong. Last night he knocked me out."

"What? He hit you?"

"Yes," I began, then saw the expression on her face. "Well, no, I mean, he did, but it isn't like you think. He wasn't himself last night."

She nodded knowingly. "Funny, he didn't seem the type. Drinker, huh?"

"No, he isn't a drinker. It is just that, oh, hell, Betsy, it would take much too long to explain."

She put her hand to her hip. "I've got the time."

I glanced at the clock. "Some other time. I'm supposed to meet him at six."

"Okay." She seemed reluctant to leave. "Just don't take any shit from him. No one is worth it."

"I know."

"Anyway, Deirdre, this was fun." She met my eyes with her customary directness. "I know you don't really like me much; no one does. I'm far too outspoken, too brash for most people to take. Some of that is a defense, I guess, and some of that is just the way I am. But I really appreciate your calling me. Maybe we could meet for lunch sometime if you're not too busy. I have a good head for business, but I just don't have the flair you do. Do you think you could help me out a bit?"

"I would be happy to do that, Betsy. But make it dinner instead. We could go to The Imperial again, I suppose. My treat, of course."

"Well, of course, you didn't think I'd pay, did you?" The ungracious words were softened by a sincere smile, and she slowly walked to the door. "Can I give you a ride somewhere?"

"No, I'll take a cab." Walking over to her, I put my hand on her arm. "Thank you so much. You've been wonderful, and I think you do have a flair all of your own. When shall I make reservations for dinner?"

"I don't know, let me check my calendar first and then I'll call you. Will you still be here?"

"Yes. Oh, and Betsy don't forget to let me know what I owe you."

"Hell, Deirdre, even you know me better than that—I never procrastinate when money is involved. Why, I'll probably write up your bill just as soon as I get back to the office." She laughed and closed the door behind her.

By the time I arrived at the hospital, I was shaking with nervousness. I paid the driver and got out, looking reticently at the front doors. Coward, I admonished myself, and forced myself to mount the steps and enter. Slowly I walked down the corridor and stopped at the nurses' station.

"May I help you?"

I was relieved to find a different nurse on duty. This one I judged to be in her early thirties, with baby-fine blond hair. She could have been pretty, but the expression on her face as she studied me was extremely unpleasant. At least, I thought, I won't have to accept countless apologies again. "I'd like to see Mitch Greer."

She looked up at me, the eyes behind her glasses narrowed and skeptical. "Are you a relative?"

"No, I'm a friend."

She removed her glasses and gave me a scornful look. "I'm

sorry, Mr. Greer is not receiving visitors this evening. Perhaps next time you could call ahead and verify visitation procedures."

"But he's expecting me. And I was here yesterday evening and there was no problem then."

She shook her head and turned back to her papers. "Well, that was yesterday, wasn't it? Tonight is tonight."

Stepping away from the counter, I stood for a second, watching her, attempting to gain my composure. "Excuse me," I said with a cold politeness, "then would it be possible to speak with Dr. Samuels?"

"Consultation hours are during the afternoon, from three to four, for family only." Each word seemed to punctuate her sudden and inexplicable dislike of me.

"Damn." I swore quietly. I moved closer to her and said in a louder tone, "Excuse me again, and I really hate to bother you, but may I use your phone?"

She pointed with her pencil toward the entrance. "Pay phones are in the lobby."

"Fine, thank you so much for your help." The sarcasm seemed lost on her; she made an unintelligible reply and returned her attention to the papers spread out on the desk. Exasperated, I turned away and began to walk back down the hall. I figured I could call Chris; he could get me admittance. But I had come to see Mitch, and see him I would, if I had to climb up the wall and break through his window.

"Deirdre?"

I spun around and faced Dr. Samuels.

"It is you, I thought so, but you look different. What did you do?"

I shrugged. "Nothing much. This is how I looked when I knew Mitch before. I thought it might help."

"You look great. Why did you ever change?"

I looked at his face, smiling at me with admiration, and smiled back. "It's a female thing," I said, knowing he would never understand my need for establishing a new identity. "Sometimes we just need to look different."

"But you're leaving? Don't you want to see Mitch?"

Although I was ready to explode into anger, I controlled my reactions. "Of course I want to see Mitch. But I was informed that I had not followed the proper procedures. I was just about to phone Chris to see if he could help."

"You could have asked for me."

"I did. 'Consultations from three to four for family only.' " I mimicked the nurse's condescending attitude.

Sam laughed. "Oh, I understand, Jean must be on duty this evening. Don't worry, I can get you in."

He escorted me back down to the nurses' station. Jean looked up at him. "Oh, Dr. Samuels, there was some woman here." Then she saw me standing behind him and stopped abruptly.

"I know, Jean. She's to be allowed to see Mr. Greer. This is Deirdre Griffin." He made a gesture of introduction in my direction, but Jean merely stiffened at the mention of my name and refused to meet my eyes.

"She's not on the list. And she's not family."

"An oversight on my part, Jean. I'm sorry you were inconvenienced. "

Then Jean gave me a long, cold stare; the scorn that she had in her eyes earlier was replaced by hatred. "There are proper procedures"—she addressed me, without any trace of apology in her manner—"and it's my job to make sure that they are followed."

Sam's voice was considerate but cool. "Yes, well, thank you, Jean. We all know how dedicated you are to your work." He gave her a token smile and nod in dismissal, and we walked farther down the hall. Until we entered his office, I could feel her eyes follow us, and her surveillance made me uneasy.

I dropped my cloak and purse on the closest chair. "What the hell is her problem?" My voice was light, but inwardly I was still seething.

Sam shrugged. "Damned if I know. She's a stickler for the rules, but will usually bend a little every now and then. Unless she's jealous of you."

"Why on earth would she be jealous? I've never met her before." And never want to again, I added to myself.

"Well, Mitch has been here for a while, and she started working only about a week after he was admitted. So I guess she feels there's a sort of tie between them; in any event, she's always been immensely interested in his case. Or so she maintains. The gossip from the other nurses are that she has a case on him."

"A case on Mitch?"

Dr. Samuels's eyes ran over my body in a quick complimentary glance. "Pretty ridiculous really. And it would have to be one-sided on her part. After having known you . . . well"—he shrugged, a look of compassion on his face—"I guess it's not pleasant seeing your fantasies dissolve right in front of you."

I looked away; his scrutiny of me was becoming uncomfortable. "May I see Mitch now?"

"Yes, of course." He moved to the door. "You want to see him, and here I stand, holding you up. He's in number seventeen, about ten rooms down, on this floor. Would you like me to take you?"

I nodded. "Please, if you would. I don't mind admitting that I'm just a little apprehensive about this meeting."

He began to walk briskly, and I followed at his side. "Everything will be fine, Deirdre. Mitch and I talked today, after he called you, and I know how much he's looking forward to seeing you. I'd be very much surprised if anything like last night occurs again."

My stomach twisted as he knocked on the door numbered seventeen. And when it was flung open, I jumped back in alarm. Sam held my arm gently but firmly. Reluctantly I lifted my eyes to Mitch's face.

He was still thin and gaunt, aged beyond the two years we had spent apart. But his eyes had lost their haunted look; they were crystal-clear and intensely blue, even more than I had remembered.

"Mitch." The name half choked me, and I was only vaguely aware that Dr. Samuels had dropped my arm and was awkwardly backing away.

Then Mitch smiled at me, and I forgot the rest of the world. There were no doctors, no nurses, no patients. There was only Mitch. His arms came around me and he held me to him tightly, possessively. I began to cry softly onto his chest; he rocked me back and forth, comforting me with the warmth of his hands, the sound of his voice. Our bodies felt as if they were fitted to each other. We had both been broken, shattered by events out of our control. And now we were one, united again, through the same chain of circumstances.

As he stroked my hair with his weakened fingers, once so strong and calloused, I knew that although I had tried to purge myself of him, tried to forget what we had shared, our bond was unbreakable; he would be forever in my blood, my soul. And as his mouth came down on mine, I realized, too, that I was lost, that I could never again leave him while he lived.

Chapter 9

"What the hell are you doing back in town?"

We were sitting side by side on Mitch's narrow patient's bed. Nothing had been said after he kissed me; he merely led me by the hand, sat us both down, cupped my face in his hands, and stared at me, searching, questioning me with his eyes. I wondered what he was looking for—did he expect to see signs of love or age, joy or sorrow? When he finally did speak, I started guiltily, not needing any words, wanting nothing but his gaze on my face.

I reached a hand up and stroked his cheek. "What strange greetings, Mitch—not 'how have you been,' or 'I missed you,' or even 'long time no see.' No, that would be too easy. Instead, I get hit and then I get profanity." I smiled at the mischievous grin that my words caused. "Do you think that's fair?"

He grew serious. "Fair has nothing to do with it. You shouldn't be here."

"And why not?"

He picked up my hand and put it to his mouth, glancing warily at the partially opened door. "For a lot of reasons, most of which we can't discuss here. It's too dangerous in this city, for you especially. Even so." He put his arms around me, hugging me tightly to him, breathing the rest of his words into my ear. "I'm glad you came. God, I missed you so. You just can't imagine."

"I think I can, Mitch." I stretched up to kiss him, but out of the corner of my eye I saw a figure in hospital whites standing hesitantly in the doorway. I tensed and pulled away as Jean entered the room. She held a plastic pitcher of ice water in one hand and a set of clean sheets were draped over her other arm. Bustling around the room efficiently and briskly, she placed the pitcher and one glass on the table next to the bed. The ice cubes clattered and the water slopped over the lip. Ignoring the spill, she stood, holding the bedclothes, staring down at us expectantly.

I remembered what Sam had said about her earlier, and I hid my half-smile on Mitch's shoulder. He kept his arm around me, not willing to move.

"Can I help you, Jean?" His voice was courteous and warm. Of course, I realized, he would have no idea of what she felt about him, or me, and I assumed that she could be a dedicated caregiver if properly motivated.

"Clean sheets, Mr. Greer." She held them forward and I could smell their fresh, starchy odor.

"But they were changed only this morning. Besides, I have a visitor."

"So I see."

He seemed not to have caught the suppressed anger I heard in her voice and he continued. "This is Deirdre Griffin, my, ah, fiancée." I glanced at him sharply for the unexpected escalation of our relationship. His only reaction was to tighten his grasp on my shoulder. "And Deirdre, this is Jean, one of the best nurses this dump has."

"We've already met."

She ignored my comment but beamed at his praise. "I do the best I can." Flushed and smiling, Jean seemed almost pleasant. Then her expression dropped and she gestured at us. "But visitors should be seen only in the lounge, and I have work to do."

Mitch's voice contained a gently teasing. "Dr. Samuels said we could meet in here. And you can change the sheets after visiting hours just this once, can't you?"

"I guess so." She hesitated a moment, then placed the sheets on the pillow, lightly brushing against Mitch's arm as if by accident. But I knew better, I saw the glint in her eye as she walked away. "Visiting hours are over at nine sharp," she said, giving the door an angry push. It banged noisily against the wall. "And all doors are to remain open."

Mitch shrugged apologetically. "I think she's having a bad day. Now, where were we?"

He kissed me again, a long and hungry kiss, and I responded in kind. When it was finished, he glared at me. "Now, why the hell are you here? And how did you know where I was?"

"Chris came for me. He said you needed me."

Mitch grimaced. "Why, that little—I expressly asked him not to contact you. When I was still coherent, I told him that you were not to get involved." He ran his hand through his hair, a puzzled expression on his face. "At least I'm pretty sure I told him. I seem to have lost track of a lot of things, including time."

"What is the last thing you remember, Mitch?"

He looked at me, and I could see the pain enter his eyes. "About three months after you left, they started coming to me. At first I thought I was dreaming because they came only at night, while I was in bed. Then suddenly they were there, everywhere, after dark, watching me, laughing at me, their teeth pointed, dripping blood." He shivered and stopped talking abruptly, staring at the bare white wall.

"Mitch?" Alarmed, I grabbed his arm and shook it. "Mitch?"

He jumped and turned to me again. "Sorry, did I drift off?"

I nodded. "Like you were in another world."

"It is another world, Deirdre. Why didn't you ever tell me?"

"Tell you what?"

"How terrible they are. How inhuman."

"Mitch," I said as softly as I could, attempting not to betray the rush of panic I felt at his words, "I don't know who they are. The only other like me that I knew was Max, and he's dead."

"Is he?" His eyes showed doubt and uncertainty.

"Yes, he is dead, Mitch. He can't threaten you anymore. You must believe that."

If he took any reassurance from my words, he didn't show it. "You see, that's just it. I didn't know what to believe anymore. Finally, I came to the conclusion that I had just flipped out, gone completely crazy. There was no evidence of what I knew, of what I saw, and yet they were there with me, inside my head, mocking and torturing. I eventually got to the point"—and he lowered his head, not looking at me "that I wasn't sure that you existed either. My memories of you were vivid, but so were the others, the ones that plagued me, the ones that no one else saw, that no one else believed in."

"But Chris knew me."

"I wouldn't listen to him; I shut him out, because if you were real, then so was all the rest of it. I think I really wanted to believe that I was crazy. It was safer that way."

"And you wrote me the letter."

"Letter? I didn't write to you. I wanted to at first, but you said six months and I waited. I guess I just couldn't hold out against them that long."

"But I received a letter from you."

Mitch shook his head. "I wish you had, but it wasn't from me. I didn't write; I know that for sure. What did it say?"

I got up from the bed and walked over to the window. "It said that you couldn't accept my life, that you could never see me again."

"Oh, God. Deirdre, I'm so sorry, I didn't have any idea."

I turned and gave him a bitter smile. "How could you have known, Mitch? You didn't send it."

"Even so, you should've known that I wouldn't have said that."

"And why not? You said so yourself, we're terrible, we're inhuman. Why would anyone in their right mind want to take that on themselves? I had no choice, but to walk into it willingly." I shook my head. "No, Mitch, it made perfect sense then, and it makes sense now."

Mitch sighed wearily and lay back on the bed. "Let's not fight about it now." He rolled over on his side and bent his knees, patting the open space on the bed. "Come here."

I settled in next to him. "You look tired, Mitch. You should try to get some sleep. I'll come back tomorrow night and we can talk some more then."

"Yeah," he agreed, stifling a yawn. "It's been a pretty busy two days."

Tenderly, I reached over and stroked his hair. The texture of it on my fingers was soothing, and the gesture seemed to calm him. He closed his eyes and gave an appreciative moan, then opened them again, sat up, and kissed me on the jaw.

"What's that for?"

"To make up for last night?"

"Oh, last night, forget it. It didn't hurt for long. But maybe you could tell me why you did it."

He smiled ruefully. "It was the only way I could be sure you were real." His expression grew thoughtful. "That, plus the fact that you're so bloody contrary, showing up when I least expected you. And when I saw your face, I felt such a strong rush of anger, not so much at you, Deirdre, as at the circumstances, at the sheer impossibility of what you are. Well, I just lashed out without thinking. Do you forgive me?"

"Mitch, my love"—I gently pushed him back on the bed and kissed him—"if you get better, I will forgive you anything. Sleep well."

I stood over him for a moment until his breathing deepened

and he began to snore softly. Then I wiped my tears away and walked out of the room, turning out the light as I left.

The door to Dr. Samuels's office was partially closed, and I hesitated briefly, then knocked. "Come in," he called. His voice sounded weary, but his smile was broad when he saw me and he gestured to a chair.

The ashtray, cigarettes, and lighter were on top of his desk; one lone, unlit cigarette was tucked alongside the blotter.

"I'm sorry, did I disturb your evening ritual again?"

"What? Oh, you mean smoking. Actually, I usually do one only before I'm ready to leave. But this"—he picked up a cigarette and rolled it over in his fingers, "this one is my third. I'm afraid that you've provided all of us with an interesting dilemma."

"How so?"

He slid a packet of papers over to me. "This represents testing done on Mitch just six weeks ago."

I looked at the tests, page after page of neat circles. "But every answer is exactly the same—he took only the first choice."

"Exactly. Did you know that some days we couldn't even get him to hold a pencil?" He didn't wait for my answer but pulled more papers from the top of the stack. "And these are the series I gave him today."

I could not read them, but saw that each question was answered with a different filled-in circle. "And the results?"

"Perfectly normal. Absolutely within the range of accepted psychological adjustment. Oh, Mitch has his fears and insecurities like all of us, but even they are normal. In many cases, fear is a healthy reaction; I like to say it keeps us from getting too cocky about our position in this world."

"And what does Mitch fear?"

Sam gave me a strange look, almost crafty. "What do you fear, Deirdre?"

His direct question threw me off guard, so much that I almost told him the truth. I fear the sunlight, I fear discovery; there are days when I am more afraid of life than death. And mostly I fear dead vampires who will not stay dead but live on in your mind and soul.

"Strangers, lack of privacy, and doctors who ask questions that they should not."

"Fair enough," he said, acknowledging my caustic tone. "I guess it's not really relevant anyway. But you must admit the fact that before you gave your very glib answer, there were darker fears that surfaced. You know it and so do I; I saw it in your eyes."

"And Mitch? After all, he's the patient, not I."

He picked up his cigarette and lit it, offering the pack to me. I shook my head and he went on. "Mitch is afraid of what he should be, especially when you consider his line of work. Senseless violence, blood, and death figure quite high in his current profile. But"—he went through his papers again, choosing one particular sheet—"when he first came here, when he was still reasonably coherent, he was very vocal about his problem." Sam took a drag on his cigarette and slowly exhaled. "Vampires. Or, as he put it 'those goddammed bloodsucking creatures in the night.' They had invaded his mind, he said, they were torturing him, punishing him for some crime."

I reached a trembling hand across the desk for the cigarette pack. "I think I will have one after all."

Sam nodded. "I thought you might. It's all pretty weird, don't you think. Why would a grown man be so afraid of mythical creatures? But you should know that through it all, while he was raving about 'them,' he was trying to protect you."

"Protect me?" My voice cracked a bit, and I cleared my throat. "What do you mean?"

"He didn't want them to find you. He said they would kill you if they knew where you were; we tried to find you, thought you might be able to help, but no one seemed to know where you had gone. Oh, Mitch knew all right, but he wasn't telling."

"Excuse me, Sam, this is all very interesting, but I'm afraid I don't quite get the point." My voice was even, but I lowered my eyes so he couldn't see the anger and sorrow I knew they must have held. "Mitch is getting better; you should be happy that he is recovering, not constantly worrying over what caused his problem."

"No"—his voice grew loud, and he got up from the desk and closed the door, standing with his back to it—"you don't understand. I am happy, thrilled, even ecstatic over his miraculous recovery. But don't you see, that's my point. In all my years of practice I've never seen a miraculous recovery. I don't believe in miracles, Deirdre. So there has to be some other answer."

"You sound just like him."

"Who?"

"Mitch," I said simply, smiling as I remembered so many of our conversations where he denied so many things, including coincidence and supernatural beings.

"Deirdre"—he crossed over to me and took my hands—"you see, that's why I need your help. You hold so much of him inside you. I need to understand what happened to you both so I can determine if he is truly healed, so that I can in good conscience sign his release. You must tell me everything. You owe it to Mitch, and you owe it to yourself."

Although I was still wary of his questions, I was moved by his argument. And if telling the story would hasten Mitch's release, I supposed that an edited version would not do much harm to any of us.

Sam stood, holding my hands, awaiting my answer. I pulled away from him and picked up my bag and cloak.

"Fine," I agreed, "but could we go somewhere else? Hospitals make me uncomfortable."

Chapter 10

When Dr. Samuels found out that I was staying at Mitch's apartment, he decided it would be a good idea to meet there. He drove; his movements in traffic were cautious and careful, a totally different style from Mitch's assured competence. But then, Mitch drove a dingy, broken-down sedan, and Sam's car was a new foreign sports model. He seemed quite proud of it, so I politely complimented him on it. When we pulled in front of Mitch's place, he seemed reluctant to leave it parked at the curb.

Sensing his apprehension, I turned to him. "Perhaps we should have taken a cab."

"No, this'll be okay, I guess. I'll just set the alarm."

"It will be fine," I assured him, "and if not, it's only a car after all. I assume you have insurance."

"Of course I have insurance. Doesn't everybody? Don't you?"

"No, I don't own a car. And I don't believe in insurance."

He gave me an incredulous look. "What do you mean, you don't believe in insurance? You must have some, life insurance at the least, or property insurance."

"I own nothing I value that much."

"Not even your life?"

I laughed. "It should really be called death insurance, being merely a bet with the company that you won't die before they get enough money from you. The only way you win is by dying sooner than they plan. And"—I winked at him as we went up the stairs—"I do not plan on dying."

"Deirdre," Sam said as I opened the door and we entered Mitch's apartment, "you are one strange lady."

"Make yourself at home," I called to him as I went into the kitchen. "But I'm afraid I don't have much to offer you in the way of refreshments. Would you like coffee or wine?"

"Coffee, I guess. And I hate to be rude, but I'm sort of hungry. Have you got anything to snack on?"

I realized that I really should bring some food into the apartment for appearance' sake, even though I would never eat it. "No," I said idly, "I haven't had time to go shopping since I arrived." I began to brew the coffee. "I hope you don't need cream or sugar in this."

"Black is fine."

I stood in the doorway of the kitchen while the coffee dripped and saw Sam studying the rows of books. "A pretty impressive collection, isn't it?"

"Yeah." He pulled out one volume. "*The Annotated Dracula*. Why aren't I surprised?"

"Oh, come now, Sam, you'll find that book on a lot of shelves. You shouldn't make too much of it."

He shrugged, then turned to look at me. "I know, how about a pizza?"

"Pizza? I told you I have nothing to eat here."

"No, I mean order one. You do have a phone, don't you?"

"Very funny." I gestured to the phone sitting on the end table. "Be my guest."

He dialed a number. "I'll have a large, um, hold on a second"—he put his hand over the receiver—"Deirdre, what do you like on yours?"

"Nothing. I don't eat pizza."

"Not at all? Why not?"

I crossed my arms and leaned against the doorjamb. "I'm allergic to tomatoes."

"This place makes a great white pizza, then. Just dough, cheese, toppings, and spices."

"Garlic?"

He smiled at me. "Yeah, lots and lots of garlic—it's wonderful."

"No thank you, I'm not really hungry."

"Okay, it's your loss." He completed his order, gave them the address, and hung up. "Why do they always say twenty minutes? Just once I'd like to call and have them tell the truth."

I shrugged, went back into the kitchen, and came back out with one mug of coffee for Sam and a glass of wine for me.

"You're not having coffee?"

"No, sit down, please." He settled into the one armchair. I sat down on the couch, took a sip of my wine, then set it back down. "Now, what would you like to know?"

"Everything you can remember would be good." He fumbled in his suit-coat pocket for a moment and brought out a small tape recorder. "Would you mind if I taped this? I take terrible notes, and my handwriting's so bad, even I have trouble reading it."

I glanced at the machine in doubt. If I should make a mistake and say the wrong thing, I would have to get the tape from Sam somehow. It would be easy to tamper with his mind, but I didn't trust modern technology; it was not susceptible to my wiles.

He sensed my hesitation. "You'll forget it's running after a while, really. And it's much better for me. Please?"

At my reluctant nod, he pushed the record button. The machine made a soft whirring sound. I picked up my wine, took another drink, and cradled the glass between my hands.

"I met Mitch three days after Thanksgiving, two years ago, at the Ballroom of Romance. He was investigating the death of Bill Andrews and wanted to question me about him."

"Bill Andrews was a close friend of yours, then?"

"No, we had just met the night he died. We were mere acquaintances, really."

"Then why did Mitch see fit to question you?"

I frowned and bit my lip. This was more difficult than I had expected it would be. Any bare telling of the story would be bound to put me in a bad light, and I could not fully explain. I gave Sam a sharp look, thinking that I didn't have to care about what he thought of me. This was all to help Mitch.

"Rumor was, around the club, that Mr. Andrews and I had shared an intimate evening before his death." My voice was dispassionate, matter-of-fact.

"Did you?"

I sighed and gently set my glass on the end table. "Look, Sam, this is difficult for me. Those few weeks were an extremely painful experience not just for Mitch, but for everyone who lived through it. And it is not a pretty story, I promise you. But it would ease the telling if you saved your questions until later."

"I'll try, but you've got to understand that it's in my nature to ask questions. That's why I do what I do."

"Then just close your eyes and pretend you're hearing a story about people you do not know, people who do not exist."

I stood up and walked to the bookshelves, stopping slightly behind him as he sat in the chair so that I would not have to watch his face. Hesitantly, I began.

"There were three more murders, two of them following fairly quickly after Andrews's, all with the same cause of death. Oddly enough, they had been drained almost completely of their blood, with no visible signs of violence other than two small punctures on their necks." I stopped for a minute, waiting for some sort of comment from him.

Sam nodded his head, and gave a clinical, "Uh-huh, go on."

"Well, since I knew all but the last murder victim, Mitch jumped to the conclusion that somehow I was involved. That I was the connecting link between them."

I paused again, editing the story, knowing that I could not tell him that Mitch's conclusion was true. That would incriminate me too deeply, raise too many questions in Sam's curious mind. "As it turns out, it was all a coincidence. The only link I had with any of it was Max."

"That would be Max Hunter, the famous 'Vampire Killer'?"

"So you do know something about all this?" My question sounded petulant; if he knew the story, why should I have to relive it?

"All I know is what was in the papers at the time. When Mitch was admitted, I did the required research, of course. I can show you the file sometime if you like. But I assume there is a lot more to tell than what appeared in print."

I gave him a skeptical look and he continued as if to justify himself.

"I was out of town, doing my internship at the time. So I

missed all the excitement. And there really was very little published about the case."

I walked across the room, picked up my glass and drained it, then went to the kitchen for more. When I returned, his eyes followed me intently. "So Mitch found this Max Hunter, and killed him. And that should have been the end of it all. But it wasn't, was it?"

I gave him a sharp look. "Sam," I said firmly, "please try not to interrupt. It's very distracting."

"Sorry, I forgot."

An uncomfortable silence enveloped us, but Sam kept his promise for a while and said nothing else, waiting patiently for me to continue.

"In between the third and fourth murder, something completely unpredictable happened that threw everyone a curve. Gwen"—I hesitated on her name—"my personal secretary, was also brutally murdered. And although her death was completely different from the others, there seemed to be a connection." I stopped and paced the room, finally ending back on the couch, not looking at him, but staring into the depths of the wineglass.

He urged me on, reminding me with a small cough of his presence. I jumped, startled, pulled abruptly out of my private retreat into the past. I had almost forgotten he was there.

"We found her, Mitch and I, in my apartment. She had a wooden stake driven through her heart." I turned my eyes to him and noticed his sickened expression. "Yes, you are right," I said, interpreting his look, "it was possibly the most grotesque display of violence I had ever seen. That alone would have been enough to drive a sane man crazy." I put my head into my hands to hide my red-tinged tears. "You cannot imagine the amount of blood Gwen's small body had possessed. It had sprayed all over the room, pools of clotting, sticky blood everywhere you looked."

As I sobbed, I felt a gentle touch on my hands; Sam was offering his handkerchief. I accepted it, blotted my eyes, rolled it into a ball, and tucked it into the side of the couch.

The doorbell rang and we both jumped. "I think your pizza

has arrived," I said, and he answered the door. While he was completing his business with the delivery man, I went to the bathroom and splashed water over my face. I was not surprised when I came out and saw the pizza sitting on the kitchen counter, unopened, permeating the apartment with its nauseating odor. Even a human with a strong stomach would have had a difficult time eating during this story.

I poured the rest of the bottle into my glass and sat back on the couch to finish the story. "It turned out that Gwen's death was unrelated to the other murders. Max did not kill her."

"Who did?" Sam asked with a rueful smile.

"A young man by the name of Larry Martin." I suppressed the shiver caused by his name. "But I don't think we need to discuss that situation at all. The only reason I told you was so that you could have a feel for the kind of horror Mitch experienced."

"And you too." His voice was sympathetic and compassionate. "Was she your secretary for very long?"

Does it make a difference? I wanted to shout at him, finding myself angry with his clinical questions. "Yes," I said curtly, "I had known Gwen for almost ten years. She and Max were the only friends I had."

"And Max? What happened there?"

"Max died the same way that Gwen did. Only this time we were present for the actual event." I looked away from him, hoping he could not hear the lies in my voice. "Mitch killed him in the line of duty. It was a case of self-defense, really. Max had broken Mitch's arm, smashed his knee, and was trying to kill him. I don't even know how Mitch managed to drive the stake in; he had lost a great deal of blood, and Max"—I shuddered now, remembering the writhing body I impaled on the door, the groping hands, the blood flowing from the wound and pooling on the floor—"Max was strong and he struggled a great deal. But people fighting for their life often do miraculous things; Mitch overcame him and Max died."

My final words echoed through the room, mocking me.

"So at the end Mitch had come to believe that Max was a true vampire."

I shrugged. "Mitch thought that Max believed he was. Max was literally a bloodthirsty killer; what difference does it make what Mitch believed about why or how Max committed his crimes?"

"And what do you believe?"

I gave him a steady look. "Max Hunter was my best friend. He had been my lover, looked after me like a father, guided my career, and was probably the single most important person in my life." My words seemed to shock him, it was incongruous to speak of a murderer in such glowing terms, but I kept my gaze on him as I continued. "He was also the most cold-hearted, manipulative bastard that ever lived. He deceived me the entire time I knew him. And I believe that no matter what he was, the world is a better place without him."

"But did either of you have any proof about him?"

"Proof? We heard his confession before he died."

"And that's another thing. If Mitch did not think Max was a vampire, why did he kill him the way a vampire should be killed?"

I gave a short laugh. "Quite honestly, the choice of weapon was just another one of life's strange coincidences."

"And what were you doing when all this happened?" He frowned as the words escaped his lips, as if he realized that they would be damning to me.

I allowed my anger to show. "I was there, what was I to do? Max was, oh, dammit, Max was just Max. I don't believe that I could say anything that could make you understand Max. He was larger than life, a romantic hero in the classical sense. Arrogant and egocentric, he often thought of himself as a god. And I'm not so sure that he was wrong. But he couldn't accept the fact that I could love a"—I just barely stopped the word "human" from escaping my lips—"another man. When Mitch and I realized that Max was the murderer, I begged him to let me handle it. Mitch was too stubborn, too proud himself, to accept my help."

My criticism of Mitch seemed to anger Sam. "And what in hell do you think that would have accomplished? What would have kept Max from killing you?"

I gave him a direct stare. "Max did not want me dead. He would never have hurt me physically in any way."

"Just the same"—Sam shrugged—"I think Mitch did the right thing, not allowing you to confront him alone."

"Had I gone alone, there would have been no confrontation." No, I told myself, there would have been no confrontation, since I would easily have succumbed to Max's demands; it was only Mitch's trust in me that enabled me to break the bonds imposed on me. "For all the good it has done me. I'm right back where I was, stuck between the two of them." I muttered the last words but did not repeat them at his request. "I didn't want the two of them to meet, would have done anything possible to avoid being involved in the death of either of them. Max had forced the issued to the impasse, so that there could be only one alternative—his death or Mitch's. And I loved Mitch. There was no other choice." I stopped on that last word; I had said too much, and if Sam had been listening carefully, he would have been able to hear my admission of murder. But he ignored my last comment—perhaps he wasn't as good a listener as he thought.

"And you left the country so soon afterward. Why?"

I stood up suddenly. "This discussion has reached its end, I think. Why I left is, quite frankly, none of your business. And I am tired."

He accepted my rebuff calmly, and nodded, finally taking a sip of his coffee. "Damn coffee's cold," he said, heading for the kitchen, and opened the cardboard box, "and now so's the pizza."

I tried to match his commonplace tone, as if I really had been telling a story about strangers, not people that I knew and loved. "There's more coffee, and you can reheat the pizza."

He began to rummage through the cabinets, opening then slamming them closed; dishes and pans rattled and clanked. Eventually, I heard the sound of the oven door creaking open. "It'll be ready in about five or ten minutes, in case you've changed your mind."

I glanced at the clock; it was only slightly after eleven. "No, I don't . . . oh, no."

"What's wrong?" Sam came out of the kitchen.

"Nothing really, but I just remembered I had an appointment this evening."

"At this time of night? With whom?"

"Victor Lange, executor of Max's will."

He gave a low whistle. "No kidding? Max left you something?"

"No, Sam." I tried to smile, but what appeared on my lips was more of a grimace. "Max did not leave me something—he left me everything."

I paused a moment while he let my statement sink in. "I suppose I should call him and reschedule."

"I would if I were you. If you don't mind my asking, how much do you get?"

Laughing, I answered him. "After all the questions you've asked this evening, another one could hardly matter. Especially in such a trivial area. I don't really know how much, but I understand it is a fairly large fortune—that is, if I choose to take it."

"Choose to take it? Why wouldn't you?" Sam's tone betrayed his incredulity.

All traces of laughter disappeared from my voice, and I looked at him with disappointment. "You heard the story, but you didn't listen, did you? It comes from Max." I turned my back on him and dialed the number of the Ballroom of Romance.

"Victor Lange, please, Deirdre Griffin calling," I said when the phone was answered.

I waited for a moment only when Victor picked up the line. "Deirdre, you're late."

"I know Victor, I'm so sorry. We'll have to meet at another time; I'm involved in another matter right now."

Victor chuckled. "I'm sure you are. Max once mentioned your proclivity, but I wasn't sure I believed him."

I resented his tone. "It's not what you think, Victor."

He laughed again. "Whatever you say, Deirdre. By the way,

there was a friend of yours here tonight, asking for you. Someone by the name of Ron. Ring any bells?"

"Damn," I said coldly. "I told him to wait for my call." I thought for a minute. "I would appreciate it, Victor, if you could discourage this kind of activity. Is he still there?"

"I don't know. Shall I check?" His voice still held amusement, and I grew angry, not so much at him as at myself for causing this situation.

"Dammit, no. I'll deal with him later."

"As you wish. Would you like to make another appointment?"

"Tomorrow night, same time, same place?"

"Fine, only don't stand me up again, Deirdre. Have some compassion for an old man."

I hung up the phone and turned around to find Sam staring at me.

"Trouble?" he said, a puzzled expression his face.

"Nothing that I can't handle, thank you." I was sorry to see that my hard tone caused a touch of pain in his eyes. With a lighter voice I joked, "Now, is that your pizza I smell burning?"

"Oh, shit!" He went for the kitchen. The oven door squeaked again. "Thank God it's not too bad. I never eat the crust anyway. I'm starving, how about you?"

"No, really, I don't—" I started to insist again, but a blaring siren sounded from the street. "What the hell?" I asked, but Sam came running from the kitchen and headed toward the door.

"It's the car alarm." He was outside before I could say anything, and I quickly followed him.

Sam stood at the curb, yelling obscenities at the shadowy figure tearing down the street; I held my ears to keep out the sound. When the thief was out of sight, he went around to the shattered driver's window and reached in to shut off the alarm. The acrid smell of blood and further obscenities from Sam's mouth assaulted my senses at the same time.

"Oh, shit, I cut myself. Goddamned car thieves. Goddamned stinking neighborhood. Goddamned stinking car."

"Shall I call the police?" My voice was trembling; the odor of his blood was so close, so compelling. "Or an ambulance?"

"No to both. Do you suppose Mitch has a first aid kit?"

"I don't know."

"Well, let's at least go inside and see what sort of damage I've done."

I glanced at him hesitantly as he came around the car and toward me; his shirt was streaked with red and his arm dripped small crimson drops. My nostrils flared, my teeth grew sharp, and the hunger awoke. "Blood," the voice inside hissed with glee. "We don't want him around anyway, do we, my dear? We could have him now; take him inside. We could answer all his questions in one simple step." Laughter that was not mine rang in my head.

"Oh, Jesus, not now, please not now, just go away," I whispered to him.

"Deirdre, are you okay? You're so pale—don't tell me you faint at the sight of blood?"

My nervous laughter echoed back from the surrounding buildings as I tried to drown out the inner urgings. "Of course not, Sam. I used to be a nurse." My voice sounded soft, breathless. I tried to pull my glance away from his arm and that precious blood dripping on the sidewalk. I didn't dare breathe as I walked past him to the brownstone's entrance. "Come inside." My back was to him and I licked my trembling lips. "I'll see what I can do."

His wound turned out to be little more than a superficial scratch. And to my relief, when his arm was rinsed in cold water, the bleeding stopped. I ran the water in the sink to flush away all traces of his blood. Then I lightly daubed the cut with antibiotic cream and wound his arm with gauze that I had found. My trembling subsided, and when I had finished I was able to give him a smile, with unsharpened teeth. "All better."

"Thank you. That was very well done. Are you really a nurse?"

"Some time ago I served as one, yes."

"Can't have been that long ago, Deirdre. You aren't that old."

"Well, it seems a long time." I shrugged. "You know how it is."

"Yeah." He looked at me and began to laugh.

"What's so funny?"

"Nothing, I guess." He continued to laugh, almost giggling. "What a strange evening it's been. As I said before, you are one strange lady."

"I am what I am."

"Yeah, well, aren't we all?"

I gave him a twisted smile. "No, actually, Sam, I don't think so."

He stared at me for a minute, all traces of his laughter gone, then he checked his watch and shook his head. "Look at the time; how did it get so late? I'd better go now. Do you mind if I take the tape home, make some notes, and talk to you later? I can't really think after midnight."

"That would be fine. I'll see you tomorrow night."

"Can you make it earlier? I have plans for the evening."

I shook my head. "Absolutely not. I have plans for the day."

"The night after that, then. But I assume you'll be visiting Mitch."

"Yes, during the evening." I laughed. "At least I will be there if Nurse Jean isn't on duty."

"Don't worry, she knows who you are now. She'll let you in."

"If you say so."

He began to make a move to the door. "Oh, Sam!" I stopped him before he could get out. "Take your pizza, please."

The disgust I felt must have shown, because he started laughing again. "You know, I don't think I've ever met anyone with such an aversion to plain, simple pizza as you."

I went to the kitchen, put it back into the box, and handed it to him with a half smile. "Enjoy."

Sam took the box, then laid it down on the table near the door. His expression was serious again. "Deirdre, I want to thank you for talking to me this evening. Everything you've told me will be a big help, and if his rate of improvement continues, I think I can promise that Mitch will be released soon."

I put my hand out, but he surprised me and put his arms around me in a brief embrace. Ignoring my gasp, he kissed me lightly on the lips, then moved away and picked up the pizza box. "Thanks again, Deirdre, and good night."

After he had gone, I closed the door, locked it, and went into the kitchen to open the window. It took almost an hour to rid the apartment of the smell of burnt garlic pizza. And by that time I had also purged my senses of the smell of Sam's blood.

Chapter 11

My dreams bring me once more to the cemetery. This time I am spared the trip through the dirt of his grave; he is waiting for me, lounging indolently against his tombstone, smiling at me, the tips of extended canines and white skin gleaming in the moonlight.

Wordlessly, I hand him the rose I carry, and with a courtly bow he takes it from me, delicately inserting it into his breast pocket.

Although I know it for a dream, I also sense that it is real; he is real and he is solid flesh once more. I find my voice and speak.

"What is it to be this evening, Max? More blood? More death, and torture, and guilt?"

He holds out his hand and I reach for it, touch it. He draws me to him. Our hearts beat to the same rhythm. Enfolding me in the black silken wings of his dark soul, he whispers to me.

"Nothing so simple, my love. You have more painful lessons to learn than that. Tonight I will show you youth, my youth and my lost innocence."

The world spins around us, a giddy, sickening whirl. A heavy, tangible mist swirls around us, and we are engulfed in that mist, then disembodied, thinned and carried by the cold night wind.

Candles are burning and a large hearth glows with the dying embers of a fire. Above the hearth hangs a tapestry coat of arms. At first I think the room empty, but my eyes are directed to a young man, dressed in fine dark velvet, who sits hunched over a piano.

No, an inner voice supplies, a clavichord; the piano does not yet exist.

The music the boy plays is sweet and pure, and something about the way he holds his head is familiar. Then, still playing, he turns his head briefly to glance at a woman entering the room. A smile curves his lips as he returns to the music, finishing it with a feverish intensity. When the last chords fade from hearing, he shakes back his long black hair and rises from the bench;

I gasp at my recognition of him, and although I have no body, no physical presence in this place, his eyes come to rest where I would be standing, as if I called his name. His face is still flushed with the fervor of playing, the eyes light and shining with an eagerness that even after years of looking on those same eyes, I have never seen before. His finely sculptured face is the work of a master, Bernini perhaps, or Michelangelo, but immature, or incomplete, as if the artist had neglected the last few chisel strokes that would imprint the true character.

Intently I study the young man, no more than fifteen or sixteen years of age, and the incongruity becomes clear. It is Max before the many centuries heaped upon his flawless features the blemishes of pride and arrogance, murder and blood—Max before the inheritance of the curse of vampirism.

"No," I cry, voiceless in this ancient place. "No." That so fine a creature could be so absolutely corrupted is an evil almost beyond comprehension.

"You see," he replies, an irony in his voice, unheard in the young one's, as he talks quietly with the other person in the room. "I was once your equal. I walked proudly in unity with my fellow men and humbly before my God." And the irony is replaced by sadness as I feel him direct our eyes to the woman. "My mother"—his tears are hot on my face—"an angel among women."

I look at her; through my vision she is a normal, middle-aged woman, her hair graying. Her thin frame seems fragile, and although weighed down with the volume of her clothing, she holds herself erect with pride and effort. Her face is creased with worry, sorrow, and laughter, and her light eyes are circled beneath with heavy shadows. But in Max's view she is beautiful, and his memories of her become mine. I remember her calm voice, her clarity of thought, her many loving acts, as if she were my mother. And I feel his pain when she coughs quietly, yet persistently, into a small silk handkerchief.

"She is dying." Max's voice confirms my thoughts. "In two years she will be gone." He turns on me in bitterness. "You are not the only one to have lost your loved ones over the centuries. But listen now, you must learn who I was to learn who I became."

Suddenly we are no longer observers to the past. We are merged with the youthful Max, buried deep within him.

"Madre." I grasp her hands within mine. "You were to rest. Go back to your bed; I will come up to say good night later."

"No, my son." She smiles, and the knowledge of her impending death saddens me. "This will be your last night under this roof as my son. When next you return you will no longer be my Maximilian, my dearest boy." She wipes her eyes. "But do not think that I am unhappy with your choice. You will do well in your vocation. You must remember to make me proud, and to celebrate your first Mass for me."

"Mother, I will."

She reaches up and gently touches my cheek. "Now play for me."

I obey and sit down at the instrument again. It is strange to look down upon hands that are not mine, playing from memory music I do not know. And yet it feels right. Max's young fingers move across the keys; the music comes from deep within me, flows through me, filling and purifying my corrupted soul with unexpected joy.

The scene begins to blur before my eyes and the mist engulfs us, pulling us away.

"Please, just a few minutes more," I cry. I do not want to leave the music or the room, filled with so much love; it could be a home for me; it *is* my home. "I want to go back."

There is no one to answer my plea, for suddenly I am in the cemetery, alone, in my own body once more, pressed against the cold earth of his grave.

When I woke, I could not remember where I was, much less who I was. "Max?" I whispered, trying to sense his presence within me. There was no response. I shrugged off the covers and walked down the hall to the bathroom. As I stooped over the sink, splashing water on my face to alleviate the confusion and grogginess caused by the dream, my stomach tightened in panic. What if I looked into the mirror and saw, not my face, but his? And would I know the difference?

Trembling, I reached behind me for a towel dried myself, and slowly dropped it, revealing to my relief the familiar features of Deirdre Griffin.

"Jesus, what a dream." Tensely I laughed at my fears. "You are you," I assured my mirror image. "Who else would you be? And Max, a priest? Deirdre, you have had some strange dreams in your life, but I believe that one will take first place." The sound of my voice provided some comfort, but my eyes quickly darted around the room, looking for the familiar ghost.

I jumped when the doorbell rang and without thinking went to answer it. Checking through the peephole, I saw Chris standing there and realized that I was naked.

"Chris," I called through the door, "I'm unlocking the door, but give me a minute before you come in."

"No problem."

I undid the latch and ran back to the bedroom, closing the door behind me. In the closet was Mitch's green terry-cloth robe and I put it on, tightening the sash. As I heard the door open, I quickly ran a brush through my unruly hair, and pinched my cheeks to give them a little color.

"Deirdre," Chris called, "are you decent?"

"No." I came out of the bedroom and smiled at him. "But I am dressed."

"Very funny." He acknowledged my attempt at humor with a weak smile, but I noticed he was furtively surveying the apartment.

"Are you looking for something, Chris?"

"No." Then he met my eyes and blushed. "Well, yeah, I guess I am. Didn't you have a guest here last night?"

"Yes, I did."

"Is he still here?"

"No, he is not. How did you know someone was here?"

He blushed again. "I stopped by last night, you know, to celebrate with you about Dad's recovery. But before I could ring the doorbell, I heard voices. I guess you decided to have your own private party." His voice sounded harsh and strained, but any anger I felt at him dissolved when I saw his sad, disappointed face.

"You should have come in, Chris. It was only Dr. Samuels, and what we talked about concerned you also. I assure you it was not what you call a private party." I mimicked his tone, and to my surprise, he laughed.

"I'm sorry, I didn't really know what to think. You know, with you being what you are and all, well, I jumped to the most obvious conclusion."

His implied judgment of the way I lived was beginning to anger me. "Chris," I said sternly, "first I am going to make us some coffee. Then it is time you and I sit down and have a little talk about what I am."

He gave me an evasive look. "Coffee'd be great, but Dad is waiting for us."

"This will not take long, and I promise you that Mitch will understand. There are things you should know, things he cannot or will not tell you."

He shrugged, but followed me to the kitchen, taking two

mugs from inside a cabinet and leaning back against the counter. "I didn't imagine that you'd drink coffee," he said with a glance that betrayed a fearful curiosity.

"Fine, we will start with that. I can drink almost any substance. I do not gain nourishment from it, but my system can accommodate it. Solid food is another matter, however. Rare meat is about the only food I can digest. Even that is not easy, but I can do it if I have to."

"Why would you have to? What possible difference could it make to you?" He sounded genuinely confused.

"That brings us to the next of the unpleasant facts of my life, Chris. Every day, every night, I am forced to deceive the rest of the world, carefully disguising my instincts into a façade of human behavior. So if socially I am called upon to attend a dinner, I must eat. Not every time, true, but often enough so that I do not call attention to my differences."

"But what are you afraid of? What can hurt you?"

I gave him a sharp glance, but his face was innocent and open, showing nothing more threatening than simple concern.

"Not everything you read in the books is true, of course. A stake through the heart worked well for Max." I shuddered as I made the statement, thinking that it really did not seem to work that well. He was still haunting me. "Prolonged exposure to sunlight would probably also do the trick. But I am not repelled by crosses or crucifixes."

"Garlic?"

I laughed. "It is true that I have a great aversion to garlic, but it was something I felt when I was still human. So for me, yes, garlic is an effective deterrent. For others like me, I cannot say."

"Still human?" He gulped on the words. "Exactly how long ago was that?"

"One hundred and twenty years ago, give or take a few. Apparently based on the information I gleaned from Max before he died, I am quite young for one of my kind."

He shivered and turned away from me.

I went to the coffeemaker and filled the two mugs, pushing one into his hand. "Here. Now, shall we go sit down?"

He nodded and we went to the living room. I sat in the armchair and he chose the couch, studiously avoiding my eyes. "Chris." I said his name to get his attention and he jumped slightly. "What I have to tell you now is the worst of it. I must ingest at least one pint of human blood each week to feed myself. This is not something I can do without. If I allow the hunger to build, the instincts will take complete control over me, forcing me to feed whether I want to or not. There is no substitute for human blood; its taking is a necessity, and cannot be overruled. This is the first and foremost commandment in my life, one you must never forget. Rest assured, however, that my feeding does no permanent harm to my victims."

He sat silent for a while, drinking his coffee, staring off into space. When he asked his next question his voice was weak, hesitant. "But doesn't everyone you bite become a vampire when they die?"

I looked at him in shock. "Good heavens, Chris, no. Where on earth did you get that idea?" My honest laughter calmed him, and his voice grew stronger.

"You know, I read it in books."

"Can you imagine what would have happened by now if that fact were true? There would be no humans on the earth—everyone would be like me. The escalation on that would surely rival the current inflation rate."

"Yeah." He gave me a sheepish grin. "I guess I just wasn't thinking."

The levity of our exchange was a welcome relief to the tension, but there was more I had to say even though I knew he would not like it.

"Chris, you must listen to me, this is very important. I love your father as much as possible given the incredible circumstances surrounding us. I will try to do nothing to hurt him while I am here. but I must feed, I have no choice. I do promise you that I will not do it here in his apartment." I looked up from my coffee cup and met his eyes, holding contact with him as firmly as possible. "You must not be jealous for him; you must not ask questions about how I take my sustenance and you must not tell anyone what I am."

"I promise."

"And you must not come back here until I have fed again." I counted back to the last night I spent overseas. "It has been five nights now, and I want you to stay safe. Tonight will be fine, I will be in total control and we can go to the hospital together. But tomorrow I will go out and do what I need to do. It does not concern you, and"—my voice grew harsh—"it does not concern your father."

"But"—Chris sounded petulant—"he's doing so well. What'll I tell him?"

"You need tell him nothing. He knows what I must do."

He nodded, drained his coffee, and looked over at me. "Thank you for talking to me. I can see how hard it is for you to talk about it, and I appreciate your honesty. Plus, I'd never have had the guts to ask you those questions if you hadn't brought up the subject first."

"You must not be afraid of asking, Chris. I will answer if I can." Setting my empty cup on the table, I stood up. "Now, give me a minute or two to get dressed, and we'll go."

In the bedroom I checked the closet, found and put on a pair of black leggings and a red knit tunic that buttoned down the front, applied some makeup, and brushed my hair one more time. My standard high-heeled black pumps were in the living room by the door. I walked down the hall and stepped into them. Chris was still sitting where he had been when I had left, his legs stretched out and his head resting on the back of the couch.

"Chris?" The tone of my voice was tentative, almost plaintive.

"Yeah?" He picked his head up, rubbed his eyes, and glanced over at me.

"Well, tonight, as I already explained, should be a safe night. I was hoping that perhaps, after visiting hours, we could go somewhere. I don't sleep well these days and would enjoy the company."

"Sure, what would you like to do?"

Eager to return to the previous relationship I had enjoyed with Mitch's son, I said the first thing that came to mind. "I thought maybe we could play some pool."

His relaxed laugh was a relief to me. "Yeah, sure, we could do that. Just go easy on me, okay? I don't like losing any more than Dad does."

Chapter 12

Mitch was dressed and waiting in the lobby when we arrived. Chris had seen him first and had run ahead, taking the front steps two at a time. I stopped just outside the door and watched them through the glass, smiling sadly to myself at their hugging and back-pounding. Only when Mitch's eyes sought mine over Chris's shoulder did I enter. Even then I held back guiltily, embarrassed somehow at the truths the three of us now shared. If Mitch had not moved away from Chris, if he had not given me the slow, sensual smile that lit up his intense blue eyes, I might well have turned around and walked away. But he held out his arms to me and I went into them willingly.

After our embrace, Mitch kept one arm around my shoulders and looked at Chris. "Well, did you bring it?"

"Oh, shit, I'm sorry, Dad. I meant to stop, honest, but I forgot."

"That's okay, Chris. I just figured that was why you were late." Mitch stopped a minute, dropping his arm from me and giving Chris a stern glance. "If you didn't get it, then why are you so late?"

Chris gave me an uncomfortable look. "Well, you see, Deirdre and I, we were talking, you know, and I—"

"I was explaining to Chris the facts of life, Mitch. Whatever it was he forgot, I take complete blame."

"The facts of life?" Mitch laughed. "He could probably tell us a few things about that subject, I bet."

Chris blushed bright red, and I felt sorry for him. "No, Mitch, the facts of my life."

"Oh." Mitch stopped laughing and nodded. "That's different. No problem, Chris. I was only joking with you anyway."

"What was he supposed to get that was so important?"

Mitch gave me a sheepish look. "My dinner—the food here is the worst. But it's really not as important as it seemed earlier, when I talked to you, Chris." He stopped for a minute, holding back the good news as long as he could. "They're letting me out tomorrow."

"Tomorrow?" Chris and I both said it at the same time.

"That's wonderful, Mitch. I'm so glad."

"But it's awful soon, isn't it, Dad? I mean, aren't they afraid you might have a relapse? Not that it's not good news or anything, but how could they have made that decision so quickly?"

"Chris, if I didn't know you better, I'd swear you were trying to keep me here. But those were my questions too. Dr. Samuels maintains that I am better. Hell, anyone can see that I'm better. And apparently he had a talk with Deirdre and she helped to ease his mind on a lot of things. I'll still have to check in on a regular basis." Mitch paused and gave a small grimace. "It's a lot like parole, as it turns out. But as long as I stay the same or continue to improve, he says that I'll be fine." He reached over and patted Chris on the shoulder. "So you see, everything's going to be okay. Now, maybe you could run out and grab me something to eat anyway. I'd like to have some time alone with Deirdre."

"Mitch, is that fair? We'll have plenty of time alone when you're released." I shot Chris a quick glance to see if Mitch's order upset him. Oddly enough, he had a huge grin on his face.

"All right, Dad! Now I know you're back to normal." Chris walked to the door, turned, and waved. "Be back in about an hour. See you then."

Mitch took my arm and steered me down the hallway. I tensed as we passed the nurses' station, but Jean was nowhere in sight. When we got to his room he closed the door, a slow smile spreading across his face. "For obvious reasons, it doesn't have a lock. We'll just have to take our chances."

"Chances on what, Mitch?" Trying to maintain a teasing quality to my voice was difficult, for the boldness of his words, his glance, almost took my breath away. I felt a rush of excitement, along with the heat of an embarrassed blush, flowing through my body. In lieu of an answer, he moved one of the visitors' chairs in front of the door to prevent its opening, then reached over and turned out the light.

Surprised at his daring and fearful of discovery, yet strangely elated, I stood quietly, half afraid to move or speak. Then suddenly I did not care where we were, or who was likely to walk in on us. Mitch was back and we were together in spite of all the obstacles that fate had heaped before us, and that was all that mattered.

His first touch was a tentative, delicate stroking of my cheek with the back of his hand. I drew in my breath, silent and shivering, as his fingers traced their way along the base of my neck. He pulled me to him and kissed me, and the delicacy of his touch was soon abandoned. His hands grew rough and demanding, exploring my body, his kisses covering my face and neck. Finally he broke away and looked down on me with a shaky smile.

"Deirdre?" The whispering of my name gave me chills, and I could not speak. But I could give him the answer we both wanted. With trembling fingers I reached up and began to unbutton my tunic. Only when I unfastened the bottom button did I look up.

Mitch made no move, he only smiled as I began to work on his shirt. My hand brushed against the heated flesh of his chest, and he flinched slightly and sighed. When I tugged his shirt out of his pants and undid the last button, he pulled the tunic down over my arms and unfastened my bra.

His mouth nuzzled at my shoulder and I gasped. He moaned quietly as he worked his way down my breasts and stomach, and knelt to ease my leggings and panties down my hips and legs. He supported me with one arm, and obediently I followed his silent urging to lift first one leg and then the other. When I was completely naked, his mouth and hands fastened on me with hunger and passion.

Oblivious of our surroundings, I called his name again and again, flinging myself against him when he stood up. His eyes, reflecting the moonlight streaming in the windows, met mine, and he scooped me up and carried me to the bed. Hurriedly he removed his own pants and we lay naked, side by side, our mouths and bodies rediscovering each other.

After what seemed an eternity, or a second, he entered me and his breath on my neck was labored and hot.

"Deirdre, oh, God, Deirdre," he said. "I've waited so long."

I said nothing, but clasped him to me, careless of his crushing weight, careless of my sharp nails and teeth. Abandoning all thought, I felt my body pulled into the vortex of passion, swirling ever upward into him, into the union of our bodies and souls. I loosened my grasp. "Mitch," I whispered hoarsely, "look at me."

He supported himself on his arms above me and opened his eyes. The merging of our glances was electrifying, a more intimate moment than any we had ever experienced. The strength of that look alone brought our building orgasms to their peaks. I shuddered and cried, feeling myself dissolve in his arms. He collapsed against me, sobbing and spent, his fingers tangled in my hair.

When our breathing returned to normal, he rolled from me and started to dress. I threw back the sheets and picked up my clothing to do the same. As I buttoned my tunic, I began to laugh, and his questioning look only intensified my amusement.

"Something funny?" Mitch sounded mildly indignant. "It's sort of an inappropriate time to get the giggles, isn't it?"

"Oh, no, Mitch, it's not that." I went over to him and put my arms around him. "That was wonderful beyond words. It's just that"—and I started to laugh again—"I was wondering if Jean would be the one to change the sheets tomorrow."

"What does that have to do with anything?"

"Nothing, really. But she doesn't like me very much and I'm sure that this episode would only reinforce her bad opinion of me." I shrugged and slipped my shoes back on. "It makes no difference to me; the thought simply struck me as funny. Now, you should probably unblock the door and put the light back on."

Mitch smiled and nodded. "I love you," he said almost as an afterthought, walking over to move the chair and turn on the lights. He had not yet put his shirt on, and when I saw him in full light, I wanted to cry at the way his body had been wasted; those years apart had been harder on him than on me. He carried the reminders of our separation like battle scars, his hair gray, his normally tight muscles, slack, and the flesh of his chest and back scarcely concealing the bones underneath. And when I saw the few reddened scratches on his back, I tensed and swore.

"Damn." I said it quietly, but he heard and turned to me.

"You've got it wrong, Deirdre. The correct response is 'I love you too, Mitch.' Try it out, will you?"

"No, I didn't mean that. Your back is all scratched. I'm so sorry."

He craned his neck to look over his shoulder. "Am I bleeding?"

"God"—I took a short breath—"I hope not. Come here."

I ran my fingers gently over him. "Does this hurt?"

"No, it feels good," he said, then winced when I came into contact with one particularly nasty-looking scratch. "Well, maybe not good, but it feels right. Sort of like getting your first hickey; you're trying to hide it when all the while you want to shout out 'Look what I got.' "

Worriedly, I checked his neck, then breathed my relief. "You're lucky in that respect, Mitch. No marks for Sam to wonder about during your release examination."

"And your examination results? Will I live?"

I put my arms around his waist and laid my cheek against his protruding shoulder blades. "Without a doubt, my love. Now, get your shirt on. Chris should be here soon."

"I like that, the way you've started calling me 'my love.' But you still haven't said it."

Giving him a small push so that he would turn around and face me, I put my arms around his neck and smiled up at him. "I love you too, Mitch."

Chris arrived with their dinner about fifteen minutes later. I could hear the rustling bags and smell the greasy odor of cooked meat long before his tentative knock sounded outside the open door.

"Come on in," Mitch called, and Chris poked his head in with a slightly curious glance at the two of us.

"I hope you didn't mind waiting. The, um, line was pretty long." He walked into the room and set the bags on the bedside table. Mitch went for them immediately and unwrapped two of the sandwiches, an ecstatic smile on his face. He held the burgers up to his nose and inhaled deeply.

"Now I know I've died and gone to heaven. What else could I possibly ask for?" His tone was smug, satisfied, and the look he gave me betrayed what had occurred while Chris was gone.

Embarrassed, I felt myself blush. "If you two don't mind, I'll let you eat in peace. I could use some fresh air."

"You'll be back, won't you?" A pleading note entered Mitch's voice, belying his former confidence. I moved over to him and kissed him on the cheek.

"Of course I will. Enjoy your dinner."

I did not go outside, but continued down the hallway. When I got to the barred window, I stopped and looked out on the night. It was snowing again and a draft came through the cracks in the molding. Inhaling deeply to remove the odor of food from my system, I saw the reflection of one of the patients, shuffling toward me. He did not enter one of the rooms as I expected, but came right up behind me and spoke.

"Nice night, ain't it?" His voice was nasal, high-pitched, and monotonous.

"Yes, very beautiful." I didn't turn around, expecting he would quickly lose interest in conversation and go about his way. Instead, he put his hand on my shoulder and said again, "Nice night, ain't it?"

"Yes," I said louder, "it is a nice night."

"You're his girl, ain't you? The cop's girl? He killed someone, did you know that? Drove a stake right through the poor bastard's heart. I was here when they brought him in. I heard him talk about it all. He's crazy. We're all crazy here, but he's worse 'n us. He believes in vampires." His hand tightened on my shoulder, his grip unexpectedly strong. He was working his way into the story and the monotone he first used had become more vivid as he continued. His deep-throated laughter caused a shiver down my spine, and suddenly the hallway seemed too long, too far from the rest of the hospital.

"He's a crazy one, he is. He believes in vampires, I heard him." I watched him through the window, his mouth working, as if chewing on his words, his eyes losing their hollow and glazed appearance, growing in cunning and comprehension. "Maybe you're a crazy one too. Tell me"—his voice deepened, becoming more cultured, more familiar—"tell me, my dear, do you believe in vampires?"

I looked again at the reflection in the window. I had never seen him before, did not recognize his face. But when I spun around to confront him, to compel him to leave, Max stood before me. It was Max dressed in the hospital pajamas, Max with his robe hanging askew, one end of the sash dragging on the floor.

"Dammit, Max, go away and leave us alone. That's all I ask."

His face acquired his usual semi-sarcastic expression. "You should know by now, Deirdre, my love, that I will never leave you. You are mine, even Greer cannot change that. Although"—he gave a nasty, knowing smile—"the sex is good, I must admit that. Perhaps that was the attraction I could not understand before. But he'll grow old, wrinkled, and impotent, as all humans must. And what will you do then?"

I made no response, but shoved past him and slowly walked back to Mitch's room. The back of my shoulder blades itched, as if his gaze on me were a tangible thing. Then the feeling retreated and his presence seemed to evaporate. All that remained was the patient's original voice following me down the empty hallway, whining, and begging for an answer. "Nice night, ain't it?"

Mitch and Chris were sitting on the bed. They had finished their meal and were talking quietly, but the conversation had stopped abruptly when I approached the door. I didn't bother to ask them what they were discussing; I had heard my name mentioned by both of them before I entered, and their nuances of tone had not been wasted on me. Both had been angry, but Chris's voice sounded defensive, resentful. Dammit, I thought, I'm getting tired of justifying my existence, of apologizing for what I am.

"Feeling better?" Mitch smiled at me as I approached him, his eyes lit with his special way of looking at me.

"Yes," I lied without much conviction, "the walk helped clear my mind. But I'm afraid that I have to go now. I have some things to tend to if you're coming home tomorrow." I ignored the way Chris tensed at my remark, concentrating instead on Mitch's expression. He seemed disappointed, but not upset.

"Well, if you have to go . . ."

"I do. But I'll be eagerly awaiting your arrival tomorrow."

I moved over to the bed, and Mitch stood up and put his arms around me. I returned his hug and gave him a light kiss on the cheek. "Until tomorrow, then, my love." I turned to Chris and held out my hand. Reluctantly he stood up and shook it, then sat back down again without saying a word. Giving Mitch one final look, I walked out the door. To my relief, the patient who had spoken to me was no longer in the hall, and I hurried out the front doors.

Chapter 13

There was a crowd standing around the entrance of the Ballroom when I arrived. The doorman I had seen previously still looked bored, but this night he was at least making an effort to examine the IDs of the patrons. I gave him a nod as I entered, and he caught my arm.

"Card?" he questioned, not looking up at me.

"Excuse me?"

"Driver's license, proof of age?"

"I'm afraid I don't have anything of that sort with me."

He gave a grunt. "Then you can't go in."

I was being jostled by the people behind me and thought that I should have gotten the key to Max's private entrance from Victor. The doorman let several people who had their cards ready go in ahead of me. Although I attempted to follow them, his arm extended across the door, blocking my entrance. I reached over, grabbing his wrist in my cold clasp, and he looked at my face.

"Now," I said with only a trace of the anger I felt, "do you recognize me?"

"No." He gave me a belligerent stare. "I don't. And I can't let you in, it's the rules."

"And, tell me"—my voice was almost a whisper, but it silenced the complaints of the crowd behind me immediately—"who makes the rules? The owner?"

"Nah, I never met the broad. I take my orders from Mr. Lange."

"Then be so kind as to tell Victor that Deirdre Griffin is here."

He laughed a bit, obviously unable to place the name. "And who the hell are you that I should run your errands?"

I leaned over toward him and smiled, not very pleasantly, into his face. "The broad who owns this place."

"Oh, shit," he said, and his arm dropped.

"Exactly. And you and I will get to know each other later. Be here."

"Oh, shit, Miss Griffin, I didn't mean to give you a hard time or anything, I was just doing my job, you know. We've had some trouble with underage drinkers, and I was to card everyone who tried to get in. No exceptions."

"I understand, and you are doing a good job of it." I let go of his arm and gave him a real smile. "Don't worry, you won't be fired."

He rubbed his wrist. "Thank you, Miss Griffin. I really appreciate—"

I interrupted. "Now, tell me, is Victor here?"

"Yeah, back in his, or I mean, your office."

"Thank you." I moved past him and entered the bar. The music from the band was deafening; I had not yet adjusted to the pace and noise of life in New York. I shook my head slightly and headed toward the offices.

Once again the eerie feeling of déjà vu overtook me, and timidly, for fear of waking too many ghosts, I knocked on the closed door.

"Come in." Victor's voice carried well into the hall.

I opened the door and went in. "Hello, Victor. I'm a bit early, perhaps that will make up for last night."

"Deirdre." Victor crossed to me and kissed my hand. "It's so nice to see you. You're looking well." His eyes glinted with amusement. "I do hope you're enjoying your visit."

"Well"—I shrugged, not meeting his eyes—"it's not so much of a visit as it is a return home. I did live here for ten years, after all."

"Do you plan to stay, then? I'd always received the impression from Max that you were a bit of a Gypsy, that you never stayed in any one place, or with any one person, too long." He chuckled to himself and walked around the desk, sitting down in front of his open briefcase.

His attitude angered me; I didn't take kindly to jokes about my lifestyle from someone I did know, much less someone who was practically a stranger. I walked to the desk, leaned over, and looked down at his face, longing to slap the smile from it. "Victor, it seems to me that you did not receive the one impression of me from Max that I would most like to emphasize." Quickly and threateningly, I slammed the lid of his case down. He jerked his fingers away and looked at me with a shocked expression. I met his eyes and continued. "The one thing that I value most is my privacy. And what I most abhor are personal questions of any kind. If you and I are to continue in any relationship, business or otherwise, you must understand this. I dislike comments or judgments about my life from anyone. Max presumed upon a long-standing relationship; you and I do not share that same history."

Victor lowered his eyes, seeming to study the grain of the leather briefcase before him. "I'm sorry, Deirdre. I didn't mean to intrude upon your privacy; that would be the last thing I would want. And I do understand that you might think we don't know each other very well. But I feel as if I do know you, through Max." He raised his face to me again and I saw a sadness in his expression. "God, the way he talked of you, he made you seem so real to me. Through his love and admiration of you, I grew to admire you, maybe even love you a little myself. And now that he is gone"—Victor's voice acquired that slight, thin edge of anger it always did when he mentioned Max's death—"it seemed natural to me that as his best friend I should proceed as he would wish, providing support for you, the only woman he ever loved."

I wanted to laugh at this archaic and trite speech, to scoff at his expression of Max's love for me, but something in Victor's tone of voice, his complete sincerity and truthfulness, caused tears to well up in my eyes. I brushed them away with the remains of my anger. "Now I'm the one to be sorry, Victor. I meant no offense, and I hope you'll take none." I gave him a smile and sat down in front of the desk, my hands folded demurely on my lap, my voice soft and confidential. "One of my biggest problems is, I suppose, a fear of familiarity. There have been too many occurrences in my life of which I'm not proud, and I don't care to have them bandied about or made into humorous conversation. Max and I shared an unusual relationship, and now that he's gone, I'm not sure that I wish to pursue another of the same sort. I hope you can understand that this is not directed at you personally, and that you can forgive my harsh words."

"Please consider yourself forgiven, Deirdre. And please, if you can, consider me your friend. I've no reason to hurt you and every reason in the world to wish you well. Perhaps we have more in common than you would expect."

I laughed at this statement and gave him a hard stare. "Like what?"

"Well"—he shrugged and gestured around the office—"we are both owners of fairly successful night spots that have managed to stay in business for years. For this city, that should be enough."

I nodded. "That may be true, but I also have part interest in a failing pub."

"There you go! I've had a few flops over the years myself. Not that it matters, of course, but sometimes the ones that don't do so well are the ones we most enjoy." He stood up and walked to the window, pulling aside the shade, then sighed and turned again to me. His eyes were guarded now; his expression serious. "But there's something else we share, something that I know you feel, deeper than anything, a tie that could bind us together if you wish it to."

I tensed at his words, unsure of the point he was making, but thinking again that he seemed to know too much about me. As before, the voice deep within me urged me to trust him; I listened to it unwillingly, wanting to get up from my chair, leave the room, and never see Victor Lange again.

He was watching me intently, as if he sensed my inner conflict. "Go on," I said with more sharpness than I intended. "What sort of bond could you and I possibly share?"

He hesitated a moment. "I don't want to bring back bad memories, Deirdre, nor"—he gave me a calming smile—"do I wish to invite your anger again." Victor laughed and rubbed his hands together. "You're pretty formidable when you're angry. I might have lost some fingers earlier, and they might not have grown back."

How odd he is, I thought, but said nothing and let him continue.

"No, I don't wish to upset you, and although I understand completely why you're so sensitive about this matter, I must speak of it."

With every word he spoke I grew more nervous. He knows what I am, I thought, but, how could he? Max would not have told him, and I was surely discreet enough in my dealings with humans that he should have no inkling of my true self.

"What we share," Victor continued, "is something more important than businesses or restaurants. You attempt to hide it, but I know you feel it too."

"Please get to the point, Victor. What is it that I feel?"

"Outrage and anger at the ending of a good man's life. Grief and loneliness now that he is gone. Our bond is Max—the loss of Max, and our love for him."

He must have mistaken my breath of relief as a derisive comment and he looked at me sternly. "Oh, I know what it sounds like when I say that I loved him, but I did. He was like my son, my brother, a comrade-in-arms, so to speak. And I know that you are grieving for him too. This we share, and just maybe we can help each other through it."

"I am over it, Victor." My voice seemed strong and confident, hiding my internal trembling. "It's been two years since Max died, and I have dealt with his death. It's time to move on."

"Are you over it, Deirdre? Truly?"

I lowered my eyes to hide my confusion. This was not the conversation I had feared, but it was painful enough. How could I possibly explain to Victor what Max's death had done to me? I didn't trust him enough to confide in him about the visions, the dreams, the nightmares. How could I explain that I regretted the death more than I would ever have expected? And how could I tell him that I would murder his friend again, given the same circumstances?

"Yes," I said. "I am over it." I glanced at my watch impatiently, seeming even to myself cruel and callous. But it was getting late, and I had to feed tonight. I was determined that Mitch's release tomorrow, and our reunion, would not be marred by my need for blood. "Now, do you have some papers for me to sign?"

Victor looked at me, his eyebrows raised in surprise. I felt even more reprehensible than before. He had poured out his soul to me and I had returned his confidence with my petty concern about an inheritance.

"Yes," he said coolly. "I have the papers. Have you decided yet whether you will accept or not?"

"No, I thought I should review them first."

Victor nodded brusquely. "That would be wise, of course." He walked over to the desk and opened his briefcase, removing a folder and handing it to me. "Here, take them with you and read them at your convenience. You should have your attorney review them also. And if you have no attorney, I can recommend one for you."

His tone was businesslike and impersonal, and I suddenly regretted my treatment of him.

"Victor," I started, "I am sorry."

"Think nothing of it, it doesn't matter."

"Oh, but it does. To me, it does. You are right, of course"—I gave him a quick glance to see if he was looking at me—he was staring with pain at the folder clutched in my hands, "blood money" his glance said—"I haven't gotten over Max's death and it would be a help to talk with someone about it. But not now, not tonight; it's still too raw, too painful. Give me some time, please."

Finally he smiled at me, a sad sort of smile that did not reach his eyes. "We can talk again, anytime, whenever you feel ready. Keep in touch." He closed and locked his briefcase and walked toward the door. He stepped out, then abruptly turned around. "And don't worry, any secrets you wish to guard will be safe in my confidence. Trust me."

I watched him walk out the door, then went over and sat at

the desk, laying the folder down in front of me. "I trust you, Victor, all right," I muttered, "but only about as far as I can throw you." I opened the folder and attempted to read the first page. It might as well have been in a foreign language for all that I understood. Deciding to accept Victor's offer of an attorney, I pushed the papers over to one side of the desk.

I opened the top desk drawer and idly rifled through its contents, feeling like an intruder in Max's office. Everything was organized, neatly lined up in little compartments and boxes which I almost hated to disturb. Nevertheless, I lifted everything out and spread the entire contents of the drawer over the desktop. Even with Max's curious black scrawl labeling some of the items, the collection was oddly impersonal; there remained no imprint of the man. I picked up the silver letter opener, remembering it as part of a gift I had given him when the Ballroom had opened, remembering a time when Max had stood, turning it over and over in his hand. When I had asked what he was thinking, he had said sadly, "Silver for werewolves and wood for vampires." I wondered now, as I did then, what he had meant. We had been quarreling; maybe he was threatening me. Or, and the new thought came into my head only because I knew now what he was, maybe he was threatening to take his own life. At the time, though, I had been too wrapped up in my own concerns to question him. So many things he could have told me, so many things I could have learned from him had I but asked; all this knowledge was lost with his death. And there was no one to blame but myself, and my complacency, my goddamned preoccupation with independence.

I laughed bitterly at my thoughts; I had never been independent. When I looked back at our relationship I could see now that Max had always called the shots, had always directed my actions, subtly and shrewdly manipulating my emotions, my habits, my view of the world. Hell, he's doing it even now, I thought, from the grave.

But he had miscalculated at the last, underestimating the love that Mitch and I had shared. A shiver went through me when I considered how close I had come to killing Mitch, how I had nearly acted on Max's order. How could he have failed to know how I would react? Max knew me, probably better than I knew myself. What fatal flaw in his thinking had led him to push me to my limits?

Two years of thoughts about Max's death, and I still had no answers. The visions and dreams of him merely posed more questions. I laughed again, humorlessly; I could almost believe they were a true contact with Max, that a portion of his soul or his being was communicating with me in this way; he was certainly as demanding, as infuriating, as when he was alive.

"And all of it is getting you nowhere, Deirdre," I said, and began putting the drawer contents away, holding out only the letter opener, a key ring, and a small black address book. I stood up and walked over to the couch where I had laid my purse, and put the items inside. Then I went behind the office bar. The shelves contained only glasses and the refrigerator was empty.

"Damn," I swore, wanting a drink to fortify myself against what I had to do this night. Somewhere out on the dance floor was a man, with warm flesh and hot blood, that I would have to seduce and upon whom I had to feed. There was no other choice, it had to be done tonight. And I knew what would happen; the darker self would take control of my emotions, and my body, so recently touched by Mitch in love, would be possessed by someone I did not know, and did not like.

It was the greatest of all obscenities, and it was the life I now led.

I looked around the office; I was wrong in thinking that Max had made no impression here. While I lived, so did he. I carried him with me as surely as I carried his heritage, his inheritance.

"Damn you to hell, Max Hunter, for all your gifts to me. I don't want any of them." I gave the bar an angry shove, and to my surprise it toppled over and hit the floor. The crystal glasses jumped and shattered, spreading thousands of shimmering fragments across the room. I walked over them; they crunched under my shoes, like the frozen grass in the cemetery where Max was buried. I took my purse from the couch, turned out the lights, quietly shut the door, and went out to the club, where a man I did not know waited.

Chapter 14

The band was not playing and most of the people that had been dancing were now gathered around the bar. I hesitated briefly, not wanting to push my way through the crowd, until I realized that, at least until I declined Max's offering, I was the owner. I stepped around the back of the bar, lifted the counter, and walked up right behind Fred, lightly putting a hand on his shoulder.

"Shit!" He jumped and spilled the drink he was pouring. When he saw it was me, he smiled apologetically. "Oh, hi, Miss Griffin. I didn't know you were here." As he talked, he deftly wiped the bar and served a new drink without batting an eye. "Busy tonight. Just like old times, huh?" I stood for a moment, watching him, admiring his technique. "So," he said, handing out another glass, "what can I do for you?"

"A drink would be nice."

He reached up and removed a wineglass from the overhead rack. "The usual?" At my nod he filled it with the rich deep red wine I preferred. I drained it while he watched and handed it back so he could refill it. "Bad day? We could talk about it. I'm good at that, you know."

"I'm sure you are, Fred. But some other time, if you please. Right now could you get someone to sweep out the office? I am afraid I knocked the bar over."

He stopped and stared at me. "You did what?"

I laughed. "Knocked over the bar in the office. There's broken glass all over the floor."

"You are having a bad day. No problem, consider it done. Anything else?"

"No, not really. I think I'll mingle for a while."

"Oh, that reminds me. Ron is here."

"Ron?" At first I didn't place the name, but Fred gave me a knowing smile and a shrug of his shoulders.

"You know, Ron, from the other night. You must've made quite an impression on him. He's been hanging around ever since, looking for you."

"Great."

Fred didn't miss the sarcasm in my voice. "I could have him thrown out if you want me to."

"No, that won't be necessary." As I thought further about the situation, I decided that Ron presented an ideal solution. I knew him already, had even gone to bed with him once. A second time would not hurt, and this time I could rectify my previous mistake, taking enough blood to leave him open to my suggestions. I smiled at Fred, feeling the tingling sensation of hunger begin. "Actually," I said, my voice husky and low, "I want to see him again very much. Where is he?"

Fred pointed him out for me. Picking up the bottle of wine and two glasses, I moved across the dance floor to where Ron sat waiting at my regular table.

"Hello, stranger," I whispered as I slid into the chair beside him. "Where have you been?"

"Deirdre." He leaned toward me and kissed me on the lips. "You are here, then. They told me you weren't here tonight. I've been looking for you."

"So I've heard. But I've been rather busy the past few days. And I told you I would call."

"Yeah." Ron reached over and touched my hair, separated and held a lock under his nose, inhaling the scent of it, rubbing it over his neck and cheek. "But I missed you. I guess I didn't really believe you would call." He stopped a minute and looked at me. "Hey, you changed your hair color, didn't you? It looks nice."

"This is my real color anyway."

"I knew that."

I jumped slightly at his remark. "How could you possibly know what my natural color is?"

He gave me a sly smile and a wink.

"Oh," I said, suddenly angry at his blatant attitude. "Of course." Restraining the urge to slap his face, I gave him a direct stare. He was grinning at me, but not maliciously and not as if he had deliberately intended to embarrass me. After all, I reminded myself, if you are going to play the tramp, you must expect to be treated as one.

I forced a smile before he could notice my uneasiness and poured us each a glass of wine.

He hesitated before sipping it. "I'd planned on staying sober enough to enjoy your company. But I guess one glass won't hurt." He held up his glass and clinked it against mine. "To the most intriguing woman I've ever known."

We talked for a while, small talk mostly. His conversation centered around his private law practice. Mine was about the sale of Griffin Designs, and a brief description of my stay abroad.

"Deirdre, I can't believe you just walked out of a thriving business. What on earth were you thinking of? Didn't you have anyone to advise you?"

"No, it wasn't that. It was time to leave, so I left."

"That easily? No second thoughts?"

I laughed a bit. "Well, not about selling out anyway. The sale itself left me with enough money to relocate and live off comfortably for many years."

"And what will you do when that runs out? Don't you have any provisions for retirement and old age?"

"My thoughts on old age, Ron, are unrepeatable. But I assure you, I am well endowed."

"I know." I blushed; his comment had nothing to do with my

financial situation. Then he gave me an appraising glance, checking out my clothes, my jewelry. "So you're rich too?"

I gave his hand a small tap. "What a question to ask, Ron. Does it make any difference?"

"No, not really." He moved closer to me, rubbing his leg against mine. "I'd want you even if you hadn't a penny to your name. But if you ever need a good attorney, you might just keep me in mind."

"Well, now that you mention it," I started to say, but stopped when I noticed Fred, standing next to my shoulder.

"Miss Griffin," he said, nodding at Ron, "your office is finished. Should I lock it up again?"

"No, I expect to be back in later on. Thank you."

"Oh, and I restocked the bar for you, including a new set of glasses." His eyes sparkled with repressed laughter. "But I wouldn't go barefoot for at least a couple of days if I were you. It was a real mess."

"Thank you, Fred. I really appreciate it."

"No problem."

Ron glanced at me when Fred left. "You have an office here? I knew you were a regular, but an office?"

Laughing, I stood up and took his hand. "It's not exactly mine yet, but that doesn't matter." He got to his feet, and I pulled him to me. I had procrastinated long enough; it was time for me to get to the point. I gave him a seductive smile, kissed him on the neck, and whispered in his ear, "I suspect that one of the sofas opens into a bed. Would you like to come see?"

We made our way down the hall, and I opened the door of the office and flicked the lights on.

Ron whistled appreciatively. "This is your office, huh? Just exactly what do you do here?"

"I don't know yet, but apparently I own the place."

He gave a small gasp and stopped in mid-stride. I caught a knowing gleam in his eye before he recovered his composure. Then he turned away and walked to the bar. "So," he said, his tone casual, confidential, "you're the one Max Hunter left all his money to?"

I was astonished at Ron's mention of that name. "Did you know Max?"

"Me?" He hesitated and looked up from the bottle he was opening. "Oh, God, no. I don't run in such rarefied circles. Of course, I've been coming to the Ballroom for a while, so I knew who he was. And he must have known me by sight at least, but it would be stretching the fact to say that we knew each other." He pulled the cork out and poured two glasses. "Did you know that every attorney in this city has been hoping to discover the missing heiress? And I run into you by chance." He laughed and walked over to me to hand me the drink.

"To the richest woman you know?" I anticipated his toast.

"Easily," he said, his voice warm and sensual. "But as I told you before, that doesn't matter. I do okay for myself. Oh, I guess I could always use a little more, but I'm not some gigolo out looking for a free ride."

I looked at him warily. "No?"

"No way. I do have ulterior motives"—he gave me a sincere smile, practiced, perhaps, but still honest—"but they have nothing to do with your money. Now, drink your wine like a good girl and turn out the lights."

I did as he asked and crossed the room, feeling foolish and dirty. I allowed him to embrace me, stood motionlessly while he unbuttoned my sweater. He put his arms around me and his hands caressed my bare skin. But I felt nothing, no hunger and no arousal. We need this man, I urged myself, we need his blood. I closed my eyes and stretched up to kiss him, trying to pretend that he was Mitch. It didn't work; my senses were too deeply developed and he didn't taste or feel the same. I nuzzled his neck, hoping to awaken my feeding instincts, and he moaned, but there was no answering response in my body or mind.

"Damn." I pushed him away from me, walking over to the window, my hands clutching the open edges of the sweater. Silent tears began to flow down my face.

"Deirdre?" His voice seemed to travel a great distance to

reach me. I ignored his presence, as if that would make him leave me alone. "What's wrong? Are you crying?"

I didn't answer. Ron came up behind me and put his hand on my shoulder. His touch was gentle, reassuring, more like the touch of a friend than a lover. Please be a friend, I silently begged him, I've had enough lovers. I needed someone I could trust, someone in whom I could confide. And although that type of relationship was impossible for me, I responded to his delicate urging, turned around, and let him hold me while I cried.

He stroked my hair, and when the sobbing subsided, he cleared his throat softly. "Feeling better?" he asked, his voice subdued. "Want to talk about it?"

"Not really." I sniffed and went to the bar for a couple of napkins to wipe my face. "I am sorry, Ron. It's nothing personal, but it's just no good. I can't do it, not with you."

He laughed nervously. "Sure sounds personal to me, but don't worry. Do I look like the kind of guy who needs to force himself upon crying women? It's just that the other night was special, different. I thought you felt the same."

"I'm glad it was special for you, but for me it was a mistake." Ron's eyes grew angry, and I tried to make amends. "No, I don't mean that the way it sounds. I like you, very much it turns out, but since I'm already emotionally involved with someone else, the entire situation is too difficult for me to handle. I'm not very good at interpersonal relationships; you can probably tell that. The words never come out right."

"If you were involved with someone else, why did you bring me back here?"

"I thought I could at first. But then, when we were talking and I got to know you better, I found that it was impossible."

"And the other night?"

"Well, I didn't know you that night, you were anonymous. That plus the fact that my other relationship didn't seem to be working out." I smiled ruefully, and rubbed my jaw in remembrance.

"So who is this other guy? Some rich s.o.b. like Hunter?"

"Oh, God, no. Not at all." I looked over at Ron and smiled shyly. "Actually he's a policeman."

He gave me a long, unfathomable look. "A cop? You're joking, aren't you?" He paused a bit, then continued. "No, you're not, are you?" He began to laugh, instantly easing the tension in the room. "No one, especially you, would joke about that. Fell for the uniform, did you?"

"He is a detective; I've never seen him in uniform."

"But you've seen him out of uniform enough times to do the trick, I suppose. Speaking of which, close up your sweater, please. If nothing is going to happen, I'd like not to be reminded of my failure all evening." He spoke pleasantly, his anger gone. "And I guess I might as well drink myself blind. Care to join me?"

I nodded, fastened the buttons, and, walking to him, accepted another glass of wine. My eyes caught his and I began to giggle, then laugh boisterously. He looked puzzled but eventually joined me, and we both stood like a pair of idiots laughing at nothing.

"I think it was the bit about the uniform," I said when I could speak. "It struck me as funny. This has been a most interesting evening." I took a sip of the wine and looked at him in a new light. He was right; he wasn't looking for a free ride. And he seemed to be someone I could trust. Walking over behind the desk, I picked up the folder containing Max's will and held it out to him. "Now, shall we get down to business?"

"Business? I thought you didn't want to."

"No, not that kind of business. I happen to be in the market for some legal advice. Can you recommend an honest lawyer?"

"I'm not sure whether it would be a wise move for me to represent you," he said as he hesitantly walked toward me.

"Why not? I'll pay you well."

"I don't need your goddamned scraps, Deirdre. I'm not some snarling mutt panting after the first bitch in heat I find." He put his arms down at his sides, his fingers tensed and splayed out. "You don't want to sleep with me. Okay, I can deal with that. But you don't have to offer me compensation. Quite frankly, I don't think I like the games you're playing with me."

"Ron." I moved around the desk and touched his arm. "I

haven't been playing games. I like you and I trust you." He pulled away from me and refused to meet my eyes, but I continued. "That doesn't happen very often. I require legal representation and I think you could perform the job to my satisfaction. You may choose to turn the offer down, but I hope you won't. I need your help."

When he raised his head, his eyes looked sad. "I've always been a sucker for ladies in need," he said with a reluctant smile. "And you say you're not good at handling people. Let me have some time to think it over, and check on the professional ethics involved. Can I let you know tomorrow?"

"That would be fine, Ron, thank you." I wrote down Mitch's address and phone number on a scrap of paper and handed it to him. "This is where I'm staying and the number there; don't lose it, I suspect the number is unlisted. Any time in the late afternoon would be a good time to call."

He folded the paper carefully and put it into his coat pocket. "I'll guard it with my life. And I'll talk to you tomorrow, then. Good night." He began to extend his hand, then shook his head with a grin and put his arms around me. "What the hell," he said, kissing me lightly on the lips. "I think you just bought yourself an attorney."

Chapter 15

The buzzing of the intercom interrupted my second attempt to read Max's will. Tentatively, I pushed the button on the phone. "Yes?"

"Miss Griffin? This is Fred. I hope you don't mind the interruption, but I saw Ron leave and figured it would be okay."

"What is it, Fred?"

"Johnny said you wanted to see him. He's about ready to go home now and said that you told him not to leave until you talked. He's a bit shook up."

"Johnny? Who the hell is Johnny?"

"The doorman. Shall I send him back?"

"Oh, the doorman, I forgot all about him." I sighed. I wasn't really ready for another personal encounter. "Yes, Fred, go ahead and send him back."

A minute later Johnny stood knocking at the open door.

"Come in, Johnny, and close the door behind you, please."

He walked in gracelessly, a gangly youth, probably no more than twenty-one or two. He seemed so much younger here in my office; not occupying the position of authority at the door had robbed him of his maturity. He had a thick crop of black hair that fell forward into his eyes as he sat on one of the chairs and stared down at the floor. Not wanting to make this meeting too formal, I walked around and sat on the edge of the desk, my legs crossed, one foot idly swinging.

"So, Johnny, how long have you been working here?"

"About six months," he muttered.

"And do you like it?"

He looked up at me, "Yeah, it's a good job. And I don't want to lose it, Miss Griffin. It's just not fair of you to fire me for not recognizing you." His face acquired a sullen expression, making him look even younger. "I mean, I didn't know who you were, I was just doing what they said I should." He glanced back at the floor as if something caught his interest there.

"I am not going to fire you, Johnny. Actually I suppose I should be flattered that you thought I was young enough to need identification." I had expected he would look up again, but still he stared at the floor. I grew annoyed at his lack of attention and leaned over the desk to see what was occupying his attention. "Is something wrong?"

"No," he said, getting up from his chair and kneeling on the floor. "But there's something shiny under your desk. Let me get it for you."

Before I could protest, he reached and picked up a rather thick shard of crystal. "Here," he said with pride, "this could really hurt if you stepped on it."

He put one hand on the edge of the desk and stood up, gripping the glass in his other hand. When he dropped it in the wastebasket, I could see the small cut on his thumb, smell his blood in the air.

"You've cut yourself," I said breathlessly.

"Yeah, but it's not too bad." He put his thumb into his mouth and sucked on the wound.

"Ah." A groan inadvertently escaped my lips, and the hunger within me that had not appeared with Ron raged like a fever through my body. My voice grew deeper, more husky. "Don't do that. Hold out your hand and let me see," I ordered, moving closer to him. Reluctantly he held his hand out and I cradled it in my own two hands. Our eyes met and he was caught. Before I even knew I had reacted, I pulled him to me. He tensed, then relaxed and smiled, wrapping his arms around me as I kissed him, stroking his thick black hair. My mouth found his neck, and my instincts reacted immediately. I sunk my teeth deep into the vein and his blood washed into my mouth, filling my body with warmth and energy.

"More, take more," the inner voice coaxed. Max's presence was strong, and his craving for life pushed me further, urging me to gorge myself upon this young body. "Drink," he whispered with a dark joy. "Take it all, take it all."

Johnny's grip on me began to weaken, and I could feel the strength fading from his limbs with each swallow I took. His body trembled against mine.

With a great effort of will I slowed on the pulling of Johnny's blood, gradually weaning myself of its intoxicating taste. Removing my mouth, shuddering at the shock of its removal, I tried to ignore the inner wail of disappointment and anger, concentrating instead on the live warm body I held against me. Johnny swayed slightly; his eyes were closed, his mouth curved into a small sensual smile. I moved away from him, held his face in my hands, and called his name softly.

"Johnny, open your eyes." When he did, I continued. "Nothing happened here. Can you remember that? Nothing happened."

"Yeah," he agreed, "nothing happened. I feel funny. Can I sit down?"

I smiled at him. "Sit. Let me get you something to drink."

When I came back with his drink, his eyes were more focused and the dreamy expression had faded from him.

"Here," I said kindly, handing him the glass, and watched him drink it in one gulp. "Do you feel better now?"

"Yeah, I guess so. What happened?"

I laughed, attempting to put him at ease. "You cut yourself, remember?"

He nodded slowly. "It's kind of funny, the sight of blood never bothered me before."

"Well"—I shrugged—"these things do happen."

"Yeah." He still sounded confused, but stood up abruptly. "Can I go now?"

I made eye contact with him again, and he showed no fear, no recognition of what I was. "You most certainly can, Johnny. Thank you."

"For what?"

"Why, for being so diligent in your work."

He returned my smile. "Gee, thanks a lot, Miss Griffin. See you later, huh?"

Hoping that would be the last of the interruptions that evening, I returned to my desk and the reading of the will. I advanced only a page, however, before there was another tentative knock on the office door.

"Damn," I said under my breath, then louder, "come in."

"Am I interrupting?" Fred walked halfway through the door.

"No, what the hell, come on in, everyone else in the world has been here tonight."

He gave me a quizzical look. "You really are having a bad day, aren't you?"

I gave an exasperated smile and pushed my hair back from

my face. "No, the day was fine. It's the night that's been a problem. Honestly, how did Max ever get anything done?"

Fred laughed. "Max never slept and was almost always here, day and night. Most places like this never see the owner; they have managers and assistant managers to handle the day-to-day affairs. But Max did everything himself. We all wondered when he would break . . ." His voice trailed off.

Max's death and the murders he had committed to earn him that death were public knowledge. That he truly was what the papers called him in jest, the Vampire Killer, had been kept secret. I knew the effect his deeds had upon my life and Mitch's, but had never given any thought to what others might think. It might prove interesting to get Fred's version of the story.

"You think it was the tension, then, the pressures of his life, that drove him to kill those people?"

Fred smirked. "I think the man was crazy; you only had to work for him for a month to see that. But I'd never have believed him a killer." He gave a small chuckle. "I wouldn't have thought he'd want to dirty his hands that way."

"So you believe he was innocent?"

"Hell, no, I think he did it. Don't you?"

"I know he did it, Fred. I heard it from his own lips, and Max, for all his faults, rarely lied to me." I laughed bitterly. "There were many things he didn't tell me, but when he spoke, he spoke the truth."

Fred nodded. "Yeah, he was like that. It was always the things he didn't say that got you." He glanced around the office and shrugged. "Anyway, I guess it was bound to happen, but it sure was strange, both him and Larry being carried out of here dead. And you know, the place was packed for months afterward, people sneaking in to visit the cellar and the office as if they were shrines or something. You'd think they'd stay away after all that, but we were turning them from the door in droves." His eyes shifted away for a minute and then came back to rest on me. "Speaking of the door, you did a good job on Johnny."

"Excuse me?" I jumped at his comment and knocked the folder on the floor. "What about Johnny?"

Fred moved down on his hands and knees to help me pick up the scattered papers.

"Be careful," I warned him, "there may still be some glass down there. Johnny found a piece and cut himself."

"No problem." He handed me the papers and I put them into the top drawer.

"What about Johnny?" I repeated, eager for his answer.

"Well, I don't know what you said to him, but whatever it was, it worked. He walked in like he was going to his own hanging and he walked out with a big smile on his face. We've had trouble with him before; he's not exactly the smartest person alive. I mean, he does pretty good as long as he doesn't have to make any decisions on his own. Anyway, I think he thought that you were going to fire him. I take it you didn't."

"No, of course not. I'm not legally the owner yet, so I'm sure that any decision of that nature would be a little premature."

"Not the owner? But Max left the Ballroom to you. How could you not be the owner?"

I saw no need to discuss with Fred the possibility of my declining Max's estate. "I haven't signed the papers yet."

"Oh, if that's all, that's no big deal. Anyway, I don't want to take up much more of your time. I just wondered if you'd like me to get the staff together tomorrow for a meeting, you know, to meet you."

"So that I won't be turned away again for lack of identification?"

"Yeah." He gave me a broad smile that I returned. "Is tomorrow too soon, do you think?"

"Probably. Tell me, who's been employed here the longest?"

"That dubious honor belongs to me, Miss Griffin. I was the first person Max hired. I've always hoped to be the one to lock up when we close for the final time."

"Look, call me Deirdre, please. This Miss Griffin address is beginning to annoy me. It makes me feel positively ancient."

He gave me a sly look. "As if anyone would think you were

old. I don't believe you've aged a day since the first time I saw you."

"Inside, I feel like Methuselah. But let's forget about age. Tomorrow evening I want to meet with you about how the Ballroom is being run and how you would like to change it. And if you have any suggestions about an appropriate manager"—I gave him a calculated look, thinking he would probably want the job, and, that even if I didn't like him very much, he would be good at it—"please say so. I don't plan on devoting my entire life to this place—one night a week should do just fine."

"Great," he said, and went to the door. He turned around again before leaving. "You know, Deirdre, I've sort of been dreading your return, hoping that you wouldn't come back. You and I never really clicked before, and I blame a lot of that on Max's attitude toward you. You were untouchable—none of us was allowed to refer to you by anything other than Miss Griffin, as if you were goddamned royalty or something. Jesus, I remember a time when a waitress was fired on the spot for some derogatory remark about you. She didn't say it to Max, of course, but he heard everything, saw everything. Lange's a lot like that too. But you seem different, warmer maybe, more approachable, or"—he gave an ingratiating smile—"maybe you're just better looking than I remembered." Then he shrugged, seeming embarrassed. "Well, anyway, that was a pretty long speech. I really only wanted to say that I'm glad you're back now, and I hope you'll stick around for a while."

"Thank you, Fred. Good night."

By the time I arrived outside Mitch's apartment that night, it was after three. The night was cold and clear and the moon was full. I rummaged around in my purse and found the crumpled pack of Players I had brought from England. One cigarette was left—it had lost a little of its tobacco, and was crooked—but I straightened it out with my fingers. Sitting down on the steps of the brownstone, I lit it and inhaled both the smoke and the night air deep into my lungs. I stretched my legs out in front of me, enjoying the feel of the tightening muscles and the warmth of Johnny's blood flowing through my body, rejuvenating and energizing. This is the best time, I thought, when the overpowering hunger is gone, the hunting successfully completed, the feelings of youth and life renewed.

I should have gone into the apartment, but the night seemed peaceful and I remained sitting on the steps. The smoke from my cigarette curled thickly into the still air; I blew on it playfully and, as the smoke dissolved into nothingness, replayed the evening in my mind.

It had been a strange night, to say the least, and a busy one. Of all the events, the one that I tried to hold closest was the fact that Mitch had indeed recovered. That, I reminded myself, was the reason I had returned. Even shouldn't things work out between us, and I still didn't see how they could, he was cured; I had helped him recover his life. His demons had been effectively dismissed, even though mine were still snapping at my heels, tearing at my throat. I sighed and tossed the burning cigarette into the street, watching the flurry of sparks as it hit. Then I stood up, brushed off the back of my cloak, and reached in my purse for the key to the door.

I was not surprised, just slightly annoyed, when I heard the approaching footsteps. "Hello, Max," I said curtly, crossing my arms and turning away from the door slowly. "I was wondering when you would show up."

I looked into the face of a total stranger; his forehead was dotted with beads of sweat, his eyes darted nervously, searching the dark street. "I ain't no Max, lady. Gimme your purse."

He grabbed at the bag; my hand shot down and held his right wrist in an unbreakable grip. "No, it's mine. But I will give you some money if you want."

"Give, like hell. I'll take what I want." He tried to wrench away from me, but finding himself securely held, he reached around and fumbled in his right-hand pocket with his free hand. I tightened my fingers around his wrist in warning and twisted his arm slightly. "On second thought"—I smiled warmly in his face—"I don't believe I have any cash at all." He shifted back and forth on his feet, his left hand still in his pocket. "I don't suppose"—I felt the cracking of bones as I continued my pressure on his wrist—"you would accept a check."

He didn't answer, but gave a feeble whimper; his face was now drenched in sweat and his eyes filled with pain.

"No." I smiled at him again and he shrank away from me. "I didn't think so." One final twist ensured that his arm would be immobilized for a while.

"Jesus, you bitch, you broke my arm." He stood his ground indignantly, cradling his wrist, tears streaming down his face.

"So I did," I said pleasantly, climbing the steps and removing the key from my purse. "You should have someone look at it. Go home now. And find another line of work." I turned away from him with an amused laugh and opened the door. "You don't seem to be smart enough to handle petty robbery."

The insult must have been the final straw. I heard the shot and felt the burning pain of the bullet enter my left shoulder. I could hear his rasping breathing, and the echoing retort of the gun. The smell of gunpowder was thick in the air.

Anger rose up within me, a terrifying, inhuman anger that I knew to be entirely my own. How dare he try to hurt me, I thought, and then, he must pay for this wound.

I spun around slowly and he was still standing two steps away, amazed perhaps that I hadn't cried out or fallen down. He held the gun awkwardly in his left hand; I kicked it away roughly, breaking his other wrist in the process. Then I reached down, grabbed the fabric of his coat, and held him up to my face. Our eyes made contact, and I smiled at him once more, this time with canines fully exposed.

"You stupid bastard," I hissed at him. "I gave you a second chance. You should have taken it and run." His eyes rolled in his head and he whimpered again. "And now it's too late."

"Whatcha gonna do?" His voice was hoarse with fright. The combination of the smells of his fear and my own blood was intoxicating; I laughed, and his answering shudder was gratifying, fueling my instincts.

I shifted my grip, holding him with one hand and stroking his greasy hair with the other. "Why, lover," I purred deep in my throat, "I only want to kiss you good night."

His terror intensified my feeling of elation and anticipation. His feet kicked feebly as I dug my fingers into his hair, roughly pulled his head over, and pierced his neck with my fangs. Although I was not hungry, my anger fueled my instincts and I fed on him for a while, leaving him with more than enough blood to survive. Then I dropped him; his limp body rolled down the steps and he groaned softly when he hit the sidewalk.

Chapter 16

When I arrived inside the apartment I went to the bedroom window. My attacker was slowly pulling himself up from the pavement, looking around, I assumed, for his gun. I knocked on the window and he looked up at me in fear, his eyes rolling slightly, then took off at a slow run. I gave a small laugh while I watched him disappear into the night. "That felt wonderful," I said, and stood for a moment, savoring the elation of my victory. "Just like being a god."

When the words escaped my lips, the joy I felt suddenly turned into abhorrence for both the deed and the thoughts that accompanied it. Was this how Max had started his killing spree, with the thrill that complete power over human beings could bring? "No," I said to my reflected image. "I will not be like Max."

I turned away from the window, wincing at the pain caused by the movement. This wound will have to be dealt with very soon, I thought, and pulling off my cloak and sweater, went into the bathroom and looked at the wound in the mirror.

There was a blackened hole in the back and a small amount of bruising on the front of my shoulder. I had bled a little, evidenced by the slight trickle of dried blood traced on my back, but my body, strengthened by two feedings, was already healing. Unfortunately, the bullet was still lodged inside; I could feel its alien presence there, a small, nagging pain that I knew would have to be removed. But, I thought as I stiffly twisted my arms around, I wouldn't be able to do it myself.

"Damn," I addressed my image, "who the hell am I going to get to do this?"

Mitch would be home tomorrow, but I hated to burden him so soon after his release. And any type of hospital was totally out of the question. I prodded my shoulder but could not feel where the bullet had lodged. If I had, I would have cut it out myself from the front.

I took off the rest of my clothes, went into the bedroom, and slipped on Mitch's robe. I picked up my cloak and sweater, examined the holes in both garments, and tossed them into the wastebasket with disgust. I jumped at the sharp twinge the movement caused me. Using my arm was painful, and I had no idea what sort of limitations the injury might impose on me. The bullet would have to come out, that much was certain.

On my way through the living room I picked up the Yellow Pages, then went to the kitchen, opened the second bottle of wine, and poured myself a large glass. Sitting at the table, I leafed through the pages of doctors' numbers. Only a very few made house calls, and I knew none of them. The only doctor I knew at all was Sam, and he could be of no help. I looked up his number anyway, and sat for a while, drinking and staring at the sky through the window. Dawn was still hours away, but I needed to take care of the situation soon.

"What the hell." I got up and went to the phone. "He owes me for the story I told him the other night." I dialed the number and a surprisingly alert voice answered on the second ring.

"Sam, this is Deirdre Griffin. I am sorry to call so early; did I wake you?"

"No, I'm on early shift this morning. But what are you doing up already? I thought you were a night owl."

I laughed nervously. "Actually, I haven't been to bed yet."

"Oh." There was a slight pause. "Is something wrong?"

"Well, yes. I was wondering if you could recommend a doctor for me. I have a bit of a problem here."

"Deirdre, if it's an emergency, you should call for an ambulance right away. Better still, I'll call one for you."

"No!" I interrupted. "No ambulance. And it's not really an emergency. But I need to find someone who makes house calls, someone who can be trusted, someone who can get here soon."

"Sure sounds like an emergency to me. I'll be right over."

"But it's not a mental problem, it's physical."

"I'm a psychiatrist." He paused, then continued when I didn't reply. "That means that I'm a physician too. And although I don't usually make house calls, I've got to admit that you've got me intrigued. I can be there in twenty minutes; can you hold on till then?"

"Yes," I said, wondering how I would answer the questions I knew he would ask. "Thank you, Sam. I really appreciate it."

"Don't mention it. Now, explain the situation, please, just so I know what I need to bring with me."

I thought for a moment; if I told him what was involved, he would never come. He would insist on an ambulance and a trip to the hospital. And that could be deadly for me. "We'll improvise; trust me, it'll all be fine."

"Okay." I could hear his reluctance. "But I'll bring my bag anyway. See you in a bit."

I hung up the phone, went back to the kitchen, and poured another glass of wine. I had no idea whether any type of anesthetic would work on me, and I could not allow him to put me to sleep in any event. We would have to do it without any sort of painkiller. I drained the glass, refilled it, and began to make a pot of coffee. Sam would probably need it.

I did not bother to dress, and when the bell rang, answered the door in my robe. Sam smiled, hesitated in the doorway, then entered, quietly closing the door behind him.

"Coffee?" I suggested timidly.

He gave me a curious look. "I thought you had a problem. Let's get to work first."

"Fine." Appreciating his no-nonsense approach, I reached up and dropped the shoulder of the robe. "I have a bullet lodged in here somewhere"—I indicated the bruise—"and it's in a bad position, so that I can't remove it myself."

He dropped his coat on the floor and looked at me in amazement. "Remove it yourself? Are you crazy? Besides, it can't be anything recent. May I?" I nodded my permission and he reached over and touched my shoulder, examining the front and back. "I can see that you were shot, but from the healing I would say that it was at least a month ago." He pulled me over closer to the light. His hands were warm and firm against my flesh. "The blood is recent though. Were you doing something to reopen it? And why wasn't the bullet removed when it happened? Jesus, Deirdre, this is even stranger than I expected. I can't just cut you open here in this apartment; you need to go to the hospital."

"Absolutely not, Sam. I will not go to a hospital. If you can't help me, then I will find a way to do it myself." I pulled the robe back up and tightened the sash. "Thank you, I'm sorry I disturbed you."

Sam laughed, but sobered immediately when he saw my serious expression. "You're not joking about this, are you?"

"No." I managed a small smile. "I am not joking. I was shot this evening"—I looked at the clock—"oh, just about an hour ago. I can show you my clothes for proof if you like."

I walked into the bedroom and retrieved my sweater and cloak. "It would not have been a problem had the bullet exited, but"—I came back into the living room and handed him the garments, wincing at the pain—"unfortunately it has not. It must be removed."

Sam poked his finger through the bullet holes in my clothes, smelled them, then looked up at me in confusion. "I guess it did just happen," he admitted reluctantly. He set the clothes down on the couch. "And as far as removal of the bullet, well, I can't argue the fact that it should come out. But I'm not really a surgeon and I'm hardly equipped for an operation. I have nothing but novocaine, and that won't do much good. And even if I had something stronger, I couldn't do anything here. What if there were complications?"

"There will be none. I can promise you that. I heal very quickly." I pitched my voice at its most persuasive level.

"But"—he gave me a doubtful look—"Deirdre, I can't. It's unthinkable."

"If something goes wrong, you may call an ambulance and have me put into the hospital. That should prove to you how certain I am that we can handle it here."

"Well, I don't know."

"Sam." I looked into his face and caught his eyes. "I could find a way to convince you. But I would much rather have you uncontrolled and free of any suggestions, willing to do this because I have asked you as a friend."

"And if I don't do it?"

"As I said before, I will do it myself. Look, I am sorry; it was a mistake to call you, I realize that now, but I knew no one else to call. Now that I think it over, I see that it is better that you not get involved in my life any further. Just forget about it. It is of no importance." I held out my hands to him, trying but failing to hide the grimace of pain caused by the movement of my arm.

"Okay, I'll do it," he said abruptly.

"You will?" I was surprised. I had expected him to question me further, but did not really expect him ever to agree.

"Yeah, I will. I think I know you well enough by now, to believe you when you say you'll do it yourself. At least this way, you have a better chance. And when the complications arise, I'll check you into a hospital, where you belong. But"—he gave me a sly smile—"if everything goes the way you say it will, you owe me a complete explanation of all of it. I listened to that tape again and I know there are things you wouldn't tell me."

I eyed him suspiciously.

"Come on, Deirdre, if you want me to do surgery here, you'll have to trust me completely. Anything you say will be kept in strictest confidence."

I still hesitated, then finally nodded. "Where shall we do it?"

Sam glanced around the apartment. "If you're sure about no hospital"—he looked at me for confirmation and I nodded again—"then the kitchen table is probably the best place."

I picked up my ruined clothes from the couch, and when we went into the kitchen, put them into the trash can there. Sam cleared the few things on the table, set his bag on the counter, and opened it. He wiped the tabletop with a piece of gauze and an antiseptic solution. When he finished, I climbed on the table and lay on my stomach, my head pillowed on my folded arms.

Sam moved my arms to my sides and pulled the robe off my shoulders, tucking it in around my waist. Probing the wound again, he gave an acknowledging grunt, turned to the sink, and washed his hands. I tilted my head so that I could watch his preparations. He wiped the counter with the same antiseptic solution and laid out his instruments. When everything was removed from the bag, he put on a pair of rubber gloves and picked up a syringe. "This will probably sting a bit, but I think I can give you enough to dull the pain. Hold on."

He swabbed my shoulder with alcohol, and I felt the needle slide into my skin, felt the warmth of the novocaine spread through the area. He gave me several shots, and when he was done, he wiped the area again. I gripped the edge of the table tightly and he gave me a small pat on the shoulder blades. "Relax," he said with assurance, "it will all be over soon."

"That's what I'm worried about." I rested my head on the table and my voice was muffled slightly.

"It's still not too late to get you to a hospital."

"No."

"Okay, then, here we go."

"There is one thing you should know before you start, Sam."

"Great, now you tell me. What is it?"

"You'll have to be quick. Make your cut as deep as possible, so that you can get to the bullet in time."

"In time for what?"

"Well, before I start healing again."

Sam laughed humorlessly. "Oh, sure, don't worry about it. Now, this will probably hurt a little. Are you ready?"

"Yes."

The novocaine had not worked, but I had expected that. His incision was sharp, clean, and painful. I held my breath and bit my lip as I felt the probe deep inside my shoulder, a cold metal intrusion. I stifled a shiver as he worked his way to the bullet; I felt his breath warm on my neck, felt the twist of the instrument as he searched.

"Ah," he finally said with satisfaction, "I've got it." He dropped the probe and the bullet into the sink. "You okay?"

"Yes," I replied, my voice wavering only slightly. "That feels much better already."

"Sure it does." I heard the skepticism in his voice. He applied pressure to my shoulder with one hand, and reached into his bag with the other. "Now, we'll probably need a few sutures here." He lifted the wad of gauze he had been pressing onto me and peered under it. "Well, maybe only a little tape." There was a long pause, and I heard him draw in an astonished gasp. "Jesus," he said, "I don't believe it."

"What, Sam?"

"Jesus," he said again, and pulled away from me.

I wiggled the robe back onto my shoulders and sat up on the table, fastening the sash, licking the blood from my bitten lips. "What's wrong, Sam?"

His face was ashen, his expression fearful. He backed away and I slid off the table and grabbed his shoulders. "Thank you, Sam. That was very well done." I smiled at him, but he simply stared at me in shock.

"Jesus." His eyes touched me briefly, then lowered, and he pushed away from me, his hands, covered still with the gloves, now coated with my blood, held extended to keep me away. "What the hell are you? You . . . you're not normal, not natural, your shoulder—"

Calmly, I interrupted him in the hope of staving off his growing panic. "I told you I healed quickly."

The tone of my voice seemed to help. He still kept his distance, but relaxed his arms. "Heal quickly, my ass. It's almost as if nothing ever happened to you, certainly no one could tell that you'd just been operated on. Hell, I'm not even sure you were, although I was the one who did the cutting." He gave me an appraising glance, calculating, I thought, what could have caused this extraordinary healing. It was almost as if I could hear the possibilities being listed, then being denied in his mind.

I stood quietly, not moving, waiting for his next response, knowing that nothing in his background or training could ever have prepared him for this moment. When he did speak, his voice was soft and full of doubt.

"Maybe I should take another look at that shoulder. I mean, the light's not so good in here; I could've been mistaken." Sam approached me slowly and still I did not move. He pulled the robe back cautiously, then whistled slightly through his teeth. I could feel his hands trembling as he examined me thoroughly, prodding at what was only minutes ago a fairly deep incision. "Does this hurt?"

"No, not at all. You did a wonderful job. Much better than I could ever have done. It was quick and clean, but"—I gave him a glance out of the corner of my eye—"the novocaine was a waste of time."

"You felt everything?" He stripped off his gloves and dropped them into the sink with disgust. His voice was strained, almost angry. "If I'd thought that you could feel it all, I'd never have done it. I'm sorry, it must have been awful."

I shrugged. "It doesn't matter now, Sam. It's over."

"Jesus, Deirdre." He swore again and slumped down into one of the kitchen chairs.

"Coffee?" I suggested again. "Or perhaps you would like something stronger?"

"I doubt that you have anything here actually strong enough to handle all this. Besides, I have to get to work soon. Coffee will be fine." Some of his natural humor had returned to his voice, and he managed to give me a weak smile as I handed him a full mug.

"I hope you like it black," I said as I turned away and poured a cup for myself. "I don't have any cream or milk."

"I know," he said smugly, "I remember from the other night that you have no food here at all. I must admit that I'm surprised you even have coffee."

"I like coffee."

"Oh." He took a sip and watched me over the rim of his cup. "Well?"

"Well what, Sam?" I tensed, anticipating his question.

"Aren't you going to tell me? You owe me that, don't you think?"

"I am very grateful for your assistance, Sam, but what would you like me to say?"

He gave a bitter grunt. " 'What would you like me to say?' " he mimicked my question. "What the hell do you think I want to hear, the goddamned weather report?" He shook his head and took another drink of his coffee, staring into the darkness of the cup. "You're not human, are you?"

"I suspect that would depend on your definition of human, Sam," I said gently. "I personally like to think that I am as human as any other person."

His head shot up. "Don't bullshit me, Deirdre. I get that every day from sick people who feel the desperate need to deny their inner selves. I don't know who you are, or even what you are, but I'd be willing to bet everything I have on the fact that you're not crazy and not human."

"Yes," I said with a sigh, sitting down across from him, "you are right, Sam, I am not crazy."

"And?"

"And I'm not human."

The silence was filled by the ticking of the clock. I glanced up at it and so did he.

"Alien." The word came out so quietly that he cleared his throat and said it again. "You're an alien, aren't you?"

"An alien?" I repeated, laughing in disbelief.

"Yeah, you know what I mean, an alien, outer space and all that. So where do you come from?"

"I do know what you mean, Sam." My tone of voice was light and teasing. "I just wasn't expecting that particular question. Actually, I come from Kansas."

"Kansas?" He seemed even more confused.

"Yes, you know, Kansas—the Midwest, farms and fields, Dorothy and Toto."

"But if you're not an alien, what are you?"

I tilted my head at him encouragingly. "What do you think? I should imagine you know enough about this situation by now to figure it out on your own."

He took a long drink of his coffee, and as he swallowed I saw the blood drain from his face. He was quick to put the facts together and come up with the proper conclusion, however unlikely and unsavory it was. He jumped up from the table and knocked his half-empty mug on the floor. "Jesus." The fear returned to his voice, and the easiness we had managed to reestablish dissolved instantly. "You're a goddamned vampire."

Chapter 17

"Actually," I said to Sam while I wiped the spilled coffee from the floor, "I am not entirely sure about the damnation, but you are correct about the other." He had retreated, but no farther than the kitchen doorway, when I had risen to get the towel. The expression on his face indicated his own internal war; part of him wanted to run, and the other wanted answers. When he spoke, I was relieved to discover that the second impulse won.

"But how could it be possible?"

I got up from the floor and threw the coffee-soaked towel

into the sink along with his blood-covered gloves. "I am afraid that I have no answer for that, Sam. I am what you said; that is a fact. But as for its possibility? I don't know any better than you."

"But a vampire is a mythological creature, a folktale no more real than the bogeyman, or unicorns, or fairies."

I gave him a serious look. "Is it so much harder to believe than the other fact that you so readily wanted to accept?"

He paused a moment and thought. "But alien visitations are fairly well documented and have been reported by so many different types of people. It seems more real somehow, more measurable by scientific methods."

"And you accept scientific methods, of course." My quiet voice took on a scornful tone. "But have you ever stopped to consider that folktales might have a basis in truth, might be the same kind of documented accounts from hundreds of years ago?"

He gave me a sheepish look. "No, not really, I can't honestly say that I ever gave it a second thought. Some things fit into reality, and others do not."

"And even now you don't believe me, because I don't fit into your idea of reality."

He cleared his throat. "I don't want to believe you. I wish from the bottom of my heart that I didn't have to believe you." Sam stared at me for a time and shook his head. "But I do believe you. Only now I don't know what I should do."

"Why should you have to do anything?"

"Well, well . . . but you're a vampire." His voice acquired a higher pitch and cracked on the last word. "There must be something I should do."

"Sam, listen to me. What I am is no danger to you or to anyone else. I lived in this city for ten years, and in all that time the blood I took was never missed." He shuddered at the mention of blood, but I continued. "Generally, I take less than you would donate at a blood bank. I do no harm to others. You can check on the facts if you want. The only people killed here in that fashion were killed by Max."

"Max." He said the name emphatically in remembrance, from my story the other night. "Max was a vampire too?"

"Yes."

"Then Mitch"—his eyes drifted to my face and stayed there—"Mitch was telling the truth."

"Yes. And you should take a lesson from him. If you were to let on to others what I am, you would be treated the same—institutionalized for years. Not a soul would believe you."

Sam laughed, more to relieve his tension than to express humor, and began to gather his instruments and pack his doctor's bag. "And does Mitch know about you?"

"Yes, Mitch knows." A smile crossed my face thinking of him. "And he doesn't seem to think that I'm a threat to the general public. Let it go, Sam." I moved to him and put a hand on his arm gently. "You can't do anything about this situation." Meeting his eyes, I drew him into me as much as possible. "And you really don't want to."

"No," he said directly, "I don't. But I want to talk more about it, document your case, if only for my own satisfaction." He smiled at me honestly, with only a trace of fear. "What an opportunity. Interviewing a real live mythological creature. I wish I'd brought my recorder."

"Well, Sam," I said with a twisted smile, "although it's not all it is cracked up to be, I will do my best to satisfy your curiosity. But it will have to be some other time." I glanced over my shoulder at the window. The first streaks of dawn were appearing in the sky. "You have to go to work, and I have to go to sleep. I'll see you out."

He gingerly picked up the gloves from the sink, wrapped them in the towel, and put them in the garbage. When he picked up his bag, we walked into the living room. He retrieved his coat from where he had dropped it on the floor and put it on. "When can I call you?"

"Later on, maybe in a few days. I'd like to get reacquainted with Mitch, spend some uninterrupted time with him. We have a lot to catch up on."

"What will you do when I leave?"

"Go straight to bed and sleep until Mitch comes home. He'll be released today, won't he?"

Sam laughed. "At this point, Deirdre, I've no good reason to hold him. Apparently, there was never anything wrong with him." He shook his head again and walked to the door. As he opened it he turned to me and his voice seemed strangely enthusiastic and youthful. "Jesus, vampires, who'd have thought?" he said, and went out.

After pulling the drapes and securing the apartment for the duration of my sleep, I went into the bathroom and removed my robe. Sam had done a good job on my shoulder, I thought as I twisted my arm around. It was still sore, but I knew that the slight stiffness and bruising would be gone by the following day; the scar from the incision, however, would require a little longer to heal. I hung the robe on the door hook, walked down the hall, and crawled into bed.

I open my eyes to an unfamiliar darkness, and the pain in my shoulder has worsened greatly. I feel the presence of others in near proximity, but I have been robbed of all my heightened senses. I am blind in this night—hurt, bewildered, and weak beyond relief. Panic strikes me and I attempt to scream; the sound that escapes my lips and lungs is a deep, rattling moan.

We are dying.

The voice echoes within my mind, and as I recognize it, I relax inwardly. Although I am still caught up in the grip of fear and pain and death, I know that I dream. And because I am Max, I know that this body I now occupy is older than the other I inhabited; it is hardened, embittered by ten long years of privation. I have served as priest and comrade on the battlefields of this holy war.

The mind of the younger Max knows nothing but the cause he has supported. He is shielded from our thoughts, from his thoughts, from the remembrance of another twenty blood-filled years of war. He is the present, I am the present. And I have served, my pain-ridden senses cry out, I have been found worthy of these deeds done for God. And now I will die. But even in the face of death there is a lightness of spirit, a satisfaction in the ministry for church and Savior. There is also a deep sadness for works that must be left unfinished; this is what I regret, not death itself.

The light from a lantern bobbles in the distance and moves toward me; I peer through the darkness to see who approaches.

"Brother," the figure addresses me in a heavily accented Spanish. "Dying is difficult when much work for the Lord remains to be done." There is an irony in the voice, but I respond to the words because they mirror my own thoughts exactly.

"I do not fear death," the whispered words rasp from my dry throat, "for I go to my God."

"But should there be a way to save you for future works, would you undertake it, though the path be strewn with hardships?"

I nod, and the pain of this movement causes my head to spin. I see the glint of a knife, but I am held by the gaze of his eyes as he makes a movement too fast for me to follow. A strong arm encircles my shoulders and holds my body in an upright position. I black out for a minute, and when next I am aware, a bitter tonic is flowing into my mouth; I choke and swallow. The medicine's taste is familiar, and something in my mind, alien, yet familiar, screams a warning.

"Do not drink," it cries, "for the salvation of your soul, do not drink."

But I cannot control my reflexes. With each swallow the taste becomes less repulsive, growing instead seductive and sweet, like the finest wine. My body blazes with heat; a healing warmth floods through my system. Infection, pain, and death all fall away from me, and I am man perfected, healthy, alive, and, the warning voice sobs, human no more.

The man wraps the sickroom blanket around my shoulders. The smell is offensive, but I welcome the warmth, for my body has suddenly grown cold. "Come with me," he says with a biting laugh. "You do not belong here anymore."

"You are a saint," I gasp, bewildered and awed by my complete recovery from death. "An angel from God, come to work a miracle. *In nomine Patris, et Filii—*"

He interrupts me with another laugh. "That is enough of that. Now, come."

Docilely, I allow him to lead me away from the life I led; he whispers counsel to me as we walk, his strong arms support me as I stumble, overwhelmed by the array of sensory stimulation I am now receiving. The stars are so bright, clearer than I had ever noticed before. I can smell so much more in the night air, and the texture of the ground beneath my bare feet is rich and firm.

I finally become aware that we are riding in an open carriage; he drives the horses hurriedly, cursing and whipping them on. When we arrive at the house, it is still dark, but I feel the approach of dawn, and catch some of his panic and fear. I do not want to enter that house, but he reaches up and throws me over his shoulder, carrying me as if I were dead. All the while, he is speaking, his voice soft and commanding. I cannot fully grasp the meaning of his words, but they frighten me and anger me. They drop heavily into my soul, and the coldness of death sinks once again into my body.

We enter a darkened chamber. I can see that it is unfurnished but for two coffins. He puts me onto my feet and stares deeply into my eyes. I cannot look away.

"I have prepared a place for you. Today you shall sleep here and tomorrow night I will explain all." He smiles and I shudder at the malice in his face, at the sharpened teeth he displays. But I obey him and lie down in the box he has opened.

When the lid is closed upon me, I want to cry out, to leave the empty place to which he has brought me. But his command holds me, and as I sense the sun rising, my eyes close of their own volition. Of his words, only one remains in my mind and I carry it into sleep with me. "Nosferatu."

A swirling inner rage overcomes me, wrests me from the transformed body of Max, and I stand again disembodied. I am not alone; for I feel his breath and hear his voice, heavy with hate and regret. Somehow the young and the old Max have merged together; the two voices combine in a cry that rings in my ears and causes a chill to caress my spine.

"I want to die. I should have died. Dear Father in heaven, let me die."

I woke shivering, echoing Max's words. Not yet recovered from the dream, I was startled by the touch of a hand on my head, stroking my hair. I sat up quickly, snarling and hissing. "You bastard," I whispered vehemently, "what have you done to me?"

"Deirdre? Deirdre, what's wrong? Wake up, please, wake up."

The name seemed unfamiliar at first, but the pain in the voice finally reached me, and I realized who and where I was. I opened my eyes to find Mitch hovering over me, his expression hurt and uncertain.

"Oh, God, Mitch, I'm sorry. I didn't realize it was you."

"I understand from Dr. Samuels that you had a rough time last night. And I really didn't want to wake you." He leaned down and kissed me warily on the cheek, his eyes betraying his fear. "But you seemed to be having one hell of a nightmare."

"Thank you." My voice was dry and rasping. I brushed the hair from my eyes, cleared my throat, and tried again. "I was. How long have you been here?"

Mitch looked over at the clock on the bedside table. "Oh, about an hour or so. It's wonderful just to have you here and watch you sleep." A loving smile crossed his face, and he sat down on the bed next to me. "You have the face of an angel, Deirdre. But when you started thrashing around, muttering and crying, I thought you'd be better off awake. You can go back to sleep now if you like; the sun won't set for a couple of hours."

"Nonsense, Mitch, now that you're here, why would I want to sleep?"

"Then do you want to talk about it?"

"Talk about what, Mitch?"

His mouth twisted, and I recognized the slight edge of jealousy in his voice. "Talk about what happened last night between you and Dr. Samuels."

"Oh, that." I reached over and touched my shoulder; as I expected, the soreness was gone, but I could trace a thin scar where there had been an incision. Then I took his hand and pulled it over so that he could feel the skin. "He told you nothing?"

"Not a word. Just that everything was okay, that I wasn't to worry, but there had been a slight emergency last night and you would probably be a little tired today." He peered at my shoulder. "So what happened?"

"Some unlucky mugger chose the wrong victim."

"You were mugged?" He lost his pout and grew instantly concerned. "Where? You really should be more careful."

I laughed, and gave him a sharp look. "You should know better than anyone that I have very little to fear from someone not armed with a wooden stake. I was right outside this apartment and he surprised me; I suppose I wasn't paying attention. But I can assure you he got the worst of the exchange. All I received was a bullet in the shoulder that unfortunately I could not dig out myself."

"Did you call the police?" He seemed personally affronted that this had occurred.

"No, I didn't."

"Why not?"

"When he left, he had two broken wrists and was missing about a pint or so of blood. I really didn't want to have to explain that to your friends at the precinct. And I believe he'll probably be a little reticent about attacking a lone woman in the future."

Mitch laughed. "I guess so. You really broke both his arms?"

"At first I broke only one. I hoped that he would take the hint and leave me alone. But then he shot me, and it hurt. I got angry and, I'm afraid, a little carried away."

"And you told all this to Dr. Samuels?"

"No, Sam never asked how it happened. I asked him to remove the bullet, and he did."

"In the hospital?"

I gave a small laugh. "You know how much I hate hospitals,

Mitch. I wouldn't allow myself to be admitted. We used the kitchen table."

"Bloody hell, Deirdre. You let my psychiatrist perform surgery on you on my kitchen table?"

I shrugged and smiled. "What difference does it make? Yes, your kitchen table. I'll buy you a new one if you like."

"No, that isn't the point. Didn't it hurt?"

"It hurt like hell. But it's over now."

"But, Deirdre . . ."

"Hush, my love." I put one finger to his lips and traced my other hand slowly up his shirt-sleeve until I reached his neck. I pulled his head toward me so that our faces were only inches apart, and smiled. "Now, do you want to talk about my operation," I whispered, "or do you want me to welcome you home?"

Chapter 18

"Deirdre?"

"Hmm?" I murmured lazily, my head resting on Mitch's chest, my fingers gently stroking the faint scars on his right arm, the visible memories of his confrontation with Max.

"I think Dr. Samuels may suspect what you are."

I raised my head and met his eyes. "Why? What exactly did he say?"

"Well, he never came out directly with any accusations. But he asked some really strange questions during our exit interview—all about vampires—did I still believe that they were real, did I have any guesses about how they would survive in modern times, how would they live, what would they look like?"

I gave a small chuckle. "And what did you say?"

He matched my smile. "I lied shamefully, of course. You'd have been proud of me. But"—Mitch paused a moment, combing his hair back with his fingers—"he seemed disturbed by my answers. He acted strange, almost as if he were disappointed that I denied everything. And from the look in his eyes, I think he suspects. It could be a problem."

"No, it will not be a problem. And you are wrong, he suspects nothing. He knows."

"How on earth could he know? And what do we have to do about it?" His voice was edged with anger, not directed toward me, I thought, but toward whatever peril Sam's knowledge might contain.

I stroked his cheek to calm him. "Don't worry, my love. I plan to do nothing about Sam. He knows only because I told him and I trust him with the truth. He is no danger to me, or to us."

"Us." His voice was soft now, he took my hand and kissed the palm. I closed my eyes and savored the sensation; his warm mouth sent a shiver up my spine. "I like the sound of that." His mouth moved up to the soft, delicate skin on my wrist. "And what do you plan to do about us?"

"An interesting question, little one." My body tensed and my eyes flew open at the sound of Max's voice. I glanced around the room and saw him, lounging indolently in the doorway. "What shall we do with your human lover? Transform him? No, I can tell you don't like that idea. Marry him? Why not? The three of us could be very comfortable together."

Go away, I urged him silently, aware of Mitch's growing confusion. Just go away and leave me alone.

Max laughed so loud that I thought it was impossible that Mitch would not hear. But he seemed oblivious of the unwelcome presence in the room.

"Deirdre? What's wrong? I don't mean to pressure you about our relationship, but I can't seem to help myself. It was hell those years without you; I can't bear the thought of losing you again. I told you before that I don't care what you are or what you've done. I love you and I want to marry you."

"Mitch." I tried to keep the anger from my voice, for it was not directed at him. "I don't want to talk about this now. Later, perhaps, when we are alone."

"Alone?" Mitch sat up and looked around. "Who else is here?" He gave a small nervous laugh when he saw nothing, then relaxed and ruffled my hair. "Deirdre, we are alone."

"I—I—I know," I stammered, upset at my error and outraged at Max. "I meant after we've spent more time together alone."

Dammit, Max, get the hell out, I thought to him. *You're not wanted. Go away and leave us alone.*

Max threw his head back and laughed, undaunted by my anger. I could do nothing in this situation but endure his presence, and he knew it. Then his eyes softened and he nodded toward me. "I'll come back, little one, look for me." His figure faded and he was gone.

I sighed and continued to stare at the empty doorway. Mitch reached over and waved his hand in front of my face.

"Deirdre, are you okay?"

I pulled my eyes away from where Max had been standing and turned my attention back to Mitch. "I've been away and you haven't been well. I think we should wait a while, take it one day at a time. A lot of things have happened to the both of us while we've been apart."

"Nothing has changed for me, Deirdre." His voice was sad. "I thought you felt the same."

"I do, Mitch, I do." I kissed him. "But, well, there are a lot of things you don't know, about me and how I have been living."

"You could tell me."

"I could and I will." I got up from the bed, pulled a pair of jeans and a sweater from my suitcase, and began to dress. "But I can't talk about it now."

"What are you doing? Are you going somewhere?" Mitch was growing angry, and there was nothing I could do.

"I have to go out."

"Just like that, huh? Welcome home, Mitch, and then you're off again?"

I walked over to him and sat down on the bed. Smoothing his hair, I held him close to me. "I do love you, Mitch. You must believe that or we'll never be able to come to terms in this relationship. And I will be back tonight. But right now I have some business to tend to."

He started to reply, but the phone rang and he answered. "Yeah," he said with a suspicious look at me, "she's here. And who the hell are you?"

He grunted and held his hand over the mouthpiece before handing the phone to me. "Some guy named Ron. Sounds young and handsome. I suppose he's the business you need to see about?"

"Jesus, Mitch, he's my attorney."

"Oh," he said, handing me the phone with a shrug and a sheepish smile. "I'm sorry."

"Hello, Ron." My voice sounded tired and irritated. "What can I do for you?"

"You know." His voice was warm and intimate and I stood up, turning my back to hide my embarrassed blush from Mitch's keen eyes. "But," he continued, "I assume that's still out of the question. Was that your cop who answered?"

"Yes."

"Thought so. He sounds like a cop."

"Excuse me, Ron, but did you call for anything specific?"

"Yeah, sorry. I just wanted to let you know that I did some checking around and I can accept your job without a conflict of interest."

"You know, Ron, I have been meaning to ask you, what sort of conflict could there be?"

"Well"—his voice sounded evasive—"there's the other night, for one thing."

I laughed. "You have a hell of a set of professional ethics if that's all it is."

"The Bar does tend to frown upon relationships with clients." He stopped abruptly, and I knew there was another reason he did not want to mention.

"And?"

"And what?" Now Ron sounded defensive.

"And there's something else. I can hear it in your voice."

There was a long pause, and Ron sighed. "Well, I have, in the past, done some work for The Cadre, and since they inherit everything if you decline, I thought there might be a problem."

"Oh." That made sense to me. "What exactly is The Cadre?"

"An international organization of entrepreneurs." The answer came readily to his lips, as if it were rehearsed, but I hardly cared one way or the other.

"So," Ron said, his tone relaxed again, "when should we get together? I'll need to read over the will."

"I have to be at the Ballroom sometime tonight." I winced at Mitch's intake of breath and glanced at the clock. "How about nine or so?"

"That'd be great." He hesitated. "Ah, you aren't bringing your friend along, are you?"

"Oh, no," I insisted. "I don't think that would be wise."

"Good," Ron agreed. "I wasn't looking forward to meeting him anyway."

"No, I suppose not. I'll see you later, Ron. Thank you for calling so promptly."

I hung up the phone and looked over at Mitch. While I was on the phone he had slipped his pants on, and was standing by the window.

"The Ballroom? Why on earth are you going there?"

I moved behind him, put my arms around his waist, and rested my chin on his shoulder. We stood there for a while, not speaking, but watching the glistening rain on the early evening streets.

"Well? Aren't you going to answer me?"

"It's the ultimate joke." I smiled and kissed the bare skin of his shoulder. "Max left everything to me in his will, including the Ballroom. I'm his sole heir."

"No kidding? Who'd have thought?"

"Not me. But he did, so now I have to struggle with that as well as everything else. He never did me any favors; even from the grave he's making trouble for us." I didn't try to disguise the bitterness in my voice. "Max is the dirtiest bastard that ever lived."

"Was."

"What?"

"Max was the dirtiest bastard that ever lived. But he's dead now, Deirdre, and he can't hurt you anymore." Mitch turned around and held me close to him. I wanted to cry, but instead I hugged him back, then broke away abruptly.

"You are right, I suppose. It's just hard for me to believe he's dead."

"Well, he is," Mitch said determinedly, "and I don't want to talk about him anymore. I thought we were rid of him two years ago. Let's quit dragging him back. Okay?"

Was that what I was doing, I wondered, causing his presence by my thoughts of him? "Fine," I agreed, trying to not let my skepticism show. "And now, the sooner I go, the sooner I can get back. Get some rest, my love." I attempted a sensuous smile. "You'll need it when I get back."

Mitch followed me out to the living room but stopped me as I started to walk out the door. "Where's your coat?"

"My coat? Why?"

"It's pouring out, you'll get soaked."

I laughed. "It hardly matters to me."

"But it does to me. It's bad enough that you have to leave just when I get here, but if you think I'm going to let you back in here dripping wet . . ."

"You can towel me off at the doorstep when I get back."

"Now, that's a tempting offer—" Mitch started toward me with a boyish grin.

"Anyway," I interrupted him, "I don't have a coat. I brought only one with me, and it's now in your kitchen trash."

"Why is it there?"

"Bullet hole."

"Oh, yeah, I almost forgot about that incident. Look, maybe I'd better come with you tonight. Just give me a minute or so to finish dressing, and I'll be right with you."

"No, Mitch, you should stay home." I tried to say it as gently as possible, but it came out as more of an order than a request.

"And what the hell does that mean? That I'm not good enough to be seen out in public with you?"

"I never said that, Mitch. I just think that you should stay home; you haven't been well." I knew he was getting angrier with each word I said, but there was nothing I could do. He could not accompany me tonight, or any night when I met with Ron. The anger he felt now would be nothing compared to what he would feel if he ever learned what had transpired between me and my newly hired attorney. "No," I repeated. "You should take it easy tonight. It's your first night home, and you need your rest."

"And that's another thing, Deirdre, while we're at it. I haven't been sick and there's absolutely nothing wrong with me. This is the second time tonight you've used my health against me. You won't talk about making a commitment to this relationship because I haven't been well. You won't let me come with you anywhere because I haven't been well."

"And all of that is true, Mitch." I held my position at the door, although I really wanted to hold him and comfort him. "You haven't been well."

Suddenly, it was as if all the anger and frustration he had been feeling for the past two years boiled over at once. "Bloody hell, Deirdre. And if I haven't been well, as you so delicately put it, then maybe you can tell me whose fucking fault it is." I cringed away from his obscenity; I knew he never used that word unless under a great strain, but he ignored my reaction. "I can tell you whose fault it is. This whole situation is your fault; you and all the other goddamned bloodsuckers out there got me into this, and now I can't ever get out. I wish to hell I'd never heard of vampires. I wish to hell I'd never fallen in love with you! I'm sick to death of the whole thing."

He stood staring at me, panting slightly, and I watched the anger slowly drain from his eyes, to be replaced by sadness and remorse. But it was too late; the words had been said and he could not unsay them. And I could not deny their truth, not to him or to myself.

There was nothing I could say, nothing I could do to change this moment. This was the moment I had spent most of my life avoiding, the inevitable moment I knew would come when I first fell in love with Mitch. Why did I ever allow it to go this far? Why did I ever let him into my life?

I could only stand and look at him, no more than three feet away from me, and more than a century out of reach. And when I felt my eyes began to tear, I turned my back on him.

"Good night," I whispered softly, and walked out into the wet darkness of the night.

Chapter 19

By the time I got to the Ballroom I was completely soaked. But the walk in the rain had cleared my mind, if not my sadness, and I felt prepared to face the evening. I walked through the crowd, ignoring the curious stares of the people that I passed, and stood at the bar.

"Fred."

He looked over at me and stifled a small laugh. "I guess it's still raining out, huh?"

"Yes." I smiled back at him. "I'll be back in the office. Bring me a towel or two, will you? And get someone to relieve you here. We need to talk."

"Sure thing." He took off his apron and headed out the other side of the bar.

"Oh, and Fred?"

"Yeah?"

"If someone by the name of Mitchell Greer shows up or calls, I'm not here. You haven't seen me and don't know when I'll be in next. Make sure the doorman gets the message also."

"You bet. I'll be right there."

Fred came to the office equipped with several large towels and a clean waitress's uniform. "I thought you might want to dry out completely," he said with a shrug, "so I brought you something to change into. Next time it rains, though, I recommend an umbrella."

"Thanks," I said. "Now give me a few minutes and come on back in." Fred closed the door behind him and I pulled off my dripping clothes, dried myself, and slipped into the uniform. It was made of lightweight black nylon, and I smiled in remembrance as I fingered the flimsy material. The last time I wore a uniform similar to this was in the early sixties at a Midwest truck stop. It was there that I had met Max, for what I'd supposed to be the first time, never knowing that he had been the one responsible for my transformation almost a hundred years before.

"Dammit, Max, you should have told me who you were. I would have gone with you anywhere and stayed with you forever. But no, you had to wait until I met Mitch before letting me know what really lay between you and me. And then it was too late."

I looked around the office uneasily, halfway expecting Max to make an appearance. Instead, there was a knock on the door and I jumped and called, "Come in."

Fred entered, followed by a waitress I did not know, who collected my wet clothes and promised to have them dried right away. Then Fred and I sat down to discuss the business of the Ballroom. When we concluded our talk, it was only a little after eight. He had agreed to take the manager's job, as I thought he might, and I was happy to leave the club in his hands. I made it absolutely clear to him that I did not want to be involved in the day-to-day routine.

"I will, of course," I said as we ended the interview, "be stopping by from time to time. And it is absolutely essential that you keep my favorite wine in stock. Other than that, you're on your own."

"Great." He beamed his delight at the situation. "This is a good opportunity for me, and I really appreciate you giving me the chance. Max never trusted anyone and"—Fred shrugged—"since he was always here, it didn't really matter anyhow."

"Fred," I said, thinking of the ring of Max's keys still in my purse, "he couldn't have been here all the time. He must have lived somewhere else. I have one of his keys that doesn't seem to fit any lock around here; I assume it's from his apartment."

"Could be," he said skeptically, "but any time of the day or night, he was here. Keeping a separate apartment would have been next to impossible. He would never've used it."

"But he had to sleep somewhere, didn't he?"

Fred gave a wry laugh. "Max never slept. Anything else?"

"No, thank you, Fred. I'll see you later."

Just before he closed the door, I called to him. "Oh, by the way, Ron will be coming in to see me around nine or so. Please buzz me when he gets in. Other than that, I would like not to be disturbed."

"Gotcha," he said with a wink, and left.

I pulled the ring of keys out of my purse. All but one was neatly labeled. There was a key for the office, the front door, the back entrance, the desk, the cellar, and a few smaller keys that were labeled "supplies." I removed the one unlabeled key and held it in the palm of my hand, putting the rest of the ring back in my purse.

"All right, Max," I said with a trace of humor, "you and I both know that you had to sleep sometime. And you had to have a secure place to do it." I stared at the key as if it somehow held the answers to his past. Then I suddenly laughed. "Dammit, Deirdre," I scolded myself, "it is absolutely amazing that you've survived for so long with so inadequate a brain."

I got up from the desk and looked around the room. There were no heavy draperies here to conceal a hidden door such as the one that existed in my office at Griffin Designs. But it had to be here. During his life, Max had as great a need for secrecy as I still did; if he secured a safe place for himself, it would be here.

I closed my eyes and thought back to the time when Max had ruled me and this place. We were always quarreling, but he always called me back. And angry or not, I would return to him. I remembered the night I had attacked him, thinking that he had betrayed me to the police as having committed the murder of his first victim. I could feel the texture of his shirt and skin shredded beneath my nails, could still taste the blood that I licked from my fingers. He had thrown the shirt away and gotten another from the closet.

"The closet. Dammit," I said, flinging the closet door open and inserting the key into the lock mounted on the back paneling. It fit and turned with an almost inaudible click. Cautiously, I pushed the door and peered into the room. The light from the office only dimly lit the area, and I looked around for a switch.

"Come now, Max," I whispered into the still air, "even I appreciate the convenience of electricity." But there were no lights here, only darkness and dust and cobwebs. I entered the room anyway and saw a small table to the right of the door equipped with a filled candelabrum and matches. I lit them and looked around.

The room was unfurnished, totally unlike the secret apartment I had maintained for years. There was a large wooden chest up against one of the walls, but the focal point was the large stand occupied by two coffins, laid out side by side. One was larger than the other and more elaborate, but there was no mistaking either's purpose.

"Oh, Max." My laughter sounded mocking in this emptiness, and the dust, stirred by my entrance, swirled and glinted eerily in the candlelight. "How very gothic of you. But why two?"

I approached the larger one. The wooden top was thick with two years of accumulated dust, but I could make out the ornate antique carving. I brushed my hand over the gold plate and leaned down to read its inscription—"Maximiliano Esteban Alveros—1596."

"Jesus," I breathed softly, almost reverently. "So old." As if of their own volition, my hands reached down and opened the casket. It was empty.

"Of course, you fool," I sighed in relief, "did you really expect him to be here? He's dead, dead by your own hand, and buried these two years." Even so, I studied the coffin's emptiness as if it contained the answers I sought. There was a faint aroma of Max in the room— the wood that had absorbed his scent for four centuries exhaled it now. Gently, I let the lid down and walked around the stand to the other coffin.

This one was newer, streamlined and modern. With shaking hands I flung the lid open. It was also empty and its aroma was one of newness. No one had ever used it. I dropped the lid, and when the dust flew from it I could make out an engraving of a single rose in the dark wood—a black rose.

"But this can't be mine." I denied the obvious. "I never slept in one of these." I shuddered at the thought of being enclosed here during the long summer days. But as I looked closer, there was no mistaking the name on the golden plate—"Dorothy Grey—1832—Beloved Wife."

My knees weakened and I collapsed on the floor, leaning up against my own coffin, not knowing whether to cry or laugh. I did a little of both. "Jesus, Max, if it weren't so damn perverse, the gesture might be touching." Whatever would have given him the idea that I would share his tomb with him? But as I considered the facts, I realized that there was a time when I would have done so, and willingly. Only Mitch's presence in my life had prevented that event from occurring. And Max had been responsible for our meeting.

I shook my head and pulled myself up from the floor. Everything in my life was becoming so convoluted, so bewildering, I hardly had any idea what to do. It had been a difficult situation when Max was alive, but now it was almost totally impossible.

"Quite a triangle, is it not, Max?" With one finger I idly traced the rose carving on my coffin lid. "The living, the dead, and the undead—just one big, happy family."

I moved to the large chest, found it unlocked, and was assailed by a musty odor when I opened it. Within were about a dozen large leather-bound books. I picked one from the top and glanced at the front page. It was written in Max's hand, in Spanish, and was dated from the early 1600s. Rummaging deeper into the chest, I found a fairly large gold locket. The light was too dim even for me to examine it; I slipped it into the uniform's pocket to view later.

"Deirdre?" A deep, soft voice in the doorway addressed me hesitantly, expectantly.

I dropped the journal on the floor, spun around, and peered through the semi-darkness. Victor Lange stood there, the light from the office outlining his body.

"I'm sorry to disturb you, Deirdre, but Fred said you were in."

"And so I am."

His voice was smooth and confident, showing no surprise at the room he was entering. "I wondered how long it would take you to discover this place."

"You knew this was here?" The voice in my head still urged me to trust him, but as he moved toward me, I backed away. "You've been here before?"

Victor respected my hesitancy and stood still. "Of course." He smiled reassuringly. "Max invited me in, oh, around twelve years ago, to show me his new acquisition." He gestured at the coffin with my name. "But it was his private spot; it's not as if he entertained here."

I ignored his last comment. "Twelve years ago? That was about the time I moved here."

"Yes." He walked over and rubbed his hand delicately over Max's nameplate. "This is a beautiful piece of sixteenth-century workmanship, don't you think?"

"But that means you know what Max was."

He laughed in amazement. "Of course I knew what Max was. He was a vampire. As you are also."

"And still you were his friend?"

I stood too far away to discern the expression in his eyes. "To a man who has lived centuries, friendship is invaluable. Don't you have friends who know you for what you are and care about you regardless?"

Slowly I walked toward him, keeping the two coffins between us. "Well, yes, but we were talking about Max."

"Was Max's loneliness, his separateness from mankind, any less acute than yours?"

"No, I suppose not." I paused and thought. "Although Max never actually gave me any opportunity to find out. The night that I realized what he was was also the night he died."

"Murdered," Victor said abruptly.

"What?"

"You said the night he died; it was murder, Deirdre. You keep referring to his demise as if it were a natural occurrence, a heart attack or an accident of some sort." He spit his vehemence at me, his anger tangible in the dust-filled air. "Never forget that Max was murdered in cold blood by some bastard cop who wasn't fit to shine his shoes. The same bastard that I understand is now out, free and easy." Victor reached across and grabbed my wrist. "Here, Deirdre," he whispered, "here is your chance to avenge Max. Find him and kill him before he catches up with you."

"Kill who?" I twisted away from his grasp.

"Mitchell Greer, of course, the bastard who pinned him up against the wall, like some insect specimen."

In the candlelight I detected a manic gleam in Victor's eyes. He frightened me, but I stood my ground. His attitude angered me; his attack on Mitch, his worship of Max, made me want to slam him up against the wall. I felt myself tense; a snarl rose up in my throat and my canines grew sharp.

"Why would I want to kill Mitch?" The words came out through my clenched teeth. "I'm afraid you don't understand the situation, Victor. And you shouldn't meddle with what you don't understand."

"I understand that Max is dead. I understand that Greer is responsible for the snuffing out of the life of a superior being, a man with the wisdom of the centuries behind him, with the prospect of centuries of life before him."

"But Max murdered four people, four innocent lives that he had no right to touch."

"The right doesn't matter." Victor's voice rose in hatred again. "He was like a god among men. Justice for him should not have been given by a human. He answered to a higher call."

The anger I held in check suddenly exploded. "Max Hunter answered to no one. He was the most heartless son of a bitch that ever lived. He deserved to die as he did. He was not a god, Victor, he was a manipulative bastard who obviously had no trouble twisting you to his purposes." I paused to collect myself. "How long had you been serving as his Renfield? What sort of rewards were you promised?" I didn't wait for his answer. "He can't control you any longer, Victor. You're free of his evil. The world is free of his evil."

He stood staring at me in shock. I walked past him and went to the entrance to the office.

"Deirdre, you can't mean that."

I turned to face him. "I do mean exactly that, Victor. And while we're clearing the air about Max, you should know that he wasn't killed by Mitch."

My comment disturbed him, and he slumped back against Max's coffin. "But if not Greer, then who?"

I smiled at him, exposing my still-sharp canines. "You knew Max, knew his strength and his power. How could Mitch ever have killed him?"

"But all the reports said—"

"I know what the reports said, Victor. But I was here when Max died, and I know how it happened. Mitchell Greer did not do it."

"Then who?" he repeated, still confused and shaken.

I laughed a small, bitter laugh. "Never count on constancy in love or friendship among vampires, Victor. I killed Max."

Confidently, I turned my back on his stricken face and went into the office. Picking up my purse, I called to him. "This has been a most stimulating talk. We should do it again soon." I opened the door. "Oh, and Renfield"—the scorn in my voice was unmistakable—"lock up when you leave."

By the time I reached the dance floor I realized that I was shaking uncontrollably. What on earth had possessed me to speak to Victor that way? It was true that he had angered me with his talk of avenging Max's murder and his vehement hatred of Mitch, but I should have gone slower and broken the news gently, not blurted it out as if the truth were something of which to be proud. Clumsily, I pushed through the dancers toward the front door.

"Deirdre, wait." Victor's voice called out over the blare of the music, and I paused a moment to glance back at him. He was standing in the doorway, watching me, not with anger, it seemed, but with compassion. The faces of the dancers blurred in front of my tear-filled eyes, and one of the gyrating bodies turned toward me and smiled. It was a mocking smile; his face and his cologne were so hauntingly familiar. Somewhere a part of my mind reacted to him with shock, but he didn't speak to me, nor did he seem to recognize me. Instead, he turned his back to me and directed his attention to his partner in the dance.

I shook my head and looked back to find him, but he had disappeared completely into the sea of bodies. Out of the corner of my eye I could see Victor moving toward me, and instantly the dancers' presence was dismissed, the nagging doubts arising within me were erased, and I concentrated only on the fact that I had to escape.

Chapter 20

The rain had stopped and I slowed outside the front door for a moment, to decide where to go. I heard the door open behind me and someone tapped me gently on the shoulder. I spun around with a snarl on my lips, but it was only the waitress with my dried clothes. I took them and stuffed them into my purse.

"Miss Griffin," she said quietly, extending another garment, "I have a coat here that someone left in the cloak room and never claimed. I thought maybe you'd like to borrow it. Fred said you didn't have one." I smiled and thanked her, threw it over my shoulders, and began to walk.

I didn't really know where to go; I couldn't return to Mitch's place, Griffin Designs did not belong to me anymore, and even had I kept a set of keys for the offices, I was sure Betsy McCain would have changed the locks over the past two years. Sam would probably be at the hospital, and I could spend some time there, but I knew he would want to hear my life story. Then I would still need to find other shelter before the sun rose. And everyone else I had known in this city was either dead or inaccessible.

But I knew I could not stay here, and I needed a place that was close and convenient. I did not want to see Victor again, much less run into that ominous figure from the dance floor. Quickly, I began to walk toward the hotel I had occupied two years earlier. Although I probably would not get the same suite of rooms, they would hopefully have something vacant.

When I got to the revolving doors of the hotel, I suddenly realized who the man at the Ballroom resembled. He reminded me of Larry Martin. But Larry is dead, I told myself, it must have been someone who just looked a lot like him. Larry was tall, well-built, and blond, a description that could match tens of thousands of men in this city. And anyone could wear his cologne. So it was nothing more than coincidence. I could not bear the thought that I might be seeing his ghost in addition to Max's. "One ghost per person is more than enough."

I went through the doors and registered at the desk. The clerk looked at my clothing, the cheap waitress uniform and borrowed coat, and his upper lip curled slightly, as if he were thinking that I did not belong here. But when I paid for my room for three nights in advance with cash, and gave him a liberal tip, his attitude turned from condescending to obsequious. When he handed me my key, I smiled at him.

"Does Frank still work here?" I asked, realizing that I had never known the doorman's last name.

"Yes, Miss Griffin, but tonight's his night off. Do you want to leave him a message?"

Two years down the road, and here I was, back where I had started from, but now I was looking for companionship from my old doorman. The thought was pathetic, and I shook my head. "No, no message, thank you," I said sadly. "But please see that I am not disturbed during the day tomorrow—no maids, no calls, and no visitors."

He agreed, and I took the elevator up alone to my single room. The first thing I did was change back into my jeans and sweater. Then I called room service and ordered three bottles of their best dry red wine. I was halfway through the first bottle, when I decided to call the Ballroom.

Fred answered the phone and recognized my voice instantly. "Deirdre, where are you? Ron's been looking for you and so was Victor. I didn't see you leave."

"Never mind, is Ron still there?"

"Yeah, he's at the bar."

"How about Victor?" My voice trembled a bit when I said his name.

"No, he left. Although I could probably get hold of him if you want."

"No." My voice was harsh. "I don't want to talk to him again tonight. But I will talk to Ron, if you would be so kind as to get him."

"No problem." I could hear him set the phone down and waited for a few minutes.

"Deirdre? Where are you? We had an appointment, remember?"

"Yes, Ron, I remember. That's why I called. What phone are you talking on?"

"The one in your office, why? What's going on? Why all the intrigue?"

I sighed and took another drink of my wine. "No intrigue, Ron. Victor and I had a slight disagreement and I just decided to leave." Slight disagreement? I thought. Now, there's the understatement of the century. Telling a man that you murdered his best friend is hardly slight or a disagreement.

"I see." Ron's voice sounded noncommittal. "Do you want to reschedule?"

"No, I thought you could come to me, if you don't mind."

Ron gave a short laugh and his voice lowered sensually. "Deirdre, you should know by now that I'm happy to see you anytime, anyplace, but"—a trace of exasperation entered his voice—"you do have to let me know where that is. When you didn't show, I called your other number to see if you were on your way. A very disgruntled and very drunk policeman informed me that he didn't know where you were, but if I found out, I should let him know. He was pretty offensive about it."

"Damn," I said softly.

"Excuse me?"

"Nothing. Are you sitting at my desk?"

"Yeah."

"Inside the top drawer are copies of all the documents we should need. Bring them with you."

"Got 'em."

I gave him my address with strict instructions to tell no one where I was, and hung up. Then I called down to the front desk to let them know I was expecting a visitor.

Ron arrived within an hour of my phone call, carrying a bottle of Merlot and his briefcase. "Fred sent this over"—he held the wine in the air—"with his best regards."

I looked at Ron suspiciously. "You told him where I was?"

"No, just that we'd be meeting tonight. He also asked me to tell you that Mitch called three times."

"Great."

Ron set his briefcase down on the table and took off his overcoat. "It doesn't sound great. Should I assume that Mitch is Mitchell Greer—the cop that killed Max Hunter? And that he's also the same cop you've been living with, the one I talked to on the phone tonight?"

"Yes, that is true." I gave him a sharp look. "What the hell difference does it make?"

"No difference to me, I guess." Ron shrugged. "I'm just trying to keep the players straight. You're not in trouble with the law, are you?"

I laughed humorlessly. "If only it were that simple, Ron. A night in jail might do me some good."

"But I'd bail you out." He sat down in the chair opposite me and opened his case, taking out the folder containing Max's will. "I read this over before I came; it all seems pretty straightforward to me. Either you take the money or you don't. All that needs to be done is to get your notarized signature saying yes or no. We can't do that tonight, of course, but I can make those arrangements at a later date. Maybe you'd like some more time to think about it. But"—he smiled at me—"as your attorney, I advise you to take it, it's a lot of money." He reached for the bottle of wine I had already opened. "May I?"

At my nod he poured himself a full glass and drank it. "You know," he said, his voice distant and small, "I guess I should've known about you and Greer."

"But I told you—"

"No," Ron interrupted. "You told me you were involved with a policeman, but you never mentioned his name. And for some reason it never occurred to me until tonight that it could be the same guy."

"I am sorry, Ron, I thought you knew. And," I repeated, "what the hell difference does it make? It's over."

"It could make a difference to The Cadre. They'll be losing a great deal of money, a fortune, in fact, to a woman romantically involved with the person who killed one of their most prestigious members. I could conceivably see that they might want to contest the will."

"Fine." I poured the rest of the wine into my glass, drained it, and opened the second bottle. "I told you before, I don't care about the money. If The Cadre wants it, then let them have it. I don't really want to discuss the will, or explain my actions to you or anyone else. And I especially do not want to talk about my doomed relationships with Mitchell Greer and Max Hunter. Right now I just want to do my damnedest to get drunk and forget that any of this complicated mess ever happened. Care to join me?"

"But what about Greer?"

"I don't want to talk about him. As far as he's concerned, he wishes he never met me."

"Then he's a damn fool."

"And so was I. Why I thought I could be happy involved with a, well, a man like him, I will never know. But we were not going to talk about this."

"That's right, we weren't." Ron hesitated, watching me intently as I drank.

"So," I said, filling another glass, "are you going to help me finish this wine or not?"

"And when that's all gone?"

"What the hell, we'll just order more. Didn't you know? I'm a very wealthy woman."

Ron and I wound up in bed together again. Not intimately this time, both of us were fully clothed and he seemed content to merely lie next to me with my head cushioned on his shoulder. Neither of us was very drunk, but we had reached a warm, comfortable high. We didn't talk much, and what we did say was not important. He told me about law school and some of his more interesting cases. I told him about England, how much I missed the quiet neighborhood pub and my favorite brand of port. I talked about books that I had read and he talked about movies he had seen. Before we realized it, it was nearly five in the morning.

"I guess I'd better get going," he said, shifting his weight slightly so that he could get up.

"Do you really have to? You're welcome to stay as long as you like. This has been very pleasant; it's been too many years since I've had someone I could just talk to. I don't really understand why, but I feel completely comfortable with you, as if you could know the worst about me and not ever care."

"Unlike some people, I assume, who know the worst about you and do care?" Ron reached over and lightly touched my cheek.

"Oh, he says that it doesn't matter, but deep down inside we both know that it does."

"And what is this deep, dark secret that is so horrible?" His voice was calm and comforting, and I was tempted to tell him.

Instead, I laughed. "It doesn't matter. So, will you stay?"

He met my eyes; his expression was hard to read. "Well, I don't really have anything pressing on my calendar for tomorrow. So, if you beg me, I might stay."

"I never beg."

He laughed. "I'm sure you don't, but you could ask me nice."

"Ron." I tried to smile at him, but began to cry instead. "Stay with me, please. I don't want to sleep alone today."

"Don't cry, Deirdre. Of course I'll stay. I told you before that I was a soft touch for a lady in distress."

"Thank you."

He moved back to me and pressed himself up against me.

"Have you ever fallen in love with someone," I asked him, sniffing a bit, my head buried in his chest, "knowing from the very beginning that it would never work out? And knowing that you would never get over them, no matter how hard you tried?"

He reached down and cupped my face between his hands, drawing my eyes to his. "And we're back to Greer again, aren't we?"

"Yes, I'm afraid so. I'm sorry."

"So am I."

We lay quietly for a long while, and I thought that he had fallen asleep. I began to drift off into sleep myself, but before I did, I thought I heard him whisper.

"Yeah, I think I have."

I open my eyes to utter darkness and I realize that my limbs are restricted, that I am completely encased in a wooden box.

But before the panic can overwhelm me, I feel the soft touch of Max's mind and recognize the experience as a dream. "Learn," he whispers; we melt down and merge together in the body lying in this coffin.

The year is 1850; it had been an uneasy ocean crossing, but I know now that we have docked and soon my casket will be unloaded. Not soon enough, I think, for I have been a long time without food. My body is hollow and insubstantial; just the slightest thought of blood causes me to gasp and bite my lips. It is no help; by now they are bloodless, dry, and cracked.

Not for the first time do I wonder why I attempted this journey, why I freely accepted this agony. I had been warned; Leupold had told me what I would suffer, but I would not listen.

Or could not listen. The truth was that I could not bear one more day in his presence and would gladly accept any torture to escape from his influence. The gratitude I initially felt when he saved my life had dissipated quickly when I discovered how he had procured that reprieve, but it had taken centuries of following in his footsteps to fully realize the brutal hatred with which I now regarded him.

I cannot even bring his face to mind; thoughts of him bring only visions of death and depravities: bloodless corpses, helpless lives lying in ruin in our wake. So I had decided to undertake this arduous journey. I will never purge myself of his evil; I had proved too apt a pupil for that, and his sway over me is too absolute to hope for my reform. There will be no repentance; no amendment of life in this new country. But at the least I will escape his constant approbation of my sins and excesses. And with that I believe can live content.

Footsteps approach my coffin and I lie still, not daring to move or breathe for fear of discovery. The scent of the living men who carry and load me onto a carriage almost drives me mad. I can break out of my confinement with one simple movement of my arm; their blood can be on my lips in seconds, but I restrain myself, not knowing if it is day or night. It would be a shame, I think to myself with a mocking laugh, to travel all this way only to disappear into a heap of ashes on the dock. Tonight, when I arrive at the house I have procured, will be soon enough.

Eventually, the coffin is deposited, none too gently, in a damp-smelling room, and I assume that all has been accomplished in accordance with my explicit instructions. Still, I wait for a while, listening to the sounds of the hoofs and carriage wheels moving away on the cobblestone streets. When all is quiet, I cautiously push up one side of the thick wooden lid and breathe a sigh of relief when I realize that it is night and I am alone, safe, and free at last.

The hunger will not let me stop and savor my freedom, but drives me out into the night in search of living prey. I wander the streets, taking careful note of the turns and twists I make so that I may retrace my steps to safe harbor before dawn.

A church bell chimes twice as I hurry past, urged on by the gnawing ache in my stomach and the unfaltering instinct that a victim is near. Quite near, I realize, as I round the corner and see the shadowy figure of a woman leaning up against a doorframe. She is, of course, a prostitute; in this day and age no respectable woman would be out alone in the night. I am well used to this type, having used them in countless brothels for sex. But my urges now are more elemental, more basic and much darker; there will be no sexual play this night. I glide over to her, giving a courtly bow; she smiles and beckons me inside the door.

The room is dingy and sparsely furnished; the bed is only a mattress set on the floor. Turning her back to me, she begins to unfasten the hooks of her bodice. Ordinarily, I would wait until she undressed, until I had possession of her body before taking possession of her blood. Ordinarily, I would not even require her life. But tonight there is no denying of what must happen if I am to survive.

I come up behind her, putting one arm around her waist, and clasping my other hand over her mouth, bend her head to one side, making her neck more accessible to my kiss. At first she does not resist, but when my teeth sink deeply into her pliant flesh, and I take my first long draw on her precious blood, she struggles, attempting to pull away. Her lips move beneath my hand, crying, perhaps in pain, calling for mercy. I have none to give.

Her blood flows into me, filling me with elation, filling the great emptiness within. I feel her heartbeat slow, then stop completely. But only when the body is drained completely do I loosen my mouth's hold on her. She hangs limp and lifeless from my arm still encircling her waist, and I drop her onto the bare mattress. I reach down to close her staring eyes gently. The words of the prayer for the dead rise to my lips as they always do when I kill, but I will not allow them to be uttered by the very mouth that took her life. Instead, I reach into my pocket, drop a gold piece next to the bed, and go back into the night.

I explore the streets of this new city until just before dawn, eventually finding my way back to my home and my coffin. As I pull the lid over me, I feel the sharp stab of pain that signals the rising of the sun, and I sleep.

Chapter 21

It took a long time to wake from the dream. I lay in bed, eyes wide open, studying the ceiling, drifting through the state that lay between sleep and waking. This dream had frightened me more than all the rest; it had been the first time that I had felt the glorious elation of draining a victim to death. The fact that it was not I, but Max, who had killed that woman made no difference. When I dreamed, I was Max; his emotions, his passions, were mine. I had never before realized what a precarious balance I maintained. That I could recognize myself in him, and that I could react so willingly, so naturally, to his murderous instincts, was terrifying.

I looked back on my life with disgust. I shared Max's guilt, shared it completely. That woman was dead because of me. It made no difference that the event had happened before my transformation. The seeds of a killer had been sown within me, and even if they did not grow to their fruition, I knew that their roots were forever imbedded in my soul. There could be no final salvation for one such as I.

Eventually I shook off the effect of the dream and pulled myself up into a complete state of awareness of who and where I was, and discovered that the sun had already set and that I was alone. Getting out of bed, I saw that Ron had left the will and the papers for me to sign, along with his home and work phone numbers, and a note.

Deirdre, it read, I *stayed all day as you asked, but had to leave around six. Tried to wake you, but you were completely out. Thanks for last night, let's do it again sometime soon. Love, Ron.* The word "soon" was underlined three times and I chuckled to myself, then sobered.

Poor Ron, I thought, he's just one more example of how twisted my life has become. I used him terribly, first for his blood, then his legal expertise, and finally for his companionship, when what he wanted from me was completely different and something I could never give him. I shook my head, picked up the phone, and called room service for a pot of coffee.

When I was on my second cup, the phone rang. I let it ring for a while; the only person who knew where I was was Ron, and if we talked, I would eventually end up spending another night with him. How long could I continue to hide out, avoiding the other complications of my life, taking advantage of a man who deserved better of me? After ten rings I answered, determined to tell him that we should never see each other again. I did not have to, because it was not Ron on the phone, but Mitch.

I could not even say hello. "How did you find me?"

His voice was quiet and sad. "If I'd been thinking straight, I would have tried this place last night. Unfortunately, I drank for four solid hours after you left, and my mind was anything but clear."

"Yes, me too. Did it work for you?"

"Other than making me feel as horrible physically as I did mentally, no. I'm sorry."

I paused, not able to speak.

"Deirdre, did you hear me? I said I was sorry, and I am. I should never have said those things to you. I'd take them all back if I could."

"And why should you be sorry for telling the truth? Everything you said was true, Mitch. What you and I have together is something that should never have happened. It can never work, and I'm glad that you've finally come to that realization. It makes my leaving much easier."

"You're leaving again?" I could hear the panic in his voice, felt my own panic rise. The thoughts of being separated from him forever tore me apart, but I knew that staying with him would be almost as bad.

"I—I—I don't know what to do," I said honestly, desperately. "I can't think straight around you; I never could. I don't know if I have the power of will to leave. But it would be much better for the both of us if I do."

"Like hell it would." He gave a tight little laugh, and I found myself smiling.

I sighed. "What am I going to do with you, Mitch?" My question was light and teasing.

"I can think of several things at the moment, and I'm sure more will occur to me when you get home." He matched my bantering tone, then grew serious. "You will come back, won't you? You can't leave me, I won't let you. If you want me to beg you, I will; I'll get down on my knees and crawl to you. I love you, dammit, and there's not a damn thing I can do about it."

"I'll come back. But we need to do some serious talking about my life and you need to do some serious thinking about how well it will fit you."

"Anything you want, Deirdre. Just come home soon."

"As soon as I can, my love. I'm glad that your mind finally cleared well enough for you to find me. I think that I must have come here so that you could."

He laughed. "Actually, I'm ashamed to say that I didn't think of it. Your attorney called and told me where you were."

"Ron called you?" That surprised me. "Why on earth would Ron tell you where I was?"

"Why wouldn't he? When he called last night, looking for you, I asked him to let me know if he located you. Or at least I think I did; everything is pretty fuzzy."

"You did; he told me."

"And he said that you were still hopelessly in love with me, that what you needed was a good kick to make you wake up and realize it."

"Well, I'm glad that Ron thinks it's all so simple."

There was a long pause, and I thought for a moment that he had hung up. "In the end, Deirdre," Mitch said finally, "I think he's right."

I gather up my borrowed coat and uniform. The gold locket that I had taken from Max's room at the Ballroom fell out onto the floor, and I picked it up and tucked it into my jeans pocket. Then I went downstairs and left the hotel.

As I walked on the streets, I had the feeling that I was being followed, a curious feeling in the middle of my back that someone's eyes were on me, watching my every move. I knew that it was not Max; there was none of his intimate touch in my mind. But it was familiar nevertheless, and I glanced over my shoulder for a glimpse of my stalker. There was a flurry of movement behind me, and I spun around, but he was gone. "Great," I said out loud, "just what I need, another haunting. Maybe everyone I've ever known can show up all at the same time and we can have a party." I laughed at my paranoid thought but quickened my steps.

When I arrived at Mitch's apartment, I was surprised to find the door unlocked. "Mitch," I called, hanging up my coat in the closet, "where are you?"

"In the kitchen."

His voice was calm and peaceful, as if no separation had taken place.

He was sitting at the table with his back to the door and I walked over, put my arms around his neck, and gave him a kiss.

Resting my head on his shoulder, I watched as he finished cleaning his gun. "The door was unlocked."

He shrugged. "Yeah, I wasn't sure if you took your keys with you." He turned around on the chair and put his arms around my waist. "Welcome home." He rested his head against my left breast, then pulled away abruptly. "Your heart is racing, Deirdre, is everything okay?"

"No, Mitch," I said with a sigh. "Not really."

"You weren't mugged again, were you?"

"No, nothing like that. But you must know that my coming back to you solves only one problem." I reached over and stroked his hair. "The problem of how I could ever live without you." I kissed him on the forehead and pulled away. "Everything else in my life is completely out of control. I don't know what to do. I don't even know how to tell you about it all."

"Well," he said, "I've a solution to one of your problems anyway." He put his gun into my hand. "This will stop you from getting victimized again."

I stared down at the revolver in my grasp, then placed it back on the table with a small laugh. "That, my love, is the very least of my problems. And I wouldn't know how to shoot it even if I had to."

"I'd teach you; we'll go down to the shooting range. I'd worry a lot less about you wandering around the city at night by yourself if I knew you had some protection."

"Mitch, I don't need a gun for protection."

"I know." He shrugged and his eyes lit with amusement. "But at the very least, you don't need to explain this kind of protection to anyone. It's a lot cleaner and simpler."

"But not as much fun," I muttered guiltily, turning away from him to look out the window, ashamed of the delight I had experienced dealing with the mugger.

"What?"

"Never mind, Mitch. It doesn't matter. If it makes you feel better, I'll carry the gun."

"Thank you." He walked behind me and put his arm around my neck, pulling my head back to nuzzle my hair.

"Mitch," I said quietly, "we need to talk."

"I know," he said, a tinge of sadness creeping into his voice. "What really bothers me about all this is that for some reason you're afraid to tell me about it." He spun me around, gripping my shoulders and shaking me lightly. "Regardless of what I said last night, I do love you, and I want you to know that there's nothing about you I can't learn to accept as long as you stay."

I met his eyes directly and coolly. "Tell me that later, after you know everything, and I will believe you."

My stare must have unnerved him; he dropped his hands and stepped back from me. I went to the refrigerator and removed the last half-bottle of wine, poured two glasses, and handed him one. "We'll be more comfortable in the other room. This may take a while."

I let him sit down first; he chose the couch, and I sat in the chair opposite him. He gave me a questioning look, took a sip of his wine, and waited.

My voice was soft when I began, tense and choked. "The first thing you must realize, before I tell you anything, is that after receiving your letter, I never expected to see you again, never expected to have to justify my life to you."

"That damned letter," Mitch interrupted. "I've been angry about it ever since you told me."

"The letter doesn't matter, Mitch. I know now that you didn't write it, and that's the important fact. Although, I wonder who . . ."

"Chris."

"Excuse me?"

"Chris wrote the goddamned thing. He said he was trying to protect me from your influence. I nearly killed him when he told me about it that last night in the hospital. He'd no right to interfere like that."

I laughed in relief, not realizing until that moment how worried I had been about who the originator of that letter might be. "Don't be too hard on him, my love. It can't be an easy thing to discover that your father's lover is someone like me. And although he has had a few problems, Chris has actually been surprisingly civilized about our relationship."

"So you're not mad about it?"

I shrugged. "Not really. And even if I were, he's your son and not mine. He did come for me when he thought I could help you, and he was right. I think that more than balances out those two years."

"And if you hadn't received the letter? Wouldn't things have been different for you?"

Mitch's question took me by surprise. With the letter I had completely accepted the fact that he did not want me anymore and my actions had been dictated by that assumption. And yet, had I not received it, I would have assumed his answer to be the same. "No, Mitch," I said sadly, "no letter would have been just as bad as the one I received. Perhaps even worse, because I would have felt that you did not even care enough to tell me your decision." I looked into his eyes and gave him a half-smile. "Now, can we forget about the letter and who wrote it? The only important thing to remember is that I accepted it as a fact."

"And that's another thing, Deirdre, how can you believe I would do that to you?" He brushed his fingers through his hair and his eyes glinted angrily. "Goddammit, I love you. Even now I don't understand why you thought you had to leave. And I'm still pretty mad about the whole thing. I was ready to share your life completely, and you ran out on me. I'm ready to share it now, Deirdre. All you have to do is say yes."

"Mitch," I interrupted him gently but firmly, "that is not what we need to talk about. We have time for all that later, but you must hear me out first. What I have to say might change your mind."

He said nothing, but I recognized his stubborn expression from the time he insisted that no such creatures as myself existed. Mitch needed hard proof to believe what he did not want to believe. I sighed and took a sip of my wine.

"Shortly after I arrived in England"—my voice trembled slightly—"I began to hear Max's voice, quiet yet insistent, from the back of my mind. Oh, it was only an annoyance at first, like the buzzing of a fly or static on the radio. But it seemed to grow stronger with each feeding, urging me to go further than I ever had before, to take more blood, more often. Almost as if he were living inside me, feeding off my body, and imposing his hungers and desires on me. As if I were possessed by Max's spirit."

Mitch gave a small grunt but still said nothing.

"I know. I don't really believe that theory either. But that is exactly how I feel. And no matter what the true circumstances are, I haven't been able to rid myself of his presence."

Mitch didn't smile, but cautiously glanced around his apartment. "Is he here now?"

"No," I admitted, "but he has been. And I'm sure he'll return. Strong emotions seem to bring him out; when I feed, when we make love . . ." I blushed and let my words trail off.

"I haven't seen him." I could tell from the tone of his voice that he was taking what I said seriously.

"He wasn't one of the creatures who tormented you?"

"No, I could've understood that. The vampires I saw were strangers, although some seemed familiar after a while. Maybe it was because they were making return visits." Mitch shuddered, then looked over at me with a half-smile. "I would've almost welcomed Max; at least I knew him, and had some experience dealing with him. Don't you have any idea about what's happening? I mean, you're one of them. There should be some sort of common bond or knowledge that would help you out of this."

I shook my head slowly. "No, and if what you saw was real, you've met more of them than I ever have."

"Can you ask around, find out who Max's friends were? Maybe they'll have answers."

I thought back about my discussion with Victor and gave a rueful smile. "Actually, I've already antagonized one of his closest friends. Do you remember Victor Lange?"

"Should I?" Mitch's face grew puzzled as he struggled with the name. "No," he concluded slowly, "I've never heard of him."

"You met him, Mitch. He owns The Imperial. We had dinner there one night."

"Really?" He sat for a while, his face expressionless.

"Mitch?" I reached over and touched him on the arm. He jumped and laughed nervously.

"Sorry, Deirdre, I was thinking. I have no remembrance of the man at all. He was a close friend of Max's? And you ticked him off? What happened?"

"I told him exactly who it was who killed Max."

"Jesus, Deirdre, why on earth would you do that? It could cause a lot of problems for us both; after all, I've gone on record saying that I killed him in the line of duty. Self-defense, remember?"

"And for that statement you spent two years institutionalized. I wanted to set the record straight with Victor for a lot of reasons. I don't believe he'll make trouble for me, and if he does, I can handle him. That really isn't the issue here."

"And what is the issue? You don't want to marry me because you see Max on occasion? You've been living with that for two years; I'm sure I could get used to it. It'll go away after a while." His voice was so determined, I almost believed him.

"There's more, Mitch. Unfortunately, Max was, or is, a creature of great appetites. As a result"—I stood up with my fists clenched and walked around behind the chair, trying to avoid Mitch's eyes—"I've been involved in a sexual relationship with almost every one of my victims since I left this city."

"Jesus," he swore in a whisper. "Deirdre."

I looked away, waiting for accusations and recriminations. When he said nothing more, I glanced back at him, curious as to why his usually rampant jealousy was not aroused. There was no anger, no revulsion in his expression, only sadness. My heart twisted and I wanted to go to him, to hold him, to tell him that none of this ever happened. But I could not.

"Mitch, I cannot justify my actions. It would be easy to say that all of this is Max's fault, but we both know that Max Hunter is dead and buried. I suppose that Sam would say that his appearance in my life is due to my guilt over his murder, and that the sexual episodes are revenge against you for turning me away."

I shrugged and put my hand into my pocket, coming across the locket I had put in there earlier. I pulled it out and held it in my hand, curling the heavy gold chain around my fingers. "And he would probably be right. But now I not only hear Max's voice, but I see him, plain as day and as real as you. And I dream of him, vivid dreams of his past life, a life that I experience as if I really were him." My voice sounded choked, panicked. "It scares me, Mitch, so much so that when I wake I'm not even sure who I am. I barely recognize my own reflection at times.

"So you see, we have two choices—that I'm completely crazy or that I'm possessed by Max. Either way, my life is not one you would want to share."

I sat back down in the chair, still idly toying with Max's locket. It fell open, and when I peered at the miniature within, I gasped in recognition and dropped it on the floor. "No, it can't be true."

"Deirdre?" Mitch's voice was surprisingly clear and decisive. "What is it?" He got up from the couch and picked up the locket. "Where did you get this? It's very old."

"It was with Max's things. And, yes, it is old, dating back to the late 1500s. The woman in the picture, I know her. I have never met her, but I know her. I know the sound of her voice; I remember the way she looked when she was young, how my hand fit so perfectly in hers."

He looked at the picture intensely. "But who is she?"

I ignored his question, and in panic bolted toward the door. "Oh, my God, it can't be true."

Mitch moved faster than I did, and blocked my retreat. "Who is she, Deirdre? And what possible difference can it make?" He grabbed my shoulders and pulled me to him.

Pushing away from him, I stared up into his face. "It's all true, Mitch, it has to be. But what can I do about it? I'll never be free of him."

"Deirdre." His voice was shaking, and his fingers dug deeply into my flesh. "What's this all about?"

"The woman in the locket; she's Max's mother. I dreamed of her. I know her. And if that is true, then I'm not crazy." I began to laugh, deeply pitched laughter that echoed off the walls and sounded so much like Max that I wanted to tear myself apart.

Instead, I flung myself against Mitch and clung to him like a small, frightened child. "Somehow, some way, Max lives within me. We may have killed him, Mitch, but he didn't die. And he won't die until I do."

Mitch calmed me then, his hands stroking my hair, his lips brushing delicately against my ears and neck. The pounding of my heart changed from panic into passion as he cupped my breast in one hand and placed the other on the back of my neck, pulling my mouth to his in a hard, demanding kiss.

The desperate quality of his embrace startled me, but my body responded in kind, the heat of his lips thawing any resistance I might have offered. The taste of him and the feel of his body on mine broke down the last of my inhibitions. When the kiss was over, we stood for a moment, staring at each other, both out of breath and frightened by the sudden strength of our desires.

"I don't care," he whispered vehemently. "I don't care whom you've been with or what you've done." He spun me around and roughly pressed me up to the door, holding my wrists against the woodwork. His eyes glowed with the intensity of his emotions. "I've lost you twice and I won't let it happen again. You won't run from me this time, Deirdre. We'll face this together. But you must promise you won't leave me. Ever. I don't give a damn about your excuses, your bloody morals about not wanting to share your tainted life. Just promise you won't ever leave."

I felt a smile begin to shape my lips even as the tears stung in my eyes. I nodded, not trusting the strength of my voice, and he dropped my hands, wrapped his arm tightly around my shoulders, and led me back to his bedroom.

It was like no other time with Mitch. His usual gentle manner was gone, his hands rough as they tore the clothes from my body. But his urgency was contagious; his passion caught me up and I surrendered completely, abandoning all thoughts of what I was, what he was, what lay between us. There existed only our two bodies, our mouths and our hands, our teeth and our nails.

"Don't hold back," Mitch hoarsely urged as he pulled me on

top of him. When I felt him pulsing inside me, hard and insistent, I threw my head back and cried out, snarling, howling. His labored moans echoed my lust; his hands grasped my waist and my breasts until they worked their way to my neck and forced me down. Our lips met, his tongue pushed its way past my sharpened teeth, and the brief taste of his blood drove me wild.

"Deirdre, Deirdre," Mitch repeated over and over again. My own blood pounded in my ears, in perfect rhythm with his frantic thrusts. My body undulated on top of his, writhing in that exquisite torment. And when his teeth grazed my shoulder, I began to laugh, manic laughter that both frightened and excited me. I was too far gone to recognize its source, too enslaved by this rapture to care. The rush of Mitch's blood into my mouth, his small gasp of pain, made me realize that my teeth were buried as deeply into his neck as he was in me.

I could not stop, did not want to stop, did not have the power of will to fight the demon. I rode on the tides of his blood, and the bittersweet taste of him rushed through my system, its intoxicating heat causing me to break into a feverish sweat. I wanted to devour Mitch, drain him completely, carry him inside me forever. As if from a distance, I felt his climax and my own shuddering orgasm. I gripped him tightly within me, and it was only my mad gasp for air that enabled me to release his neck from my bite.

Rolling from him, I felt the trickle of his blood on my chin and wiped it away in revulsion. Mitch sighed and moved toward me, nestling against me, his hand resting lightly on my hips, his mouth breathing into my ear. "That was incredible," he whispered weakly. "Absolutely incredible."

"Jesus," I swore at him, hiding my tears. "Incredibly dangerous is more like it. I could have killed you, Mitch. That can't happen again."

But he didn't hear me. His shallow, labored breathing had already relaxed into a more normal pattern. He was asleep, beyond any comprehension of my panic, leaving me alone and sated with sex, blood, and guilt.

Chapter 22

After an hour, I slid the covers from me and quietly got out of bed. The panic that I had felt had not subsided, but continued to build deep within me. I knew that if I did not escape the room, the situation could quickly get out of hand. I found my clothes in the dark and began to dress. Mitch should sleep well, and with luck he would never know that I left. But the metallic hiss of my zipper roused him slightly.

"Deirdre?" Mitch's sleepy whisper made me jump guiltily and spin around.

"Go back to sleep, my love." My voice was soft and reassuring. "I'm just going out for a little air. I'll be back soon."

"Why're you always leaving?" His petulant question only heightened my desire to leave.

"Hush, Mitch, and sleep. After all"—I walked back to the bed and smoothed his hair—"I promised. And I always come back."

By the time I finished dressing, his breathing was deep and regular again. Silently, I slid through the apartment and out the door into the night streets.

Two blocks down I found a taxi and gave the driver the address of Mitch's hospital.

A quick survey of the parking lot revealed Sam's foreign sports car, and I breathed a sigh of relief. I didn't know whether he could help me or not, but I decided it was worth trying. I couldn't live my life as it was now, torn between two men, one dead and one living, but both central to my existence. And, I thought with a sarcastic smile, he would be more than pleased with the opportunity to delve into my unusual psyche.

With my customary shudder I entered the front doors of the hospital and walked to the nurses' station. When I saw that Jean was on duty, I almost turned around and left, but she looked up from her papers and her face darkened in recognition, her expression a challenge. Formidable as she is, I thought, she's still no match for me. I smiled my sweetest smile and was rewarded by her most hateful glare.

"Good evening, Jean," I said courteously. "I wonder if I might talk to Dr. Samuels."

"Not in," she muttered. "I'll leave him a message."

"Oh, but Jean, I saw his car in the lot. And I'm sure he would be happy to talk with me. Be a dear and tell him I'm here."

She bristled at my tone, as I had expected. "And who exactly are you?"

Suddenly I grew tired of her games and reached over the counter, grabbing her chin in my hand and pulling her up to eye level. "You know damn well who I am," I said through clenched teeth. "Just call him—now."

Jean's eyes held their defiant stare for a few seconds, then dropped in failure. As her hand went for the phone, I loosened my grasp on her. "Dr. Samuels"—her voice admitted defeat—"Miss Griffin is here to see you."

"Great." I could hear the response from his office. "Send her right down."

"Thank you, Jean," I said in a softer tone. "Now, that wasn't so hard, was it?"

I walked past her, but she reached a hand out to touch my arm. "Miss Griffin?" I felt her fingers tremble slightly. "How is Mitch?"

Behind her still-obvious dislike of me I could see tears glistening in her eyes and some of my animosity toward her dissipated. "He's doing well, Jean." I smiled honestly and her expression lightened, making her seem younger, prettier. "I'll be sure to tell him you asked."

"Thank you."

I patted the hand still resting on my arm. She held it there for a minute, then moved away from me and back to her desk. Shaking my head in disbelief—it was hard to imagine that Jean had a softer side—I entered Sam's office.

"How's the shoulder?" He got up from the desk and took my hand briefly. "No complications, I trust?"

"It's fine, thank you so much." I sat down and looked around doubtfully. Now that I was there, I was reluctant to talk about my problem, not so sure now that Sam could help me.

"And how's Mitch?"

"Mitch is fine too. I left him sleeping peacefully."

Sam nodded, walked back to his desk, and sat down. He smiled at me, exhibiting just a slight bit of uneasiness. "Then what on earth are you doing here?"

"I needed to talk to you." I paused, not knowing how to proceed. I had already pushed the limits of Sam's beliefs; my next admission would probably be going too far for him.

He went into his top drawer and pulled out the cigarettes. I took one, lit it, and inhaled deeply. Closing my eyes, I leaned back in the chair and nervously licked my lips. When I raised my head, I saw that he was watching me patiently, tapping his lighter gently on the desktop.

"Do you believe in possession?" As I blurted out the question, my voice sounded light, as if I were making a joke.

But Sam knew me better than that; he glanced at me in concern. He got up, looked out into the hall, then closed the door. Taking a deep breath and exhaling loudly, he leaned back against the wall and gave a small, humorless laugh.

"Three days ago I didn't believe in vampires. Now I don't know what I believe anymore. Do you mean by possession the taking over of one person's body and mind by a hostile spirit?"

"Yes."

"And that person is you?"

"I think so." I looked down at the cigarette in my hand, took one last drag, and stubbed it out in the ashtray. "I know you can hardly be an expert on the subject, but I had nowhere else to go, no one else to confide in."

"What about Mitch? Did you talk to him about this?"

"I tried to, Sam. But he seems to think it's all an evasion on my part to avoid making a commitment to our relationship. And that is in itself another totally different problem."

"Your relationship?" Sam walked back to his desk and took a cigarette for himself. "You and Mitch are having problems?"

I threw my head back and laughed, then looked him directly

in the face. "What do you think? How could we have anything but problems?" I got up from my chair and went to look out the window. "Damn," I said softly. "I was a fool to return. And I was an even bigger fool to promise to stay."

"But you love him and he loves you. I know that's true. I see it in him and in you." Sam's voice acquired a sharp edge, almost accusatory in tone. "You can't leave him again. You do him so much good."

I felt a surge of anger but repressed it as much as I could. "But that's not why I'm here. I don't mean to involve you in my relationship with Mitch. It'll work out or it won't. Either way, it has nothing to do with you."

"Sorry." He accepted my rebuke politely, professionally. "So, why don't you tell me why you think you're possessed?"

"Max." I whispered the name as I brushed the condensation from the windowpane. "He never died. Max Hunter still lives."

"But you said that Mitch killed him. A stake through the heart, the only thing that works with vampires. How could he be alive?"

I walked back to my chair and sat down again. "I don't know, Sam, but I know it's true." Reaching over, I removed another cigarette from his pack but didn't light it. "And he's with me, inside me. I see him, I hear him, I feel him. I dream of his past life; I know things about him I could never know otherwise: his real name, how he became a vampire, the sound of his mother's voice. I'm afraid to sleep, afraid to do anything that might draw him out."

Sam looked over at me, his expression concerned but detached. "And you feel he represents a danger to you?"

The question seemed such a complacent textbook response that suddenly the rage I had been suppressing broke loose. I rose to my feet and leaned over him, looking him full in the face. "Don't humor me, Sam. Why will no one take this situation seriously? No, he is no danger to me, he's already done his worst to me." I closed my fist over the cigarette I had been holding and crushed it, sprinkling the shreds of tobacco and paper over his desk. "But he's a danger to everyone else I meet. Why don't you understand? Max Hunter was, or is, a bloodthirsty murderer and he can control me. I've been walking the line between reason and insanity for these past two years. And . . ." I turned my back to him. My voice trembled as I felt tears well up in my eyes. "I don't know how much longer I can keep him at bay."

"Deirdre." I felt Sam move up behind me and lay a gentle hand on my shoulder.

"No," I said, spinning around to confront him. "Don't touch me. I have to go now. I can't stay any longer. You're not safe with me here and alone. I don't want to hurt you."

Sam backed away from me. "Deirdre, don't go yet. I'll try to help you if I can. But I'll need more details to get anywhere." He sat back at his desk and opened his drawer, removing a file folder. "I could hypnotize you, maybe talk to this presence you feel. Find out why this has happened, give you some control over it."

"What is that?" I pointed at the file. "Is that about me?"

"Deirdre, calm down. All my files are kept in strictest confidence, no one but me has any access to them."

"Destroy it," I hissed at him, going to the door. I turned the knob, opened the door, and saw the patient of the other night shuffling down the hall, past the nurses' station and into the recreational area. "Jesus," I swore to myself. "Oh, not now, not again." Panicked, I slammed the door and leaned up against it, breathing hard.

Sam was staring at me, his expression a mixture of fear and hurt. I sighed, regretting my brutal treatment of him. He had done nothing to deserve it, and I had gone there looking for help, not enemies. "I'm sorry, Sam," I said with a trace of a smile, pushing back my hair from my face. "I didn't mean to frighten you. Walk me out?"

"Yes," he said slowly, "if you have to go."

"I do." I stood back while he opened the door and escorted me out. "But I can come back. Some other night perhaps."

"Tomorrow?" He sounded strangely eager for my return visit.

I shrugged. "We'll see."

"Well, I'll have some time for a little research, then." He laughed. "Though God knows where I'll find anything remotely concerning all this. As I said the first time I met you, you're a strange case, Deirdre. But I'll do what I can."

We walked down the hall and stood for a moment in the waiting room inside the front doors. He extended his hand to me, and I took it carefully. "Good night," I said softly. "And thank you." An awkward silence ensued, broken finally by raucous laughter from the recreation room. Sam looked embarrassed but kept my hand in his.

"Time for me to get to work, I suppose. Sometimes, I wonder how any of us manage to hold on to our sanity. It's a crazy world."

I nodded in response to his statement and he gave me a searching look. "Are you feeling a little bit better, having talked this out with someone?"

I thought for a moment. "Yes, I think so."

"Good, that's what I'm here for." He hesitated, still holding on to my hand, and cleared his throat. A smile crossed his face briefly. "Now," Sam said, meeting my eyes, "you say you came here for my help. Will you accept it even if you don't like what I say, even if my opinion doesn't coincide with yours?"

"Try me."

"Okay, here goes nothing. I think that your basic problem is the fact that you spend too much time running from your problems, running from commitment. This feeling you have of being possessed may stem from your denial of life. You're alone and you try to avoid loving people because you're afraid you might harm them. Your relationship with Max was the closest you ever allowed yourself until you met Mitch. And when Max died, you left immediately so you wouldn't hurt Mitch."

I pulled my hand from his. "I suppose from one point of view all that is true, Sam, but . . ."

He gave me an exasperated glance. "Don't interrupt the doctor, Deirdre. The human mind is capable of going to almost any length of self-deception." He looked around us to see if anyone was near, then lowered his voice slightly. "A good part of you is still human despite your denial of that fact. And humans aren't meant to be alone, so you've manufactured a companion, a conscience almost, to be with you. You need someone, so you take the safe way out and fall back on your unhealthy relationship with Max. The fact that he is dead and appears only periodically works out even better. But it's all gotten out of hand. Your conscious mind is no longer in control of your fantasies."

"Then I am actually crazy?"

"No, I didn't say that. Surely you know by now that insanity is a relative term. You being what you are"—he looked away for a minute—"who's to say what's the normal psyche for a vampire? The bottom line is that you must begin to live the life you've been given. And Mitch has offered to share that life with you."

"But it'll never work." My voice trembled slightly. Sam's common-sense approach and rational explanations upset me more than I wanted to admit, because I could see that he might be right.

"You asked for my advice. That's a dangerous thing if you don't want to follow through with it." Sam reached over and took both my hands into his. "Deirdre, work it out with Mitch no matter what. If any two people are good together, you two are. We can talk through more of this later, but don't throw away what works."

I nodded and pulled my hands away, then delicately grabbed his shoulders, reaching up to give him a soft kiss on the cheek.

He put his hand up and touched the place I had kissed with a shy, pleased expression on his face. "Good night, then, and I'll see you soon."

"Thank you." I turned my back on him and hurried out into the night.

"Well, where to, lady? The meter's running."

I had flagged a cab and gotten in but did not give the driver any destination; instead, I sat silently in the backseat. His question finally pulled me out of my brooding. "You know," I said, almost thinking out loud, "if I were smart, I would go straight to the airport."

"The airport? You sure?" The driver seemed confused by my ambivalence.

I laughed softly to myself; why should he be any different

from the rest of us? "No, I'm not sure. Just drive around for a while and let me think."

"It's your call." He shrugged and moved the cab from the curb into the street. "As for me, I don't much care. I'm on all night and it's your money."

Although I was watching out the window, I became aware that he was studying me covertly in the rearview mirror. When our eyes met, he showed no embarrassment, just curiosity. I gave him a small smile, the encouragement he was waiting for.

"You visiting someone in that hospital?"

"Well, you might say that. I know one of the doctors."

"Your boyfriend? You two have a fight?"

"No, no, nothing like that. It's more complicated than I could explain, even if we drove around all night."

"Suits me. You're better looking than most of my fares. Probably safer too. This city is getting crazier every day."

I said nothing, but he continued. "You meet all types in this job. You probably wouldn't believe some of the things I've seen from up here. But I can tell you're sad about something. And it seems a shame that a pretty little thing like you shouldn't be happy. Why, you should be living in a nice house in the suburbs, with three or four little ones running around, happily married, not cruising this city with an old, worn-out cab driver."

I looked at his license. "Are you married, Bill?"

"Was. Almost fifty years, but she died."

"I'm sorry."

"Yeah, me too." He stretched his neck up so that I could see his smile in the mirror. "Probably a lot sorrier than you. When she died I was devastated. Didn't hardly know what to do with myself. It's been three years now, and I still miss her like it was yesterday."

He fell silent and I went back to the window. He stopped at a traffic light and turned around. "You decide where you want to go yet?"

"No, just keep driving. But do you mind if I ask you a question?"

"Sure, goes with the territory, you know?"

I nodded and leaned forward in my seat. "When you were married, did you and your wife ever have differences of opinion, things that you couldn't reconcile between the two of you?"

He snorted a bit. "Hell, yeah. Women and men couldn't be more different if they were two different breeds. So things that seemed real important to her didn't matter to me. And vice versa."

"But you still stayed together."

"Yep. It's a nasty world out there if you don't have someone to love."

"Then here's another question for you. If you had known, when you first met your wife fifty years ago, that she would die before you, would you still have set yourself up for it?"

"The loss, you mean?"

"Yes, would you have married her regardless?"

His reply was so quick, I knew that he had put no thought into what I had asked. "Of course," he said in an injured tone, "I loved her. And how could you ever know for sure?"

"But let's say, as a hypothetical situation, you had known for a certainty that you would have only, oh, fifteen years with her and not fifty. And that when she went, you would have nothing. That you knew you would never find another like her no matter how long you lived."

"Hypothetically?"

"Of course."

He thought about it this time; I could see his eyes narrow in the rearview mirror. "Yeah, it would've been hard to deal with that certainty, but I would've married her even if I knew we had only one year." He paused for a minute. "Your boyfriend sick or something?"

"Yes, I suppose you could say that. I know for a fact that I'll outlive him by quite a few years. But that doesn't seem to bother him."

"And it bothers you?"

"Yes, it does. I've already lost one husband; I have no desire to lose another."

He gave a low whistle and a chuckle. "At the risk of sounding sarcastic, lady, I gotta tell you it's a tough life. You got to take chances or you're nowhere. Marry him. You might be surprised how it'll turn out."

I sighed and settled back into the seat again, smiling to myself, watching the passing pedestrians, studying the buildings, the shops, the bars. It was the same city as ever, but suddenly, as if my eyes had been cleared, as if the city and I had been washed clean, everything changed. I realized with a deep conviction that I had a home, not just a room, but a place where I belonged, where I was wanted, loved. Like all revelations, it seemed so simple, so true, that I wanted to laugh with joy. Instead, I tapped Bill gently on the shoulder. "I know where I want to go now. Thank you." I gave him Mitch's address. "And hurry, please. I'd like to get there before dawn."

Chapter 23

The following evening Mitch and I were married. I still had my doubts as to whether it was the right thing to do. But the revelation I had been given the night before was still clear in my mind. Sam was right, the cab driver was right; I was tired of running from commitment, sick of living from day to day in loneliness and fear. And the look of complete happiness that crossed Mitch's face when I finally agreed was more than worth any problems that might arise later. I hadn't seen that look on a man for over a century, and it felt good.

"Are you sure?" He had gripped my face in his hands and searched my eyes.

"Yes, Mitch," I said, growing more confident in my decision. "I've never been surer of anything in my long life."

"Good. We'll do it soon, okay?"

"What's the hurry?"

He laughed and leaned over to kiss me. "I'm afraid you'll change your mind."

"But don't these things take time?"

"Yeah, but you forget I'm a cop. And although I've been out of action for a while, I still know a few people who owe me big favors; they can hurry it along. And we can get our blood tests tomorrow."

"But I can't take a blood test, Mitch. Have you forgotten?"

"Oh." He had looked disappointed, then shrugged it off. "We'll figure out a way. I assume your passport is up-to-date."

I nodded and he smiled. "Well, then you get some sleep and I'll start making calls right away."

True to his word, by the time I awoke all the arrangements had been made. Sam had been enlisted to produce a valid blood test for me; his only stipulation was that he be invited to the ceremony. Mitch had even managed to produce a wedding gown of sorts, apparently with the collusion of Betsy McCain, another self-invited guest. Before I hardly knew what had happened, I was standing nervously in an anteroom at the courthouse, waiting for the arrival of the judge, wondering, as the small bridal party assembled, why the hell I had ever agreed to this situation.

Mitch reached over, took my hand, and smiled. "You know, when Betsy brought that dress this afternoon, I had my doubts. But it looks great on you."

I looked down at what little there was of my bridal gown. It was white satin sheath covered entirely in white lace. True, it did have long sleeves, but it was an off the shoulder line, and I was afraid to move too quickly for fear of losing it entirely. Laughing, I gave a tug on the too-short hemline. "Well, if you ask me, Betsy tries too hard to save money on material. There's practically nothing here."

Mitch's eyes lit up mischievously. "Yeah," he said with an exaggerated sigh, "but what's there is wonderful."

"If you had only given me some time, I would have gotten something a little more appropriate."

"Liar." Mitch's smile never left his face.

"That is not a lie."

"Yes, it is, and you know it. If I had given you more time, you'd just have found excuses to put this off. I'm not getting any younger. I've had visions of you pushing me down the aisle in a wheelchair. Or"—he pulled me to him, serious once again—"visions of you disappearing again, this time for good."

"Mitch," I whispered, "I promise you I will never leave you."

"Okay, you two, break it up." Betsy McCain bustled into the room balancing several florist boxes. "You're not married yet, and you can't get married anyway without the maid of honor. And"—she flourished the boxes and set them on one of the chairs—"certainly not without flowers. Although on such short notice I had to make do with what they had."

"Whatever they are, I'm sure they'll be fine," I told her. "It was a very nice gesture." I gave her a smile as she took off her coat and hung it on the rack by the door. She looked different to me, and it took a while to recognize why. She had abandoned her normal tailored suit, donning instead a dress cut very similar to my own but with less lace and completely in black. "And you look great."

"Thanks." She shrugged off the compliment and opened the flowers. "Here." She handed me the bouquet of white roses, then removed one in black for herself. Then she stood looking at me. "On second thought, and if you don't mind breaking from tradition . . ." She handed me hers, took mine from me, and stood back, squinting critically. "I like that better—there's more contrast."

I looked doubtfully at the black roses, then began to laugh until tears formed in my eyes. "Oh, Betsy"—I choked out the words—"you could never know how much more appropriate these are."

Mitch frowned, then lightened as Betsy went to him and pinned on his boutonniere.

"Now," she said, armed with one more flower and a deadly-looking pin, "where's the best man?"

"He should be here soon." Mitch looked at the clock on the wall. "He'd better be, he's got all our paperwork."

"Chris has our paperwork?" I questioned in surprise.

"Chris," Mitch said, his mouth tightening slightly, "won't be coming tonight. Dr. Samuels has volunteered to stand up for us."

I felt a flush of sudden anger. "Chris was too busy for his father's wedding?"

"No, Chris was not too busy, he just won't be here."

"But Mitch—"

"Deirdre"—he interrupted me with finality—"let it go. I don't want it to ruin our evening. He'll come around eventually."

"Stepkids," Betsy said with disgust. "There's nothing worse than sulky little brats who don't want their parents to be happy."

Mitch shrugged, but I instantly rose to Chris's defense. "He is not sulky and he is not a brat. There are issues involved that you don't understand, Betsy. And"—I softened my voice—"Mitch is right. We shouldn't let it ruin our evening."

"Okay, okay. And speaking of the evening, did Mitch tell you where we're eating after the ceremony?"

"No. Actually this entire event is pretty much of a surprise."

"Well, then," Betsy said with an obvious wink at Mitch, "I can keep a secret too."

"Secrets?" Sam came through the door, a white envelope in his hand, "who's keeping secrets?"

"Everyone," I said with a warning glance softened by a small smile and hug. "Thanks for coming, Sam."

"Not to worry. I had tonight off. And I wouldn't miss this occasion for all the world."

Betsy sidled up to Sam and extended her hand. "Betsy McCain, Griffin Designs. And you must be the best man."

"John Samuels." He shook her hand and accepted his boutonniere, then turned to Mitch and clapped him on the shoulder. "In this case, though, I suspect the best man is really this lucky dog. Mitch, I can't tell you how overjoyed I am about all this. You must tell me how you managed to get her to agree."

"I will when I figure it out myself," Mitch started to say, and all three began to laugh.

I stood for a while, watching their mirthful exchange, feeling a total stranger in their midst. What did I have in common with these humans other than the calling of their blood to my hunger?

"It is what you chose, little one."

I snapped my head up and saw Max, shadowed in the doorway, beckoning to me. Aware but uncaring of the others' astonished faces, I pushed through them to where he waited in the hallway.

I heard Sam's startled voice call my name, Betsy's "what the hell," and with relief I heard Mitch say calmly, "Let her go, she'll be back," but none of that seemed important.

Max was leaning against the wall, just out of view of the door. "I might have known you would be here," I said bitterly. "Have you come to talk me out of it?"

"Not at all, my dear. I've come to a grudging respect for Greer over the years, and since he has accepted my presence in your life, I can do no less."

"Accepted your presence? How on earth could he do that? He's never seen you."

"Are you totally sure about that, Deirdre? He's a lot closer to understanding than you think. And he loves you anyway. How could I stand in the way of a relationship like that?"

I laughed softly. "It never stopped you before. So, am I to believe that you are here only to wish us well?"

"Believe what you like." Max leaned over and gave me an icy kiss. "Maybe I came to give away the bride."

"Deirdre," Mitch called from within the room, "the judge is ready."

I moved into the doorway. "I'll be right in," I answered, but when I turned back, Max was gone. "Damn," I swore softly, and ran my fingers over my lips, still cold from his touch.

The ceremony went smoothly. Sam must have done a good job faking my blood test, since apparently the paperwork was in order. Although tempted, I did not run screaming from the room, and if Max was present, he at least had the good grace to stay quiet and out of my line of sight. Twice during the short time we were there though, the door had opened. The first person to enter was Chris, the second, a woman who seemed familiar, but at the time I could not quite place her and did not want to stare. I had held my breath expecting one or the other of them to interrupt at the appropriate time, but nothing had happened.

". . . I now pronounce you husband and wife," the judge intoned, and Mitch pulled me to him for a kiss passionate and long enough to make everyone in the room slightly uncomfortable. And then it was over.

Chris walked up to us, shook Mitch's hand, and hesitantly kissed me on the cheek. After the introductions were made, I looked around for the woman who had accompanied him, but she must have left at some time during the ceremony. And there was no time for questioning him; Betsy hustled us into the limousines she had rented. On the way I found out, to my dismay, that she had arranged to hold the wedding dinner at The Imperial. When we arrived, the driver came around and opened our door.

"Well, Mrs. Greer," Mitch said, smiling at me tentatively, "shall we go in?"

I touched him softly on the shoulder. "Mitch, did dinner have to be here? After my last run-in with Victor, I doubt that I'll be welcome."

"Just a minute." Mitch motioned to the driver and closed the door. "I knew it wasn't a good idea, but Betsy made all the arrangements. I called after she told me and found out that Victor won't be in tonight. He's out on important business. So you should be safe."

"I'm not really hungry. And I can't eat anything they serve in there anyway."

"I know." Mitch reached over and patted my cheek. "But I'm starved. And the wedding dinner is almost as important as the ceremony itself. What else did you want to do?"

"Well, I thought we could just head on out to the airport; we could go anywhere you like."

"After dinner, Deirdre. Betsy was so excited to set this up, and I'd hate to hurt her feelings. She's been a real help to me. Besides, this'll give us a chance to work things out with Chris."

"Oh. I almost forgot about Chris." I sat quietly for a minute, then leaned over and kissed Mitch on the cheek. "Fine, we'll go in, but right afterward we're going to pack some things and get out of this damn city for a while."

"Great. Now, don't you think we should go in? They'll wonder what we're doing."

"Let them wonder." I took his hand and gently stroked his palm with my thumb, then held it up to my lips. "Mitch, this may sound crazy, but did you happen to see Max tonight?"

"See him, no, but I knew he was around."

"How?"

"For one thing, by the way you acted. You get this distant look in your eyes, this distracted expression when you say he's present. Now I know what that means, and when it happened tonight, I tried to pay attention. I thought I could actually feel him there, and I could almost hear something, far away and indistinct." He smiled at me. "Don't worry about it, Deirdre. It's a little spooky, but I'll get used to it." Mitch reached for the door handle, then pulled away. "So, what did he want anyway?"

"To give the bride away."

To my surprise, Mitch threw his head back and laughed. "That's what you get for putting 'Father' on his gravestone. Come on, let's go in."

We caught up with the other three in the lobby. Betsy was talking to the maître d'; Chris and Sam were carrying on a whispered discussion in the corner. They looked up guiltily when we walked in, and I knew they had been talking about us. But since Chris seemed more at ease, and smiled more freely at Mitch and me, I didn't really mind. If Sam could help him deal with this situation, it would make our lives a lot easier.

Our table was ready and Betsy claimed Mitch's arm and followed the waiter. I touched Chris gently on the arm; he barely suppressed a shudder, but Sam nodded at him encouragingly. "Everything will work out all right, Chris." I smiled at him. "I promise." He gulped slightly, tucked my hand around his arm, and escorted me to dinner.

"Deirdre, I'm sorry I didn't come sooner. Dad asked me to be best man, but I just couldn't. He was really angry, read me the riot act on the phone."

"But you finally did come," I reassured him, "and that's what matters."

Chris slowed down and looked doubtfully at the back of Mitch's head. "I hope so. He can be real stubborn sometimes."

"Tell me about it," I said with a small laugh. "Why do you think this happened at all? For all that I love your father, and I do love him, I was not entirely convinced that this marriage was a good idea. But, Chris, it was what he wanted. He's been alone so long." As have I, I added silently, but he seemed to understand.

"I know this'll be good for you both. It's just that you're a"—he had the grace to blush slightly—"well, what you are, and that'll take some getting used to."

"Fine, we have a lot of time. But keep it to yourself tonight, kiddo. Betsy doesn't know and I'd like to keep it that way."

"And what doesn't Betsy know?" She bounded over to us, her eyes gleaming almost maliciously, acquisitively. "More secrets?"

I sat down next to Mitch and held his hand. "Only that I married the best man in the city."

"Oh, that," she said disparagingly. "I knew that. But you've got only one, Deirdre"—she settled Sam in on one side of her and Chris on the other—"and now I have two."

Chris looked embarrassed, but Sam laughed. The waiter brought and poured the champagne. I wanted to ask about the woman who had entered the courtroom and then quickly departed, but I hated to spoil what was left of the evening with an interrogation of Chris. Betsy had no such compunctions.

"So tell me, Christopher, who came in after you tonight? And why didn't she come along? One more person wouldn't have been a problem, would it have, Deirdre?"

"No, absolutely not." I glanced at Mitch, who suddenly seemed nervous.

"It was Jean," Sam interjected.

Mitch nodded and said nothing, but glared at Chris.

"Good God, so it was," I blurted out with a funny choked laugh. "I must have been really nervous not to recognize her. But who the hell invited her? She was the last person I expected to see." I looked at Sam. "Do you think she listens in on your phone calls?"

"No, she was off duty this afternoon; she works only nights. And I know I didn't mention it to her."

"Don't look at me," Mitch shrugged. "I haven't seen her since I checked out. And anyway, what possible difference can it make?"

"Who is Jean?" Betsy asked, sounding slightly annoyed at being left out of the conversation.

"A nurse at the hospital where I work," Sam said. "And like Mitch said, it's not really important, just curious that she should have shown up like that."

Chris cleared his throat. "I stopped by there this evening, looking for you, Dr. Samuels. I couldn't find you, but Jean was there and I asked if you were going to the wedding. Nobody told me not to say anything. And when she asked herself along, well, what could I do? She stayed until it was over, then slipped away before I noticed she'd gone."

Nobody said anything, and he continued in her defense. "She took good care of you, Dad, better than any other nurse there, and if she wanted to see you married, I can't see what harm it'd do."

"No harm, Chris." I reached across the table and touched his arm. "We just wondered how she knew. I think it was sweet of you to bring her along. Now, let's just drop the subject, shall we? How about some more champagne?"

By the time everyone's glass was refilled, dinner arrived and the conversation turned to other matters. I sat quietly through the meal, picking at my rare prime rib, trying to ignore the waves of nausea caused by the varied aromas of the food around me. When the waiter finally cleared the plates and provided coffee, I sighed in relief.

Mitch caught the hint, paid the bill, and got up from the table. "Thank you for your help today, Betsy and Sam. It was wonderful. But we have some packing to do before we leave on our honeymoon."

"Honeymoon?" Betsy asked blearily, the champagne having taken its toll on her. "I didn't know you were going away."

"Oh." I stood up and rubbed my head against Mitch's sleeve. "We just decided on the way over here."

"Where are you going?" Sam smiled up at us over his coffee.

"Ah, we don't actually know yet, do we, honey?" Mitch kissed the top of my head. "But we're heading straight out to the airport. We'll send you a postcard."

I walked around the table and gave them all a hug. Mitch shook Sam's hand, kissed Betsy, and clapped Chris on the shoulder. "See you later," he called, and we left the restaurant.

The limos were nowhere in sight, so we flagged a cab and when one finally stopped, we snuggled in the backseat.

"That wasn't so bad, was it?" Mitch asked me as we arrived at his apartment.

"No, it was a lot of fun, actually."

"You see, you should've married me two years ago."

"Yes, I guess so. Mitch, we have some things we still need to work out."

"I know, but it can wait, can't it? Let's enjoy the next few weeks before we get back to the harsh realities. And speaking of enjoying, we don't need to rush right off to the airport, do we?" His one hand tightened on my shoulder while the other played with the lace on the hem of my dress.

"No." I turned to face him. "We have a little time."

"Good." He kissed me, his lips crushing mine, his hand delicately moving up my thigh.

"Actually," I said breathlessly when he removed his mouth, "tomorrow night would be soon enough to leave."

"I was hoping you'd say that." The rawness of passion in his voice made me gasp, and like the night in the hospital made me forget where we were. Had it been a longer drive to his apartment, we would have made love right there in the cab.

As it was, the driver coughed and discreetly announced our arrival. When Mitch paid him, we ran up the steps of his apartment clutching each other and giggling like teenagers. He unlocked the door and picked me up to carry me in.

My head was nestled into his neck, so when he dropped me abruptly, I was taken completely by surprise by the three men, Victor Lange, Ron Wilkes, my attorney, and Fred, the Ballroom's bartender, standing in Mitch's living room. More surprising still was the fact that both Ron and Fred held rather large handguns, aimed directly at us.

Chapter 24

"Close the door, Greer," Victor ordered. Mitch slumped for a minute, then did as he was told. He leaned up against the door; his eyes were glassy and his breathing came in short, panicked gasps.

"Mitch." I took him by the shoulders and called his name but he didn't hear me; he was absorbed in studying the faces of the men.

"What the hell is this all about, Victor?" I turned around and faced the three of them, attempting to block Mitch's body from their guns. "Are you planning to shoot me? Well"—I bared my teeth unpleasantly—"you had better give it your best shot the first time. It will be the only chance you get."

"Now, Deirdre," Victor said calmly, "we don't want to hurt anybody. And of course, if we did, it would be Mitch we would shoot. So if you'll just move away from him slowly, everything will be fine. We can talk this out like reasonable beings."

"Reasonable beings do not break into people's apartments and threaten the inhabitants with guns. What is this all about? And what have you done to Mitch?"

"Nothing. I assume he's having a little flashback from his recent mental problems. It will pass." Victor motioned to the couch. "Come here and sit down, my dear. Ron and Fred will take good care of Mitch."

I looked steadily into the faces of the two men. Fred met my glance defiantly; Ron lowered his eyes, but not before I caught a glimpse of sadness. "You I can understand, Fred, you've always been a self-serving little bastard." He said nothing, but continued to smirk, so I turned to Ron. "But what are you doing here, Ron? I thought we were friends."

Victor laughed and beckoned me to the couch again. "As you so succinctly put to me not that long ago, 'Never count on constancy in love or friendship among vampires.' " His emphasis on the last word caused me to draw in a sharp breath that he ignored. "Ron and Fred both work for me."

"All three of you are vampires?" I dropped onto the couch with a small, humorless laugh.

"Just so, Deirdre."

Mitch made a small choking sound and slumped down onto the floor, his back resting against the door, his eyes still focused on the faces of the men.

"Ease up on him a little, boys. We don't want him passing out, do we? I think Deirdre will cooperate with us."

Some of the fear left Mitch's face and his breathing deepened a little. He managed a weak smile that wrenched my heart.

"Mitch," I said quietly. "I'm sorry. But I always said you were better off without me."

"Be that as it may," Victor continued, "he's now involved in this situation if only by association. And speaking of which, I understand congratulations are in order."

"Congratulations?"

"On your marriage." Victor's voice sounded amused.

Fred snickered, calling my attention to the two of them where they stood, their guns no longer pointed at Mitch, but still very much in evidence. Ron gave me one brief, angry glance, and his shoulders tightened. When he did speak, his tone was flat and bitter. "You don't date the meat."

"Excuse me?" But Ron made no response, so I turned again to Victor. "And how did you know we were married?"

"You'll discover that very few of your activities are unknown to me. I make it my business to know these things. And there is one member of our group to whom you have not yet been properly introduced. She's a little insecure, being only newly one of us, and I wanted her out of the way if there was trouble. But you'll be reasonable, I know." Victor smiled, not maliciously, I thought, but as if he were enjoying a joke. "And you may find out that you share many things in common; one might even say you were from the same family. Come out, Jean."

Jean stepped out of the hallway, where she had been concealed from us. One look at her pinched face and white uniform and I began to laugh, sounding a little hysterical. "Jesus, Victor, this is entirely too much. Is everyone I meet in this damned city a vampire? How many of you are there?"

"Don't you mean how many of us?" He did not wait for my answer. "We'll let that go for now. I completely understand that your ignorance of our existence was Max's doing. Ill-advised, as I said before, but Max did what he liked. And you were his responsibility."

"I take care of myself, Victor. I always have."

"And that is an admirable sentiment, my dear, one which we all admire in you. To answer your questions, there are approximately one hundred of us in the metropolitan area and no, not everyone you meet is a vampire. But of course Ron and Jean were planted, carefully cultivated for their roles. Granted, Fred had been with Max practically since the Ballroom opened. But Ron was engaged to keep tabs on you when you returned and Jean was put into the hospital to monitor our punishment of Mitch." He looked away from me. "I must apologize for that, Greer. We had thought you had killed Max. We'll make what amends we can."

"Can you give him back the two years he lost in the institution? Can you give him back an unaltered mind?" A surge of anger flowed through me; these people were worse than Max—he at least had a personal interest in my life. And his manipulations were understandable from that point of view.

"No," Victor said gently. "But I can allow him to live, under certain circumstances, of course."

Jean gave a small gasp, then cleared her throat nervously. "Mr. Lange," she said hesitantly, "do you need me anymore? I have to be back at the hospital soon."

"No, thank you, Jean. That will be all."

She went to the door and gave Victor a sidelong glance. He nodded slightly and she looked down at Mitch. "I'm sorry, Mitch," she said, and slipped past him.

Her subservient attitude annoyed me. "This is quite a nice setup you have, Victor. Do all the vampires here serve you so willingly, or is this group your private little army?"

"No, Deirdre, you misunderstand the situation. They do not serve me so much as they serve The Cadre. But since I am the head of that venerable institution, I do command a certain amount of respect."

"The Cadre? That's the organization that inherits Max's money if I turn it down, isn't it? Is that what all this is about? Money? You can have it all; I've never wanted any of it."

"I wish it were that simple, Deirdre. The money is not the issue here. The murder of Max Hunter is. The other night you admitted to that crime; do you want to change your statement?"

I have him a short, vicious smile. "Would it do any good?"

"No, my dear. Eiither way you must appear before the judicial board of The Cadre. We have no choice." Victor checked his watch. "And we must go soon; they're waiting for us."

"And if I refuse?"

Fred turned around, displaying a delighted grin and brandishing his gun. "Then we shoot Greer."

I had no doubt that he would do as he said. I stood up and smoothed the skirt of that ridiculous wedding gown. "Well, then, I can hardly refuse such a polite invitation. Shall we?"

Mitch struggled to his feet. "She's not going anywhere without me."

Fred laughed unpleasantly. "Of course, you get to come too, you're our insurance that Miss Griffin, or shall I say, Mrs. Greer, doesn't bolt."

I gave him a cold stare. "You don't need insurance, Fred. I will not bolt, as you so cleverly put it. Mitch stays here."

Fred shifted uneasily under my gaze and looked at Victor for confirmation.

"I trust you, Deirdre," Victor said with a frown, "but I'm afraid Fred is right, even if overly anxious on the trigger. Mitch will accompany us, but you have my word that he won't be harmed and that you'll both be returned here before dawn. This is merely a preliminary hearing. Certain allowances have been made for you, since you are what we call a rogue, and are unschooled in our ways. You'll be given every chance to prepare for the trial, and although you will be under surveillance, you'll still have a chance to spend a few weeks together before the final decision." Victor gently took my arm and moved me toward the door. As he opened it, he looked deep into my eyes, his eyes a curious mix of anger and sympathy. "That is the most I can promise you."

Once again Mitch and I were loaded into the backseat of a limousine, and once again our destination was The Imperial. But this time we entered through the back and rode an elevator down two floors.

Victor reached out and pushed a button on the control panel. The elevator stopped but the doors did not open. Then he turned to Mitch. "Mitchell Greer, you have been brought to a place where few humans have ever been; fewer still have left alive." His tone was formal, rehearsed. "You are here for several reasons. One, you must be cleared before the panel for the murder of Max Hunter so that others do not attempt your punishment on their own. Two, you have married one of us"—Victor glanced over at me, his eyes sparkling—"even though she will not admit that kinship. The Cadre is an ancient institution and has much respect for traditions and sacred vows. So you have been given leave to attend unharmed. But"—his voice deepened, darkened—"you must not interfere in any way. Your assistance or defense of Deirdre under any circumstances can only harm her and will not be tolerated."

"I understand." Mitch's voice matched Victor's solemn manner, but I noticed the dangerous glint in his eyes. "You've been more than fair, I suppose, given the situation. But you've also got to understand that I'll do my damnedest to keep you, or any of your thugs, from hurting her. Quite honestly, Victor, without her, my life is worthless. And I'd happily give it for the chance to take a few of you with me."

They stood appraising each other for what seemed a long time. Finally, Victor smiled and held out his hand. "You have my word," he said as they shook hands.

"Deirdre will not be killed, and you won't be required to fight us for her." He took his finger from the button and the doors opened. "Despite what you might think, we're really quite civilized."

We entered a large meeting room, thickly carpeted and illuminated only by candles and torches. At the end of this room a long table stood, occupied by eight people, four on each side of the two vacant chairs in the center. On the wall behind the table, a large tapestry was hung depicting a dark night sky over a medieval-looking city. Ten small golden plates, each about six inches in diameter, resembling family crests, hung from chains on either side of the tapestry.

Victor stepped forward, motioning Fred and Mitch into chairs along the wall, and Ron moved up beside me to take Victor's place. Slowly, ceremoniously, Victor walked down the center aisle and the people seated at the table rose and bowed to him as he approached. Their eyes shone oddly in the light; none of them looked familiar to me. Victor nodded his head and walked around the table, removing two of the crests from the wall. One, he hung around his neck; the other was draped over the center of the table. He raised his hand and the others sat while he remained standing.

"Deirdre Griffin"—his voice was soft but powerful and the echoes filled the room—"born Dorothy Grey, remade in the house of Alveros in the common year of 1860, come forward."

Ron gave me a soft push in the small of my back. Trying to

match the pace Victor had set, I approached the table, my hands at my sides. As I walked I kept my eyes on the center crest, recognizing it with surprise as one I had seen in my dreams of Max. Damn you, Max, I thought, searching for his presence and finding nothing, why the hell did you get me involved in this?

When I got within one foot of the table, Victor gave a slight nod of his head and I stopped. He raised his hand again. "Deirdre Griffin is brought before us on charges of murder. Do any of The Cadre wish to speak for her?"

I opened my mouth to explain that I would speak for myself, but caught the almost imperceptible shake of Victor's head and heard the footsteps behind me.

"I ask to speak for her." Ron stepped up beside me and gave me a small smile. There was shock and surprise on the faces of some of the panel, including Victor's, but when he lowered his arm, he looked strangely pleased.

"Ron Wilkes, your request is granted. This woman stands before us accused of the murder of the founder of the house of Alveros. How will she answer?"

"She cannot answer at this time. As the distinguished houses know, she is a rogue, unused to our ways. I ask that she be given two weeks in which to prepare her answer."

Given Victor's promise to me at Mitch's apartment, this defense did not surprise me. The panel members nodded and Victor raised his hand again. "Deirdre, you have been given that for which you have asked. Mitchell Greer, human, and husband of this vampire, come forward."

Ron pulled me gently to one side and back a few steps as Mitch approached. He stood facing the panel, and I admired the determined way he held his shoulders and head.

"Let it be known among The Cadre that this human, who had previously, by certain evidences and by his own admission, been judged guilty of the murder of Max Hunter, is at this moment exonerated, and is to be held exempt from further punitive actions on our part, until such time as his true involvement in the crime can be ascertained."

"It has been witnessed," a female member seated to Victor's right agreed, "and it will be communicated."

"Then," Victor said, "we are adjourned."

The formality of the panel instantly dissolved at his words and everyone became more relaxed. Victor walked over to me and smiled. "See, I told you we were civilized. Now, can I offer you a drink?"

Mitch shook his head and put his arm around my shoulders. "No, but we'll take a ride home."

"Fine," Victor agreed. "I'm afraid we have rather interrupted your wedding night. Ron will call you tomorrow evening and begin your education, Deirdre. Until then, you can pretty much do what you want. You can move about the city freely and continue your activities but"—his eyes grew stern—"stay away from the airport. Any attempts to leave town will result in your incarceration until the trial. I don't want it to come to that." He took my hand and kissed it. "Good night, Deirdre." Releasing me, he nodded. "Mitch."

We followed Victor to the back of the room, and when we reached the elevator, Fred stepped in behind us, his gun still in his hand. "Fred," Victor said, the disgust evident in his voice, "your obvious delight in tormenting your fellow beings is sickening. Put your toy away. And drive Mr. and Mrs. Greer home."

Chapter 25

Fred remained subdued by Victor's reprimand only until we stopped at a traffic light a few blocks away from Mitch's apartment. "Good hearing, huh?" He turned around in the driver's seat and smiled at us maliciously. "You're pretty quiet, Deirdre. Don't you have any questions to ask?"

I gave him a long, cold stare. "You want questions? Fine. Just where do you fit in, Fred?"

"Oh," he said, returning to his driving, "same as you—house of Alveros. Common year 1922. There aren't many of us left from that house." He gave a cruel laugh. "And in two weeks time there might be one less. Although"—he met my eyes in the rearview mirror—"Victor seems to like you. Maybe he'll let you live, provided, of course, you give him the proper encouragement. Play your cards right and he might even let you establish the house of Grey someday. Compared to most of Max's children, you're positively ancient. Me, I like my women younger, less experienced, if you know what I mean."

I felt Mitch tense up next to me, and putting a calming hand on his arm, I warned him with my eyes to keep his temper. I knew that Fred was merely baiting us, hoping to provoke an angry response. And I wondered how much of his self-confidence came from the weapon he carried and how much was inner strength. He was younger than I; perhaps he was weaker, perhaps he could be bent to my control. I glanced at Mitch out of the corner of my eye and shook my head almost imperceptively. He understood, and gave my knee a gentle squeeze.

I took a deep breath and leaned forward in my seat with a feigned eagerness. "So, Fred," I said, touching him softly on the shoulder, "you are one of Max's children. I suppose that makes us related: cousins, perhaps, or maybe even siblings." I lowered my voice to a sultry whisper and ran a finger along his cheek and jaw. "You must tell me," I breathed, "what exactly are The Cadre's rules on incest?"

He tensed at my touch, clenching his teeth together, but encouraged by the jump of his pulse, I continued.

"There is a lot to be said for experience, Fred. I may be over sixty years your elder, but those were sixty years spent in experimentation, pushing the natural limits. You might be pleasantly surprised at the kind of things I could teach you."

"Quit playing games with me, Deirdre." Fred's voice was curt, but his breathing quickened.

"It is no game," I whispered to him, gently nuzzling the side of his neck. I saw that we were back at Mitch's apartment. "Stop the car, Fred."

He pulled over to the curb and turned off the engine. "That's right," I encouraged. "Why don't we let Mitch go in first? We don't need him here right now, do we?"

"Get out, Greer."

I nodded and Mitch left the car. I waited until he was up the stairs and in the door before I made my next request. "And now, Fred, you can give me your gun. We won't be needing it, not now. I can give it back to you later on, after we have completed our business."

I felt his hesitation. "Please, Fred," I breathed in his ear, "give me the gun. You don't need it, not for me."

Quickly, he vaulted over the seat, landing next to me; his hands flew up to grip my shoulders. I met his eyes. "The gun, Fred. Give me the gun."

He reached into his pocket and produced the gun, handing it to me with a guttural moan. I put it into my purse and reached over to him, holding his face in my hands. "Thank you, Fred." My eyes bore into his, until I felt that I was deep inside his mind. "It's too bad that you lost your gun on the way over here. That was very careless of you. Now, open the door and let me out of the car."

Fred shuddered slightly at my intrusion but obediently opened the door for me. I smiled and, bending over, kissed his cheek lightly. "Thank you, Fred," I said again. "I will see you soon."

"Good night," I heard him call, his voice faint and confused.

Laughing at my success, I ran up the stairs, opened the door, and bumped into Mitch, who had apparently been standing at the entrance, watching. "What the hell was all that about, Deirdre?"

I looked behind me and saw Fred pull the car into traffic and drive away. "I merely wanted to see if he was controllable."

"And?" There was a slight tick in his cheek, as if he were trying not to smile.

I reached into my purse and, with a grin, produced Fred's gun, dangling it back and forth on my finger. "Like candy from a baby." I took his arm and rubbed my head against his sleeve. "Let's go inside, love. I think we'll be safe from Fred for a while."

Mitch unlocked the door and we both sighed in relief when we saw that his apartment was empty. "You know, Deirdre," Mitch started to say, removing his suit coat and tie, "I still don't understand why you felt you had to play that little scene with Fred."

I slid out of my heels and sat in the armchair, stretching my legs out in front of me and flexing my feet. "I had to know what sort of power I possess. It was not important before, because I never had to deal with beings like myself. But now . . ." Shrugging, I curled my legs underneath me and settled back. "It's important to know what I can do."

"And if it hadn't worked? If you hadn't been able to control Fred, what do you think would have happened?" Mitch came over and sat on the arm of the chair. Although he put his arm around me tenderly, I could feel the tension in his body and sense the anger he was keeping tightly in check.

Attempting to lighten his mood and diffuse his anger, I joked. "At the very least, I would have had to hire another manager at the Ballroom." Reaching up, I stroked his cheek and ran my fingers over his lips. "And at the most, there would have been one less member of the house of Alveros for us to contend with. You know as well as I that had he laid one hand on me, you would have killed him."

"Damn straight." Mitch gave a tight little laugh and kissed me on the forehead. "Now"—he stood up and began unbuttoning his shirt—"let's get changed and start packing."

"What?"

"We're supposed to leave for our honeymoon, remember? Now that you've gotten rid of Fred for the evening, I suspect that we've got enough time to get out of the city before The Cadre exacts their vigilante justice on you. I won't stand by and let them prosecute you, Deirdre. After all this time and the way I had to live without you, and after . . ." Smiling, Mitch ruffled my hair. "You finally came to your senses and married me; I won't let anyone interfere, not the bloody pretentious Victor Lange or even his goddamned precious Cadre."

I chuckled at his accurate summation of the scene we had just been put through, then grew serious. "But Mitch, I can't leave. I promised Victor. Besides, what sort of life would we have, running and hiding from them wherever we go? The life I already lead is bad enough, but to have to avoid them for the rest of eternity?" I shook my head sadly; the decision to marry him had been an easier one to swallow, but the commitment I had finally made to face up to my problems and not run away applied as much to this situation as to my relationship with Mitch. "No, we can't run. It really doesn't matter for me, but you, you're a different matter completely. I will not have them punish you again for something I did. And if, in the process, they were to hurt you, or drive you completely insane, or kill you, I'd be forced to take revenge on them." I sighed and wiped away a tear. "Mitch, I love you, I want nothing more than to stay with you for the rest of your life, but I'm tired of running away. I can't exist any longer at odds with the entire universe. It will stop here. Like it or not, I'm one of them and I'll accept their terms and their justice, no matter what."

To my surprise, Mitch was not angry at my statements. Instead, he smiled at me, his blue eyes almost aglow in their intensity. "Deirdre, we'll beat them, together. We can get you off this charge, I'm sure of it. And if not, I'd put down money that you could take them all on single-handedly and come out unscathed."

"I wish I could be so sure. Fred was easy, but who knows how long my control over him will continue? And as for all the others, I have no experience against which to gauge their power or their reactions."

"But don't you see?" He pulled me to my feet and held me to him. "You're a rogue to them, a wild card. They have no gauge of you either. And they've all been tutored, led along the easy path, while you had to struggle and fight every inch of the way. You have an inner strength and conviction that none of The Cadre, with all their ancient ceremonies and rites, can match."

I moved an arm's length from him and smiled. "I never thought of it that way. You may just be right. But"—I nestled up against him, sliding my hands under his open shirt, savoring the warm texture of his bare skin against my fingers—"let's not spend the rest of the night discussing this. I thought we were supposed to be on our honeymoon."

Shortly before dawn I lay entwined with Mitch, admiring the shine of the street lights reflecting onto my wedding ring. A simple gold band, it was only a little too large for my finger. I smiled and, for those last few precious minutes of the night, watched him sleep. It has been too many years, I thought, since I allowed myself to love someone fully. And yet, he was worth the waiting.

When the sky began to lighten, I got out of bed, pulled down the blinds, and drew the heavy draperies across the window, then slid back under the covers, pressing myself against his warm body.

The dirt road I walk seems familiar somehow; a voice in the back of my mind recognizes this place even though I've never been here. I shrug the feeling away, a habit that I've become quite adept at through the centuries. What I don't understand I tend to leave alone. A soft rain is falling, and the wheel ruts in the road well up with muddy water.

I have been traveling with no purpose for some time now, ever since Leupold made the long ocean journey and found me. He remains in that city, excited by his new life and slowly building for himself a dynasty of other beings like us. I managed to convince him that I wanted no part of his empire, but helped him to locate those that I myself had transformed. There are only a few still living; whether they choose to join him or not is their decision. I have not yet met one I would be willing to spend the rest of eternity with. I tell myself that I prefer my loneliness to their inane society, prefer to commit my atrocities with no audience other than my own belabored conscience.

I hear the carriage approach long before it comes into sight. Having left a dead body behind in the closest town, I wish to remain unseen and melt into the surrounding trees. I watch them drive by, the man and the woman inside the closed coach. They are talking and smiling, and I feel a strange twinge of jealousy for a life I will never have.

When they are farther down the road, I step out of the concealing brush. I continue walking, but suddenly a bolt of lightning strikes a nearby tree. There is a deafening crash and it falls and catches the rear end of the carriage, which overturns on the road.

I wait a minute, watching the upper wheels of the carriage spin in the air. The horses rear and scream in fright, perhaps they are spooked by the lightning, perhaps they sense my unnatural presence.

The smell of blood falls upon the air, hypnotizing, tantalizing me, and although I had already fed, the deadly hunger engulfs me again. I discover the man's dead body under the lower wheels; he lies in a crumpled heap, his neck twisted, his body crushed and his blood uselessly mingles with the muddied rain.

But the woman, ah, the woman still lives. As I open the door of the carriage and reach in for her, she opens her eyes. There is happiness in her glance, as if she had been waiting for me. My heart twists when I realize that it is probably only relief at being rescued. But still I pull her out of the wreckage and hold her warm body close to mine, carrying her farther up the road.

She welcomes my embrace at first, responding eagerly to my caresses and my kisses. Then she looks deep into my eyes, and her fear becomes apparent. Feebly she attempts to push me aside, and I would gladly let her go, but the feeding instinct has been triggered and cannot be denied.

Her body tenses when my teeth sink into her neck; she is powerless to stop me, but still she fights. God, I think, admiring her perseverance, she is strong. As I drink, I feel a sharp pain in my own shoulder. She has clawed her way through my clothes and is answering my assault with one of her own. My own blood flows and she drinks, pulling upon me with a hunger almost as great as my own.

In my surprise, I laugh and stop feeding upon her, allowing her to drink of me. Eventually, she slows and stops; her eyes flutter shut. But I continue to hold her, cradled in my arms, until I hear the approach of another carriage. I do not want to leave her, but I have no choice. I cannot permit myself to be seen.

Reluctantly, I lay her down on the road and she opens her eyes to me once more. "If you survive, my little one," I say before fading into the night, "we will meet again."

Chapter 26

When I woke, Mitch was not in bed. I got up, wrapped a robe around me, and opened the closed bedroom door cautiously. There was no natural sunlight in the hall, so I guessed it would be safe to venture farther. Mitch was in the living room, sitting cross-legged on the floor, sorting through a box of papers. "Good morning," I said, my voice dull and lethargic. He turned to me, smiled, and I asked, "What time is it?"

"A little before four. Sunset'll be soon, but you can sleep more if you like."

"No, I'm awake now. But how about you? You should be tired. You were awake practically all night also."

Mitch shrugged, running his fingers through his hair. "I haven't yet adjusted to sleeping all day. I guess it'll come in time. How'd you manage?"

"I had no choice, remember? It was not a conscious decision to become nocturnal. And you have no reason to adjust to it."

"No, maybe not." His voice was calm, noncommittal, consciously avoiding, I thought, this particular issue that would need to be dealt with eventually. I welcomed the development with relief, not needing another argument to further complicate our lives. Maybe this was how we would survive, avoiding the painful subjects completely until they became unimportant.

"Deirdre." Mitch's voice pulled me out of my thoughts. "Would you like some coffee?" He stood up, and at my nod went into the kitchen and brought out a full mug.

I sat down on the couch, taking a sip, and looked at the papers strewn on the floor. "What is all this?"

Mitch sat back down on the floor at my feet. "I stopped over at the station today and picked up the personal files they had kept for me in storage. It's been so long, it seems much longer than two years, and I thought I'd refresh my mind on some of the details of the Vampire Killer case. Thought maybe I could find something in here you could use in your defense."

"And?"

"Nothing yet, but who knows? The next page may just be what we need. I won't let them hurt you, Deirdre."

I sat silently and sipped my coffee. When I finally spoke, my voice sounded far away. "I had another dream."

"Max again?"

I shuddered. "Yes. This one was so real, so horrible. They're not frightening in content, but they utterly terrify me. In the dream I become a part of him, and it robs me of my self. Robs me of my defenses, of any feelings for him but sympathy and love."

Mitch looked at me questioningly, and I continued. "It's strange. I hated him for so long, never completely understanding him. But now that he's dead, I know him so much better. And when I wake, I feel empty, almost as if I've been torn in half."

Mitch reached over and stroked my leg, then laid his head on my thigh. Idly, I ran my fingers through his hair. "I just don't understand any of this situation with Max. Will I have to live with it for the rest of my life? I'm not sure I can handle that; eternity is too long anyway." Then I laughed a little. "Did you know that Sam thinks it's all my imagination, that I've invented the entire situation to alleviate my loneliness, my guilt?"

"Yeah," Mitch said dryly, "and he thought I was crazy too."

I nodded. "I guess he can't always be right. But he sounded so sure, so authoritative."

"Forget about Sam." There was only a slight tinge of jealousy in his voice. "He can't really help you. But you should ask someone else about it, someone who might be able to give you an answer that makes sense. Victor Lange, maybe, or your attorney."

"Maybe I will."

Mitch went back to sorting his papers, methodically putting them into small stacks, glancing at each page. "Well," he said, waving one particular sheet in the air, "this one doesn't belong with the rest." He went to put it into a separate pile, then stopped and read it in more detail. "Son of a bitch, I don't remember this at all." He shook his head slightly as if to clear it, then looked up at me, an odd expression on his face.

"What is it?"

"A morgue report."

"On Max?"

"No, on Larry."

At the mention of the name, I shivered as always. "What about him?"

"Nothing much, and it's not really that unusual. Sometimes they just lose track of the final disposition papers." He read it again, slowly and thoroughly. "That must be what happened."

"What do you mean, Mitch, final disposition papers?" A cold stab of fear entered my abdomen. Vaguely I remembered the familiar face on the Ballroom dance floor. Was I destined to be haunted by everyone I touched? "Larry too?" I wasn't really aware that I had spoken it out loud.

"Larry too, what?"

"Nothing."

"Well," he said, giving me a questioning look, "I'm sure it's just an oversight. After all, he was dead. He couldn't have just gotten up and walked away."

"Are you sure?" My voice trembled. Larry's death had been nagging at me for years; something didn't seem right.

"Of course I'm sure. I shot him, remember? He was dead, all right. I suspect they shipped his body out to his next of kin and just forgot to fill out the forms. Sloppy practice, but it happens all the time."

"If you say so, Mitch." His words reassured me only slightly, but I did have other worries to occupy my mind. "Did anyone call?"

"No, you expecting someone?"

"I thought maybe Ron would set up an appointment to talk about my case."

"Deirdre, it's not sunset yet. He's probably still sleeping."

"Oh, yes, I forget." I laughed gently. "I still don't quite believe that he's like me. That any of them are like me. I've been alone in my species for so long. I wish I had known that they existed years ago."

"I don't."

"Why not?"

"Because, if you'd known others of your kind, you'd never've fallen in love with me." He sounded a bit defensive when he said it. I looked at him for a long time, studying the lines of his face, the strength of his shoulders, saying nothing. I wanted to imprint him on my mind so that after he was dead I would never forget the fineness of him.

"What?" He smiled tentatively at me, seemingly unnerved by my stare.

"None of them could ever compare with you, Mitch my love."

"No?" He ducked his head a bit, and busied himself with his papers to hide his pleased grin.

"No." I got up from the couch, went over to him, and sat next to him on the floor, taking his hand in mine and holding it up to my cheek. "Let's do this paperwork later and take advantage of the time we have now."

By the time Ron called, we were out of the shower. And when he finally knocked at the door, we were dressed and composed, although I was perhaps smiling more than someone accused of murder should have been.

"Hello, Greer." Ron shook Mitch's hand at the door and walked in. He nodded at me where I sat on the couch. "Deirdre."

"Would you like a cup of coffee, Ron?"

He set his briefcase on the top of Mitch's desk and opened it. "I actually prefer tea, if you have it."

I moved to get up, but Mitch stopped me. "I'll get it, Deirdre. You stay here."

I heard him running the tap and filling the teakettle. Ron removed a sheaf of papers and sat down on the chair opposite me. "Before we get started," Ron said with a wary glance at the kitchen, "I'd sort of like to apologize for my involvement in this whole affair. It's not actually my sort of thing, threatening people with guns, spying on them, you know. But Victor calls the shots, and although he seldom abuses it, his power within The Cadre is absolute. I'm too new to the life to be able to make waves."

"You don't need to apologize to me, Ron." I lowered my voice to a level that I thought Mitch could not hear. "I just wish that I had known the kind of games you were playing those nights we spent together."

"I resent that, Deirdre. And it's not really what you think. True, I was under orders to keep you under surveillance, but I had absolutely no idea why, or even who you were. I thought maybe you were being considered for admittance to The Cadre, or were romantically involved with a member. I didn't actually realize who you were until that night in the Ballroom, when you told me you were Max's heir. But no one asked me to seduce you into my confidence. I liked you, and"—he gave me a sharp look—"as I remember, you were more than willing."

I felt my cheeks redden, from embarrassment and anger. "But that was only because I didn't know what you were. You weren't entirely honest with me and you had me at a disadvantage. And the other night, you could have told me what you were."

"And you could have told me."

"But you already knew everything about me. You lied to me through your silence, and you betrayed my trust in you."

He gave me a hard, quelling look. "No more than you did. Imagine my surprise on finding you married to a man you were never going to see again."

"But you told him where I was."

"Yeah, I did." Ron stared at me for a moment, then shrugged. "Look, Deirdre, we could talk about this all night, but we'd get nowhere. It's over and done with, so let's try to forget it and go on."

"That sounds like a good idea," I agreed. "So, what's on your agenda for tonight?"

He handed me a set of papers. " 'The Establishment of The Cadre,' " he read, " 'and the Laws and Rules Thereof.' "

The teakettle whistled, and Mitch called out, "Water's ready. How do you want it?"

"Plain will be fine, thanks."

"And how about you, Deirdre? Do you want more coffee?"

"Just bring the pot out, Mitch, and join us. You don't need to play host all night. I'm quite sure that Ron is capable of helping himself."

"There's no doubt about that." Mitch came out of the kitchen, glaring at us and balancing two mugs and the coffeepot. He handed the tea to Ron, poured himself a cup of coffee, and sat down on the couch next to me, setting the pot on the floor. Ron handed him a set of papers identical to the ones I was holding.

We all read in silence for a while until Mitch groaned and pitched the papers across the room. "Jesus, is everything The Cadre does this bloody pretentious? I don't see where a history lesson on the holy organization will do Deirdre much good at this point?! Can't we get down to the facts without having to wade through a goddamned written lecture?"

Ron looked at him in surprise, then gave a small chuckle. "I guess the material is rather dry," he admitted, "but I thought you might want some of the background before we started preparing your case. Keep them anyway." He looked over to me and shrugged. "Read them later on, when you feel like it."

"Thank you, Ron." Actually the origins of The Cadre were of interest to me, but Mitch was right. Knowing how it started really did not help my case.

"The facts we really need to know"—Mitch glanced at me and I nodded my acquiescence—"are the sort of extenuating circumstances that are acceptable in the killing of other vampires and the type of punishment possible if she's found guilty."

Ron gave Mitch a look that could have been admiration. "Fine, I appreciate your no-nonsense approach. And I can answer the second fairly succinctly, so let me start there. There is no death penalty provided for by The Cadre. We're not a vigilante group out to subject the world to vampire justice. We banded together for protection and preservation of the species; as you know, our reputation among humans is deplorable. We might have a thirst for blood"—he gave a funny, twisted smile—"but we are not bloodthirsty in the way that you think. Punishment, even for the murder of one of our own, can range anywhere from exclusion from the group to a period of supervised incarceration and starvation."

He stumbled a bit over the last word, and I glanced at him in surprise.

"Starvation? That sure sounds like a death sentence to me." Mitch's voice was soft, but I could feel the anger flowing beneath.

"Actually, it isn't," Ron said, shaking his head. "No vampire has ever died from a starvation sentence. But"—he shuddered—"it is extremely grueling for both the prisoner and the keepers. A starving vampire is someone you would never want to meet or be, I promise you that. In fact, many under the starvation sentence choose suicide instead."

"How?"

Ron looked over at me again, his eyes sad. "The most accepted way is to go to a secluded but open area and simply wait for the sun to rise. Even should you change your mind, there is hardly even enough time to find shelter." His voice trailed away.

"But some take the starvation?"

Ron's voice took on a more definite tone. "And they survive it. After the time's up, sustenance is provided so that the weakened individual doesn't need to hunt for a while." Ron shuddered again, his eyes gaining a far-away look. Then he seemed to shake himself free of his thoughts and smiled at me. "Very few of those who've gone through the starvation need to be disciplined again. Actually"—he gave Mitch a wary look from the side of his eyes—"it's a much more humane and effective deterrent than your human judicial system."

Mitch laughed a bit uneasily. "You'll get no argument from me on that. But I don't want Deirdre to go through it regardless of the results."

"Of course." Ron nodded his agreement. "We'd all like to avoid the starvation sentence if we can. So we need to work on your motive for the murder, Deirdre. Why did you kill Max?"

I took a sip of my coffee, warming my hands as usual on the mug. "Max was out of control. He had murdered four people, and was threatening Mitch." I stopped and shook my head slowly. "No, that's not exactly true. What he did was much worse. Max attempted to coerce me into killing Mitch." My voice broke and my hands trembled, splashing coffee on me. I set my cup down and stood up, rubbing my hands on my jeans. "I understand from Victor that The Cadre does not consider the murder of humans to be a terrible crime. But I had lived all my many years hurting no one, human or otherwise. I would not even have killed Max unless he himself had brought the situation to such an impasse. He knew how I felt about Mitch, and yet he persisted. He gave me no choice." I walked around behind the couch and massaged Mitch's shoulders, easing both his tension and mine.

"Can anyone else substantiate your evidence?" Ron's expression included both interest and surprise. Apparently he had not heard the true story of Max's death. But then, I thought, no one actually had.

"I ask only," Ron continued, "because the killing of one's maker, and the founder of a house, is a serious charge, maybe the most heinous crime a vampire can commit, and yet, if you had made a case before The Cadre at that time, and told us of Max's deeds and his attempted coercion of you before you killed him, then the outcome might have been different."

"I can testify to what happened," Mitch said firmly. "I was there."

"Sorry, Greer." Ron's voice was condescending. "We can't accept the testimony of a nonvampire. You wouldn't help her case much anyway; there are too many who are opposed to marriage with humans. The fewer who know about your involvement, the better. At this point it'd be much better if you just laid low for a while. I'm stretching the rules as it is to allow you to be present at this briefing."

"And God forbid I should make you stretch the rules." Mitch stood up and walked around the chair to me, kissing me lightly on the cheek. "Deirdre, I've got to get out of here. Your attorney says so." His voice sounded calm and reasonable; only the glitter of his eyes and the set of his shoulders betrayed his anger. "And I could use a little night air to clear away the stench of The Cadre. I'll be down at the pool hall. Join me when you're done with Mr. Wilkes."

"Mitch"—I touched his shoulder—"you don't have to leave. Ron has no jurisdiction over you."

"That may be true, but I don't think I can tolerate his presence much longer. I've met him before. You see, he used to supervise some of my little trips into insanity. And every time he opens his mouth, I find myself longing for a wooden stake."

Ron shifted in his seat. "That's not really funny, Greer."

"I know. It wasn't meant to be." Mitch kissed me hard on the lips, put on his jacket, and left the apartment.

"Good," Ron said with finality as the door slammed shut, "we can talk freer now that he's gone. His presence really complicates things."

I looked over at Ron, taking in his expensive suit, his flawless features, the manicured hands that looked as if they had never done a day's work. I thought about how he had befriended me to serve The Cadre, about how he was a part of the group that drove Mitch into madness. Trying to control my temper, I turned my back on him and silently counted to ten, gripping my hands together, telling myself that he did not know any better, that none of this was his fault. But it did not help. I spun around and confronted him, feeling anger rise uncontrollably through my body.

"Goddammit, Ron," I snapped at him, moving quickly around the couch and grabbing the lapels of his expensive suit. "You have no right to order Mitch around. You all seem to be overstepping your bounds these days. All your regulations, all your questions, don't you understand that they mean nothing to me? I never knew about the goddamned Cadre, never even knew who Max was until the night he died." He attempted to rise, but I pushed him back down in the chair and held him there. Ron glanced around the apartment in a panic, licking his lips in fear.

"Deirdre," he gasped, "don't do this. Violence won't help your case any."

"I am not looking for help, Ron. Nobody has ever helped me. Where, at any time in my long, miserable life, was your precious Cadre to give me guidance, to read me a list of their bloody rules and regulations? And where was Max? No, you were all quite content to stand on the sidelines and let me struggle with what I had become all by myself. And dammit, I struggled and I survived, no thanks to Max or you or any of The Cadre. Mitch has been the only being to care for me, to truly love me, for a very long time, someone who stayed with me without being ordered to." Ron winced slightly at that statement, but I ignored him and continued. "And yet you feel you have the right to order him around as if he were your servant. He is ten times the man you will ever be, regardless of your superior powers and attitude. Have you ever seen the scars caused by his confrontation with the beloved and much-revered founder of the house of Alveros? Did you ever look inside the mind you tortured to find his goodness, his intelligence, his love? No, of course you didn't. Mitchell Greer deserves better treatment from you, from all of us."

Suddenly the anger I felt drained away, leaving me empty and sad. I let go of Ron, noticing as I did so that my nails had made long gashes in the lapels. He looked down at his coat in dismay, and I laughed softly. "You're a lucky man, Ron; it could have been your skin."

"Yeah," he said, his voice quavering only slightly, "but the skin grows back."

"I am sorry, Ron. Send me a bill and I'll buy you a new suit. And I apologize for my temper, it was not directed at you so much as at the entire situation. You see, I'm in a difficult position. Had I known of The Cadre's existence, my life might have been quite different. And Max might still be alive. But it's a little late for hindsight at this point; I cannot change what happened. And neither can The Cadre. So let them mete out whatever punishment they feel is necessary. I've survived worse, I assure you."

"Deirdre." Ron got out of the chair and stood in front of me, meeting my eyes squarely. "I'm sorry, too, that it should all come to this." His voice lowered. "The last thing in the world I want to happen is to see you hurt, to know myself partly responsible for that hurt. It's just that there are conventions to be satisfied, and two or three of the other house leaders are calling for blood. Your blood. But they are bound by The Cadre's decision. That's why Victor urged you to accept our justice, why he tried to impress upon you the importance of this trial. Once you have been tried by The Cadre, and their decision has been rendered, they cannot retaliate in any way, or they face the same punishment themselves."

"I suppose," I said with a twisted grin, "that Victor is one of those calling for my blood."

"No, he's not." Ron sounded so confident, and I found myself almost believing him.

"No? But he and Max were so close. Or at least that is what Victor has always claimed."

"Well," he started to say reluctantly, "they were close. But Victor was not blind to Max's faults and knew that there would come a time when Max would be held responsible for his misdeeds."

"Trial before The Cadre?" Victor had hinted at that the evening I discovered Max's coffin.

Ron nodded. "It wouldn't have been the first time for Max either. I'm sorry to say this, and I mean no offense, but there's something strange about those in the house of Alveros; they tend to be more headstrong than most, more determined to do things their own way, more vicious. Maybe it's just in their blood"—he looked away from me—"although some of us think that it's more from the tutelage they've had."

"Fred mentioned that I was one of the oldest, that there were only a few of Max's breed left. Do you have any idea of how many?"

A look of concern crossed his face. "Fred shouldn't have told you that." With effort he pulled his eyes away from mine, "And I've probably said too much myself. I'm not sure how much I can actually help you, Deirdre. I don't even know why I volunteered to speak for you."

I smiled at him. "I know why; you can never resist helping a lady in need."

"Yeah"—he smiled back at me, obviously not holding a grudge about my previous actions—"that must be it. Now, I think we've covered more than enough material tonight. I'll want to look back through our archives and see what kind of loopholes there are. Maybe there's a precedent." I could see his mind working on the problem, turning over the possibilities. "If only we had a feel for what Max was trying to do with you, what purpose he thought was being served by keeping you unaware of your birthright, well, maybe we'd have a stronger case. As it is, it's only your word we have to go on."

"My word is good."

"I believe you, and I think Victor does too. But unfortunately we have eight other houses to convince." He walked over to the desk and closed his briefcase. "Well, let me see what I can do. I'll call you tomorrow evening, if that's okay."

"That will be fine, Ron." I walked over to the door with him and shook his hand. "And I am sorry that I let my temper get the better of me tonight. I won't allow it to happen again."

"I don't mind so much." He winked at me. "I like a lady with spirit. Just promise me you won't get that carried away in front of the panel, okay? They won't take it quite as well as I did." His lips brushed my mouth briefly in a light kiss and he went out the door.

Chapter 27

Mitch was at the pool hall, hunched over a beer at one of the tables. I pushed past the crowd of people at the entrance and sat down next to him, lightly touching his hand. He looked up at me with a grimace. "I'm sorry I ran out on you. But I wasn't joking. Every time he opened his mouth I wanted to kill him, or maybe just smash his perfect face in."

"You have no need to be jealous of Ron, my love. He means nothing to me."

"Even though you and he spent nights together?" He emphasized the plural with vehemence.

I opened my mouth but did not know what to say. His name was all I managed to get out. "Mitch."

"I know," he said after taking a long drink from his bottle. "You thought I couldn't hear your discussion. And I wasn't deliberately listening in, but it's my training. When people drop their voices to a whisper, I'm naturally curious about what they must be saying. No wonder he was so quick to jump to your defense. You're a fast worker, Deirdre, only in town a few weeks and you have an instant champion for your cause. I guess I should be happy you have someone to stand up for you, but under the circumstances . . ." He took another swig of his beer and his eyes met mine defiantly. But under his anger I could see a deep sadness.

"Mitch," I said softly, "do you know that Max once said the same to me about you?"

"Really?" His voice sounded harsh and sarcastic. "And how did you answer him?"

I touched his hand softly. "I told him that I loved you more than I had ever loved anyone before. And it was true, then and now."

Mitch stared at me as he drained his bottle. "And how will you answer me?"

"Ron means nothing to me, never did and never will."

"But the same can't be said of him, I'm afraid. I've seen the way he looks at you. And I recognize that look." He signaled the waiter for another beer, then glanced back at me. "Dammit, I should recognize it. I've been wearing it around you ever since we met."

The waiter came over and brought two bottles and one glass. I didn't use it. When he left, Mitch looked at his watch and held up his beer. "Cheers," he said with no expression on his face. "Here's to a little over twenty-four hours of wedded bliss."

"Please don't do this, Mitch. I warned you what marriage to me would be like. As I remember, you didn't care at the time."

"I lied." He studied the wet bottle rings, drawing his finger through them, idly tracing designs on the tabletop. "So, when did you and Ron enjoy your little trysts? And when do you plan another?"

"There will be no other," I said firmly. "One of the nights I saw him, well, that was the first time I visited you at the hospital. You do remember, don't you?" I rubbed my jaw. "That wonderful welcome-home gift you gave me?"

Mitch looked at me with a trace of a smile. "Oh," he said hesitantly, then gave me a full grin. "Ouch, I remember. I'm sorry, are you still mad about that?"

I returned his smile. "I was never angry with you, just hurt and discouraged. I believed that was how it was going to be between us, thought that everything was over. What difference did it make whether I went home with Ron or not at that point?" His smile faded, and I joked to bring it back. "A girl's gotta eat, you know."

"Yeah, well, I guess I can understand that, but how about the other nights?"

"There was only one other night, after you very succinctly told me that you wished you had never met me. And all we did was talk."

"Okay, maybe I'll believe that one too. But I still don't like it."

"No one said you had to like it, Mitch. But you may have to get used to it. However much I would like to, I cannot exist on your love alone. But we were not to discuss the grisly details for a few weeks, so let's drop it."

"But a few weeks is all we may have. I don't know about you, but I'm not sure I believe that The Cadre is as humane as they keep trying to convince us they are. I still say we should get out now, before they get their hands on you."

"Shame on you, Detective. Urging a criminal to jump bail and leave town." I shook my head at him, and he laughed. Then I picked up my beer and stood. "Now, I know this is not exactly the honeymoon we anticipated, but do you want to play a few games of pool before we go home?"

"No." Mitch stood up too and threw a couple of bills on the table. "Let's just go home."

He put his arm around me and slowly we began to walk back to his apartment.

"So, what did Ron have to say for himself?"

"He's going to do some research, check the archives, see if he can find any precedents. I doubt that he'll find anything. The Cadre seems to keep a strong grip on its members."

"And if he can't find anything?"

I snuggled against him for comfort. "Well, then it becomes a case of their trusting my story. I doubt that will help much either." I gave a small, bitter laugh. "If only I could get my wayward ghost to make an appearance. They would probably be more easily convinced if they had a glimpse into his . . . damn!" I stopped dead on the sidewalk.

"What is it?"

"A glimpse into Max's mind. He left a huge stack of journals behind. It's possible they may hold some answers."

"Where are they?"

I grimaced. "At the Ballroom, of course, the last place I ever want to go again. He had them stored in a chest in his secret sleeping place. I found it and them the other night, but Victor came in and interrupted me." I shivered, remembering what else that room contained, and gave Mitch a dubious look. "I don't suppose you would like to take me out dancing tonight. I really don't want to go in there alone."

He shrugged. "I don't want you going there at all, even with me, but if the journals can help, we should have them. But let's take a cab, I'm getting cold. How about you?"

I agreed, not bothering to remind him that I could not get cold. "That would be fine, Mitch."

Johnny was working as doorman again that evening, slumped against the entrance with the expression that I now recognized as his normal surliness, but he straightened up and smiled as we approached. "Hi, Miss Griffin. How're you?"

"Fine, thank you, Johnny. Listen, is Victor Lange in tonight?"

He shook his head and grunted no.

"How about Fred, then?"

"Nope, neither one's here tonight. You want me to call 'em for you?"

"No, actually I don't." I looked around; very few people were waiting for admittance. "Has it been busy tonight?"

"Nope, it's been pretty slow."

"Thank you, Johnny. Oh"—I indicated Mitch—"by the way, this is Mitchell Greer, my husband." I smiled to myself at the strangeness of that phrase, and its sweetness. "So if he ever stops by without me, you should let him in."

Mitch extended his hand and Johnny shook it, smiling. "Congratulations. It's nice to meet you." Then he dropped his hand as if he had been bit. "Wait a minute, ain't you the cop that shot the last doorman? Larry, um, what's his name?"

"Larry Martin," I said, my voice tight and nervous.

"Yeah, that's him." Johnny cringed against the door, pushing aside with one hand the lanky bit of hair that always seemed to fall into his face, rubbing the side of his neck with the other. "I don't know, Miss Griffin." He lowered his voice and glanced at Mitch with a panicked stare. "It don't seem right to let him in, not tonight."

"Calm down, Johnny. Mitch is not going to shoot anyone, especially you. I promise you."

"Well, I guess if you say so, it's okay."

"It's okay, Johnny." Mitch spoke confidently, calmly. "Larry Martin was shot while he was trying to kill Miss Griffin. I don't think you're planning to do that, are you?"

"No way, Mr. Greer."

"Then you're perfectly safe." Mitch took my arm and led me through the door. We crossed the dance floor and entered the hallway that led to my office. "What the hell is his problem?" Mitch asked when he thought he could be heard over the band.

"Who? Oh, Johnny. He's not very bright, I'm afraid. But he seems to do a good job. On the other hand"—I opened the office door—"being unaware is an asset in this place. He's much better off not knowing about half the things that go on around here."

Mitch closed and locked the door. "Do you think he's one of them?"

I thought about that for a moment. "I doubt it, Mitch."

He gave me a humorless chuckle. "Yeah, but you couldn't tell about Victor or Fred or Ron or Jean either."

"You're right, of course," I said with only a trace of sarcasm, "but now that I know about them, I can recognize the signs. There's something about their mannerisms, their directness, their overbearing arrogance that makes them stand out. Johnny, poor boy, has none of that."

Reaching into my purse, I found my ring of keys and opened the closet door, then the secret panel. "Here you go," I said over my shoulder, "just let me light the candles and we'll go in."

Victor had apparently put everything away that night we had met there. The candelabrum and the matches were back on the side table where I had initially found them.

"Candles?" Mitch's voice echoed through the empty room. "What's wrong with electricity?"

I laughed, my voice shaking a bit. "Max was a traditionalist in more ways than one, it appears." I held the candelabrum up so that he could see the two coffins on display.

"Damn." Mitch cautiously approached the stand and bent over to read the engraved plaques. "He slept here?"

"Apparently."

"But who does the other one belong to?"

My voice was soft in the dusty darkness. "It was for me."

"Damn." He walked around and lifted up the lid of the smaller coffin, then let it down gently. "Did you ever . . ."

"No." The distaste I felt for the idea was apparent in my voice. "I never knew that this was here, how could I? Max never told me anything."

"I know that, Deirdre. What I meant was, did you ever sleep in one of these?"

"Oh, no."

"Why not?"

"By the time I had figured out what I had changed into, I had been managing to sleep quite comfortably in bed with the curtains drawn. Why on earth would I want to lock myself up in a coffin day after day?"

"I wonder why Max did?"

I could tell from Mitch's tone of voice that the question was a hypothetical one, but I knew the answer anyway. "Max was tutored, taught from his first day to choose this as his refuge. The habits of centuries are very hard to break."

"You sound pretty sure of that. How could you know?"

"I dreamed it. But let's get what we came for and get out of here. This place unnerves me." Carrying the candelabrum with me, I walked across the room and opened the chest.

"Dammit." Slamming the lid of the chest down, I swore again. "Goddamned son of a bitch."

"Deirdre, what's wrong?"

"Somebody else has been in here. The journals are gone, every goddamned one of them."

"Are you sure they were here?" Mitch questioned me patiently, as if I were a child or an idiot.

I gave him an angry glare that he was probably unable to see across the dimness of the room. "Yes, I know they were here. They were real, tangible; they weren't something I dreamed up. The box was full of them, all nicely dated, all written in Max's hand. And now they're gone."

"That's strange."

"It's more than strange, Mitch, it's goddamned convenient. My one chance to find a motive for Max's actions, something that might enable me to prove that my killing him was justified, vanishes practically overnight. How wonderfully convenient for The Cadre and that bastard Victor. All this time spent trying to convince us that they're playing fair, that they're not out for my blood, and then they do this." I brushed my hands on my jeans to remove the coating of dirt that had come off the chest, and made a move to sweep the remaining dust away with my hand.

"Don't touch it." Mitch's voice was stern and commanding; I obediently backed away. "I'll come back tomorrow during the day and see if I can get fingerprints. At least that way we could tell who else had been in here."

"Only if our thief was previously printed. What are the odds on that?"

Mitch laughed. "I've got your prints on file, remember?"

I nodded; he had taken my prints right after my secretary, Gwen, had been murdered by Larry Martin.

"Well, you can't tell me that The Cadre as a whole and Victor in particular are so careful that they haven't had some run-in with the law during their long lifetimes."

"I don't know, Mitch. It seems like such a long shot."

"It can't hurt, Deirdre. And if I come during the day, none of them can bother me."

"I'm not sure I like the thought of you being in here alone."

"Jesus, Deirdre, I'm a grown man. I was able to keep myself safe and alive before we met. I'm not your child or your pet that you need to protect. And I'm going crazy with all this happening to you and not being able to do something. This I can do; it's what I good at. And you can't stop me." He was extremely angry, angrier than I had seen him for a long time. But I was not upset, for, other than our lovemaking, it was the best sign that the man with whom I had fallen in love had returned.

I walked across the room and put my arms around his waist, hugging him tightly to me. Then I smiled up into his face. "I love you, Mitch. And I'm sorry if I was treating you unfairly. You do what you want, but be careful. You carry my life in your hands."

He seemed surprised but pleased by my reaction, and his mouth came down on mine in a crushing kiss. Then he pulled away from me abruptly. "What did you mean, I carry your life in my hands? You don't think I would ever do anything to hurt you, or your chances at beating this rap, do you?"

When I had reached the decision to marry Mitch, I had also decided that I would stay with him until he died and then kill myself. But I didn't want him to know that, and even if I did, this was not the time to discuss it.

"Your life is my life, Mitch," I said softly, offering no further explanation. "Now, let's get out of this tomb and go home."

Chapter 28

The next two weeks went quickly. Ron and I worked evenings preparing our case, but without Max's journals, there was no proof available as to the state of his mind and Ron did not have any luck turning up a similar case in The Cadre's archives. Victor bemoaned the theft of the journals, admitting that they could have helped my case, but assured us that his organization would never operate in such a fashion. Mitch had found fingerprints on the chest other than mine and had spent a long time at the precinct trying to match them up with their current files, but had been unsuccessful. And both Mitch and I had, however unhappily, come to the conclusion that since Victor knew about the existence of the room, a match of his prints wasn't substantial proof that he'd been involved in the theft.

For the three nights prior to the trial, I fed. Each time, I chose a street person from different locations in the city, forcing myself to take more than I needed, to prepare for the sentence of starvation that seemed sure to follow. But I felt no elation in these feedings, no exhilaration, no rejuvenation. Instead, I felt cheapened and unclean, and the fresh, warm blood that I stole from their veins tasted more bitter than ever before.

"Have you ever wondered," I questioned Mitch when I returned from my third victim, "whether a condemned man enjoys his last meal?"

He was sitting at his desk, poring over the files he had brought home from the precinct, and he must not have heard me enter, for he jumped when I spoke. "No," he said distractedly, "I can't say that I have." Then he shook his head and smiled. "I'm sorry, Deirdre. This whole case just gets stranger and stranger. Did something go wrong tonight?"

"No, something went wrong over a hundred years ago." I did not try to disguise the bitterness in my voice. "Now my life is just one eternal picnic."

Mitch got up and held me to him tightly, stroking my hair while I sobbed on his shoulder. “It’s okay, babe,” he crooned, “we’ll get through this. And after it’s all over, we’ll go away and forget that The Cadre ever existed. Don’t get discouraged now; we can beat them.”

I sniffed a bit. “I suppose you’re right. But, God, I’m so tired, Mitch, so tired. I feel as if I could sleep for a hundred years.”

He kissed me on the top of my head. “Then go to bed. I’ll be just a little while longer here, and then I’ll join you.”

Obediently, I went back to the bedroom, stripped off my clothes, and crawled into bed, not even checking to see that the curtains were drawn for tomorrow’s dawn. But I did not sleep. I wanted no dreams tonight, no visits from Max, no glimpses of lives not mine. I lay on my back and stared at the ceiling for an hour until Mitch came in.

When he settled next to me, I rolled over, pressing myself against his warm, human body.

“Hey,” he said with a catch in his voice, “you’re supposed to be sleeping.”

I didn’t answer, but put my mouth to his shoulder, taking gentle nips, my hand exploring his chest and his muscular thighs. When this preliminary love play brought no response from my feeding instinct, I grew bolder, kissing his nipples and tracing my tongue down his stomach. Shifting my position so that I lay between his thighs, I continued my attentions and he groaned softly and whispered my name.

I looked up at him for confirmation, and he nodded slightly, his eyes glittering in the darkness, but with passion, not fear. Grasping his buttocks in my hands, I took him fully into my mouth, something I had never done before for fear of my sharpened fangs. I did not think of blood or feeding, I knew only that this was Mitch, a man I loved more than anything else in the world, and I wanted to please him, tonight of all nights. It might be our last together.

So I continued, licking and kissing him, coaxing him time and time again closer to climax. Finally, when he moaned and pulled my head away from him, I crawled up his body and smiled. "How was that?" I said, kissing the side of his mouth.

"Jesus, Deirdre," he gasped, "you make me crazy. I can barely catch my breath."

Then he rolled me over and entered me quickly. I began to cry from the sheer beauty of the unity we shared, and the painful thought that we might soon be parted. But I laughed too, and whispered encouraging endearments to him in the darkness, until half an hour later we both pulled apart from each other, sated and exhausted. Mitch's body and mine were slick with his sweat. Playfully, I licked the salt from his neck and he shuddered.

"Enough," he half laughed, half groaned, "or you'll kill me for sure."

Then he snuggled into me, draped a hand over my breast, and we fell asleep.

Mitch woke me at five the next afternoon with a cup of fresh-brewed coffee in his hand. I pushed my hopelessly tangled hair from my face and sat up in bed, taking the mug from him. "Thank you," I said after my first sip.

"Good morning, my love." He had a smile on his face that not even The Cadre could remove; I knew because I wore the same smile.

"I'm sorry to get you up before sunset, but I thought you might want a shower."

Setting the coffee cup down, I stood up and stretched. "Yes, I do. How about you?"

Mitch shrugged. "Oh, I had mine hours ago, but"— his eyes lit with a mischievous grin—"I'll keep you company if you like."

We got into the shower together, and Mitch soaped me all over as if I were a child. He shampooed my hair, then stood back and watched me while I rinsed it. "You're so perfect," he said, his tone of voice almost reverent, "and I love you so much. I can't even begin to explain how much you mean to me, how special our time together has been." Then he reached around me, turning off the water, and kissed me full on the lips. But he did not touch me, or hold me in his arms, nor did we make love.

It was as if our experience of the previous night was such a strong bonding, cementing us so firmly to each other that we never needed to make love again, but could stand forever, naked skin against naked skin, heart against heart, always together.

The phone rang and we both jumped.

"Wouldn't you know it?" he said with a twisted smile, and wrapping a towel around himself, climbed out of the shower to answer it.

I toweled my hair, then dried my body and put on Mitch's green robe, tying the sash tight around my waist. By the time I reached the living room, his phone conversation had grown animated, almost angry.

"What the hell do you mean, you don't remember? You were on duty in the morgue that night; I have your name on the log sheet. Goddammit, Harry, I've heard you recite the list of corpses you've handled over the years, including the dates and causes of deaths, and the names of their next of kin. And all that after putting away a six-pack or two. How on earth could you forget this one? Jesus Christ, Harry, he had a hole in him large enough to stuff your fist into, for God's sake."

Mitch paused for a minute listening to the agitated voice on the phone, then he nodded, discouraged. "Okay, okay," he attempted to pacify the caller, "if you don't remember, you don't remember. Thanks anyway." Nervously, he shifted the towel around his waist. "Yeah, you too." He slammed the phone down impatiently, then sat down on the couch, running his fingers through his still-wet hair.

"What's wrong, Mitch?"

He looked up at me, startled. "I didn't know you were out here. Look, I'm sorry. I really meant to tell you about this last night, but you came in so upset. And then"—he gave a reminiscent smile—"you sort of distracted me."

"Tell me about what, Mitch?"

"Larry Martin. There's no report on the final disposition of his body, and the morgue guy can't even remember seeing him."

"Does that really matter at this point?"

Mitch's eyes shifted away from me for a minute. "I think it

does. Maybe not ultimately to your case with The Cadre, but it does matter, very much. You see, I finally found a match for the fingerprints in Max's room."

"And?"

"And they were Larry's."

I must have stood staring at Mitch for a full minute, taking in his statement. And when I found my voice, it was soft and desperate. "But Larry has been dead for more than two years, Mitch." Even as I said it, I realized it could not be true. Here, then, was the explanation for the sick feeling of dread I had whenever I thought of him, the familiar face on the Ballroom dance floor, maybe even for the fright on Johnny's face the other night. Larry Martin was still alive. More than that, Larry had gotten from me what I had not ever wanted to give to anyone: immortality in the form of vampirism.

"Damn," I swore softly, and sat next to Mitch on the couch.

"Is there something you need to tell me, Deirdre?" Mitch sounded stern, remembering, I thought, of how I denied him what Larry had received.

"I didn't know, Mitch, and it wasn't on purpose, believe me. When you shot him, the bullet went straight through him and into my shoulder. I couldn't tell you; you would have taken me to a hospital, and that was totally out of the question at the time. You didn't know what I was then; how could I let you find out in the emergency room?" I stared unseeingly at the floor. "It never really occurred to me, but I suppose that enough of my blood could have mingled with his to enable the change." I put my hands over my face, then looked at him. "Jesus."

We sat silent for a few minutes. Then Mitch spoke up. "We've got to find him, Deirdre. He was unstable, crazy, and I don't believe that two years as a vampire could have improved him any."

"But why would he want Max's journals? How would he know they were even there?"

"Larry Martin always made it a habit to find out what he wanted to know. As to why take the journals, I suspect that he is none too pleased with you and he did it just to hurt you. Or maybe to hurt me. Or maybe just for the hell of it, because he could. You once told me you couldn't explain the ravings of a madman. What makes you think I can?"

I shivered and Mitch put his arm around me. "I'm sorry," he said again. "I shouldn't have said anything, I guess. But don't worry about it now, nothing is going to happen. And tonight, after all this is over, you should ask Victor. Maybe he knows something; I really think he owes you that much."

As if on cue, the phone rang again. This time it was Victor. "I will be there in one hour to escort you and Deirdre to the hearing." His voice was completely audible to me, even though Mitch had answered.

"We'll be ready."

Several days ago, and much to Mitch's amusement, Ron had already surveyed my wardrobe and dictated what I should wear to the hearing. After he had made the selection and left, Mitch had started to laugh.

"What's so funny?" I had asked him.

"Obviously the breed runs true no matter how much it's transformed."

"What?"

"Ron Wilkes may be a vampire, but he's still one hundred percent attorney." Then he had sobered and looked at me intently. "I've known a lot of lawyers in my day, and I can tell he's good. I guess I'm grateful that he decided to speak for you, whatever you had to do to get him."

Now, clothed in a basic black dress, black hose, and a low-heeled pump, I had to agree that his choice was a smart one. Unfortunately the skirt was slightly shorter than I felt comfortable with. "Damn Betsy McCain," I muttered when Mitch joined me in front of his mirror.

"What's wrong? You look great."

"Damn skirt is too short, like everything else she designs."

"Oh, well," he said, patting me slightly on the hip so that I would move out of his way while he tied his tie, "maybe they'll get one look at your perfect legs and decide to let you go scot free."

"Chance is a fine thing."

"What?"

"Just an expression I picked up from Pete in England. I guess the American slang would translate into fat chance."

"Who's Pete?" By now it was easy to recognize the slight twinge of jealousy in his voice.

"My partner in England. I own half of a failing pub over there."

"Great," he moaned, "just what we need. Another bar owner. Don't you meet any other types?"

"But you would like him." He gave me a dubious look and I continued. "No, honestly, Mitch, you would. He's like a second father to me."

"Good God," he said, crossing the room and slipping on his suit coat, "and that's another thing we don't need. Speaking of fathers, heard from Max lately?"

"Not since that last dream."

"How typical of him. He's perfectly capable of getting you into this trouble in the first place, and then he bails out when you need him. You're not much of a judge of character, are you?"

"Oh, I don't know." I went to him and wrapped my arms around his waist. "I've done pretty well for myself this time."

"And don't you ever forget it, lady." He kissed me on the tip of the nose. "Are you ready?"

I looked in the mirror again. "I think I need some jewelry; basic black is nice, but too funereal, even for this occasion." Opening the top dresser drawer that Mitch had cleared out for me, I went through what I had. I hesitated over the ruby necklace and earrings that had belonged to my mother, when the glint of antique gold caught my eye. "This would be perfect." I opened it up and looked at the portrait of Max's mother and smiled to myself.

"Do you think that's wise?" Mitch asked doubtfully. "After all, somebody there might recognize it, might feel that you're flaunting it."

"No," I said, hanging it about my neck. "I think Max would want me to wear it. It would appeal to his ironic nature. Besides, it is a beautiful piece and she was a beautiful woman. She deserves to be remembered."

The weight of the locket pressed between my breasts was somehow comforting. I chose a simple pair of gold button earrings to match, and we went to the living room to await our escort.

Chapter 29

Victor arrived promptly in a limousine accompanied only by the driver, who to my great relief turned out not to be Fred.

Mitch shook Victor's hand, greeting him in a pleasant voice, but his smile only thinly disguised his deep animosity, and when he spoke, all the illusions of pleasantry vanished. "Traveling without your thugs tonight, Lange?"

Victor chose not to take offense. Solicitously, he helped me into the car, then turned to Mitch with a friendly smile. "There's no need for thugs, as you call them, Mitch. Deirdre is a woman of honor I know, and I'm sure you will not attempt any useless heroics. Anyway"—he glanced in at me knowingly—"Fred has been replaced. He has proven untrustworthy as well as unnecessarily vicious."

Mitch climbed into the seat next to me and Victor walked around to get in the other side. "No, Fred will not be bothering you anymore, Deirdre." He carefully adjusted his expensive suit coat before he sat down aligning the creases of his pant legs. "But I'm afraid you'll need to hire another manager for the Ballroom."

"Where did he go?" I was glad of Fred's absence, but also briefly angry that Victor would have released him without my consent.

"He was selected to do an overseas assignment for The Cadre. It seemed best to get him out of your way. Especially"—Victor lowered his voice confidentially—"since he was so susceptible to your powers. That was a nice bit of control, but your timing was bad. I don't advise a stunt like that tonight, my dear."

"No stunts, Victor, I promise. Just the truth."

"Thank you." He reached over and patted my knee. "And can I assume I've your promise too, Mitch?"

"Yeah," Mitch said abruptly. "I'll stay out of it."

"Actually, you will not be allowed to be present at the questioning." Victor gave an elegant shrug. "I did my best, but too many of us are still prejudiced against your kind. Ron did explain the procedures to you, didn't he?"

"Yes." I reached over and held Mitch's hand. "I'm to be questioned by each house individually, with you acting as an impartial arbitrator."

"Not exactly impartial, Deirdre. Should the houses be divided on your decision equally, the final vote belongs to me. Hopefully, it will not come to that."

I glanced over at Victor to get some feel for what that comment meant, but his face was expressionless. Mitch's hand tensed on mine, and I leaned over and gave him a small kiss on the cheek. "It will be all right, my love," I whispered.

"It damn well better be," he muttered as the car stopped in front of The Imperial. His jaw was set stubbornly and his lips were pulled tight. "Or there'll be bloody hell to pay."

Ron met us as we got off the elevator in The Cadre's warren. The large assembly room in which we had met previously was empty and dark. I looked over at Ron questioningly.

He responded as if he had read my mind. "Oh, we won't be meeting in here."

"But this is where our paths part, my dear." Victor took my hand and kissed it in his characteristic fashion. "Mitch and I will be waiting upstairs."

Mitch put his arms around me in a brief hug. "Knock 'em dead, Deirdre," he whispered to me, and gave me a quick, hard kiss. I watched the two of them enter the elevator, and when the doors shut, turned to Ron.

"Let's get this over with, shall we?"

All the founders of the houses of The Cadre had their own individual offices, furnished in their own unique style. Any other time I would have found my surroundings fascinating and pleasant. The founders were gracious and courteous, and their manners and emotions were kept in careful control, so much so that many times I was forced to remind myself that these meetings were more than social visits. Studying the eyes of each one as I spoke to them, I found myself wondering which ones had been calling for my blood, and which were perhaps more sympathetic. But their faces might as well have been masks; they were unreadable, unfathomable, giving me no hint of their true feelings beneath.

They had each been provided with my written testimony on the death of the man I had known as Max Hunter, as well as a short biography of my life to date. Ron and I had spent most of the past two weeks preparing this document, and he assured me that it would be read carefully and in great detail, as the founders took their judgment responsibility very seriously.

I did not recognize any of my eight judges, and their names were not given. Most of them simply asked me questions about the night of the murder, clarifying details that seemed to me to be extraneous. But the last one, one of the two female founders, was much more interested in the biography of my life than in any details concerning Max.

"And so you woke up, in the hospital, with no idea of what had occurred?" Her voice was soft but powerful, with a suggestion of a lisp and a slight foreign accent. She was seemingly young with an amazing mass of blond, curly hair piled into an intricate fashion on the top of her head. If I had to give her an age, it would be early to mid-twenties, at least several years younger than I had been at my time of change. But the intensity of her eyes belied this apparent youth, as had the eyes of all the others.

I glanced over at Ron; none of the other interviewers had been interested in my life. He gave me an encouraging nod, and I answered her question.

"Well, I knew that there had been an accident. I knew of the loss of my husband and unborn child. And I sensed the change in my physical and mental makeup, but any memory I might have had of the transformation and the encounter with Max was buried. All I had to go on were my dreams. And"—I gave her a small, wry smile—"the fact that my father was a great lover of dreadful gothic literature."

She returned my smile briefly, then arranged her face once again in its neutral expression. "And you managed to survive long enough to piece together the facts of your vampirism without anyone to guide you or to provide you with what you needed to live?"

"I provided for myself. There was no one to help."

"You were either very lucky or very resourceful—I suspect a little of both. A pity, really, for with a mentor you could have become very powerful indeed."

I said nothing, expecting that no response was required. She nodded absently, as if to herself, then her eyes moved quickly over my features, finally fastening upon my eyes as she spoke again.

"And you had no contact with Max"—did I detect a note of scorn in that dispassionate voice? I wondered—"until the mid-sixties, at which time he still did not make you aware of who he was?"

"That is correct. I had no idea who he was, or even what he was, until the night he died. And then, of course, it was too late."

"Yes," she said impatiently. "I have read your testimony." She picked up the document in question and dropped it into the wastebasket by the side of her desk. Then she looked at Ron. "I am the last, is that right?"

"Yes," he responded.

"Well then, I don't want to hold up these proceedings any longer." She gave a low chuckle. "I have other fish to fry this evening; a particularly delicious bellboy is waiting for me at my hotel."

Ron and I moved to the door. "Wait," she called after us. Ron tensed, but I turned around and smiled at her. She came around her desk and walked over to me. Then, ignoring Ron's gasp of surprise, she put her arms around me and gently kissed my lips. "My true name is Vivienne. You may count me as a friend, Dorothy. Walk softly this night."

"And you," I said solemnly, sensing the last as a ritual goodbye.

Her eyes searched mine again, and she smiled fully. "Your instincts are excellent. Good night." Ron stood rooted by the door, and she nudged him. "Well, go ahead, Ron, get her out of here. She shouldn't be kept waiting any longer than necessary."

Ron took my arm, and I felt him trembling, but he said nothing until we arrived at the designated reception area. When we got there, he went straight for the bar and opened a bottle of wine, pouring two glasses and handing me one before draining his completely.

I stared at him over my untouched wine. "Something wrong, Ron?"

"She surprised me. She wasn't supposed to touch you, or respond to you in any way. And she was definitely not to tell you her name. Next to Victor, now that Max is gone, she is the oldest among us."

I sat down in one of the overstuffed leather chairs. "What difference should any of that make? You know her name, why shouldn't I? I thought she was easily the most agreeable of them all."

"And that worries me too. Vivienne has always held herself aloof from our politics. Actually, she has very few dealings with any of us; she attends when she is required and avoids us when she can. And she has always been very determined on the subject of rogue vampires." He poured himself another glass of wine, his eyes avoiding mine.

"In what way is she determined, Ron?"

"Well," he began hesitantly, taking another long drink, "she has been quoted on occasion as saying that the only way to deal with rogues is to have them killed, quickly and cleanly." Then he shrugged. "Maybe she's mellowed on the subject."

"But you don't think so, do you?"

"No, but she kissed you. And told you her name, not the name she goes by now, but the name she was born with." He shook his head as if to clear his mind. "Jesus, I wish I knew what she was up to. Victor will want to know."

I took a small sip of my wine. "Well then, tell him."

"No, I can't. It's another one of the rules, you see. Anything that I heard or witnessed must be held in complete confidence. Even you are not supposed to divulge anything about the interviews. The judges are free to speak of it, although they seldom do." He filled his glass again. "This really puts me in a bad situation."

"I'm sorry, Ron. I would help you out if I could. But other than Vivienne, how do you think we did?"

He looked at me with a rueful smile. "Honestly, I haven't got the slightest idea."

"Great," I said. "Just goddamned great." Holding my glass out for him to refill, I crossed my legs. "So I guess we just sit here and wait."

We had just finished the first bottle of wine and started a second one, when someone knocked on the door. Victor walked in and Ron hastily placed his glass on the bar. "They've decided so soon?"

Victor inclined his head and handed him a slip of paper. Ron looked at it, then back at Victor for confirmation. Nodding slightly, Victor dismissed him. "That will be all, Ron, thank you." Ron left without so much as a backward glance at me, closing the door softly behind him.

"Ron is a good attorney," Victor said without preamble, "and he did his best for you. The papers were prepared properly, with all the right nuances and emotions. Even your biography was a masterstroke, portraying you as a romantic heroine of epic proportions, single-handedly learning to survive and grow as a vampire." Nonchalantly, he studied the bottle of wine we had been drinking. "Not a bad year, not the best, of course, but still good."

"I know you aren't here, Victor, to discuss the wine or Ron's quality as an attorney." I finished my drink and got up from the chair, walking over to the bar. Looking him directly in the eye, I set my glass down. "They didn't buy it, did they?"

He gave an odd laugh. "I really do appreciate your directness, Deirdre. But you're wrong; half of them did buy it. That's why I said Ron was good. Your odds going into this situation were not that favorable. Now, the other half . . ." Victor's voice trailed off and he sat down. "Well, I'm afraid it's a stalemate, my dear."

"So the deciding vote is yours after all. What's it going to be, Victor?" I tried to keep all emotion out of my voice but succeeded only in sounding stilted and antagonistic.

"Sit down," he said in a sad voice. "We need to talk this out."

"In the first place," he began as I settled into the chair again, "I want you to know that I have always liked you, admired you, and I thought that Max was an ass to keep you so uninformed. But I do not have the freedom, as the other judges did, to decide this on my own emotional responses to you. As leader of The Cadre, I have responsibilities and I cannot afford to have it rumored that I decided a case of this magnitude on personal feelings. Nor, on the other hand, can the decision be made out of a desire for vengeance on my part." He gave a charming smile and shrugged again. "Quite honestly, Deirdre, I'm not sure what I should do."

I laughed softly. "I could tell you, but that would hardly be fair, would it?" As I sat back down in the chair, the chain on the locket I was wearing came loose and it fell to the floor. I picked it up and examined it, refastening the catch, and put it back on. When I looked back at Victor, he was staring intently at the locket.

"Where did you get that?"

"It was in the chest in Max's room. It seemed appropriate that I should wear it this evening. Mitch didn't think I should, but I thought that she should be remembered." My voice softened a bit as I stroked the gold. "Max would have appreciated the gesture."

Victor looked at me with a strange expression on his face. "Do you know who that is?"

I snapped the catch open and glanced at the portrait, feeling a reminiscent smile cross my face. "Of course," I said confidently. "It's Max's mother. Did you know her? She was a beautiful person."

"I never knew her." Victor's voice was flat and even. "But Max spoke of her often. He loved her very deeply. He never really seemed to get over her death." Then he stopped and gave me an intent glance. "When did she die? And how?"

I knew the answers as well as I knew my own family's history. "She died two years after Max entered the seminary, a year before the Thirty Years' War started. As to what she died of, I assume it was what we now call tuberculosis, although, in my century we would have called it consumption. What you would have called it, I have no idea."

"And when did Max transform into a vampire? And who was responsible?"

"Ten years after the war had started. He had been wounded and was going to die." I closed my eyes to avoid Victor's burning glance and to bring the memory of the dream to the surface of my mind. When I spoke, my voice was soft and not entirely my own. "We were saved by a vampire. We were going to die, but he came along and promised us eternal life. I thought he was an angel; he worked the miracle and I thought he was an angel." I snorted angrily. "I was naive, too immersed in my religion to understand the ways of the world, and I didn't know any better. Can you believe it? I thought he was a goddamned angel. But he wasn't! He was Nosferatu; then I was Nosferatu." The word came out like an obscenity. "His name was . . ." And I paused, searching deep within me for Max's residual memories. I knew that somewhere beneath the loathing and the depravities, past the countless dead bodies and the long centuries, there lurked a face that he had blocked from my view. Or perhaps I had blocked its recognition. Whatever the reason, I struggled to tear away the veil that obscured that identity.

Finally I found that for which I searched, and my eyes opened wide on Victor's astonished face. "His name was"—the voice speaking was my own again—"Victor Leupold." I paused again and matched the face before me with the one my memories held. "Victor Leupold . . . Victor Lange. It was you who turned Max into a vampire."

Chapter 30

Victor's face turned even paler than usual. "Max?" he whispered, searching the room as if he thought he could see him. "Max is still with you? He must be, how else would you know of these things you have told me. Why didn't you tell me that Max was still with you?"

"I have had dreams of him for years now. I have heard him and seen him. Quite honestly, I thought I was just going crazy. And I did not know it would matter to you whether he was haunting me or not, or believe me, I would have told you sooner."

"I have read of this phenomenon." Victor's voice was eager, full of emotion. "How if the bond between two vampires is strong enough, one will linger even after his death. But I never really believed it. And no vampire living today has ever experienced it. What is it like?"

"Do you want the truth?" I looked at him shyly, feeling ill at ease.

"Yes," he said without hesitation. "Of course."

"Well, there are times when he is a comfort to have around,

but most times it is simply hellish." Then I laughed, surprising both myself and him. "He is actually more of a bastard dead than alive."

"But I must speak with him. Can you summon him?"

I laughed again, this time with more humor. "Have you ever known Max Hunter to come when he was called? Or to do anything merely because you wanted him to?"

Victor looked at me skeptically for a moment, then suddenly his expression lightened and he laughed himself. "No, Deirdre, I suppose not. I can't imagine that even death would change him that much."

"So, what are we to do?"

Victor stood up and poured himself a glass of wine. He gestured with the bottle, and at my nod, poured one for me.

"There is a way." He hesitated. "Not without risk to you, nor, for that matter, to me, but a way in which I can speak to Max. He must have stayed with you for a purpose."

"Other than to devil me, you mean?"

His eyes showed amusement only for a second. "That would be one reason, of course. But somehow we both know that it goes deeper than that. If I can ascertain his purpose, then maybe it'll help us both out of the awkward situation we are in."

"What are the stakes?" I was curious about why he wished to pursue this avenue so avidly.

"Your mind, maybe even mine."

"Look, Victor," I said determinedly, "I know I haven't been taking this trial as seriously as I could. But I hardly see that a few weeks or even months of starvation on my part would be worth the prospect of losing my mind. Or justify your wish to risk yours. Why not just take the sentence? It can't be so terrible, can it?"

For the first time since I had met Victor, I saw a clear, readable emotion in his eyes. It was fear, complete and utter terror. "Maybe Ron wasn't that good an attorney after all. What kind of sentence did he tell you to realistically expect?"

"A set time of incarceration and starvation. But he did emphasize that it would not result in death."

"He took it as lightly as that?" Victor looked surprised.

I thought for a moment. "Well, no, he seemed very upset at the prospect, and gave me the impression that it was a fate worse than death."

"And so he should have."

"But I don't really see—"

Victor interrupted me angrily. "What he forgot to mention is that the starvation sentence for this particular crime is rarely any shorter than fifty years. Normally it is almost twice that."

My eyes opened wide. "One hundred years?"

"Exactly so. Think it over carefully, Deirdre. Do you still wish to take your chances with The Cadre's sentence?"

I really didn't have to think very long. A hundred years was almost the entire duration of my life as a vampire. Even the mere contemplation of living those years without sustenance was painful, unthinkable. "No." My voice was shaking. I understood why Ron had neglected to tell me that one crucial fact. Had I known it at the onset, I would have been long gone, the rules of The Cadre be damned. "What do I need to do?"

"Have you fed recently?"

"Three nights in a row, actually." I gave a short, cynical laugh. "I thought I was preparing myself, you see. As if it would have done any good."

"Well, your instincts have still served you well. That will help you. Finish that"—he gestured at my glass—"in fact, finish the whole bottle. You need to be relaxed and at ease. I will do the same."

He went behind the bar and opened another bottle of dark red wine. But instead of bothering with the glass, he drank it straight from the bottle. I giggled nervously; the gesture seemed so incongruous, so out of character for someone as elegant and polished as Victor. He gave me a stern look; I shrugged and followed his lead draining my bottle shortly after his was emptied.

"Now," he said, pulling his chair forward so that our knees were touching, "relax and don't fight me. I need to enter into your mind and find Max." He held my hands in a tight grip and looked into my eyes. At first I felt nothing except for his cold hands on mine, then delicately at first, growing stronger and more persistent, I could feel his first tentative intrusion into my mind.

A chill crawled up my spine, and I felt the hair on the back of my neck rise. A wave of panic swelled within me, and I longed to run from this rape. But he held me, cruelly I thought at the time, with hands and eyes. And there was no escape.

"Easy." I heard his whispered thought as if it were mine. "Easy. Don't fight me."

I heard him and acknowledged the wisdom of his words, but couldn't relax, couldn't stop my fighting. I screamed, and tried to pull away from him. His hands had become shackles on my wrists; his eyes were swords driven deep into me. "No," I said. "I can't."

Then I felt a presence that was not Victor, and I struggled less, being more used to his occupation of my mind.

"Trust him," Max's familiar voice urged from deeper within my being, caressing me and calming my terror. "Trust him and let him in."

I took a deep breath and suddenly Victor's penetration became, not rape, but a warm and loving presence, like a return to a lover's embrace. I felt his gratification in his success, and his eagerness to pursue Max was as strong as my own.

I lead Victor down the paths of my life, pausing briefly at the points at which Max and I intersected. There is the carriage and the shadowy figure that carries me from the wreckage; he hurries away and we pursue him, stopping again at a small midwestern truck stop. Here he stays longer, and we almost catch him making love in an empty field on a star-filled night. But he is farther ahead than we are. We quicken our pace to find ourselves in his office at the Ballroom of Romance. He is impaled on the door, and we watch in horror and sympathy as he bleeds out his life by my hand. Then the room blackens and we seem to be nowhere.

I call his name and suddenly we are at the same cemetery that I have walked in my dreams. But this time I do not need to search the stones for Max's name, for his blood calls to me, his being calls to me, and when we arrive he is waiting for us, as I knew he would be, leaning against his tombstone.

"Hello, Victor," Max says with a twisted grin. "It certainly took you long enough to find me." He beckons to me, and as always, I go to him. He pulls me to him, holding me closely against his chest. "Although Deirdre and I have been living such exciting lives, I sometimes did not wish it to end. But now that you are here, I know it's for the best. I'm tired." He brushes his eyes and the soft drops of his tears on my upturned cheek burn. "God, I'm tired and I'm more than ready for my rest."

"Max." Victor's voice sounds hurt; I can feel his pain. "Why didn't you come to me?"

"Ah, old friend, that hurts, doesn't it?" Max's voice is hard and cruel. "You feel betrayed, I suppose. It could even be a betrayal of the magnitude I experienced many centuries ago when you took my humanity from me. I hope so. I would be very thankful to know that I was capable of inflicting similar pain on you."

"But I saved your life." Victor is crying, his voice jagged with emotion. "I gave you everything I had. You were strong, you were powerful, you were immortal. And you owed it all to me. I loved you like a son, like a brother."

"That's true; and I was grateful, for a time, for what you gave. But over the years I learned it could never replace what you had taken." Max's arm tenses around my shoulders and his anger echoes from the surrounding graves.

"I was a man of God and with the taste of your blood I lost my one chance for salvation. There were compensations, of course, many wonderful compensations: the women, the blood, the sensations of life. But as I sunk deeper into a depravity that you encouraged, I began to hate what I was. Began to hate you. And powerful as I was, I was powerless to change.

"Then"—Max's voice becomes tender, loving—"Deirdre came to me. As trusting and as innocent as a child. She taught me to love again, not in the pure way that I loved as a priest, but as a man. How could it be a pure love? I was so depraved, so degenerate. But I did love her. And I hesitated telling her who I was; I was ashamed of my excesses, knowing that she could not forgive them, or me. I tried to guide her along the paths I had taken with you. 'Revel in your power, revel in your life' was the message I wanted her to accept. 'Be as a goddess among humans.' " Max choked out a small, cynical laugh. "It didn't work."

"Max, I'm sorry." I find that I am crying now too.

"Little one, you don't need to be. If you had accepted that path, I think that deep down I would have been disappointed. But I had to take my chance. And when I finally came to the realization that you could never accept life on my terms, I found quite simply that I did not want to live." Max sighed, then laughed. "I suppose it could have gone either way that night. You could have killed Greer and come with me. But that wasn't really what I wanted."

"Then Deirdre is innocent?" Victor stares at Max in disbelief.

"Innocent?" Max shrugs. "Oh, I don't doubt that there was a part of her that wanted me dead. Can you blame her? But I wanted to die, Victor, and I hadn't the courage to face the sun. So, as usual, I took the coward's way out, the way of least resistance, and forced her to kill me. By doing that, she gave me what I most wanted, rest from my wicked life. But her grief and remorse and love held me here." He smiles, the cynical expression that enters his eyes is so familiar, it tears at my heart. "To be honest, I really didn't fight too much, it was an interesting two years. But that time is past, and I must go." He reaches out and grabs Victor's shoulders, giving him a kiss on the cheek. "Good-bye, Victor. Walk softly this night."

"And you." Victor puts his hand to his face, then turns away, walking down the cemetery paths, leaving me alone with Max once more.

My lower lip trembles and tears stream down my face. "Max," I plead with him, "why did you never tell me?"

He holds me close to him one last time and I feel his being envelop me like black, silken wings. "And what would you have done, my little one," he whispers into my hair, "if I had?"

"I would have loved you."

"Ah, thank you for that, Deirdre." I feel his body shake slightly and look up to see that he is laughing. "I almost wish it were true. But when you met Mitchell Greer, there was no longer any room for me in your life. You had grown beyond me. You would never have given him up willingly, nor I you. And so neither of us had any choice, did we?"

"No," I say, knowing the truth of his words, "but it should have been different. You should not have died."

"Deirdre." He cups my face in his hands and kisses my mouth gently. "Victor gave me eternal life, and for that I will eternally curse him. You, my little one, you gave me death, and I will love you forever." His next kiss is longer, more passionate, but I feel a pulling away, a parting of our unity. I look deep into his eyes.

"Rest easy, my love," he says, "and sweet dreams."

"And you, Max."

He smiles. It is one of the truest expressions I have ever seen on his finely sculptured face, not mocking or cynical, but honest and sweet and loving. It is the smile I had seen the younger Max wear in my dreams. I feel despair, for I will never know that man. He touches my cheek softly and then he is gone. I am left alone once more, crying over his grave. But this time, I know, will be my last visit. The man that I know as Max Hunter, who is more than a father to me, and more than a lover, the man born as Maximiliano Esteban Alveros so very long ago, is finally dead. God rest his soul.

Chapter 31

"God rest his soul," I whispered the prayer to darkness and I woke in a strange bed and a strange room, my head throbbing and my eyes hot and tired. Eventually I focused upon the shadowy figure sitting by the side of the room, his hands pressed over his face. My heart jumped slightly. "Max? I thought you had gone."

The tortured face of Victor Lange looked up at me, sad and aged. Startled by this perception of him, I blinked my eyes. When I opened them again, I realized that his features had not changed, but his manner and stance made him appear older. The weight of his many centuries seemed to hang about his neck.

"He is gone, Deirdre."

I could not tell whether he spoke the words aloud or if some portion of him still remained in my mind. But the result was the same; I felt his pain and his loss as keenly as if it were my own. And, although my empathy for him was enormous, I knew I could do nothing to help him.

"Victor, I am sorry," I started to say lamely.

"No, do not be sorry." He managed a vestige of a smile. "It was what he wanted."

Silence wrapped us for a while in its dark softness. Then we both tried to speak at the same time.

"How long have I . . ." I began.

"You've been found . . ."

We both laughed nervously. "You first, Victor."

"You've been here for well over a day. There's about three hours until dawn and you're completely free to leave whenever you want to. I sent Mitch back home when the verdict came through; he did not want to go, but I explained that you would be here for at least a day. He sat with you for a while, but when the sun rose he left." Victor waved his hand feebly. "He said something about a celebration when you got home."

"And the verdict was?"

"Guilty, but with just cause. No one could deny that yours was the hand that dealt his death. And yet, with what I learned, I could not see you unjustly punished. You do, however, have one small penance to perform. Mitch agreed to assist you if necessary." Victor stopped for a moment as if to collect his thoughts. "He's a good man, Deirdre," he said grudgingly. "Although I can't help but wish that you had chosen Max, I suppose you just did what you thought you had to."

"Victor," I began, but he did not let me continue.

"It won't help, you do understand, don't you? Nothing you can say or do will bring him back. But"—he straightened up in his chair—"as I said before, I cannot let my personal emotions interfere with my leadership of The Cadre." He looked at me again and his eyes seemed weak, drained of the energy they had always shown.

I did not try to offer my sympathy again. We were bonded so closely by his entrance into my mind, by the blood we both shared, I felt his overwhelming sadness as if it were my own. I also felt that there would be no cure for Victor. I got out of bed and walked over to him, taking his hand and silently touching it to the tears on my face.

He nodded, then smiled again. "So, your penance is this. You are required to perform one service, any service named, for The Cadre at any time we should choose to request it. May I have your promise?"

"Certainly, Victor. I'll do what I can."

"You may never be called on it, you understand. But you'll need to keep in touch with us, let us know where you can be reached at all times."

I nodded. "I can do that."

"There's one more thing." He stood and absently brushed his suit jacket, taking the pose of his former elegance. "We've a vacancy on the judicial board. As the eldest unhoused member of

Alveros, you could petition to occupy it. At this point, you could even petition for establishment of your own house."

"Victor," I said slowly and deliberately, "I do not wish to take Max's place, nor do I wish to set up my own dynasty. Is it required?"

"No, no." He smiled at me again as he opened the door. "But let me know if you change your mind. Go on home to Mitch now and have a nice celebration." The final word seemed to choke him and he said no more, but walked out the door, his shoulders slumped.

I found my shoes, coat, and bag and prepared to leave. When I entered the hallway outside the room, I realized that I was still in the warren of rooms that constituted The Cadre's quarters. I recognized many of the rooms I passed from the interviews I had undergone the previous evening. The thick gray carpeting cushioned my footsteps and I moved silently, though not silently enough for the occupants of these rooms. When I reached the door that was Vivienne's, she stood there, waiting for me.

"Deirdre." She smiled at me. "Congratulations on such a favorable verdict." Her hair hung in a mass of unruly curls to her waist, and she was dressed in a filmy black negligee that left little of her lithe body to the imagination. I looked away, extremely embarrassed by her blatant exhibitionism. "I'd hoped you might join me for a drink before you leave. Who knows when we will meet again?"

I glanced back at her and the expression on her face was friendly and earnest. She seemed so young, so untouched by the life that she must have led, that it was hard to believe she was like me. But the power in her eyes, the strength and glow of her body, spoke the truth. I wanted to refuse her offer; I did not trust her, did not trust any of The Cadre, but I knew that they could not hurt me now, so I returned her smile and nodded.

"Yes, thank you, that would be nice."

"Come in, then. I promise I will not keep you any longer than an hour or so, but we've so much in common that I thought we should have a nice long talk." She moved to one side as I entered, but not so far away that I could not smell her perfume.

"You see, I don't visit here very often. I find the ways of The Cadre confining at times, and I much prefer to be on my own."

She directed me to a room behind the one in which our interview had been held. It was expensively furnished with beautiful antique furniture and lit by many candles. One corner of it held a large ornate coffin much like Max's. I shuddered when I saw it, then shook my head.

"Do you all sleep in one of those?"

Vivienne followed my stare and gave a small shrug. "So we've been taught. And you don't."

"I've never found it necessary."

"And you don't fear the sun's penetration?"

I laughed a little nervously. "Of course I do. But not so much that I care to be confined the entire day. I'm careful to protect myself in other ways."

"Ah," she said, "that is most interesting. Please make yourself comfortable and I'll pour you a drink." She indicated a brocade sofa and I took off my coat and sat down. "White or red?"

"Red, please." I watched while Vivienne worked at the sideboard that apparently doubled as her bar. Her hands were small and delicate, but the nails were quite long and highly lacquered. Not wanting to appear ill at ease, I kicked off my shoes and casually curled my legs beneath me, wondering what purpose lay behind her invitation. Ron had said she didn't like rogues, but she knew what I was and still had asked me here. Her mind was completely inaccessible to mine; I had no experience in dealing with this situation. I should just go home, I thought, and try to forget that The Cadre ever existed.

Vivienne turned around, two glasses of wine in her hands. "I will not keep you long, I promise," she said as if she had read my mind. "I'm sure you want to be back as soon as possible with your Mitch." I smiled to myself. His name pronounced in her French accent sounded so exotic, so different. Crossing the room with an almost sinister grace, she handed me a crystal goblet. "I think you will find this a marvelous vintage. I've had it set aside for many years for a special occasion."

I took a sip; Vivienne was right, it was wonderful, rich but slightly biting. I took a long drink and sighed. "Thank you." I smiled at her. "It is very nice."

"I hoped you'd like it." She settled onto a chair opposite me. "I've several others just like it, enough to last quite a while." She made a move as if to pull her negligee closer to her body, but all she managed to do was cause it to drop from one shoulder.

I felt extremely uncomfortable. "So," I said, trying to make my voice as friendly as possible, "what house are you from, initially?"

She looked at me over the rim of her glass, then took a sip but said nothing.

"I'm sorry, is that a forbidden topic? I'm totally unaware of Cadre etiquette."

"No," she laughed, but I relaxed only slightly. "I was just wondering how it could be possible you didn't know."

I sighed again, setting my glass down on the end table and pushed my hair back from my face. "Vivienne, quite honestly, I know nothing of any of this. And"—I slipped my shoes back on, stood up, and reached for my coat with a twisted smile—"somehow, I suspect I am much better off that way. Thank you for the drink."

"No, Deirdre, don't leave yet." Vivienne jumped up from her seat to prevent my retreat; her voice was low and urgent. "I forget that all of this is new to you and that you've been under a terrible strain these past few weeks. I didn't mean to make you uncomfortable; it's just that there are so few of us, female vampires, I mean, and I thought we could become friends."

I studied Vivienne as she stood in front of me; her eyes glistened in the candlelight and she seemed sincere and honest. I fully understood her feelings; I, too, missed female companionship.

Sensing my weakening, Vivienne pressed on. "As far as my lineage, I don't mind discussing that with you. It's not forbidden and it's no secret." She leaned forward and traced her nails down my cheek, not pulling her hand away when I tensed, but grasping my chin delicately yet firmly. "I'm also from the house of Alveros," she whispered to me, an odd smile crossing her face. Her face held a strange mixture of longing and loathing, desire and hate.

I moved away from her so abruptly that she almost lost her balance. "But Deirdre," she continued, straightening herself, touching my arm lightly, "please consider. I could do so much for you. You could have power and wealth in The Cadre. After all, you and I are sisters in blood."

I met her eyes squarely and surely. "All the same, Vivienne," I said, shrugging off her touch and moving to the door, "until I know what sort of game you are playing with me, I would prefer to remain an only child."

To my surprise, Vivienne took no offense, but laughed, a light metallic laugh, so charming and inhuman, so like her. "Bravo, Deirdre," she called after me as I left the room. "Have a nice evening."

There was no limo waiting for me outside, so I walked to Mitch's apartment. I dismissed the strange episode in Vivienne's room, knowing that I didn't need to worry about her, that she was no threat to my life. With my trial before The Cadre finally over, I felt freer than I ever had before, and hummed to myself, smiling at the few people I passed.

There was no trace of Max in my mind or on the street, and although I missed his presence, I felt relieved and at peace. I would no longer be tortured by thoughts of him, for by his own admission I was free of the guilt for his death. For the first time in over a century, I did not need to fear my dreams. The demons of my sleep had finally been exorcised and were put to rest.

When I had gotten to within three blocks of Mitch's apartment, I felt a cold stab of fear and stopped dead on the sidewalk. The way the recent events of our lives had worked out seemed too simple. Would it really be possible for Mitch and me to enjoy our lives together, unencumbered by demands of the outside world? Well, why the hell not, I reassured myself, I deserve a happy ending the same as everyone else.

I counted our assets in my mind. I had enough money to last us several lifetimes, not even counting the fortune I had inherited from Max. We could go anywhere, live anywhere we liked. Freed from guilt, freed from the sentence of The Cadre, I was immortal and Mitch, well, Mitch was young, strong, and in good health. He could conceivably live another forty or fifty years. They would be good years, I was certain, filled with love and happiness. And when death finally came to claim him, I would follow. But finally, after over a century of running away, I would be living a normal life, the life I had been denied the first time around.

I started walking again, quickly this time, for all my rationalization could not allay the terrible feeling that something wrong had happened. No, I corrected myself, beginning to run, ignoring the sharp pain of fear entering my stomach and washing over my entire body, something wrong is happening right now. Right now.

I kicked off my shoes and ran the rest of the way, shouting his name, brushing past surprised predawn walkers and joggers, the buildings and cars that I passed blurred with speed and tears.

I was almost prepared for what I faced when I arrived home. I bounded up the steps, noticing that the main door was hanging open and askew, and that one of the hinges had been torn off. Mitch's front door was battered and lying on the living room floor. The remains of a bottle of wine that he must have opened for our celebration lay in pieces on the floor. I walked over them, not heeding the pain from the broken shards beneath my bare feet.

I stopped and held my breath. "Mitch," I called tentatively, my voice quavering, "are you here?"

I heard an odd laughing sound from the bedroom, then the crashing of glass. Running down the hall, I felt the icy blast of wind from the broken window, smelled the tangy, warm scent of fresh blood, and a tantalizingly familiar man's cologne. "Larry Martin," I whispered, and knew that I could follow him out the window and easily catch up with him. But when I arrived in the doorway, the sight of Mitch occupied my complete attention.

He was bruised and badly beaten, clutching his gun with one hand and the open wound on his neck with the other. I dropped to the floor and knelt beside him. His eyes fluttered open and focused weakly on my face. His skin had the bluish-gray color that meant he had nearly been drained of all his blood. Taking his pulse confirmed this.

"Jesus, Mitch, what the hell happened? Who did this?" My voice sounded calm but inwardly I was raving; damn The Cadre and all its members! The time I had spent in Vivienne's room might well have caused Mitch's death. Even the few minutes I had spent on the sidewalk planning the perfect life would have been all the time Larry needed. And if I had been here when Mitch was attacked, I could have prevented this.

Tenderly, I touched his cooling cheek. "Mitch, talk to me, please. Oh, God, you can't die. I won't allow it."

He stared at me for a moment and coughed weakly.

"Deirdre." It was the only word he could manage, and even it cost him too much strength.

I did not think of the consequences of my actions; all I could think was that he would die too soon and leave me alone. I could not bear the thought. Taking his shoulders in my hands, I shook him until his eyes opened again and focused on me. "Do you want to live?" I said to him. "Do you love me enough to live?"

He nodded weakly, a small spurt of blood came from his neck, and he managed a ghost of a smile.

"Are you sure?"

"Yes."

Picking up one of the broken shards of glass from the window, I cut into my wrist deeply, and forced it to his mouth before the wound could heal. "Drink, Mitch drink."

There was no pull on my blood at first. He's dead, I thought, he's truly dead. "Drink, Mitch!" I screamed in desperation, not knowing or caring if he could hear me. "You must drink."

Oh, God, I raged inside, I spent so much time away from him and we had so little time together. Don't let him die, I prayed. Don't let him die!

Finally after an eternity of despair, I felt the delicate movement of his lips at my wrist, feeble at first and then with greater strength, as he pulled deeply on my blood. The gray color began to fade from his skin, replaced slowly by an internal glow and the appearance of health. I watched as his bruises healed before my eyes and still he drank, until I began to feel the emptiness of my own veins. Then ever so gently I pried myself away from him. He choked, spitting a small swallow of my blood back to me.

His eyes opened briefly, then closed as his body shuddered once, then again, as if adjusting to its new life. His chest moved visibly as he breathed, and I knew he would live. I got up from the floor and looked out the window. There was no one on the street below, no sign of who had broken in here. All I could see was the lightening sky. Panicked, I pulled the curtains shut, but the wind blew them back, splashing the street light on to the floor where Mitch lay.

"Damn," I swore, wondering how I could move him, how I could keep the sun from him. Then I noticed the tall dresser in the corner of the room. It would cover the window and he would be safe. Frantically, I ran to it and pushed it across the room to block the light. The noise of this movement caused Mitch to awaken and sit up.

"Deirdre." His voice sounded strong but confused. "What happened? I can't seem to remember anything. And I feel so strange, light-headed." His eyes sought me out and linked with mine. I had always thought that their strength and intensity were one of his most attractive qualities. But nothing could have prepared me for the shock of their depth—their complete and utter transformation; I knew his eyes, but never had they bored so directly into mine, never had they been so searching, so relentless. I choked back my tears and went to his side again.

"Hush, my love," I said to him, cradling his head on my lap the way I had over two years ago, trying for his sake to hide my despair. "Everything will be fine. Sleep now."

"But I need to remember what happened. Someone broke in while I was waiting for you. He told me not to remember and I can't. Then you came. And now everything is different. What happened? Tell me, please." The urgency in his voice almost broke my heart. How could I explain in the few remaining minutes until sunrise the life to which I had doomed him? That in my fear of losing him, I had done what I had resolved never to do?

"Sleep now," I repeated. "We'll have all the time in the world to talk later."

We tensed at the same time, reacting to the rising of the sun.

His body writhed in agony and his eyes met mine. They were clouded now with fear and confusion, and in spite of my resolve, I began to cry.

"What's that?" he demanded, his voice deeper and stronger than before. "What's happening to me, Deirdre? Why are you crying? And why do I feel so different?"

"It's only the sun, my love." I put as much reassurance into the words as I could and my fingers stroked his grayed hair, trying to calm and comfort. "Now is the time to sleep."

He looked up at me one more time. His eyes were undeniably the eyes of a vampire. Then they slowly closed, the lids falling as if of their own volition, and Mitch fell into the trancelike sleep I knew so well.

And I was alone again for a time, to mourn the death of the man I loved.

Epilogue

As soon as arrangements could be made, Mitch and I went to England. We told no one what had occurred that evening in our apartment, explaining only that we would be gone for a while on an extended honeymoon. Mitch needed time to learn, time to adjust to his new life, and I needed time to calm my panic over what I have done.

Before returning to my house and the pub, we decided to travel through the country, seeing the sights at night. Stonehenge was wonderful, and we crept past the guard and the gates and lay in the center, whispering to each other, making love on the dry, cold gravel. At Mitch's suggestion, we even stopped at Whitby. From our hotel bed we listened to the waves beat on the rocks and read aloud from *Dracula,* pointing out to each other the inconsistencies of the book compared to the life we knew. As always, at the end of the story I cried when the stake pierced the count's chest, remembering with a shudder exactly how it felt to kill a man of great power and age. And he laughed and kissed away my tears.

We have found that Mitch has a great instinct for hunting, his senses having been finely honed by his many years of police work. He is as good as I, or perhaps even better, at the post-feeding suggestions, but he still approaches the feeding and the victim timidly, tentatively, as if he had no right to their blood. He senses this hesitation as a liability, and I console him that he will get better with practice.

As for me, I don't dream much anymore. When I allow myself sleep, it's become like a small death, silent and mindless. Mostly, I lie awake and watch him sleep, wrestling with his own private demon of dreams. He moans and quivers, his eyes rolling within his closed lids, and he wakes covered in sweat. I never ask who appears in his dream, with whom he fights daily, what figure haunts his sleep. I fear his answer, sensing deep inside that I already know, not wanting to hear him say that I am the demon. So I lie, my mind pure and emptied of all former ghosts, holding him while he writhes, tormented and struggling in the darkness that is my eternal gift to him.

[redacted]